RISE

OF THE

WATER MARGIN

A Novel of the Near Future

by

CHRISTOPHER BATES

ĭnter-fās

To my parents, genetic and memetic, Woody, Jean and Sunnie

Table of Contents

SPRING

Don't call me anything. Better not to deal in names. What is your name?

Did you know your name is the anchor point of programming? And the programming began at birth, with tricking you into having a name. And you now identify with language instead of your True Nature. No words can encompass your True Nature. They are just limiting constructs. So, no, don't call me anything.

This story is not about me, anyway. I am just at the center of it, like the eye of the typhoon, but the center is not where the action is. It is from my perspective at the center, at the calm, I could observe and communicate this whole story. Or at least as much as the limiting construct of language and words would allow.

CHAPTER 1

"MILI, ARE YOU WITH US?" THE HUMAN RESOURCES ADMINIS-
trator called out in the front of the meeting room from where she delivered
a sermon on the ways the National Security Agency was adopting new federal policies for workers with disabilities.

Mili Parekh opened her eyes and concentrated to speak as clearly as possible, "Yesh, I am wesh you." She frequently thought with her eyes closed,
either deeply considering what the other person was saying, blocking out
extraneous sensory inputs, or as in this case blocking out people and subjects she deemed a waste of her time.

She looked across the room filled with wheelchairs, crutches, white
canes, and their owners. It was not filled with a commensurate number of
limbs and eyes, she calculated.

Many of the people here were veterans wounded in foreign wars, some
by improvised explosive devices, others by gunfire or helicopter crashes,
and had lost legs or arms. Others had different disabilities. Blindness, au-
tism, developmental challenges.

She supposed she fit in this latter group. Cerebral palsy brought on by
perinatal oxygen deficiency during her birth had left her semiparalyzed
and confined to a chair. She refused to let it define her and what she was
capable of, yet here she sat in this meeting called by HR.

It is all well-meaning, she thought struggling to keep her eyes open and
look attentive, *and for sure veterans deserve proper opportunities after*

their sacrifices. The new policies will help, she judged. *However, I don't have my job at the NSA because of policies for workers with disabilities. I am here because I am the best at what I do, and right now I've got bigger things on my mind.*

As chief of the attribution section within the NSA, she had a specific and, she felt, crucial role.

The NSA conducted intelligence gathering on foreign governments, businesses, and individuals to preempt credible threats, thwart nascent attacks and get sufficient dirt on people to push Uncle Sam's way in the world. She was not a part of these activities at all.

The NSA also sought to intercept foreign intelligence incursions into the US and otherwise identify and neutralize national-security-level cyber threats. This was also not her job.

When a threat had been identified, it was important to try to attribute it to a source, be it a government, a movement, a syndicate, or an individual. Decision makers wanted to know with whom to go to war. This was her job, or more precisely the job of her shop.

She had built a team of seven groups, each with about ten data scientists. The seven groups were Russia, China, Iran, North Korea, Terrorist Groups, Hacker Groups, and Rest of World (RoW). There were functional specialists on each team focused on threats to military, infrastructure, and financial services.

Attribution had been an extremely complex, unreliable, and thorny craft until Mili Parekh came along. There were thousands of hackers and "bad dudes," as a former president had labeled them, out there, and cyber threats left only the faintest of fingerprints. How to create a forensically reliable methodology to categorize and identify the culprits?

Before she joined the intelligence community, attribution had been conducted by documenting intrusion sets. The assumption was that the style or approach used by perpetrators could be identified, their modus operandi as it were, and repeated in future attacks. This could be used to at least narrow the list of suspects.

Her approach, developed in her PhD dissertation at Columbia, had been to apply memetics to attribution.

The evolutionary biologist Richard Dawkins had famously proposed the idea of a meme, a distinct unit of information shared between people that would spread, propagate, and evolve if it was accepted, or die. It was seen to be like a gene, distinct in its construct. This had taken on a popular life of its own as the internet bred new "memes" daily, which were not really memes at all, just punchy, memorable bites of life or satire to which a wide swath of people could relate and click Thumbs-Up.

Mili created a systematic path and a progression of algorithms to analyze how information is transmitted with heredity and selection and trace generations of memes back to a root. She had not called it attribution and working for the NSA had been far from her mind, but NSA wonks read Mili's conference papers, found her, and convincingly proposed that within their four walls the research could best be put to work.

They had been right.

The NSA's databases with millions of examples of code and their vast resources, not to mention the variety of threats analyzed, provided a fully equipped laboratory within which to test her theories.

The dissertation had taken three years to complete, but within four months at Fort Meade she had refined both the process and the algorithms several evolutionary steps beyond those she originally documented. She then ran an analysis of the database of codes through the sieve and cataloged them in a meaningful and searchable way. Memetic analysis was to intrusion sets as DNA testing was to an awareness of modus operandi.

A test of Mili's prowess came early in her tenure. A billion-dollar program trading scheme on Wall Street had gone awry triggering a crash on the London Metals Exchange, siphoning off hundreds of millions of dollars in a single turbulent morning of trading before it was shut down. In the aftermath there were suicides, bankruptcies, and lawsuits, and the American and British publics cried out for retribution.

FBI and Treasury Department investigations quickly disposed of the possibility that the brokerage firm itself had something to do with the mishap. Clearly their system had been breached and used by an outside party. The possibility existed that a foreign entity had perpetrated the crime, and the NSA never refused an invitation to get behind the firewalls of the financial services industry, so they sent in Mili to analyze the digital detritus.

She isolated the unique signature of the author of the code that had precipitated the meltdown and then followed a subtle trail of elements of that signature backwards in time to the initial incursion and forward in time to the disposition and disappearance of funds. More importantly, she performed a comparison of the signature elements of the coding to those in the database she had already cataloged and narrowed the origin of the style down to one person, Eunice Stravinsky.

A young math and computer genius doing a PhD at Cal Poly, Stravinsky was from a family with a fine reputation (everyone knew of the composer in the family). She was convicted of hacking into the financial markets for fun and profit and sentenced to life in prison. No evidence of a crime was found on her computer, and there was no evidence that any of the funds siphoned off had found their way into Stravinsky's hands.

The main evidence presented was a sanitized, FBI-generated version of Mili's forensic analysis.

Eunice consistently proclaimed innocence and in the years of appeals first claimed someone had gotten hold of her artificial intelligence research and used it to create the crash. Later she claimed that the AI program itself had done the crime. Because she was the author of the AI program, the appeal was dismissed as frivolous.

The event had occurred five years ago. Eunice was arrested four and a half years ago, convicted three and a half years ago, and was behind bars and denied access to computers or smartphones. That was precisely the "bigger thing" Mili had on her mind as she struggled to look engaged and interested in the HR administrator's presentation.

Parekh's system had flagged Eunice as the source of a new cyber threat just that morning. Like following evolutionary patterns in a gene pool, Mili's system could track adaptations of someone's coding style or if someone sought to combine or imitate a style to their own ends. This was neither. It was purely Eunice Stravinsky's memetic coding style observed in the LME meltdown, which meant there was a glitch in Mili's program, a very rare false positive.

The HR administrator had arrived at the final slide of the presentation. Thanking all the disabled attendees to the meeting for their contributions at the NSA to the nation's security, she pledged to continue supporting their needs. She invited them to stop for coffee and donuts outside the meeting room.

Mili tugged the electric wheelchair's joystick and steered it nimbly between the attendees, trying to make a dash for the door before the exit was clogged with people rolling, ambling, or limping toward the snacks. She got to the elevator and struggled to get her ID card near the reader with her good hand. Then she pressed the button for the fifth floor and took a breath, exhausted with the effort. She had some diagnostics to run before she would tell anyone about this.

For the time being it was a low-level threat to which no one else was paying attention. She would crack this. "A dog with a bone." That is how her dad had described Mili's spirit. Half of her mouth curled up in a smile.

ᗡ 人 ᑕ

LIN CHONG PACED UP AND DOWN THE ROWS OF YOUNG contenders muttering, "Tick-Tock . . . Tick-Tock," as they hammered away on keyboards. With annoying irregularity, he rapped a wooden pointer on the cubicles just to keep them rattled. The examination room was dark save the glow of flat-screen panels on which the aspirants struggled to focus despite Lin's distractions. "The enemy is going to launch, going to launch, launching," he taunted. "Break the code, break the code, save your friends."

Three thousand contenders had been whittled away to this cohort of thirty. They hailed from every corner of China. The fastest and best five of them able to crack this software challenge first without losing their cool would be offered a slot in the People's Liberation Army Unit 61398. Known to its adversaries and foreign rivals under various names, such as Advanced Persistent Threat 1 and Byzantine Candor, this unit was the tip of the spear of China's cyber warfare efforts.

These were no ordinary times, but commander of Unit 61398 Major Lin Chong was no ordinary warrior.

A stalking, nocturnal predator, he padded among the contenders facing the challenge: to save China from destruction. He lived this mission every day and counted on some of them to be tough enough, resilient enough, smart enough to contribute to the cause.

China, the center and apex of civilization for so many centuries, had stumbled 200 years ago. Humanity's struggle out of colonial exploitation and hegemony toward a system in which nations established their right to coexist as equals defined the 20th century. This, Lin knew, was no less true for China which convulsed for a hundred years of unequal treaties, revolution, warlords, invasion, and liberation, and thirty years more of ill-executed economic and political reforms. Hundred Flowers, Great Leaps, and Cultural Revolutions left the Chinese people exhausted, impoverished, and ready to start again from the ashes of the hundred years of humiliation.

Looking about the room filled with the glow of advanced computing systems, Lin Chong was proud China had stood up to bullies; it had not cowered in the face of American wars in Korea and Vietnam. It had developed its own nuclear deterrence, its own capacities to protect itself.

With market opening, the floodgates of investment released a torrent of cash into China. Factories sprouted like bamboo thickets across the eastern seaboard exporting shiploads of "stuff" for global consumers who themselves were now making lower wages and welcomed the opportunity to buy cheaper Chinese products. Money filled pockets, money filled coffers, spilling over into the government and the military.

The financial crisis of 2008 and the quantitative easing in the US and Europe released a tsunami of cash surging across the Pacific and washing up on the shores of China. More investment in manufacturing, infrastructure, and lifestyle but also more inflation, more pollution, more crowding in the coastal cities. So huge, so sustained, was the wave of cash hitting China that it naturally began to flow back across the Pacific. China consumed large pieces of the Treasury-bill pie baked by the US Federal Reserve. Chinese companies acquired Western companies, and US West Coast real-estate prices surged as private Chinese money sought underpriced assets and safe havens for excess currency.

All this bought China a seat at the big table of wealthy nations and a chance to reassert its centrality to the civilized world. It had taken almost 200 years, but China was back. Lin's mission, and the mission he would press upon the best of these aspirants toiling to join his team, was to make certain China could not be bullied and maintained its newly minted stature in the world.

Lin Chong had studied China's rivals. He did not deem them to be enemies. He hoped that it would never come to war; indeed, there was no reason for war, as China's long history was not expansionist.

China demanded to be respected and not harassed. The mission, the cause, was that simple.

China's chief rival was the US. He knew his American counterparts would find his views on historical materialism, the deep connection to the past and to cultural roots, quaint, perhaps ridiculous.

As he walked the room and whispered distractions into the ears of the hopefuls, he recalled the initiation lecture Major Lu Da, his former commander and mentor, had given when Lin was inducted. "Americans have an overinflated view of their future and virtually no connection with their past. Indeed, the US does not have much of a past. China was prosperous and civilized for ten times longer than the US has been in existence. American 'culture' is no culture, an amalgam of all the different kinds of people who settled there and sorted out their beliefs in a free-for-all tussle of ideas.

"This tussle and the emergence of winning ideas is certainly a strength for the American economy, but these ideas are rarely rooted in a deep commitment to American culture per se. That is why we can beat them if it comes to that. Just like the American-born Chinese Bruce Lee eschewing his roots in traditional Chinese martial arts in favor of an Americanized experimentation with many styles. Lee ultimately proclaimed, 'My style is no style.' Abandoning his cultural identity for expedience, rather than mining the strength of it. Imagine how great he could have been if he had respected it."

Despite the hypermodern weapons Lin designed and deployed, his perspective was rooted in the past. The core of his being was Chinese. It meant something to him to be part of this culture, this nation, this tribe identifying themselves as Chinese. It was something of value to be lived, preserved, defended, and improved, not neglected to be eroded, be scrapped, or be eclipsed. The actions he took today were to improve and enhance what it meant to be part of that culture in the future. Defending it for the future was why he was here, why he was a Chinese patriot.

Lin Chong's eyes inspected the field of contenders struggling to crack the problem. He had read the dossiers of each one. He knew that they had been raised under circumstances quite different from his own. *Take this wannabe here,* he thought as he passed the desk of a pudgy, bespectacled fellow not yet twenty years old, whom he recalled was surnamed Wu. *A product of the one-child policy doted on by upper-middle-class parents too busy to spend time with him, so they bought him everything. "Just deliver the grades from school," they had no doubt bribed and controlled him. Wu had submerged himself in online gaming, then deconstructed game code and written his own games. Until his grades plummeted. The parents fought, got divorced, and Dad had left Mom with zip, just a spare apartment. Little Master Wu showed talent in coding, but would he crack now, or be able to deliver? Would this upbringing make them more, or less, reliable when things got tough? Only time and the effort I put into the final recruits to forge and temper them will tell.*

His grandfather had been a soldier during the Communist Revolution and had been among the thousands marching in front of Chairman Mao at Tiananmen Square when he proclaimed the foundation of the People's Republic of China in 1949. He had stayed in the military, married a tall, handsome Manchurian woman while stationed in Northeast China during and after the Korean War and soon thereafter had one son he was proud to raise, Lin Chong's father, who also went into the military.

Lin Chong was born after market opening. He had never lived in a centrally controlled, totalitarian China like those under Chairman Mao. In his life, he had seen shantytowns, fields of crops, and vistas of single-story brick dwellings give way to flocks of cranes pulling skyscrapers out of the ground like long elastic worms, McDonald's, foreign cars, a cellphone in every hand, and virtually full employment.

He too had been a single child, doted on by his parents only until he reached school age, then trained to follow father and grandfather into the military. They disciplined his body and spirit with martial arts training under the best coaches, and his mind with studies of Chinese chess, Chinese historical classics, math, and science.

It was in this last area that Lin showed the greatest academic promise, and the authorities shunted him into a program for gifted math students. Here he also began to learn English and computer programming and soon won national competitions for programming challenges.

He was awarded a scholarship from the PLA to attend Tsinghua University at the age of sixteen for his undergraduate degree and then the PLA Academy of Military Science for a master's. At age twenty-two, he was recruited into Unit 61398 as a young officer and was sent under an assumed name to Oxford for a year of computer science studies. On return, his climb within the unit had been steady and punctuated with numerous milestones and victories.

A raucous warning buzzer pealed in the test room rousing Lin Chong from his reverie.

The first of the recruits had cracked the code. The annoying sound further rattled the nerves of the remaining recruits pushing them on to complete their work before they were knocked out of the competition. Thereafter in brief succession, a second, third, fourth, and fifth buzzer went off and then the overhead lights came on. The test administrator entered and ordered the twenty-five failing recruits to file out. *They will no doubt go on to become e-commerce sensations,* Lin Chong reflected on the losers hanging their heads low and exiting the room.

The remaining five stood at attention, bodies taut, eyes still alert, saluting Lin Chong.

A flush of pride filled Lin's heart as he appraised the five. Little Master Wu had made the cut, he noted. They were the best of the best, and he led them. Woe to China's rivals. He saluted back crisply, turned on point, and marched out of the room.

ㄅ 人 ㄈ

ZHANG ZHENNIANG WAS RELIEVED SHE HAD ARRIVED ON TIME at the health club. The late afternoon spinning sessions were the best, the instructor the most skilled at motivating the riders, and it fit well with her schedule. She had booked a seat in the session a week before, but today she and Lin Chong had fought the afternoon traffic to get there, and as the minutes in the slow line of cars dragged on, she became anxious she would miss her spot.

The club was the finest in Shanghai, the monthly fees a bit beyond their means, but it was clean and bright, equipped with the newest machines, well maintained, and only the best people were members. Lin Chong had wanted his wife to take up exercise, and her condition had been that it be at the best club, not some dank, sweaty, iron-pumping house like the PLA gyms he was used to.

At the afternoon spinning session, women occupied eighteen of the twenty stationary bikes. The instructor prepared her bike, guided new riders on how to use the machines, and adjusted the surround-sound speakers pumping out pop music for the intense ride ahead.

Zhenniang turned back to lean over and adjust the height and position of the saddle. On the bike next to Zhang one of the two men in the session sat. He was ogling her, no doubt removing the remaining clothes she wore for the workout. He was a thin, pallid man a little older than her who tried to look hip by binding a balding pate into a tight ponytail. He continued staring. She finished setting up the machine while scowling at him and turned to mount the bike.

The instructor got the class moving, putting them through five minutes of warm-ups, then several three-minute sprints alternating with three-minute hill climbs. Zhenniang tried to get into the spirit of the class, tried to push herself, raise a sweat, and get her heart rate up, but she felt as if any fun, any positive excitement had been sucked out of it. Glances to the side revealed the man still looking at her. She began to regret every decision she had made in preparing to enjoy the class, wearing the lime-green sports top that revealed her cleavage and the choice of the tight, form-fitting cycling shorts that hid nothing from this man. But she persisted, she did not want this person to spoil the moment here, so her attention focused on the instructor, the shoutouts to give war cries, the flashing of the lights, and the pace of the music to put the unwelcome attention out of her mind.

At the end of the class, she gathered her things and went out into the weight machines area as she headed toward the women's showers. A voice from behind asked, "Miss, did you drop this?"

She turned around and looked to see the man proffering a scrunchie. She felt back at her bun. The scrunchie was still there. She looked up from his hand to his face and frowned as she took in the hungry look of lasciviousness on the prowl. *Best to disengage quickly and firmly from Uncle Creepy.* "It's not mine. Thank you anyway," she said turning to resume her path to the showers but running into a man wearing a track suit and sunglasses blocking her way, arms akimbo, a smirk on his face.

The man with the scrunchie reached out and took her shoulder firmly, but not threateningly, and turned Zhang around to face him. "I know it's abrupt, but could I invite you for coffee?"

She did not answer him, but her eyes took on a concerned look as her focus shifted to something behind *him*.

A large hand clamping on his shoulder spun him around firmly *and threateningly*, and he looked up into fierce eyes to appraise the interruption. Tall, over 1.8 meters, and broad with the physique of a wrestler who had turned to bodybuilding, he wore a tight tank top stained with the sweat of his workout exposing sculpted biceps and lats. The shirt was emblazoned with the emblem of the PLA Academy of Military Science PE Department. The hair on his head was closely cropped, but he did have a goatee. His eyes glared with fierce intelligence, and he said, "You need to learn to be polite to other men's wives."

The man measured the situation as his bodyguard, the one who had impeded the woman's retreat, stepped forward, and he beckoned him to stand down with a small flourish of his hand. *If I backed off every time some man thought to get in the way of my conniving, I would not have enjoyed many women indeed.*

He looked at the emblem on the sweaty shirt and the man again. *Probably still in the military, maybe special forces, in the Shanghai area as they are club members, so undoubtedly someone under my father's bootheel.*

"Ah, such chivalry. And you are?" he asked while his eyes darted to the security camera high on the wall near them alerting the potential assailant to its presence.

"Her husband. Lin Chong. *Major* Lin Chong," he said, taking his wife's hand and pulling her to his side.

"I was merely trying to return something I thought she had dropped. My father, General Gao Qiu, would be pleased to know he has such stalwarts in his troops."

Lin Chong heard the name, and his eyes narrowed.

He knew General Gao Qiu had beaten out rivals when the PLA had reduced seven military regions to five. In the ensuing musical chairs, two rivals had been retired and Gao had been elevated to command the new Eastern Region. The territory included the massively wealthy and modern Shanghai-Nanjing corridor, an economy so enormous that were it a country, it would be the sixth largest. So, yes indeed, Lin was one of "his troops."

That means the skinny philanderer facing me must be Gao Yanei. Born to the general's mistress and adopted by him, he's a "princeling" sent to the US to study at the best schools that money and his father's influence could get him into. Word has it the wastrel played a role in the father's jockeying for leadership of the Eastern Region.

"My regards to your father," Lin said sullenly as he pushed through the man and led his wife safely to the entrance of the women's locker room.

⊃ 人 ⊂

GAO YANEI'S BODYGUARD WAS AN EX-SPECIAL FORCES SERGEANT named Fu An who had run into trouble when his image was caught in a mobile-device video of a Tibetan Buddhist monk self-immolating at a monastery in Sichuan.

It was so unfair, Fu often groused to anyone who would listen. *I didn't light the match, I didn't want to be in the picture, I wasn't there to do anything particularly bad to the monk. But some tourist caught me in the cellphone video, it was uploaded immediately, pushed out to several dozen Buddhist prayer websites and local social media, viewed an estimated fifty million times before the Ministry of Public Security's Golden Shield had contained it, and I was the one who got burned.*

Forced into an early retirement, he had welcomed the offer from General Gao Qiu to take on a private assignment as a bodyguard to his son.

The old general doted on the son of a mistress, but with good reason, Fu thought. The son's real name was Gao Shide, Worldly Virtue—certainly that was a joke, he mused—but everyone knew him by the more appropriate cognomen Gao Yanei, the Insider. Leveraging status as a "princeling," he was now a junior partner at the famous Wall Street investment banking

15

firm SilvermanFuchs's Shanghai office. Through the young man the father had no doubt sequestered millions, why stop at that, probably billions of yuan in currency in the form of payoffs and kickbacks, and moved them off-shore or hidden them in China. So the old man wanted tabs kept on the son, and Fu was well paid to do so.

He observed that in the week since Gao Yanei had encountered the filly at the health club and her old man, Gao had been quite preoccupied. He had called in sick to work twice and spent long hours online digging out information about the woman.

All this Fu An had noted. And all of it he had reported to the General.

Besides making sure his charge was not kidnapped, accosted, or approached by foreign spy organizations, Fu had also been taught to look for signs of fixation and melancholy in the young man. Yanei refused to take medication saying it interfered with his sex drive but was known to have gone into deep depressions in the past rendering him unfunctional. Fu felt it was time to intervene and donned a therapist's hat.

"Hey, Flower Lord," he employed yet another of Gao's sobriquets to cheer him up. "How about we go find some young buds to deflower?"

"Aiyo, Dried Pecker," Yanei spat in defeat, using Fu An's nickname denoting his gnarly foreskin. "I can't get this woman out of my head. I mean, I can taste her, I can feel the warmth of those tits in my hands and that tight, hot, wet twat, over and over again. But for naught. I've got to get a piece of that."

He knew "this woman" referred to Lin Chong's wife—Zhang Zhenniang. "There is the matter of the husband to deal with," Fu noted, trying not to put too fine a point on it.

"When has a husband ever been the real issue? The real issue is whether the woman wants to give me what I want. Once she wants it, she gives it; the old man is never a problem."

"So how do you get her to want to give it to you?" Fu An knew that active scheming was better for his charge than just letting him mope.

"I'm working on it. She plays violin for the Shanghai Symphony Orchestra. I kinda wish it was the clarinet," he winked at Fu An, "but I guess it means she is good with her fingers instead. SilvermanFuchs is a sponsor of the symphony. I am leveraging that. You want to bet that within two weeks I'll be inside those panties?"

"I never bet against the Flower Lord," Fu An chuckled encouragement.

⊃人⊂

ZHANG ZHENNIANG SMILED THROUGH CLENCHED TEETH AS THE director of the Shanghai Symphony prepared to deliver the bad news she could see was coming.

"Ultimately, ours is an entertainment, something people pay to come and see. And they come to see something...special. You haven't picked up your game, Zhenniang, and I have had this conversation with you before. So, for the upcoming program of Vivaldi's Seasons...we are considering bringing in Cherub Liu as the featured soloist."

Cherub Liu?!? Cherub Liu!?! Fuck your mother! Zhang screamed inwardly. *How can a seventeen-year-old Canadian-Chinese "prodigy" get the opportunity to steal my big chance, the piece I have spent a lifetime preparing to bring to an audience?*

Responding to a pout, the director continued, "You deserve to know why she is even being considered. You might think it's because she's hot. Because she has a recording contract. Because she has already traveled the world soloing and brings in the crowds. No. Frankly, our key sponsor has connections with Cherub and can arrange it. They think it might be good for the symphony, and I find it hard to resist the logic. They are, however, dedicated to promoting and featuring local talent, so they have proposed a meeting with you to discuss it."

Zhang calmed herself. *Ok, I can do this.* She had not clawed her way to be the leader of the first violin section to let the spotlight be turned on some foreign kid. "Excellent. The sooner the better. What do they want to know?"

The positive attitude relieved the director. "They're investment bankers. They bank on people, invest in talent. So they just want to look you in the eyes and know that you are willing to go the distance to bring glory to the symphony. Of course, it wouldn't hurt to lay on the charm either. Cherub *is* mighty cute, but you're not bad yourself," he smiled encouragingly. "If you are amenable, they are proposing a private dinner meeting at the Les Saisons Hotel this week, Thursday. I told them we have neither performance nor practice that night, so I guessed you could go."

"Alright. I will bring my violin and give them a private performance to remember."

ᗐ 人 ᑕ

THE GRAY, POLLUTED LANDSCAPE SMEARED PAST THE WINDOW of Lin Chong's seat on the high-speed rail heading from Shanghai to Nanjing. He sat thinking about how perspective changed things.

If he looked far beyond the window into the distance, objects there were still, distinct, defined, and identifiable. A little closer and objects started moving, and shifted in relation to one another, something closer appearing to move in front of something further. Nearer still and they began to visually smear together until objects closest to the train elongated and mixed, no longer distinct, defined, or identifiable. And if one's eyes darted to track the nearby object, the distant ones smeared. But it was all just a visual illusion caused by velocity through this landscape.

Those objects were not moving, their outlines did not change, they did not merge with other objects. It was his own speed, perspective, and the limitations of his vision that created this illusion.

A distinctly Taoist observation, he reflected. In order to be able to observe reality and not distort it as one hurtled through life, one needed to clear one's mind of preconceptions, of false fixed perspectives, and perhaps slow down. Preoccupation with any one object or thing could make one lose sight or awareness of other important things, impeding flexibility and change.

Of course, his former commander, mentor, Buddhist promoter, and occasional drinking partner and hell-raiser, the Playboy Monk, retired Major Lu Da, would claim this was a *Buddhist* observation, and that Lin Chong was "becoming a cultivated man...slowly."

Indeed, over time Lin felt he had eschewed false fixed perspectives. He no longer blindly consumed the Communist Party pabulum and regurgitated it to his officers. There was China, and the Chinese people, and then there was the Party. Despite all proclamations to the contrary, the Chinese Communist Party was not synonymous with China or the Chinese people.

This realization had not made him safer or more prosperous, but he followed the maxim of Deng Xiaoping, the chain-smoking, bridge-playing dwarf of a giant whose big thinking had liberated China from the limiting and self-serving perspective of Chairman Mao. Chairman Deng had urged to seek truth, or reality, from facts. The facts at that time had been that Soviet-style centralized planning and State ownership of all assets of production had failed the Chinese people. It was time to try something else.

After market opening in the early 1980s, the CCP served a beneficial purpose acting as a governor on the engine of the economy and market liberalization. It ensured that growth was not runaway, rampant, or rapacious and that Chinese people benefited from economic contact with foreign markets. In recent years, the facts showed the CCP was no longer

Communist at all. Although it still had some well-meaning ideologues, it was infested with self-serving and corrupt politicians who owed their seat on the gravy train to the Party, not the people they represented.

Lin Chong was not sure if one person-one vote, multi-party democracy would work yet in China, but it was clear that the Party's interests were no longer absolutely and benignly aligned with the interests of the people.

He kept his thoughts on this deeply hidden, but no doubt the psychological profile tests he had taken for security clearances and promotions would have revealed this proclivity. He imagined this was why his career was shunted into the military and not Public Security.

The military's primary mission was to protect China from foreign aggression and prevent any repetition of the country's humiliation of recent centuries. The secondary mission was to stand up against domestic uprisings and divisive elements.

Public Security, on the other hand, had the opposite mission. Ostensibly Public Security enforced the laws of the People's Republic of China. Together with the Ministry of State Security, its real primary role was to quell any domestic dissent at its inception, any opposition to the CCP. Its forces included beat cops, plain clothes investigators, "black site" undocumented prisons where troublemakers could be held while cases were developed against them, real prisons, and "reform through labor" camps. Electronic aids included a sophisticated and highly integrated CCTV domestic surveillance network deployed in all major cities even within internet cafes and, of course, the Golden Shield, known abroad as the Great Fire Wall of China, monitoring all usage of the internet and mobile telephony and "protecting" citizens from unfiltered information from outside.

Old-style censorship and boots-on-the-ground observation were replaced with a massive, ubiquitous architecture of surveillance. Public Security was well on its way to integrating a gigantic online database with an end-to-end surveillance network incorporating speech and facial recognition, CCTV, smart cards, credit card records, automobile movement, and internet surveillance technologies.

Lin Chong's beliefs strongly aligned with his mission of defending China through the military, but he was at best uncommitted to, and at worst deeply questioning of, the role of Public Security.

As the train started its deceleration on arrival in Nanjing, he turned his thoughts to the meeting into which he was heading.

Nanjing was the headquarters of the Eastern Region military command, a large, white marble, heavily guarded information fortress nicknamed White Tiger Sanctum. On a quarterly basis, he met with colleagues from Public Security and State Security to share information on cyber threats and best practices for security, surveillance, analysis, response, and preparedness. They would rotate locations every quarter and request the host of the next quarter's meeting to prepare a special presentation for the group's consideration and discussion. This time it was the military's turn as host, and Lin Chong had been requested after the last meeting to prepare an analysis of North Korea as a cyber threat to China.

After hustling through Nanjing's modernized train station, a soldier saluting crisply and bearing a sign with Lin Chong's name on it greeted him. They walked to the car, and he settled into the plush seat of the sedan for the twenty-minute ride. On arrival at the "White Tiger Sanctum," he surrendered a mobile phone. All employees and visitors were required to either carry old-style mobile phones made with neither camera, Wi-Fi/ Bluetooth, nor removable memory card, or were required to surrender their devices. At the same time, any tablets, notebook computers, digital cameras, and memory sticks had to be surrendered at the reception. Lin Chong agreed with the precautions and had instituted even stricter rules at Unit 61398. Nevertheless, here violations of this inspection could cost one a career, or worse.

He was given a green-colored digital tag allowing him to enter the building and access a limited number of doors and elevators and was escorted to the large conference room he knew well. A long oval table beautifully made of solid wood could seat about thirty-six, and the room would be full.

The host organization, in this case the People's Liberation Army, normally occupied the third of seats closest to the digital screen at the head of the room with the Public Security representatives on the left and the State Security officers on the right. Lin Chong took the seat at the head of the table as he would chair the meeting. He was only a major, and technically only deputy commander of Unit 61398; however, the commander himself was a Party apparatchik not *au fait* with cyber warfare, and hence of no real use in this gathering.

Lin Chong greeted his comrades and got the conference under way on time. After a brief review of the last meeting's minutes, each group gave a presentation on their current efforts in cyber vigilance, reviewing new tools, tactics, and outcomes they had employed or come up against in the prior quarter. These presentations were always interesting for what was shown, and what was not shown. The question on everyone's mind was, "What are they holding back, not showing us?" There was never free and unrestrained sharing of information.

The existence of Lin Chong's crowning glory, the Centipede, was unknown to anyone in this room save Lin Chong, and he had never revealed its full potential to anyone, ever. As far as a limited number of officers senior to Lin Chong were aware, Centipede was a weapon that could be activated to selectively turn off any device that was equipped with a semiconductor into which the link was deployed.

Public Security reported on a worrying rise in encrypted social networking messages. They had picked up on it when they found random digital images being shared daily between sites or individuals they had flagged for observation and vigilance. One day a fluffy kitten with a file size of 135KB, one day a car in a junkyard being crushed and 158KB file size, one day a political cartoon of the American president mocking a South American leader with 123KB file size. There was no pattern or meaning. They had deconstructed the digital images but found nothing lurking between the lines. They postulated that dissidents had created an encryption tool that would take a message and scour the internet's billions of images to find *the* one that, when the message was turned into coded pixels, matched the image. So far, they had not been able to decrypt any of the messages.

On a more upbeat note, they reported success in linking street cameras, facial recognition, and license plate recognition to be able to automatically acquire and track individuals consistently during a journey the route of which was not known to the system. To do this, they had juiced up the technology developed by a start-up in Beijing to which they had provided seed capital.

To demonstrate, they put up a series of images of Lin Chong emerging from his apartment block that very morning. The images followed him entering the subway station, crossing the turnstile, entering the subway car, transferring to the high-speed rail, sitting on the high-speed rail, being greeted at Nanjing Station, getting into the sedan, and arriving at the White Tiger Sanctum.

There was general applause. Lin Chong forced a good-natured smile as he wanly clapped hands. He was not amused.

State Security reported on successes detecting an NSA probe into China's National Space Administration servers. They noted with humor that the acronym was also NSA. Apparently, they were pfishing for information on China spy satellites launches but had been detected and repulsed.

After a tea break, Lin Chong presented a report on the cyber threat assessment of North Korea. Ostensibly allies, China had viewed Pyongyang as a foil to American adventurism in Asia, something to keep the US preoccupied in a never-ending, fortune-depleting stalemate. However, China increasingly eyed Golden Fatty the Third as a major liability, more trouble than he was worth in the best of times, and in case of brinksmanship leading to war, a true disaster for China and the region. As the squeeze was put on the fat brat and foreign exchange reserves were depleted, North Korea had stepped up cyber theft efforts to steal funds from the international banking system. They had had limited success, and so far, had not targeted China.

Lin Chong concluded that if China's security services focused on stopping more highly skilled Russian, Israeli, and US hackers, they would remain vigilant enough to staunch any North Korean effort. He also proposed that State Security employ some of the remaining goodwill between their nations to send a "technical exchange" team to Pyongyang to assess their skills and perhaps even propose some cyber war-gaming trials to test them.

Over lunch, Lin Chong sat next to Cai Jing, Chief of the Technical Department of the Ministry of State Security, who continued to gloat over their coup in stonewalling the NSA. "So, Lin Chong, when war finally comes between us and the Americans, are you really going to be able to do anything to them? Or just leave it up to us to stop them at the border?"

"You, and they, will be surprised at what we have hidden up our sleeves."

"This isn't a card trick," Cai Jing chided.

"Nor am I referring to cards, more like a concealed dart we can spring to pierce their heart. They won't know what hit them." Lin Chong trusted the power of the weapon he had created, the Centipede, unknown to Cai Jing.

Cai Jing turned the phrase over in his mind to try to figure out if Lin Chong was revealing anything new and useful or whether it was just fluff. He decided it was just fluff. "If you actually have such a weapon, perhaps we should evaluate it for use against domestic enemies."

"I'll wait for the request to filter through proper channels. Should be fun." Lin Chong yielded in such a way that he knew the attack would fall into emptiness, and he would remain unscathed.

ㄅ 人 ㄷ

ON THE APPOINTED THURSDAY EVENING, ZHENNIANG ARRIVED at the Les Saisons Hotel Shanghai.

She was dressed in a tailored, black, silk, bodycon shift that exposed sufficient thigh and cleavage to be captivating, but not cheap. High heels boosted a tall Northern Chinese frame to nearly 170 cm and set off the whole slender, buxom package. Lin Chong, usually not one to comment, had expressed surprised awe at her appearance and wished her luck in the meeting.

She carried the Guadagnini violin, Ex Contessa Cristo, in its case. It was not actually "hers." A benefactor in China had acquired it on the advice of his wealth manager, heavily insured it, and provided it to Zhang. The case and its contents were a talisman, something that made her strong and invincible, and confident that tonight's meeting would go well.

She inquired at the concierge and was told to proceed to a room on the eighth floor. Taking the elevator up, she walked to the room and knocked on the door.

An attendant admitted her into a large suite of rooms and led back into a large meeting area furnished for the meal with a table, chairs, rolling buffet, and bar, a bucket with champagne on ice waiting to be uncorked. A man rose from the table to greet her. It was Gao Yanei, alone.

She let neither surprise nor disappointment show. He liked that. Keep it neutral.

"Miss Zhang, you've come," he said sweetly. Gao was dressed in a tailored shirt and pants, collar open, with imported loafers, gold cuff links, and a Patek Philippe watch. His Lamborghini smartphone was on the table.

She assessed the situation. *So, this was the game.* It would not be the first time she had navigated a conductor's or director's or maestro's interview couch and come out on top without sacrificing her dignity. "Dinner *is* better than just coffee," she opened. "When we met before I didn't know you were a patron of the arts."

"Ah, well, at SilvermanFuchs I sometimes just luck out on the assignments. When they asked me to vet you for the soloist this season, I had no idea you were the vision of beauty I met at the health club. That makes me feel luckier still."

"So, can I play for you or would you like to eat first?"

Playing with her or eating her succulent, honeyed peach? What a delightful choice, Gao mused. "Let's at least taste our first course. Have some champagne."

Three courses with wine, coffee, dessert, and cognac later, Gao felt he was falling in love. *This woman is pure class. Smart, gorgeous, talented, and aloof. All the more challenge equals all the more satisfaction with triumph.* As his lines of inquiry began to close in for the final grasp at her panties, he asked, "Cherub Liu, what do you think of her?"

"Bringing true passion alive through the violin, or any instrument, requires experience. She's a cute teenager with great technical competence, yes, but she is not a woman who has mastered her craft. Can I show you the difference?"

Gao could not believe how well this was going. He was rock hard. "Yes. Yes, please."

"Give me a minute to freshen up." She rose and walked to the toilet. He knew it would only be a minute or two, and she would be standing there in full view for him to take.

When she returned, he was disappointed to see she was still fully clothed. She had the violin tucked under her chin and bow at the ready, standing in bare feet.

She did not announce the piece she would play. She knew now he understood absolutely nothing about music, but might appreciate a difficult piece.

As he sat on the couch, she stood above him staring into his eyes and launched into Ernst's "Last Rose of Summer" violin solo. As the bow rose and fell, her big toe rose and fell keeping time on the carpet, and he imagined it brushing his thigh, keeping time on his crotch, and he closed his eyes, appreciating her performance.

Four minutes into it, he could swear he heard two violins playing and had to open his eyes slightly to see that a twin had not joined her. *Look at her soft, delicate hand sliding up and down the neck of the violin,* he mused, *the instrument ejaculating its notes in joyful fits.* Once he tried to slide a hand up her inner thigh, but without missing a beat, she rapped his knuckles with the bow and continued playing.

At the conclusion, she stepped back, looked at the audience of one who appeared spent, and wiped a drop of sweat with her wrist. He stood up and stepped toward her expectantly. She dropped the tip of the bow and lodged it in the pit of his throat stopping his forward momentum instantly. He coughed, stepped back, and rubbed his neck.

"Don't even think about letting Cherub solo. Much more powerful and wealthier men than you have given me much more for much less than my performance tonight," she said, punctuating the statement with a pluck on the string of Ex Contessa Cristo. "As long as I am a married woman, you can't have a piece of this."

She turned, stepped into her high heels, picked up her case, and walked for the door.

⊃ 人 ⊂

GARBAGE. I BUILT MY LIFE ON GARBAGE. LI JUN USED TO THINK that said something negative about him but not anymore. *When I was twelve, I embarked on this grimy, crime-ridden, dangerous, self-serving journey that has improbably brought me here. Here, to this clean, sterile, law-abiding place where I am, proudly, responsible for a mission to save the world.* He inwardly smiled.

Staring out into the bright, tropical, Singaporean sunlight unstained by pollution, he recalled that day long ago, back in China. Back in his home-town of Hefei, a secondary city of nine million souls growing faster than its infrastructure and job creation could manage.

Shortly after his mother died of a flu going around and his father failed to return from a factory job in Shenzhen, Li Jun, who was a good student, had been thrown out of middle school for fighting and unruly behavior. Destitute, he was educated by the academy of the street together with a gang of buddies that had gravitated to him.

They all got high scores on their tests. They had already learned that collecting and recycling garbage could earn enough for instant noodles. They graduated from that course when they figured out that certain types of garbage were worth more to recycle than others.

This led them to study garbage, which garbage paid best and where to look for it. They passed this course when they realized they needed a ve-hicle to cover the distances and haul the types of garbage they knew were most precious. They found several discarded bicycles and salvaged parts and begged an uncle with a car repair shop and a welder to show them how to convert it into a three-wheeler with a platform on the back to haul stuff.

On this day, a month before his thirteenth birthday, he would pass the course in which they were currently enrolled, Expanding and Defending Your Turf 101.

Li Jun was tall for his age, already 1.7 meters, which may have been why shorter peers gravitated to him. He was also sprouting wiry facial hair, and his voice was deeper than theirs. Because he was a keen swimmer, his nickname was River Dragon, but he did not have much time to enjoy that anymore. Besides, the lake in the center of the city was too polluted, and he had no spare coin to invest in a trip to the municipal pool. Dressed in a pair of green, army-surplus shorts and a white singlet stained with sweat and grime, foam flip-flop sandals on his feet, he now got exercise pedaling the three-wheeled truck. He hauled his three friends on the back in the mornings and heaped it with their findings in the afternoon.

Today they were scouting out a new area in which to rummage. They rode up and down the residential streets between rows of gray apartment blocks built a generation before, bamboo poles slotted into brackets hanging out the windows drying laundry like some ragged, storm-torn schooner. At the end of each block was a garbage depot.

"I gotta' tell ya, Tiger Pubes, I didn't believe you before, but I think you were right," Li Jun said as they dismounted their ride.

Ni Yun did not care for the sobriquet he had acquired when his first three chest hairs had all come out with different colors, tawny, red and black, but the name stuck, and the gang persuaded him it was manly enough. "Yeah, yeah, I told you so. This part of town may look the shits, but the people living here are all upgrading their apartments inside, chucking out all kinds of goodies."

They climbed into the dumpsters to survey the bounty. The useless, wet-food garbage dumpster was easily avoided though they had long ago become accustomed to the stench. There was some separation of materials in other dumpsters: paper, plastic, glass, cans that made their job easier if they wanted to focus on just squashing cans with the can-crusher they had mounted on the truck bed.

Even better, there were heaps of discarded VHS and DVD players, televisions, flat screens, set-top boxes, personal computers, and the like.

"Gold mine!" Di Cheng squealed. He was still working into his nickname, Thin Faced Bear. He was skinny and had sunken cheeks, but with a voice that certainly had no growl to it.

"Jackpot!" echoed Bu Qing, the Flood Dragon, so named because he still wet his bed.

Kilo for kilo they got the best bang for their effort with printed circuit boards. A man they had run into one day rummaging for PCBs had told them that he would pay the urchins top dollar for old electronics and double the amount if they disassembled the stuff first. He dissolved the PCBs in large glass vats of nitric acid to extract the precious metals. The metal and plastic cases he sold for recycling.

The boys had each bought used rechargeable drills and bits at the secondhand hardware market, which they carried proudly when making their rounds. They got them out now and set upon the discarded technology, ravaging it efficiently, quickly building piles of metal, plastic, and green circuit boards. One by one, their tool batteries died, and they reached the limit they could carry on the tricycle, so they started to pack up their loot.

Around the corner of the apartment block ambled an old woman and her grown son. The woman was stooped and worn out, gray and wrinkled, yet she pushed a heavy hand trolley half-full of recyclable materials. She looked at the boys and their tricycle with suspicion and concern.

Li Jun returned the stare at the odd couple. The man was tall and able-bodied, yet he let the old lady push the trolley. Looking closer Li Jun could see the man was not right in the head. On the lower lip of a slack mouth dangled a cigarette, and his eyes were vacant.

"Scat," the old lady shouted, "We work this patch."

"I don't see any signs with your name on 'em," Li Jun replied defiantly.

He could see the man was getting twisted up inside, hands clutching at his shirt, and he looked down into himself, mouth grimacing like he had just swallowed too much bitter melon. "Ma?!" the man-boy said seeking direction to the conflict within him.

"I told you boys to scat, now scat!" she threatened, taking a coarse broom from the top of her pile and brandishing it like a pike.

"Fuck off, lady, and your retard son, too," Li Jun upped the ante as his three friends stood shoulder to shoulder with, if a little behind, him.

The son released whatever anger, confusion, and misunderstanding he was wrestling with, and half ran, half stumbled toward the boys, bellowing a loud, unintelligible shout. He did not touch the urchins, but took their tricycle, overturned it, and stomped on the spoked front wheel warping it out of round.

Li Jun loved that tricycle and became enraged. He had custom-built the masterpiece and had mounted a PVC tube section onto the downtube of the bicycle frame into which he had slid a forearm-length piece of iron pipe kept handy to ward off aggressive dogs.

Seizing the pipe, Li Jun turned and set upon the man with it, first taking out his legs, then pounding onto the arms of the man guarding his head from injury.

The old woman cried out and placed herself over the son, protecting him. "Please, no, stop. No more. We shouldn't fight over garbage!" She collapsed and wept, embracing her only son, back turned to Li Jun.

His spirit emptied out, and he felt the pipe go slack in his hands. "I'm sorry, old lady. Just let us take our stuff and go. We will leave you to this patch," he said as he looked at the sullen friends who all nodded their heads in agreement.

The old woman, still hugging her son, back to Li Jun, reached behind toward him, her hand gently but uncertainly grasping at the air until she found a wrist, which she followed to hold his hand and pull him gently towards her. When he was close, she put her arm around him. The three other scatterlings came and joined the sobbing scrum.

When they had all cried a while, each with their own thoughts, longings, and regrets, the old woman loosened her grip on them, and turned and faced Li Jun. Wiping snot and tears on her grimy sleeve, she looked him in the eye. "I am Mama Fei. This is my son, Fei Bao. What's your names?"

They each introduced themselves and their nicknames with some machismo.

"Well, my son is also called the Red Bearded Dragon," she said tugging playfully on his sideburns. He smiled with the attention. "So, we have three dragons here, a tiger, and a bear. That must be good luck in some universe. Are you boys living rough?"

"Yes, Fei Mama," Li Jun said, eyes turning to his feet.

"Well, why don't you take in with us then? We have a roof, not much of one, but between us we can probably do okay collecting stuff. I care for my son, and he helps the best he can, but there are limits. I am a good Mama, and maybe I can help you boys that way, too. Serve us all good."

Eyes squinting in the bright, Singapore sunlight, Li Jun reflected on the twenty-three intervening years. Fei Mama had organized them, kept them out of trouble, and seen to it that they got vo-tech educations relevant to recycling. She had died eight years ago, but not before seeing Li Jun and his friends all grown and gainfully employed and sending her some monthly stipend, which she socked away to care for Fei Bao.

Li Jun had joined a large plastics recycling company in Jiujiang, Jiangxi, and risen to be the general manager before his thirty-third birthday.

Then came a call from a recruiter. He found this curious because he did not have a résumé, did not seek a change in jobs. But the opportunity was compelling. A Western company was going to build a special plastics recycling plant in Singapore and needed someone who understood the process end to end to manage the construction and operation.

The recruiter was a woman named Eliza Eurisko, who, he judged, spoke remarkably good Mandarin for a foreigner. She knew that Li Jun had worked at every level of the recycling plant. Despite not being an engineer, he had designed and built custom modifications. He could repair machines and adjust formulations just as well as he could lead the teams. He was exactly the person she was looking for, a deeply experienced "all-rounder," and she added, "by the way, the job pays twice your current salary with a substantial bonus program." Li was not married, he could use the money, he thought the idea of travel and the free English lessons offered in Singapore sounded good, and the company allowed, even encouraged him, to bring his team along.

When he arrived in Singapore, the true scope of the entire project was revealed to him. Rather than feeling he had been duped, he was awed and inspired.

A philanthropist in Europe had bought three used and idle semi-submersible offshore oil rigs and towed them to Singapore. Infinity Shipyards was contracted to join them together and refit them as a floating, integrated, plastics recycling plant. Infinity was not the biggest shipyard in Singapore, but it was one of the more advanced and built its reputation on delivering retrofits and upgrades on time and on budget. Li Jun would be the Chief Project Manager overseeing the retrofit on behalf of the shareholders.

For two years, under Li Jun's watchful eye, they had focused to bring this day to fruition. With today's christening, the monstrous machine would be towed to the Western Pacific Garbage Patch, a circulating gyre of discarded floating plastic estimated to contain 35,000 tons of debris and growing exponentially.

The firm making the investment had been tight-lipped about their source of funds or business plan. Some analysts speculated that with zero cost for feedstock, zero cost for energy, no government oversight or regulatory compliance costs, zero taxes (they were Panamanian registered and operating in international waters) the business would do quite well and would go public. Others said it was a wasted effort doomed to fail either because the rigs were in the Pacific Typhoon Alley just begging to be destroyed, or they would rapidly consume the plastic patch, running out of source material long before they had made a profit.

A crowd of dignitaries and press was gathering for the christening of the new platform. For such a newsworthy event, the general manager of the shipyard had demanded that everything be spic and span for the day. Infinity Shipyards' vast concrete and metal production area lay out at the extreme Western tip of the small island city-state of Singapore, past the harbor, past Jurong, all the way out in Tuas facing the Straits of Johor. In this hypermodern, highly regulated, tropical city priding itself on cleanliness, law and order, and punctuality, even the shipyard was clean, neatly laid out, efficient, and sparkling. The intense noonday glare reflecting off the water added to the sterile, highly organized appearance. Even the stately, miles-high pillars of cumulous far out across the waters and slowly moving in for an afternoon downpour seemed timed and orderly.

On a dais up above the gathered crowd stood Li Jun, recently promoted from chief project manager to chief operations officer. Next to him was the captain, a Myanmar mariner named Aung Win, and his first mate. Behind them stood Li Jun's right-hand men, the chums from the garbage pile, the "brothers" Di Cheng, Bu Qing, and Ni Yun.

The speeches had all been given, the interviews all finished, and the only thing that remained was the finale.

The investor had declined to come to the christening and told them to bask in the glow of the public relations effort. Tasked to do the honors, Captain Aung Win took the champagne bottle attached with a long cord to one of the legs of the forward-most rig. He passed it ceremoniously to the deputy prime minister of the city-state and shook his hand as final photos were taken. The DPM threw it, but not directly at the leg. The bottle of champagne looped around disappearing behind the leg like a ribbon on a giant maypole, then appeared on the other side and smashed against the steel, a burst of foam and glass. A banner was dropped revealing the name of this unique, enormous machine.

The senior team standing on the christening podium all wore proud smiles as the Leviathan was released to the ocean.

⊃ 人 ⊂

IT HAD BEEN RARE IN THEIR MARRIAGE FOR LIN CHONG TO BE able to surprise his wife. He was just not that kind of guy. Those glorious, tear-welling moments of joy women most appreciate, he believed, having watched romantic comedies on occasion, when the man in their life goes the extra distance to be there for them at that special moment. He planned to try.

Zhang Zhenniang had won the prized soloist role in Vivaldi's *Four Seasons*. He knew that she had fought for the role, but thought it was just the usual politics in the symphony about which she had groused frequently.

For several weeks, she had been thoroughly preoccupied with practice until her fingers ached nightly. He correctly surmised that the stress being put on her joints was not unlike the martial arts hand conditioning in his youth. He got out a bowl of hot water and a bottle of liniment, the secret herbal and grain alcohol formulation inherited from his teacher. At the end of each day, before they slept, he soaked the aching hands in the hot water to enhance circulation and open pores, and he coached his precious to breathe out into her fingertips while he gently massaged the liniment into the joints.

Every morning she thanked him for this tenderness that truly helped her stay on top of the piece she was reviewing, and sometimes at night she would reward these devotions with the rapture of her body entwined in his.

Zhang Zhenniang had long ago stopped providing him with tickets to performances or expecting him to go to them. She knew he loved her, but this was a job, and she thought that eventually it must be like going to the office to visit one's spouse. Okay, once or twice, but sooner or later, no fun. This time, however, Lin Chong had managed to get tickets to the opening night without telling his wife. They were not good tickets and there would be no way she could see him in the crowd. Indeed, he had brought binoculars to see up close her ferocity as she tore into the piece.

As the curtains pulled back and the symphony warmed up, he waited for the conductor to come out and invite the night's star performer, his precious Zhenniang, to enter.

She took the stage wearing a stunning silk dress patterned in green, yellow, red, and blue, the progressive colors of the seasons, high-heeled spikes lengthening her tall and slender form.

He was so proud when she entered, his exuberant ovation exfoliated half the petals of the bouquet he had brought. Embarrassed, he put the bouquet on the ground between his feet and anxiously awaited the piece to begin.

As he had tended to her sore hands each night, she had described to him what to listen for in each of the four concertos. He felt he could appreciate this piece more than others she had struggled to share with him in the past. He could hear the rain when there was rain and thunder when there was thunder, the barking attentiveness of the shepherd's dog, the festivities of peasants celebrating a good harvest, and finally, the violin solo's cruel blast of winter wind in the fourth concerto.

When the symphony reached its finale, Lin Chong rose with the audience to encourage the three rounds of standing ovation. As the musicians vacated the stage, Lin Chong looked down and saw that he had trampled the stems of the flowers when he stood for the applause. They no longer looked fresh, romantic, or even congratulatory. He decided it was the thought that counted and picked them up as he made his way from the distant perch, through the crowds, into the theater to the backstage access. This took him several minutes.

He negotiated with the usher, the smart military uniform convincing the man that he was, indeed, the star soloist's husband, and worked his way through the halls until he found her dressing room. Steeling himself for squeals of delight, congratulations, and a round of hugs when she saw him, he fussed momentarily with the mangled flowers and then pushed the door open.

The room was a sea of grand bouquets and people. He could not find her for the crowd and pushed his way in. There were mothers with their daughters seeking autographs and encouragements to practice harder, there were well-dressed society matrons seeking to take their picture with the ingénue, and there were lots of men. He waded through people and flowers denser and more beautiful than his bouquet had ever been and finally could see Zhenniang through the throng, standing with a glass of champagne in hand and clinking the glass with another. He followed the stem of that glass up from the hand to the face of Gao Yanei.

Gao's face lit up in a triumphant smile when he saw Lin, and he toasted the man as he called across the room, "Isn't she something!" Zhenniang then caught sight of Lin Chong, and for the briefest instant, the delight that had shown on her face flickered out and was rekindled.

Lin pushed the way up the final meters to his wife's side and took her hand, putting the offering of flowers in her arms. She smiled up at him and kissed him on the cheek, "You came! What a wonderful surprise!"

Gao Yanei broke the moment, "We meet again! Seems your flowers have seen better days, friend. Luckily, she has plenty more with which to remember the night. Now, Zhenniang, we have a photo op to get to and an interview with the press."

Zhenniang looked to her husband searching for approval, or at least not a bad end to what had been a stellar evening.

"Shall I wait?" he asked, looking at the two of them.

"We are going to a party after the interview. Would you come with me?" she pleaded.

"I am just back from a conference; it has been a long day and I have an early start tomorrow. I better head home. See you there later."

"Thanks for coming," she said as he pulled his hand from hers and headed for the door, looking back at his precious with a smile of acceptance, but feeling like he had just been kicked in the solar plexus.

⊃ 人 ⊂

TYPICALLY, MILI PAREKH ORGANIZED HER DAY AND TIME IN three buckets. There were emergent situations that needed immediate and conclusive attention. There were the initiatives of the teams to identify perps. And there were her own projects to improve the tools she had brought to the NSA.

The false positive on Eunice Stravinsky had become a mini project. Ultimately the exercise had forced Mili to consider a further iteration to the package of algorithms. She had looked at each of the markers that had led the system to conclude that the code was written by Stravinsky. The conclusion was correct, but it couldn't be.

So she dug deeper. It just did not feel like the same person had written it. As she sat one day with her eyes closed, deep in thought, she tried to imagine other situations when something she had perceived to be from the same source had been altered by an intermediary. She imagined her mother's cooking, a simple recipe for dahl, which her sister could imitate, but never replicate. The sister could use the same ingredients, and she had the written recipe to follow, but it never tasted exactly the same. But neither Mili nor her sister could identify how to replicate the recipe.

She reached a dead end with this line of rumination. She thought about a nerdy programmer who teased her once at grad school. He had shown her a Land O'Lakes butter carton. With a few simple folds, the image of the chaste Native American maiden proffering the gift of ghee became a bare-breasted, buxom squaw. This new image looked like it had been done by the same artist; indeed, the lines, colors, contours *had* been done by the same artist, but folded in on itself, it was no longer the artist's work.

She had decided this was sufficiently like what she had observed in the Stravinsky coding to warrant further investigation. Was it possible to fold

33

coding within itself in such a way that it would appear to be from a particular coder, but not be? For several days, she had an analyst developing her idea and just noticed that a Post-it note she left had been read and discarded.

This was one concession Mili leveraged due to her mobility-challenged status. Neither by temperament nor agility was she inclined to "manage by walking around." She preferred to observe and comment to keep things on track and productive.

With the open understanding of her team, she had set up everyone so that she could log on at any time to see their screens, what they were working on, and leave virtual Post-it notes on their work. She would get a report on any Post-it notes read and/or discarded.

She had one large screen and two smaller ones in front of her and regularly circulated through the screens of her team members. Of course, at the NSA, it was understood someone might be secretly watching your work at any time. The difference here was that Mili's observation was not secret, and therefore not resisted by the team, who accepted that it would be difficult for her to circulate among them. For face-to-face discussions, team members came to her office.

She went to the coder's screen and looked at the work. Progress was being made; she understood the tack the analyst was taking in incorporating Mili's observations from the note.

There was a knock on her door. As was the habit for security, she blanked out her screens and looked over to see Hugh Chang Hsuehliang waiting at the door.

Hugh was like Mili. His parents had come to the US from Taiwan and worked, like her father from India, at a Silicon Valley software start-up. Hugh was a second-generation geek, dual schooled in the American educational system, and with weekend cram-school learning in Chinese language, history and culture. He had won coding competitions in his youth and dropped out of grad school to follow a friend's dream of start-up riches. The friend had worked Hugh to the bone, but the company went bust. Hugh became disillusioned and attended an NSA cocktail reception at a White Hat conference. Now he worked for her on the China team.

"Hey, boss. Got a minute?" he asked sheepishly.

She was painfully aware that minutes with Hugh turned into hours. She did not want to dismiss and discourage him, but to keep the meetings succinct she had learned to ride him. "Yesh, Hu, I have a moment before my nesht meeting."

"I wanted to give you a quick update on Persistent Threat," the code name for China's Unit 61398. Although her team was not allocated any resources for gathering information from the field about enemies, they were sent relevant intel her analysts might be able to turn into insights useful to the attribution team. The Chinese were skilled at keeping NSA hackers at bay, nor was she aware of any human assets within the Unit. They relied on her analytics to keep track.

"They have had a new intake of talent. We have identified three so far."

This was not surprising to Mili. Persistent Threat, like the NSA, was constantly recruiting to bring in the best talent not motivated purely by money. Nor was it surprising that Hugh's team had identified the recruits. Top talent in China, like elsewhere, left samples of their work in the public domain before they went dark at Persistent Threat. Memetic coding styles were analyzed early on while they could still be attributed to individuals. When new threats were identified with similar, but not exactly the same, coding styles as previous threats, Mili's algorithm could usually match the changes to an individual previously noted in their database.

"We have completed scans for these three people on the internet. Two of them have disappeared. One is still active."

A way of double-checking whether her program was accurate was to determine if the previously identified coder was still active in social media and other online activities. They had noticed that any recruits to Persistent Threat soon became invisible, their previous online identities erased with no new postings, at least under the usernames they had previously employed.

"Wish one ish still active, where?" Mili drilled down.

"He has dropped off all social media but is still logging onto his alumni website."

"So pretty mush all three have dropped off the grid."

"Yes."

"Good work. I've got that meeting to prepare for now. Thanks, Hu."

ᴐ 人 ᴄ

IT WAS A SUNDAY ONE WEEK BEFORE THE TOMB SWEEPING FESTIVAL, and Lin Chong wanted to avoid the rush. Thus, he found himself amidst throngs who had the same idea, swarming through crowd-control corrals to make it to the elevators admitting him to the upper floors of the twenty-story communal necropolis, home to the memories and ashes of 300,000 souls.

The Penglai Funerary Center was located east of Shanghai, south of the giant airport, near the sea. It was a traditional, opulent, white marble and blue-tile-roofed building modeled on the Temple of Heaven in Beijing, but four times taller and with just a touch of Suzhou architectural flavor to make it more acceptable to local eyes.

A good son, Lin had bought space here for both his mother and father next to each other. He could not afford space on the top floor but had gotten two cubbies side by side at eye level on the sixth floor, which was supposed to be a good, lucky space. He hoped his parents knew how much he loved them.

To reduce massive amounts of pollution, the government strongly discouraged some of the traditional observances. When his parents died, he had burned paper mansions, cars, computers, mobile phones, playing cards, and other things they had enjoyed in life, as well as "billions" of spirit money notes. The doors of heaven opened more easily, failing which the fires of hell burned a little cooler, if one could grease some palms. It had been several years that he had not been able to make further remittances to them this way. Now, all mourners were limited to one short, paltry stick of incense they were encouraged to burn at both ends as they made their prayers.

Having navigated the lines, Lin now stood with the lit stick held up near his forehead, eyes closed. It was his commitment to stand and commune with his parents until the stick burned down and told him it was time to go.

He sent out his prayers that mother and father had found each other in paradise and apologized one more time for not having had any children yet. He thanked his mother for having brought him into the world, raised, fed, and cared for him. He told them about his life, and Zhenniang's life, and how his career was going well so they would not worry about him.

His thoughts turned to his father and one of the last conversations he had with the man. "Dad, I have been given a big new assignment. Kind of stuck on it." He could not give the old soldier any details, nor was his father cyber-savvy, but he was a strategist and a warrior.

He did share with his father that intelligence about the Stuxnet virus deployed by the Americans and Israelis to hobble Iran's uranium processing centrifuges had been revealed. His commanding officer, Lu Da, had ordered him to develop a conceptually similar piece of code.

"I don't know where to start, Dad."

Despite being treated for lung cancer at the time, his father took a long drag on a cigarette and looked into the distance. He exhaled a plume of smoke, then coughed. "Okay. The way I see the future of intelligent warfare, whatever you are designing, think of it as your soldiers, not just a weapon. Not just a tool. It is something you can command. Right?"

"Yes, Dad." Lin was surprised he had not thought of this before.

"Then remember the maxim of the Grand Strategist."

Lin knew this was always referring to Sun Zi, the canny and deceptive general from 500 BC whose tome on the art of war resonated through the millennia, never proven wrong. "Which maxim, Dad?"

His father took another long tug on the cigarette with eyes closed. Lin could smell the sickness in his father within the smoke he exhaled.

"The acme of deploying troops is to make them formless; formless, spies cannot detect them and even the wise cannot counter them."

As Lin Chong stood in obeisant prayer in front of his parents' cubbies, the smell of the incense reminded him of his father's cigarette. "Dad, the help you gave me that day, I learned from it. I have tried to be a filial son. Your advice worked."

His solution took two years to deploy and another five to ramp up but was elegant beyond description and to the delight of his commander went far beyond what was requested. It was so deeply embedded as to be virtually undetectable and would give China an unparalleled opportunity to disrupt most any digitally controlled device. By now it was spread across the globe, even in space. The Centipede was born.

His father's comments had set the process in motion. After thinking long and hard about Sun Zi's advice, Lin Chong ordered a team to define the lowest, most elemental, most formless target level at which they could insert code, or a virus.

The Stuxnet approach, he learned, was to circulate a remarkably simple instruction in a virus form that would only be recognized and acted on as a command by a specific brand and type of device, a motor speed controller used in centrifuges. Through the controller the virus commanded the motor to spin at increasingly high RPMs until it burned out at great cost and embarrassment to the Iranian nuclear material program.

His team rejected a similar approach because it relied on chance circulation and was very device specific. Instead, they sought to move further upstream. After attending a semiconductor design, testing, and manufacturing trade show and symposium in Shanghai, he proposed to the team to look at electronic design automation tools as an entry path.

Semiconductors, the engines of the information economy, had long ago become so complex that humans alone could no longer design them. After attending the conference, he briefed the team. "Imagine an architect drawing a building blueprint by hand. One man alone could design a house, maybe a building, with perhaps a maximum of two or three dozen rooms. The rooms serve different functions and are connected by hallways and passages, not to mention the wiring and plumbing in the building. When you multiply that by a million rooms, or now a billion rooms, each with their own purpose and interconnected by passages, on several stories, it would take humans an eternity to design. Then, imagine squeezing the complexity of that building into the size of a kernel of corn and imagine the difficulty facing chip designers."

Electronic design automation (EDA) software tools had been developed to speed up the process. EDA enabled improvements to continue in processing speed, memory capacity, integrated functionality, reduced power consumption, and reduced price.

When the team understood the complexity, and how some extra code might be hidden in several of the billions of rooms, he got them to focus on the target company.

"The American firm Précis Industries is the leader in EDA tools with a market value of over $40 billion. We will infiltrate Précis and create some add-ins to their software. Rather than try to plant some virus into software on an ad hoc basis, our fix will surreptitiously add our own back door into masses of semiconductor designs. The back door will be hardwired into the chip."

His team now had their target and set about developing a strategy for infiltration.

For several months, one group tested whether breaking into Précis servers and working remotely would be a possibility and concluded this was a dead end. The company was too well prepared, guarded its intellectual property encrypted within the vaults of its IT systems too well, to make penetration likely or to go undetected. Another group launched into identifying human assets within the company that could be leveraged to facilitate the work.

This was never a preferred fallback because human assets were expensive, unreliable, and left a trail. As Lu Da had coached him, "You can't buy loyalty because you never know when it's paid for."

The team identified three potential weak links. An American, by which Lin meant a Caucasian, PhD EE from Rensselaer Polytechnic Institute, with massive student debts he had tried to pay off by gambling, compounding his problems. Like dropping boulders on someone who has fallen in a well, the Chinese saying goes. He was in a bad way, could be bought into cooperation, but otherwise seemed an unreliable horse on which to bet.

The second was a Taiwanese woman with a green card, also a PhD from Stanford, well placed within the organization. Further digging revealed that her family had no strong roots to China they could leverage, and she was a supporter of the main Taiwanese party opposing reunification with China. Unlikely to be turned.

The third weak link was from China, also a green card holder, who had done his master's degree at Tsinghua and PhD at MIT. He had been at Précis six years without a promotion, worked in the team developing next-generation design tools, and had recently been circulating his résumé on jobboards in China.

The team decided to concentrate on this third candidate, Dr. Wang Bo-lai. He turned out to be readily approachable.

Posing as an executive search consultant firm for the high-tech industry in China, they approached him about a job with a confidential client and recorded several internet video conversations with Dr. Wang.

They learned that he was well positioned in the organization, claimed to have access to the level of program they would need, and felt that as a Chinese he would never be selected to lead the team he was in, hence had not been promoted. He groused he was underpaid, and on top of all that, Précis had declined to help him apply for a visa to the US for his fiancée in Shanghai. Dr. Wang had heard about an Israeli in another department who received this assistance for his fiancée, so Wang felt this was just another example of a racist bias against him.

Still posing as executive search consultants, they said they had interested the client in Dr. Wang's background and asked when he planned to be back in Shanghai and could meet them. He confirmed a visit six weeks hence and continued to exchange emails, his excitement growing over the prospect.

During the six weeks, two groups worked in parallel under Lin's direction.

One group tracked Dr. Wang's email and mobile phone communications to learn more about him and his level of commitment to the trip. They also investigated the background of Dr. Wang's parents and the fiancée to see if any further leverage could be applied through them. They found out the fiancée was the niece of a Party member, well educated, and had high expectations around her standard of living but did not speak English. Dr. Wang's mother had suffered a stroke several months prior and was not expected to recover use of her legs.

From this they surmised that a multi-pronged approach should be used to encourage Dr. Wang's cooperation. Cooperation would lead to a guaranteed, high-paying job in China, with great face and promotion prospects. There would be no need to force his wife to adjust to life in a strange country with a language she did not understand, and it would give him more time with his mother, who would be well looked after. All this icing was layered thickly onto a patriotic cake: "you will be providing invaluable service to the Chinese people."

The second group tackled a deep dive into EDA tools, how and where they might best hide the code they needed to embed. Several team member alumni from a top local university called on the professor of semiconductor engineering to ask if they could test out the sample EDA software tool Précis had provided the university as a promotional strategy. They told the professor that they had a backer willing to provide seed funding to them if they could present a business plan to replicate Western EDA tool programs. "There is no need for China to bleed money for these products if we can create our own industry," an opinion the professor shared. He granted them access to the tool and for two weeks they experimented, chipping away at layers of programming, and obtained a sufficient understanding that they would sound competent when they talked to Dr. Wang.

Having made thorough preparations for his visit, they were well armed with lots of carrots, and a couple of stout sticks.

Wang had told the fiancée he would be interviewing for a role during his visit to Shanghai. She subsequently told him that she had heard (from her uncle) it was an important role he should be eager to consider. They did arrange for him to interview with China's largest server manufacturer, whom they knew was building a team to do their own semiconductor design. He received a verbal offer to join that company with a salary more than double what he was making at Précis and managing a team of PhDs. His mother had received a visit from a specialist at the Veteran's Hospital, who prescribed an improved treatment for her.

A dinner was arranged between Lin Chong, the leaders of the two groups who had been conducting research, and Dr. Wang. Lin revealed that he represented the government, who took an interest in his return to China. They wanted him to know that only in China could he find a prosperous future, and that China's prosperity relied on talents returning to the Motherland. They had, however, one significant request to ask of him to make all this happen, or not.

At first, Dr. Wang squirmed. He wanted to leave Précis on good terms, was what was being proposed ethical, would it get him fired? They deflected these questions reminding Wang that "the US has taken a racist swing toward reactionary, conservative politics. It is not even safe or affordable for you to raise a family there. The shabby way Précis treats you exemplifies this, denying support to your fiancée, paying you half what you are worth, not seeing your potential to manage a team, indeed not even giving you a promotion in six years. So where are the ethics in that? Time for payback."

In the end, Lin's team did not even have to strongarm Wang with doctored videos of his interviews skillfully edited to exaggerate what he had revealed, ready to be delivered anonymously to Précis and the FBI.

He asked them what they wanted. The technical challenge they communicated intrigued him professionally, and they began to discuss how it could be done.

That was seven years ago.

Dr. Wang stayed at Précis for a year and delivered on his promise, inserting a set of deeply embedded instructions into both the existing and next-generation EDA tools. During a chip design program these instructions would alert the operator to errors in the circuit routing of the chip. The error codes denoted small problems. The designer would be encouraged, as was the EDA tool's function, to accept the proposed solution. When the designer accepted the solution, the program embedded the back door into the system. If the operator did not accept, which was rare, the bug would try again at a later stage alerting to another problem. The instructions only activated for design programs of chips made to communicate externally through nearfield, Bluetooth, Wi-Fi, or ISDN.

A year into the program, they were to be able to show that chips designed with Précis EDA tools were being fabricated with the back door. They then targeted two other major competitors of Précis, succeeding in achieving the same infiltration at one of them. The weapon, code named Centipede, was deployed.

Now, seven years on, they estimated that at least seven billion infiltrated semiconductors had been sold into the market, and the number was growing by 1.5 billion a year. Thus far, besides testing later generations of chips to make sure their infiltration was still secure, China had never employed this weapon. Lin Chong did not think they would need to, but it was good to know they could knee-cap an enemy at any time without firing a shot and without spilling a drop of unnecessary blood.

Dr. Wang had moved to Shanghai, gotten married, taken the job at the server company, and continued to make great contributions there. As far as anyone knew, Précis was none the wiser.

Lin Chong could feel the ash of the incense stick close to his fingertips, and the reverie of past years since his father talked to him dissipated, returning him to the Penglai necropolis. He bowed thrice more to his parents. "Thank you, Mom, for having suffered to bring me into the world and raising me with all your love. Dad, your words, your teachings, have made me everything I am." *And your wisdom embedded into the Centipede now protects China, the country to which you devoted your life.*

CHAPTER 2

RETIRED MAJOR LU DA, THE PLAYBOY MONK, held a Bohemi-an, cut-glass tumbler of Japanese single malt up to the light and appreciat-ed the mellow, golden tone, within and without. There was a golden purity to the nightclub's chandelier lights refracted through the carefully crafted liquid. And there was a relaxed, golden purity to the peaceful, easy feeling he felt inside as an Eagles' song played in the background, and he smelled the sweet pungency of a cigar being smoked by a businessman with a host-ess at the next table.

He took a long, slow, deep breath with eyes closed. He was at that tipping point where the influence of the alcohol made him feel like he was actually getting somewhere in his meditation, his mind poised between the dis-tracted anxiety of a normal state of awareness and the fuzzy oblivion that would come with several more shots. Semiretirement and a new gig as a cyber dick agreed with him, he thought as he exhaled.

On retiring from the PLA's cyber corps, his first foray into commercial cyber investigation had generated him considerable unexpected fame.

A muckraking reporter, Dao Yi-pa, accused a large, publicly listed meat packing company by the name of Willow Holdings of shoddy quality con-trol, contaminating whole meat with a paste of fat and scraps, and having public health officials on the payroll. Willow's Chairman Zheng vehement-ly denied any such charges and to overcome negative public opinion doubled down on his advertising sponsorship of a popular, nationally televised singing competition.

Two things brought Zheng into Lu's crosshairs.

Firstly, the reporter turned up dead in a Suzhou canal leaving behind a social media suicide message expressing his shame in making a living at the expense of other people's reputations. His death was not treated with suspicion, and the authorities closed the case after it was revealed the reporter was on antidepressants, and a girlfriend said he was frequently despondent that his degree in journalism from Columbia had not been put to better use.

Secondly, Chairman Zheng abused his clout as sponsor of the singing competition to nail one of the contestants, Jin Cuilian, known by her adoring fans as Jade Lotus, a nymph not even out of high school. He had lawyers put the full-court press on her to sign a recording contract.

The first two or three months, Jade Lotus and her family were treated lavishly, put up in five-star hotels, dined in the best places, making appearances all over the country squired from city to town in a limo with a retinue of guards, marketing people, and coaches. Then, Zheng presented the tab to her family for this largess. According to the details of the contract they had signed, they were now RMB4 million in debt to him and how would she ever repay. . .?

Her father, a righteous man, retired soldier, and Great Proletarian Cultural Revolution teen rustication mate of Lu's, reached out to him to report these woes "Butcher Zheng" had inflicted on his family. Lu took immediate action. With copies of some email correspondence between Jin and Zheng, some social engineering, a little dumpster diving, and a bit of creative hacking, he was able to secure a convincing trail of evidence.

The company regularly hosted health inspectors' "training vacations" at cathouse resorts in Shenzhen and Macao. Alarmed by the impact the reporting would have on a new round of funding raising, Zheng had ordered adulteration of the meat to boost profits. He had received an email from SilvermanFuchs advisors telling him to "shutter the reporter or we will pull our investment". Then, there was the funds transfer to the security detail at a cold storage trucking company known to be a money-laundering investment of local organized crime. Orders were noted on the remittance to "*song dao gua*," a play on words meaning to deliver death to Dao. Finally, there was also proof Zheng had ordered bribes be paid to the reporter's girlfriend.

In advance of an exposé based on his investigation being published by *JingCai*, the top economics and business weekly in China, Lu established a brokerage account in Jade Lotus's name. He made a highly leveraged short bet against Willow Holdings on her behalf.

The exposé, "Uprooting the Willow," featured Lu Da's investigative efforts. Short term it resulted in the tanking of Willow's share price and long term with the arrest, trial, and conviction of Zheng and several other company officials.

Jade Lotus held a press conference for her fans announcing her return to their embrace, her ability to pay off the nefarious debt to the "Pig sticker Zheng," and getting out of her contract with him. She attributed this lucky turn to her canny belief that such an evil man and company could not sustain stock value growth long term. The press ate it up and propelled her to new highs.

Business streamed in for Lu Da as well. The money and satisfaction of working in the private sector was surely a draw, but Lu Da sometimes missed his "army days" when he had been a mentor to Lin Chong. The recruit had been the best talent he had ever led: intelligent, ultrafast in coding, cool in response to threats, and a principled leader of his team. He continued to hold a soft place in his heart for the lad and was always ready to lend an ear to the boy.In their last evening of drinks and chat, Lin Chong shared worries that another man might be trying to seduce his wife. Lu knew Zhang Zhenniang well and felt she would live up to her name, True Maiden, if only because the pursuit of musical perfection permitted her no mundane distractions, and she reveled in the primal, physical passion Lin Chong ignited. He reassured Lin Chong and urged him to stay focused.

Tonight's meeting was on a different subject altogether.

A week ago, a total stranger had approached Lu Da. In a world where everyone had some digital identity, some contrail of cyber-condensation, this man had none. Nothing, no biometrics trail, no spending trail, no social or academic trail that Lu could detect. Nothing. This made the man's story even more convincing. He said he had something that could only be delivered into the hand of Lin Chong. Could Lu Da arrange a meeting? After coming up with nothing on the man and conferring with Lin, they had agreed to meet at the Club Beamer.

Prompt to the minute, both men entered the club at the same time, walked back into the relative darkness toward the private booth Lu occupied, and when they were standing by the table side by side, looked at each other, saying together, "You must be . . .," then laughed as they sat down.

Lin Chong broke the informality. "I have taken this meeting based on the referral of my old friend and mentor, Major Lu Da. I understand you have something for me. I trust it will not waste his time or mine. Firstly, since you know who we are, who are you?"

"Who I am is unimportant. What I am is marginally important. What I have for you is *vitally* important," the man said as a waiter brought two more shots of single malt in the cut- glass tumblers and a bucket of ice. The man, ordinary in every way except for eyes that vacuumed in all the details of his surroundings, stopped talking until the waiter had finished and retreated from earshot. "I have been serving State Security in a deep undercover operation for several years. The mission has been open ended. Infiltrate a group of cyber-criminals known to be tied to Taiwanese gangsters and determine if they are linked to any other foreign interests or political activists. Through the years, some arrests have been made you will have read about, some big Taiwanese and Chinese call centers in Africa that were defrauding our people out of their retirement savings. A bunch of extraditions."

Both men nodded.

"Recently, I have been on the run with this group, still undercover, and learned that they have, indeed, joined up with some foreign interests. In fact, they have a detailed plan to disrupt the next Party Congress."

Wannabes were always thinking about disrupting the Congress, and State Security was always far ahead of them. Both officers raised their eyebrows skeptically.

The stranger noted their disdain. "It's different this time. I've seen the plan, I have a copy of the tools they will use to disrupt it, I know how and when."

"So why not turn it over to your handlers at State Security? You be the hero," Lin Chong prodded.

The man looked left and right, then leaned in towards them, head tilted askance. "This plan, it relies on the cooperation of some heavy hitter in State Security. I don't know who I can trust. It doesn't seem to include people from the military, so I trust you guys. And it's the US that supplied the hacking tools to do the disruption, calling it Operation Broadsword. That makes it a foreign attack on us, so you guys need to know about it."

The two majors looked at each other trying to read what the other was thinking. "Okay. What do you propose we do to help?" Lin Chong asked.

"I have everything you need here on a thumb drive. It should be delivered only into the hands of General Gao Qiu. No one else."

"Then why don't you do just that?"

"I can't get anywhere near him without State Security having some record of it. I am all in for saving our country, but I am not going to be offed by some traitor as thanks for my effort." He looked at the two men letting the words sink in. "The files are encrypted. Only General Gao can open them, and only three tries on the password, or the files are dumped."

"So, you know General Gao?" Lu Da asked.

"He won't remember me, but our paths have crossed. The password is the name and rank of the first guy who ever served as Gao's full-time driver, back when he was a colonel. Five characters."

"Is that you?"

"No, but I knew the guy. The General will remember it." He placed his palm on the table and slid it toward Lin Chong. Moving the hand aside, he left a key-shaped thumb drive. "Remember, deliver this only into the hands of General Gao, no one else."

ꓤ 人 ꓛ

HIT THE GROUND RUNNING, NANCY NILLSON REMINDED HERself as the meeting with the Chinese prepared to enter "Round 2." That was how the US president's chief of staff had characterized her mission.

President Mick Coin had been sworn in two months ago, and Nillson's appointment was a catch-up position. She had been fast-tracked to the top of Coin's pick list based on the strong recommendation of his pastor, Ronny Roper. And the pastor, on the board of the Devon Alliance, had put her at the top of *his* list because she had what he called the "Three Ts": she was talented, telegenic, and theological. She had completed her master's in environmental science at Georgetown, so she could be called an "environmental scientist" in the press releases. The Devon Alliance had given her a full-ride scholarship at the Evangelical University of the South to write her PhD dissertation applying Justice Scalia's yardsticks for constitutional originalism to the debate over the Dominion Mandate, or Genesis 1:28.

During the campaign, she appeared frequently on talk shows defending then-candidate, now President, Coin's views on environmentalism. Her full-throated support of policies to "resist the Green Dragon" did not go unnoticed.

He ran on a platform that the environment was a place where people lived, that God gave man dominion over the earth and all its plant, animal, and mineral resources. The fundamental purpose of environmental policy was to support man's efforts to be fruitful and multiply. Efforts of green movements ignored God's will and placed man in a subordinate role to be tyrannized by nature, a reversion to pantheism.

"Hitting the ground running" meant boarding a plane to Beijing three days after confirmation of her position as advisor on environmental science and policy to the president.

The state of Alaska was seeking punitive damages against China. Scientists in the state had documented rising pollution levels, and five years prior had predicted this would begin to have impacts on Alaska's pristine environment. The "canary in the coal mine" were lichens and mosses growing in Alaskan aboriginal forests. They had begun to die-off. Their further investigation determined it was specifically airborne pollution from China that caused the die-off. Impacts to the Alaskan tourism and logging industries were being estimated in the billions of dollars.

Having run on a platform of standing up to Chinese Communist atheist bullying, Coin wanted to turn the pressure up on all fronts and dispatched Nancy to Beijing.

She sat across from Meredith Cummins, the Commissioner of the Department of Environmental Conservation for the great state of Alaska in the Beijing hotel coffee shop and watched Cummins pick and frown at her breakfast.

Cummins fumbled with the slippery dumpling on the plate. "Nancy, can't you just *not wait* to get out of here?" she opined. "I mean, between the unbreathable air, the rude crowds, and what passes for breakfast! Really!?!"

Nancy stared back, her steely gaze competing with her polite smile and thought, *We're here to do a job. To negotiate as hard as we can to get some benefit for the people of Alaska. I am way too much on point to worry about the food or pollution. I am much more worried that you and your team have not prepared well. Normally, if a state is lucky, someone from the State Department might be interested enough in your case to lend an ear. Today the weight of the White House has been invested in you by sending me. Wake up, get ready, and do your. . .* she willed her mind from using the F word *. . .job.*

Nancy's forced smile won out as she voiced, "Chin up, Meredith. They can smell your anxiety to return home and use it to push us to make unnecessary concessions just to be able to leave. I am only an observer, here to lend weight to your case, but you need to drive this."

Meredith considered the woman sitting across the table. Half Meredith's age, gorgeous, with sculpted, honey-colored tresses hanging to her shoulders and green eyes, conservatively but attractively dressed, she was confident beyond her years. Meredith gave in to the jealousy she felt. *How could this woman have achieved so much so fast, working in the Oval Office, and I am at the end of my career, old, undistinguished, constantly stretched, pulled, and abused by the environmentalists and the resource companies? What has she got that I didn't have?* "Yeah. You're right. Just like sharks smell blood," she conceded. "Okay, let's go back and try to get something out of 'em."

They got up from the table, walked out of the hotel into Beijing's crisp, dry, hazy air and crossed the street filled with ultramodern architecture, none of the buildings smaller or older than Anchorage's largest or newest, not to mention Juneau's. Meredith felt like a poor country cousin visiting the rich city folk and asking for a hand-out.

つ 人 ⊏

LIN CHONG FROWNED AS HE ADJUSTED HIS TIE AND MEDALS. HE wanted to look spot-on the professional soldier today. Gazing in the mirror, he satisfied himself that he had not forgotten anything he went out into the breakfast area. Zhenniang was attired in a négligée drinking a cup of coffee at the dining table. Shanghai's hazy, orange, morning sunlight came through the window as a beam and fell right onto her body, illuminating each secret curve and proud promontory.

"Do you have to go out so early today?" she pouted playfully as she twirled a curl of hair around her fingers. "Can the soldier come and play?"

He looked at her and smiled. The night before had been electric, and he regretted he could not succumb to her tease this morning. "Precious, nothing would make me happier. But if I am late today, the general will cut my nuts off, and then where would we be?" he laughed.

"So today you are meeting the big man?"

"Yep, cleared it through his aide. Got to make the 8 a.m. to Nanjing. I'll grab breakfast on the way." He walked over to where she sat, looked down at her looking up, her negligée's bodice open to his view, and leaned over and kissed her on the mouth, their tongues briefly chasing each other in a hot flutter. "My lady, I must be gone, but save that thought for me." Lin

Chong put on an officer's hat, stood ready at inspection before her for a moment, then turned on point and left.

Lin Chong was normally not anxious about meeting senior officers. He knew he was the best at what he did, and his contributions were appreciated by his commander and useful to the defense of the country.

Today was different. His stomach was queasy, and the breakfast he had taken onto the high-speed rail did not sit well. He was meeting General Gao Qiu, the head of the Eastern Command, a man who could make or break Lin's career prospects, and he was being summoned. The day before, while trying to hack the password and open the files on the key- shaped thumb drive to gauge their worth before passing them on, he had a call from General Gao's aide, a man named Lu Qian. The aide said the general had become aware Lin Chong recently acquired a "precious broadsword," and being a collector of such things, the general wanted to see it. Lin Chong was requested to come the next day to Nanjing. Lin Chong was surprised by the call, not expecting that the undercover agent would have used a back channel to close the loop and wondered if Lin himself was the one being tested here. *For what? Reliability, loyalty, some new mission?*

On arriving at the Eastern Region military command, Lin once again admired the clean, modern lines of the new, white marble building. It reminded him how great China was, and of the importance of defending the homeland. The pride he felt settled his stomach, straightened him up, and put a snap in his stride as he entered the building and stopped at the reception.

Captain Lu Qian came to the lobby. "Major, welcome to the Eastern Command. Let me escort you in."

The receptionist requested that Lin Chong surrender his mobile phone and other devices. Lin took out the phone and gave it to them. He was issued a pass to wear around his neck and noticed that the color coding was different from those given to him for the quarterly conference meetings denoting a higher level of security clearance. They proceeded through the security check. Lin removed keys from his pocket and got them back after the scan.

"I thought we would be meeting General Gao here in one of the meeting rooms?" he asked.

"No, Major, he doesn't meet people *here*," the tone of the answer communicating "here" was beneath the general's dignity and that he expected to impress or intimidate those he met on his own turf.

Entering a bank of elevators, Lu Qian went to one that did not have call buttons, only a card scanner. This was an express elevator. "Does this go straight to General Gao's office?" Lin asked.

"No. It goes direct to the floor below his office. He has a private elevator. Visitors must take the stairs the last floor to see him. A precaution, you understand."

This also subliminally communicated the subordination of any visitors to General Gao; they had to walk the last stage, had to climb to his level under their own power, none could gracefully glide into a position on par with him.

As the elevator doors opened, Lu Qian extended a hand through the portal and said with a smile, "Welcome to the *real* White Tiger Sanctum."

Lin Chong stepped into the room. On each side of the elevator were armed guards at attention. Though their uniforms and helmets were highly polished, refined, showy, and symbolic, the weapons they carried (safeties off, he noted) were practical: the QBZ-95 5.8mm Bullpup Assault rifle and pistols, as well as several flash-bangs, tear gas, and grenade canisters each. The large room was darkened with most light coming from flat-screen monitors on desks and a large bank of them covering one wall over thirty meters long.

A quick scan of the visuals on these suggested to Lin Chong that the information was roughly divided into five groups. There were screens visualizing the activity level, state of readiness, deployments, and logistics of each of the three major branches, army, navy, and air force. One other section seemed to rotate between other areas of the service while the last was focused on threats. Here, he imagined, was where the big decisions would be made if it ever came to war. The thought of it both thrilled and repulsed him.

"Follow me," Lu Qian said as he walked to the side of the room and started up a stainless-steel spiral staircase. At the top of the stairs were two additional armed guards. Lu Qian held his pass to be scanned and when the door opened led Lin Chong in. "General Gao will be with you in a moment. Please wait here." Lu Qian walked to the far side of the room, used his pass on a scanner, and the general's private elevator door opened. He entered it, the door closed, and Lin Chong was left alone.

The office was a contrast to the dark strategy room a floor below. It had a wide, tall window with a view of the countryside in the outskirts of Nanjing through which morning sunlight spilled into the room. The furnishings were modern, expensive, hewn from solid, tropical hardwoods. It was carpeted and on one side of the wall was a bookcase filled with accolades General Gao had earned through the years, some antique Chinese swords, and some maps.

Against another wall was an aquarium with one large, solitary Arowana fish, its iridescent golden scales subtly changing hue as it lazily breathed and fluttered its pectoral fins. He knew these fish represented strong male energy and could sell for up to $600,000 and imagined this specimen to be representative of the finest. There was a small plaque on the aquarium saying the fish had been a gift from the King of Thailand. He shook his head at the extravagance. *Not my father's PLA.*

Lin Chong's leisurely examination of the room was interrupted by the sound of the elevator door swishing open. He snapped to attention and saluted as he watched General Gao emerge from the elevator, walk toward the desk, place an attaché case down, and then turn to face the room hunched over papers on his desk. Lin Chong remained rigid in his salute, his face the mask of a ready warrior, and waited silently for recognition.

Momentarily, General Gao looked up from the desk and started, his body launching backward with the surprise, and spat, "Who the fuck are you!?"

Lin Chong was confused. "Sir. Major Lin Chong, Unit 61398, reporting as ordered, sir!"

Gao stepped back to the desk and pressed a button on the phone console. "Guards! Emergency!"

The look of the ready warrior on his face crumbled into one of shock and dread, but Lin Chong remained saluting. "General, sir!?!"

The door slid open and the two guards bounded in, rifles raised, and crossed the room to Lin Chong, one standing to his left and the other ahead of him, between the general and Lin Chong.

"This man has no business being in my office. Search him," the general ordered.

The man to Lin Chong's left stepped behind him and forcibly yanked his arms out of the salute he was frozen in and handcuffed him behind his back with a plastic pull-tie. He then frisked him. Finding nothing hidden, he emptied out the pockets of Lin Chong's pants. The only contents were a wallet, some coins, and his key chain.

"Sir, there is nothing here, sir," the guard reported to the general. "His military ID in the wallet says he is Major Lin Chong."

"He told me he is with Unit 61398. Check the key chain carefully," Gao ordered.

"General, sir," Lin Chong spoke up. "Your aide, Captain Lu Qian, called me and ordered me to come here today.He brought me into this room!"

"My aide's name is Colonel Yu Zhi. Not Lu Qian. If such a person brought you here, he must be your coconspirator."

The guard was busy complying with the general's order, taking each key and examining it. One key, though, was not quite right, and he pulled on the bit of the key. It slid off to reveal a mini-USB connector built into the shoulder of the key. "Sir, he is carrying a hidden memory stick."

"So, we have a spy here. Take this man to the stockade. He is not to speak with anyone, *anyone*, without my express authorization. Tell the stockade to await my orders to have him transported off-site."

Lin Chong slumped, his massively strong legs gone weak, formidable arms gone limp. The guards put a black bag over his head and dragged him out of the room as his voice weakly protested, "General, sir?"

⊃ 人 ⊂

TRAINED AS HE WAS IN INTELLIGENCE GATHERING, KEEPING hidden, and ferreting out those who were hidden, Lu Da always had a back-up plan. Besides the Playboy Monk, Sagacious Lu was another sobriquet he was known by, for precisely this reason. Wisdom was being able to go on living in the here and now even as one was prepared for the come what may.

Lin Chong had kept him abreast of preparations to reach out to General Gao and of the unexpected phone call summoning him to the White Tiger Sanctum. He knew that the meeting was to have taken place yesterday morning, and Lin Chong had promised to reach out to him on the back end to let him know all had gone well, and the general was pleased with his proactive efforts on behalf of the State.

That call had not been received. And now, Lu Da noted he was under increased surveillance and control.

Today his desk-top computer no longer allowed access to sites he had regularly trolled. The receptionist guard in the lobby of his apartment block had been changed since the day before to someone looking much tougher, experienced, and alert. Despite being an impediment to traffic, a black sedan with darkened windows was parked across from the exit of the apartment car park and in sight of people walking out the front door.

Finally, Zhenniang called him and said Lin Chong had not returned home, had not returned her calls, did Lu Da know where he was?

So, "come what may" had come, he decided.

He went to his closet and took out a backpack prepared for the unforeseen. In it was everything he hoped he would need to disappear.

He took the elevator to the car park, got into his BMW 5 series, and pulled into traffic, noting that the sedan soon started up and kept pace behind him, replaced after three kilometers by another car. He headed across the river to Puxi in the old part of Shanghai and parked the vehicle in a multilevel car park serving the tourist visitors to the Yuyuan Garden district.

Leaving the car, he walked north along Old School Road crowded with tourists from across China and the world. They were milling slowly, sorting through the long rows of shops selling tourist bric-a-brac, souvenirs, snacks, handicrafts, jewelry, and purported antiques. Yuyuan Garden and its environs had been built in the Ming Dynasty and, even then, was a tourist draw with its temples, gardens, shops, and eateries. It retained its traditional flavor despite now having a Starbucks located right at its heart.

Lu Da had not seen anyone following him but the same crowds that obscured him, obscured them as well. He ducked into a deep, poorly lit "antique shop" and combed its depths, eyes on the front of the store. He slung the pack off his back and removed sunglasses, a Chicago Bulls cap, and a folding, white, fiberglass cane from it. In one smooth move, he removed and reversed his windbreaker from its bright-red side to its navy-blue side, put the pack on his frontside, pulled the windbreaker back on, and zipped it up over the pack.

He limped slowly out of the store, now an old, fat, blind man, struggling with his girth. Another 50 meters ahead, at the intersection of Old School Road and Yuyuan New Road, was the Mount Wutai Pavilion, a shop selling high-quality Buddhist art, prayer accessories, statues, and incense, as well as some cheap related items for tourists, such as wide-brimmed straw hats and sandalwood fans.

Lu Da had been introduced to its owner by Zhao Yuan-wai, a wealthy and pious man who had taken the young singer Jade Lotus's hand in marriage. He was a patron of the shop and instructed the owner, Zhizhen, to treat Lu Da with respect. Lu had visited the store several times to discuss principles of Buddhist logic with the owner. The shop had a front and side door as well as a private office space. Lu entered the shop and asked cheerfully if the boss was around. The clerk nodded with her head to suggest the boss was back in his office. Lu walked in and rapped on the doorframe. "Master Zhizhen, can I trouble you?"

"Sagacious! How are you?" the older gentleman returned warmly, ushering him in and closing the door.

"Well, friend, I have had better lives." They both laughed at the allusion to reincarnation.

"Anything I can help with?"

"The less you know or help, the safer. Better yet if I was never even here. I am still working on my Karma, and evil from my past is pursuing me."

"Enough said. Let me know anything you want or need, otherwise, you were never here. Do you want me to let Squire Zhao," the aristocratic nickname of the man who had wed Jade Lotus, "know you need his help?"

"Not yet, thanks. Right now, all I need is fifteen minutes in your bathroom, for you to turn off and erase any security cameras you might have on, and for you to give me the largest sedge hat you have for sale and a pair of monk's slippers. Size 42 will do."

"Easily done. Give me a moment." Zhizhen turned around and erased that week's security camera file and turned the system off, then left the office closing the door behind him.

Lu Da stepped into the small toilet and stripped to his underwear. He took an electric hair trimmer out of the backpack and began to shave his head. He was midfifties and proud of a full head of dark hair. It pained him to take the tonsure but getting out of this fix was going to require more than just a haircut.

He pulled on a pair of loose-cut gray trousers drawn in at the ankles and unrolled from the backpack and donned the gray robes of a Chinese Buddhist monk. The prayer beads he always wore around his neck were pulled out from under his T-shirt to be displayed in front of the robe. He pulled a brass singing bowl and its mallet from the pack.

He turned the pack inside out converting it from a backpack to a monk's haversack with prayers embroidered on the outside and down the single shoulder strap. Remaining in the bag was a wig, his street clothes, the folding cane, and three unused mobile phones, and concealed in pockets RMB50,000 in cash, eight taels of gold, three sets of identification papers, and a dozen stored value cards for the subway and train network.

Zhizhen returned with the slippers and hat, a tourist version of a grass, conical rice farmer's hat with the characters for "Long Live Chairman Mao" printed in garish, red letters. As soon as he saw Lu's metamorphosis, he said, "Nope, wrong hat," turned around, closed the door, and came back a minute later.

This time he was carrying a rustic and authentic antique traveler's hat, conical to be sure, but with a brim the size of a small umbrella and woven from wicker and long, golden, dried leaves. "A true pilgrim's hat, that's what you want."

"Thank you, Master Zhizhen. Please forget I was here. I will trouble you no further." He clasped his hands together in prayer and bowed to the man, who returned the obeisance, then exited quietly through the side door.

For the remainder of the day, Lu Da stood near the entrance to the Starbucks, facing the pond and the Huxin Pavilion, his singing bowl in his palm, the haversack and a small plate at his feet, the wide hat on his head sheltering his face from the sun and onlookers, but allowing him to see 180 degrees. Whenever some kind person dropped a coin on his plate, he would recite a sutra and slowly rub the mallet around the circumference of the bowl letting its pure tone send a prayer to heaven on behalf of the generous soul. He was passed by thousands of people that afternoon. Only five heard the bowl sing for them. *Such was the spirit of people in Shanghai, nay, all of China*, he lamented. *Truly, the righteous and kind have no quarter here.*

⊃ 人 ⊏

IT TOOK A DAY FOR LIN CHONG TO GATHER HIS WITS. ONE DAY of ruminating in a depressed slump about his condition. *What have I done to deserve this? How can I see justice served?* Finally, pieces to this hellacious puzzle fell into place.

He had been taken to the stockade in the basement of the Eastern Command building and thrown into a cell with the black bag still on his head and wrists tied. His requests for water and to use the toilet were denied. But he did not have long to wait.

After what he guessed was two or three hours, two men were ushered in with orders from General Gao to transfer him. They hauled him into a van and drove about an hour. Finally, they stopped, and he heard them talk into a speaker and the creak of a metal gate swing open.

The van pulled in only a short distance and did not go onto a ramp of a covered carpark. He was hauled into a building and down a flight of steps and cast into a dark room. He could smell the moldy dank of poorly set concrete.

From all this, he guessed he was in a walled compound inside a relatively small building, not a high rise, and that it was either fairly new, or poorly built.

But who runs it? Am I in a formal military stockade awaiting formal military proceedings? Or is this one of the privately run black houses used to silence critics and complainers while cases are built against them? Or am I completely off the legal grid?

Who is Lu Qian, and why was I set up by the guy who passed me the thumb drive? Doesn't matter, I am in hot water. Even if I am being detained within the military court system, they can hold me for thirty-seven days without charges or telling anyone, and at the end of that time, if they still suspect me of wrongdoing, they can hold me indefinitely while a case is built. What am I talking about, building a case?! I've been fucked over. I have "broken the law" and they can prove it. I can prove nothing.

On the evening of the first day, the door opened, two men walked in the darkened room, removed the black hood, and left the room turning on the lights. He was in a bare, concrete space with no windows. In its center was a 30 mm diameter steel pipe running from floor to ceiling and anchored sturdily. Next to it was a student's chair with a folding desk attached.

Shortly, the two men returned, and without saying a word they answered his vexing question. It was Captain Lu Qian and a tough he vaguely remembered from the run-in with Gao Yanei at the fitness studio some months before, whom he later learned was named Fu An.

He wished he had gone to his grave not knowing this answer; better that they could have just killed him with the black hood over his head. Better not to believe, even for a moment, that his Zhenniang somehow conspired with Gao Yanei to get him out of the way. That ripped into his heart like no shock he had felt when he was arrested in the general's office.

He crumbled once again, inside and out.

They dragged him up, let him relieve himself in the toilet, and brought in a steel tray with a scoop of rice and a mix of vegetables and pork on it. His hands were then cuffed in front of him with his arms around the pole in the center of the room. The handcuffs had a long chain connecting them, affording enough freedom to carefully feed himself sitting at the desk, still sobbing.

The two louts sat in earshot smoking as he tried to force down some food. "What a chickenshit toy soldier," Fu An, the ex-special forces sergeant, quipped. "Fucking blubbering mess."

"Ah, he's just in shock is all. I have seen his kind before. Little Red Guards following all the rules in the Little Red Book, sanctified Communist proles. They pretend to be hard as steel and passionate as fire. The world has changed, but they just don't get it," said Lu Qian tiredly.

"He certainly softened up since the first time I saw him," Fu An chuckled. "Now that her old man is a traitor, I hope the wife does, too. She's had a steel vise clamped over that cunt of hers and just won't let The Flower Lord come a knockin' on her jade gate."

"This hare-brained scheme of yours better work," Lu spat. "I don't know how you persuaded the general it was a good idea, but. . ."

"You have no fucking idea what's at stake," the sergeant brusquely interrupted the captain. "Yanei fell hard for this filly, and it's like he'll die if he can't mount her. It's become an obsession for him, and all the work he does for his father is at risk. You're just lucky to have been selected for a 'special mission.' Do the old man a solid. Trust me, he'll owe you."

"Only when we finish," Lu grumbled, "only when we finish." Looking at Lin Chong slumped over the food tray, he stood up and walked over to gather the remainder.

Lin Chong continued looking despondent, an empty, wasted vessel. But now it was just an act. He had learned all he needed to know. These bastards of whores were working for General Gao so his philandering son could sport with Zhenniang. Lin had done nothing wrong, they were treasonous dogs, and Zhenniang remained true to him. He was outside of the formal legal system, and they would no doubt seek a way to dispose of him. *Well, I am not known as the Panther Head for nothing*, he resolved.

⊃ 人 ⊂

THE SURVEILLANCE SYSTEM ERECTED IN CHINA WAS SOPHISTIcated, extensive, and elaborate, hard to evade but not impossible. Sagacious Lu found a place to hunker down, gather his wits, call in some favors, and try to find out what the hell had happened to Lin Chong.

First was finding a haven. All normal hotels and guest houses were required to copy identification papers and report them to the authorities. He avoided that option and instead reached out to Squire Zhao via an internet phone app. "Squire, how goes it? Sagacious here, and I need a hand in a delicate situation."

"Sagacious. Nice to hear from you. What's up?"

"I want to take a vacation today in the Shanghai to Nanjing area and want some peace and quiet. No disturbances. I know you have a bunch of places and wonder if I could trouble you."

Zhao grasped the meaning of everything Lu had said and responded jovially, "I bought a place in Nanjing and furnished it quite lavishly, but frankly I have never even visited it. Shame for it to go to waste. I'll text the address and door and Wi-Fi passcodes to this account you are calling on. You just show up, the guards will be expecting you, well, expecting *me* actually. They'll treat you fine. This is a luxury, one percenter high-rise building for people who expect deference, discretion, and privilege. Should be perfect for you."

"You're the best. My regards to Jade Lotus. I heard her new record online the other day. It's a winner."

"Yes, it's heading straight to the top of the charts. No worries on the apartment. Use it as long as you want. See you again soon."

Even that simple outreach on a mobile device was fraught with the danger of detection and interdiction especially if, for some reason unbeknownst to Lu, Zhao Yuanwai was himself under surveillance.

There were internet cafés. However, by law all internet cafés were required to register one's identity card number and had video surveillance. Additionally, the Golden Shield automatically monitored new café registrants, what they viewed online versus their origin in China, search terms and words being used. If the system detected anything that it might deem suspicious, it would automatically, without the intervention of a human, order a wider investigation and surveillance of the person of interest. If Zhao was under surveillance, callers would automatically be similarly investigated until the system determined they were not people of interest. This would make use of that bogus identity harder for him.

The system was designed to detect and monitor the activities of "bad actors," meaning law breakers, terrorists, criminals, and organized gangsters, to give the security authorities a leg up in preventing crime. That was all well and good for the country and keeping people safe. But when "law breakers" include someone grousing about a new policy of the Party, pointing out a fundamental contradiction between policy and execution or between yesterday's Party line versus today's Party line, that was, at best, questionable. Worse still was the situation Lu Da was in. He was acting out of self-preservation to avoid extrajudicial harassment.

Technically, all mobile phone SIM card accounts and internet accounts had to be registered with the authorities. He had three mobile phones registered to bogus identities. Each was fully enrolled for electronic payment with a generous balance of cash to burn, search tools, internet phone and messaging, and an encrypted online storage account in which he kept back-up files, contacts, tools, and past cybercrime investigations reports he had produced. Similar to using internet cafes, he had to be cautious about what he searched for, which websites he passed through, who he contacted, lest these identities be flagged by the Golden Shield for further monitoring.

Then there was the problem of physical movement. If his facial identity was being sought by the authorities, he needed to disguise or trick the recognition software. Not easy, but not impossible. He also needed to avoid having his face associated with any new identity. This could happen as easily as buying a train ticket with a new burner phone's electronic payment at the ticket queue in the train station. The system automatically recorded the face of each ticket purchaser and would cross-check the database facial identity.

This meant the highly automated and surveilled rail and air travel were out. He would rely on car-sharing networks with which his identities were pre-registered, taxis, buses, and subways.

On departing from the afternoon of begging at Yuyuan Garden, he had called Squire Zhao, then taken public transport to the inter-city express bus terminal. After buying a ticket from Shanghai to Nanjing and before boarding, he went into the toilet a monk and emerged the fat, old, blind man with a limp. He arrived at Zhao's apartment block, the Seven Treasures Manor, in the late evening.

Zhao had not been exaggerating. The building was in an unbeatable location with Xuanwu Lake at its foot and the Bell Mountain Scenic Area at its back: green, quiet, and with never-to-be-obstructed views yet only ten minutes to the city center. His unit was a generous, four-bedroom penthouse that had sunrise views of the scenic area and sunset views of the lake beyond a twenty-meter infinity swimming pool. It was furnished with modern, Scandinavian, teak furniture, not made in China but imported from Scandinavia. The electronics and entertainment equipment included a cable- and internet-connected, eighty-inch flat-screen television in each bedroom, and the living room media center further boosted with a Bang & Olufsen home theater audio and karaoke system. The kitchen and dining room were fully equipped, but there was no food in the fridge or shelves.

Zhao's internet router accessed the internet through a VPN. Although not the prophylactic it was purported to be—the government was easily capable of breaking into it— the virtual private network provided a modicum of safety and obscurity to online searches and communications. He telephoned out for some food delivery and got right to work.

He made three calls, each one at some risk to himself, with old comrades still in the system who trusted Lu completely or who held grudges against General Gao. The third call yielded useful intel. He reached Sun Ding, a senior law clerk attached to the military courts for the Eastern Command. His job was to check and forward paperwork for those arrested and under investigation.

Prior to General Gao's ascension to the top leadership position, Sun had been a defense counsel representing those arrested. He was punished and demoted when he had over-zealously and effectively defended someone who had crossed General Gao. His nickname was Siddhartha Sun due to a known propensity for compassion and justice.

"Siddhartha, Sagacious here, long time no see."

"Indeed, Sagacious. A long time, but not as long as everyone else who seems to have forgotten me after my demotion," he said sullenly. "At least you've visited a couple of times."

"Anyone who forsakes you is just a fart-sniffing insect with their nose buried high up someone's butt cheeks." General Gao's surname meant "high up."

Sun harrumphed at the subtle cleverness of the barb. "To what do I owe the honor?"

"I am trying to catch up with a friend of mine who visited yesterday."

Sun implicitly knew that Lu was thus inquiring about someone who had *not* returned from a visit to the White Tiger Sanctum.

"Funny you should ask. A former acolyte of yours visited yesterday. I processed some transport and accommodation paperwork for him requested by the old man."

"Do you know which hotel he's staying in?"

"I should be able to find the details."

"You live up to your name, Siddhartha. Many thanks. If you could send me the details, it would be much appreciated."

"The least I can do. Don't be a stranger."

The next morning, Lu's mobile device pinged with an incoming message from Sun, simply a link to a Baidu map address. Lu clicked on it. It was a residential district in the city of Saddle Mountain, an hour's drive due south of Nanjing. The community was a neighborhood of upper-middle-class, walled villas called Wild Boar Forest.

He set out for Saddle Mountain in a GoGoLyte carshare vehicle. In the outskirts of the town, he stopped in a hardware store and bought a large, cheap, folding sunhat, a high-visibility street worker's vest, a spade, a broom, a dustpan with a handle, and a pair bolt-cutters. He drove closer to the Wild Boar Forest residential development, found a parking space in a surveillance blind spot, and walked in the rest of the way, a hat and high-visibility vest on, broom, spade, and dustpan over his shoulder.

As he approached the street indicated by Sun, he put the spade on the curb and started sweeping up the street. Slowly, meticulously, he tended to the trash, dust, and gutters. When he got to the number of the street Sun had sent, the place did not feel right. The gate was open, and a pair of children about four and six years old played in the yard under the watchful eye of their mother, whom he observed through the window working in the kitchen. This could not be the place.

The next unit, though, was more promising. The gate was closed, there was a camera mounted at the gate and on the telephone pole across the street pointing to the gate, and the wall had razor wire looped along its top. This was the place. Siddhartha Sun must have sought to avoid raising suspicion by looking up and sending the location of the unit next door to the black house.

Lu swept up the dust, plastic bottles, wrappers, and cans he had accumulated into the pan. Across the street was an elementary school, quiet on this Saturday afternoon. He approached the dumpster in the school and deposited the collected litter, then snuck upstairs to the open balcony walkway fronting the classrooms and facing the black house.

He took out one of his burnable mobile phones and mounted it on a cheap, hand-sized, tourist tripod with mobile phone clamp. He clipped on a 12x mobile phone telephoto lens and focused it. He activated the device to deliver a continuous recording of the black house to a cloud storage account. He plugged the phone into a wall outlet and left it.

He reckoned he had at least eighteen hours before the device was noticed, and the elementary school janitorial staff would probably assume it was left by the detective of a deep-pocketed wife seeking to get dirt on her husband and pinch it for their own use. He came out of the school, swept his way up the other side of the street and back toward the car, picked up his spade, and returned to Nanjing.

The video feed Lu Da had set up worked surprisingly well for something slapped together on the fly, and he was very pleased with himself. It was both being continuously saved, and he could tap in and watch the current feed. When he got back to Nanjing, he logged in to the cloud drive and started a fast-forward review of the video. Save its razor-wire-topped walls, the house was nondescript and very similar to the rest of the homes in the district.

Once in the afternoon, a van with its windows blacked out had pulled up, the driver had spoken into the intercom, and the gate had opened. Two soldierly-looking men, armed only with extendable batons and perhaps tasers, came out and picked up some cases of food and bottled water from the van, which then left.

With sunset, Lu Da could see slightly more into the illuminated rooms of the house. The rooms on the second floor remained unlit the whole night, meaning Lin Chong was being kept in the dark there or was being kept downstairs or in the basement. By watching the circulation of people, he counted a total of four attendants on the ground floor. Again, Lin Chong never came into view.

With this intel, Sagacious started making plans: how to extract one person while fighting off four and get away undetected, all without any special equipment.

⊃ 人 ⊂

DURING THE COFFEE BREAK, NANCY NILLSON HAD TRIED TO rally Team Alaska's spirits and stiffen their spines a bit, but even she was knackered. Besides Meredith, the team consisted of the Chief Investigator-Environmental Crimes Unit, an assistant attorney general from the Department of Law-Office of Special Prosecution and Appeals, and one environmental science staffer with a bachelor's degree. They shuffled like chastened detainees into the meeting room for their last afternoon session with their Chinese counterparts.

Across the table from them were twenty seats. Twelve of them had been filled consistently by central government representatives of several ministries and departments, including Foreign Affairs, Environmental Protection, Justice, Commerce, and Industry and Information Technology, plus a passel of PhDs with relevant expertise. The remaining eight seats had been filled on a rotating basis with other special guests and representatives of other ministries. Some important-looking people came in, listened, made some comments to the Chinese team that were not translated, and left without being introduced.

Neither China nor the US were members of any environmental court or tribunal, a fundamental impediment to this dialogue. They were at the mercy of their counterparts to recognize that damage had been done. If no solution was suitable or the other side reneged on an agreement made, there was little opportunity for recourse. Retaliatory threats were only as good as the possibility of their being implemented and doing real damage.

Team Alaska had started with a presentation of the scientific case for their claim. They presented readings from Anchorage and Fairbanks showing an increase in pollutants. They chemically traced this pollution to industrial pollutants and showed a concomitant increase in particulate from the deserts of China, matching the crystalline structure of the sand to that blowing into Beijing from further west. Finally, they correlated the specific rise in pollution with die-offs of lichens and mosses.

The Chinese side had several PhDs refute this, arguing that increases in population and tourism might have caused the increase in pollution.

Team Alaska pulled out another deck presenting evidence that in the far western reaches of Alaska, far from cities, industry, or tourism, the same pattern was observed with the same proof. This was a move Nancy had contributed to Team Alaska, coaching them to restructure their presentation in anticipation of this counter from China.

Nancy was pleased to see this put the Chinese team on the defensive, but they quickly recovered. No correlation could be drawn between the increase in sand particulate being blown from the deserts of China and the source of the pollution, which could have come from Japan, Korea, or Russia.

She felt particularly uncomfortable when the chief negotiator of the Chinese side said, "We have had the desert on our western regions for millennia, and sandstorms blow in and blow out. Surely *you* will appreciate, Ms. Nillson, that this is an act of God."

Really!? This coming from a Communist atheist? The statement only demonstrated to her how thoroughly briefed the Chinese side was on the US negotiating team and their beliefs. She knew nothing about them beyond titles and sometimes diplomas.

In that morning's session, China had proposed a joint research effort to conduct a five-year study to "investigate deeply into the causes of this change to Alaska's environment".

Nancy pulled Meredith aside and unloaded her view. *This was just a kiss-off, acknowledging no culpability, providing no recourse if the research determined China was the culprit. It pushes any satisfaction for Alaska many years down the road. It would be pure torture, death from a thousand cuts.*

Team Alaska had replied vociferously, if a bit toothlessly, that they had provided the proof, they were in Beijing seeking redress, so what was Beijing willing to put on the table?

In the final session, Nancy was concerned that they had gotten nowhere, were no closer to having a substantive proposal on the table, nor even a workable framework for further discussion, and that she would come away from her first challenge at the White House with nothing to show.

Shortly after reconvening, a new person was ushered into the room, sitting between the representatives from the Commerce and Foreign Affairs ministries. He was introduced as representing the National Development and Reform Commission.

The representative from Foreign Affairs spoke, "We want to thank the delegation from Alaska for making the effort to come to China to state your concerns about the environmental degradation taking place in Alaska. We want you to know that, as a responsible global citizen, China shares your concerns about the state of the environment in the world. We feel much more research must be conducted to pinpoint the source of the pollution. Indeed, is the die-off of lichens and mosses being caused by the immediate effects of a localized increase in pollution, or by more global trends, such as changes in temperature and humidity? We note your concerns that your claims are not being immediately addressed, but we must insist on first conducting a more thorough study and would like to propose a timetable for a next meeting to discuss setting up this study."

Nancy was pleased that they had not explicitly spoken the G word, "global warming," as this had been deleted from the White House dictionary of acceptable terms to be used in press releases, correspondence, or negotiations. She was less pleased with the general direction of the statement painting them back into the "paralysis by analysis" corner. She was frankly pissed that she and the White House were not acknowledged at all.

The Foreign Affairs representative continued, "We also want to thank President Coin for dispatching his representative, Dr. Nillson, to participate in this discussion. This shows a laudable focus on maintaining a healthy, high-level dialogue between our two friendly nations on issues important to the American people. China would like to convey an invitation to President Coin through you to make his first State visit since the inauguration, to China. At that time, we would like to formally propose and discuss the possibility of extending our One Belt One Road initiative eastward, with great benefits accruing to the state and people of Alaska. We would ask that your team not make this invitation public until President Coin has had a chance to respond to us."

Nancy was stunned and looked over at Meredith, who was gazing at the quality of the manicure received the night before at a spa near the hotel and had either zoned out or did not understand the implications.

This was an entirely new game. And one which Nancy was now invited to play. Nancy gathered her thoughts and responded, "I will report your invitation to President Coin. Thank you for extending it. Of course, we will keep this confidential until both sides deem it appropriate to make a public announcement. We would appreciate an opportunity to hear more about your thoughts on extending the One Belt One Road initiative eastward so I can also give the president a briefing on what this might entail."

The balance of the afternoon was spent watching several well-prepared presentations orchestrated by the Commerce and Foreign Affairs ministries and National Development and Reform Commission, who, they learned, oversaw the OBOR initiative.

The initiative was conceived as a modernized expression of the ancient Silk Road, binding cultures, communities, and nations closely together with commerce, technology, and social intercourse. China had offered soft credits and built high-speed rail connections, south into Myanmar and Pakistan, west to Turkey and Europe, and even into Africa. The initiative was bold in its conception and rapid in its execution, and its detractors were mostly those countries that had not benefited from it, or those who fell behind in their repayment of loans.

Nancy could not determine if the initiative being pitched was doable or who would pay for it, but it was certainly an inspiring, audacious "moon shot." This was the kind of effort that might appeal to President Coin, create thousands of jobs in America, and open new areas of the economy.

China had mapped out a new high-speed rail network linking China to the east coast of the United States, from Beijing to Harbin to Vladivostok, through Siberia's Magadan and Naukan and over to Alaska. It branched in

Canada, south through Vancouver, Seattle, San Francisco, and Los Angeles and east through Edmonton and Winnipeg to Minneapolis, Chicago, and New York. It would carry passenger and freight cars at speeds exceeding 200 mph, and in a bit of hyperbole they promised "going from Fairbanks to Russia in three hours" and "moving cars from Detroit to China in a quarter the time and half the cost of ocean freight."

She asked how they planned to cross the Bering Strait.

A high-definition CGI animation was played. A tunnel would be bored from Naukan to Big Diomede Island, a Russian territory onto which they would deliver a modular nuclear power plant. This alone would ignite new growth in Siberia *and* power the train from Canada to China. From there, the tunnel would continue to Little Diomede Island, a US territory, and on to Wales at the western coast of Alaska. Each hop would approximate the length of the Channel Tunnel. In short, a new wonder of the world.

The Chinese side concluded the meetings by presenting Nancy with briefing materials on the One Belt One Road initiative. The representative of the Ministry of Foreign Affairs came to shake hands in farewell. "Thank you for coming to Beijing, Dr. Nillson. Your opinion on this initiative will be vital to its success."

She knew when she was being stroked, but it still felt good.

⊃ 人 ⊏

SO FAR, LIN CHONG WAS NOT TOO IMPRESSED WITH THE INTER-rogations. They had not really tried to torture him in earnest.

They started by demanding him to "confess to your crimes." Nothing specific was accused. The tortured were expected to figure out to what they should confess. They would make the demand, sometimes softly, sometimes loudly, but always accompanied by a light to medium slap in the face. Three or four times a minute. For hours. And hours. Perhaps a day. The light always on. Relentlessly.

He knew that if they were bothering to exact a confession from him, they felt they needed something substantial enough to assassinate his character and put him away for good, thus freeing up Yanei to pursue Zhenniang. He only gave them the satisfaction of name, rank, and identity number.

He focused his ire into the charcoal tips of burnt matches, with which the guards had lit their cigarettes, writing a poem onto the cement floor:

Just is Lin Chong, Loyal to the People.
Renowned in the demimonde, a hero of the nation.

Fate has cast him adrift, his glory forsaken.
But someday his will be done, and Mount Tai will bow before him.

He gazed wearily at this and read it over and over, an ember of strength and solace kept faintly glowing.

The interrogations got worse, though, when they said they were going to "let him get cleaned up." He figured they were euphemistically talking about water boarding, which he had succeeded in beating during army training.

Instead, they made him lie facedown on the floor with shoes and socks off. They then slowly poured a steady stream of water just off the boil onto the YongQuan Bubbling Spring acupuncture point on the soles of his feet. Though only one small point on each foot was being scalded, the feeling of his entire body being burned from the inside out agonized him.

"Listen to this ingrate!" Fu An derided. "Usually, the prisoners serve the guards. Here we are giving this turd the luxury of a footbath and he screams, 'Bloody hell, the water's too hot'. Boo-hoo."

Lu Qian shook his head and chuckled at the cruel joke. "Here, let me scrub that foot clean," he said, as he took a steel bristle brush and zealously went at the soles of Lin's feet, layers of skin coming off with each pass.

Lin Chong gritted his teeth, screamed, and passed out.

When he woke, he was weak from the pain, which had left his body and now was concentrated in his feet, which felt like he only had two raw stumps left. He looked and was relieved to see the feet were intact, but the soles were badly blistered, raw, and bleeding.

He dragged himself up into a sitting position on the floor, back against the steel pole, and collected himself. *How to get out of this? Trying to escape would be a disaster, I can barely walk, let alone run. Confessing to anything won't be a route home. It'll only lead straight to conviction and execution, solving none of my problems.* He began to rock back and forth in misery, sobbing, his chest heaving, and a new sensation came to him. The steel pole against which he leaned was not as stiff or secure as he had first imagined.

He stood up painfully on the scalded feet and grabbed the pole with both hands near its center bottom and top. He pushed and pulled it experimentally to gauge the flex. Perhaps if he used "fajin," which he had mastered in Form and Intent Boxing, a martial art style, he could lodge it free.

At that moment, what sounded like the report of a gun went off outside, somewhere in the compound, and he heard shouting and rapid footfalls. Without further thought, he widened his stance and with a deep breath relaxed his entire body. He imagined the Horse form of this martial art, the wild animal rearing up on its hind legs, striking out with its front hoofs, and dropping its weight into twin explosive blows. The intent of the form exploded out of him, his body instantaneously going from full relax, to full tension, left and right palms driving into the pole, which flexed and broke from its mounts above and below.

He grabbed the pole and ran to the hinge side of the door as he heard people running down the steps. The door burst open and in bound Fu An. Using the Splitting form, Lin swung the pole like an axe square onto the top of Fu An's head, felling him dead in his tracks. Lu Qian ran in, stumbling in his haste over the body of his comrade, and turned to face the armed prisoner. He snapped out a metal baton and took a guard position.

Lin Chong lunged in, thrusting the pole like a spear. Lu Qian deftly sidestepped the thrust and snapped the baton to parry the weapon left to right. However, Lin Chong expected this, wanted this, and circled the tip of the pole counterclockwise, gathered momentum, and snapped it down hard on Lu Qian's right forearm, breaking the radius bone and making him release his grip on the baton. Without losing any advantage, Lin Chong again marshaled the explosive, twisting thrust of the Drilling form and drove the pole into Lu Qian's throat, impaling him crudely, painfully, and fatally against the cement wall.

Using the pole as a crutch, Lin hobbled up the steps. There was still a commotion going on, and he did not know what to expect. He entered the living room just in time to see a man wearing a black balaclava dispatch the second of two guards with a garden spade.

"Thank..." Lin Chong erupted, but the man waved him silent and shook his head, then gestured for Lin Chong to follow him. Noting the trail of blood Lin Chong's feet left on the floor, the man in black ran to the bathroom and came back with two towels. He quickly tied them around Lin's feet, then bade him to drop the pole and use the spade carried by the man to hobble with him. Staying in shadows and evading the known positions of the security cameras, they left the compound, passed through the campus of the elementary school, and got to a car in an alley a block away, behind the school. They heard police sirens responding to the commotion they had caused as they closed the doors of the automobile.

Once they were safely in the car, the man in black spoke up and Lin Chong immediately recognized the voice of his friend and mentor, Lu Da. He reached over and yanked the balaclava off his face and embraced the man. "Sagacious, how? How did you find me?"

The older officer wiped the young man's embrace away. "Hey, I'm driving. Hands off." He straightened up. "When you went missing, I figured we were both in trouble. Pulled in some markers, got the information I needed."

"I heard gun shots. Where is your backup?"

"You think I could get backup to save *your* skinny ass?" he chided. "This was a solo mission. I set up a box of fireworks on the front wall with a stick of incense to light them, giving me about five minutes. Went to the back of the compound and scaled the wall and razor wire with my spade and a blanket. Then I waited and got ready. When the 'shots' rang out, I took out the guard who came to respond, went in, and dispatched the second. Don't think I killed either but put them out of commission for a while. From the blood and guts on that pole you were carrying, looks like you took care of the other two, am I right?"

"Yes. Dead for sure," Lin responded with the first sense of satisfaction and security he had felt in several days.

"Good, then we were in and out clean in less than four to five minutes. With no one to talk to them, the local police will get a slow start on this case, then it will be hobbled a little when they realize they are looking at a black house, and military intelligence steps in. Let's use this time wisely, switch vehicles a couple of times, and make tracks. There's a first aid kit in the black bag on the back seat. See if you can take care of your feet."

As Lin Chong busied himself with hydrogen peroxide, antibiotic salve, topical pain killer, and bandages, he distracted himself from the pain by talking. "Zhenniang. I have to reach her."

"Negative on that, Major. She did call to ask if I knew what happened to you. We can find a way to tell her you're alive, but my advice is to tell her to forget you. You are radioactive, my friend. Any contact with you will just hurt her."

Lin Chong was not happy with the answer, but knew it made sense. "Where are we going? It's going to be hard to evade security for long."

"I'm working on it. There is a group I know of, hard to describe, let's just call them a bandit cult. I think we can take refuge there. Do you have any identities squirreled away?" Sagacious had always given his mentee the advice that in the case of a foreign enemy attack, they had to be prepared to go underground to defend the Motherland.

"Yes, but accessible? Not easy. They are in a locker in Suzhou," a city located between Nanjing and Shanghai.

"Ok, it could be worse. We are heading in that general direction. You get some sleep. I will wake you when we need to change cars."

Lin Chong was more than happy to comply with this order and through closed eyes saw the flash of streetlights under which they passed glow on his eyelids. Comforted by this gently familiar and nonthreatening pattern, he was deep asleep within a minute.

⊃ 人 ⊂

WHY WAS THIS A PROBLEM? MILI PAREKH REFLECTED AS HER car picked its way through morning traffic on the commute from home in a Baltimore suburb to the NSA campus. She looked up at the traffic lights and pondered their programming. Clearly there had been no improvement in *her* commute time. *Probably too far down the list to rate an upgrade*, she mused.

A hacker or hackers (no one had taken credit) had broken into the traffic control systems of major cities across the nation and made changes, improvements, to the sequencing of traffic lights. This had resulted in reductions of 10-15 percent in commute times during rush hours, particularly on surface roads, and a measurable reduction in traffic accidents.

The hack was very sophisticated. It was not simply a change in algorithms to modify traffic light signaling. It incorporated real-time sources of data not previously employed by the original systems to make its decisions.

A consulting company would have charged upwards of nine figures to take on the risk to its reputation of diving into this data morass and making sense of it. *Nine figures per city*, she reappraised. After all, if traffic did not improve, heads would roll. Yet this was done quietly, with no fanfare, gratis. It had not even been revealed to the media.

The car decided to change lanes. Although autonomous, self-driving cars were still vastly outnumbered on the roads by conventional, human-driven vehicles, she had gotten an early license for one. Cases like hers were preferred. Technically, she could have passed the driving exam with a specially built vehicle. Licensing and insurance authorities wisely decided that people like Mili would be the best to avail first of the new technology, deeming the autonomous driver safer than her own skills could ever be.

The minivan was equipped with an electric door and ramp for a wheel-chair. She could now come and go as she pleased, just like anyone else. Once she was secured inside, she instructed the on-board computer, by voice command or through her mobile phone, of her destination. Then she could sit back and relax.

And think about problems. *Why was this a problem?* she asked herself again. *Upwards of a billion dollars in taxpayer money saved on consulting fees, no new infrastructure investment required to implement the enhance-ment, and measurable benefits to the people living in those cities.*

This hack had not been revealed to the media for a reason. A program-mer with the DOT of New York City had noted an improvement in his com-mute and, satisfied he had done a good job on something, dug in to see which subset of the control system was optimizing flows. To his horror, he found that the graphic user interface and dashboards provided to human users were unchanged, humming along smartly and reporting the health of the system, but behind the dashboards, the entire system was new. He reported this up the chain of command, and it was brought to the attention of Homeland Security.

Mili had not yet been called on to try to attribute the provenance of the hackers but read about this in a weekly classified briefing she was autho-rized to receive.

It might be a problem, but it is not my problem, she thought as she ar-rived at the main entrance of the NSA. She disembarked from her car and ordered it to park in her reserved space. She now took control of her own vehicle, the wheelchair that she still enjoyed driving manually, and headed through security, into the elevators, and on to whatever emergent situa-tions awaited.

⊃ 人 ⊂

LI JUN STARED OUT AT THE WEATHER. HE DID NOT NEED TO BE a meteorologist or mariner to know that the situation did not look good. The wind was picking up, the seas were getting heavier, and the swiftly moving gray mass on the horizon was foreboding. Standing on the obser-vation deck of the first, leading platform, the howl of the wind buried any other noise of man or machine, an intense warning: *You Don't Belong Here.*

The Leviathan was halfway through a slow, tugboat-impelled, 5,000-kilometer journey from Singapore to international waters southeast of Japan at the convergence of currents concentrating plastic garbage. The day before they had passed the northern tip of Luzon and headed out of the South China Sea into the open ocean.

They had targeted a springtime departure date precisely to avoid the typhoon season, but for naught. Li Jun shook his head. The first typhoon of the season, Diwata, was a monster of a storm and early by several weeks. It had formed quickly southeast of the Philippines in unseasonably warm waters and was now 1,100 kilometers in diameter with maximum windspeeds of over 250 kilometers an hour. And heading straight for the Leviathan.

The modified, semi-submersible platforms had their own motors used for positioning and travel of short distances. Even with the assist of the six tugboats, they only made a speed of ten kilometers per hour. It was not a speedy vessel that could run and hide.

Bu Qing tapped on Li Jun's shoulder and stood close, shouting into his ear, "Boss. Everything's ready for inspection." The Flood Dragon was wearing a full set of foul weather gear, plus the required safety kit of life vest and harness to attach to guy wires.

"You know this is all *your* fault," Li Jun shouted with a smile.

Bu Qing did not get the joke.

"You're *the* Flood Dragon, right? The spirit responsible for regulating this kind of crappy weather. Put in a good word, will you!" Li Jun clapped his old comrade on the back, and Bu laughed and shook his head.

With news of the intensifying storm, Li Jun had ordered the operations crew to secure all production equipment and make sure everything was properly stowed.

They were starting the inspection on the first platform, called the Mouth. Once fully deployed, the Mouth would lower 200-meter-long jaws facing the oncoming stream of plastic detritus. The Jaws were a set of two booms, each anchored to one of the jack-up legs, which would capture a 300-meter-wide swath of incoming floaters. The incoming plastic would be automatically sorted, processed, shredded, rinsed, and dried on the Mouth.

Li Jun and Bu Qing walked the top three decks of the Mouth. "I don't like the look of the Jaws," Li Jun said pointing up through the rain at the retracted booms supported and lashed to one hundred meters of platform leg, yet sticking up another hundred meters into the sky, wind, and rain, unprotected and unsupported.

"I hear you, Boss, but nothing we can do about it now. They are rated to take a considerable load. We just have to hope the platform doesn't rock with the waves too much. Could snap them."

Li Jun pulled out a walkie-talkie and radioed the captain, urging him to keep the condition of the Jaws in his calculus when he made course corrections to accommodate the storm.

They braced themselves against the wind and rain across the bridge to the second platform, nicknamed the Gut. Here was a processing plant where separated material was blended, melted, pelletized, and bagged for sale. This space was the least exposed to outside elements, so Li Jun focused attention on making sure the team had double-checked that all equipment was properly secured in place and would not shift during the storm.

He and Bu felt the storm had already intensified as they took the next bridge to the third platform, called the Sphincter. Here finished goods were to be stored, ready to be off-loaded into freighters that could be docked there. It also included a facility to produce coarse fiber from material not suitable for recycling that would weave and press the fiber into sheets, cut and sewn into bags to hold finished product.

"That crane needs to be parked," Li pointed out.

"Right on it. We've been moving some items," Bu said. He caught the attention of the man operating the crane, circled his right hand in the air, and dropped it to point to the deck, signaling the man to conclude the work, park the crane, and return to safety.

The storm was intensifying, the first arm of the typhoon sweeping over them, a process that would repeat itself hourly now.

"Let's make our way back to the captain's bridge on he Mouth. First, I want to check out the solar panels," Li Jun ordered.

Once it had arrived at the garbage patch, the entire rig would deploy a floating "mesh" of 2xSolar floats, so-called because their surfaces were covered with solar cells, and the floats were connected by swing-arms that turned generators built into each float as waves passed underneath, bobbing it relative to its neighbor. The field of floats would extend far beyond the Jaws, further coaxing a wider swath of material to find its way to the Mouth. The power generated was expected to be sufficient to run the sorting machines, desalinization plant, processors, extruders, and bagging machines.

"Fuck, how come my instincts are always right?" Li shouted at Bu through the howl.

The solar panels had slipped through the cracks, literally and figuratively. His operations team had focused on the machinery, and the mariners had focused on battening down the vessel. No one had ventured here to make sure this critical, future power plant resource was safe.

Cables were strewn about, and several stacks of panels had overturned, one stack dangling over the side and smashing repeatedly into the framework below. "Call all the team over. We got to get this in order fast," he shouted to Bu and set to work himself.

This deck was the lowest, closest to the waterline, and the panels were exposed to the storm. "Captain said we might get ten-meter waves. That means they could wash up here. Tell them to haul ass."

Li Jun secured his harness to the safety guy ways and leaned out over the water trying to see what could be done about the stack of panels dangling below. He looked high above to catch a glimpse of the Jaws. They were being whipped back and forth but seemed to be holding up.

He did not hear the robust strapping on a stack of solar panels near him give way with a *snap*. Hearing a crash, he turned and dodged out of the way as two tons of solar panels slid past him and went over the edge.

Li Jun looked at Bu Qing and theatrically wiped his brow. "Dodged that one," he shouted and beamed a smile.

The Flood Dragon did not laugh in return. Instead, his eyes narrowed and, speechless, he pointed forcefully at Li's feet.

Too late. Li had stepped into a loop of scattered steel cable next to a length that was rapidly playing out as its caught end plummeted with the solar panels. Fast as a bandsaw and just as surgically, the loop closed on his leg just above the ankle and neatly removed his foot, flinging it overboard.

The last thing Li Jun remembered was seeing the corrugated sole of the steel-toed work shoe he was wearing and wishing he had opted for the high-top work boots instead.

CHAPTER 3

DURING THE CAMPAIGN DEBATES, CANDIDATE MICK COIN HAD made light of "frivolous, government-funded, egg-headed research when the real, hardworking American just wants a reduction in government spending and government interference." As president, he wanted to show the voting base that he was on point with this issue and ordered all his advisors to review government-supported research with a view to reduce it by 20 percent.

In what Nancy would learn was characteristic of President Coin's imprecision, he did not specify if he meant a reduction in the number of projects funded or the quantum of funding. He did make clear that the reductions were to be achieved by eliminating research into programs he deemed "wasteful, wrong-headed, or with no foreseeable benefit for the good people of the United States."

In the waiting lounge at Beijing Airport, Nancy finished the report for the president regarding the Alaska negotiation and summit invitation from China and then dug into the spreadsheet of government-supported projects that fell into her purview to assess.

Some items were easy to nix. She did a search for projects that had "environmental impact" or "endangered species" in the title. She was able to make a recommendation "not to continue support" on 95 percent of the several hundred projects that came up from this search between her first and second drink at the lounge. She could see in each synopsis that most of these were looking at the impact of human activity on the local environment or native species. Not of interest.

The 5 percent of projects spared the knife focused on the danger to human populations from localized severe pollution or major earth-moving activities. To avoid future liability and litigation, she knew these studies needed to be completed.

Some projects warranted a second look, but within two to three minutes she was able to determine that the private sector could handle the investment in research or that the American people and industry were unlikely to benefit. For example, some people who had left DARPA were adapting microdrone surveillance technologies to perfect artificial pollinating drones. If they succeeded, they would become Silicon Valley billionaires. No need to seed them with taxpayer money.

Then there were "possibly interesting" projects. An example was research being done in Northern California mapping the extent of communication between giant redwoods through the mycelial network linking them. A Cal Poly professor by the name of Dr. Aléjandra Chavez was leading the team. Chavez's approach was interesting, incorporating mycologists, biochemists, botanists, evolutionary biologists, computer science grads, and remote sensing of chemical and electrochemical signals. A proposed benefit of the research was the possibility of determining what signals to the trees would switch on an accelerated growth gene. This would benefit the timber industry, but would the benefits accrue soon enough?

She marked this "continue six months and revisit." The researchers would be notified they were on a short leash and urged to "get cracking."

Altogether she was able to determine the fate of 1,200 projects before dinner was served on the flight and, just to be safe, was beating the 20 percent reduction Coin called for both in number of projects and quantum of funding.

She then turned her attention to a "bigger" problem.

Bigger in size, as it was expected to be as large as the state of Rhode Island. Bigger in public relations impact, as the opposition would be certain to latch onto it and inflate the global warming bogeyman dummy with their hot air. And a bigger chance to turn lemons into lemonade, from Nancy's perspective. NOAA and climate scientists in Antarctica were warning that a new, larger, and at present landbound, chunk of the Larsen ice shelf was starting to show signs it might break off and slide into the ocean.

She had some ideas she wanted to flesh out with engineering friends before she went to the president. She fired off a half dozen emails and then knocked herself out for the remaining nine hours of the flight. She did not want to miss a beat when she alighted in DC.

ㄥ人ㄈ

ZHANG ZHENNIANG SAT ON THE CARPETED FLOOR OF HER apartment, their apartment, Lin's and hers. The mirrored doors of the closets reflected a pathetic form: broken, broke, distraught, and disheveled.

It had been the worst day of her life; indeed, it could not get any worse. Four days after Lin Chong had gone to meet "the big man," four days after what was supposed to have been an opportunity for triumph and promotion, four days after he had disappeared without a trace and three days after she had reached out to Lu Da, who went silent, she had at last heard from Lin. Sort of. She received a WeChat message from one of Lin Chong's alternate accounts.

The message came from Bao-zi, and the avatar was a pair of dice. Bao-zi meant "leopard spots" and referred to a role of two at craps. It also alluded to his handle, Bao-tou, or "panther head." It read:

> Dearest Zhenniang,
> Our sweet life together was just begun, but fate has torn us apart.
> I love you more than anything, but to protect you, I must make the sacrifice never to see you again, at least until I am able to find some justice. I will not blame you if you forget me, go to the marriage bureau, and divorce me. Tell them your disgraceful husband was arrested by the military and disappeared. They will understand and grant your wish. But know this. This is the doing of 'the Insider' and his father.
> I am with Sagacious. Do not worry about me, just forget me.
> I will make any sacrifice to find justice for us.
> Bao-zi

That message had started the morning. Stunned, she had called her father.

Before she had gotten too far into the story, he told her to stop talking and arrange to meet him face to face. She knew he suspected the phone to be tapped. He was a day away, so she would not be able to see him until the morrow. She felt so vulnerable.

She dialed the HR director of the symphony to call in sick for that day's performance. The call was shunted to the director.

"Thanks for phoning, Zhenniang. Actually, I wanted to speak to you today. I am afraid I have some unhappy news, and I hope you won't take it too badly. The symphony will be letting you go."

"What?! Letting me go where?"

"We are canceling your contract."

"Why?"

"We don't need a reason according to our agreement with you, but since you ask, you have fallen out of favor with our sponsor. They are willing to set up a meeting with you to discuss this. An exit interview, if you will."

Zhenniang was silent, the churn of her emotions crashing between hurt, rage, and bewilderment.

"You can come in any time before the end of the week to clean out your locker and make-up space. After that, we will just discard anything left."

"That's it? You just tell me on the phone? You dickless turtle egg!"

"Well, you did call me. In any event, this conversation is over. You will be receiving an email confirming our discussion shortly," he said and hung up curtly.

She looked about the room in shock. The phone rang breaking the stupor. "Hello?"

"Zhenniang, it's Gao Yanei. I got a message from the symphony. Is there anything I can do?" he asked sweetly.

She was dazed and confused. "Gao? Do you know what's happened?"

"I got word the symphony had released you from your contract."

"That's all? And you didn't have anything to do with it?"

"Heavens no!"

"What about my husband?"

"What about him? Is he taking this badly? I can talk to him if you like."

"He was arrested at the Eastern Military region command headquarters."

"No? Not really? Wow. Do you want me to ask my father about it?"

"You're so full of shit. If you had anything to do with this, then make it right. Otherwise, you're dead meat."

"Now, Zhenniang, dear, I know you are distraught. But I am here for you. When you are ready to talk, or if you need anything, I am here for you."

She hung up on him and slumped to the floor of their bedroom sobbing as she disregarded some text messages Gao sent.

She and Lin had bought their apartment on credit in a community that was beyond their means, counting on a two-income family and real-estate inflation to keep them afloat. Now her beloved was gone, and she was unemployed. They had not saved for any such setback, Lin trusting that his job in the military was rock solid. She knew it would be only a matter of weeks, months at most, before the bank came inquiring about the security of their loan. She could lose it all.

The phone rang again. She was reluctant to answer it. She'd had enough bad news for one day. But the ringing insisted she answer, and she knew the day could not get worse.

"Hello."

"Is this Zhang Zhenniang?"

"Speaking. Who is this?"

"I am the secretary to your benefactor, Mr. Xu Wenhui. We understand that you are leaving the Shanghai Symphony. As you know, the violin you use is on loan to you, with the condition that you remain employed at the symphony. Mr. Xu and our insurers request that you return the Guadagnini violin. Are you with the instrument now at your residence?"

"...Yes?"

"Wonderful. A courier will be arriving shortly to pick it up. He will provide you with a proper receipt of delivery to discharge your obligations to us. Please sign that and retain a copy for your records. Thank you, Ms. Zhang." The line went dead.

Zhenniang's head slumped between her knees, and she felt the tears drizzling her thighs as what was left of her world collapsed.

⊃ 人 ⊂

IT WAS TIMES LIKE THIS CHAI JIN WAS GLAD FOR THE REPUTAtion he enjoyed.

He was three generations Red, the grandson and son of high-level party cadres who had built Modern China and a very wealthy and successful real-estate investor in his own right. It was said he had an "ironclad carte blanche."

This was not quite true. He could not oppose the Party chief, or engage in undermining the State, but otherwise he was free to build wealth, support the needy, and oppose injustice when it was the result of corrupt, middle-level functionaries not acting on the will of the president or the Party chairman.

A handsome man in his forties, he had acquired land and built cities from dust bowls and marshes. But his passion was the ideal that the Party represented building a New China and seeing that justice be done.

Lin Chong sitting before him certainly fit that description. The day before, he had received a call from Sagacious Lu asking whether he could leave a friend in his care only telling him Lin had been "grievously wronged." Sagacious had other matters to attend to. Chai assented.

Over a private lunch served in Chai's manor, Lin Chong recounted his tale. The devotion to his country and role in protecting it, Gao Yanei's efforts to seduce his wife, the mysterious outreach to deliver the "Operation Broadsword" files into the hands of General Gao Qiu, his arrest, torture, and escape with the help of Lu Da. "I was able to retrieve my things in Suzhou, and Lu Da said he had arranged a place for me to convalesce, and here I am."

Lin looked strangely savage, Chai thought. He had used a black permanent marker to draw the Chinese character for gold 金 on his face in heavy lines and looked tattooed. The first and second strokes of the character 人 dropped down from the peak of the hairline to the breadth of his eyebrows. The third and fourth strokes 二 were drawn across the ridge of his eyebrows and from the point of his left cheekbone across the face, over his nose, and terminated at the point of his right cheekbone. The fifth stroke | dropped vertically, bisecting the face from the center of the eyebrows to the point of his chin. The sixth and seventh strokes \ / dropped diagonally from the tips of his cheekbones to the corners of his mouth, and the last stroke — was horizontal from the right jaw across the chin to the left jaw.

Lin had remarked to Chai that this branding would be sufficient to redefine the features of his face rendering previous facial recognition records of him obsolete. He would be invisible until, for any reason, the new image was tagged for further review, and a deeper, more time-consuming run of facial recognition algorithms was conducted.

A servant entered and sought to serve Lin Chong more dessert fruits after their repast.

"Really, no more. It has been a meal I will never forget. Your kindness ... is overwhelming."

Chai Jin shook his head, waved a hand, and said with deep sincerity, "Thank *you* for coming. It is a rare privilege for me to meet a man like you, someone I can truly admire."

Lin Chong had heard that Chai Jin's nickname was Lord Chai, and given the royal lunch he had enjoyed and the grandeur of the manor, he felt comfortable mimicking the formality of that language. "Your Lordship has been too kind."

Chai had a quiet word with the servant, who went out and ushered in a new visitor. Chai said, "Lin Chong, I would like you to meet someone. Professor Hong, this is Lin Chong, quite the expert in system penetration. Lin, this is my head of IT security, Professor Hong. I thought you should get to know each other."

Hong scowled and took the seat next to Chai, not the one proffered by Chai next to Lin Chong.

Lin took measure of Hong. *If he is respected by Chai, it would be best to give him face.* "A professor. Respects. I never got past my master's; I imagine there is much you could teach me."

Hong did not find the bait tasty. He turned to Chai and said, "Lord Chai, why do you always let these stray dogs in the house? I have heard of his reputation. He is being hunted by PLA military police. I am in danger just being in the room with him, and so are you."

Chai was annoyed by the insolence of the employee to a guest. "This gentleman is no ordinary person. He led Unit 61398. Legendary."

"Respectfully, I think you are taken in by too many people with sad stories. They use you. My team is fighting to keep your network secure day after day as all manner of criminals, hackers, and industrial spies try to break in. Look at him, he is a jock-meathead, handier with his fists than with his fingers on a keyboard. He is just an army bureaucrat."

Lin Chong remained silent, but Chai Jin spoke up, "Best not to judge people from appearances. He is not one to be underestimated."

Hong scowled and issued a challenge. "Ok, if he is so good, let him take a whack at our network security. If he can break into it, I will be the first to kowtow."

Chai liked this idea, having gotten quite tired of Hong's bluster and riding rough on the IT team, who hated him. He raised eyebrows to Lin seeking an answer.

"I would not presume," Lin started to reply.

"I insist," Hong goaded.

"Let's make it interesting," Chai interjected. "If Lin Chong can demonstrate that he has broken into our network by tomorrow morning, then let's consider it his victory, and if he can't, you are the winner, Hong. And to the winner will go a five-tael gold bar. Sorry I don't have any cryptocurrency, but this is worth about the same as a bitcoin. And to make it even more interesting, let's first retire to the lounge and have something to drink. Lin, do you enjoy cognac or whiskey?"

They descended the two steps from the dining area into a lounge, Lin still hobbling on scalded feet. They were in the penthouse of Chai's Eastern Manor, an integrated shopping, office, and high-rise living complex in the Hong Qiao district of Shanghai. From the fifty-ninth floor they watched the world go by while Lin and Hong traded stories of hacks executed and hacks foiled, college days and family, while imbibing several snifters of Chai's best VSOP.

Lin Chong got up. "Got to use the toilet. And is there somewhere I can go online?"

Chai waved for the servant to escort Lin in the right direction. Lin took up his backpack and left the room.

He came back in twenty minutes. "Ah," he sighed comfortably. "All done."

Hong, who was well into his fifth cognac, thought it amusing that Lin would announce he had successfully taken a leak and said so.

"No. The hack is done," Lin smiled.

"You're blowing the bull."

"No. Check your mobile device, Professor Hong."

Hong logged in. The screensaver image had been changed to a close-up photo of a pair of hairy testicles and a large but relaxed penis. Not his screensaver.

"Your phone requires network security log-in. It is part of the system with access to the system."

"How the f ..."

Chai interjected, "Ho! Good work, we have a winner!"

⊃ 人 ⊂

IDRUS SUKABUMI HAD TO KEEP IN MIND THAT HERE HE WAS just another person; he had no special status. However, he was having difficulty keeping his temper, maintaining composure. In Indonesia, he was the minister of the environment and forestry, an important man. Here in Singapore, he was just another client of a bank, a rich one to be sure, but not the richest.

"I am really having trouble understanding what you are trying to tell me. What do you mean, all my funds have been transferred out of the account? I have come here today to discuss doing just that."

The client management officer, a Chinese Singaporean surnamed Ng with an awkward Singlish British accent, took in the short, nut-brown elder wearing a *peci* on his head and a fine, hand-printed batik shirt the color of burnt sugar, its cuff hiding most of a gold Audemars Piguet Royal

Oak watch but not Idrus's hand, revealing a large, pigeon-blood ruby cab-ochon ring. Ng knew he had to handle this delicately. His quarterly bonus depended on it.

For decades, Singapore had milked its image as the Switzerland of the Far East. A conservative, tightly run government of technocrats brooked little corruption at home, making it punishable by brutal caning, fines, and prison. However, at best it turned a blind eye and at worst encouraged corruption in its neighbors by providing private, confidential banking services. Originally marketed to individuals in ASEAN, China, and Taiwan seeking a safe, low-tax haven to hide assets out of their home countries, wealth had flowed into the island republic. Billions of dollars.

Ng could see the minister had been a client for twenty-five years. Slowly, Idrus Sukabumi had amassed great wealth, over $300 million's worth. Not a bad haul for whatever it was he did, or did not do, to earn it.

Such ministers could make a businessman wealthy or bankrupt, success-ful or stillborn, with a comment or the stroke of a pen. It was worth it to court their favor. Agreements were needed to access primordial rainforest timber, to avoid pollution issues building a smelter or tire factory or bat-tery plant, or to build a resort in an animal sanctuary.

It was not Ng's job to judge where money had come from, only to make sure that the bank's reputation was not damaged by anything the bank did with the funds on behalf of the client. That was the problem they were facing.

Idrus had called several weeks before and said he was preparing to re-tire. He would enjoy his dotage in Europe, had already secured a Swiss passport, and was planning to move his funds.

The bank explained delicately that ever since 9/11 the US government had put a death grip on any bank worldwide that wanted to do business in the US. Major compliance hoops had to be jumped through, records main-tained, and reports made on interbank transfers beyond a certain, minus-cule limit. Prior to this, Singapore was the regional laundromat for dirty money. The US Treasury had made this all much more difficult.

The Indonesian was an old client of the bank, so they had maintained his accounts and had urged him to avail himself of their "wealth management services" to better disguise the extent and location of his assets.

Idrus had rejected this advice, believing it to be self-serving, fee-gener-ating gouging on the bank's part. After their most recent phone calls, he confirmed via email he was planning to come to Singapore on this day to discuss the removal of funds and closure of his account.

Ng told him once more that yesterday, Idrus had logged in following all the proper protocols and had initiated transfers of the entire balance into six separate overseas accounts in Hong Kong, Amsterdam, Zurich, the Cayman Islands, Panama, and Dublin. The money had been successfully remitted.

"Bapak Idrus," Ng started respectfully, "here is the print-out of your password-verified demands to make the transfers yesterday. While we regret to lose your business, we understand your desire to move your assets."

"I did not demand, authorize, or even log on yesterday. In fact, I can prove I was on an airplane flying here during the time shown on your print-out."

Ng swallowed. "Give me a moment to arrange some more senior representatives of the bank to meet with you. Could I get you a cup of coffee in the meantime?"

Idrus stewed for half an hour with a paltry serving of Nescafé in a paper cup before three Singaporeans reentered the private meeting room. He was introduced by Ng to the branch manager and the vice president of legal affairs.

The lawyer spoke up first, "Bapak Idrus, our records of your log-in are clear and without error. According to our agreement with you on terms of service, *you* are responsible to maintain the security of your passwords and log-in credentials."

"Impossible, I have never shared my details with anyone. You are liable, and I will prove it," he said, voice rising.

"Sir, before we discuss that, there is another problem that has been set in motion by your transfer of the funds out of Singapore in this way." He paused for effect. Idrus stared coldly and silently back at him.

"We have, through the years, sent you information about the evolution of global banking regulations. Most recently, as you contacted us about closing your account, we reiterated that this must be done with proper care so that your identity can remain private and so as not to be seen as money laundering." He paused again.

"Your wholesale transfer of such large sums of money ... Well, it has triggered our own compliance regimen, and we are now absolutely obligated to report this to the US Treasury. Your name, the sums, and the account numbers you transferred the funds into will be transparent to the US Treasury. As you are from a predominantly Muslim country and are yourself

Muslim, it will, no doubt, prompt their interest in you. Although our bank will vigorously resist efforts of the US government, they will no doubt seek records from us on the source of your funds. Just looking at the past ten years, I see that deposits have been made from all over ASEAN and with increasing frequency from China."

Idrus stared coldly at his fingers spread out on the table, the paper cup between his hands, and counted the digits one by one slowly, as he took a deep breath, something his *Dukun* faith healer had recommended when he felt like his heart was ready to explode.

"Sir, if past experience is an indicator, the US Treasury's Financial Crimes Enforcement Network will reach out and share this information with your government's internal affairs investigators. You should be prepared to... Are you well, Sir?"

Bapak Idrus Sukabumi slumped face forward into the remains of the cup of coffee. After heroic efforts to revive him failed, he was declared dead of a massive heart attack that afternoon at Mount Phillip Hospital.

His death caused a minor flap in relations between Singapore and Indonesia. Ng did not get his quarterly bonus.

⊃ 人 ⊂

LIN CHONG GOT OFF THE SUBWAY AT THE END OF THE LINE. HE had been the sole passenger remaining on the vehicle for the past two stops, and no one was waiting on the platform to get on the car for its return journey to Weifang, a prefectural city in Shandong Province.

Unlike the larger, busier stops further up the line, this station was only half-alight, dusty and litter-strewn, and was not adorned with the bright, colorful, urgent courtesies of advertisers. One set of motionless escalators led to the sunlight, and he trudged up the steps toward the surface. This was *ShuiHuZhan*. The Water Margin or Waterside Station, so-called because it dead-ended into the Huang He estuary, known to Westerners as the Yellow River, one of the mothers of Chinese civilization. Lin Chong noted wryly too that these words, *ShuiHu*, water margin, denoted the end of the line for a man. He had fallen so far he was in a place of no return.

Chai Jin had been a kind and attentive host, but their time together came to an end. Chai had called his personal physician to attend to Lin's feet, fed him well, and let him use the private gym where Lin could release torrent after wave after landslide of anger and frustration into the weight stacks and heavy punching bags. Lord Chai also enjoyed long conversations with

Lin about politics, philosophy, and justice and finally told him about a place where he felt Lin would be safe.

In the tabloids, Little Tornado was the preferred nickname for Chai Jin. He had been skilled at planning real-estate acquisition campaigns from a distance, without arousing the kind of local speculation known to generate hold-outs and price wars. Having done his homework, he would swoop in and, like a tornado, suck up everything in a targeted area. Among the many real-estate investments his company YiDa Properties had made, not all were immediate successes, though.

From Chai's perspective, a few were just ahead of their time. *They will turn a profit soon*, he told himself. From the perspective of the press and Western news agencies who loved to highlight the possibility of failure, they were "ghost towns," expensive mistakes and misallocations of capital that would drag companies like his, and possibly the whole banking system, down.

The ghost town into which Lin Chong alighted from the subway was called Mount Liang and was designed as a green, eco-friendly, integrated residential, shopping, services, and commercial complex. The shopping mall and two high-rise podiums had been completed along with a hydro-electric generator in a tidal estuary before any buyers lined up to purchase units. Chai decided to halt further construction of schools, clinics, and government service buildings and wait for the population pool to seep out further into the countryside, closer to Mount Liang's location.

From Chai Jin's perspective it was an investment swamp into which he had poured tons of capital, and he hoped, maybe, if he was lucky, to break even. In private to friends but never to investors, he referred to it as *Liang-ShanPo*, the Mount Liang Marsh.

Rather than let it go to complete waste, and so as to discourage vandals and squatters, he had quite unofficially and, with no paper trail to substantiate it, assented that certain guests take up residence there. These people were inclined to be of a particular type, which is to say, vagabonds but not beggars, wanted by the government for questioning or trumped-up crimes. They tended to be nonviolent offenders and those who had religious affiliations the government felt threatened by. Many of them were hackers.

Lin emerged from the subway station into an elaborate pedestrian square devoid of pedestrians at the center of the two podiums and in front of a shopping mall, largely free of stores. He saw one small restaurant on the ground floor selling noodles and dumplings and could see steam rising from the pot, so he knew someone must be around. He walked over and was greeted by the proprietor, Zhu Gui.

"What's recommended?" Lin asked.

"We have noodles and dumplings. The dumplings are popular, unless you prefer noodles," Zhu Gui replied elliptically.

"Give me fifteen dumplings, some cucumber pickle, and a stewed egg."

"Serve yourself the pickles. Get a beer from the fridge if you're thirsty," Zhu said as he busied himself with the dumplings, which he brought to the table after a few, short minutes together with the hard-boiled, stewed egg cut in half. He took a stool next to Lin Chong and stared at him as he ate.

Lin disregarded the annoyance and said, "Not a lot of customers, I see." He stared back at Zhu Gui. He was handsome, with prominent cheekbones, and had dyed blond his hair and beard.

"Nope, you're the first this afternoon." He looked out at the empty plaza. "Might get busy at dinner time."

"Hungry?"

"Thanks." Zhu Gui beamed as he slid the plastic cover off a pair of disposable chopsticks and helped himself.

Surprised by how familiarly the proprietor behaved, Lin Chong said, "Friend, I am here looking for the leaders of Mount Liang Marsh. You know where I can find them?"

"Why do you want to find that lot?"

"I am, as it were, on the run."

"Well, you need an introduction. They don't meet just anyone."

"I have one, from their benefactor in Shanghai."

"You mean the Little Tornado?"

"Yes, Lord Chai Jin. How did you know?"

"He is on excellent terms with the leaders. When two of them were on the lam, Chai Jin put them up at his place. And he lets us use this property development for free. We owe him big time."

Lin noted the "we." "Seems I have been blind all along. *You* are one of the leaders!"

Zhu Gui smiled. "Here I'm known as the Parched Earth Crocodile. You need to meet our 'executive committee,'" he said euphemistically. "Wang Lun, Song Wan, and Du Qian. I run the canteen here on the ground floor. I sniff out who is looking for whom and why. Then I let the ExCo know."

"So, can I meet them?"

Zhu took a bosun's whistle from a shirt pocket and gave it a loud toot. Lin Chong looked on wondering what that was for.

Shortly, he heard the quiet whine of a drone descending from floors above. It glided into the restaurant, approached the table, looked at Lin Chong, and flashed a green light, then sped out of the canteen and disappeared upward.

"Yep, we can go." Zhu Gui smiled.

Zhu Gui led the way to the emergency stairwell. "We have a bit of a hike."

"Why not take the elevators?"

"We want to conserve electricity, only use the power generated by the tidal estuary, totally off the national grid, as it were."

"But this place is empty. Surely you are not consuming all that power?"

"You'll see," Zhu Gui said smiling. "Also, we want anyone who comes a-knocking to have to hike a bit, including pesky officials or Public Security. There is nothing important on the first twenty floors. Did you notice that the two podiums are linked by skywalks on the twentieth floors?"

Lin nodded that he had.

"That is the center of our world, as it were. Not the ground floor."

They had ascended the stairwell in the furthest-east podium. When they got to the twentieth floor, a slightly winded Lin Chong followed Zhu Gui into the building. Expecting to see the residents of the building, or at least their apartment doors, he was greeted by a dark room filled with rows and rows of what looked like racks of computer server blades, the hundreds of cables all well labeled, organized, and air-conditioned, their green, red, and yellow LEDs flickering in the darkness like a field of fireflies in the summer.

They crossed the skywalk to the west podium. At its center, near a bank of unused elevators, was a larger community meeting room with a sign over the door inscribed, "Righteous Fraternity Conference Room."

Inside was a long boardroom table around which sat three men who looked askance at Lin Chong when he was led in by Zhu Gui. The man in the center was shorter than the other two and bookish, wearing an ill-fitting white track suit and thick glasses. The two by his side were quite tall, a good hand taller than Lin Chong, and had penetrating stares.

The man in the center spoke first. "I am Wang Lun. My handle is White-Clad Scholar. These two colleagues are Song Wan, known as Heavenly Diamantine, and Du Qian, known as Thunderhead Diamantine. Together with

Zhu Gui, whom you have befriended, we are the leaders of this merry little band of like-minded men and women. And you are?"

Taking the lead from Wang Lun, Lin Chong replied with the formality characteristic of China's demimonde, the world of Rivers and Lakes. "I am Lin Chong, major and deputy in command of the Unit 61398 cyber warfare unit of the PLA, at least until several weeks ago. My handle is Panther Head. I fell under the radar of General Gao Qiu, whose bastard son coveted my wife. He arranged to have me dealt with, disgraced, ruined. I have escaped the dogs who were going to kill me, offing them both, and carry a letter of introduction from Lord Chai to you."

"How is the Little Tornado?"

"He is well. I have never met a man like him before, so prominent and seemingly so willing to risk his reputation to seek justice."

"Well, the family background provides him with that 'ironclad carte blanche,'" Wang Lun mused.

"I am grateful for his help, but I worry that someday he'll overstep even the boundaries of *his* protections."

"What can we do for you? We aren't seeking new members. We don't have anything to offer. Really, you would be better off going somewhere else." Song and Du's eyes both questioned Wang's statement.

"I am not seeking anything but to be of service and to join your group. I saw that you have a lot of computer hardware. I can definitely be handy."

"No doubt, but we don't even know you. You might be a government spy, for all we know."

"I am a man on the run who has been ruined by despicable louts. Why should you suspect me?"

Song Wan spoke up for Du and Zhu, "Lord Chai has vouched for him. We owe Chai our right testicles for all he has done for us. I don't think we can really afford to spurn his request."

"Okay, "said Wang, "but entrants to our fraternity must make a pledge."

"I am very literate. I can write quite an earnest pledge," Lin Chong responded.

Wang chuckled at the naiveté. "You were never a member of a university fraternity, were you? No. You must make a pledge to get into this group; you have to successfully complete a task we assign you."

"Name it. If it is within my power, I'll do it."

"You need to deliver someone's head to us on a platter. Figuratively speaking. We have a list of enemies, people who are unjust bullies the world would be better off without. Destroy one of them and bring us proof."

"That won't be hard."

"In three days."

"And what does your fraternity do, exactly?"

"Time enough to discuss that later," Wang Lun stood up and ushered Lin Chong toward the door. "Zhu Gui will show you to your quarters. Your room has a high-speed internet connection. Please take precautions in how you use it. There are a couple of places you can grab a meal, including Zhu's, if you are willing to take a hike."

As they walked to his quarters, Zhu Gui saw Lin Chong was a bit disappointed with the outcome. "Cheer up. Wang Lun's just that way. You need to get to know him. He was a respected student who did a master's at Oxford and then was sent overseas to do his PhD in computer science in Japan. He published the first papers describing blockchain and cryptocurrencies under a Japanese pseudonym. You might know him as Nakamoto Satoshi."

Lin Chong's eyes widened. No! Not the mystery man who had created Bitcoin. But yes, the characters for Nakamoto Satoshi were 中本哲史; Nakamoto can mean "Originally from China," and Satoshi meant "Wise Scholar." Fuck me.

ⴱ 人 ⊂

"IF THE TREES COULD SPEAK, THEY WOULD THANK YOU. IN THIS case, let me do so. Thank you, so much." Dr. Aléjandra Chavez hung up the phone, stared out the office window, and just soaked in the San Luis Obispo California sunshine. She wanted to remember this moment forever, just like this, and so she savored it, prolonged it. Perhaps a bit too long. Her TA, Luke Jennings, grew concerned and interrupted her reverie.

"Professor? Everything okay?"

"Yes, indeed, Luke. Everything is just fine. Better than fine." Chavez picked up the phone again and pushed an extension number. "Tony, get in here right away and prepare for some serious celebrations."

Tony Millard, a postdoctoral mycology researcher, rushed over and gripped the doorframe to whip himself into the office. "What's up, boss?" he said with characteristic energy and enthusiasm.

"You both know that I have been under some pressure the past week or so."

The two men nodded sympathetically.

"You know I got this letter from the government telling us to be prepared to show results in six months or lose our funding. It's really been weighing on me. We built this great team, and you all have done great work, but science takes time, and you can't schedule a breakthrough by circling a date on the calendar."

They nodded again.

"Well, some weeks ago I was approached by a new investor. New to me, anyway. Have you heard of Grönland Capital? No? Me neither. They are an SRI firm." The two men stared back blankly. "Socially Responsible Investing. Now get ready. I spoke to the CEO a couple of times, a woman. I submitted details about our current endowment. So, she says to me last week, 'What would you need to double the people you have on the project, increase the range of the sensors and number of networks being monitored, and put another hundred acres under research?' I sandbagged an estimate, enough to put the most sophisticated and sensitive gear that's ever been in a forest and sink that into every two meters square, plus fund full-ride scholarships for all existing team members and have enough left over to double the team with full rides."

Their eyes widened.

"She just said, 'Yesssss.' To the full endowment." Chavez beamed.

"Just like that, no strings?" Tony asked incredulously.

"We'll look at the boilerplate they send over, but what she is talking about are insignificant, positive strings, in a sense. First, she wants the network linked to a data center they own. They won't own the data; we just use their facilities and store the data there. Second, she said the concentration of the research can be on the inter-species and intra-species communication. Focus on what is communicated, how it is communicated, and how reciprocity works to the benefit of all the forest species. Finally, we *don't* have to come up with how to tell the trees to grow faster. Not even on their wish list."

Tony smiled. Although that was a possible benefit to the research they were doing, he had always been uncomfortable stating that in funding proposals. "Anything else?"

"They own a stand of old-growth timber in Northern California. They want one hundred acres of that put under the scope of the research, too. Jordan's lawyers are reaching out to our endowments office. She said she wants this to get underway as a high priority for their team."

Tony had been disappointed by fickle endowments funding for past scholarships and could not help but be pessimistic. "Any chance it won't happen?"

"Of course, it might not happen, but right now I want to savor the moment and look forward to when I can tell the Department of the Interior threatening the grant that they can kiss my Costa Rican ass."

The two men were unsure whether it would be more offensive to laugh, or not to laugh.

⊃ 人 ⊂

AFTER LIN CHONG HAD SETTLED INTO AN EMPTY APARTMENT furnished with a desk, two chairs, a mattress on the floor, a small fridge, hotplate and microwave oven, and minimal lighting, Zhu Gui had delivered to him through the Righteous Fraternity's dark web board a document bearing the list of targets. No email addresses and no real names were used on the dark web board. Only the sobriquets each hero had chosen. The list was encrypted and could be opened by those who knew the real names of the person who had posted it.

Lin Chong dug into the list. Most targets were individuals. People whose unjust, corrupt, maligning abuses of power stood out in a sea of people living afloat in an ocean of misery. *KuHaiYuSheng*, Lin thought. Alive in the Sea of Bitterness and Pain.

The list included information about the malicious evidence of their wrongdoing, links, private details, etc. Lin Chong was impressed at the depth of the intelligence gathered and collated. Besides individuals, the list included some organizations and some events. Events could be targeted to cause embarrassment or disruption to a malicious person, thus shining a spotlight on them of which the media or some upright official might take notice.

The file also included a map of nodes: how any of the people on the list were connected to others on the list, or common links between them who might or might not be innocent but were important to both. Nodes extended outside of China to people in places like Hong Kong, Thailand, Indonesia, Vancouver, Silicon Valley, and New York. Clicking on any node opened the file on that person.

He explored the map. There were thousands of nodes, but one caught his attention: Cai Jing, Chief of the Technical Department of the Ministry of State Security, with whom he had interacted at the last quarterly meeting.

He opened one of Cai's direct connections, Liang Shi-jie, Cai's son-in-law and Party secretary in a third-tier city. Intelligence collected in the file demonstrated that Liang was setting up a sweetheart deal, bluffing and cajoling some peasants off their land, which he knew was rich in rare-earth minerals vital to China's semiconductor industry. Mining rights would go to a company of which Liang and Cai had substantial back-door ownership.

Lin Chong clicked on another node connected to Liang, a man named Yang Zhi, code-named Blue-Faced Beast because of the large port-wine birthmark that extended from his left eyebrow to chin. He oversaw intimidating the locals and delivering the "gift" to Liang and Cai, though his official job was as a local member of State Security.

An event connected to the nodes was a negotiation soon to be held.

Lin Chong decided to dig into this target. To avoid detection, he worked through the dark web, entering through a local VPN and connecting to a second VPN service in tandem within the dark web, re-emerging from another location. He deployed a tool to break into the servers of the geological survey company whose name was mentioned in correspondence between Cai and Liang. He rummaged within it until he could download the survey results of the land in question, its mineral content, and an estimation of the yield to a mining company.

A couple hours' more research and he was able to make an estimate of the real value of the land to the mining company, forecast the impact on the share price, and identify members of the peasants' negotiating team and their relatives, including one son studying law at Beijing University, and members of the press focused on rural rights, the environment, corruption, and social equality.

He spent another hour packaging the data into a credible presentation and, of course, exposing the roles of Yang Zhi, Liang Shi-jie, and Cai Jing. This package was sent from "a friend" to all concerned. Then he crashed, sleeping through the day.

It took twenty-four hours, but impacts started to be evident. The law student at Beijing U got busy on social media, news reports began to be published, and reporters showed up in the small, dirt-poor village. Lin Chong knew that whatever Liang had hoped to finagle, the plan was exposed to the sunlight and foiled.

He reached out to the Exco and requested a meeting, granted quickly, and descended the two stories to the twentieth floor and the Righteous Fraternity Conference Room. The four Exco members were there, Zhu Gui,

Song Wan, and Du Qian surrounding Wang Lun. Wang Lun started, "So whose head have you delivered?"

Lin Chong walked them through the node he had focused on, saying he had chosen an event rather than person, the information he had sourced and analyzed, the presentation he had sent to interested parties, and the response thus far. He then asked if they had any questions.

Wang Lun was the first to respond again. "Normally, we expect some tribute, some return, something that pays the bills, in short some money or cashable value to accrue to the fraternity through these pledges. I guess I need to make everything clear to you, huh?" he said dismissively.

Lin Chong had half expected a "congratulations," "welldone," or "welcome to the club," not a kick in the balls. His eyes narrowed, "Has anyone done better at their pledge in three days?"

Zhu Gui stepped in. "Frankly, no. Well done, Lin Chong. I think the White-Clad Scholar's point is, we need funding to survive, to do what we do here. So be mindful of that in the future. Any objections to Panther Head joining us?" He looked around the table.

Everyone nodded in agreement.

"Welcome to the Righteous Fraternity!" he said and clapped him on the shoulder. "You asked in the last meeting, 'What is it that this fraternity of yours does exactly?' Time to find out. Song Wan and Du Qian, do you mind taking him on the grand tour?"

"With pleasure." They beamed and stood up. "Follow me," Song Wan said.

Lin Chong bid Zhu Gui and Wang Lun adieu and followed the two tall fellows out and across the skybridge to the Western podium, which he had not yet completed visiting.

The twentieth floor was enclosed but unfinished, walls and doors had not been installed, and it was just one large, concrete, open space filled with over a hundred desks, each set up as computer workstations in various states of nonconformist informality. The individuals working at the desks were as distinctive as the workspaces. Some were heavily tattooed and pierced, others as clean cut as fresh military recruits. Some were buff stalwarts, others looked to be anemic drug abusers. Coifs were every style, from poufy to butch, and every color. Each ten meters was punctuated by a hive of beanbag chairs, some occupied by groups of two or three in lively discussion or competition in an online game, some occupied by solitary burnouts, sleeping to recharge enough to hit the keyboards again.

"This is where most of us work," Du Qian said. "The nodes you tapped to do your pledge are the collective output of these heroes. They read, they observe, they connect, they tap, they spoof, they pfish. They get information and squirrel it away, connect it to other people, make sense of what is obscure. They shine a light on that which the corrupt or powerful want hidden, they deliver truth to those being treated unjustly. Depending on the person being dealt with and the situation, they shame, ruin, hound, or impoverish the perp. Impoverishing them is one way we keep thriving. That means outright stealing from them or threatening to reveal their secrets, and when they try to buy our silence, we use the information we have to steal everything from them," he snickered.

"And the other wing I saw when I arrived in the Eastern podium? Is that the database?"

"Ah, no. That is a cryptocurrency mining operation. That is also where we generate additional revenues for our operations. Zhu Gui mentioned to you the White-Clad Scholar's other Japanese nickname, right? Here at Mount Liang, we have created a new cryptocurrency called Taelspin."

"I've heard of it." This also explained their sensitivity to take power generated independently of the State grid, Lin Chong thought. Cryptocurrency mines were huge power drains, and a blip like that on the power grid map would draw attention.

"We mined most of the early packets out of it. As you know, each succeeding packet gets harder to open, so we are letting the world at it now. The value has increased nicely, about US$3,000 per packet presently, and we hold 200,000 packets give or take, with 500,000 in circulation. We estimate the price will go to at least US$10,000 before we want to start selling off some of it."

"Impressive. I was never into cryptocurrencies, but I'd love to learn more about blockchain," the universally diffused, encrypted ledger system that made the ownership and value accounting of cryptocurrencies possible.

"No problem. Wang Lun is the one to talk to. I know, he likes to lord it over people, but he *is* a fucking genius. He will test you to see if you can keep up with the maths involved. If you pass that test, no worries."

Lin Chong raised his eyebrows and nodded, willing to take on the challenge. "Where did the team come from? How did they find their way here?"

"They used to be white hats, black hats, coders, some game developers. One by one, they fell afoul of some law, or someone, and had to disappear. One by one, they found their way here. Some came from other groups, like us." He could see Lin Chong did not understand. "We are not the only such fraternity in China. There are other enclaves. Guess you didn't know that, huh?"

"I am still not sure I understand what you *do*, though. Is this all just about revenge, balancing scales? What?"

"Let's go upstairs." They led Lin to the stairwell and hiked up two floors. "Are you a spiritual man, Panther Head?" asked Du Qian.

"I reckon I am a Taoist by training, temperament, and my experience of life," hoping that would answer the question.

"And what do you mean by that?"

He thought for a moment. "I try to understand how nature and natural laws are at work at all moments in my life. Tao is a proxy word for the operation of objective reality."

"Good. Not too far off from our understanding." They exited the stairwell and entered a large open space, not furnished, but finished off as a temple. Concrete columns had been painted in a deep vermillion and topped with colorful patterns of cloud and sky, earth and tree, and with images of the all-seeing eye. It was illuminated only with candles bathing the space in golden light, diffused through a thin haze of incense smoke. Row on row of meditation cushions filled the area leading to a dramatic display of statues along the back wall. In the center was a statue of the Maitreya Buddha, gilt and seated peacefully, his aura radiating out. Punctuating each of the rays of wisdom were other small Buddhas, each with their own auras radiating out, and at the intersection of these radiating lines were tinier representations of the Buddha, and so on.

"This is why we are all here. This is the center of Hua Yen."

Lin Chong had, of course, heard of Hua Yen but knew it by the name the government chose to label it, the "evil cult Hua Yen." China's constitution espoused freedom of religion, but religion did not include heretical cults, any movements seeking to indoctrinate the masses with a zealotry born of faith in some foreign idol or never-to-be-realized future. The Communist Party, Lin Chong thought darkly, wanted to reserve this mind space for themselves. Many times in China's long history, central power and stability had been challenged by religious zealots, to no good end. He did not think it odd or wrong that the government would take this line.

"You have heard of us, no doubt," Du Qian said, and Lin nodded. "Well, there is of course a big divide between what they tell the world about us and what we are really about. Mostly, we are about meditation on the nature of the Dharma, what you have called the Tao, or the operation of objective reality, which we see as a pattern of cause and effect, with effects returning to reward or punish those who caused them. For those who create evil in the world, we seek to accelerate the return of the effect to them."

Song Wan continued, "We also find that clearing our minds in meditation makes us better coders, so we hope you will join us!" and clapped Lin Chong on the back.

⊃ 人 ⊂

MCDONALD'S OR BURGER KING? I CAN'T BELIEVE HE ASKED ME that, Nancy Nillson brooded with a patient smile. *This is a first date, we are dining in an okay restaurant, what kind of quiz is this?*

"Fries or burgers?" she asked dryly seeking more detail before committing to an answer.

The handsome and earnest man her mother had urged she meet when he was visiting DC looked confused for a moment, then understood the game and said, "Both."

"Burger King for burgers, McDonald's for fries."

"It was a trick question!" he laughed. "Of course, the answer is In-n-Out," followed by a loud guffaw.

"Ha haaaa," her laugh trailed off almost into a growl. *Another handsome, earnest moron*, she lamented. *How come all the interesting guys I meet are either evil, gay, or atheist?* She had begged her mother many times to vet the men she was recommending, but it seemed the only criteria her mother had was their Christian credentials.

"So, Tom, tell me more about what brings a farm machinery distributor to DC?" she gushed while tuning out his answer, throwing out occasional fawning smiles, "Really?" and "I never imagined" to encourage him to continue talking.

She filled the gap in mental stimulation by replaying her meeting that day with the president. It had been only ten minutes in the Oval Office, but what a ten minutes. "Nancy, I want to start the meeting by telling you what a great job I think you are doing," Coin had said at the get-go. "I have communicated with President Zhao in China, thanked him for extending the invitation for the state visit, and tentatively accepted it. Good job. Also, you were the only one who stepped up to the plate the first time and got my message about reducing wasteful spending."

Coin was known to be a people person, at least if you were white and Christian, and this was characteristic of his style. "Thank you, Mr. President. Have you had a chance to review the briefing paper I sent?"

"Yes, but I want you to walk me through it." Coin had only read the first-page executive summary and had liked what he saw.

"Of course, Sir. Similar to the event of 2017, another large section of the Larsen C ice shelf in the Antarctic appears to be about to break off. The 2017 chunk was the size of Delaware, but was already submerged, that is to say, not landbound when it broke off, so it did not create an appreciable rise in ocean level. It was, however, a media bonanza for the climate change crowd." She looked into his eyes to make sure he had not zoned out. He remained attentive.

"This time, the piece is expected to be the size of Rhode Island, and it is mostly landbound, which means it will measurably, if minutely, impact ocean levels. My proposal is to absorb a potential feeding frenzy about climate change for the liberal media and co-opt it into a bigger, feel-good, moonshot for your administration, the American people, and the world."

Coin nodded; he liked her priorities.

"Antarctic ice represents a tremendous store of clean, freshwater, something in desperate shortage in some parts of the world. We will not let that go to waste. Some engineering friends have responded to me with some *very* preliminary reactions on my idea, but so far, they say it is feasible to sail the ice block. We will drop concrete masts 200 feet tall, pre-rigged with sails, solar cells, and transponders onto the ice mass. They estimate if they are dropped from a height of 600 feet, the base of the mast will impact the ice and penetrate to a depth of eighteen to twenty-five feet, rendering them stable. NOAA computers will model wind and current conditions real time and, once underway with sails unfurled, will make coordinated corrections to sail direction, angle, and trim to optimize navigation and speed, which will be slow, but measurable."

"I like your idea to sail it to South Africa," the President interjected, demonstrating he had at least seen that idea. "That's a Christian side of Africa, right?"

"Predominantly so, Sir. The country has been undergoing a prolonged drought and its export-oriented agriculture is threatened."

"I love this idea. As a nation and a civilization, we are trying to win friends and markets in Africa effectively under attack by China. It's bold and hopeful. I can see the headlines , 'Green in the Sahara,' and pictures of well-fed children eating fresh vegetables they just picked."

"Absolutely, sir. However, just to be clear, the Sahara is in North Africa. Definitely there will be pictures of children romping in well-irrigated fields full of vegetables."

"What's your estimate on the probability of success and what will it cost?"

"Firstly, if we do nothing about it, the probability of failure is 100 percent; the ice shelf will slide off and melt, and any negative outcomes will be blamed on those who did nothing and the 'big, bad polluters.' Early estimates are a better-than-50 percent chance that at least half the water mass can be salvaged and utilized. As for cost, there will be tens of thousands of masts. We expect to sell advertising on the sails. Progress of, let's call it NOAA's Ark, will be beamed twenty-four seven to the world. 'Who is making the world a better place, who is trying to save the world, who is part of this grand project to make people's lives better?' The answer will be 'The US and the Advertisers.' One of my advertising friends estimated we could actually turn a profit, but I won't put that in the bank. Then there is the cost of preparing the bay into which the ice will be sailed to capture freshwater melt."

"Doesn't really answer my question. What will it cost, first pass, ballpark?"

"Just shy of a billion."

"Okay. So, let's put it in perspective. There was a 500-million-dollar ad-spend at the last Super Bowl. That was during a four-hour period. Yes, high viewership, etc., but we are talking about spreading ad donations out over...?" he looked to Nancy for help.

"A year, sir, to sail it to Africa."

"So, we could probably defray half the cost through selling advertising, easy. Another chunk of it can come out of our foreign aid budgets. I like it. Even if it never makes it to Africa, at least we tried to make the world a better place. The goodwill generated by being a leader in the world, priceless. I want you to reach out to NOAA and the Army Corps of Engineers as a first step. Bring them together with your engineering friends. This is not a 'think about it and get back to us' situation, but a 'don't tell me it can't be done, tell me how it can be done and do it immediately' situation."

"Yes, sir. Thank you, sir."

Coin looked at his watch and saw he had one more minute allocated to the meeting. "Nancy, this reminds me of that entrepreneur who is putting up 600 million of her own money to fund that plastics recycling platform in the middle of the Pacific. Ballsy."

Nancy had read about it and, like the president, admired the initiative.

Nancy gathered her thoughts into a response. "Yes, sir, it certainly is similar. Like what you achieve with the ice shelf: a big, inspiring effort to make lives better. The owners did comment that they benefited from not having any government or authority looking over their shoulders or having to make approvals."

"This is an example of what I always say, the least government is the best government. Just get the hell out of the way and let business solve problems. But in the ice shelf case, I don't think business will take care of it, so let's save the world!" the president said in conclusion.

Nillson emerged from thoughts of the meeting that day to the dreary date underway. Tom had continued talking, following crumbs of encouragement she sprinkled in as they worked on their main courses.

When she had finished and parked her fork and knife as a signal to the bus boy, who came and took her plate, he said, "So, tell me about yourself, Nancy. Your mother says you work for the government somewhere?" so she had to answer substantively.

"Yes, I do work in the government. I work for the president," she said mustering a genuine smile.

"Oh... Yeah, she did mention that. What's he like?"

He doesn't even remember my mother told him I work for the president!? And when reminded, he doesn't ask what I do, just shifts to the president. If I only had a bitcoin for each brain-dead suitor my mother introduced, I might be able to attract a man worthy of me.

ᗐ 人 ᗕ

"OKAY. BETTER!" THE FILIPINA REHABILITATION NURSE COAXED a pained Li Jun as he hesitated to place his weight one more time onto the new foot prosthesis while he gripped handrails to support himself.

This was the first time he was trying out the device and liked neither the idea nor the feel of it, but knew he had no choice. Best to get on with it, he pushed himself. He took several tentative steps. He had been told to expect discomfort and perhaps some phantom limb disturbance. "I think

I can manage the pain," he said, swallowing it instead. "It will get better with time."

The nurse smiled, "Yes, it should. Let's take it off now, and you can try it longer tomorrow."

Several weeks earlier he had woken up in this hospital in Makati, Philippines. After passing out with the loss of his foot, the medic on board the Leviathan had kept him in an induced coma until the typhoon passed, and they could get a helicopter ambulance out to the rig to pick him up. The Filipino emergency medical system was already stretched thin coping with the devastation wrought by Typhoon Diwata, so he had not been flown to the mainland until almost four days after the accident.

It took the doctors in Manila several days to stabilize him and get an infection under control. He had agreed to an operation to saw off another inch of shin bone to clean up the mess at the end of the stump and an osseointegration to insert a metal pin. Another two weeks were needed before they could fit him for the foot. The doctors told him he was young and strong and healed rapidly.

It was now a month since the accident. He had held a teleconference with his team on board the rig almost daily since he had been brought out of the coma. The team had gotten the solar panels stowed before further damage took place, and the Jaws had survived the storm, he was relieved to find out. When they had arrived at the gyre, they sent him video of the expanse of floating garbage surrounding them even though there was no land on the horizon in any direction for hundreds of miles.

Bu Qing had been put in control of operations, and on each call Li Jun shared thoughts with him about what next steps should be. Both knew this was as much for Li Jun's spirits as for any necessity, and both were glad for the opportunity. The prior week they had deployed the 2xSolar floats and sent him video of the sight, the scarab-colored solar panels an undulating field hundreds of square meters in size and, as expected, generating more power than needed. Two days ago, they had deployed the Jaws, and the captain positioned the rig in a direction such that wind, currents, and the amount of incoming detritus would be optimized.

His morning call was about to start, so he wheeled himself back to his room and propped up a tablet computer on the adjustable table. The screen flashed on alerting him to the incoming call.

"Hey, Bu Qing," he greeted. He could see sitting around the Flood Dragon Di Cheng and Ni Wan, along with the captain. "Hey, guys, nice to see you all."

"Everything okay with you?" Captain Aung Win asked.

"A little better. Tried on my new foot today. Felt okay. I will be walking the deck in no time!" he said cheerfully.

The men on the rig looked at each other and did not comment.

"We did a test run today, Boss," Bu Qing said. "End to end worked fine, sorting, washing, drying, crushing, extruding, pelletizing, bagging. One hundred percent across the board. Only problem we might have is that we have no control over the mix. Our capacity is weighted toward PE, PET, some PP, some nylon. We seem to be getting more nylon and styrenics than we expected. Anyway, it is early days."

"When will you start full production?"

"Another week. We are planning for the first delivery in another fifteen days."

"Well done," Li Jun congratulated. "When is the next supply vessel coming out from Naha?"

"Departs Okinawa in ..." Bu Qing looked to Aung Win for the answer.

"Three weeks," Aung Win finished.

"Well, I will talk to my doctors and see if I can make it on to that ride."

Again, the men looked at each other. "Take care, Boss. See you soon," Bu Qing said.

"You, too. See you soon."

On disconnecting from the teleconference, the tablet screen lit up again prompting him to take a new call from the CEO of the company making the entire bet on the whole Leviathan project. He was not expecting this. "Good morning, Orö. It is quite late where you are."

The blond-haired, forty-something face of Orörd Jordan appeared from her office, the window behind dark with the Scandinavian midnight sky, her face slightly grayed from the blue light of the monitor at once illuminating and capturing her image. She shrugged her shoulders and smiled. "Money never sleeps, Li Jun, so alas, neither do I. How are you doing? Doctors treating you well?"

"Yes, ma'am. Good doctors. I got your flowers and the books and magazines you sent." He turned the tablet so she could see the huge, colorful, tropical bouquet of fragrant flowers that had arrived the week before.

It was the third "cheer-up care package" he had received under Jordan's name.

"Looks lovely. Glad they did a good job on it," she said.

"I just talked to the Leviathan. Deployment is proceeding as scheduled. They ran a full system test yesterday. I am going to try to catch the next supply vessel out to the rig from Okinawa in three weeks to join them. I should be up to it by then."

Orö looked into his eyes, paused a moment, and said, "We need to talk about that, Li Jun. I know how much this project means to you. You were there at the start of the planning for retrofit in Singapore, you pushed and shoved and sweat and moved mountains sometimes to get Leviathan out to sea, to do this important clean-up. But I feel you have sacrificed enough for the project. I do not want you to return to Leviathan."

"Ma'am, I am, or I will be, fit for duty. I really want to return. Like you said, I was there at the start. I want to see it through."

"I know you do," she said in a tone that reminded him of the consoling Mama Fei had succored him with as a young man experiencing setbacks. "But it is not entirely my decision either. You know we provided a generous insurance package for you. In addition to an immediate payment of one million dollars for loss of your limb, you will also get 110 percent of your salary for life, so long as you cannot resume the work you were insured to do. And since that work was defined as COO on a floating recycling plant, and there is only one in the world, it means you could still work a job on land, draw a full salary, and take the other salary and sock it away. I hope you see that as good news." She paused to look at how he took the message.

"More importantly, due to the increased risk of another accident, the same insurance company refuses to re-insure you for service on the Leviathan."

"But. But I would be willing to work there without insurance," he said, the disappointment visible to her.

"I know you would, Li Jun. You are a strong, fearless man. And compared to the circumstances you grew up around, life on the Leviathan is gentle, orderly, and fulfilling." She laughed, hoping he would understand the humor. "But on this I must insist. I would personally be devastated if you were further injured or lost your life to this project."

"I understand," Li Jun said with resignation, head held low.

"Now, cheer up!" she said commanding attention and making him raise his head to face her again. "You are too wonderful a person, too action oriented a manager, too loyal to the mission, and too reliable to be retired or dismissed by me. I value you too much. When you get clearance from the doctors, I am flying you to Beijing to take on a new role. Instructions will be awaiting you when you get there. The job is more important than Leviathan, and I want you to oversee it."

"I am... overwhelmed. Thank you."

"Don't thank me yet. The job is every bit as important, every bit as dangerous, as on board the Leviathan. My team will be sending you some things to read and online courses to prepare you. You up for it?" she said rousing his spirits one more time.

"Yes, ma'am. I am. Thank you."

⊃ 人 ⊏

TWO WEEKS WENT BY FAST FOR LIN CHONG. THE NORMALITY OF life had disappeared. He no longer lived to a schedule, rising together with Zhenniang, leading his unit in the day and returning home in the evening, to repeat the cycle again and again. No one lived a well-defined pattern here at Mount Liang. Or at least it was completely different from the old pattern. He welcomed this. It helped to keep his mind off that which he could not change and place his mind deep into coding or meditation.

Hua Yen, the Crowning Glory of Profound Understanding, was a sect of Buddhism that had flourished 1,300 years ago at the end of the Sui and beginning of the Tang Dynasty, he had learned. It derived unique strength from its four patriarchs' analysis and exposition of meaning in the Flower Garland Sutra, an ancient text over a million words in length.

Its last major patron, or in this case matron, had been China's only empress, Wu Ze-tian. Perhaps because of the misogynist vilification of Empress Wu after her reign, it had fallen into obscurity, but not disappeared completely.

Heavenly Diamantine and Thunderhead Diamantine, the Buddhist handles of Song Wan and Du Qian, had come from Xi'an, an ancient capital of the Tang Dynasty, and from an early age were initiated into the sect by a venerable monk in a small, inconspicuous temple, a caretaker of the Way. He raised them from babes after their parents were killed at the end of the Cultural Revolution. The two of them had sworn to the monk to restore the former glory of the old school, but as soon as they began to attract converts, they also attracted the unwanted attention of the government and were driven underground.

Lin Chong was initiated into Hua Yen's detailed metaphysics and logic as explained by the founders. The sect combined elements of both the Hinayana philosophical approach and the Mahayana religious approach. The school's Sudden Teaching method rivaled Zen's approach to satori's sudden, indescribable, intuitive enlightenment. A believer was to be ever vigilant in differentiating conventional reality—the reverie-filled haze of distraction in which most humans existed—from absolute, objective reality, or truth, which one had to strictly clear the mind of habituation and programming to perceive. At the same time, one focused on the paradox that even in conventional reality one could find absolute reality, and vice versa.

Lin had not devoted considerable time to seated meditation. He had trained in Taoist martial arts to a level where he performed them spontaneously. The ancients said "naturally" or "synthetically," free from distraction or a programmed mind. This ability to immerse himself, to discipline mind to focus, had served him well in his chosen field. He could sit at a computer for hours, reviewing lines of code until he found the weak link. When writing, the code flowed from a well-defined intent. Hua Yen meditation acted on him like an even more concentrated mind booster.

There were meditation sessions twice a day, two hours per session, in the morning and evening. Either Du Qian or Song Wan would deliver a sermon on some aspect of Hua Yen Buddhism, something to be visualized and concentrated on during the meditation, or an aspect of self to dive into, explore, expose for its falsehood, habituation, or karmic attachment to misery, and then dissolve.

After sermonizing the message of the day, they all did a breathing set in which each meditator would take slow, deep inhalations, then project energy from the sexual center straight up the body's line of chakras to the superior center by a tonally bursting "Hap" at the start of the exhale, then relaxing the body as the rest of the breath was released, "Paaaaaaaa," then repeating for one cycle of the rosary, 108 breaths. Breaths were regulated to three per minute, so one cycle took thirty-six minutes.

The room then fell into silence as each meditator cycled through the rosary again, this time seeking to slow the breath to two per minute. With each exhalation a part of a sutra revealed in that day's sermon was repeated. With each inhalation the lesson of the sutra was visualized as being installed or activated on a cellular level throughout one's mind and body.

Today, Du Qian had spoken about the nature of the times in which they lived, how the world is such a fucked-up place, but this is the blessing of difficult times.

If all was right in the world, it would be hard to see how Dharma, the laws of the universe, operated, because the wheels of Karma would turn slowly. The desperate state of the world, though, roused one to action, outside and inside. The lesson was not to take delight in feeding or exercising the resentful mind, a habitual characteristic of the human realm. Instead, he exhorted all to work with mind, then speech and actions would be tamed, bearing the fruit of peace rather than war, kindness rather than cruelty, compassion rather than revenge.

The Maitreya Buddha, the Future Buddha, was coming back, and maybe now was the right time; maybe he was just waiting for the situation to be primed. Then all would be well. All sentient beings would shed their mortal coils, and those that had perfected their souls would join the Buddha in an enlightened Pure Land, while those that had not, well, have compassion for them.

But today, Lin Chong's mind was on the topic introduced the day prior in the sermon—interpenetration—the connectedness or mutual reflection of all phenomena in the universe. This was a cornerstone of Hua Yen and was an observation from the Buddha's first sermon after reaching enlightenment.

This interpenetration was called Indra's Net and came from an ancient parable of a jewel-encrusted net that spread across the universe. Each jewel reflected the image of all the other jewels in the net with sublime perfection.

Any piece of the universe reflected the whole, and the properties of the whole existed within the fragment. At any fractal scale, one could go up a scale or down a scale and find the same principles in operation. This was depicted in the mural on the wall behind the grand Maitreya Buddha in the meditation hall. The thousands of smaller and ever smaller Buddhas all interconnected by the intersection of the beams of wisdom radiating from their auras.

Interpenetration was not just symbolic of the scalability of Dharma and Karma, but also of the wisdom inherent in the fabric of the universe, the potential for great awareness when one gave up the singularity and discrimination of me-you and us-them, and realized that one is connected intimately to the whole. Infinite wisdom would be known if one shattered the false barrier of the singular, isolated ego and released it to be fully sharing with, compassionate of, and learning from the entire universe.

As his breathing and heart rate slowed and attention held fast to his cinnabar field, the area below and behind the navel in the center of his body where the aorta bifurcated, he reached a stasis at the end of an exhale. He was in no rush to inhale, and when he did the air was drawn in as if through a small straw, a thread of breath. Without warning, but without surprise, attention shifted from the cinnabar field to his third eye like a firework skyrocket had been launched. And like the skyrocket, when attention shifted up, ascending into the inner heavens of his experiential universe, it exploded in a chrysanthemum starburst, and as those bursts expanded outwards, they had secondary starbursts and then tertiary starbursts. His field of experience was filled with the image of complex interconnectedness.

When Lin Chong opened his eyes again, the meditation room was empty save Du Qian, who sat nearby. "Brother Lin, you have been away awhile."

"Really? How long?"

"The group finished about an hour ago. Good session?"

"Wow, I can't imagine it's been that long. Seemed only a moment. Yes, very strong, very clear. I saw something in a way I had never seen or imagined it before."

"Well done."

"Actually, I saw something I created for the military, a weapon called Centipede, but it was different. It was Indra's Net."

"Hmm. Perhaps something will come of it."

"Perhaps," Lin Chong said, his mind already deep in thought.

⊃ 人 ⊏

MILI STARTED EACH WEEK WITH A MEETING OF ALL THE GROUPS in her shop. Each of the seven groups would be represented by its leader and one other selected by the leader to attend that day, usually chosen because there had been significant or unusual activity the prior week or an ongoing emergent effort that needed to be acted on. This kept the meetings fresh, not exactly the same faces each week, allowed for beneficial exchange of knowledge, gave more junior-level team members face time with Mili, and also kept the size of the meetings manageable at fourteen plus her.

These meetings also required total concentration. She listened to a range of new information from different parts of the world and possible attack nodes and relied on herself to see connections, threads, "stuff" that the individuals siloed in their domains did not see or connect.

That had not yet happened today, and she guessed it was too much to expect that she would have insights and revelations each week. Or perhaps she was just tired. She had not slept enough and not slept well that weekend. She had spent too much time wandering through virtual environments. In sleep, her breathing had been troubled. The doctors had always said, well, that she was frail. Never mind.

The Russia group lead, Alex Comiskey, was concluding his discussion of some worrying signs that Russian signal intelligence had cracked into NATO communications networks. His team was trying to identify the group or groups that had done the work. The signs were not conclusive but were worth highlighting.

"Thanks, Alexsh. Hu, what have you got today?"

Hugh Chang perked up. "Yeah. Something interesting in China, not certain if it's a 'thing' or not. It seems that the head of Persistent Threat has been removed."

"Removed?"

"We can't say what yet. As you know, we have no HUMINT resources in Unit 61398. However, the CIA sent a terse message to us that a source within the Eastern Military Command reported a meeting between the head of the unit and General Gao Qiu at the command headquarters. Afterwards, there was a flurry of activity at the Unit. We are not sure if the former head of the Unit has been given a new assignment or what. The CIA has yet to determine who the new leader is."

Mili knew as much as anyone about who Hugh was talking about, but for the sake of the group said, "Can you give ush some color on the former head of the Unit, Hu?"

"Sure. His name is Major Lin Chong. Third-generation PLA. Early admittance to TsingHua University, master's in computer science at the PLA science academy. There were not many samples of his coding identified prior to joining Persistent Threat, but based on the limited samples and the memetic analysis, some of his early work after joining was the sniffing tool we called BotSniffer and the spoofing tool Scooper."

"What do you think has happened?"

"We can wait to see if he re-emerges somewhere, but my guess is he has been assigned to another unit, maybe even deeper cover with a new mission."

"Keep an eye on it."

"Yes, ma'am."

"Jill, what have you got?" Mili called on Jill Barnes, who covered RoW, Rest of World. She had brought the new head of her FINSEC, financial security, desk.

"I want to turn it over to Bill. He's got something."

"Bill" Bilaval Singh stood up, all six feet, four inches of him, not including a Sikh turban. He was a newer recruit to the team not aware of the meeting protocols, and he wanted to show proper deference to his boss and Mili, who smiled and said, "You don't have to be formal, Bill. Pleege take your sheat."

"Thank you, Dr. Parekh, Jill. Several weeks ago, you may have heard about the diplomatic row in Singapore. The head of Indonesia's environment and forestry ministry keeled over and died while meeting with a bank in Singapore. The row was over the purpose of the meeting. The Indonesians jumped to some conclusions and started trying to pry open the doors to get any ill-gotten wealth returned to the nation. The bank denied any of the minister's funds were there. Technically, this was correct at the time the bank said that. However, alarm bells had been ringing at Treasury about this huge transfer of funds. Treasury went back to Indonesia and said, according to records, around $300 mil was remitted to six banks. The Indonesians went in and seized the minister's computers and files. The bank then said, 'Like we said, when he died in our office, there wasn't any of his ill-gotten wealth *in our bank*.'"

"And what ish the NSA interest in thish?" Mili interjected to move it along.

"For one, Minister Idrus Sukabumi did have substantial contacts with radical clerics in Sumatra and had sponsored the construction of a Madrasah after the 2018 tsunami in Sulawesi. He may have been siphoning off funds to support the ISIS caliphate or others. After being remitted to the six banks, the funds were then remitted again, with less traceability this time. They have disappeared."

"Let me clarify, what ish attribution's interest in thish today?"

"Because of the special circumstances and the diplomatic row this was creating, the bank cut through a lot of red tape and surrendered records of the transfers, password log-in records, etc., and the Indonesians shared the activity logs and hard drives off the minister's computer. We had a chance to analyze them. Eunice Stravinsky's fingerprints are on this again."

"Well," Mili sighed tiredly, "that *ish* interesting."

⊃ 人 ⊂

TODAY WAS JUNE 20. THE LAST DAY OF SPRING. THE ANNIVER-sary of the day Zhang Zhenniang had consented to be his bride and Lin Chong had taken her hand in marriage, meant to be a joyous day in Lin Chong's life.

They had been wed in Shanghai, and her father, a retired veteran of the PLA, had arranged a full military honor guard at the wedding. They had walked under the Arch of Sabers and cut the cake with his sword, every-thing. Members of the Shanghai Symphony had played at the wedding ban-quet for which they had twelve tables, 144 guests, in a swank but not too over-the-top restaurant that catered to events like this.

Their honeymoon had been spent in Hainan, known as the Hawaii of Chi-na, at a resort where they had their own bungalow, walled garden, and hot tub. The lovemaking had been amazing. Lin remembered and shook his head back and forth, eyes closed, head hung low, thoughts dark.

Today would have been their third anniversary. In that time, they had grown together as a couple, ever stronger. She knew his work was import-ant and secret and did not ask him about it but comforted him when he was stressed or seemed concerned, just letting him know she was there for him. He listened to her whenever she needed to share ambitions and challenges to achieve stardom at the symphony and let her know he sup-ported her, giving advice on navigating the politics. They had tried to have children time and again. They stopped worrying about it after the doc-tor said that she was still young and later, when career stress abated, she could try again.

Lin Chong stared blankly into the computer screen, finger tapping on, but not pressing, the "enter" key.

Those three years had been magical beyond Lin's expectation, imagina-tion, or deserving. He was so in love with all that Zhenniang embodied. Her skill and passion for music enriched his life. He had never studied music and could not play an instrument, but lying on the couch, his head in her lap as she listened to favorite pieces, he could learn of and love her pas-sion. And she had followed him to the fitness center to maintain her figure and vitality and had developed muscle where she did not know she had any, becoming all the more desirable for it. Lin Chong felt nothing but love for Zhenniang, this miracle who had entered his life.

Today Lu Da had sent a text message to one of Lin's burnable phones requesting that they speak urgently on a messenger service. Lin had passed through a VPN and called him.

"Lin, my dear boy, I have some terrible news, but I wanted you to hear it from me rather than by chance from someone else."

"What? What is it?" Lin asked, bracing himself.

"Zhenniang is dead. She committed suicide last night, sometime in the middle of the night."

Lin was silent for a long time, then asked simply, "How?"

"It seems she hung herself. She used the waist sash of a robe she had, tied it to the water pipe in the bathroom." Lu Da waited for a response from Lin. "I'm sorry to give you the news this way. Her note said that after she lost her job and sponsorship, the Insider kept up the pressure on her, and the bank had reached out about the mortgage on the apartment." He paused again. "Do you need me to come to where you are? They treating you okay?"

"No, Sagacious. No need to come. It won't change anything," he said, voice devoid of emotion, digesting the bitterness in the pit of his stomach. "They have treated me fine here. Thanks for letting me know, but I need some time to process this. Bye."

Lin Chong had sat in the darkness and skipped the meditation practice.

He knew he was to blame. *If I had been a real man when Gao accosted her at the gym, the bastard would have thought twice. And then there was the night at the symphony when I could have insisted to accompany Zhenniang to her after-concert party. The sash of the robe she hung herself with was what she was wearing the last morning I said goodbye to her. I bought her that silk robe on a trip to Hangzhou. And the upstairs neighbor's drainpipe hanging in their bathroom ceiling that together we had painted a sunshine yellow, turning its obnoxiousness into a bright, humorous architectural detail, became her gallows. Zhenniang is signaling me, telling me, blaming me. It is all my fault. I could have prevented this. I should have prevented this. It is all...my fault.*

His thoughts turned to others. *How can I blame myself alone? We were so in love. No one could come between us. But someone had tried.* He saw Gao Yanei's thin, pallid face in front of him and visualized crushing it like a melon in his hands. He imagined the diabolical meanderings of that wastrel's mind and the depths he had sunk to in order to wrest Zhenniang's love from him, to no avail. He replayed the staged and feigned surprise and urgency as General Gao called the guards into his office and accused Lin of being a traitor. He relived the taunting and torture of Fu Yuan and Lu Qian, briefly celebrating a flare of solace in recalling their smashed and pierced bodies at the end of that steel pole he had wielded. *No, others were to blame, too, and some have yet to see justice.*

But Zhenniang took her life in desperation, under pressure from others. How could they all have been so cruel? The symphony dumped her like some used toilet paper. My Zhenniang, so talented. Her benefactor had demanded return of her violin. She had earned the right to use that instrument, they belonged to each other. How could they just seize it? Her audience, didn't they long to see her perform again, or had they abandoned her, too? And the mortgage company, just being the soulless wretches they were destined to be. No. There was a gallery of the guilty, faceless, out there waiting to be punished.

After his deep meditation the prior week, he had realized that if the interpenetration of the Internet of People and the Internet of Things could be actualized, it would create a complex web, a true, real representation of Indra's Net. He had worked several days toying with this idea to write a program linking all the nodes of the Centipede.

This morning, Lu Da had contacted him with the crushing news. It was now late at night. During the past fourteen hours Lin had sat alone at his terminal. Thinking, tinkering, ruminating, fuming, coding. He started by opening the file he had created as a useful exercise after meditating on Indra's Net. As he worked furiously all day, the benign thought experiment he had toyed with was strengthened, given teeth, armor, and self-organizing direction.

With the creation of the Centipede, he had written a bot that would ping devices and determine if they were embedded with the Centipede. The response was cataloged in an ever-growing file at Unit 61398. He did not have access to it. But he did not need it. He did not seek to push the button on a rocket or pull the trigger on a gun he pointed at someone guilty. He wanted to see justice done organically and perhaps hasten the pace of karmic retribution.

The revised program would seek to secure its fidelity and permanence by adapting blockchain. It would seek purpose through what it could learn once it realized what wisdom was to be gathered from complete interpenetration. Now he sat in the dark, within and without, a scowl on his face, right index finger touching, tapping, teasing the "enter" key, the launch key.

Lin Chong knew he could not conceive what would emerge as Indra's Net was released into the wild, what terrible actions it would take against the guilty. Seeking revenge was contrary to the compassion of the Bodhi mind. However, what was Karma but the cosmic guarantee that all wrongs would come back on those who perpetrated them? Better to launch this agent of retribution now, right now, while his rage was hot, and he had the courage.

He would have his revenge. Against someone. Against anyone. Against *everyone*.

SUMMER

JUNE 21, THE FIRST DAY OF SUMMER.

I know. Everyone was looking forward to holidays: summer fun, picnics, camping, block-buster movies, binge-watching favorite shows. Stuff like that you all enjoy.

But anyone who was anyone in the IT industry woke up to an unhappy surprise that day. It was like the World Wide Web had sprung a leak, and no matter how much bandwidth was thrown at it, enough was siphoned off to make the internet feel sluggish. Individual companies' information security departments speculated that the impairment of traffic to their site was due to a weak, distributed denial of service attack on their networks, which their systems were foiling. *Hurray for us!*

Later, everyone realized the impacts were universal, but no one could identify a single point of attack, or reason, or outcome. Eventually, it was speculated that this drag on the internet was caused by the ubiquity of social networks and search engines sucking up data about everyone twenty-four seven. They denied it and indeed could prove that they had not started any new efforts or programs that week to cause the additional burden.

You all never did figure it out. You had to be told.

CHAPTER 4

PERCHED IN THE CHAIRMAN'S BOX AT THE BEIJING OLYMPIC
Bird's Nest Stadium, President Zhao Ji had a perfect view of the field as
the Beijing National Security Football team battled it out with the Jiangsu
Suning team in the finals for the national Super League championship. He
felt comfortable in this moment.

The stadium was packed. Eighty thousand fans screamed, shouting encouragements of "step on it" to their favorites or "you stupid cunts" at the
team they deemed unworthy of victory. The score was tight. It was the beginning of the fourth quarter, and the teams were tied 3–3. Each goal had
been hard won. Either side could still win. No one was giving in.

Zhao loved this game. Indeed, once upon a time he had been pretty good
at it. But there were no pro leagues when he was that young, and his dedication to the Party would never have allowed him to try to make a living
from it. Still, he loved the game.

It helped that China could trace historical records 2,500 years back to
a team sport of kicking a ball around a field. He did not really care that
Egyptians could claim evidence of a ball being kicked around a field 2,000
years before that; theirs was clearly not a team sport. China had invented
football.

He raised bushy eyebrows and focused on the field for a moment as Suning forwards attacked the National Security goal but were repulsed after
an aggressive challenge from the right fullback.

Within an arena of constant change, disciplined and tireless excellence were necessary to win, to defeat an opponent, or to come out on top. This he had learned on the football field. This he had internalized and brought with him to his work in the Party. This he tried to instill in *his* team.

Modern coaches also had teams researching their competition's players, styles of play, formulas for success, and strengths, as well as weaknesses, foibles, and gaps in teamwork. This he had also learned from, keeping an eye on his team. For he was the chief coach, the commander in chief, the president and the chairman, of China. For life, if he willed it.

For now, he did will it. China was an arena of constant change, with old reactionary forces and new radical forces pulling centrifugally at the seams as the nation changed course and continued its arc of historical restoration. He had to keep the nation bound together tight, preventing fragmentation into a dozen shards all moving away from each other to their own agenda-gravitated orbits. That would be a disaster.

Then there was the unfinished business of Taiwan, restoring national integrity and sovereignty before the tumor of Taiwan's multi-party democracy could metastasize in the body politic of China. Democracy was one of the core values espoused by the Communist Party. But by that, he did not mean a one person-one vote, multi-party free-for-all driven by corruption and immoral or amoral interests.

Even the flag bearer for democracy in the twentieth century, the US, was now questioning its own dedication to it in the twenty-first century, was being split by money politics on the left and the right in a tug of war for the center. The center, losing its grip on the two sides, struggled, confused and enervated.

He was sure China was not ready for that, and he was sure he was right about it. *Democracy meant promulgating just policies enabling all to benefit in the progress of the nation so long as each citizen was committed to the progress of the nation, not plotting its destruction or disintegration. And the Communist Party alone represented those interests.*

He knew well that on the football pitch as in government, corruption, bribery, nepotism, cheating, and other forms of rot that diminished the meaning of any progress had to be eradicated. Too many football players, coaches, referees, and sports officials had been convicted of illegitimate player selection, selling berths onto national teams, bad calls on the field, and match fixing.

This rot, this flabby bloat of greed-driven antiperformance, does not produce excellence, and the proof is in the results. Our teams have never made it into the finals of the World Cup. One point three billion people and corruption does not let the cream rise to the top, he darkly reminded himself.

The Chairman's Box was filled with those he had personally invited to attend this event. They were the face of success, wealth, and fame in China. Select members of the People's Consultative Political Conference, many tech company CEOs, and today a famous Hong Kong kung-fu actor-turned-shill for China rubbed shoulders with senior members of military, provincial, and Party leadership. He knew that connecting these people in this way might be an invitation to the kind of corruption he was seeking to eradicate.

Two things led him to take this contrarian action.

Firstly, every person in this room knew that Zhao's priority was to wipe out corrupt practices. He was expressing absolute confidence in each of them that they would never be tempted to personally profit from taking a short-cut. Aligning interests and working together for the greater good of China was to be promoted.

Secondly, also present in the room was his person in charge of the National Supervisory Commission, Su Yuanjing, the man leading all efforts to ferret out graft. On paper he reported to the minister of supervision, but no one was above suspicion, and Su reported to President Zhao. He and Su went back several decades to a time when Zhao was provincial governor of Guangdong, and Su was in Hong Kong prior to the 1997 retrocession.

Su was a straight arrow, and one Zhao had nocked on his bow and dispatched many times to investigate and take out people who were targeting Zhao or his policies for their own personal gains. Tall and urbane, Su had stood down many a threat in the past and was as adept at sniffing out foreign intrigue as he was taking a deep dive into the forensic analysis of a company's ownership and finances.

He watched today as Su worked the room. Always friendly and smiling, he disarmed strangers and those who knew his reputation alike with charm and warmth. Everyone here knew he had the president's ear and confidence, but they also knew that to prick the smallest suspicion of impropriety would be to trigger an investigation from Su.

Some men and women who had attended previous such rarified functions were not found in the ranks today for precisely this reason. They were to be found in uncomfortable prisons, or worse, in undistinguished graves after being convicted of corruption in a court of law and sentenced to death.

These cases were not secret. They were publicized for a reason. The common man, the old hundred surnames, needed to know that Zhao was on their side. No one was above the law. And those who contemplated such villainy needed to know there were stark consequences if he was crossed.

Again, the crowd in the stadium roared, and the attendees in the Chairman's Box gasped as a National Security challenge on the goal was repulsed. The Suning goalie ran to the edge of the box and rolled the ball to his defender, who was attacked by a National Security forward swooping in from behind him.

After a ferocious clash the ball was stolen, passed across field, and then lofted back to the center to a National Security striker poised to smash the ball just out of reach of the goalie into the left top corner of the net. The score was now 4–3 with two minutes remaining.

The striker who had scored jumped, ran, and pranced in jubilation, arms outstretched, embracing the love of the crowd, all eyes and cameras on him. The microchip embedded in his jersey received a command from the advertising auction site licensed to sell ad space for broadcast football. The successful bidder for that moment's share of mind would have their logo and message displayed.

Healthy Chef Instant Noodles flashed vividly on the front and back of the shirt for three seconds as the striker celebrated. Being a tie-breaking score from the favored team within five minutes of the end of the game, all of which were factors in the valuation calculus of the exposure, the ad's placement cost was twenty times that of a score made halfway through the second quarter. Three hundred thousand of revenue had just dropped into the pocket of the Beijing National Security football team owner for three seconds of prime exposure to an audience of 200 million. Looked at that way, it was a bargain.

A group of generals made their way over to Zhao smiling broadly and clapping each other on the shoulders. General Gao Qiu spoke up first, "General Chen's team is certainly kicking ass today!" he said. General Chen San was Gao Qiu's counterpart in charge of the Northern Theater Command, so Beijing's National Security Football team was jokingly "under his command." Actually, the YiDa Real Estate group owned the team and paid a licensing fee to the military for use of the name.

"You can always count on us tall, northern lads to teach you southern shorties a lesson!" General Chen rejoined hoisting a mug of beer and clinking it together with those of his comrades.

They turned and looked to the president, who stood, as usual, without a drink in hand. He had never picked up the habit of drinking socially and now was seen to discourage it by his abstinence. He took up a glass of tart haw juice and toasted them. "A great end to the season, comrades. Rejoice tonight. But remember, *our* work is not done."

General Chen raised his glass higher with this cue. "To restore the Motherland!"

The other generals and President Zhao repeated the pledge, then cleared their drinks, the last gulp swallowed as a horn blew signaling the end of the game. National Security had won.

As the individuals began to leave for their evening plans, some heading to post-victory soirees, others to more private rendezvous, Su Yuanjing approached Gao Qiu and touched him on the elbow. "Old Gao, how are you? We didn't have a chance to chat this evening. I feel hurt."

Gao's face was all relaxed smiles and goodwill as he turned to face Su. This was a hard act to put on. To begin with, he was insulted by Su's effrontery of calling him "Old Gao" like they had been school chums for the past forty years. *The impudence!* Second was the "I feel hurt." Su was not a man on whose list of resented encounters one wished to find oneself. Gao's blood ran cold. "Eh? Commissioner Su, there you are! Quite a game, wasn't it? Right down to the wire."

"Yes. Quite a game. Exhilarating. Say, the president would like to have a word with you before you are off. Do you have a moment?"

"Of course."

Su kept a hand on Gao's elbow and gently guided him in the direction of the president. The people saying their farewells to Zhao understood immediately to clear a path to the president and backed away, leaving Gao to face Zhao with Su at his side.

"General Gao, how is the Eastern Command treating you?"

"Sir, I am fine, working hard. The real question is, How am I treating the Eastern Command? The metrics show I have increased operational efficiency by 15 percent, operational readiness by 20 percent, and ..."

"Yes, I read the reports. Spending is in line, but requests for budget increases are way ahead of your counterparts."

"When viewed from the perspective of the size of the population and economic assets under the protection of the Eastern Command, our requests are actually less than my counterparts. I will have my staff work up an analysis for you."

"Yes. Do that. And remember, I endorsed your candidacy despite some opposition. Do me proud."

General Gao crisply saluted Zhao and barked, "Commander in Chief, sir!" then felt a tug on his elbow as Su gently pulled him away.

ᗡ 人 ᄃ

MILI'S CONDO WAS MORE THAN AN ABODE. IT WAS A LIBERATING sanctum.

She had learned to deal with the looking away, the shunning, or the overly solicitous manner of the public at large. The inconvenience of her physical condition and people's reaction to it could be left behind here.

Most of Mili's considerable salary she sank into the one place that could provide freedom she could not enjoy elsewhere. Here she roamed within virtual reality. Acoustic walls and ceiling, surround sound system, and an automat galley that would deliver cooked, preordered food and drink wherever she was in the flat had been the first additions. In the center of the largest room was a state-of-the-art, eight-*tsubo* Wander Floor made in Japan allowing endless navigation in any direction and inclines of up to ten degrees when indicated by the design of a virtual environment she had entered, all within the apartment. Everything—the sensors, telecommunications, the Ol-Factory-brand pheromone and scent generator, the refrigerator, automat galley, Wander Floor—everything was online with her substantial computer, which had a small airconditioned room of its own. The term "living room" had taken on a new meaning.

On arriving home each night, she would don virtual reality mirrors, a term popularized by the Mandarin term "electric mirrors," *dianjing*, used to describe VR goggles in the country where all such products were manufactured. China had become the leading manufacturer and innovator of mirrors. No one could compete with them for quality, resolution, leading edge design, or especially price. The United States, Japan, Netherlands, and Taiwan rapidly abandoned manufacturing and instead had their designs implemented there.

In Mili's case, she had top-of-the-line gear, no longer goggles or even glasses, but contact lens screens with tiny filaments connecting them to a light, nylon cap that held a power supply, six degrees of freedom sensors, and processors with wireless connection to her computer.

The space was decorated any way she or the computer wanted it. From where she sat, one window looked out over yesterday's actual scene from Mount Fuji, another a quiet, fog- bound day in Maine, and yet another overlooked a small alley in Paris from where she could espy the pretty women coming and going from the chic perfumerie across the street. She had created that scene. Window Shopping, she called it.

Where to go, where to go? she puzzled. Her calendar chimed a reminder of a midnight revelry in Stuttgart. The invitation had made it sound interesting.

She called for a mirror and a white space of wall turned silvery and began to reflect her image.

She looked at herself in the virtual mirror. There she stood on two good legs, not bent, not drooping, tired, or sick, the wheelchair erased from the scene. There she was, standing tall, in a tailored saree in the style of her Mumbai Hindu roots. *Not bad. The curvaceous, Bollywood looks get 'em every time*, she thought wistfully. A full head of black hair draped in rolling curls halfway down her back. Eyeliner and mascara accentuated the mystery of intelligent eyes and glossy lipstick the sweetness of her mouth. Sufficiently full breasts revealed themselves discreetly from the top of her tight blouse that left stomach and navel exposed, a thin, gold chain circling her waist.

She looked more closely at the stomach muscles. Not quite pronounced enough. She reached out and stroked the lines of her stomach on the mirror as she said, "More definition." Immediately the ladder effect of muscle was enhanced.

She called for the closet to open. From a seamless wall emerged a panel and a clothes rack. The rack moved a chain of clothes within her sight, such as an old dry-cleaning shop paternoster would. "I want that piece I bought from Sulaiman," she ordered.

Sulaiman, the hottest fashion designer on the cyberscene, mixed Asian and ultramodern motifs and changed patterns with the environment and the emotions. It was said that "If clothes make the person, Sulaiman's creations make the person honest." The underlying software expressed itself quite independently of the bearer of the clothes. Très chic, très cher, très cyber. His design applied to the saree's *pallu* draped over her shoulder depicting two open hands, the right hand in front of the heart palm out and fingers up in a one-hand prayer, the other palm up in front of the navel.

Mili once met a boor at a cy-bar, a real creep, the kind she felt had no place in virtuality. This fellow would have been better off sticking to limited personal relations on a dimensional plane.

He kept badgering Mili, invading the space of her image and generally being rude, bordering on racist. If Mili had not been enjoying the company of another gentleman at the time, she would have left. But that night she was wearing the Sulaiman creation.

The fuzzy logic generating the clothes measured the temper of the situation. As Mili tried to ignore the boor, the left hand printed on the shirt slowly animated, turned, and pointed at the man while the right hand rotated and closed into a large erect middle finger. "Fuck you, too," the man said in a huff and stormed away.

Satisfied she had selected the right outfit for the evening, she ordered, "Okay. Dress up." Immediately clothes that were floating beside her reflection were worn by the reflection. "Mirror, mirror, on the wall, make me the fairesht of them all," she said with a chuckle.

She called for the menu that emerged from the floor beside her. "Do you have the connection for the party?"

"Yes. Do you want to be connected now? The cover charge is one thousand credits plus time."

"Yesh, yesh," she said gruffly. *It is not that I am unwilling to pay for a good time. And god knows someone has spent good time to create the party world I am entering. But a thousand clicks! Pretty steep. Better be worth it.*

"You are connected," the computer told her.

The scene evolved into an evening soiree around a beautiful pool. The plaza around the pool was marble, and fluted columns held up the stone framework of what might have been an ancient temple. Nevertheless, the pool and the party were open to the sky above, which was cloudless, clear, and filled with stars and a bright white moon. That was rare. The moon she remembered was usually a creamy yellow.

The crispness of the air and its fresh, clean scent suggested she was high in the mountains. She was standing at the entrance above the party, behind a column. Such entrées to cyberscenes were designed so that one did not emerge suddenly out of nowhere startling the guests who had already arrived. It also allowed one to make an entrance with appropriate flair. She came around the column and emerged into the light. A man was waiting there for her.

"Hello, may I help you?"

"Yes, I received an invitation to attend this party. Menu, please give it to the maître d'." The computer corrected any slur to her speech, but otherwise left her voice, language, tone, and accent intact.

The invitation appeared in the man's hands. "Yes. Thank you very much for attending, Dr. Parekh. You are an honored guest. The cover charge is being waived for you."

Mili smelled a scam. *Maybe they're trying to sell timeshare condos in Mogadishu or Calcutta.* "What's the deal?"

"Oh, so sorry to alarm you with our offer. Is this not a beautiful scene, though?"

"Quite nice. And?"

"Frankly, this is the graduating project of the Stanford/Stuttgart class matriculating in information and cyberspace design. We have many distinguished guests here this evening, yourself included, and the rest are the students. Please mingle with your counterparts from industry. Relax, enjoy, and remember the quality of our work if you receive any résumés or portfolios."

Disappointed as she was that she had been snookered into this scene, she was impressed with the quality of the effort and the details.

She could hear frogs croaking in a small pond at the edge of the plaza. She could also hear a cricket to the left in a planter. She walked over to the planter to take a look, the Wander Floor converting the direction and speed of her wheelchair into the pace of her avatar. True to its nature, the cricket quieted, not allowing Mili to find it.

In a hack job of scene emulation, the students would have remembered to have cricket sounds, but on looking for the cricket one would find the sound source, but no insect. She was impressed.

She descended the ramp (stairs were taboo in virtual architecture unless visitors were expected to fly down them) to the pool. People stood and sat in groups. Beautiful people, all dressed in beautiful clothes. Some were talking, some just looking about absorbing the tranquil elegance of the scene.

Who should she talk to? Who were real people and who were not? It was always a conundrum, even for a pro like Mili. Unless they were specially marked, one could not tell well-designed virtual people from real by just looking. She had to talk to them. Ask a few questions. Gauge their answers. Then she could take a guess. It was considered bad form to ask one's menu to verify, unless one wanted to insult someone known to be a real person.

She looked for interesting people. The novelty of creating strange and unusual avatars—luminescent blobs, evolved dinosaurs, giant hands with eyes in the palm, and the like—had worn off long ago. The fashion now was to be as detailed a person as possible.

There was someone in a toga who looked like Aristotle addressing a crowd of admirers hanging on to his every word. Standing by the pool at the far end were some formal-looking executive types who were as likely immersed in a discussion of Tibetan golf courses (where the balls flew further due to the thin atmosphere) as they were talking about stocks and shares. On her side of the pool, a straight shot away, a handsome young man caught her eye.

He was dressed in a tight, batik shirt open at the collar and some khaki chinos. A full head of black hair was oiled back, and he had a day's growth of beard drafting a masculine shadow on cheeks and chin. A dark cloud of chest hair loomed over the definition of his stomach, and a gold chain hung around his neck with a small medallion dangling from it. He explored Mili with bold, intelligent eyes.

When she entered the environment she was visiting, it had communicated with her server, detailed the extent of compatible hardware within her environment, and begun to tailor the experience. The environment had assessed the contents of Mili's bar and automat, habits and preferences, and had ordered up the delivery of a beer. In cyberspace, Mili saw the approach of a butler dressed in tails and black tie. "Your drink, mademoiselle." Mili had set the default personal status to "unmarried" whenever entering social settings.

The default status also said she was a software design authenticator at an intellectual property law firm in the DC area, a cover provided by the NSA so that she and other employees could continue to have an online social presence without being pestered or visible as NSA human resources.

Mili reached out to pick up the glass. "Thank you."

"My pleasure, mademoiselle. Can I help you at all?"

"Yes. Who is that person there?" she nodded toward the man in batik.

"Yes, Mlle Parekh. That man would like to meet you."

"Really? And how do you know this?"

"You were on his invitation list."

"You still haven't told me who he is."

"I can introduce you."

The mysteriousness of the exchange with the butler piqued Mili's interest. "Please, then."

She followed the butler toward the man. His eyebrows rose as the butler prepared an introduction.

"May I present Dr. Mili Parekh. Dr. Parekh, this is Vaughn Neumann." His duty discharged, the butler turned to other guests leaving the two strangers facing each other.

"Vaughn," Mili began but was cut off by him.

"Dr. Parekh. It is indeed a pleasure," he said with hand extended, the fingers an open V between the ring and middle finger.

Handshakes were virtually impossible, and bowing was too easy. Cyber etiquette called for two parties meeting to interlock the Vs without violating the visual space of each other. But rather than withdraw then, he took his time, so as not to overlap her cyberspace and to give her a chance to catch up, and directed Mili's hand to his lips, in true continental fashion restraining a kiss at the last moment. She strained to raise her hand and follow his, and just managed to keep up with his unexpected move.

"Bravissimo!" she praised in a whisper. She realized this might create a new trend in virtual etiquette, at once testing her grace in this environment and demonstrating his gallant mastery of it.

"It is I who am overwhelmed," he said. "Indeed, there is not one person in ten thousand who could have taken my cue and tracked the movement of my hand to my lips without violating my space," he flattered.

Is he for real? she wondered. "Are you here as a guest or ...?"

"No. I am one of the graduating students from the Stanford side. This is partly my doing."

"Really? Which part?"

"I was the project leader. I directed conceptualization and refinement, and did the detailed implementation for several areas of the environment."

"For example?"

"Ummm. I noticed you stop at the entrance and look in the bushes. You didn't find the cricket, did you?" He waited for an answer. "I did the entrance and the maître d'."

"Well done. What's your background?"

"Mathematics and geometry, then I got into simulation and environments. I graduate magna cum laude this quarter."

"Extraordinary."

"Not as extraordinary as you. I mean, I don't want to sound like a groupie, but really, having a chance to talk to *the* Mili Parekh. Excuse me if I gush on."

This is a first, she mused. "Please do. It's nice to be appreciated every now and again. Do you know my work?" Mili asked with some surprise.

"Of course, I remember in high school reading about you in the student magazine Stanford sent me trying to attract me to apply. Your ability to immerse yourself in the conceptual framework of complex problems when others would get lost in the morass."

"Oh that!" She had shunned the article when it came out because it seemed to pitch her as the Stephen Hawking of programming.

"When I did get into Stanford, I dug up your dissertation. Brilliant."

"Did you have any problems with the numbers?" Mili asked, as she recalled laboring an obstinate but ignorant dissertation advisor, the head of the department, through the proofs.

"No, should I have? Pretty straightforward."

Mili found herself liking Vaughn more than she was comfortable with. "Well, perhaps if it was that easy you didn't really grasp it."

"Well, I mean it was brilliant stuff. Not flawless, but brilliant."

"Not ... flawless?" She was not sure the nuanced edge in her voice would be conveyed correctly by her cyberself.

"Menu," Vaughn called out. "Source the Stanford archive for Mili Parekh 'Memetic Tracing of Heuristic Evolution' page ... eighty-seven, if memory serves."

She remembered the page and the coding in the footnote.

The page appeared on his menu, which he turned to show to her, a glowing slate suspended between and visible only to them. "It's the footnote. It was bold of you to refute the theorem provided by Wolfitz, but you missed a factor. Right here." He pointed to a line of code that lay deep in a maze of algorithms. "Maybe just slipped your attention."

She still did not see what the beef was.

"You don't see. Okay. Wolfitz *was* wrong. You *are* right, but your demonstration does not prove it. Menu, bring up my rework." It appeared instantly. "You see the difference, yes?"

Mili looked deep inside herself to find the humility to admit he was right but could not find it. "I'll have to think about it. Can I copy this and look it over at my leisure?"

"If you pinky promise to take a copy of my résumé, too," he winked and wagged his right pinky and thumb.

"Menu, copy both, please," she ordered. "Tell me, Vaughn, what is your best creation so far?"

"I am," he raised his eyebrows and flashed a coy smile. "Oh, excuse me," he broke off. "There is another guest arriving. Hope to see you again," he said turning away.

Mili did not want him to leave so soon and reached out to his form as he walked away, her hand passing through a shoulder violating his space. "Goodbye," she muttered.

She turned dejectedly away and looked out across the pool. Her eyes passed from one person to another looking for an interesting conversation to join. She recognized some of the people, hoped she could avoid them. Others she did not know, but they did not look interesting. *If you can't make yourself look interesting even in cyberspace, you have no hope.*

An odd couple across the pool caught her eye. They were engaged in a feisty discussion. She thought she recognized them, but that did not mean much in cyberspace where one's appearance could change with a word to the menu. Still, they looked like people Mili had read about before. Personalities. Interesting people.

She decided to try to join their conversation, or at least listen to what they were so absorbed in talking about. As she walked around the edge of the pool, she called for the menu. "Who is the lady I am looking at?"

"She is Dame Margaret Merriweather."

"Elaborate."

"She is the British bestselling novelist who made the transition to Hollywood screenwriting and who did the first virtual novel to be written by a professional novelist rather than a computer hacker."

Mili recalled her, had not met her, and thought she would be interesting. "And the man she is talking to?"

"Dieter Shaffer."

"Elaborate."

"German, naturalized American citizen, world-renowned industrial designer, known for a variety of products, Cappella luggage, Pen-B penbased computer revolution. The corporate identity, advertising, and car design for the start-up Alset Automotives was done by his company, Recycledesign, privately held by him. Deceased, early last year. The subject of a case on the current docket of the Supreme Court."

Mili recalled this man's story receiving considerable coverage in the popular, VR, design, and legal press. Indeed, he had been the most famous designer on the planet. Alset Automotives, a joint venture between a Silicon Valley industrialist and a Kyoto ceramics and specialty electronics company, had been the first to produce popular, workable, enjoyable, and relatively trouble-free battery-powered cars. Shaffer had personally worked on all phases of the design for mucho credits and ego gratification. He was already famous; this just made him more so.

Three years ago, he had been diagnosed terminally ill with stomach cancer. He had immediately invested a small fortune in the latest neural networking computer with a biological memory system. This he had installed in a purpose-built office complete with emergency generator and advanced security system to prevent tampering. The computer was linked to all major databases, digital libraries, and the CNC machines and 3-D printers in Recycledesign's modeling shop. A corporation was formed with its address at this office. The last six active months of his life had been spent working with a computer on a machine-learning, artificial intelligence entity.

When Shaffer died, the will was probated to determine the future ownership of the company. To the dismay of his top design managers worldwide, and his female companion for the last five years of his life, he had left them not one share of stock. Some cash, houses, and cars, yes, but not the company. The shares had been willed to the new holding company he had incorporated. His explicit instructions were that this holding company, with the estate lawyer named as a board member and another commercial lawyer named as executor and chief executive, should manage Recycledesign in his absence, taking day-to-day instruction only from the computer.

Recycledesign management staff were summoned from each continent to meet in cyberspace about the future of the organization. To their shock and surprise, Dieter strode into the scene, in the pink of health looking fifteen years younger, and in his famous style trashed the design they had done in his absence since he died.

All the design managers quit following that meeting. "How can that thing, that poseur, design for real people?" one was quoted by the news. But Recycledesign paid top dollar to attract the best talent, and young designers were eager to fill the void. With Shaffer out of the way, they supposed they would finally get credit for any good designs that emerged.

They were wrong. Shaffer had not died, he had just moved onto a new plane. His cyberself had taken on all his talents and foibles. He was still as creative, as demanding, as egotistically perfectionist, as rough on clients and staff who did not share his aesthetic. If anything, his media appeal blossomed.

Mili drew closer to the man and woman who continued their animated discussion. Margaret Merriweather was what people referred to as "handsome": fifty-ish, slightly overweight, with salt-and-pepper hair and a face that beamed with matronly beauty. She wore a grand evening gown of black silk spotted with diamonds in the shape of constellations. Dieter Shaffer appeared to be forty, well-tanned, athletic, and mustachioed. He was very casually dressed in slacks, moccasins, and a rugby shirt.

He turned to Mili and said, "Dr. Parekh, yes? Please join our talk. This woman wishes to trivialize our world."

Mili realized that Dieter knew her name without asking who she was, and indeed had immediate access to every bit of public information about anyone he met. He must be an intimidating negotiator, Mili thought, conjuring up ideas for a new business to create cyberselves for business executives to use in their international negotiations, which more and more frequently took place on a cyber-plane.

"Mili, meet Dame Merriweather."

"I know of you, Mili. I was kicking around for an idea for a screenplay and read about you in some college alumni magazine. I worked it up into a treatment, turned out to be sort of a reverse Porgy and Bess, but couldn't generate interest in the story."

"We never met," she replied simply.

"No."

"How could you write a screenplay about me without having met me? The result would have to be pretty far off the mark," she said with mild contempt.

"Happens all the time in Hollywood and journalism. Anyway, looks like I had you all wrong. I never saw you in the Bollywood mold," she said appraising Mili's avatar.

Mili remembered herself, and her cyberself, and shut up. *This is a can of worms I don't need to open.* "Dieter, pleased to meet you. I've read so much about you."

"Mutual."

"As you may gather, she has trivialized my world already. What is the topic now?" Mili asked.

"The very validity of cyberspace," said Dieter as if there was no rational need for further discussion.

"Validity. Authenticity. I'd say it's a slam dunk. I mean, to say I do not accomplish valid work efficiently in cyberspace would be absurd. Cyberspace is a playground and office environment where the biological brain and the electronic brain can meet on the same plane. Not only through keyboard, pen, or cursor. God forbid we should have to go back to only manual input of data. Of course, we all work more efficiently here."

"I quite agree," Dieter said cutting off a comment about to be made by Dame Merriweather. "My efficiency has improved ten-thousand-fold. Let me tell you how it works, and you tell me if this is valid or not. Cybertel came to me to do a new virtual-conferencing system."

"You designed the new System 9000?! Phreakin' hell!" Mili exclaimed.

"Thank you. They wanted a product with optimized ergonomics in virtual, augmented, and limited reality. They had a competitor who had been working on a device for six months, so Cybertel knew they had to shake a leg. We met, reached an agreement on the fees, and signed. In that moment, their computer downloaded all the hardware specs and dimensions and credited my account for the deposit. I scanned several hundred research reports about hardware in the virtual environment, crystallized the findings, did a demographic survey of the target group, made conclusions about their lifestyle, developed five concepts, and presented them as workable, three-dimensional objects in virtuality and as fully engineered, costed, and scheduled product blueprints, all while the executives from Cybertel took a pee break. I gave them a presentation that knocked off their mirrors, and we closed the session with a decision on one of the concepts. I transferred the plans to their cad/m network, and they started to tool up. Meanwhile, I shifted into the model shop. We delivered a detailed, full-scale prototype, printed via 3-D technology in three days for them to ogle. In three days... They beat the competition to market. Crucified them. Valid or not?"

"Thank you for the enlightening marketing presentation on Recycledesign," Dame Merriweather jumped in with her cool and mature British accent, "which, by the way, I find to bea very prescient name in view of your personal ... circumstance. However, you have been debating the wrong word. I do not question the validity of cyberspace, but the reality of it. As you may have read, Mili—may I call you Mili?"

She nodded her agreement.

"I have always referred to cyberspace as enhanced fiction."

"But that's where you earn your living, not ..."

"Let an old lady have her say, now. Ever since man's consciousness evolved beyond that of the primates, he distinguished himself primarily through the retention of information. Animals are limited in what they can pass on to the next generation. All they can pass on is through their genes or instinct. Some higher-level mammals can teach the next generation, group hunting skills, for example, but they have no record of the instruction that survives independent of the animal itself.

"Man was able to pass on experience. I have long felt that it is not our thumb and toolmaking capacity that made us greater than other animals. It was the ability to pass on information in ways other than direct imitation. Since those most early times, man developed 'virtual reality.' It started with cave paintings. It became oral history, storytelling, songs, plays, puppet shows, opera, ballet, theater, biographies, how-to books, cinema, television, video games, and then enhanced electronic fiction. Man has always yearned to live vicariously without risk through the experience of others. The ascent of man has been the long, slow evolution of our capacity to improve and enjoy 'virtual reality.'"

Mili and Dieter looked at each other, each waiting for a rebuttal. Mili spoke first. "Are you saying the world I live in is a fiction?"

"Are you saying that the world you live in is this?!" she begged the question, waving her hands through Mili's body, rudely violating her space.

"Ask him," Mili countered, pointing at Dieter.

"Madame. All I can say is, I am more alive than I ever was. I meet with clients and staff daily all over the world, frequently in many different meetings at the same time. The quality of my design has actually improved since I died," he huffed with pride. "And the manifestations of my work populate your world of limited reality. People shop for them and use them every day. I am no fiction."

"This is truly an amazing conversation," the jovial Merriweather said. "I am talking with a woman whom I know to exist in flesh and blood insisting that this dimensionless void of electrons in which she now projects herself is her world. And I am talking to a skillfully written piece of software who insists it exists as a man impacting on the real world."

"Madame," Dieter growled. "You are cutting close to the bone."

Merriweather's brow arched as she looked closely at the figure. "Touched a nerve, did I?" she taunted. "Mili, what say you?"

"I believe you do not appreciate what either of us do for a living." She immediately realized the conundrum her choice of words created but continued. "I wonder as I see you here whether you are just denying your own situation. I mean, the very fact that we are meeting you *here*, doesn't that say something about this as a medium of reality?"

"I would say 'touché' if you were closer to the mark. No. I was invited here, because as you know, I write fiction to be experienced in virtuality. To do this I enlist the aid of talented designers such as those who are graduating from this class. I enjoy my visits to cyberspace much as I enjoy a good book or a classic movie. But I always return to the real world. I always close the book."

Trying to move the subject to something with which she was less uncomfortable, Mili changed tack, "Very thought provoking. Dieter, has the internet slowdown affected you at all?"

The avatar feigned the slumped face and slur of a stroke victim, twitched his chin erratically, and said, "No, why do you ashk?" and Merriweather looked on aghast.

He resumed a normal face. "Actually, I have felt what people are describing as this burden, but so far it has not impacted my performance."

Mili was used to the callous disregard of people for others and gave his unintended taunt a pass. "How is your case proceeding in front of the Supreme Court?"

A petty squabble of would-be heirs fighting over the crumbs of a dead man's estate had grown from a novelty in the lower courts into a major constitutional challenge on the nature of corporate personhood and First Amendment rights thereof. Ever since Citizens United, the Supreme Court's 2010 decision allowing unlimited corporate and union spending on political issues, and subsequent rulings granting corporations freedom of religious expression, the personhood of corporations had been strengthened. The plaintiffs in this case argued that a corporation's shares could not be owned by the holding company as an entity, that ultimately a human being had to own the holding company shares in order for the corporation to be endowed with personhood.

"Well, my lawyers have instructed me not to comment substantively on this. I can say I am confident in the outcome. There are two ways we can win. SCOTUS agrees with me. That's a big win. Or they say that it is not a constitutional question for them to decide. As I have won already in the lower courts, this is a victory, too. Actually, the case I am more interested in is the Second Amendment case on the docket."

"What's that about? Sounds interesting. Second Amendment cases never survive the court," Dame Merriweather chimed in her interest.

Mili had read a good deal about the case and offered, "S. Jones v T. Smith. Jones and Smith were two people who squabbled online. Smith was viciously attacked on his own website by Jones. Smith deployed a precisely targeted malware to eradicate Jones from the internet. Jones claims damages and that federal authorities should also prosecute Smith for a cybercrime. Smith claims a Second Amendment right to bear arms to defend himself."

"Really!? Now there's a story." Merriweather said. "What do you think is going to happen?"

"The case is being made that Smith's internet presence had economic value and was a real, equivalent extension of his personhood, fungible, to be defended, especially on his website. The weapon he deployed did nothing other than 'kill' Jones's internet presence posing no threat to any other third parties. The NRA is going to bat for Smith to prevent erosion to the right, and I have even heard a gun manufacturer licensed from a software company a line of cyber-guns and bullets for such self-defense. They are just waiting in the wings for product launch if Smith wins."

Dieter jumped in, "I would buy such products to protect myself. I'm in Smith's corner."

"Margaret, Dieter. Nice to meet you both. Got an early start tomorrow." Mili turned and walked away.

This was no fun. This was not the kind of night out she was looking for. First, she meets a hunky man who outdoes her own math and walks off, then she joins the wrong conversation and is left asking questions she thought she had reconciled in her heart long ago. The reality of her situation could not be measured only in what she got done. Of course, she got work done quickly in virtuality. Everyone did. To her the litmus test was, "Where am I happier?" The answer was that she had never been happy before, save when she was buried in a book, a programming problem, or a virtual environment. She decided to leave the party and bed down.

⊃ 人 ⊏

I AM NOT A FAN OF POP MUSIC. NANCY NILLSON WILLED HERSELF to clear her mind in preparation for an important meeting. But the song she had heard only three times by chance on car radios when she was in transit from here to there was now firmly embedded. And it had just played once again on the taxi's radio as she rode to the White House. Going through security, having her bag scanned, taking the employee access tunnel to the West Wing, and emerging into the blue-carpeted halls, she could not shake it.

The band named Gront, US disc jockeys called them Grunt, was unknown. It had just sprung up out of Scandinavia early in June, and its first hit was briskly climbing the charts. She had no idea why the tune appealed to her. It was dark and lyrical, but poppy, and told the story of an alien race that has polluted its home and detects a beautiful, pristine planet orbiting another star to which they can migrate. The journey takes centuries, and as they travel they observe the deterioration of the planet they approach. By the time they arrive it, too, is uninhabitable. The destination is Earth.

Seeking to cleanse the song from her mind, she lectured herself on it instead. *The song is preposterous. God created life on Earth. That was it. Man was His crowning, if disappointing, creation, whose sin and stain had to be cleansed through the embrace of Jesus Christ my Savior in order that redemption could be earned. Inspired by God's heavenly kingdom, man created the State with its monopoly of force to deliver impartially rendered justice, the righteous and wise rule of law.*

Within those bounds, and living according to God's law, all humans are born with one mouth, but have two hands and a brain, endowing each and every one with the capacity to produce more than they consume. That was God's design: produce, consume, be fruitful, multiply, repeat. Environmentalists were just satanic deceivers with a sweet, green message leading only to the subjugation of man under nature, a reversion to paganism and pantheism, a road to damnation. Even the atheist Ayn Rand had warned of this.

She became aware her internal sermon was delivered to the tune of the song she was trying to shake from her head as she sat outside the Cabinet Room waiting to be called in. *Focus. Focus. Focus*, she told herself, but found the words pulsing to the beat of the tune.

She began to pull out her briefing materials in hopes of a beneficial distraction, but the aide came out and motioned that the time had come. She gathered up presentation materials and a voluminous, black, woven leather Bottega Veneta tote she had treated herself to during a conference in

Milan, and followed the aide into the Cabinet Room, her first foray into the Den of Lions.

As was the intended design of the room, her eyes first caught sight of the president, to whom she bowed her head briefly. She took a place at the head of the room next to the large flat-screen monitor already displaying the first page of her presentation. NOAA's Ark was beginning to get some momentum, if not physically at least in the mind of the body politic, and its ramifications touched on foreign affairs, budget, military, commerce, and environment. The president wanted to keep the cabinet up to speed on progress and talking points.

"Nancy, what have you got for us today?" Mick Coin warmly invited her to begin.

"Thank you, Mr. President, cabinet members." She forwarded the slide to a satellite picture of the Larsen ice shelf. "The calving of the ice shelf that took place thirty-six hours ago surprised some NOAA scientists. They had predicted it, but its occurrence was a little faster than predicted. And, as I predicted, the left-wing media is having a field day with this but has been stymied by our response. All news channels, not just Linx News, have embraced the message and intent of NOAA's Ark. The president's numbers are up 6 percent on this." Everyone in the room knew this. She emphasized it to fuel support for what was to come.

"We have made astonishing progress in several weeks by parallel tracking a number of efforts on technical, engineering, sourcing, and diplomatic fronts. There is confidence now that it can be done."

She forwarded to the next slide showing an iceberg, crystal-blue freshwater melt on its surface, and in large font "Minimum 30 Percent Freshwater Retention." "An iceberg *can* be nudged to sail in a course we set. Estimates as to how much freshwater can be captured range widely depending on how long it takes to sail it, how many pieces it breaks into, and the quality of the preparations at the target site. However, the lowest *realistic* estimate is 30 percent. This represents millions of tons of freshwater. Of course, nay-sayers estimate that zero percent of the freshwater will be able to reach the target."

"Nancy, what is the basis for the naysayers' pessimism?" The question came from the attorney general.

"There are natural reasons. For example, during the 2017 event, the Delaware-sized chunk of ice shelf became caught on an elevated ice promontory called the Bawden ice rise, where it remained for a year, melting. If this happens, well, we won't have much control. That early in the voyage, very few masts will have been dropped, and little sail power will have been applied to the direction and steering of the berg.

"Then the human-induced reasons. Some glaciologists have speculated that our masts will act like 10,000 chips with an ice pick, breaking up the shelf into smaller, melting 'ice cubes.' If we imagine the scale of your everyday ice pick as equal to our mast and put this into perspective, the chunk of ice would be four feet thick, forty feet wide, and 200 feet long, and our 'icepick' will penetrate less than an inch. Our engineers do not agree that the impact or strain of the masts will break apart the flow."

She looked into their eyes for questions. None. She continued. The next slide revealed a computer-generated conceptual illustration of a mast being dropped from a helicopter onto a glacier set in a bowl between two mountains.

"Military pilots have been practicing the past two weeks dropping increasingly heavy payloads. This is not something they are trained for. They have been trained to lift tanks or Humvees, but it was considered a disastrous emergency if the cable snapped or the payload had to be released midair. So far, no accidents, God bless, and they are optimistic that the procedure can be perfected. Within the next two weeks a test will be made with five functional mock-ups of the system released from different heights over the ice field, two mounted with drogue chutes to see if that improves the impact profile. We want to make certain we have the correct impact speed approximated. We will fine-tune the drop height over the actual ice floe. The mock-ups will be masts outfitted with furled sail, booms, solar array, batteries, GPS, and actuators. After deployment, they will be tested to unfurl the sails, position them, and make sure the sensors and electronic systems survived impact and are working. They will then be retrieved back to the lab, examined for damage due to the deployment, and final design modifications will be made. We are still trying to figure out how to build them fast enough and do it in America. Any thoughts or suggestions would be appreciated."

She paused, then advanced the slide to a picture of moth-balled merchant ships. "Logistically, we have an inventory of category B ships in the National Defense Reserve Fleet that can be deployed within 20–60 days. Several of the ships would be adequate for transporting materiel from supplier factories to the assembly ship. We will need help from the Navy to deploy a helicopter ship to travel with the factory ship. Discussions are already underway with Admiral Meixner's staff to see what can be done." She nodded to the secretary of defense, who nodded back.

"The gap in our plan has been finding a sufficiently large vessel to act as the center of operations, to be a factory ship on which sub-assemblies are put together, and fully constructed masts are positioned for lift to the ice. There is nothing in our inventory suitable, and of course a custom-built solution would take years and cost a bomb." She paused for dramatic effect waiting one, two, three seconds. "We think we have found an elegant solution."

She switched the slide to a picture of a large, rather tired-looking fish factory ship. "Those of you from the maritime community may be aware of this vessel and its current status. It is the Penglaishunhao, Russian flagged and owned by a Chinese food consortium partly owned by the Chinese military. Sailing under the name Old Glory, it was detained by the Peruvian government three years ago for illegal fishing within its territorial waters. The owners have refused to pay the $38 million in fines awarded by the Peruvian high court and have sought international arbitration. This has been dismissed by international courts. We have had initial discussions with the Peruvian government to buy this vessel and pay to have it retrofitted to our needs at one of their budding shipyards, which are underutilized and eager to help.

"The vessel is built to be out of port for months, years, at a time, designed to be able to group with supply vessels mid-ocean and on-load catch and off-load product. Our engineers have looked at it. Stripping out the freezers and packaging lines will open up an interior space large enough to assemble the masts. There is plenty of space for work-in-process inventory. Well-placed cranes are already installed to right the finished masts and position them for pickup."

"What is 'elegant' about this solution, Nancy?" the secretary of commerce asked. "Looks like a pretty scruffy scow that's going to take a lot of work."

"Several things, sir. One. It was christened only twelve years ago with a price tag of close to a billion dollars, with a B. The Peruvian government is willing to sell it to us for the thirty-eight-million-dollar fine owed by the Chinese plus forgiveness of $50 million in debt Peru has with us. That's a small fraction of their total debt to the US, and they want our commitment to have the retrofit done by Peruvian yards, which looks like it will cost under $50 million. All in all, a bargain! My people say the retrofit can be completed with a crash program ninety days after we push the button on it. Two. The loss of the vessel has got to hurt the owners, by that I mean the PLA, but it's their fault for dragging their feet on paying the fine. Three. There is a feel-good story here too. This vessel and its detention by the Peruvian authorities was lauded by green activists. If you look at the blogs, they are rabidly calling for its destruction, sinking it as an artificial reef. Repurposing it for the biggest green mission on the planet, NOAA's Ark, would confound them. How are they going to attack us on this?"

"What about the response from the Chinese? The summit they proposed is just two weeks away, and it's supposed to coincide with numerous announcements about their investment in the Siberian and Alaska extensions to the One Belt One Road," the commerce secretary continued.

"As far as international law is concerned, they have exhausted avenues to try to get the factory ship back, save paying the fine. Also, we will acquire it and fly it under the flag of our Army Corps of Engineers. They won't dare try to reclaim it on the high seas."

"Sounds like an invitation for a bidding war," the commerce secretary groused.

"While it is always possible that Peru will use this to squeeze a better deal out of China, I am told by our commercial attaché and ambassador that they seem keen to be part of our mission. As for impacts on the extension project, they want it more than we do. I don't think they will jeopardize it over this. However, if they bring it up as an issue, we could always offer to proclaim that China is contributing, give them some face; hands across the water and all that."

She paused for further comment, then progressed to the next slide, a map of Southern Africa with several points along the coast highlighted. "Perhaps the thorniest problem we are working on: where to deliver the bounty of freshwater. Ideal locations into which the ice mass can be steered will be proximate to areas of drought and deep-water bays that are also at the mouths of rivers. One such location is Alexander Bay on South Africa's border with Namibia. It's knocked out because of its proximity to Richtersveld World Heritage Site, basically a desert park. We expect that NOAA's Ark would make that area bloom, but as a World Heritage desert nature site, no way. Next site along the coast on the Western Cape is St. Helena Bay. Geographically ideal, it is an eleven-mile-wide mouth abutting a river; however, there is a growing, wealthy, White vacation community there who will resist this project. The next ideal location is between Cape St. Francis and Blue Horizon Bay in the Eastern Cape. Same issue as St. Helena, only more so: Black plutocrats, kleptocrats from neighboring countries, and Middle-Eastern money have bought in to it, all NIMBY's." She saw the attorney general's brows furl. "Not in My Backyard—they will resist having their view spoiled. Finally, the last great option is up at the southern tip of Mozambique, sandwiched between Swaziland, South Africa, and the Indian Ocean; Maputo Bay. Despite occasional monsoon flooding, the country is also experiencing drought, it is predominantly Christian, and Maputo is not home to a lot of wealthy vacationers, all plus factors. It would, however, represent an additional 960 miles of sailing, which means more melting, calving, etc. And Maputo is in an area where the prevailing currents are running south along the coast; we would be 'swimming upstream,' as it were. There is a recirculation current that I am told might work, but it is a much trickier navigation."

"I know you have had contact with our people in Pretoria, what do they tell you?" the secretary of state asked.

"They have been very helpful, thank you. Yes, the drought in the region is severe causing major issues for agriculture, tourism, employment, and the enhancement of under advantaged communities ..."

"What does 'enhancement of under advantaged communities' mean, anyway? Drop the diplo speak here, okay."

Nancy bridled a bit under the secretary's withering statement. "Indeed. We are talking about Black shantytowns promised the enhancement of running water, but who do not yet have it; there is a water shortage, why install water pipes? So, your classic," she paused to refrain from using the word 'shithole,' "cesspool. Imagine a 'town' of one or two hundred thousand souls, no running water, spotty electricity, in 100-degree weather. NOAA's Ark would help resolve these issues. At the national level, South Africa will rejoice at this boon. The investment will create jobs for the Black population. The water will help White farmers thrive. The government will deal with the coastal communities."

"What about the Mozambique option?"

"Our people say having an alternative to South Africa is better for our negotiation with them, and their negotiation with South African stakeholders. We keep it on the table."

"What's happening with the possibility to fund it through ad sales?" the president asked.

"Yes, your thinking has played out. Recouping our investment is possible. It depends on several factors. One is the receptiveness of Americans, the world and the target country to the whole process. If this continues to be a feel-good, save-humanity-and-the-planet story, then advertisers will bid up the value of the available space. Two is how many early adopters we can get to cough up the adspend and how much they pay for each space. The more competition for the early spots, the higher the initial value, and this will set the trend for a sliding scale until at the back end, we probably won't be able to sell spots. One issue is the logistics of designing and delivering customized sails bearing the advertiser's message. We are still looking at that and might end up having a team on board the factory ship perform the customization."

"What are next steps?"

"Yes, sir. As soon as the tests of the masts are completed and we have proof of concept, let's say three weeks from now, we need to be able to finalize the discussions with the Peruvians to acquire Old Glory. Then we will need a budget to start ordering materiel."

The president looked about the room. His cabinet knew he liked the idea of this project. Many shared his zeal. Those that did not kept largely silent, their support tepid but support nonetheless. No one met his eyes with a question or challenge. "Before you are off, Nancy, any word on the environmental impacts of the One Belt One Road extension project?"

Nancy thanked herself for having anticipated that question and made some calls to get updates. "Yes, Mr. President. It is more about the impacts of the *environment* on the *extension*," she said with a chuckle and a wink to let all know there was humor to be mined there. "Challenged by such harsh conditions, can a high-speed rail line be built, operated, and maintained *at all*? These are engineering questions, though, not my worry. The impacts of the initiative on the environment can be minimized. The main concern is the annual migration of the Western Arctic caribou herd. It is one of the biggest migrations on the face of the planet and moves across the path of the proposed rail system. Especially for a 150-mile stretch between Brevig Mission and Kovuk, it will have to be elevated or buried frequently to allow the caribou to pass."

"And we need to accommodate the caribou because...?" the president asked.

"ANILCA—Alaska National Interest Conservation Lands Act—established by Congress in 1980 in cooperation with Indigenous communities, the state, and industry and its correlated Western Arctic Caribou Herd Cooperative Management Plan. Native communities rely on the migration for their subsistence survival."

"Subsistence survival," he scoffed. "We are talking about an initiative to catapult them into the twenty-first century. Frankly, if I were them I would be offended if the only thing the government was trying to guarantee was my *subsistence*. Jill," he said, alerting Jill Masterson, secretary of the interior, that his comment was for her. She looked up from notes she was taking.

"Yes, Mr. President."

"You make sure this is not going to be an issue. I don't want a bunch of starving Eskimos on national TV shooshing their way up to the Hill on dog sleds to tank the deal."

"Yes, sir."

"Thank you, Nancy."

As she exited the room the first slide for the next person up appeared, "Status Update on GIBA Investigation." Global Internet Burden Anomaly was the name that had been given to the generalized slowdown of the internet in the past several weeks. It had not impacted Nancy in her work, but it was certainly getting considerable press, and she knew the financial markets were going batty over it.

Watching the stock market news, she had heard the secured, dedicated, ultrahighspeed and bandwidth connections the big investing houses used to interconnect their offices and markets providing them millisecond advantages over common investors felt their networks wobble and deliver uncertain speed. Wall Street was ringing a clarion call to shore up the internet and demanding that the federal government act.

Nancy left that thought behind as she exited the room. She had something else on her mind; the Grunt's earworm tune had started playing in her consciousness again.

⊃ 人 ⊂

LIN CHONG SAT IN MORNING MEDITATION. YET AGAIN HE WAS finding it impossible to clear his mind, to empty it of thought, to remain still and focused only on the sensation of breath. Arisings and mental formations continually sprouted into his field of awareness.

In the weeks since he learned about Zhenniang, he continued to ruminate on her death, on the nature of suicide. Was her choice an act of courage or cowardice? Of desperation or liberation? Of compulsion or free will? Of protest or surrender? Of strength or weakness? Of deliberation or abandon? Compassion or despair? Each day's rumination brought him no closer to an answer. It only made him wish she had not made her choice, for whatever reason.

The scriptures instructed him to place his mind in the now, where the ghosts of old wrongs do not abide. The wishing always dragged his mind back to the old wrongs. In recent days it had led him to castigate himself for a total lack of any capacity to fight back for her.

After releasing the retooled, repurposed, weaponized version of Indra's Net into the wild, he had watched and observed… nothing. He knew he had made it autonomous, he had not known with any certainty what it would "do," but he had yearned for the world to immediately come to some bad end.

Instead, just a long, tired yawn. The internet slowed to a drag about that time. He was not sure whether this had anything to do with Indra's Net or was just a coincidence. Even if it was his doing, it was such a non-event that he felt Karma was mocking him. *So what, I slowed down the worldwide pace of kitten video enjoyment, search requests, chat-bot replies, porn torrenting, avatar responses, bank remittances, police monitoring of suspects, GPS updating. For what? It is not delivering justice on a global scale.*

He took another deep breath and exhaled some frustration. *Give it time. Maybe it is still learning.*

He wished he had been able to take direct action like his brother-in-arms here at LiangShanPo, Wu Song, one of the programmers in the corps. Wu Song was not an anemic, nerdy, skinny reed like many of the people at the redoubt, but was a tall, broad-shouldered oak, vital like Lin Chong, and they had made fast friends.

Wu Song had risen to some prominence as a video game champion whose moniker was Tiger Slayer. On the back of that fame, he had started a video game house and mastered programming. The first title was "Heroes of the Iron Shirt," a hand-to-hand combat game for which he personally trained in earnest in mixed martial arts to know how to lend realism. His brother had provided the seed capital and backed him and let him live with him and his wife while he started up.

The tabloids had a field day with the bloody scandal that then unfolded. Wu Song's brother, Wu Dalang, had a nickname picked up by the papers, Three-Inch Nail, referring perhaps to his inadequate manhood, and a gorgeous but frisky wife, Pan Jinlian, the Golden Lotus, who would not be satisfied getting nailed by him. With the help of a neighbor, she had carried on a steamy affair with a rich and well-connected stud until Dalang discovered them together. On the way back from that confrontation, Dalang was the victim of a hit-and-run, succumbing to injuries at the hospital despite doctors' opinions that his wounds were not life-threatening.

Wu Song smelled a rat. In the past the sister-in-law had coquettishly displayed herself before him and suggested that what was the brother's was also his to enjoy. He knew she was capable of treachery and confronted her, eventually beating a signed confession out of the vixen that she, her lover Ximen Qing, and the old crone busy-body who stoked the relationship had all played a part in Dalang's death at the hospital. Ximen Qing had run him down in his car, and the crone was a retired nurse who injected air into the intravenous feed. When he started to shudder and shake from the embolism, Golden Lotus had suffocated him.

If Wu Song had stopped with the confession, perhaps the court would have been more lenient. Instead, he silenced her permanently, strangling her before he went to the apartment complex owned by Ximen Qing. When he was finished with his sister-in-law's lover, the man was beaten to meat paste: ugly, bloody, and dead. Wu Song called Public Security, waited for their arrival, and confessed to the crime.

The judges in the case felt merciful for Wu Song and perhaps clinging to some atavistic Confucian ethics had not condemned him to death but delivered a hefty prison term. They were less merciful for the woman the tabloids called Granny Wang and skinned her alive with their sentence of death by firing squad to be carried out immediately, her organs to be harvested to pay for court costs.

During his transfer to a remote prison location, the guards had been delinquent for a moment at a rest stop, and Wu Song had seized the opportunity to escape. The tabloids had been light on those embarrassing details. Wu Song, too, found shelter with Chai Jin, snuck to a hacker enclave known as Twin Dragon Mountain but did not like the company there, and eventually, like many other unfortunate worthies, found his way to LiangShanPo.

Lin Chong had read about Tiger Slayer Wu Song in online tabloids but was pleased to get to know the man in real life. Lin's story would never be the subject of a tabloid exposé, his work had been too secret and the people who laid him low too powerful. But he found the idea of some direct and bloody revenge to be a satisfying distraction.

Since nothing had happened after the release of Indra's Net into the wild, he was relieved he had not told the executive committee about it. Otherwise he would have to face the embarrassing explanation of what was *not* going on and why he was *not* generating any tithes. He turned his mind to work on the next sting. It would be prominent and public and had the potential to net a significant chunk of change. If he could pull it off.

⊃ 人 ⊂

MILI HAD HIT A ROADBLOCK, AND WHEN THIS HAPPENED IT WAS her habit to divert attention from whatever was obstructing concentration. Sometimes just five or ten minutes of distraction was enough. When she approached the obstruction again, she would then see a way through, over or around it, or identify the missing piece that had eluded her before.

Favorite distractions were trips to the tea and coffee dispenser; going to the toilet was too much effort. But on her desk was a half-consumed mug of tea, and she had already had three that day.

She recalled the titillating encounter with Vaughn Neumann and idly relaxed into the memory of his handsome, sexy intelligence. His comments on the Wolfitz calculations intruded on the warmth of the recollection. She spoke to her computer. "Retrieve off my server the file copied over from Vaughn Neumann."

The file appeared on her desktop. She clicked on it. The document was simple. For context it excerpted several pages from her dissertation, discussed Wolfitz' theorem, showed her work on refuting it, then swiftly and conclusively punched a hole in her work and finished up with an elegant rework that proved her challenge to Wolfitz was correct. There were some charts that when clicked on would cycle through an animation of the calculations and changes. She was impressed. She had seen PhD dissertations with less substance than this grad student demonstrated in seven pages. *Definitely someone the NSA might look at attracting*, she judged.

"Pull up the résumé he gave me, Vaughn Neumann."

The document opened and appeared on her desktop.

"Pull up any papers and the GPA for Vaughn Neumann."

"There is no grad student enrolled under that name. The search was conducted for both Vaughn and Vaughan spellings."

"Former graduates or try undergrads and PhD candidates."

"I have Vaughn Neumann, graduating class in chemical engineering 1952."

"No."

"That is the only record."

"Okay, the party I wash attending was sponsored by the Stanford and Stuttgart graduating class. Maybe I got it wrong. Check at Stuttgart."

"No record."

Well, Mr. Neumann, you certainly blew a chance to impress a future employer, she thought. *Better luck next time, Vaughn.*

⊃ 人 ⊂

THIS WAS GETTING NOWHERE, GENERAL GAO QIU FUMED AND fidgeted. Attending the meeting in the White Tiger Sanctum by video conference on an encrypted line was Cai Jing from a State Security office in Beijing and Gao's foster son Yanei, the philandering wastrel with whom his finances were inextricably entwined. *The boy isn't useless, but between the pursuit of any snatch his erections point at and his depressions, he is fucking high maintenance bordering on a liability.* "So, you are saying there has been no progress in determining who stole the birthday tribute?" he directed at Cai.

The "birthday tribute" referred to the rare-earth minerals claim they had been trying to finesse from peasants to boost the value of their ownership in a mining company. Gao and other members of the investing syndicate were testing Cai out as a possible member.

The syndicate was secret; the power of their collective intel leveraged across investments required it. Not getting caught in President Zhao's dragnet and executed for corruption also demanded stealth. Gao was disappointed. The day before final negotiations had been expected to grab the land, Cai Jing and Liang Shijie had been publicly broadsided. Gao's interest in the enterprise was hidden within a maze of shell companies in and out of China that Gao Yanei's SilvermanFuchs buddies had set up. Cai Jing was not so protected; the public revelations had named him and his son-in-law Liang. These "spurious reports" had been quickly quarantined by the Golden Shield, but the damage may have already been done. The National Supervisory Commission was known to monitor the internet and capture discussions and reports of anything that might smell of corruption before it could be removed.

"There is a limit to the resources I can put on investigating it without drawing attention to myself," Cai commented.

"That cake is already baked and spoiled." Gao shook his head. "You have to assume attention has been drawn."

"The fucking Beijing University law student from the village was making the biggest stink, but he was arrested last week for campus agitation." Cai paused for effect. "That didn't have anything to do with *me*," Cai said, winking at them both. "I don't think the kid pulled this off. He wouldn't have the

148

resources. He claims he was delivered a complete package of information on the entire deal. A forensic analysis of his computer corroborates that. People I have had digging into this say that the trail leads back to Date-Merchants.com, an online pimping website disguised as a dating app. They have been raided as part of the investigation, but from there the trail is cold. Someone accessed their servers from the dark web and used them to distribute the information. Dead end."

"What about the guy you had working locally on this, Yang Zhi, had that wine-stain crap on his face?" Gao grilled.

Cai was hesitant about how much to reveal. "He's gone to ground."

"Gone to ground?! Disappeared or 'been disappeared'?"

Cai knew the difference. "Disappeared."

"Fuck his mother. This just gets richer."

"Is it possible Lin Chong had something to do with all this?" Gao Yanei asked.

His father gave him a cold stare and, unable to kick him in the virtual shins under the table, determined his glare should shout "Shut... the fuck up ... you idiot" with no ambiguity. *Cai doesn't know the real reason Lin Chong is gone, you fuck-bag, and you are not supposed to know anything about the existence of such a person.* Yanei had been told Lin Chong killed Fu An, and the general thought the lad had the sense to keep silent. The new babysitter Gao had found for his son, a Special Forces retiree named Xue Ba, was finding Yanei to be a handful.

Cai narrowed his brows tucking the provenance of the question away in his thoughts for further examination. The story was Lin Chong had been caught trying to insert a virus into the IT systems at White Tiger Sanctum, had been arrested, and escaped by killing two guards and severely injuring two others while awaiting trial. He was on the run and wanted. He looked at the two Gaos. *What's the back story here? Could Lin Chong be the one who did this?* "Lin Chong is capable, certainly, given resources. But on the run and avoiding surveillance, I think it is highly unlikely. Too risky, and for what?"

"I have military police working on finding Lin Chong. He'll turn up. Meanwhile, you work your end, Cai. Son, you cover the fall-out on the investors' side through one of your partners."

"I don't have much I can put on it now," Cai offered. "With the summit between Presidents Zhao and Coin starting tomorrow, everything is diverted to circumventing online coordination of protesters and critical commentary. The country is locked down tighter than a virgin's pussy."

Gao Yanei smirked at the reference. *Only that tight, huh? Easy, like eating white cabbage.*

ⵑ 人 ⊂

POMP. IF THERE WAS ONE THING HE DETESTED IN BEING PRESIdent of the United States, it was the formality of receiving and being received as a dignitary.

Mick Coin campaigned as a populist, and for him it was not just a slogan or an air he put on to win votes. He deemed himself a regular guy: a no-nonsense, Christian conservative, six-feet-two-inches-tall veteran from a family of veterans and Iowa farmers. He was educated by experience. He had only a bachelor's in business from a state school, did not have a big degree from a hoity-toity institution, and counted that as an asset.

When the family farm had been threatened by the 2008 Great Recession, he had decided enough was enough, ran for, and won a seat in the House of Representatives. His ascent from that point had been rapid. He talked straight, made friends fast, made decisions even faster. The liberal media and late-night talk show comedians attacked his principles, but he reasoned they could not attack that he was principled.

One of those principles was that he avoided idle chitchat and grandiosity. Since he had stepped off Air Force One onto the red carpet covering the tarmac at Beijing Capital International Airport, shook the hand of President Zhao Ji, and walked to his respective limousine, the minutes had all been stage-crafted, media-friendly pomp and grandeur. He had even instructed his translator to say to President Zhao that "now that we are talking directly, let's talk directly." It had changed nothing.

The city appeared to be all hustle and bustle but was on alert. He had a briefing from his team on the efforts the Chinese Communist Party made to ensure his visit went well.

There would be no protests. Instead, there had been lines of school children along some of the avenues alternately waving Chinese and American flags. Some dissidents had been rounded up and put under house arrest. Internet chatter had been squelched.

Early on a code phrase with negative connotations for the summit had been corralled. Wags had called the summit between Zhao Ji (趙佶) and Coin (KangNing康寧) as being held between Zhao Ji著急/Anxious and Irritable and KangNing/Peaceful and Calm. Despite the impacts it

150

had on pharmaceutical companies selling antidepressants and mood drugs and any company that had the peaceful, calm characters in their name, the Golden Shield forbade access to pages with these references and recorded the locations of anyone trying to look them up.

Contrary to the horror stories he had heard about China, there was no pollution. Blue skies prevailed. This, however, was the result of all polluting industries being shuttered for a fifty-kilometer radius and strict enforcement of automobile alternate-day rationing for four days prior to his arrival. Local press and televised news had been full of feel-good support for the great work President Zhao was doing to build strong relations between the two largest economies on Earth.

The first session with Zhao had been just smiles, crafted talking points, and handshakes in front of cameras, with the Chinese president standing in just such a way that to the local media cameras positioned to the left, he appeared bigger than Coin. Then there was the state dinner at ZhongNan-Hai next to the Forbidden City.

The beef and duck had been good. The crispy fried, whole mother carp in spicy bean paste sauce was okay, though he could have done without the orange roe cooked in the belly that popped like gritty little bubble wrap between his molars. He could handle some of the vegetables, but he was not a fan of the sea cucumber in brown sauce. When told the dessert was steamed snow frog ovaries in rock sugar syrup, he and the First Lady together simply put down their spoons and requested a cup of coffee.

But now was Sunday morning and his time. The event he attended was on the itinerary, it was planned and staged, but at least it was something he had inserted into the schedule, something he wanted to do.

He and the First Lady sat in the first pew of the Church of the Savior, a cathedral built in 1703 on land given to the Jesuits by the Qing Emperor of China after their medicine cured him of an illness. The church had survived the siege laid on it by the Boxer Rebellion zealots in 1900, and that is where the story got personal for him.

At the time, Coin's great-grandfather had been a Methodist missionary in Tianjin with a wife and daughter. They had barely escaped a mob that torched their home and killed several converts. Fleeing to Beijing, they hoped Imperial sanity and rule of law would prevail, but alas, the xenophobic flames were being tacitly fanned by the Qing court itself, and they soon found themselves in grave danger, begging to be let into the haven of the Catholic Church of the Savior.

During the two-month siege the church sheltered several thousand church members, foreigners, and local converts. His great-grandfather had died during an explosion that killed twenty others. His grandmother, just a girl of ten, nearly starved to death, her weight plummeting from seventy-four pounds to only fifty. She counted herself fortunate. She witnessed many other children succumb to illness and starvation around her.

When Coin was a boy spending many weekends with his grandmother, her Sunday stories were as much about the evil inflicted on man by heathen religions as they were about Christian love and charity. This was family history. His biographers and the press had not gone back that far to look at his early influences and only focused on the bucolic, hardworking Christian upbringing. *Just another example of the press not doing their job and reaching false conclusions based on incomplete information*, he thought.

Coin was not aware that the only English mass normally held was on Sunday afternoon at 14:00, and that his coordinators had seen to it that an English mass would be held instead at 08:30 when he wanted it. He was not a Catholic, did not believe in the pope's remit, did not understand the strained relationship between Communist China and the Holy See, and if he had he probably would have sided with Beijing. However, he prayed to the spirit of his great-grandfather, was grateful this sanctuary had been opened to his ancestors, his grandmother had survived, and ultimately, he had been born and raised. The world would be a better place for it. As president, he could bring morality back to that office. And stand up to aggressive, heathen nations.

⊃ 人 ⊏

LI JUN HOBBLED HIS TALL, MUSCULAR FRAME THROUGH THE door of the brand-new office space in a brand-new office-tower-cum-residential-complex overlooking the Ritan Park in east central Beijing. The fortieth-floor office was fully equipped and furnished, but not manned. The landlord handed him the keys the day before when Li arrived in Beijing from Manila. At the same time, he received the keys to a fully furnished, deluxe apartment in a middle floor of the same building.

For the past several weeks in Makati, he had spent his time equally devoted to rehabilitation, getting used to his prosthesis, stretching, and strengthening all muscle groups that had grown weak or tight during the convalescence, and with the online courses Orörd Jordan's team had sent him.

The courses, all in Mandarin, were an odd assortment, but he had time to kill. He was intrigued by what job he would be qualified for that would require him to learn how to keep his digital presence anonymous; how to evade the tools of the surveillance state; global trends in environmental policy; the history, strategies, and tactics of nonviolent protest; and how to leverage social media.

Before departing Manila he received a final gift from Orörd by courier. In the box was a package and a card inscribed, "The River Dragon is at home when quietly active beneath the surface, but all mankind feels his presence. Enjoy your new assignment, Orörd." He was not sure he had ever shared his sobriquet with her. Indeed, he had never met his boss face to face and supposed that Bu Qing or one of the lads had told her.

In the box was a special mobile device that was preloaded with numerous tools he had learned how to use. He was instructed to always keep it on, always keep it charged, and not to lose it.

Though far from alarmed, he was beginning to wonder why Orörd had pressed him with increasing urgency to get to Beijing. It was a Sunday morning, but he had been told to get into the office first thing. Surveying the office, no sign on the door, he was guessing his job was with some foreign NGO that had not gotten around to proper registration in China and needed a local to keep a seat warm while they ironed out the details. What was the rush?

He walked into the office and looked at the seat that needed warming. His hand played over the smooth upholstery and polished stainless steel. He guessed it was at least an RMB10,000 business chair. His desk was arranged with two curved, one-meter UHD monitors arrayed one on top of the other and a tiny, sleek desktop computer. On the floor, light green carpeting flowed to wood paneling and up to pleasing, indirect lighting. He had his own toilet, and he had seen a galley when he walked in from the entrance.

"Enjoy it while you can!" he said aloud to himself and wishing Mama Fei could see him.

He swiveled around in the chair to look out the floor-to-ceiling window overlooking the Ritan Park and diplomatic district in the distance. The air was uncharacteristically clean for the US president's visit, and the Sunday morning traffic flow was light. Quite a sight.

He swiveled back around and faced the desk. He took the mouse in hand. A voice asked him to touch his fingerprint to a black spot on the computer's bezel. His fingerprint was recognized, and the screens became active. A clock on the screen read 09:00.

A message arrived on the computer's desktop and onto his mobile device at the same time with a chime. He opened it.

> Please take a taxi to the Tiananmen Subway Station East Exit. Arrive before 10:00. Bring your mobile device and earpiece. We have arranged a welcoming ceremony for you to Beijing!
> - Team Green

He smirked and spoke to the empty office. "Where are you, Team Green? Okay, I will go along."

He called a taxi.

"I'm new in Beijing. How long will it take to get there?"

The cabby looked at him in the mirror. He replied to Li in heavily Beijing-accented Mandarin, which he only half caught the gist of, "Don't worry, traffic is light."

He alighted from the vehicle at 09:38 and his phone chimed, inviting him to walk west a minute and stand in front of the entrance to the Forbidden City, under the huge portrait of Chairman Mao, and just keep a watchful eye on the square. He stared out at the crowds for ten minutes. There was nothing to note. No one approached him; there were no large groups. Just the large plaza with what he assumed was a normal amount of people from all over China visiting, milling, hawking. He began to fidget, his leg stump angry at him for just standing there. He did not like games, and he did not like to just stand around idly. He told himself he would give it until 10:05, then walk to see more of this city he had never explored before.

⊐ 人 ⊏

AT THE END OF THE MASS, PRESIDENT COIN ROSE IN THE PEW, looked one more time around the church, and took the First Lady's arm, and they walked solemnly to the line of limousines awaiting them, a phalanx of secret service agents shielding them from a press of clearly agitated Chinese Public Security officers brought in for crowd control and the crowd of Chinese onlookers being controlled beyond that.

Unless he was attending a friendly rally, Coin had learned not to pay attention to the posters and signs carried by protesters. And in this case, he could not read the anger written on the signs, nor did he realize that this kind of protest was not supposed to happen here. Not now and not in front of a foreign dignitary.

The convoy proceeded to his working meeting with President Zhao. Along the way, the US ambassador to China sat with the president and his wife. "Mr. President, a moment, please."

Coin nodded that he had his attention.

"I have received reports and conveyed them to your security team. That protest we just witnessed outside the church was highly uncharacteristic. Normally if there is a protest against a visiting foreign dignitary, it is orchestrated by the government and focused on the foreign party. This was a flash protest; it congregated out of thin air, was highly critical of both US and China policy, and got considerable foreign and local press coverage. We have also started getting reports of China's Golden Shield having difficulty keeping dissenting opinions about the summit under wraps this morning. Your security team is evaluating the situation and will keep you informed. I just don't want you to be startled if there is a change of plans."

"Well, Sanford, thank you. The crowd outside the church seemed pretty tame. Guess the CCP is going to have to get used to some dissenting opinions sooner or later," Coin said with a wry smile.

"Indeed, sir."

The limousine entered the gates of ZhongNanHai just west of the Forbidden City and Tiananmen Square and pulled up to a stately, century-old, Western-style building overlooking a Chinese garden and pond on which several pairs of ducks swam. The door was opened by a secret service escort, and he and the First Lady were greeted by President Zhao and his wife, a petite woman with salt-and-pepper hair and a sharp, knowing smile. She took the arm of the First Lady, and together they walked toward the garden with their translators while Coin was led into the building. He hoped that during this "working session" he and Zhao would finally start to chew on the meat and potatoes of their discussion.

He and Zhao were led into a large room that was empty save heavily upholstered chairs lining the walls and a densely woven, Chinese, wool carpet on the floor. Two chairs bigger and heavier than any others in the room sat side by side at the center of one wall with a delicate table in between them, on which two cups of tea and a plate of Xinjiang grapes and honeydew melon cubes was placed. Zhao stood to Coin's right in front of their respective chairs. After a handshake photo shoot, the press and aides were led out, and the two presidents were left with their respective translators.

"President Coin, our two nations are now the biggest economies on Earth. The burden of maintaining global market stability while pursuing virtuous and ethical aims for national prosperity falls on the shoulders of men like you and me. Thank you for making your first state visit to meet me here to strengthen the understanding and friendship between our countries."

It was a summary of the message conveyed by the speech and toasts during the prior evening's banquet.

"In this setting, please call me Mick. And what can I call you?"

During private English lessons he had taken decades ago while governor of Guangdong Province, the teacher had given Zhao the name "Jim." He had never since used the name, and no one knew about it. "You may call me Jim," he said with a toothy smile in accented but clear English. His translator smiled broadly and clapped her hands.

"Well, now, Jim. I must be careful what I say around you. It seems you are fluent in English," Coin said jovially.

Zhao looked to his translator, who interpreted for him, then smiled broadly and replied in Mandarin that was about all he could say.

"How was your visit to the Church of the Savior this morning? I understand the location has special significance for you,." Zhao asked in Mandarin.

Damn, Zhao's people had briefed him well. Coin was quite surprised, almost disturbed, that Zhao knew of his ancestry. It was not public knowledge. "It was very moving. Yes, the last time my family members were in China, the armies of the Eight Nation Alliance were on their way, marching up from Tianjin to lay waste to palaces here in Beijing as payback for the Boxer Rebellion." He waited for that to be translated. "My great-grandfather died at that church."

"A sad chapter for all in the history of the world, best learned from and not repeated. This hall in which we sit, the Hall of Cherished Compassion, had been the Empress Dowager Ci Xi's residence, but was seized by the commander of the Eight Nation Alliance Armies, German Field Marshall von Waldersee, as his residence during their occupation and rampage."

Unmoved by the history lesson and disturbed by Zhao's intel on his family, Coin decided he wanted to try to push his buttons back. "I couldn't help but notice outside the church this morning that there were hundreds of protestors, and they were angry not just at America, but at you, too. And somehow your Great Internet Wall of China seems to have crumbled this morning." As this was translated, he tried to read the expression on Zhao's face but got nothing.

"We allow freedom of expression that does not conflict with socialist values or endanger the peaceful security of our communities. I think this must have all been in this spirit." He took a sip of tea. "We feel that at this stage in world history it is important that we build bridges of understanding. That, ultimately, is the objective of our proposal to extend the One Belt One Road project eastwards."

Finally, some straight talk, Coin thought optimistically. "I think you know I am excited by big ideas and big possibilities, and I have thrown my support to this. But my team tells me that the numbers do not add up. What they are telling me is that the proposal tabled by your side, when we dig into it, is basically the US putting up a boatload of cash, land and tax incentives in order to enable Chinese construction companies to use Chinese technology and labor to build a transport system enabling the economic shipment of more Chinese goods to the US and even European goods to the West Coast. I need some good incentives to sell Americans on the benefits. Cheaper baby bibs and bicycles at the local store won't cut it." He realized he had gone on too long, and Zhao's translator was trying to catch up.

When he had assessed Coin's comments, Zhao took a breath, prolonging a pregnant pause. He leaned forward, as he had seen other Western leaders do, shortening the physical distance between the two of them. "I have explicitly instructed our side that the agreement must be fair and balanced and told them to consider incentivizing the assembly or manufacture of some of the rolling stock in the US if our investment is approved in your manufacturing sector, as well as using US crews in the construction. I will make sure your views are understood." He waited for that to be translated. "But speaking of 'boatloads of cash'," Zhao said, to make sure Coin would know the translator had correctly conveyed both the intent and flavor of what Coin had said, "we continue to support the US economy with the purchase of your treasury debt, yet word has come to me that the US has sought to interfere in our ongoing negotiations with Peru over a maritime matter."

As the translator spoke into the president's ear, both men were distracted by the sudden flood of light from a door to an outside hall that opened unexpectedly. The foreign minister and the US ambassador entered the room and paused at the entrance. Zhao waved them over, and they were followed by two secret service agents and two presidential guards. Zhao and Coin looked quizzically at each other wondering what had brought the meeting to an abrupt end.

Sanford Townsend leaned over and spoke into the president's ear, "Sir, there is a massive protest that has gathered outside on Tiananmen, and it looks like it'll get nasty. The secret service recommends an immediate evac."

He looked to President Zhao and could see in his eyes that the same message had been conveyed by his foreign minister. They shook hands and were shunted to the door by their respective security details.

When he and the First Lady were secured in the limo, the ambassador spoke up. "I apologize for breaking up the party, but the shit really seems to be hitting the fan." He could see the president did not like the use of foul language. "Apologies, sir. But a massive protest has appeared, like, out of nowhere. One minute it was not there, the next minute it was a full-blown protest: posters, banners, and drones transmitting video of the whole thing to the web. The plain-clothes and uniformed security people just got drowned out. We expect a more robust military response, one hopes nothing like 1989, but your security people decided not to wait around to find out."

"Any idea what they are protesting?" Coin asked as they pulled out of ZhongNanHai and turned right to avoid the square.

Just then, civilians jumped out onto the street in front of the limo, and posters and banners were hoisted. Several large plastic bags of coal dust powder were hurled at the limousine breaking on the windshield and roof, pouring over the windows, and obscuring their view of the outside.

Despite not being able to see clearly, the driver shouted, "Brace!" and hit the accelerator.

A Molotov cocktail was hurled at the passing car, smashing on the roof, spilling the burning kerosene, and igniting the coal powder. Two civilians hit by the car flew onto the hood and rolled off to the side, their clothes catching on fire.

Free of the crowd, the retinue continued to accelerate and took a ring road north and then east, heading to the airport.

The ambassador took a call on his mobile phone and then informed Coin, "Okay, they are getting Air Force One ready for take-off. They have not planned for departure today, so the galley is not fully stocked. The press corps are not going to be able to make it back to take off with us, but the steward says it doesn't matter. You are good to go straight back to DC."

"Again, Sanford, what is this all about?"

"Sorry, sir. Okay. I am just spitballing based on a couple of data points. The banner the protestors unfurled just before we were hit by the crowd had a play on words. In Mandarin, America is *MeiGuo*, the Beautiful Country. The banner called you the *MeiGuo*—Coal Country—president and demanded you go home."

"So, let me get this straight, Sanford. This protest is in response to the clean coal sales my *predecessor* negotiated to help balance the trade deficit? Seems like a day late and a dollar short, to me."

"Well, there is something else I just learned. I don't think it is a coincidence. At *the same time* this unfolded here, a flash protest materialized on the mall in DC. It's just past 22:00 there. Hundreds of thousands of people, a couple of hundred Athabaskan natives with them, protesting Alaska wilderness destruction. And a full-page ad in tomorrow's *New York Times* was previewed online by a group calling itself Demeter."

"So?"

"Sir, I am just speculating. But the group apparently has very unsympathetic things to say about you and Zhao. Their message seems coordinated with those here in Beijing. These are," he paused to choose his next phrase, "harsh words for the two presidents they say are leading the desecration of the planet," Sanford Townsend the ambassador, the diplomat, offered, putting it mildly.

CHAPTER 5

Sagacious Lu was not feeling wise today. He was putting trust in people of questionable character to seize control of something he was not sure he wanted or needed. But such was life since coming to the aid of Lin Chong and dropping off the grid. Wise choices had evaporated.

Across from him sat Sun Erniang, her husband Zhang Qing, and another man on the run who had entered his orbit, Yang Zhi. A sordid group indeed.

Sun's reputation preceded her with a nickname in the underworld: the Witch. While this could have spoken to her short, stocky, muscular body, pendulous breasts barely concealed by a silk halter top, and face, ugly in a fierce, masculine way, it was in fact referring to her ability to brew potions. She was a master chemist and ran a lab producing the purest, pharmaceutical-quality Ecstasy. Her brand of this illegal, rave pleasure drug was called Madame Ma or Mdm Ma, because of the chemical abbreviation of the drug, MDMA. She had a reputation for drugging enemies, either in food and drink, or, if she was under attack, with an aerosol she carried.

No fan of the illegal drug trade and the devastating, nation-destroying impact it had had on the country 150 years ago, Lu had read that Ecstasy was relatively benign and nonaddictive, so he just held his nose on this one.

Zhang Qing ran a microbrewery tavern in the coastal city of Qingdao, but otherwise served as Sun the Witch's muscle. He had been adopted and mentored by her father as a street tough, and the old man had encouraged their marriage. His nickname was the Vegetable Gardener because of the number of slain enemies he had dumped into fields to fertilize the plants.

Yang Zhi was the third spoke on this strange, warped wheel. Yang stood out because of the port-wine stain splashed across the left side of his face. Until recently he had been working at the direction of powerful officials to finesse mining rights away from some peasants, but when news had gone public, he knew his masters would not forgive him, so he had dropped out of sight.

Lu had run into Yang as they both approached the same destination seeking shelter, a hacker's enclave called Twin Dragon Mountain. Both had heard from different sources that the leader, Deng Long, was a detestable martinet hated by those he led. Both had reached their own conclusions that the enclave was ripe for a hostile takeover. Serendipity had brought them together at Zhang Qing's tavern, where they both recognized by their accents that they were "not from around these parts."

It had been a quiet night in which they were the only two customers being served by Sun and Zhang. As they jousted with large mugs of pilsner, they warily began to share their stories about what brought them to Qing-dao, and soon Sun and Zhang joined in the conversation.

The two locals confirmed to Lu and Yang that Deng Long was indeed a dick hated by the crew. Sun and Zhang did not like him either and had their own reasons for wanting to see him taken out. Lu had already tried the courteous approach and been rebuffed by Deng. Among the four of them, they hatched a plan over several days to oust Deng and install Lu and Yang as the leaders, peacefully if possible, violently if necessary. Tonight was the night.

Yesterday, Sagacious had accessed his toolkit on the cloud and down-loaded an exploit called "Ball Buster." It was a typical ransomware attack. When triggered, it would encrypt the victim's hard drive and demand a ransom. If the victim failed to pay, all their data would be lost forever.

Standard antimalware tools were already able to spot and stop Ball Buster, so Sagacious tweaked it. He based his tweak on the concept of binary explosives, two chemical mixes that are themselves safe and nonexplosive and can be carried separately through bomb detection systems, but when combined become volatile. He split the Ball Buster coding packet into two benign packets and inserted them into other exploits, both of which would have to be opened for the Ball Buster to reconstitute.

These exploits were files attached to an offer of hacking tools to be sold at auction. He mimicked the style and content of a well-regarded hacking group thought to be Russian or Ukrainian called Shaggy Dog, who had a solid reputation for offering the best tools, and only once, to the highest bidders. The two files were ticklers, or freebies, a usable taste of what was in the rest of the auction lot. Invited bidders had twelve hours to evaluate before bidding started.

Twelve hours ago, Lu Zhi-shen had uploaded the offer to a Twin Dragon Mountain bulletin board on the dark web and waited. Five hours ago, both of the file attachments had been opened. Ball Buster reconstituted itself and immediately replicated the two packets onto the largest capacity servers on the local area network first, then branched out to smaller servers, desktop computers, notebooks, and tablets. Within two seconds, every computer and server within the local network of Twin Dragon Mountain had the two packets. A half a second later, all the information on them imploded into a dense, encrypted black hole of 0's and 1's. All that was left was a screen that said, "Hope you enjoyed getting kicked in the balls. I will see you at 20:00 hours. Better let me in this time and be prepared to be generous. The Playboy Monk."

Two hours after he had posted it, though, something happened that concerned him even more and made him doubt the wisdom, or at least the timing, of his gambit. Reports about the collapse of the summit between Presidents Zhao and Coin began circulating without any restraint.

The Golden Shield should have sequestered these reports, especially the news the US president's retinue had been attacked with firebombs at the same time as a major protest in Tiananmen. No Americans were hurt, and the president and his team had gotten to the airport and the safety of their plane, from there to depart immediately to the US. Two Chinese protestors were severely injured by the president's limousine, however, and a high-definition video was circulating widely on the Internet. By noon rioting had broken out, and one group estimated to be 25,000 people marched east on the boulevard to the embassy district and started throwing bricks and Molotov Cocktails at the US embassy.

How could this have happened? he thought. *Who could have pulled it off? A foreign government? Locals? What did it take to orchestrate it and keep it secret?* The videos being replayed online were captured by a drone sent skyward at 09:59 showing a quiet, normal, busy, local tourist scene at Tiananmen. Precisely at 10:00 a.m. things changed. By 10:01 it looked like everyone and their dog were protesters. It took an hour for a surprised military to mount a response of armored personnel carriers approaching the square from west, south, and east. Drones were capturing the images of the military's assault on Tiananmen and broadcasting it live within and outside of China. There must have been dozens of the drones, some no longer flying but hidden in elevated perches, capturing the melee from all angles. *How could Public Security have been unable to shut down transmission?*

Curiously, the faces of protestors were being obscured real time before transmission, while the close-ups of any soldiers or officers were enhanced so that their faces, names, and units could be seen by all.

Today, at 10:00 a.m., his clean, unshared mobile phone pinged with an incoming message. In the room around him phones lit up and pinged as well. They were all the same message from an organization calling itself in Chinese *DeMeiE*. The three characters were not normally seen together like this. *De* meant virtuous and was an abbreviation for *DeGuo*, Deutschland. *Mei* meant beautiful and was an abbreviation for *MeiGuo*, America. *E* meant sudden and was an abbreviation for *ELuoSi*, Russia. DeMeiE's message was an inflammatory call to take to the streets to protest China and America's environmental policies.

He knew better than almost anyone the resources invested to control the internet and undesirable content on it. He knew this breakdown of control went far beyond anything they had gamed out or anticipated. Though he was now sitting on the other side of the fence, he could not help but feel a twinge of patriotic sadness. The loss of control was going to cause considerable suffering to the masses as the government sought to assert itself.

And sitting on the other side of the fence was his main cause of concern right now. *The government is gonna come down like a hammer on anything or anyone that they learn, ferret out, or even guess might have played a role in this. If Deng Long played any part in orchestrating this, the government will spare no resources to arrest him. Do I really want to take on a band of cybercriminals today of all days?*

He shared his concerns with his small team.

"Don't be a pussy," the Witch said coldly.

"Ditto," rejoined the Vegetable Gardener.

"I understand your concern, Sagacious," said the Blue-Faced Beast, "But since you knocked on their door, Deng Long already knows who you are. If the government goes after him, he *will* drag you in. You might as well take them over, build up some firepower. And in the end, I think the chance Deng Long had anything to do with today's events is remote."

"Okay," he resigned himself. "Saddle up then."

They left the tavern, got in Zhang's Mercedes SUV, and headed across town.

The Precious Pearl was a huge video game arcade located on the ground floor of the Twin Dragon Mountain Mall and two-podium, high-rise apartment block. The second-tier mall had never taken off, there was no major anchor tenant, and the occupancy rate was 60 percent . The apartment block was only 30 percent sold out, and many floors had been enclosed but not finished awaiting buyers. The video game arcade was a front business run by the Twin Mountain Dragon enclave. The wake of its power and bandwidth requirements allowed the needs of the ten apartments in the first podium occupied by the digital scammers to go undetected.

The four ascended a lift in the second podium to the thirtieth floor, where they crossed a skybridge through a defunct restaurant that had counted on patrons being willing to pay a premium to eat and see Qingdao at night. The grimy, soot-streaked windows, hazy air, and low visibility outside made the restaurant a non-starter. They then descended the fire stairs to the twentieth floor. The stairwell reeked of stale cigarette smoke, the intensity of which increased as they reached the target floor. Here were strewn a dozen cans brimming with the butts of spent smokes.

Lu stopped the group at the fire door with a wave of his hand and an intense look. He then pointed to each of them to ready their weapons. They were not heavily armed but did not expect much resistance and hoped to finish the evening without bloodshed. Lu had a service, semiautomatic QSZ92 pistol in the officer's configuration with twenty 5.8mm rounds. Yang Zhi was equipped with the similar, standard-issue, fifteen-round 9mm version. Zhang was a traditionalist and carried a hatchet: blunt, to the point, wieldable in close quarters and, by throwing, at long range. Sun the Witch carried a spray bottle and several concealed, wood-carving chisels, their U channels crusted with chemicals of her own devise.

Zhang opened the door covered by Lu and Yang, who advanced in, guns raised. "Good evening, comrades. No cause for alarm. We are here to see Deng Long about your little computer problem."

Lu Da looked about the room. Fifteen or so coders were lazing around. No reason to be at their keyboards, all the screens displayed the same "Hope you enjoyed getting your balls busted" message.

One of them waved a languid hand shooing them in the direction of a door to an adjoining apartment. The coders got up and followed the four into that room, crowding in behind them, and even more joined from other rooms. Lu was encouraged by some whispers he heard among them, "About time someone took out this asshole" and "Fucker can't even keep our work safe, what good is he?"

Deng Long was positioned at a large, ornate desk and fancy chair, a gun displayed on top of the papers in front of him, within reach. He sat there in the far end of the room, facing the door, back to the picture window overlooking the cityscape. He was a thin, greasy man with dark circles under his eyes, a pock-marked face, and graying ponytail. To the left and right of the desk were two burly attendants, clearly armed but not yet with weapons drawn. He sprang up from his chair and growled, "Mangy dog. Fuck your mother—what did you think you were doing, pulling this cheap trick?"

"Ah, friend, it won't be a *cheap* trick. I told you so," Lu countered.

"Fuck your mother. Give me the password and we'll let you leave alive."

"Really? So rude? And so unrealistically demanding. What a dick! Anyone else agree?"

Sagacious raised his own hand and waved the barrel of his pistol in circles, encouraging the coders to feel free while his three compatriots joined in and raised their hands as well.

"Looks like we have a quorum," Lu said with a calm smile looking at the forest of hands that had sprouted around the room. "I am taking over Twin Dragon Mountain for the good of all. You're dismissed, Deng Long. Don't come back, and don't think you can rat us out. I am far better connected than you."

Deng was seething, the veins bulging in his neck and forehead, his lips pulled back from his grimy teeth into a snarl. "Get 'em!" he ordered his attendants on each side of him.

They looked at him and each other, then raised their right hands casting their votes.

Panicking, Deng reached for his gun but not fast enough.

Lu only had a moment to act, but it was a moment full of thought that passed in slow motion. From where they stood, if he let Yang Zhi take out Deng with the 9mm, the slug would likely blow right through the skinny hoodlum, shatter the window behind, and continue until it hit the building next door. High probability to create a police response.

Lu lunged to the side, his left shoulder crashing into Yang's right as he brought Deng's abdomen into sight and squeezed off a 5.9mm round.

Deng crumpled forward onto the desk, the window behind him intact.

Lu advanced a step and pulled the trigger a second time, this shot penetrating the top of Deng's head and burying itself in his spine behind his lungs. Lu let out a breath slowly to calm himself, then looked at the attendants. "Are we good? No problems?"

They both nodded their agreement.

"Good. You know how to dispose of bodies?"

They shook their heads.

"Shabby cunts," Zhang Qing swore under his breath, knowing the honors would fall on him. *Good thing I brought the hatchet*, he grimly humored himself.

Lu looked at Zhang with an understanding smile. "Please instruct these stalwarts in the fine art of vegetable gardening, won't you?" He turned to the assembled coders. "Who is the *real* leader here, the go-to guy for all of you?"

Three dozen pairs of eyes searched around the room and began to coalesce on one person who stood off to the side leaning against the wall, arms folded across his chest. His eyes found the eyes of those staring at him. He straightened himself up. "I guess that would be me."

"Wonderful," Lu smiled. "And your honorable name is?"

"Song Jiang at your service. People call me Timely Rain."

Lu Zhi-shen looked about the room. "Okay, enough excitement for one night. Everybody get a good night's rest. Tomorrow we start fresh and new. New rules, new incentives, new management, maybe even a new mission. You all get that mess cleaned up," he directed to Yang. "Song, please hang on a bit. I've got some questions for you."

Lu and Song moved into another room and closed the door. "I'll look forward to learning more about you in the coming days and weeks, Song, but first a couple of urgent things to attend to. The coding to deactivate the Ball Buster exploit is on this thumb drive. As soon as we are finished here, insert this into one of your servers and execute the file. It will do the rest and unlock your systems."

Song took the thumb drive in hand.

"Second, did Twin Dragon Mountain have anything to do with the protests in Beijing?"

Song raised his eyebrows and looked puzzled. "No. That's not our gig. But we *have* been watching the shit hit the fan with great interest. Why do you ask?"

"Just wanted to know what kind of avalanche of crap might be coming my way. So, third, what *is* your 'gig'?"

"Seasonal scamming. Right now, we are focused on taxes." He could see Lu wanted more. "We feed profiles and contact details to a call center. They call up these people claiming to be from the tax bureau. 'Such and such tax hasn't been paid, you have disregarded earlier notices, if you do not pay immediately while we are on the line, it will result in a further fine of X tens of thousands of Yuan due'. Smart people just hang up. Clever people ask for a number to call at the tax bureau to verify. Concerned people listen and ask for more detail. Scared, stupid, or cowed people cave and make remittances through their phones from their banks to the call center bank. Somewhere around 3 percent hit rate. We get 40 percent of any 'tax' collected. Last year it was about RMB60 million. We've broken through that level already this season."

"What are the other 'seasons'?"

"There's the 'your child is in the emergency ward, I am a hospital administrator' season, then the 'there is a problem in processing your retirement pension payments this month, please give me your account details and password to verify your identity' season, and finally the 'your child has been admitted to the best local high school program but you need to pay the deposit today to reserve their space' season. We get about 15 percent hit rate with that one. Each season takes a huge amount of research to prepare for. The better our profiles sent to the call center, the higher the hit rate."

Lu found the whole setup repugnant. "Would you prefer not shit on the little guy and make some real money for a change?" he asked with a mischievous smile.

Song grinned. "I'd love to. Just point the way, Captain."

"Major," Lu Da corrected.

⊃ 人 ⊂

MICK COIN STARED AT HIS TEAM AND GROWLED IN A MOST unpresidential way, "I want   ANSWERS."

Arriving in Washington, he had called for a meeting with his national security advisor, the heads of the NSA and CIA, his secretary of state, and special advisor on the environment. So far, they were giving him bupkis.

"For Pete's sake, my limo was firebombed, and the First Lady was scared witless. I expect more from each of you. Now start over, what do we *know*? Not the cable news version, I've heard it, and I'm not paying you for that."

Indeed, the twenty-four-hour cable news cycle had already sliced and diced the events in Beijing and Washington for just that length of time. A five-second clip of the presidential limo had been shown countless times on television news programs around the world and viewed hundreds of millions of times on social media. It showed the limo with Stars and Stripes flying on the front right bumper and the seal of the president on the door, making it unmistakable, being hit with the bag of coal dust, the exterior of the car erupting into a bright- orange flash of smoky flames when the Molotov cocktail hit. The vehicle was seen to surge forward as the driver hit the accelerator, the bodies of two protesters flying like struck ten pins as he ploughed through the crowd.

Opinions of every political stripe about who, why, where, when, and what had happened had already been aired. But they were just opinions, and being of every political stripe, they clashed, conflicted, and contradicted. All the opinions could not reflect the same reality. Facts, details, the *knowns* were as yet very few.

Secretary of State Clarissa Roy waded in. "We have some knowns. The two Chinese protestors hit by the limo were admitted to the hospital. Both are expected to make it. Some broken bones and burns. The angry crowd that witnessed the limo hitting the pedestrians and the bombing of your entourage swelled to about 50,000 people by the time they got to our embassy. They did not try to breach the walls. Main buildings on the property are set back a safe distance from accessible public areas. Eventually they used slings to loft bricks and Molotov cocktails over the wall and far enough into the compound that some minor damage was done to sculptures and the moat. Two marine embassy guards sustained minor cuts from falling glass. They are fine. Today calm has resumed in front of the embassy due to the massive response of Chinese Public Security and military forces."

"I have been in contact with the foreign minister. He has extended his country's deepest apology, but otherwise his wording was rather bland. 'Rest assured the people responsible will be brought to justice' kind of thing. He did not share any substance."

"Except for your call with the foreign minister, I have heard that all on cable news," Coin interjected. "Dick, how about your people?"

Richard "Dick" Vesuvio, director of the CIA, was most comfortable when he had deep, personal knowledge of the topic about which his boss was inquiring—like when he was briefing the president on the MiddleEast and Islamic threats to secular governments. Now, he was very uncomfortable. He did not have depth in China but carried with him deep suspicions of a foe his father had fought against in Korea in the 1950s. "Mr. President, the knowns remain few. However, I attended a spirited debate this morning about how we should be interpreting the movement on the ground in China." He looked to the president for encouragement to continue. Coin nodded his approval to continue.

"My people are coalescing into three camps and are hashing it out to try to determine what the situation really is. One group says that the protests were a sign of a crack in Zhao's vice grip control over the military and Public Security. That this might be stage one of a reform attempt or a coup."

Nancy Nillson's ears perked up. *What about Demeter?*

"Had such a faction been identified previously? Do we have any reason to attribute this to such a faction? Indeed, are we sponsoring anyone?"

"We are aware of some generals who are uncomfortable with Zhao's zealous purge of corrupt officials. Puts a crimp on their activities. Very indirect, very informal contacts have been maintained. Did we have intelligence that this was planned or play any role in the outbreak of violence? Absolutely not. No advance warning."

"And the other two camps?"

"One argues that this is the work of a foreign government, the other that it is the work of a nonstate actor either within China or overseas."

"By foreign government, you mean Russia?" Coin asked pointedly.

"Yes, or possibly us," he said shifting his look to the director of the NSA.

"Whoa! What the F!" William Hollister, the director of the NSA, interjected. He paused to contain himself, then continued. "You'd best focus on your other two theories, Dick. We did *not* launch this, had *nothing* to do with it, and would *never* put the president in harm's way."

Coin had seen this behavior play out between his heads of CIA and NSA since he appointed them, and it was a concern. He had asked the national security advisor to look into the background of this animus between them but had yet to get an answer.

Dr. Marlene Wheaton, the national security advisor, could see the look in the president's eye and took it as her cue. "What does this camp say about Russia?"

Vesuvio continued, "Although Russia has been cooperative in the discussions with China about the One Belt One Road Eastern extension project passing through Siberia, indeed it would be a boon to them, they are perennially paranoid about being encircled by a deep friendship between the Western Alliance and China. The fact that the protest on the Mall started at exactly the same time and way would also suggest it is not stage one of a coup in China and is more likely interference from Russia."

"Bill, any signal intelligence out of Russia support that camp?"

"None that has been reported to me, sir."

"So that leaves the possibility of non-state actors. What group would have the resources to do this?" Wheaton asked.

Nillson squirmed in her seat and restrained raising a hand like the excited kid she used to be with an answer to the teacher's question.

"Frankly, none that we are aware of. This is far beyond the capability of any group we have looked at in the past, such as Wikileaks or TruthBTold-Net. If it is a non-state actor, it is not one we have identified before."

"So, you have concluded that the Beijing and DC protests were linked?" Coin queried.

"No, sir," Vesuvio conceded. "This is, as yet, one of the unknowns."

"Nancy, what do we know about this group Demeter that printed the BS in the *Times*?"

Now that the spotlight turned to her, she was concerned the answer would disappoint. "I am afraid, sir, that I have never heard of them. An online search for information about the group yields nothing dated earlier than the day before yesterday. This is itself strange and concerning. We only have their proclamation or manifesto or rant, whatever you want to call it, in the *Times* to go on."

Nillson had been shocked by the blunt, bold, full-page placement in yesterday's paper, copies of which were also sent to everyone's smartphone. The text was surrounded by pictures of polluted skies, acid-rain-scarred trees, waifs sifting through mountains of garbage, dead whales rotting on beaches, flooding, parched earth, and thin, starving animals. It read:

Citizens of the World

Presidents Mick Coin and Zhao Ji preside over the two most environmentally reckless nations on the planet, one measured by absolute pollution (China) and the other by both absolute and per capita pollution (USA). Together, they pollute more than the next seventeen countries combined. This is a crime against the planet.

These leaders pursue policies that despoil and rape the environment with ever more effectiveness. Citizens of China, the US, and the world will pay the price with increased health risks from smog-and-vector-borne diseases, destruction of natural habitats restorative to the human spirit, and erratic weather patterns, with flooding and droughts leading to famines and mass dislocations of human populations.

Starting *today*, *we* the concerned scientists, artists, politicians, students, warriors, activists, first responders, hackers, priests, managers, doctors, factory workers, mothers, fathers, and young and old at Demeter, *we* are holding Coin and Zhao to account. *We* will no longer tolerate their willful ignorance or self-serving stupidity. *We* will expose them on every occasion and in every forum where they and their minions lie, obfuscate, or ignore the facts. *We* will take them to court, *We* will obstruct their policies. *We* will support grass-roots efforts and student-led movements. *We* will give money, time, and effort to encourage the political ambitions of candidates who share the vision of a world with reduced pollution, reduced consumption, and reduced burden on the planet.

We, all of us, citizens of the world.

America, you have made a grave mistake electing Mick Coin as your leader. His policies invite nothing but environmental ruin. Exercise your will at the ballot box, vote his party out of office, punish them for their lies. This Green Dragon has teeth.

China's citizens, you did not have any democratic say to determine the path and policy your government takes on the environment. It is time to exercise your will in the streets and make your voices heard for you and your children. The days when you can breathe clean air should not be restricted to when a foreign president is visiting or your cities are on epidemic lockdown. Someday your will be done, and Mount Tai will bow before you. Please join us to be a part of the future.

Demeter.Org

Nillson composed herself to continue, "I cannot speak to their strength, resources, origin, or intent, but the fact that the ad singles out China and the US and was previewed online at exactly 22:00, when the flash protest started on the Mall and likewise in Beijing, would strongly suggest that they are indeed responsible. I am no expert, but the English does not seem to be completely American to me. The tone is decidedly international."

The president pursed his lips tapping them with his index finger. "I think you hit it on the head, Nancy. We need to know the 'strength, resources, origin, and intent' of Demeter. If they are a foreign entity, then any efforts they make to interfere in our elections can be prosecuted. If their intent is hostile, we can then strangle their resources. Nancy, I want you to co-ordinate my talking points about our environmental policy with the press secretary. Keep us one step ahead of these rabble-rousers. Clarissa, keep China's feet on the fire about this. I want to know what they know." He looked at Wheaton, Vesuvio, and Hollister. "Figure out which one of you is supposed to know about things like this non-state actor, Demeter group, and give me a report tomorrow."

Vesuvio and Hollister looked at each other. Hollister spoke up, "Sir, it's probably the FBI's purview."

"Figure it out," the president said, his voice dripping with disdain. "And *never* bring whatever petty crap has gone on between you two into this office again."

ⴲ 人 ⴱ

TWENTY-EIGHT MILES, FORTY MINUTES' DRIVE, AND A WORLD away from the White House, Mili Parekh sat in her Monday meeting. The format for today's meeting was different. She had directed the teams to double down on research to reach some useful conclusions about the issue that had been nagging her; was her memetic attribution methodology and tool reliable?

She had directed one team to try to create a tool to fool her system. She directed the other team to interview the creator of the code that was being replicated to determine whether there was anything to be learned. Today both teams were presenting their conclusions.

Jill Westerhoff had been selected to lead the first team, and Mili consid-ered her a great pick. Jill was a PhD in analytics from Columbia and had been on track to be director of the attribution group before Mili had been identified by the NSA and brought in to adapt her work to their needs. Westerhoff had recognized the brilliant efficiency of Parekh's approach and stepped aside without rancor when Parekh was put in charge. The two of them had created a strong working relationship, which meant they felt free to question the rationale or direction being pursued by the other for the good of the team and the output.

"Okay, Jill, you're up. Letsh shee what you got," Parekh said with the best smile she could muster. "Bring it on!"

Westerhoff returned the smile and took the floor. "Yeah, well, we'll see. We used a Generative Adversarial Network, or GAN, approach to try to create code that would fool the system that it was written by some other known coder. This is a dialectic iterative method.

"Briefly, imagine someone who wants to create a forgery of an artist's style, a new painting in the style of an artist that will fool experts. The memetic attribution tool you created is the 'expert' in this scenario, also called the Discriminator Network. It knows what the real artist's work looks like and what characterizes it as distinctive and original. When it sees an image offered up of a painting, it evaluates it and delivers a 'yes' or 'no' answer back to the forger."

She flashed through a series of fifteen slides with the original *Mona Lisa* on the left and various forgeries and cartoonish adaptations of it produced through the centuries. As the slides progressed, the pictures became closer and closer in appearance and style to the original. "The forger has an idea of the style of the artist but does not have the skill and knowledge of the discriminator. Over time and repetition, the forger gets better, gets closer to something that fools the discriminator, which is also learning during the process."

A slide appeared with the *Mona Lisa* and a similar work titled *Mon Luigi*, a picture of a man of the period dressed in period clothes with the left-handed hatching, copious curls in the hair, and sfumato technique of Da Vinci blurring some of the distant landscape. "Eventually, the discriminator system recognizes the work on the right as by Da Vinci, because it matches the style of the *Mona Lisa* in all respects. The forger has fooled the expert."

"Sho, you *were* able to create a GAN that fooled the shishtem?" Parekh hoped aloud.

"The executive summary, no. Unlike most instances of GAN applications, where the forger/generative system catches up with the expert/discriminator system and delivers an image that fools the expert, your memetic expert system is separately analyzing the forger's work as having its own memetic attributes and continually learning to distinguish it. The forger is never able to conclusively fool it."

"After how many iterations?"

"Several million."

"Would these advanced iterations fool mosht attribution shishtems?"

"Well, they fooled *my* system," Westerhoff conceded with humor and grace.

"Did you ashk the forger to try to generate the Stravinshky coding shtyle?"

"Yes."

"And?"

"Same result. Your system was never fooled, mine eventually was."

Parekh looked around the room. "Any thoughts? Next shteps?"

From a dark corner of the room a timid hand rose. It was Harley Barrows, the latest hire. He was a thin, shy young man with blue eyes and receding blond hairline. Based on the brilliance of his coding and analytic skills, it was evident he had turned many introverted hours alone into a productive haven for himself.

"Does everyone here know Harley?" she welcomed him to the group and everyone turned back to look at him. "What ish your thought?"

"Well, um, I was reading your original paper on memetics. And thinking about the origin of this whole idea with Dawkins being from genetics and all," he paused like that was the whole thought, as if everyone would grasp his point and conclusions self-evidently.

"And?" Parekh drew him out.

"A clone is not a forgery."

It was a simple statement, true, at once penetrating and illuminating. Mili pursed her lips. *This guy is good.* "Ok. What follows?"

"Your method analyzes the digital DNA of a coding style. What would happen if a tool were created to analyze a coding style as you have, but with the intent of cloning the style, not just identifying it. Would your expert system, or one like it, be capable of fooling your expert system?"

Mili looked to Jill and raised her eyebrows. "That ish a good idea. Jill?"

"Seems like cheating. I mean, if the forger has all the resources of the original..."

Mili interrupted her, "No, not a forger. A genetishist seeking to clone. A scientist, not a thief. Though their goal may be similar, they start with different tools and methodologies."

"I suppose we could rewrite your program so that it takes the memetic analysis of a coding style as the start of its work to create new programs that embody the imprint of the original. Wouldn't this require lots of resources to pull off?" Even as the words left Westerhoff's lips, she knew the question was lame.

"Our enemies *have* the reshources," Parekh answered. "Jill, I want your team to pull in Harley and test out his idea. Shee if *we* can beat *me.*"

Westerhoff looked to her team and nodded in agreement.

"Ok, now for part two of today's double feature we have Bill Singh's presentation. Bill drew the short straw and won the chance to fly to beautiful Dallas/Fort Worth for a couple days of interviews. Bill, it ish all yours."

Bill moved his lanky frame to the head of the table and took up the laser pointer remote. "A quick recap. Twice in the past four or five months the system has flagged threats as having been written by Eunice Stravinsky. Problem is, we understand she has been incarcerated and denied access to computers since before these threats emerged. The latest threat surfaced when I was analyzing the hard drives of Idrus Sukabumi, the Indonesian minister who died visiting his bank in Singapore.

"Mili tasked me to dig into this, find out where she is held, talk to her lawyers, and try to interview her, see if we could get any clues."

He forwarded the slide to a photo of the inmate C1956-426, Eunice Stravinsky, clad in orange, her eyes distractedly wandering to the left, hair cut short, no trace of emotion on her face. She appeared overweight, pasty, and enervated.

"Yeah, if my trip taught me anything, it's 'I don't want to break the law and wind up like her.'" There was nervous laughter in the room. "I mean, she could have worked here, had every bit of the smarts, but now she's reduced... I get ahead of myself," he said shaking his head.

The slide forwarded to a picture of the Federal Medical Center, Carswell. "The US doesn't have a supermax prison for female inmates, so this is the facility where women considered to be threats to national security are remanded. The entrance looks pretty friendly, like a drive-up, drop-off point to an old folks' home, and I suppose as prisons go, it is 'nice.' However, the terms of her incarceration strictly deny her access to computers or any devices with access to the internet.

"During her trial she was held without bail, but she was indeed able to hack the prison system and be released into the custody of a phantom person for work-leave community service. She got as far as the parking lot, too, when her lawyer pulled up for a visit, saw her, knew this was not good, and persuaded her to turn around. She denied any knowledge of the hack, no charges were added, but afterwards the authorities were more cautious.

"It was a tough negotiation with her lawyers to get her consent to meet me. On the one hand, we cannot reveal anything. On the other hand, her lawyers do not want to allow their client to incriminate herself in any new crimes. Basically, I had to play stupid. It was 'I am a federal investigator looking into a new financial crime like the one she was convicted of. Her cooperation in understanding the methods used by the criminals would be appreciated and might result in a "good behavior" comment in her prison file.'"

"It turns out that this medical center is the right place for her. They also house female inmates suffering from mental disabilities." He forwarded to the next slide, on which he appeared sitting across from the inmate and her lawyer in a spare, antiseptic meeting room. Her legs were in shackles, and she had a black notebook on the table in front of her. He clicked on the arrow key in the middle of the photo starting the video playback. "This was our interview."

"Thank you for meeting with me today. You and your client's cooperation are most appreciated. For the record, can you state your name?" he said turning to the prisoner.

Eunice sat silently, her head turned slightly to the left and looking up, staring at the sunlight coming in from a high window. She rocked back and forth.

"Eunice, can you answer the question?" her lawyer encouraged.

She looked forlornly at the edge of the table in front of her and slowly shook her head back and forth to the rhythm of her rocking.

"Eunice, this man has come a long way to see you. He knows you are a brilliant computer scientist, and he needs your help. Can you answer his questions?" the lawyer said as if talking to a kindergartener.

She looked up and, biting her lower lip, continued to shake her head back and forth.

"I see you have brought a notebook today, Eunice. Is that for me to see?" Bill asked encouragingly while looking to the lawyer for approval.

She bit her lip harder, and tears began to well up in her eyes. They coursed down her cheeks as she slowly pushed the notebook across the table toward Bill. Again, he looked to the lawyer for a nod of approval, then picked up the book and began to flip through it.

He took a packet of tissues from his pocket and passed them to Eunice. "This is amazing, Eunice. Did you write this?" Bill asked in the tone of a school marm gushing over a crayon drawing.

She nodded her head as she wiped her tears, blew her nose, and wiped a drop of blood from her lip.

"Do you have more notebooks like this?"

She nodded her head again up and down slowly.

He looked to the lawyer as he said, "Could I see those, too?"

She nodded.

"Can you tell me what I am looking at, Eunice? I am not a computer scientist like you," he lied.

She sat silently.

"Is this the work you were doing that was lost off your system?"

Stravinsky nodded tiredly.

"How many more notebooks do you have?"

She spread the fingers of her right hand and the index finger of her left hand open on the table.

"Six notebooks? This is wonderful work. Can I see them, Eunice?"

She nodded, and her gaze drifted off to the window again.

She responded to no further questions.

"Eunice, you have been extremely helpful. Thank you for your time."

The video stopped and returned to the starting picture of the three sitting at the table.

"Stravinsky had six notebooks. Her lawyer had them copied for us. The earlier notebooks have some rants about her innocence and worries about her eroding sanity interspersed with lines of code. The later notebooks are only filled with lines of code and references to books she had read—pages and pages of code, notebooks filled with it. I have not been able to dive into it yet. With her mental condition and whatever meds they have her on, it might all be gibberish."

"Bill, well done. What about the hack of the jail she was in during the trial? Did you get to shee that?" Parekh asked.

"I am ahead of you on that, boss. I did reach out to the jail system in California. I was able to contact someone who remembered the incident. The IT guy who was in charge at the time has since left. They are not sure if he took the files with him and have promised to try to dig them out for me, but it is not a high priority for them."

"I just thought it might provide another shample of her coding."

"Got 'cha."

"Bill, pleege turn over the notebooks to Harley. You and Jill take a look at what's in them," she said turning away from Bill to face Harley. "Ish it gold dusht or bull shit? If it ish gold, use it in your experiment to further analyze and clone her coding."

Harley perked up. *This is going to be fun.*

⊃ 人 ⊂

CAI JING WAS ONLY HALFWAY THROUGH A DAY THAT WAS proving to be grueling. President and Chairman of the Communist Party of China Zhao Ji demanded answers. Heads *would* roll. So far, his was not on the chopping block. *Who sitting around this large conference table will not make it?* he wondered.

The flash protest had caught China's security apparatus off guard at all levels and all branches. Public Security, State Security, and the military were left to sort out who had dropped the ball, who had "let this happen," who had not anticipated that it could even be done.

Today's meeting was to try to sort through the mess, or at least to determine how it had been done and, if possible, figure out who the likely perpetrators were. The president had sent his watchdog, Su Yuanjing, to oversee the meeting. That did not bode well.

In the morning, Public Security with an assist from State Security investigators delivered their interim conclusions on the physical evidence. Tiananmen had been locked down during and after the protests, and a sweep of the plaza had netted 378 drones. These had been launched from a flatbed, tractor-trailer truck that had pulled into the center of Tiananmen at exactly 09:55, the same time Public Security cameras in the area had gone dark. The trailer had been parked overnight at a truck stop in the outskirts of Beijing on the road from Tianjin. On early Sunday morning, an autonomous tractor-trailer truck had pulled up to the trailer, coupled with it, and departed for Beijing.

More importantly, the flatbed trailer had been highly customized. Besides the charging docks for the drones, all laid out in a ten-by-forty drone grid on the trailer, it was also equipped with a gas-powered generator, its own cellphone signal tower, a wind weathervane, and a substantial computer and networking system. Quick work by Public Security had identified the company that did the customization, a local computer systems integrator in Tianjin. The owners claimed total ignorance and cooperated fully with investigators. They had received an order from a US company two months prior for three flatbed trailer systems claiming it was contracted to design and build them for an amusement park in China.

All the components had been delivered to the Tianjin subcontractor who had done the systems integration. Once it was ready, they had been ordered not to test it, only put it online and let the owner make a remote test and diagnostic. This had been conducted three days before the delivery. The Tianjin firm said that the tests went well, systems all came online, all the drones were activated and rotors revved, camera images tested, and cell tower signal power tested, and then it powered off. The systems integrator had turned over to investigators all correspondence with the US company including drawings and specifications, delivery orders of components, and payment details.

The Tianjin firm got an email from the US contractor confirming the test, and the balance of 40 percent of payment for the work was remitted as promised into the Tianjin company's account. The trailers were parked as ordered to be towed by the contractor's driver, who signed off on delivery. The driver had towed one trailer to the truck stop where he had orders to leave it. The other two trailers were fetched by autonomous vehicles. The driver was a local nobody with no record of any criminal or political activity. His orders to do the pickup and delivery had been received and paid for through normal channels. He had no reason to suspect or report anything. The other two trailers had disappeared.

A member of Cai Jing's team was next up to present. The State's capacity to capture and recognize the faces of the people in the crowd had been corrupted or circumvented. The facial images of individuals were blurred out. Only the images of police remained well defined. How this had been done was the subject of a different investigation. In seeking to determine if there were other ways to extract intelligence from what remained in the video feeds, Cai Jing had reached into his organization to get a team working on analyzing the crowd. He was happy to have his team present the results netted to the group. He chose an articulate Captain Zhang San to explain.

"Our team works on detecting abnormalities within crowd behavior," Captain Zhang said by way of introduction. "We do this using both canned and proprietary algorithms we have generated to look at crowd-density estimation, motion detection, tracking, and behavior recognition. The algorithms can be divided into three groups: people counting, people tracking, and crowd behavior analysis. Our algorithms work whether we have the facial details or not because they are more focused on what can be learned from the aggregate behavior and the outliers.

"Typically, our system is employed to analyze incidents. For example, the riot at the vegetable market in Ürümqi last month. Human visual inspection of the security camera footage as well as the firsthand accounts of security personnel suggested that the riot was a spontaneous outburst, the result of a dispute at one stall. Our analysis of crowd behavior, and of outliers, suggested the riot was instigated. This was later corroborated by the confessions of those arrested.

"We have had less than twenty-four hours to work with the feeds, and analyzing Tiananmen Square is several amplitudes more complex than the market in Ürümqi, but we can report some anomalies and areas worthy of further investigation."

As Captain Zhang spoke, Cai Jing looked to Su Yuanjing to make sure his attention was still held. The older man's eyes were intently focused on the screen.

An image of the square appeared. It had been artfully constructed by a computer from multiple image sources. "Within the image area are 412 security cameras." Four hundred twelve tiny red arrows depicting the location and direction of the cameras was overlaid. We analyzed the movement and pattern of behavior of each individual and as a member of a crowd. According to the analysis, little evidence of abnormal 'crowd behavior' manifested before 09:58. That is to say, as a mass, the people were acting as a crowd of strangers." Zhang manipulated both the perspective and timeline. "Flows within and around each other were normal. Some normal subgroups were detected," several hundred small, orange circles appeared overlaid, "such as families or small tour groups.

"At 09:58, we can see the drones deploy." The truck bed was highlighted, and the video reconstruction showed drones, colored in green, rise and spread out.

"At this point, our program starts detecting a change in crowd behavior." A wave of blue spread across the entire surface of the square enveloping the orange circles. "Within this ninety-second period, what appeared to be a group of strangers with no common intent became a crowd with one purpose. You can see that the small groups we had flagged before in orange start to move out of and away from the crowd, signaling they were not part of it to begin with.

"Analysis of the crowd behavior using our most advanced tools could not detect a 'leader,' instigator, center, or head of the crowd, at least until after the fire-bombing of the American motorcade when the witnesses of that event moved east toward the square and picked up mass."

Commissioner Su signaled with his right hand he wanted to interrupt and asked, "What conclusions have you reached that you can share with us?"

Captain Zhang looked from Su to Cai and paused a moment. "Yes, sir. I mentioned before outliers. We then ran the behavior of each person captured in video to try to isolate those whose behavior was different from anyone else. When the protest occurred ..."

Su interrupted him, "We are not referring to this as a protest."

Zhang cleared his throat, "Sir, when the spontaneous upwelling of the people's fervor occurred, these people neither joined in nor departed, neither became part of the crowd nor detached themselves from it." Highlighted on the screen were about one hundred dots.

"We then analyzed the actions of these individuals in the time leading up to the outpouring of fervor." All of the dots save one, standing in the northern part of the square under Mao's portrait, disappeared. "Our algorithms have highlighted this *one* person as a significant outlier."

The image zoomed in to a man, tall judged in comparison to those around him, standing with his back to Mao facing the square. The computer stitched images of the outlier together from various angles and created a 360° walkaround image, all with the face blurred.

"He arrived at the square at 09:38, took a position in this spot, and waited. He was flagged as an outlier because once he arrived he did not move, he did not talk to anyone, did not buy anything, and when the action in the square started, he remained where he was, neither interacting nor departing. Finally, when the crowd surged past him on the way to the embassy district, he followed them, never joining them, never leaving them."

Cai Jing spoke up, "Captain Zhang, what can you tell us about the outlier? Who is he?"

"Nothing of significant value. But what we have not learned has precisely led us to conclude that *this* outlier is, if not the leader of the," he paused, "people's fervor, at least he is closely associated with the leaders."

"Explain," Su said.

"We tried to trace him through the car he arrived in, but the license plates of the taxi were also obscured. Tracing the taxi's prior movement, where the outlier was picked up, was a dead end. He walks with a limp. Interestingly, when we tried to isolate observation of all men in the city who walk with a similar limp, we came up with images of several hundred, but the facial images of all were blurred."

Cai spoke up, redirecting Su's attention, "We are at work to determine a way to identify him real time through his gait. I will report to you as soon as we have anything of substance."

Financial Crimes Investigation branch of Public Security was next up to report on the payment of the services to the subcontractor and payment for components delivered to the subcontractor: the drones, computers, signal tower, generator, etc. The presenter looked to be a fresh graduate, Cai Jing surmised, perhaps sent by her boss as a diversion or cannon fodder. He thought she was attractive and bright looking, bringing a fully professional sexiness to a crisp, blue uniform with silver buttons, long black hair pulled back into a ponytail at the back of her head, and no makeup but no need for it either. The name tag, facing toward the ceiling as it lay atop substantial cleavage, indicated she was Li Shishi, and the one silver button on her epaulet signified her rank of superintendent first class.

Her brisk presentation of evidence and research kept their attention. "All of the vendors and contractors received their purchase orders from one US firm." Pictures of all the purchase orders displayed. "This turned out to be a real-estate investment trust solely focused on building and operating data centers. Their operating headquarters is in Northern California, from where the purchase orders were issued, but their ownership is murky. The company was incorporated in Panama with the lawyering and corporate secretarial work done by a local legal firm, Jürgen & Mora, specializing in helping people hide offshore wealth. From there the trail runs cold. No information about owners, investors, when it was set up, capitalization, or where they operate data centers, nothing. A call to the switchboard of the headquarters was shunted to an answering machine."

She advanced the slide to a picture of an unadorned, unmarked building. "We had an operative embedded in the San Francisco Chinese Consulate take a drive up the coast to the headquarters' address. He drove around this large, unmarked, white, three-story property 200 meters square. It has a full rooftop solar array. It is surrounded by a double row of fences, both barbwire topped, every other pole mounted with a security camera. At the back side is a guard house and entrance leading to a deliveries ramp and a small parking lot with space for only ten employee vehicles.

"Requests to talk with management or visit the site were denied. In fact, local police showed up while our operative was on-site to say the property had reported a disturbance. With diplomatic license plates and a story that he wanted to discuss buying server space, the police let him go without any further harassment." Then she got to what was on everyone's mind. "The ownership pattern obscured through opaque holding companies is reminiscent of overseas operations conducted by the CIA or NSA; however, the purchase orders being issued by the HQ in California seems a sloppy twist."

Su interjected, "Thank you, Superintendent Li. A question for those who have not presented yet. Does any of your evidence gathered also suggest this is a US attack?"

Cai Jing raised his hand, happy to be able to score some points. "We have analyzed the software used to control the drones. It was developed by Telint, the US semiconductor company, for the last Olympic opening and closing ceremonies. They created an artificial firework display with the co-ordinated flight of 1,200 drones. They had wanted to highlight the power of their processors and networks. This software is not commercially available, so it was either stolen by the perpetrators or provided to them."

"Teams are working to try to determine how so many participants were coordinated to arrive and begin the protest at that moment without having been detected. We have not been able to determine how they gained control of our security surveillance network to deactivate the cameras in Tiananmen and overcome our attempts to block their signals. Within minutes of the flash protest video transmissions starting, Public Security teams were on it but were unable to block the transmission signals. We are still doing analysis of the software in the transmission tower. What is clear is that that this was a well-funded, highly orchestrated, technically sophisticated operation. I think it could only have been pulled off by Russia or the US."

"Perhaps the US government is trying to tell us something," Su offered up. Everyone in the room wondered if it was a question or a statement, not sure whether to take his lead or respond to it.

Cai swallowed and continued, "Then there is the message from the organization calling itself DeMeiE, identified as Demeter in its circulation overseas, that was transmitted across China at the time the protest erupt-ed. Based on the time stamps on the messages we all received, this message was sent at exactly 10:00 a.m. Beijing time. We know that it was sent on all mobile networks, and all email pathways. It is estimated that three billion devices or email accounts were sent the message from accounts within China. So far five thousand source accounts have been identified, all dummies set up for the transmission of this message and not used since. We must assume that every man, woman, and child with access to digital messaging, which means 93 percent of the total population, received the message.

"Our preliminary analysis of the breach indicates that similar tools were used to orchestrate the flash protest. Again, it was a well-funded, highly orchestrated, technically sophisticated operation. I think it could only have been pulled off by Russia or the US, or possibly by Israel or North Korea, but that is less likely."

"A state-sponsored attack," Su said. Again, his words walked the line between a question and a statement leaving everyone in the room trying to determine which line would be prudent for them to support.

To Cai's surprise, the flower vase, pretty Superintendent Li, stepped in with a level of confidence that took him off guard. "I agree that Israel is an unlikely perpetrator, unless they are just acting as running dogs for the Americans, in which case we are still talking about the Americans. North Korea, however, should not be written off just yet. They would have much to gain by destabilizing our relationship with the US, and I reviewed a presentation of their cyber warfare capabilities done by our own PLA indicating that their skills are considerable.

"The bigger question is, if this is a state-sponsored attack from the US, why would Demeter be attacking the administration of President Coin as vociferously as that of our President Zhao?"

"The Coin administration and its talking heads frequently raise the specter of the so-called 'Deep State' thwarting their initiatives. Perhaps this is it taking action," Su said.

Li countered, "I think it is too early to conclude. To the extent moderate US politicians recognize the existence of anything resembling a 'Deep State,' they feel it has a governing influence on the ship of state preventing excesses in either direction, not perpetrating excesses that are destabilizing. No, I know I stated that the shell company setup of the data center firm that paid for the flash protest suggested a CIA or NSA modus operandi, but it is not a conclusion. Multinational corporations also use these fronts for various reasons. It may just be an MNC with an agenda."

"Can anyone tell me to what these two lines of the Demeter statement refer? The ones addressed directly to Coin and Zhao." Su Yuanjing pulled out his smartphone and read, "'This Green Dragon has teeth' addressed to the US people, and 'Someday your will be done, and Mount Tai will bow before you' addressed to the Chinese people." The Chinese translation of the Demeter message used the characters *Qinglong* to represent "green dragon." This carried several meanings in Chinese. "I assume it is neither referring to the Taoist guardian spirit of the East nor a well-endowed man after a Brazil wax."

Uneasy laughter rippled through the room.

"The West always refers to China as the Dragon, much as Russia is always represented as the Bear. Perhaps it is more China-baiting, bullying and blaming us for their problems as usual," Li said.

"I have a lead on the Mount Tai reference," Cai interjected. "I am trying to run it down now."

"Okay. Superintendent Li, I want you to work closely with Chief Cai on this. Report directly to me," Su ordered.

A tea break was called, and many attendees went out to the lobby to retrieve the personal devices they were denied use of in the secure conference room.

Cai was busy fingering through his emails when he looked over to see Li Shishi approach him. Su's request had come as an unwelcome complication.

Li held a mobile device in front of her like a drawn knife, her ponytail swinging in time with the sway of her hips. "Let's connect on Skylink," she coaxed him like a freshman at orientation to link up on China's encrypted social network. She shook the phone back and forth in front of his to activate its mating function like she was parrying strokes of a sword. His phone pinged its recognition of the invitation.

He considered this an awkward intrusion, but unlike many people his age, he could not feign ignorance and fumble with the device, a liability when one was the head of technology at State Security. He harrumphed, squirmed, and opened the screen that confirmed his facial recognition, then pressed the screen button to accept her invitation.

"Thank you, Chief Cai. This is such an honor for me!" Li gushed in a spritely, girlish tone.

"And what would interest Financial Crimes in the reference to Mount Tai?" Cai asked mustering an innocent tone.

"I don't know. When Uncle Su calls for something done, I just say 'yes,'" Li Shishi said with a twinkle in her voice.

Uncle Su?!? Cai *really* did not welcome this complication.

ꓤ 人 ꓛ

THE WHITE-CLAD SCHOLAR WAS APTLY NAMED. LIKE A university don, Wang Lun was particular and precise—some said prickly and persnickety. He did not suffer fools and made even the most intelligent of partners feel like he was condescending. Most people then caved to his will and way of thinking, even if they did not like it.

Not so Lin Chong. *This cat is different*, Wang Lun judged looking across the table in the Righteous Fraternity Conference Room at the disgraced major. Lin Chong was clearly gifted; he was by far the most artful coder the White-Clad Scholar had met. He was clearly intelligent; he had grasped Wang Lun's deep dive into blockchain like it was a trifle of rudimentary maths. He was clearly motivated; on the run for espionage, treason and murder, how could he not be? He was a leader, quickly integrating into the network at LiangShanPo, making friends, helping people, supporting teams.

So what was it that bothered Wang Lun? He had to admit he felt threatened by Lin Chong. Every bit as skilled as Wang Lun, he was twice the leader. So far Lin Chong had respected the chain of command like a good soldier should. But the White-Clad Scholar was an academic, not a soldier, and had an inborn distrust of those who lived off might over right. He knew that was unfair to Lin Chong, but there it was.

Lin Chong had not delivered on the tithes as expected. Yes, he had helped others with their work and several stalled programs started bearing fruit with his management of their tasks, but he was expected to create new programs, new stings. So far there was nothing to show. That was the topic of today's review session.

Ten days had passed since the protests in Beijing occurred. They had all been enraptured by the elegance and audacity of the attack and the mysterious perpetrator. They had many meetings, both formal and while chatting over meals, about what had happened in Beijing. Why couldn't the stalwarts at LiangShanPo also have done something like this? Were they thinking too narrowly? Did they not have sufficient resources, or was it just a lack of imagination? Wang Lun felt upstaged, like a loser, like someone had taken glory meant for him. Perhaps if people like Lin Chong had been pulling harder, LiangShanPo would have attained more renown.

He looked to Zhu Gui, Song Wan, and Du Qian for support, then said, "Panther Head, what's the deal? It's clear you are skilled, but I feel you are holding back on us. Yeah, you have helped some coders achieve their objectives, but we aren't seeing anything come out of *you* yet. Your desk has a cost, you know?"

Lin Chong had had sensed such a conversation was coming and was truly uncertain how to respond. He respected the executive council at the community, and he liked most of them. However, he felt Wang Lun was in it a bit too much for himself. Not self-aggrandizing, as he seemed to lead an austere life, but certainly in a self-promoting way.

"You gentlemen have all been fair and welcoming. I thank you for that. I am sorry I have been unable to return your generosity with major contributions." He paused, and the expressions on their faces told him they wanted more.

"There has been lots of talk over tea about what's happening around us. Seems to be a new world. Someone has taken a bold initiative to disrupt the old order. The question is asked, 'Why wasn't it us?'" Nods around the table showed a consensus. "Whoever this Demeter group is, they do not seem to have done this to make money. It would have taken considerable resources to do what they did. And unless they were gaming the stock market or something, I feel it would be hard to make coin out of it. No. The group acted on principle. Just on principle."

Wang Lun interjected, "And, yes, we all believe that you, Lin Chong, are capable of big, great things, like this Demeter group pulled off."

Lin Chong stared the White-Clad Scholar dead in the eyes. "Not so long as we are distracted by the imperative to make money out of our hacking. That is a principle that seems to come directly from you, and it detracts from the group's potential. We generate funds, savings, investments. The group can sustain itself for what? Six months, twelve months, without making a single yuan. If you want outsized results, something that will truly put your mark on history, then you can't be stingy about it."

Zhu Gui looked uncertainly at Song Wan and Du Qian. No one, absolutely no one, had ever challenged the White-Clad Scholar like that. He looked to Wang Lun.

After a pause, Wang Lun said, "Touché. I will think deeply about this. In the meantime, what are you working on for us?"

Zhu Gui sat back in his chair and let out a quiet breath. He had been girding himself to see the fur fly.

"I do have a scheme I am working on. It will completely align with our principles, and it should generate a sizable sting, netting you more than you have pulled in before."

"Would you care to elucidate?"

"No. I don't think I would."

⊃人⊂

SUPERINTENDENT LI SHISHI DID NOT HAVE TO SPEND LONG with Chief Cai Jing to take his measure. She knew he underestimated her. To him, she was a flower vase, an object of beauty, empty, vacuous, to be kept on the shelf and admired, or taken from the shelf and filled with the stems of a man's desire, but not to be respected. She had met many men like Cai Jing and learned to use them to her ends without disabusing them of their misperceptions. This was a soft strength. They never suspected this flower of being anything but an object of longing, unfulfilled.

She had, in fact, graduated first in class at Beijing University law school and rejected a lucrative offer from a foreign law firm to follow her family's profession, close-knit loyalty to the Communist Party in service of the people. For three generations, the family had been Red and humble. After market opening, they had eschewed all opportunities to profit in myriad ways from their positions and insider knowledge. They were known as honest and incorruptible, loyal to the Party and to China. When she graduated, her real uncle, who had raised Li after the untimely death of her parents, reached out to Su Yuanjing, whom their family affectionately referred to as Uncle Su, inquiring if she could serve the Commission. He had seen to it that she was placed within the Public Security Financial Crimes desk, and she regularly reported to him, especially after orders came from on high to squelch inquiries of people or organizations she or her colleagues were investigating.

Su's team had provided Li with several useful tools to pursue the covert work. One tool mimicked the mating invitation of Skylink with other smartphones. When the link was accepted, she could mirror the target's phone, view and download its files, emails, and call records, listen to calls, and track its location. She could probably learn everything she needed to know from Cai without shadowing him, but she could learn so much more and embed herself more completely within his organization if she stayed close to him, observing, listening, and capturing more target mobile devices to mirror.

Shortly after they had left the meeting and she continued to tag along close behind, he had said dismissively, "Look, I have many other things to be looking into. Why don't I give you a call when I have gotten to the bottom of this Mount Tai reference?"

"But Commissioner Su told us this *is* the priority," she pouted. "I just have to see it through. You don't want Uncle Su angry at me, or you, do you?"

When it was clear that she was not going to leave his side, he called an aide and made an appointment. Since his conversation with General Gao Qiu and Yanei, he had put his own investigator on the Lin Chong incident to try to learn what they were not telling him and started to see some of the results come in. One thing stuck in the back of his mind, but he wanted to reconfirm.

They got into the backseat of his car, a Shanghai-assembled Audi with a driver, and pulled out into Beijing traffic heading to the State Security headquarters. He looked across at the young woman. Flawless. Not a hair out of place. Fair, smooth skin. Double eyelids fluttered over large, brown, doe-like irises. Her uniform cut to regulation specifications, crisp and clean, but tailored to accentuate her very feminine form. She smiled innocently across at him, and as she breathed slowly, he could see the rise and fall of her blouse. "Are you married yet, Superintendent Li?"

She blushed, "No sir. I have not met the right man. Perhaps I will be lucky enough to meet someone worthy working for you. *Yuanfen*, destiny. You can be our matchmaker!" she squealed joyfully and clapped her hands. "How about you, sir, do you have children, grandchildren?" She found that asking the matchmaker and grandchild questions always helped to tweak the right perspective with such men as Cai. They might still lust but knew that she regarded them more as respected elders than potential lovers.

"A married daughter and boy, in high school," Cai replied, his ardor deflated.

"What is he interested in studying?"

"Not Public Security. I hope he can get a business degree and a high-paying job, make a boatload of cash, and not have to work so hard like his old man."

She noted the chief's sour reflection on his own financial returns. "Surely there must be great rewards in what you do?"

Cai looked askance at her, realizing that he should not relax into a casual conversation with Li. "Of course. The State has invested heavily in creating and rolling out the most advanced surveillance tools in the world. I am privileged to lead great people who have a great sense of mission." The car pulled into the State Security headquarters.

"I would have thought your offices were in Xiyuan?" she queried, referring to the area in Northwest Beijing where State Security maintained a secretive campus. The headquarters was a three-block-long, white, marble building near TianAnMen.

"Apologies. You are not authorized to go there. We will meet someone here."

They got out of the car and were ushered through the lobby and into a meeting room on the ground floor. Li observed that the room was plain, small, and not part of the inner rooms. Clearly, she was being held at arm's length. Tea was served, and shortly they were joined by another man. He was tall and well built. Although he sported a beard and had a manly look, his voice was soft and somewhat high pitched.

"Superintendent Li. Please meet Tong Guan."

"Tong Guan, nice to meet you. What unit are you with?"

Cai interceded, "You do not need to know that, Superintendent Li. Tong Guan is a trusted advisor to the government and tireless investigator who supports me." Indeed, Cai did work closely with Tong Guan, but usually it was when he needed work done off the record, either for personal affairs and investments or for the government's interest. Nicknamed the Eunuch because he had survived testicular cancer by having his balls removed, Tong Guan had been an able general who lost his commission early.

Tong Guan's eyes darted to Li Shishi with some suspicion and certainly no attraction to her charms. "Who's she?" he asked bluntly.

"She works on financial crimes at Public Security. Commissioner Su has asked that we try to understand the significance of something related to the unrest in Beijing."

"So why am *I* meeting her?" he asked, ignoring Li completely.

"I have asked you to bring the research you have been doing on that traitor who is under investigation. I want to confirm a hunch. Can you pull up the photos from the crime scene?"

"You think it is related?" Tong asked petulantly.

"Look, I have told Commissioner Su I have a hunch to try to confirm, and he asked that she stick with me on this. So, can we get this over with quickly?"

Tong frowned. He used a remote to turn on a flat-screen panel then pulled out his mobile device and waved his finger from the device to the flat screen. A photograph appeared of the compound located in the Wild Boar Forest residential community of Saddle Mountain Township.

"Some context," Cai said to Li. "A PLA cyber corps major was arrested several months ago on charges of treason. He was detained in this black house and undergoing interrogation when he killed two officials and severely wounded two others. He escaped and is on the run." He urged Tong to continue advancing the photos.

The next shot revealed bloody footprints and a steel pole on the tile floor, its end also covered in flesh and blood. "Some of these pictures are quite shocking, Superintendent Li, hope you don't mind."

She pursed her lips by way of girding herself and nodded for him to continue.

The next picture was of a person lying awkwardly on the floor next to a wooden staircase, head caved in, brains spilling out onto a concrete floor.

The next picture showed yet another man seated on the floor, his back to a cement basement wall with a long, red smear behind him where he had slid into this position, his throat a large gaping puncture, the chest of his white shirt wet, dark crimson.

There were pictures of the basement, some implements presumably used for torture. An overturned chair in the center of the room and a broken mounting where a pipe had been affixed and torn out. The next slide showed a close-up of the overturned chair near the broken mounting, and there were words scrawled on the floor. "That's what I want to see," Cai jumped in. "I read it before, but just zoom in on it."

Written in charcoal from spent matches was a four-line poem:

Just is Lin Chong, Loyal to the People.
Renowned in the demimonde, a hero of the nation.
Fate has cast him adrift, his glory forsaken.
But someday his will be done, and Mount Tai will bow before him.

"We have our culprit," Cai Jing beamed, knowing that Lin Chong was fully capable of the offense and that blame for letting the Beijing protests occur could be placed on him, deflecting any criticism of Cai and the State Security team.

"Who is Lin Chong?" Li Shishi asked aloud. *More importantly*, she wondered, *why did he feel so wronged as to have written this poem? And why is State Security investigating a PLA matter, anyway?*

ɔ 人 ᴄ

AUGUST 31 WAS A DATE MOST PARENTS LOOKED FORWARD TO IN China. It was the last day of summer vacation from schooling. The day the children went back to work, and mothers and fathers did not have to scramble with grandparents and aunties to try to get their own work done while worrying about who was minding the little ones.

This summer had been different and the end to the school break, even stranger. Everyone was on edge. Though State media painted a rosy picture, conversations were dominated by talk of what had happened in Beijing and of the message virtually all Chinese had received from a mysterious organization calling for young and old to hold their leaders to account about the dreadful pollution in China. Especially in Beijing, after an initial crackdown, it had been uncharacteristically quiet. Beijingers had expected mass arrests, if not bloodletting, but in conversations among themselves, few people spoke of missing relatives. It did not seem like people were disappearing.

Stock markets, however, had taken a drubbing. Wags in the teahouses proclaimed that their relatives weren't disappearing, but their savings were. The government had stepped in several times to try to shore up the market, and after a 26 percent drop, they claimed to have staunched the decline. Breast-beating Securities and Exchange bureaucrats loudly proclaimed that they would go after nefarious foreign investors who had shorted Chinese markets heavily. Real-estate prices followed, and many middle-class and wealthy investors soon found themselves underwater on their mortgages.

Parents had another growing concern. It had begun as a welcome summer distraction for their children, which they believed was sponsored by the government; an effort to co-opt and redirect a potential enemy's initiative, a typical Communist Party strategy, parents reasoned. A month earlier, on the last day of school before summer break, students across China had gotten a message on their mobile phones. It was tailored to their age, gender, location, and in the case of college students, their major, but the intent was the same. It was written with proletarian fervor and frequently quoted past speeches from Communist party leaders, including Mao, Deng, Jiang, Zhu, and President Zhao Ji, citing the drive to create a just, democratic civil society that respected nature and encouraged green initiatives. It had all the look and feel of a communication from the Communist Youth League. In fact, all 110 million members of that organization had received invitations, too, and because many of them had been peeved by President Zhao Ji's efforts to curb the Youth League's power, they responded with interest.

For any student who read the message and responded, an app was downloaded and installed. It gave specific instructions on what to do next. Within days, college students had organized teenagers, who had recruited middle school children, each having been communicated their rank, role, and lists of activities to support. Hundreds of thousands of these cells sprouted across China. Every day they received new reading materials, new instructions. They learned about alternative lifestyles, the evils and limitations of consumerism, the pain, death, and destruction wrought on the planet by rampant consumption, the role of environmental activism in other countries through a democratic process, and how to initiate, execute, record, and broadcast nonviolent protest.

They were called Green Guards, and many of them quickly bought bright-green mobile phone covers that they waved in green fields of passionate arms when they gathered by the tens of thousands. They quickly ran out and emptied the secondhand and military surplus clothing marts of the old, green, cotton trousers, Mao hats, and shirts, which became their uniform.

They also received credits on their phones each day to pay for travel, supplies needed to drive the green revolution, mobile communication expenses. College students got enough that they could distribute the excess to on-the-ground, spontaneous initiatives. They were encouraged to document and report these initiatives with their mobile video links. Those who were creative, made the effort, promoted the cause, or went beyond the call of duty found even larger stipends waiting for them the next day.

If a Green Guard used these credits for other things, like hanging out with (non-Green Guard) friends at a fast-food store, buying an online game, or going to a movie, they would get a reeducation message the next day. The message did not explicitly mention their transgressions but would seek to galvanize further effort and shame them for their lack of commitment. There would be readings about recruiting friends into the movement or efforts Green Heroes had exerted the day before with their time. Or how someone or some animal or some river had suffered the day before because of pollution, habitat destruction, or illegal dumping. That day's stipend would also be withheld. Other members of that person's cell would also be educated to put positive pressure on the recidivist.

The Green Guard app was encrypted end to end, and messages were customized to each participant and cell every day. The authorities could neither stop the movement of messages using keywords nor could they discern the greater aims of the movement by seizing one, two, ten, or a thousand mobile devices.

Initially, parents welcomed the distraction. Their children were given an educational summer activity and pocket money that they reasoned could only be afforded on such a massive scale by the government. Before the government could respond with media messages warning about Green Guards and the app it employed, it was too late.

A generation of Chinese, 260 million strong, between the ages of ten to twenty-four, had known no revolution, no class struggle, no spirited reason to serve the greater good. They had been raised by their parents and the examples of the successful around them to chase income opportunities and wealth, and thereby the ability to consume through education, self-betterment, *guanxi*, and if necessary, bending or breaking rules and stepping on the heads of those less fortunate . The message taken to heart by many who read the daily green missives was in equal parts fresh and new, hopeful and urgent.

As the first day of school approached, fifty million Green Guards were on the march.

CHAPTER 6

LI JUN SAT IN HIS OFFICE, FIVE FACES STARING BACK AT HIM through the dual screens, awaiting his answer. He worked a tense kink in his neck stretching to the side and digging his thumb into a knotted trapezius muscle, buying time and some comfort. He did not want to appear obtuse or indecisive to his team, but he needed more information. "Tell me what happened again, and what you are proposing."

The team of five reporting to him daily were designated as Gold, Water, Wood, Fire, and Earth, the five elements of the Daoist physics concept of mutual generation and destruction. He had never met them face to face nor did he know their real names. He accepted that as a proper security precaution.

Fire jumped in to respond. "We successfully pulled off 2,200 protests across the country yesterday. Multiple protests in each province, over 600 each in the Beijing to Tianjin, Nanjing to Shanghai, and Pearl River Delta corridors. This represents a doubling over the past week. Average participant rate was 173 Green Guards per protest, and the largest was 1,700."

Fire appeared to be in his late twenties and described himself as Chief Instigator. He set up protests and made sure they were recorded and distributed. "We have been able to keep ahead of the authorities. They were not prepared for any of these events and have neither been able to capture clear security camera footage to track Green followers, nor prevent the distribution of our protest videos."

Li Jun had observed several of these flash protests unfold himself. None were as large or dramatic as the event at Tiananmen. All were highly targeted to protest companies in flagrant violation of environmental regulations, or offices of the government turning a blind eye to the rapacious behavior. They were short in duration, to prevent sufficient time for an organized police response, but lasting in impact since mobile device footage from the many participants was skillfully edited to make it seem the crowds were larger, the passion inspiring, and the environmental threat real. This was launched daily into *weibosphere*. The Great Internet Wall had been able to consistently block redistribution of the videos after a period of time, but not the initial shots.

"So, what is the government's change in tactic we are dealing with?" Li Jun asked.

"Several changes. Since we have been able to catch the authorities off guard, they have generally not been able to make arrests at the site of the protests. Some clever police officer got the idea to video emergent protests with her mobile device, and then feed that into the facial recognition database. Public Security has now issued a standing order to do this whenever a flash protest happens."

"What else?"

"With the facial recognition, they are swooping in later, after the protests, to make arrests. There has been a significant increase over the past week of arrests being made of Green Guards."

"How many?"

"Six thousand one hundred thirty-five, judging from the number of Guards who pushed the panic button."

Built into the Green Guard encrypted app was a function that could be activated by pushing a red button on the log-in screen, or by repeating a self-selected and recorded password spoken, or in many cases screamed, by the Green Guard when they were being roughed up by Public Security and their mobile device was seized. This would trigger immediate erasure of all Green Guard participation on the device and would start recording and transmitting whatever was said within earshot of the device and the device's GPS location until it was shut off or the battery died. It would also promote the next in line to lead the cell or assume new duties while letting the members of the cell know to lay low.

Over 6,000 today. Li shook his head and thought of the cost to their futures these young people had borne. The average age of Greens was only eighteen. He dug into the tight spot on his neck again and tried to relax it without success.

"So, yeah, I'm pissed," Fire said, his glare reaching out of the screen. True to his element, he was rash and easily irritated. Several times, Water had helped Li by stepping in and cooling Fire's temper.

"Ideas? How do we protect our Guards or get them out of this?" Li asked the brain trust.

"I want to double down," Fire said. "I think if we keep anteing up, the government will capitulate, start to respond to our movement."

Earth sat with her chin resting on a steeple of fingertips like she had been praying. "It is the youth who have the most at stake if the environmental degradation continues, but also the ones who have most at stake if their future lives are ruined by having done 'the right thing'. We cannot let them become disillusioned and turn their backs on the movement."

She was an older woman, professorial by demeanor. Li thought she might have been from Kunming in the far south. She gave direction to the group, setting the tone philosophically for the movement and activities.

"I agree, I don't want you to raise the stakes, Fire, until we have a strategy to help out those who have already followed us to their arrest. Ideas, people. You are resourceful. How can we leverage some leniency for our Greens?" He looked from face to face.

Water spoke up. She was a younger woman, a wiz at digital marketing and PR. "I could double down on the online side, with the extra communications focused on the plights of the detained. Get the message out one more time about what they were trying to highlight to the authorities and how unfair their arrests are, with details on police stations or black houses to put pressure on."

Li knew she was effective in this job because he felt readily persuaded by her. Sincere and energetic, she appealed at once on an emotional and rational level to him. The accent and style with which she dressed suggested she was from Shanghai.

The capability and resourcefulness of the team Li Jun had inherited was a source of consistent amazement. He knew not how they were able to muck around with the State's digital security apparatus, helping him evade detection, posting video online, and coordinating millions of Green Guards. He had asked once how they did it, and the response had been basically "Don't ask, we have teams of thousands working for us." All he knew was that when they had hashed out an idea or a strategy one day, it was ready to implement the next.

"Wood, if Water delivers double the messaging, can you grow your channels to deliver?"

Wood oversaw operations; whenever materiel or logistics, physical or digital were required, he got it done. In other circumstances he would be known as a fixer. But Li reflected that they were all fixers, operating, as they were, outside of the law. Wood was about Li's age and had a Southern accent, possibly from Guangdong.

"Sure thing, boss."

"Don't worry about the cost," Gold said preempting Li's next concern. Gold was a fellow who appeared be about forty-five years old and was, for lack of a better word, the CFO. He had a ruddy complexion, a prominent mole on the right side of his chin with three long, coarse hairs growing out of it, and was balding. He helped control access to and the flow of funds. Li could not make out his accent, but supposed Gold was from Xian or thereabouts.

"I don't think upping the ante on the PR is enough," Li said. "For various reasons we can't reveal ourselves and go out and hire lawyers for these people." He looked at both Earth and Gold, who shook their heads in agreement. "But I suspect we can help leverage information about the incarcerated to get them a better deal. Shine a light on their cases, as it were. Thoughts?"

"We could leverage the recordings of the police being made after incarceration," Earth said.

Wood chimed in, "Well, we have about 10,000 hours of recordings since yesterday. Some devices have been shut off or placed in evidence lockers where the recordings are just silent. But we do have several thousand hours already documenting the outrageous treatment being meted out. We can correlate it directly to the Green Guard who activated the emergency button. In some cases, voice pattern recognition will allow us to identify the individual police speaking. Otherwise, we know which station they were taken to."

Water picked up the thread. "We could make mini-documentaries, 'Profiles in Courage,' based on data we have already collected about the activities of individuals arrested. Something like this," she said, and a screen opened up in the bottom right corner of Li Jun's lower monitor.

The camera slowly zoomed in on the image of a Chinese flag waving to strains of the orchestral Chinese anthem. The zoom continued into the main golden star in the upper corner and morphed into green with an image in black background of the face of a young woman smiling and laughing with friends, her name, and the title of the series, *Chinese Profiles in Green Courage*.

The voice of a male presenter, who Li Jun thought sounded like the men reading the news for the national broadcasting network, spoke about the young woman's life, schooling, and love of nature. The monologue was accompanied by photos and videos of her growing up, and copies of glowing school reports floating across the screen.

The story segued into a description of a semiconductor chip packaging company in the girl's hometown that was a notorious violator of environmental regulations and showed reports about the toxic effluent it discharged into the river, as well as the ethereal rainbow reflection of sunlight off chemicals at the surface of the water.

There was a video of the young crusader pumping up the fervor of her cell of followers as they rode to a protest and then the event itself, peaceful but loud and accusatory at the gates to the factory as the owner's limo drove up. He opened the window and flung a cigarette butt at her, then drove through the gates, which closed behind him. The presenter described the peaceful dispersal of the protest and showed the young woman making a relaxed selfie video with a friend later that day when they were grabbed by two Public Security officers.

With the cry of the young woman shouting her emergency password, the video shut off, but the audio continued as the presenter described that she was arrested and taken into custody in blatant disregard for her rights. The mistakes made by the arresting officers were highlighted as the audio played out.

The video stopped, and Water spoke up again, "You get the picture. We have enough information that we could put these together for several thousand of the incarcerated. Then we pump them through the internet."

Li Jun liked it. It was well presented and even patriotic, but he worried that not enough of the right people would see it to make a difference, and then there were the fates of those whose stories were not told.

"This can be one prong of a multi-pronged effort. It may raise more public awareness about these 'enforced or involuntary disappearances.' I can't believe the UN even has a formal name for such shit. However, I think we can go further. We need to escalate presentation of their stories on up the ladder. Someone, at some level of the Party, has got to care about this, has got to see that it is wrong and not aligned with the interests of the Party and the Chinese people. We just have to make sure the unadulterated message gets to them."

Fire shook his head impatiently, "It's not enough to tell them what's happening and just hope. We have to hammer these assholes so they know if they don't wise up, there is a price to pay."

"We can dig for information on up the line, all the touch points, guards, prosecutors, judges, and Party leaders, and give them a taste for what we know, what will be made public, if they do not back off and start doing their real jobs. Same with people like the factory owner," Wood shared.

"No person is perfect. No doubt we can dig dirt up on anyone with our resources. However, before we threaten people, we should first determine if they have sympathy with our cause. Otherwise, we can really alienate them," Earth said in her measured way.

"Okay, let's do this," Li Jun said. "For each protest and each individual incarcerated, let's do an analysis, as you said, all the touch points on up the line. Let's start with the humanitarian and legal appeal: what the guards are doing is only what the government, the Party, should be doing, seeking the enforcement of environmental justice already embodied in our laws. If we see no softening, then we suggest that the selective enforcement of laws only against our Greens will have repercussions. Suggest there is a hammer. If they still don't act, then we get the hammer out and strike. I think we will find if we go high enough up the ladder that touch points from all the protests and geographies will coalesce around several individuals. People with power and influence. If we can turn them to our cause, then we can create real action."

Li Jun looked at Fire. "Is that a plan?"

Fire nodded, satisfied.

"Yes, boss," the others chimed in.

Li Jun thought of Mama Fei and how she had been a lioness whenever he or the gang had gotten into some trouble. "I have another idea I want you to flesh out. What do each of these incarcerated people have in common?"

The five hesitated, looked at each other. Earth said, "Their commitment to the environment?"

"More basic than that. They all have parents, presumably who love them and care about their futures."

The faces nodded. Water's eyes perked up, and she smiled. "Leverage the parents?"

"Yes, more than that. I want you all to look at creating an extension of the Green Guards. Let's call it the Gray Guards, maybe. Parents of Green Guards who have been arrested. It can start with an outreach like the biographical documentary you showed us, Water. Let the parents know their child was involved in something important and that they were valued and respected. Then we let them know what has happened to their children, where they are, and explain their rights. Finally, we network parents who opt in to the organization and financially support their effort to seek justice. Can do, Gold?"

"Can do. We will work together on the plan and the financials, let you know if there are any hitches."

"Okay, let's meet tomorrow and give me an update on this. I have to get to my rehab appointment." The people waved a goodbye, and the screens went blank.

So, this is what power feels like, Li Jun said to himself. Since Team Green's flash protest "welcoming" him to Beijing several weeks before, he had tasted power, and he did not like it. He could see how seductive it might be to other people, lulling them into an addictive need to continue growing it, and how it could be felt as necessary by the weak seeking revenge or security. He felt neither need.

In his years growing up at the margins of society, he had frequent run-ins with people who had a little power and wanted more, through government imprimatur or money or brute force. Ever since knee-capping his future "brother," the Bearded Dragon Fei Bao, he had eschewed violence unless in self-defense. He had never been rich, seized power through force, or been granted power from an outside authority.

He *had* resisted corrupt power many times, though; government officials and party hacks, local hoods, even ill-informed or misled environmental groups seeking kickbacks to shut up. He had dealt with each in their own way, neither caving to unreasonable demands, nor going to war with them. And he had also seen the examples of goodness in people, like Mama Fei, and even in some well-meaning and upright government people. He sought to learn from them.

When general manager of the recycling plant, he felt he had been fair and balanced, not coercive, corrupt, or overbearing. The loyalty of those who worked for him in the past, the gang of Bu, Ni, Fei, and Di, spoke for itself.

They gravitated to him as a leader because they trusted him, not because they were forced to.

All of which made the current circumstance stand out in his reflections. He had not sought this job, and chance alone had put him into it. But in his honest feelings, losing a foot was a small toll to pay Fate to recruit him to this new mission, well worth the sacrifice.

The team had been able to take decisive action without him. The massive protest at Tiananmen was proof, as was the stymied government response. But he knew they benefited from his direction, his experience, and his commitment. Together they had built the Green Guards, yet none of the Green Guards knew who they were.

Here, in this role, he was not just cleaning up the garbage of faceless people thousands of miles away, even as those same people continued to dispose of ever more garbage. Here he was building a movement for good in the largest polity on the planet. Changing perceptions, changing behaviors, eventually changing legislation and making a difference for every person here. All 1.4 billion.

The tools his team wielded were powerful and not to be used lightly, but he had heart.

⊃ 人 ⊂

Zhao Ji lay on his left side in the golden afternoon glow spilling through the curtains and took a deep breath to appreciate this moment, from which nothing could detract. Not the feeling of gravity pulling a loose paunch. Not the reflection in the mirror of a thinning pate. Not the agitation in the country that enemies exploited to suggest his leadership was faltering. Not the self-admission that he had come before his lover, again. Nothing could detract from this moment because she was the perfect partner *for* this moment.

His body was aligned with her back, and he inhaled youth and freshness, his left hand under her, reaching around so that his forearm created a balcony for breasts ample and firm, right arm draped down across her belly, hand on her mound. Every inch of his body felt this woman; all senses invested in her.

As his hands explored, his mind returned to his youth when he was sent to Northeast China to be rusticated by the Party.

Rustication meant being sent far away from home, from the people and customs he knew, far from whatever class or status or education normally protected him from seeing the people, their needs and suffering. He had become a man in that land, and his deep commitment to the Party grew. He helped with crops, with gathering and chopping firewood, with educating the ignorant and listening to the native knowledge of the tough but gentle people living there. Winters were dead hard, days were short and cold, and he suffered along with them on meager rations of pickled and fermented vegetables that had been put up for the winter, potatoes, noodles, and the occasional unlucky rabbit or helping of pork.

The people rejoiced in spring as life was renewed to the land. Sunshine, wildflowers, animals, insects, migratory birds returned along with his spirits. He recalled hiking through the ripening blueberry bogs, a cheerful, red, plastic pail used for washing his clothes in his hands. Walking amidst the bushes, his eyes became tuned to detect the largest, bluest, ripest berries. His hands learned to gently coax only those berries most willing to yield to his touch leaving their stems on the branch.

Although the local peasants chided him for never picking as many as they did, they conceded that his pickings were of higher quality, with fewer stems or fewer unripe berries.

His reverie of days gone by sharpened into a focus of the here and now as he became aware of his fingers caressing the center of his woman's pleasure. She shuddered and let out a slow, satisfied breath.

She turned to look into his eyes. A face so beautiful, not marred by age or decline, cynicism or avarice. Long, straight, black, silky hair; a proud, straight, Northern Chinese nose; prominent cheekbones tapering gently to a round, friendly chin; intelligent, penetrating eyes; the hint of a satisfied smile on lips pink and full.

This woman was like no other he had enjoyed since he and his wife had been young lovers. But now his wife was busy enjoying the benefits of being First Lady. Not in a corrupt way, but he knew she made the rounds. She had encouraged him to take advantage of his position as leader of the largest country on Earth, soon to be the largest economy on Earth, indeed stressing to him that as first among men, she would scorn him if he did not take what was offered to him.

In his bones, Zhao Ji did not want to "take advantage." He was not an emperor. He was not like Chairman Mao, who had warmed his bed with countless nubile acolytes.

The adoring masses had indeed presented Zhao with many opportunities. He had resisted temptation. The invitations had come loaded with traps. He could see the cynicism or avarice in their eyes and avoided them, or had seen no deep intelligence, only vapid longing, and rejected them.

That had changed when he met this woman. *Woman? She is so young and so beautiful; she is more of a fairy.* She had given a presentation at a Communist Youth League meeting he had attended during an anniversary celebration. Afterward she had shaken his hand in a line-up.

When she looked up into his eyes and saw his interest, she had averted her gaze, and a winsome smile sprouted.

He squeezed the young woman's hand a moment longer than protocol suggested, placed his left hand over hers in a two-handed shake, and said, "You spoke very well today. Thank you for your dedication to the Party and the Motherland."

The response had been simple and yet burned into his heart. "*You* are my inspiration, Chairman Zhao."

He had not rushed, coerced, or bribed her to bed. He did not want her that way.

He confided his interest to Su Yuanjing, who had done a background check on the girl.

Her mother had died in childbirth, and she was raised by her father, a factory worker in a textile dyeing mill so poor he had fed her bean milk instead of infant formula. He too had died thereafter of a broken heart, or from exposure to the toxins at the mill (though this was never proven), leaving her an orphan. The orphanage turned out to be a step up in life as she was exposed to books, other children, and learning. She excelled at studies and in middle school and high school had graduated top of her class earning admission into Beijing University's law program. There she was active in the Communist Youth League.

As she approached graduation, her uncle reached out to Su Yuanjing to ask if a role of service to the nation could be found for her within the National Supervisory Commission. Placed instead into the Financial Crimes section of Public Security, she had done fine work there and been enlisted by Su to confidentially report anomalies to him and President Zhao.

And so, Li Shishi had come to spend frequent moments with Zhao Ji. She could sense his longing, the feeling of isolation, and need to relieve himself of deep concerns. She felt his ardent dedication to the country, the people, and the Party and was further inspired by that.

She too felt a longing to be with him. If she had analyzed it, she would have dismissed the desire as seeking to replace a father figure gone too early from her life. Instead, she indulged the longing and the intense fantasy of being *the one* to help relieve Zhao's isolation, longing, and anxiety. One evening after she had presented a briefing, and Su had absented himself, she looked up into Zhao's eyes. "Permission to speak, sir?"

"Please."

"That day in the line-up after I gave my speech and shook your hand. You took my hand in both of yours. I felt so secure, so protected in that moment. I felt there was a special spark between us."

Zhao looked at her and did not speak. He held out his right hand, and she took it to shake it as she had before. He placed his left hand over hers again, his clasp firm and gentle, his palms a warm, secure retreat. She tugged gently away, as if to withdraw her hand. He did not let go, nor did he pull her toward him. But with her tug, she yielded her body closer and then her lips to his.

That was months ago, and many liaisons passed during which they had enjoyed each other's company and sated each other's needs.

Today, she felt he had been distracted and needed even more care than usual. Yes, he had come first, but she wanted him to be so excited he could not stand it. That increased her excitement, allowing him to release high tide in other satisfying ways. After, they would talk about the country, his head alongside hers on the pillow. He would share his concerns or seek a younger person's read on how the youth of China responded to him and the Party's leadership. This also served their mutual satisfaction and endearment.

"Old Zhao," she interrupted using the name she spoke in private. "What's troubling you?"

"This Green Guards thing. It's snowballing. How does one prevent being inundated when faced with this?"

They both enjoyed practicing Taijiquan, China's ancient, meditative combat exercise, and he appreciated references to it. She felt there was relevant wisdom to be imparted from its application, but first she had to acknowledge his concerns. "Yes, it is a movement, formidable and growing. Many of my peers have spoken to me about it, or I have overheard them at coffee shops, restaurants, and on the metro. Even the ones who have not joined the movement are awed by what it has achieved. Some suggest that it is just the first salvo toward a democracy movement. Once the tiger is seen to have no teeth, they will be emboldened."

Zhao looked deep into her eyes. "Since the first protest in Beijing, which my people are only able to circumstantially connect to the Green Guards, there have not been other mass protests. Instead, thousands of mini-flash eruptions across the country, with no specific pattern allowing us to predict the next one. Aiya," he let out a sigh. "They are quick to form, quick to make their point, and then to melt away, but always with live video coverage from multiple mobile phone cams distributed rapidly across the net. So even if I ordered the tiger to chomp on them, where does he bite?"

"The tiger is not the enemy of the people. He shouldn't bite them," she said tickling his cheek with a lock of hair. "Whoever is leading the Green Guards, they have been exceedingly careful to couch all their proclamations and agitations in the words of Party leaders, including your words. I think you have a great opportunity here."

Zhao arched a bushy, skeptical eyebrow.

"Yes," she insisted. "In Taiji we absorb the energy of the opponent's movement, obliquely if we must, to avoid being crushed, and make it our own, return it or use it to take on other opponents."

A second eyebrow raised higher wrinkling his forehead.

"The things that the Green Guards are agitating against are all things that you want to see done. Reduced carbon footprint, less conspicuous consumption, clean air and water in the countryside and cities, no corruption associated with environmental degradation. If anything, when you get on the right side of this, you can co-opt the power of the movement, surface your enemies, and with the power of the movement, destroy your enemies."

He knew that Mao had created the Red Guards to weaken and destroy his enemies within the Party, who found themselves standing on quicksand and struggled to maintain any solid footing. However, the legacy of the Great Proletarian Cultural Revolution and the Red Guards spawned therein was one of cultural destruction, lost opportunities for the nation, and a delicate balancing act for loyal Party leaders like Zhou Enlai, who had tried to maintain cool heads without getting them chopped off by Mao and his minions.

Zhao ruminated on his tenuous grasp of complete control. *This indeed is the crux of the issue and always has been in China since time immemorial; a ruler with absolute power can only retain it so long as he or she maintains absolute power. When you are at the top, the only next step is down, down, down. And when you are out of power, the new victor is free, nay incentiv-*

ized, to go after you, destroy you, your family, your family's family. This was where Zhao Ji found himself now. He could remain standing at the pinnacle of power... or fall.

She sensed the concern. "Unlike Mao, you didn't create this movement. You can be overrun by it, or you can absorb its energy and endorse it to your ends. If you do nothing about it, your Party enemies will use your per-ceived weakness against you. As for keeping control over the movement, Mao *lost* control over Red Guards. You are starting from a fundamentally different situation; you *have* no control over the Green Guards. I think ab-sorbing and endorsing their energy is the only option."

Zhao Ji was silent for a long while, his eyes closed, his body feeling hers next to him. The proposal was not new to him. He had been toying with the idea. It was a very fine line he would have to walk in order to pull it off. And failure for him would be catastrophic, not to mention whatever conse-quences instability in the nation would wreak on the masses.

"I'll think about it" was all he said before changing the subject. "Any more information about the poor sap on whom State Security is trying to pin responsibility for the mass protest?" He felt it improbable that one man, no matter how skilled in cyber warfare, could have pulled off this stunt.

"I said before, I suspect there is more to the story than meets the eye regarding this Major Lin Chong, but details are hard to dig out. I was both-ered that State Security is looking into the investigation being conducted by the PLA. I have determined that, indeed, no case file has been opened at State Security on Lin Chong. The investigator Cai introduced to me, Tong Guan, is not on State Security payroll, which means that Cai is looking into this personally for reasons unknown."

Zhao squeezed Li in his arms one more time enjoying the plasticity of their flesh melding together at all touch points. "Thank you, Little Li," his nickname for her. "Keep Su in the loop on this."

⊃ 人 ⊂

RAPPER, CULTURAL ICON, AND ENTREPRENEUR KY WAS HOLD-ing court at his hacienda-styled mansion in North Beverly Park in the hills above Los Angeles.

He was not a happy king. Before him were his vassals, people to whom he paid good money for their flawless advice. Lawyers, marketing and market analytics team, media team, producer, and manager all had failed him.

He drummed fingertips on the glass table, the digits heavy with gold rings adorning each of them and stared out beyond the infinity pool to the relative wilderness of the Franklin Canyon Park behind his home. He was tired of the parade of musical-chairs excuse making.

KY, a stage name chosen "because all d'bitches be wet when they 'round me," was born Joseph Louis Joyner to middle-class parents in an upscale neighborhood in Atlanta. Gifted with good looks and athleticism, a clear singing voice, a strong work ethic, and genius IQ, he had advanced into one of Atlanta's talent-magnet high schools, excelling in dance, choral, and drama and graduated a year early.

Nixing a scholarship to Berklee College of Music, he headed to LA and planted his flag, staking a claim by inventing the Rap Funkadelic style. His first album had gone gold, the second and third had gone multiplatinum. He had owned the summer hit slot the prior two years.

That was precisely the problem for which he was seeking answers from this crew of slackers and hangers-on facing his wrath today. At age twenty-four and with somewhere north of $20 million in the bank and no debt, he felt he had made all the right decisions, yet things had not gone his way with the fourth album. The summer hit entry had dragged itself into an anemic, distant second place to a song that held tight to number one. Someone must be to blame.

"The damage is done. This is supposed to be a team effort. Y'all failed me in the run-up to this dénouement, now you're failing me again in the postmortem. None of you have told me what went wrong. Why are we not at number one?" Despite his trash-talking, ungrammatical, urban-sex-machine public persona, in private KY was nothing if not articulate.

They had been reminding him there was no shortage of things the team had done right. KY had been everywhere in the run-up to launch. Hyper-profiling had identified 90 percent of internet users in the US who were fans of, or predisposed to be fans of, KY, and they were carpet bombed with messages, invites, teasers, trailers, and samplings. If anyone watched major cable and broadcast media, they would have seen KY and known the event was about to happen.

Based on the deep understanding of the target fan, the data analytics team had driven the sound and lyrics of the tune. Of course, he had massaged KY magic on the lyrics to gel the song into something of which he was proud. The result was a hard-driving but optimistic message-song about mass shooters and gun control in which the "gun" in the end is identified as a man's penis, with a warning about the casualties of unwanted pregnancy.

208

The team had negotiated exclusive content with each of the streaming services to drive clicks and had registered over ten million downloads per hour for the first twenty-four hours of its release.

His eyes scanned those of the vassals looking for anyone who averted his stare to pick on. He found the head of the analytics team with her eyes closed. "Mellissa, is my demanding quest for truth and perfection tiring you?"

She opened her eyes, and her lips trembled. "No, KY, sorry. I was deep in thought about your question. We have done an analysis of contributing factors to the deficit, the twelve-percentage-point spread, that separates your hit from the number one."

"And?"

"We attribute 2 percent of the spread to changes made to the lyrics proposed by the algorithm, specifically the less-than-normal use of expletives you chose, and music, specifically the counterpoint rhythm you insisted on."

"So, you are saying it's my fault?"

"Of course, we will never know if the original lyrics and tempo would have done better, but our analysis says that the changes impacted the fitness of the song on the landscape of survivability of all competing songs." She knew KY had read up on fitness landscapes as applied to marketing and required no explanation.

"What else reduced the fitness of my song to beat out all others?"

"It seems the problem is less what we as a team did *wrong* and more what the number one song did right. Our analytics of that band's launch, the song selection, lyrics, music, and promotion, all were flawless."

"But who the fuck are these kids?" KY's voice raised a notch. "Grunt! WTF kind of name is that! Have you ever seen them play, no. Have they toured, no! They come out of fucking nowhere, literally and figuratively, some small shit town in Sweden where no one has ever heard of them, and never had a hit before, no contract with a label, no Euro-Vision contest winning, nada." He made a zero with his thumb and forefinger and waved it in the faces of his team.

"They could not possibly have a team like you behind them. So, are you saying they just lucked out?" He waved his hands in the air grasping for luck that was not there. "You guys negotiated my *Saturday Night Live* season finale spot to launch the song, for Christ's sake. That was a big boost the previous two summers for me. These kids don't have that kind of fire-power."

The lawyer looked at KY's manager, eyes saying, "Do you tell him or do I?"

The business manager spoke up. "Well, actually, *SNL* told us they were trying to get Grunt to appear instead of you. We thought this was just a ne-gotiating tactic. Then they came back to us with open arms. I had a tête-à-tête with their people. She indicated Grunt refused to do live performanc-es."

"Fuck me," KY muttered.

"It happens, KY. They lucked out with a catchy tune and lyrics that are classic earworms. And their Angst Electropop appealed to a broader de-mographic. Adolescents, 'tweens, teens, college, adult, male, female, white, ethnic, domestic, international—analysis shows fairly equal download rates, and radio time was also spread pretty evenly across stations appeal-ing to each demographic. Did you read the cover story in today's *Rolling Stone* about Grunt ..." the manager stopped mid-sentence as KY's eyes grew large and ferocious.

The entertainer took a deep breath, closed his eyes, and pulsed his palm in front of him as if testing a cold fire or pushing away an unappetizing plate of risotto. Finally, he said with undisguised sarcasm, "No, I did not know *Rolling Stone* did a cover story on them. What does it say?"

"Not much. Most of the article is about the author trying to catch up with the band, get some face time, and learn more about them so he could write the article and always coming up with nothing. All he got was a phone call with them. More of a mystery story than a promotional interview. What was interesting is that he learned the song has inspired teens and college kids going back to school to set up Save the Earth clubs. Looks like it will be a big thing this fall."

Convinced the team had not dropped the ball and that greater effort next time would pay off, KY decided to move on. "Okay, guys, what's the update on the fall tour? And since we know Grunt doesn't play live, I am not taking any Grunt excuses later for less-than-perfect performance, planning, exe-cution, and ticket sales. Am I clear? Grunt, grunt!"

The team all smiled and nodded, feeling relieved and ready to deliver.

⊃ 人 ⊂

CHAI JIN, THE REAL-ESTATE TYCOON WEALTHY BEYOND ANY need or want, held his dying uncle's hand and realized once again that all the money in the world could not buy one more breath of life when one's time was up.

The day before, in the middle of a heated negotiation with the officials, Chai Huangcheng had keeled over, left hand clutching right shoulder. The heart attack had done *its* damage before the ambulance arrived, and the stroke had done *its* damage before they got him to the hospital.

His uncle's second wife made an urgent call to Chai Jin informing him the elder had endured a massive stroke. When Chai Jin arrived, his aunt had breathlessly filled him in on details before he entered the hospital room to see her husband. "This past week local officials led by Yin Tianxi, you know who that ratbag is, he is the brother-in-law of Gao Lian, that's who," she spat, "stormed our new property development, Gaotang Gardens. They've given us a laundry list of bullshit, trumped-up hassles: permits not gotten, engineering and public safety deficiencies, complaints from the community. Most serious is the claim that title to the land on which the Gardens were built was never correctly transferred to our company; it is still owned by the PLA, aiya! Heaven is far from us, but your uncle's grave is close at hand, I fear."

The elder Chai now lay before Chai Jin, the left side of his body limp, face slumped, and he held the nephew's hand with his right hand, still strong, and pulled him in, the good side of his face contorted in a half-twisted scowl. He slurred his last words, "Nephew. Seek justice. I know you well, and I know you will. From the Nine Springs of Hell, I will thank you."

Chai Jin squeezed the old man's hand in affirmation, thinking no words were necessary, but regretted it as the elder's hand went limp, and the rhythmic message of the patient-monitoring equipment was interrupted by a long, shrill warning and nurses rushing in to intervene without success. His aunt also ran in, and he took her in his arms and led her out.

As he held her and handed his handkerchief over to dry her tears, he said, "Auntie. Do not cry for Uncle as he had a good, long life. Do not cry over worries for your future. I will take care of this current mess, and you will not want for anything."

"Chai Jin. Your uncle said I could count on you to get even with these bastards," she looked up at him, determined eyes piercing through the pools of tears.

"Yes, Auntie. Count on me." As Chai Jin consoled her, he looked over and beyond her to his hulking aide-de-camp and bodyguard, Li Kui.

"Use your influence to bury these shits. You are three generations Red, for heaven's sake; you can't be touched. They are clearly Party scumbags just trying to get something for nothing."

"Yes, Auntie, I will go now to meet with them and set this right." He flicked his eyebrows signaling to Li Kui it was time for them to make a move.

The two men headed through the penthouse level, high-net worth portion of the hospital with its private medical suites and via a private elevator to Chai Jin's waiting 7 series BMW. Climbing in, Li Kui spoke first, "Seems like it's time to wield the axe."

"Patience, friend. We need to meet with this Yin Tianxi and see what he's about. We may be able to work it out. Otherwise, the law is on our side, and we go to court."

"The rule of law, peh!" he spat. "We know there is no real rule of law here. Who knows who, who has more to pay, or it's the 'State's' interest always winning over the individual's. Better to whack him now, let him know it's personal and dangerous for him. Then let *him* complain in court."

Chai Jin knew Li Kui's mettle well and knew he could count on him. Among those who were close to Chai Jin, he was referred to as "the Little Tornado" while Li's sobriquet was the much more ominous "Black Tornado." Tall and built like a walking, talking brick, his complexion was indeed dark. Li even speculated that his grandfather may have been a Black American soldier with the SeaBees stationed in Shandong after World War II.

Short on temper, Li was given to visible rage that cowed most opponents before resorting to blows and long on skill in protecting Chai Jin. He had, after all, mastered the martial art of Bagua Palms into his heart and soul, an art perfected two hundred years before by the bodyguards to the Qing emperor. Li had also served as a go-between for Chai and the leadership committee at Water Margin Station.

"Let's see what Yin Tianxi has to say for himself," Chai said, calming Li.

Chai ordered the driver to stop at a prayer supplies store. He bought a coarse, black, burlap armband that he pinned to his shirt. This concession to traditional mourning attire symbolized he was willing to suffer wearing rough clothes during the next forty-nine-day grieving period.

Chai's secretary called him. He had texted to ask that she find out where he could find Yin. "Hey, boss. I got what you needed," she said with characteristic, cheerful efficiency. "Yin Tianxi is waiting to meet you at the bar in the ground floor of the Gaotang Gardens. Seems he is expecting you; I didn't even need to wrangle an appointment. Sort of strange."

"Ok. Anything else."

"Yes, I sent you a document I was able to put together from internet references about Yin Tianxi. You should have it now."

"Thank you, you're a gem."

"Anytime, boss." She hung up.

He opened the document. Councilor Yin Tianxi was a member of the local Party and on the City Council. He was married to the daughter of Gao Lian, who was governor of the province, which seemed to be Yin's only distinguishing trait. And Gao Lian was the cousin of General Gao Qiu.

Chai Jin drew in a slow breath, taking in the stench of this nepotistic cesspool. He would have to swim carefully.

As the limo pulled up the Black Tornado stirred his index finger in a circle signaling to the driver to make one slow circuit around the Gaotang Gardens building complex before stopping. He had downloaded the plans to the building and looked at points of danger, avenues of safety and refuge, potential sites for egress and exfil, and where the best place to park the car might be in order to make a spirited retreat. He now was looking at the reality of the building from the outside, eyes searching for points of confirmation or contradiction to what the plans had told him.

Another large building was under construction adjacent to the complex. Festooned with safety banners and pictures of what the completed skyscraper would look like, it was now just a hole in the ground with a webbing of I beams latticed through it where a carpark promised to be in another month. A large dump truck was about to leave with a load of water-logged earth, and workers supervised it as it pulled out into traffic.

Around two corners opposite the side with the new construction, he espied a tractor-trailer truck parked with a dark black container on its bed. Neither the truck nor the container had commercial markings on them, which he felt was strange, and he pointed this out to Chai Jin.

Rather than enter the underground parking lot, Li Kui instructed the driver to pull up to the main entrance, which had a VIP parking space adjacent to it. "Keep the motor running. Be ready to leave at any time. And if I send you the alert, depart immediately, head back to headquarters without stopping unless you get further instructions from me or 'Lord' Chai."

The two men stepped out of the limo and walked into the building, the first two floors of which were devoted to retail and restaurant outlets including the bar, a faux Irish pub called Lucky Charms.

The bar was empty in the early afternoon, and as they entered, they could see Yin Tianxi seated in the rear, his back to the wall, facing the entrance. As they approached, a tough dressed in an ill-fitting suit emerged from the bathroom, left hand tucked into the right breast of his suit, and joined Yin. Chai and Li looked at each other and continued to the table.

"Councilor Yin, thank you for making time to meet us," the Little Tornado said with a congenial bow of his head.

"Which Chai are you?" Yin rejoined rudely.

"I am Chai Jin, the nephew of Chai Huangcheng, at your service."

"Peh! And why the hell hasn't your family cleared out and handed over the documents requested? What's the delay? Fucking lazy squatters."

Li Kui curled his lip and inched forward, but Chai Jin touched his arm.

"As you can see, I am wearing a black armband. My uncle just passed away this morning. Give our family the forty-nine days of mourning he deserves, then we can discuss again and put this behind us. Does that sound fair?"

"Like I give a shit about a squatter's death, has nothing to do with me. Rules are rules. The court isn't going to wait for your fucking mourning period. Clear out now."

Li Kui took a half step in, but Chai's tug on his sleeve was insistent. Chai Jin spoke up, "My friend here is very loyal to our family, and your words are hurtful. Surely, we can just focus on the business matter at hand and talk this through without resorting to name-calling and threats."

"This trained monkey with you looks like a fucking King Kong," Yin sneered the racial taunt alluding not only to his size but his hint of African blood.

Li Kui stepped in and pointed his right hand at Yin, about to berate him. The tough standing to Yin's left and Li's right drew a pistol in his left hand and pointed it square at Li's temple, the safety off but his trigger finger touching the outside of the trigger guard. Without thought or hesitation, Li Kui responded with an emergent modification of a Bagua palm sequence he had mastered, Flower Concealed under the Leaf.

Keeping his right hand pointed at Yin motionless, his left palm snaked under it missing the chance to grab the pistol, but finding the tough's left wrist and jerking it up. The tough squeezed the trigger letting off one round that hit the mirror on the wall behind Yin Tianxi.

Li's right hand now followed up the left arm of his opponent and chopped for his face, the tough frantically blocking the blow, which was then seized

214

by Li's right and jerked across the man's body tying him up. A second round was fired, this one hitting Yin in the neck, the flesh erupting in a crimson spray.

Using the man's right arm over his left as a lever and unbalancing him, Li twisted the wrist holding the pistol toward the hapless thug. A third round went off, this one hitting the tough in his right thigh shattering the bone. Li finally wrested the gun from him, kicked the man away, and emptied the remaining four rounds into Yin and the guard.

Dazed and spattered with blood, Li Kui turned and grabbed Chai Jin's arm to lead him to safety. Chai tugged back and put his hand gently on Li's. "No, friend. Let me deal with this. Go to the swamp."

Li narrowed his eyes. "Going to the swamp" was a code phrase Chai Jin had told him before. In the event Chai gave this order, Li was to drop anything he was doing, no matter what, and head to LiangShanPo to inform the management committee of whatever had happened. He was not to wait, he was not to stop to help Chai, he was not to stop until he got to LiangShanPo. He pulled on Chai's arm.

The man shook his head, "Go. Now!"

Li put the gun back in the tough's hand, looked up to get his bearings, and ran for the kitchen, behind which he remembered was an exit leading to a Basement 2 loading dock, from where he could gather his wits and find a way out.

Chai Jin watched the stalwart who had just risked everything for him make his retreat and was grateful to know such men of high skill. He would be relying on him and other stalwarts to get him out of this jam. He slumped into a seat and pressed an emergency button on his phone that told his driver to leave without delay and go back to headquarters to report. Then he gathered his thoughts and waited.

In the unmarked, black shipping container parked by the Gaotang Garden development, weeks of investigation and surveillance, some lucky breaks, and calling in some tabs were coming to fruition. They had narrowed down the paths leading to Lin Chong. Gao Qiu and Cai Jing knew they were not there yet, but they smelled they were getting closer.

The investigations run by the two men had made the educated guess that Retired Major Lu Da had aided in Lin Chong's escape. General Gao Qiu alone knew Lu had been present at the bar the night Lin Chong was recruited to deliver the Operation Broadsword thumb drive to Gao. He told investigators to look at Lin's former mentor and commander. Lu had gone ghost right after Lin Chong was arrested, and that drew more attention to him. Interrogations of the guard who had survived the assault on the black house where Lin Chong had been detained described a man of Lu's age and physical description setting on him with a spade, but the face had been obscured, and he had said nothing.

Although careful to hide his tracks and relying on cash or stored value cards to pay for expenses, Lu Da had slipped up several times. His face had been recorded by surveillance and stored in memory, including when he drove into the Seven Treasures Manor in Nanjing, bought some hardware at a shop in Saddle Mountain City and, after Lin Chong had made his escape, in Shanghai at the mall entrance to the Eastern Manor highrise shopping office and luxury residential complex. There were no more sightings after that. Research showed that the Eastern Manor was owned by Yida Real-Estate, and that meant Chai Jin.

Both Cai Jing and Gao Qiu reviled Chai for his holier-than-thou attitude and shared the same thought: *Someone that wealthy could not possibly make it in China without being corrupt.* They knew Chai was tight with the Communist Party leadership, some said untouchable, so they knew they had to catch him in the act to bring him in.

Gao Qiu decided to work through his cousin, Gao Lian, and put a squeeze on the Chais until they screamed "uncle" quite literally. Gao Lian's son-in-law, who did dirty work for him, was called in to front the effort, and they knew that Chai Jin had been dispatched to the city to help his uncle.

Today was the day. The noose was tightening. The video was recording. Li Kui had threatened Yin, and Yin's guard had stepped in to protect his boss. It was perfect. And now there were gunshots and blood spattered on the hidden camera lens they had installed, the monitor showing the carnage in vivid color.

What a fucking mess, Gao Qiu thought as he barked orders to the tactical squad of military police he had brought with him to race into the building and surround the crime scene. "Take Chai Jin alive!"

⊃ 人 ⊏

I SURE KNOW HOW TO PICK A THOROUGHBRED, RICHARD McCAL-lister, of the Kentucky McCallisters, considered as he waited in the plush, red-leather booth of the Dupont Circle Brasserie waiting for his dinner companion. Whether choosing a stud to sire a future Triple Crown victor or a hot-to-trot filly to warm his own bed, he had instincts that he relied on. His instincts had guided him to grow the family business from coal into natural gas and then into shale oil fracking.

Along the way, the family went from being millionaires to billionaires. Just like Senator Robinson had said when presenting the American Heritage Patriot Award at ceremonies the night before, McCallister "had helped America, God's country, to wean itself of the petroleum from mullahs in the Middle East and commies in Venezuela, staunching the torrent of US dollars into their foreign pockets. Americans could now cook, light their homes, get to work, and indeed enjoy their lives more cheaply and without sending an endless stream of money to immoral peoples bent on destroying our way of life."

He believed to the depths of his soul that success was a sign of the Lord's grace shining on him, that God's munificence was evidence of the approval and direction of a Higher Authority. Indeed, his instincts were charismata, gifts bestowed on him by God to enable him to do God's will. As such, while his wealth expanded, he was ever more determined to spread the Lord's word, to educate those who had not heard the word or who demonstrated false ideas and false ideals in the error of their ways. It was in this spirit that he had formed and funded the Devon Alliance.

The Alliance had sought to keep a low profile. Its Green Dragon Manifesto had detailed the ways in which environmentalists were simply modern pagans, bent on making Man subservient to nature and along the way encouraging all manner of unGodly behavior. The alliance had encouraged good Christian and some Jewish lawmakers, clergy, rabbis, and opinion leaders to endorse the Manifesto. They had created political action committees to direct messaging, supporting candidates who had signed the Manifesto and destroying candidates who were pro-Green policy advocates. They had raised many more millions of dollars than McCallister had donated from likeminded Evangelicals and business owners and with that, the Alliance's influence behind the scenes expanded.

Though the Alliance name did not appear in the credits, they had funded the filming of the documentary "All That's Green is not Gold" about the spurious claims made by "scientists" from such fields as meteorology ("they can't tell us what the weather is going to be tomorrow, how can they con us that they know what will happen in thirty years?") and biologists ("most of the methane is produced by belching cows and farting beaners, it's not our cars"), which had not won any awards, but had reminded people sympathetic to their message why it was an important fight.

McCallister knew he was at the Right-wing fringe, but the polity had to be dragged in his direction. The very capitalist and Christian fabric of mainstream America, that which had made America great and therefore that which God inspired and rewarded, was under attack. The Green Dragon had to be slain, lest it lend its strength to other godless movements: globalism, identity politics, moral relativism.

Taking a seat at the Dupont Circle Brasserie booth was another of the thoroughbreds his wise instincts told him to bet on. The race was now being run, she was in it, and he had to determine she had the willpower to sustain the effort, even as emergent competing interests were on her tail. This visit to DC was not overdue, but it was due.

"Nancy, you've been a stranger since joining the White House. I'm hurt," he started with his Kentucky gentleman's drawl.

Nancy Nillson smiled politely and looked across the table at the aging philanthropist, not sure how to treat the intrusion into her schedule. His secretary had not taken "no" for an answer and pestered until she had pried open an hour to do a dinner. "Not at all, Richard."

She doesn't call me Mr. McCallister like she used to.

"Just occupied trying to fulfil the president's mandate," she continued. "You can't imagine how busy I am. Every day I have a choice to make, either to see people I would like to see, or get the important work of the people done. Seems I always fall on the people's side of the fence. My apologies. To what do I owe this honor?"

"Indeed. You have gotten off to a good start. This NOAA's Ark, epic, biblical. Dissing the Chinese by taking over their super ship, inspired. And you are handling the tone and communications just right. 'Make Africa Green Again for Africans.' I like it. MAGAFA, Ugama Bugama,"he said, parroting how he imagined some cartoon savage in the jungle might cheer. "MAGA but keep 'em over there," he chortled. "McCallister Energy was one of the first to buy up advertising space on the sails, did you know?"

"Thank you for your support."

"Indeed. But we are a bit worried for the president about this whole Demeter thing. Frankly, I've been able to learn not one bit about them, but they seem to be all over the place. How about you?"

"Richard, I can't share anything confidential with you. You understand." Little was known about the group that was not already public. "The day the ad was placed, Demeter registered itself as a 501(c)(4) social welfare group. As such, it's not required to disclose its donors, can accept unlimited contributions, and can spend, spend, spend as much as it can to advocate its issue. The only people we've been able to associate with this dark money group are the lawyers who did the registration."

"And they are?"

"Look, Richard, we have significant resources digging into this. But as Demeter does not appear to have broken any laws here, certain hands are tied."

"Well, that's the charm of the situation. My hands are *not* tied. And I will *always* come out swinging for Mick Coin. I want to help you and the president find out who's behind this. It's not right that they can clog the media with their poisonous message and give voice to candidates whose platforms are so stridently anti-American."

"Actually, their support of candidates seems to be channeled through a separate Demeter super PAC. The 501(c)(4) places limits on electioneering." It was not lost on Nancy that these legal funding devices that the Right had long ago developed to support its initiatives were being mobilized effectively by the Left.

"Who's the law firm? Let me do some digging. Find some bones, find some skeletons, find out where all this money is coming from."

Nancy thought for a moment. It shouldn't take him any time to find out who had done the registrations for the super PAC through public channels, but she could just give him a heads-up. It was not a secret, just not yet widely known. "Goldman, Waters, Greenbaum, Feuer, and Erdman."

Such a typical Jewboy law firm name, he chuckled to himself. He would get his people digging right away. "If we find things to discredit this Demeter group, you'll know." *Failing which,* he mused to himself, *we could always precipitate some crisis to pin on them. That would work just fine, too.* "Now, what would you like for dinner? The steak is excellent."

⊃ 人 ⊂

ONE BY ONE AND IN PAIRS, THEY BEGAN ARRIVING AT LIANG-ShanPo.

First, in order not to raise alarm, was Sagacious Lu Da. Then came the Witch Sun Erniang with husband the Vegetable Gardener Zhang Qing in tow. Timely Rain Song Jiang, who had turned out to be an able lieutenant, arrived next with the Blue-Faced Beast Yang Zhi followed by several teams from Twin Dragon Mountain.

Each were greeted at the dumpling stand by the Parched Earth Crocodile Zhu Gui, until he had a full house, but Lu Da alone was allowed to ascend to the thirtieth-floor Righteous Fraternity Meeting Hall to have an audience with the committee.

When he entered the room his face lit up on seeing his mentee, Lin Chong, sitting among them. Lin, too, smiled, crossed the room, and pulled the friend in, refraining from a hug, but slapping him on the back. "This is the fellow who saved my bacon, Lu Da, also known as Sagacious or the Playboy Monk!"

With a nod of their heads, Du Qian and Song Wan both returned smiles to Lu. Only the White-Clad Scholar remained taciturn. "Why are you endangering us with your unwelcome intrusion?" he demanded.

Lu took measure of the heat in the room: the relative postures, positions, body language, tone, and seating order of the men facing him. *The thin, bespectacled man dressed in the white tracksuit not welcoming me is seated furthest from the door at the end of the table, clearly the leader. But the other two, who at least gave me a smile, turned their backs even further from this douchebag when he was rude to me. Lin Chong seems to have created some status for himself here. In any event I can count on him.*

"Truly, gentlemen, my apologies for the unexpected arrival. We can't exactly broadcast our movements, but I think I bring good tidings."

Silence filled the room begging him to continue. "Right. I think it is time for us to band together. I have brought my team of thirty plus to join yours. They are all good and solid, and together we can do so much more."

"We have only followed the activities of the Twin Dragon Mountain community very loosely. What happened to Deng Long?" Wang Lun asked pointedly.

"Don't tell me that ratbag was a friend of yours? He refused an offer I made him. In the end his team voted to run with me. He is, as it were, dead."

Wang Lun squirmed with the news. *First, Lin Chong, now this Lu Da, both ex-military types on the run. And if he had taken Deng Long out, am I next in his sights?* "We were not fans of Twin Dragon. Their hacks seemed to lack... virtue."

Lu smiled, "I'm glad we agree on that. The first thing I did was put an end to the scams they were running."

Wang Lun bristled. He was not aware he had to entertain this lout's agreement with him on anything. "So why *are* you here and why should we let you *stay*?"

"Three reasons really. Mobsters who had been milking that data gravy train got pissed off big time when I pulled the plug on supplying intel to them. They decided to make things tough. We defended ourselves pretty good, but still I knew that it was time to disappear and regroup. At the same time the heat turned up from the government side. We could detect they were looking for something, probably me, and again it was time to disappear and regroup. Finally, Lord Chai Jin spoke highly of you all and said he hoped I could join you someday. So, here I... we are. The team is solid, they are keen to stick it to the big guy and work on the kind of noble hacks for which you, the White-Clad Scholar, are renowned."

To the surprise of his confederates in the room, Wang Lun said, "I think I have to put this to a broader vote than just this committee. The people you brought with you...let's just say they have history with my team."

Lin, Du, and Song looked to Wang for clarification.

"Yes, for example, Lin, part of Sagacious's entourage is Yang Zhi. You remember him, don't you, the so-called Blue-Faced Beast who was fucked over so elegantly by your exposure of the scheme he had been asked to orchestrate by on high. You think he is going to be a congenial partner?"

Lin thought for a moment and decided to let instincts side with confidence in Lu Da. "I'm okay with it if Yang is."

"Well, then what about Wu Song? I know you hang with him a lot, Panther Head."

Lin Chong raised his eyebrows.

"Yes, together with Lu Da are the Witch and the Vegetable Gardener. They aren't hackers, they're just lowlifes. Did Wu Song ever tell you how he escaped? The marshals stopped with him at a pub while taking him to prison, if you can believe it. Seeing an opportunity to do their usual mischief, Sun and Zhang drugged them all. Under the haze she put them in, the guards emptied their ATMs for Sun." Wang Lun looked about the room to make sure all eyes were on him. "But Wu Song's a big guy, she didn't get the dose right, and he grabbed the Witch, took her to the floor, and was doing a reverse choke when Zhang Qing came in. Wu said he would break her neck if he didn't back off and let him run. So, they let him go and pointed him in the direction of Twin Dragon Mountain, too. He came here when he couldn't stomach Deng Long either."

"So, Wu Song owes his escape to them?" Lin asked.

Not used to looking at it that way, Wang Lun frowned. "I don't know how he feels, but I bet he won't be happy to see them. They don't belong here."

Silent to that moment, Du Qian took an opportunity to step in. "Actually, Sagacious, we have something pressing on the table that we were discussing when you all started to trickle in." He paused and looked around the room. "It may be why we seem a bit tense. I'd like to hear your thoughts on it, though."

"Please. Anything we can do to help. We are all brothers."

"We'll see," Wang Lun took control again. "Yesterday, Li Kui, you might know him as the Black Tornado, showed up. He looked like shit and is resting now. He reported that Chai Jin has been set up and arrested. Chai gave Li the order to come to us. So, we are now debating what to do."

"There *is* no debate. We go and get him out," Lu Da proclaimed without hesitation.

Du, Song, and Lin looked at each other and then to Wang. This voiced their sentiment, and it was not one not shared by Wang. Wang looked back at them uneasily. "Attempting to free him must be exactly what they want! They want us to expose ourselves."

"And that's supposed to deter us?" Lu Da rejoined.

Wang Lun did not like that the decision-making tree had already become "us." "I think the Little Tornado would want us to keep low until such a time as..."

"They execute him?" he was cut off by Sagacious. "No. What did Li Kui say? What are his instructions?" he ordered.

"He's just a bodyguard..."

"No, he was the right hand to Lord Chai entrusted to carry out this last mission. And from your description he had quite a time getting here."

Cut off once more by Sagacious, Wang Lun was now red in the face.

Du Qian stepped in. "Chai and Li were drawn into a confrontation, things got out of control, Li capped a couple of people, but Chai Jin wanted to take the heat and ordered him to come here. Prison break or revenge or both are on Li's mind. He escaped from the area in a dump truck covered with mud from a neighboring building. Never really got cleaned up, was several days on the run in a zigzag until he made the final move here."

"Well, I and *my* team aren't going to sit on our hands," Lu declared. "I don't know about you, but if I did nothing, I couldn't sleep knowing that he is taking whatever torture they are hitting him with, trying to find out where *you* are, which they clearly haven't because he hasn't caved. No, he invested in us for a reason. Not because he expects we *owe* him, but because he knows we are not the type of people to let the corrupt triumph without a fight."

Wang Lun knew when he was beaten. "Okay, so what resources can you muster? Lin Chong had been developing an idea that we can apply once we know where Chai is. Lin?"

"You well know the mechanics of ransomware attacks."

"Even recently," Lu Da grinned.

"We lock up the resources on a computer or a server and demand money to unlock it, right? Well, I have been thinking bigger, much bigger. Even bigger than the hack on the UK healthcare system that Russia did. Imagine doing this on a grander scale, collapsing entire systems, an airport, an airline reservation platform, a food factory, a power plant, or regional grid, and holding it to ransom. Done right, this would net hundreds of millions per hack. So, in this case, I try to do it for the prison where they are holding him. Just, we don't know where he is yet."

"Hmm. I'm radioactive now, but the same guy who helped me find you might be able to give us a hint. I'll try to reach out to Siddhartha."

⊃ 人 ⊂

DR. ALÉJANDRA CHAVEZ AND HER TEAM SAT AROUND THE speakerphone in the conference room of UC San Luis Obispo "waiting for the damn thing to ring," Chavez said with a nervous smile to the group. Almost three months had passed since she had hung up the phone on the Grönland Capital conversation, starting a whirlwind of rejoicing and activity.

True to the promise made by the CEO of the investment firm, their lawyers took quick action. All concerns of the university's endowments office had been handled with alacrity, and within weeks not only had funds arrived, but materiel as well. She knew from experience that some of the things she needed were hard to obtain and had long lead times. Somehow, Chavez's needs had been bumped to the front of the queue.

One of the conditions that the university's endowments office had predicated was that the team be required to give an update every two months to the benefactor. The university wanted to make sure that they demonstrated oversight, responsibility, and gratitude for the investment and that benefactors could see the results of their donations. The endowment office also knew that happy and engaged benefactors frequently invested even more.

In four minutes, their first two-month update report was to commence. Nervous that the first meeting go well, Chavez had coached the team. "Besides their lawyers, the only person I have spoken with is their CEO, Orörd

Jordan. She has been nothing but nice, understanding, and supportive. She has not dictated what we are to present to her today, set no expectations for the meeting. That makes it easier in some ways, and much harder in others."

"We have your back, Alé," Tony Millard said. "We are ahead of schedule on almost everything and the quality of the metrics we are gathering is improving every day. We are prepared to speak to their questions."

"What about the people she has sent to help with implementation?"

"They seem qualified and well motivated. They've delivered on their commitments, and we have no issue with them."

"What about them with us? We don't want bad, back-channel reports going to the investor."

The team looked around the table at each other to see if anyone's eyes belied some undisclosed friction with the advisors who had been gifted to the effort.

Tony spoke up, "They have pushed hard on some time issues. Mostly how long it took to increase the head count on the project. But they expressed understanding and even helped us on that count. And data collection is off the charts, much more robust than before."

"Where are we in setting up the second research station in their stand of redwood timber?" Chavez looked to Mike Liao, a grad student in computer science and networking who had an assistantship covering his tuition in return for supporting the project.

"Almost good to go. The sensor grid has been laid out and installed. Cabling is almost ready. The central monitoring unit is being assembled by the systems integrator, should be delivered next week. Then we just flip the switch. I told the group about some hardware upgrades their people insisted on. Not sure what they have in mind, but it's really overdesigned. Anyway, it's their nickel, and you signed off on it."

The conference call speaker at the center of the table rang, and the flat-screen teleconference panel flickered to life jarring everyone's attention to it. Chavez raised her eyebrows, smiled at the team, and pressed the green "accept call" button. "Hello, Aléjandra Chavez here. Is that Grönland Capital?"

"Yes, indeed, Alé, this is Orö. How are you today?" The face on the flat-screen panel was illuminated from the light of a notebook computer screen, rendering the colors off and the textures vague. She was middle-aged, blond, and well-kept, her hair pulled back revealing fair skin and

224

ears sporting one diamond stud in each lobe. The voice was warm, feminine, and professional with a slight Oxford Cambridge accent deflecting a native Scandinavian tone.

"Fine, thank you. It must be very late where you are."

"It is late, but money never sleeps, so I never rest," she laughed.

"I have the whole team here. We are all grateful for the support Grönland is providing and look forward to this presentation. I was wondering if you could perhaps introduce yourself and Grönland?"

"So, I have fifteen minutes set aside for the update call. Can you tell me how things are going the first ten, then I have something to talk about in the last five?"

That was a bit of a worry, Chavez thought, but replied, "Absolutely, do you have the PowerPoint open in front of you?"

"Yes. It's all clear. Can we focus on pages four, seven, and nine?" The voice on the other end of the line directed them to the pages regarding head count onboarding, upgrades to the system, and the execution schedule for new acreage.

Chavez was proud of the team's response. They presented their respective bits clearly, gave positive, proactive answers to questions, and responded well to the suggestions returned. Orö complimented each of them in turn.

"So, what is Grönland?" Orö continued. "It is an SRI, a socially responsible investment firm, with several dozen billion under management. It is part of our charter to devote a significant chunk of our profits to research and activities expected to protect or restore the environment, or expand our understanding and awareness of it. Besides endowments like the one we have provided you, we are very active globally supporting green initiatives. You know, Alé, we are impressed with your enthusiasm and responsiveness. Your first update report has strengthened that impression."

"Thank you, Orö."

"We also think your research is critically important to an understanding of ecosystems, biodiversity, and the earth itself."

"We share that passion," Chavez said, gratified, but not sure where this was going.

"We also think that it is the type of research that is scalable, indeed, that it is better done in multiple locations at the same time to enable comparisons, a larger data set, varying climates, and different stresses being put on the landscape. You can imagine the benefits."

Indeed, Chavez could imagine the benefits to the study, but she was a professor in a publish-or-perish world. It was critical personally, professionally, and to the team that she maintain control, that her name be front and center on the release of any findings.

Orö continued, "We would like to propose expanding the research globally. Russia, Brazil, your home of Costa Rica, Kalimantan, and Uganda as a start. There are academics in each location who follow your research. They respect you. We would predicate any expansion and support of them on their agreement that all data they collect is copied to you real time. They can write about the findings within their location, but only you and your team will have all the data from all the locations." Orö paused to let it sink in.

Chavez's mind raced ahead. She had visited forested regions in each country mentioned, she could see where, how, this could work, and in some cases she even knew who might be the collaborating academic. So far, Grönland Capital had kept all its promises and more. Still, she had to guarantee that she maintain control. *How to test Orö on this without sounding greedy or self-serving?* Chavez digested for a moment. "You are no doubt aware that in science, in experimentation, it is important to maintain a standard of tests and data collection. All too many environmental studies are debunked by the obstinate ignorant when they claim the data collection tools or methods varied so widely as to render comparisons useless. They claim the data is garbage, no cross-study conclusions can be made."

"I know what you are talking about, yes."

"If you want to expand this, then my team sets and monitors the standards and methodology for all sites. All sites are equipped with the same sophistication. All data is collected into the same formats. If other researchers in the field have suggestions or improvements, we can of course evaluate them here, and then back-fill them to all the locations, but we can't have a bunch of ants running in all different directions."

"Of course, I agree, although I am sure you know better than me that ants never scurry about uselessly. They are always working to a purpose."

Chavez regretted the lame expression. "Absolutely. So, do we agree on my team here being the Queen Ant?"

"It's what we want. Glad you share the same thoughts."

"Timing?"

"Our lawyers have had preliminary discussions with your university. It's not the first time they have worked on a global research project, so we don't foresee any issues there. We think that Russia is the only place we expect approvals to take a little longer. Otherwise, we believe all the agreements can be done and dusted within a month. However, we will be ordering the equipment now, right away. In a nutshell, A-S-A-P," she spelled it out. "And I am sure your next question will be whether this includes scaling your team. Absolutely. Let me know what you need and the budget."

Chavez cast her eyes at the table, feeling that she had somehow been out negotiated, railroaded, snookered, or fallen into a bright and beautiful trap, the dangers of which she had yet to fathom. She wrestled with conflicting feelings and enthusiastic gratitude for the boon.

Orö spoke up, "Everything good, Alé? I want you to be comfortable with this. It is, after all, *your* life's work."

Chavez looked up at the woman on the screen, this woman who could sense concern even over a teleconference line, address it, and reassure others just like that, and she decided to trust the woman. "It's just so much good news to digest," she said flashing a big smile at the screen. "Yes, we're good. More than good. Thank you, Orö."

⊃ 人 ⊂

LU DA TURNED ACROSS THE AISLE OF THE NONDESCRIPT COMmercial van to look at Lin Chong, who sat with his eyes closed. Was he sleeping, meditating, thinking? "Panther Head," he said in a loud whisper.

Lin Chong opened his eyes wearily. It was dawn, and he could see they were back at the vacant plaza next to Zhu Gui's dumpling shop. It had been a long day, but at least he had the consolation of a mission accomplished.

The LiangShanPo heroes found Chai Jin in a black house known as "the Well" by State Security. Once enemies of the State were dropped into it, they rarely emerged. A week of interrogation and torture had beaten the wind out of the Little Tornado Chai Jin. But for now, he was safe and being tended to by Li Kui, who had brought along emergency medical supplies. A drip was feeding and rehydrating Chai and supplying painkillers and antibiotics to his as yet unconscious body wrapped in a blanket, lying on the floor of the van.

It had taken elements of all their many resources to extract him. The easiest part had been Lu Da's request to Siddhartha Sun for a heads-up on Chai's location. With just a little hesitation because of the blowback from the Wild Boar Mountain black house penetration, the upright official had come through with the name and location of the black house for Lu in the same way as before, the address of a neighboring residence in Gaotang.

Wang Lun had released substantial anonymous and untraceable bribes paid to melt some weak links in the chain.

Lin Chong had tapped into the IT and security systems at the black house, including opening the front gate and door, giving them both access and clear surveillance of the property.

Sun the Witch had unpacked several cylinders of compressed, odorless gas of her concoction that she said would render anyone in the house useless. She had mischievously failed to add that those exposed to it would be hallucinating for anywhere from six to twenty-four hours. *Oops*, she had said later with a cocky smile.

Lu Da and Li Kui, wearing full tactical gear and gas masks, came in through the front door at 03:00, halfway through a shift of the guards and an hour after the valves on the cylinders had been cracked open to evacuate their contents. Song Jiang had suggested that they embroider their uniforms in the front and back with the words "National Supervisory Commission" to increase confusion and fear among the elements holding Chai Jin and delay any response to his escape.

Lu and Li, lightly armed, met little resistance. One guard was walking around, his face a delighted mask of illusion looking up at the swarm of stars and planets playing on the ceiling, hands waving upward trying to orchestrate the dance of the universe unfolding before him. The other guards and staff were seated or lying on the floor, their eyelids closed or, if open, their eyes rolling back and forth trying to track the story their minds created for them, occasional gasps, giggles, shudders, or frothy, choking gurgles being heard to emanate from their mouths.

They had found Chai Jin in "the Well", a small, windowless room at the bottom of a narrow, steep staircase. He was stripped naked, badly bruised, dehydrated, and malnourished. And though not exposed to much of the Witch's concoction, he was clearly hallucinating. They grabbed a blanket from a bedroom on the main floor, wrapped it around him, and carried him out, making sure they let the security cameras record the image of his wracked body and their boldly identified uniforms. Then they stole away into the pitch darkness of a new-moon night signaling the approaching end of summer.

ᗤ 人 ᗥ

GEORGE BROKENFEATHER LOOKED OUT THE WINDOW OF HIS OFfice at the Sutter County California emergency services office and stared deep into the coming weather. Sunset, which meant it was around 8:00

p.m., and to the northeast of Yuba City he could see flashes of lightning illuminate thunderheads dispensing unseasonal rain onto Lake Oroville. It was beautiful, and he loved to see nature "do its thing," but it was also a cause for deep concern. The prior winter and spring had seen a huge amount of snow deposited onto the mountains serving the headwaters of the Feather River, that river which, when it was dammed up in the 1960s, gave rise to his family's change of name. The spring and summer melt had filled Oroville Dam to capacity. These torrential rains were heavy icing on, as it were, a shaky, crumbly cake.

The Oroville Dam had a history of instability. In the spring of 2017, heavy rains forced the dam managers to utilize the emergency spillway designed to evacuate overflow conditions on the reservoir. However, suffering from age, poor maintenance, and perhaps poor initial construction, the spillway eroded in its middle and broke away, like a large chunk of road that washes away in a flood. Then, as water is wont to do, torrents of spill water dug their own new 300-foot-deep channel down the slope.

The managers had shut off the spillway, but with the commensurate increased risk of dam collapse ordered the evacuation of 188,000 residents until the risk was reduced. It took years and millions of dollars to restore the spillway.

Brokenfeather had been around then, albeit not in the current role of chief communications officer, and recalled the dread and anxiety of those days, not knowing if family, friends, livelihoods, homes, businesses, and farms would be wiped out.

This summer Brokenfeather had been scanning the daily assessments provided to the county from the dam as the reservoir neared full capacity. His alarm increased when these assessments pointedly reminded him of the water levels that would trigger use of the rebuilt spillway, the need to be vigilant, and suggestions that emergency services do a dry run (an ill-chosen term, Brokenfeather felt) or game out an emergency evacuation just in case. His office had received communications from the California Governor's Office of Emergency Services and the Northern California Regional Intelligence Center urging the same, but the state was not allocating budgetary support.

His boss said, "The muckety-mucks in Sacramento are just covering their asses with an email trail." His bosses had no resources to allocate to it; tax dollars were stretched too thin. A dry run was a *No Way José*.

Turning his eyes back from the window and another display of lightning that had crossed the horizon from right to left, he looked at the computer monitor on the desk. "Fuuuuuuuck," he gàsped. A message framed in bright red was flashing on the screen from the Integrated Public Alert Warning System. He clicked on it to display the message content:

> From: Oroville Dam Emergency Management Team
> 20:17:32 PST
> To: IPAWS Alerting Authorities Butte County, Yuba County, Sutter County, California Governor's Office of Emergency Services, California Highway Patrol, Northern California Regional Intelligence Center, FEMA
> RE: Imminent Collapse of Oroville Dam   EMERGENCY ALERT
> The dam has suffered a catastrophic internal failure. We are estimating there is no more than a half hour before the dam fails completely. THIS IS NOT A FAILURE OF THE SPILLWAY. THIS WILL BE A CATASTROPHIC FAILURE OF THE ENTIRE DAM WITH FLOODING UP TO 10 FEET DEEP IN THE FLOOD ZONE UP TO 90 MILES DOWNSTREAM.
> We recommend immediate distribution of this warning to all news outlets and immediate mobilization of police, fire, emergency medical services, and first responders to initiate
> IMMEDIATE EVACUATION. All dam personnel have been evacuated.

Before he had even finished reading it, a wireless emergency alert arrived on his mobile phone with a similar message, this one addressed to "Residents in the Expected Flood Zone." Anyone with a mobile device in the impact area was receiving the warning, he guessed. "Holy shit," he muttered as he opened a folder on his computer desktop marked "Dam Collapse – Emergency Management Priorities" and looked at the list of those action steps prior brainstorming and FEMA coaches had suggested would result in the greatest impacts to save lives and property.

But first, he called his wife, instructed her to take the emergency management box he had packed in the garage, their children, and dog, get into the SUV, and drive east, stopping at an ATM to raise cash, and continue without stopping into the hills where her sister lived.

⊃ 人 ⊂

DANIELE SMOTHERS, DEPUTY CHIEF ENGINEER OF THE EDWARD Hyatt Power Plant located within the base of the Oroville Dam, was working the night shift and keeping an eye on the weather, figuratively speaking. From her office deep in the cavernous facility, she could look out to see the plaza housing the six turbines, but the storm was several hundred feet above. The weather-monitoring app displayed on the computer screen confirmed the deluge had deposited three inches of rain onto the headwaters area above the dam and was now dumping directly into the reservoir.

Based on the reservoir management team's models, the level of the water would rise an additional eight inches in five hours. That was approaching the limit where they would have to consider using the emergency spillway. According to routines established after the 2017 incident, she knew that in the event the reservoir managers called for utilization of the spillway, she would commence a temporary shutdown of the power plant and removal of the personnel until after the viability of the rebuilt spillway was determined.

Her power plant was special. It had a total of six giant turbines, each weighing more than 140 tons turned by the pressure of over 500 feet of water above them at a speed of ninety rpm generating clean, renewable energy for Californians. That was not what made it special. Three of the six turbines could be switched to pumping mode, to move water back up into the reservoir during low demand hours so that during peak demand hours output could be maximized. That was special. With the reservoir nearing overflow capacity, that function was not being used tonight. All six turbines were busy humming along, producing power, some of which was excess on the grid, but no matter.

Smothers put on a hard hat and earplugs and struggled with her overweight frame down the short flight of steps to walk the floor. Fresh air, sunshine, and exercise were not part of the job. Nevertheless, she loved this place.

She loved the hum of it, the smell of it, the purpose of it. And she ran a tight but amiable ship. She had observed and absorbed that skill as a submariner and power plant technician on board the nuclear submarine USS New Hampshire. After two deployments, she had worked at the company that built and serviced the turbines here as a maintenance contractor and made the transition in-house a decade before, working up the ladder from the plant floor and into the deputy chief engineer's role.

She knew the power plant inside and out. Her team said, "If the turbines hiccup, she knows how to burp 'em." Far from a sexist comment about a mommy working a "man's" job, she took it as a truth she was proud of. Damn Skippy!

She shuffled toward a man in blue overalls and a yellow hard hat carrying a clipboard and a portable vibration sensor. "Hey, Jim. How's it looking?"

"Shake and Bake, chief," his standard, easygoing reply for normal vibration readings.

At the same moment both of their mobile phones, remote from any phone service provider signal but connected to the plant's Wi-Fi, buzzed in their pockets, and they reached in to take them out.

"What the F?" she said aloud and turned back to face Jim, who had a panicked look. The wireless emergency alert read:

> From: Oroville Dam Emergency Management Team
> 20:18:45 PST
> Imminent Collapse of Oroville Dam   EMERGENCY ALERT
> The dam has suffered a catastrophic internal failure. We are estimating there is no more than a half hour before the dam fails completely. THIS IS NOT A FAILURE OF THE SPILLWAY. THIS WILL BE A FAILURE OF THE ENTIRE DAM WITH FLOODING UP TO 10 FEET DEEP IN THE FLOOD ZONE UP TO 90 MILES DOWNSTREAM. INITIATE IMMEDIATE EVACUATION TO HIGH GROUND.

"Jim, you gather up the team and come to my office." But she could see that other members of the shift had received the alert, panic on some of their faces as they emerged from whatever corner of the facility in which they had been busy and looked at their phones. She waved for all of them to head to the office.

As she exerted her way back up the stairs, she dialed the reservoir management team. "Will, what the fuck? Why are we just hearing about this now?" she shouted above the sound of the turbines as she closed the office door behind.

Will Wright, her counterpart at the dam, shouted back, but more in panic, "Daniele, I don't know what the hell is going on. We don't even have an IPAWS authorization to send out these alerts. There's nothing wrong with the dam that a few dry days won't solve. Really, all our sensors are green, no crisis."

"So, what do I do, Will, stay here, or shut down?"

"Under the circumstances, that call is for *your* bosses on the utility side to make," he said, prodding the buck for any costs of a stoppage back to her side of the table.

"Jeez Louise, Will. I got my crew to think of," she remonstrated.

"We are not showing anything wrong with the dam, that's all I can say. You gotta do what you gotta do. I gotta go and figure out what to do with my crew!" he hung up.

She turned to look at the team and did a quick head count. All were present. "Will says the dam condition is solid green lights. He doesn't know why the alert was sent out."

No sooner had she uttered this than the floor shuddered beneath their feet. The look on everyone's face asked the same question, Earthquake? But Daniele knew from the sound that it was not an earthquake, it was the vibration of #1 turbine being slammed into reverse, from power generation to pumping mode, something that should never, ever happen. After a second, it stopped and resumed proper flow.

She was preparing to say "We gotta run a diagnostic" when #3 turbine sent a shock through the bedrock as it too locked up and reversed flow. Again, after a moment it resumed proper rotation, and the shaking stopped.

Before she could respond, #5 turbine locked, reversed, and resumed. This was not good. As the cycle started to repeat itself, she gave orders to the team, "Ok, all of you evacuate. Head to the monitoring center. You should be safe there. I have to stay here and figure it out."

"Boss!?" Jim asked.

"Go on, get outa here. I'll be ok. Call Will Wright and tell him what's happening. And make sure you capture the data as I send it to you, just in case." Like a goose herding gosling, she spread her arms and moved them as a group toward the exit and the elevator. When the door of the elevator closed and the cabin departed on its 700-foot vertical journey, she turned and went to the control room, every fourth step made unsteady by the shaking of the floor.

Priorities, priorities, her mind analyzed. Should she try to shut it down, or try to figure out what was happening? Shut it down, she decided, but first call the boss, Chief Engineer Sam Hodgkins.

He picked up right away, "I was just about to call you. Have you evacuated?"

"You're talking about the emergency alert. Yeah, I evacuated the crew, but I am still here. The dam says this is a false alarm. They're trying to figure it out. I'm calling about something else, Sam. We have a situation here. Turbines 1, 3, and 5 keep locking up, reversing flow and going back to normal. Permission to shut the system down, sir."

He paused for a moment. "Yes. Do it. I'm getting in my car now. It will take me twenty minutes to get there and join you."

"Righty-O. Thank you, sir."

She settled at a control console and took a binder marked "Shutdown Procedures" off the shelf above the console. The instructions were clear. She had to access a bank of programmable logic controllers through the computer and enter a code, and the PLCs would do the rest of the work.

The pattern of shock, vibration, and abatement continued, each time shaking the console. Pens left in a cup rolled about, and a mug of coffee abandoned by a team member had long since slurped out half its contents over its lip and onto the console.

She navigated the graphic user interface to find the PLCs and highlighted those for turbines 1, 3, and 5, then clicked on the highlighted group. A menu of commands appeared. She selected "Emergency Shut Down." A box appeared prompting her to enter a code. She referred one more time to the binder making certain she had the right digits, then entered the six-digit code into the blank and pressed "enter." The system prompted her to reconfirm the action, yes or no. "Here goes nothing," she muttered as she confirmed.

Hitting the "enter" key coincided with a temporary abatement. She held her breath while the calm continued. Her heart slumped as the pattern resumed. "No, no, no," she pleaded to no one.

Okay. What to do? Flashing red warning lights had been activated, and an emergency siren had gone off. The noise, the shock waves, the intensity, and frequency were all increasing. There was a changing pattern to the shocks. It had started out as turbine 1 then 3 then 5. Now it mixed and blended, sometimes even locking up two at a time and with changes in the frequency of lock and release. She had to ensure that this was recorded.

She turned to the monitoring systems. They collected data from throughout the plant and related parts of the dam, head pressure, turbine rotational speed, power output, vibration, seismic, and hundreds of other measurements, as well as all commands entered by the personnel. However, these continuous measurements were only backed up once per hour, on the hour, to an outside server. She wanted to make sure, come what may, that there was a real-time record of this event. She entered in the commands for a manual override of the automatic data backup, confirmed the order to back up immediately and switch to continuous real-time transmission to the outside server. The system responded with a confirmation.

Back to business. So the PLCs are not responding. How can I shut down the plant without using them? With eyes closed she traced her imagination through the system. Turbines 1, 3, and 5 needed electricity, a lot of it, to lock up and enter pumping mode. *If I can shut off the power to them, it should stop the phenomena. Okay.* Her mind's eye continued its tour of the facility and came to rest on a bank of high-voltage switches. She could manually crank the spring release on the switch and unlock it, breaking the circuits going from Turbines 2, 4, and 6 supplying power to 1, 3, and 5.

By now, the event had been underway for over eighteen minutes, and cracks appearing on the floor were widening. She had a good football field of space to traverse to get to the circuit panel, so she set off. She took out her phone and plugged in a set of noise-canceling earbuds, then dialed home. Her daughter answered. "Hey, honey, it's mommy here. Is daddy home?"

"No, but he called to say he would be home soon. Mom, what's this alert that came up on my phone? Is everything ok? I'm scared."

"Mommy's working on it. You don't have to worry, we live high up behind the dam. But listen to your dad when he gets home, okay?"

"Yes. When are you coming home?"

"As soon as I take care of a problem. Got to go, honey. Give a hug to daddy for me. I love you."

"Me, too."

Daniele disconnected the call and put the phone away. Looking up, she noticed a drop of water on the visor of her helmet. Turning to the ceiling high above, she saw a fine spray spreading from a crack. She picked up the pace and got to the heavy door leading to the switch room. Hauling it open she dropped the door prop to keep it swung wide so she could keep an eye on the plant plaza and turned to the long array of switchgear panels, each the size of a large, double-doored refrigerator.

She thought for a moment back to the training many years ago on operating a switchgear and looked at the panel. *Yeah, they were dangerous. Yeah, they used to explode sometimes, or operators got fried. But that was in the past. This one is clearly laid out, well engineered, well marked. Totally mechanical and not connected to or controlled by a computer or online systems.*

"Thank you, engineers, for being the good people you are," she praised under her breath as she looked around the side of the first panel for the "key."

The key was actually the size of a large, X-shaped tire lug wrench, and she found it hanging on the right side attached by a small chain, which she broke off. Turning to the front of the panel clearly identified for Turbine 1, she moved a control gate lever up into the switching mode. This allowed her to insert the key into the feeder switch.

Hefting weight into it, she was able to rotate the key until she heard a loud *chunk*, and a symbol on the panel physically moved to show the circuit was broken. She removed the key and moved the control gate lever to the earthing position, put the key in the earthing slot, and again heft the switch until she heard another *chunk*. One turbine down, two to go.

She turned to look out into the plaza. There were now multiple jets of water coming from the ceiling with pressure exceeding that of a fire hose, and she could see chunks of concrete and rock that had sheared off and fallen to the plaza floor.

She got to work on Turbine 2 and looked behind again when the operation was complete.

She had lived the life and risk of a submariner on two deployments. The possibility of the sub imploding, of suddenly surrendering to the tremendous pressure of the water outside, was a consideration they were trained to mentally handle. Yes, it could happen, but it was not likely. She had never believed *that* possibility would follow her into this land job. She smiled briefly at the foolishness and shook her head as a wall of water, rock, concrete, and rebar flattened her against the third panel killing her instantly.

Outside, as torrents of rain lashed from the sky, Sam Hodgkins pulled into the employee parking lot above the dam, the tempo of windshield wipers keeping *prestissimo* time yet barely able to clear the glass.

It was a new-moon night, dark and shrouded, but under a prolonged flash of two lightning strikes, he was the first to witness Oroville Dam crumble away, its arms no longer able to hold back the goodness of one trillion gallons of water. It released them from their bondage, unrestrained to the earth below and beyond.

"God's Holy Trousers," he muttered in awe and in defeat.

AUTUMN

You remember the words to the old Dylan song, "Blowin' in the Wind," right?

How many gentle reminders are disregarded, how many nods to the danger of a coming tipping point go unheeded, how many clear shoutouts are willfully categorized as inconvenient falsehoods, until the warnings themselves, lest they be further ignored, become nearly as dangerous as the outcome being forewarned.

CHAPTER 7

MICK COIN PREFERRED TO KEEP BEN FRANKLIN HOURS, EARLY to bed, early to rise. His youth on the farm had dictated it. The arduous work expected by his Lord demanded it. And the fine people of the United States of America deserved it. But this evening, disaster had woken him just as he and the First Lady had gone to sleep.

The mobile device on the nightstand was programmed to ring during rest hours if an emergency call was coming in; other calls would just vibrate. For his first seven months in office, it had never gone off at night. When it did go off this evening, it was loud, urgent, and flashing red and dragged him back from the first moments of dream sleep. He was disoriented and dazed, fumbling for the device to quiet it as much as to respond to it. The time and date were flashing on the screen: 00:01 September 22

"Yes," he said in a daze.

"Mr. President, this is Jerome Mitchell. Approximately 20 minutes ago, a catastrophic dam failure occurred in the state of California. We have set up an emergency response war room at DHS headquarters. This is going to be a major disaster, sir, and I think it would be best if you were here to lead the response."

Mitchell was the secretary of the Department of Homeland Security. That told Coin something right off the bat. FEMA was already reeling under the enormity of what had happened, whatever it was, and had punted to their parent, DHS.

"Is it an earthquake, terrorism, what? How bad?"

"We have no confirmations as yet. Only that the Oroville Dam collapsed at peak capacity during a heavy storm."

Coin trusted Mitchell, but this was the first major emergency he had dealt with and thought his pick for the job might be responding from panic. "If the situation is as bad as you suggest, I think I should stay here to lend whatever weight I can to the federal response and assure the people. We'll set up in the Situation Room. You have your people link up whichever intel feeds you think are most important for us to track. Keep us in the loop, and anytime you feel you are hitting a roadblock, let me know."

"Understood, Mr. President. Thank you."

Coin hung up and placed the phone back on the nightstand. He knew it was going to be a long night and day ahead, but the first thing that weighed on him was his wife. She was a Valley Girl from Los Angeles, but had aunts, uncles, and cousins in the area below the dam, wealthy farmers.

"Honey, is everything okay?" she asked, touching his arm.

"There's an emergency. The Oroville Dam has collapsed. I think you better call your kin and make sure they are alright. I have to get to the Situation Room."

"Goodness. How could that happen?" she wondered aloud, shaken.

"I don't know, dear, but we'll get to the bottom of it. Someone'll pay. First, we have to determine the extent of the damage and get rescue operations underway. Now, you make those calls and let me know what you learn," he said patting her hand.

He got up. His valet had been alerted to the emergency and was ready in the anteroom with a selection of clothes. Coin put on a pair of blue trousers and a dark blue polo shirt with the presidential emblem on it then headed to the Situation Room. He remained there for two hours, frustrated as his cabinet trickled in, but substantive, reliable intel did not. It was night, there was a heavy thunderstorm underway, lots of excuses.

He left them with instructions that he would return at 06:00 and expected details when he got there. He wanted to have a press conference at 08:30 to let the nation know what had happened and reassure the markets before Wall Street opened at 09:30. And he was very specific that he expected them to have some good news or at least something inspirational to tell the American people.

When he returned to his bedroom, the First Lady was still propped up and awake flicking through news feeds on a tablet computer. He sat and put his arm around her shoulder. "Were you able to reach your folks?"

"Some of them. They said that they had gotten good warning and headed for high ground. They said they had reached the others and thought they were okay, too."

"Let's pray that *everyone* heeded those alarms." He and the First Lady got off the bed and kneeled on the carpet, their arms on the mattress, their hands both clasped in prayer and clasped with one another's: hers, his, hers, his. They remained there for ten minutes deep in concentration, their souls reaching out for wisdom, for humility, for strength. Then they got up without a word and went back to bed.

When morning broke and Mick Coin strode into the Situation Room, he faced a more organized response. The team was in place and functioning. It was still 03:00 in California, but they had assets on the ground that had been able to report back and begin to get some intel. The news channels were also bringing in reports and visuals that added to the story.

Jerome Mitchell was cued up on the screen to give an update, and a battery of other screens showed what he would be talking about.

"Good morning, Mr. President. We have a substantial update to give you. I want to draw your attention to monitor #1 first. What you are seeing is a simulation of flooding based on a catastrophic failure of the Oroville Dam. The collapse took place at 20:45 Pacific Standard Time, which was 23:45 for us here."

The color simulation was overlaid on a topographical map and showed in ten-minute increments the location and expected depth of floodwaters. It cycled through the process several times allowing Coin to see the blue of the water release, expand, and fill in most of the area south and west of the dam to Interstate 5 in the west and State Road 90 south and as an eastern boundary. The floodwaters were not expected to hit Sacramento.

The simulation paused.

"This is where we are now, sir, six hours and fifteen minutes since the event. These small towns just southwest of the dam were inundated. But the waters have not reached more major population centers like Yuba City yet."

"Was this simulation shared with the locals in the past?" Coin asked.

"Mr. President, the simulation was generated this evening. A staffer at FEMA plugged the basic data into a stock tool they produced in the past; it shows the adjacent damage simulation."

"Were those small towns evacuated?"

"We do not have a count on missing people. However, what we *can* say is that the timely warning issued by the dam authorities and the disaster communication system FEMA had set up worked admirably well. Many, if not all, of the people in the immediate vicinity of the dam did evacuate. Emergency services are reporting effective evacuation efforts further down in the path of the expected flooding."

"What do we know about the cause?"

"We haven't ruled out anything yet. The dam was nearing overflow capacity. After the dam had been ordered to be evacuated, seismologists measured tremors in the vicinity of the dam prior to its collapse, but they were only just measurable, not major. These coincided with an anomaly at the power plant. Its vibrations may have caused the tremors picked up by the seismographs. We have people on the ground doing interviews right now to collect more information."

"Any sign it was destroyed rather than just collapsed?"

"No, Mr. President, but it is not ruled out at this point either."

"Damage estimates?"

"It is too early to estimate the death toll and human casualties. One hundred eighty-eight thousand souls live in the projected flood area; 20,000 in the area already flooded,where we estimate casualties will be higher. I am told to expect a minimum of 6,000 deaths. Property damage is expected to be north of $29 billion. There is a greater impact on the general economy of California.

"Beyond the immediate flood area damage, the economy will have to cope with the loss of power generation capacity, and much more importantly, the loss of distributed irrigation waters that feed the agriculture industry in Central California. Over time, this will have hundreds of billions of dollars of impact on the local economy and of course hit every American in the pocketbook when they go to the grocery store."

Coin sat in thought absorbing this last statement. As a farmer, he knew how dependent his livelihood was on nature, and how taming some of nature's erratic excesses, such as with damming and irrigation, allowed him to reduce or eliminate a variable, moving the farm one step closer to being an industrial business and not a casino crapshoot.

His heart went out to those people who, he could see, were at risk of losing it all. "Insurance coverage?"

"Less than 10 percent of the properties in the hundred-year flood plain are insured against flooding. The dam and the power plant have insurance, but the liabilities could drag the utility and their insurer both into bankruptcy."

"Any good news, something inspirational to bolster the people's resilience?"

"Sir, Tammy Jones and Troy Masters are working on it," he said, referring to the press secretary and the President's speech writer.

"Okay, continue to feed details to them as they come in."

Coin looked over and called to his secretary to get the governor of California on the line. After four minutes she called back to him that the call was waiting.

He picked up the receiver and punched the button of the flashing extension. "Bill, Mick Coin here. I know you are back to back with people needing your help, but I wanted you to know we are all assembled here, and you are not facing this alone."

"Mr. President, sorry to make you wait just now, but yes, I have been up all night. Thank you for calling," the tired and anxious voice of Guillermo Garcia answered.

"Is there anything you know that you need right now that I can help with?"

"No, Mr. President. FEMA has responded quickly. They tell me they have sufficient resources originally planned for an earthquake emergency in Southern California that are being mobilized as we speak. Portable hospitals, temporary shelters, food. I have mobilized the National Guard out of Sacramento to ramp up for response and coordinate with FEMA."

"Good. What are you hearing from the front line?"

"One thing that has been repeated is how fortunate we are the team at Oroville sounded the alarm when they did. Tens of thousands of lives were saved by that alone. People's property can't be saved, but lives were spared. And the sacrifice at the power plant. The engineer on duty sent her crew out while she remained to try and shut it down. Cost her life."

"Do you know her name?"

"Smothers."

"Family?"

"Yes, sir. A husband and a daughter," he solemnly replied

"I am sure the extent of damage we are facing will be more evident with morning light. I am declaring a state of emergency. That will be made public at 08:30. But we are here, we will back you, and when appropriate, I will make a trip out to lend a hand and support awareness."

"Thank you, Mr. President, from me and the people of California."

"I will call again towards the end of the day to check in with you, if not sooner. Goodbye, Bill."

Coin got up and asked where he could find his press secretary, then went to her office, where she huddled with Troy Masters, their dazed faces staring at the few scenes the cable news channels had picked up. In heavy rotation were repeating images of buildings and homes being swept away in the dark, rain-lashed landscape. Local reporters stood on high ground commenting on things they did not understand and events they could not see, of which they had no firsthand knowledge.

His staffers looked like deer caught in the headlights of this catastrophe, unable to move as the scenes repeated themselves over and over.

"Morning, team," he greeted as he strode in.

Jones and Masters straightened up and shook off their funk. "Good morning, Mr. President," they said struggling to stand up but failing to do so before he had placed himself in an open chair.

"As you were. You're working on my statement to the American people for 08:30, right? What have you got so far?"

They looked at each other. Jones moved a document off the computer desktop onto a larger, flat-panel screen mounted on the wall that was showing the news feeds.

Coin read it. They were struggling. "It's a start," he said with more positivity than the piece deserved, "but I want to make sure you get three elements right."

He outlined things he wanted to have emphasized. "Garcia mentioned to me a story from the power plant, the engineer in charge, name is Smothers, saved her team, sacrificed herself. Try to get some more details on that. Bring me the next draft at 08:15."

He got up to leave, turned, and looked back at them with a silent nod and a confident look that told them "I believe in you, we will get through this," and then left the room.

⊃ 人 ⊂

GAO QIU GLARED AT HIS COUSIN GAO LIAN. IT WAS ALMOST 17:30 in the afternoon. He had come as soon as he was notified of the escape or capture or rescue or whatever they should call this tits-up Chai Jin mess.

"It was really quite simple, wasn't it? Interrogate Chai Jin, get a confession and location for Lin Chong, and turn him over to State Security. How could you have fucked it up?"

Cai Jing watched on through his mobile device video connection. He was still not sure what had transpired between Gao Qiu and Lin Chong in the past, but Cai was now inextricably linked into this whole mess, seeking as he was to prove that Lin Chong was behind the flash protests in Beijing and who knows what other mischief. "Governor Gao, you said this was not a jailbreak. Why?"

"It wasn't a bunch of gangsters busting through the walls and crashing this guy out of prison with no regard to the lives of the guards," Gao Lian said, standing his ground with his cousin. "No. It was well planned and executed, very sophisticated. The black house was gassed, all the guards were knocked out, not killed. Just tripping their brains out for twenty-four hours. These people had gained remote access to the gate and main door. But they did not deactivate the video surveillance."

Cai Jing had watched the video a dozen times. Fully armed, tactically clad gunmen in black sporting the bold characters for "National Supervisory Commission" on the backs of their uniforms were seen to enter wearing gas masks and helmets, their faces obscured. "Is there any reason to believe that this is not the work of the NSC? Because if it is them, that opens a whole new world of problems for us. I, for one, was not aware the NSC even had this sort of armed response team."

"If it's not the NSC, Chai Jin could definitely afford the best to break him out and make it look like them, but I don't think even he has the balls to stand up to the government that way," Gao Lian remarked.

"We're screwed either way," Gao Qiu lamented. "We can't just ask the NSC, 'By the way, we think some imposters broke a prisoner out of our custody wearing your uniforms. Care to comment?'" he spat sarcastically. "If it was them, it just pushes the shovel a little deeper into the grave for us. If it wasn't them, then they start to inquire, 'Why do you ask?' If we keep up our search for Chai Jin, and they actually have him and come knocking on our door asking 'Why, didn't you see our uniforms in the video?' we look even worse."

"Did your people get *anything* out of Chai Jin, anything that might help us capture Lin Chong?"

"Nothing. He held firm. No locations, no names, no admissions. When he *was* conscious, he just scowled at the interrogators, cobbed on them sometimes, told them they would pay dearly because he had the ironclad carte blanche, and said that his uncle's soul was waiting for them in hell."

"Any luck on Li Kui's whereabouts?" Gao Qiu asked, hoping for some shelter in this shitstorm.

"No, he got away clean. A ghost," Gao Lian said.

"Okay," Cai Jing tried to drop the curtain on this circus. "We'll redouble surveillance on Chai Jin's known staff and accomplices. See if we pick up any clues as to where he is."

"Meanwhile, need I remind you I am out one son-in-law?" Gao Lian asked. "My daughter is not going to let this go. Funeral expenses, mortgages, and raising kids. What are you going to do about it?"

"I'll deal with it," Gao Qiu growled, his tone neither generous nor sympathetic.

⊃ 人 ⊂

BY THE TIME 08:30 EST HAD ARRIVED, MICK COIN HAD SHAVED, changed clothes, breakfasted, been briefed a second time, watched as Jerome Mitchell spoke with FEMA and DHS lieutenants on the West Coast, and reviewed, revised, and approved his statement.

He sat behind the Resolute desk in the Oval Office, as his broadcast director stood to the left of a camera and silently counted three-two-one with his fingers, and the light on top of the camera went from red to green.

Mick Coin, confident and steadfast as he looked straight out to millions of his fellow citizens, connected to them eye to eye, and said, "My fellow Americans, good morning. Last night at 8:45 in the evening in the great state of California, as families finished their dinners or gathered around their television sets and children worked on homework, while stores finished up their day of work, disaster struck our nation. The Oroville Dam, the tallest dam in the United States, bigger than even the mighty Hoover Dam, collapsed.

"The sun will not rise on this scene of devastation for another forty-five minutes, so we have few details to report to you. What we *do* know is that emergency management authorities and first responders have been busy through the night, their brave and swift actions have saved many lives, and the alert systems federal and state authorities have put in place to safeguard American lives worked extremely well.

"A full half an hour before the collapse of the dam, our Integrated Public Alert Warning System sounded an alarm that was swiftly and effectively communicated through various media and to all police, emergency services, and hospital responders. They acted immediately, as did many families that had received the warning.

"At the dam itself, the lives of all on-duty personnel were saved by the quick action of management, save the life of one that *was* taken. That of Daniele Smothers, deputy chief engineer of the hydroelectric power plant located in the dam. This veteran, a former submariner, wife, and mother, ordered her team to evacuate the power plant while she remained behind to monitor abnormal behavior in the turbines and sought to shut them down. Smothers' brave and selfless actions will not be forgotten, and the data she preserved will help investigators determine what caused the collapse.

"The Oroville Dam had a history of issues that will need to be reviewed. Federal, state, and local officials will coordinate efforts to identify how and why this collapse occurred, accountability will be established, and what we learn from this will improve safety, monitoring, and warning systems across the industry.

"I have spoken to the governor of the state of California, Guillermo Garcia, and assured him of the complete support of federal authorities. The Department of Homeland Security and its Federal Emergency Management Authority have immediately mobilized regional resources to take action in the area impacted by flooding. I have declared a state of emergency to streamline federal aid response and support.

"To the people of California and the impacted area, I want you to know that our hearts and prayers are with you, as is the full effort of the US government. To the people of the United States, I want you to know that our engineering, our systems, and our technology remain the envy of the world. When an isolated incident like this occurs, we learn from it, we get stronger and better. We are a resilient people. We thrive in the face of challenges.

"God bless you all, and God bless the United States of America."

⊃ 人 ⊂

IN A CONSERVATIVELY APPOINTED MEETING ROOM ADJACENT TO his quarters in Zhongnanhai, President Zhao Ji met with Su Yuan-jing and Li Shishi. Against the wall, an old, ornate pendulum clock gifted from the King of Prussia to the Qing Emperor chimed gently the call to nine p.m. The mood in the room was somber, each in their own thoughts. His secretary had notified them of the appointment that morning, but much had happened in twelve hours.

"I can't imagine the devastation if the same thing occurred at Three Gorges," Zhao shook his head wearily referring to the giant hydroelectric dam project that had reshaped the Yangtze River and powered a percentage of the country. "Hundreds of millions would be wiped out, destitute if not dead."

There was silence. Su and Li just looked on; the unthinkable had humbled them.

"I reached out to the American president right after the address to his people and extended my condolences and hopes that the devastation is less than feared. Our Red Cross has offered to airlift supplies as soon as they know what will be needed. Anyway, that's not why I called you in."

Su and Li looked up at Zhao, supportive determination in their eyes.

"I have all my ministers, party members, generals, advisors. But I can never be sure whom to trust. I trust both of you completely. These are dangerous times. Times when we must stay the course, but there are reactionary forces at work. Though I can't determine who for sure is part of the Shanghai Clique, I know they are out there. And they are gunning for me.

"The Tiananmen demonstration, the public ridicule of me personally by this Demeter group, the Green Guards. Is this all a coordinated effort to embarrass me, show my weakness, topple me? To give free rein to dark, corrupt forces here, panicked by my efforts to expose their perfidy?"

Su looked to Li. She was intelligent, it was true, but she was also too young, or perhaps too doe-eyed about the ways of the world, to always understand the danger of speaking her mind, of grasping at the prickly, or of saying what needed to be said when others kept their mouths shut. For this he was grateful.

Li Shishi stepped into the void as he had hoped. "I have no doubt the Shanghai Clique is exploiting the government's response to these emergent situations to their own ends. The newspapers and media outlets aligned with their propaganda stance daily send up trial balloons to test how far they can go, damning you with faint praise. But so far, have we seen any evidence that they instigated these situations? Demeter and the Tiananmen protest seem to have their roots abroad. The Green Guards, though, seem to be homegrown. You know what *I* think should be done about them."

Su shared Li's view that Zhao should try to co-opt the movement. But the details determine the outcome. How to do it? "If you can co-opt the movement, it may force the hand of your hidden opponents. Draw them out."

"I could simply go on record supporting the group, but without having any way to channel communication to them, I think I am just setting myself up. I don't know which security apparatus I can trust to help me influence them directly. They haven't been able to get Green Guards under control, nor wipe them out. Meanwhile, the parents of arrested Greens have organized and are making their own petitions. So, is the security apparatus truly unable to get a handle on this group, or is that just part of the effort to embarrass me?"

"Not to change the subject, but my gut is telling me that this Lin Chong affair is tied into the Shanghai Clique somehow," Li said. "I have been able to piece together some more details, but the picture isn't complete yet." She looked to Zhao for permission to continue. He flicked his eyebrow.

"Lin was a highly decorated officer in the cyber corps and based in Shanghai. Third-generation PLA. He had no black marks in his folder, and psych profiles suggested high integrity and loyalty to country. Some question as to Party loyalty, but we must remember that he, like me, was born after market reform.

"Out of the blue he is caught trying to infect the computer systems at the White Tiger Sanctum. For what? I looked into his finances. Pretty standard: wife, mortgage, comfortably modest sum in the bank, no conspicuous assets to red flag, no apparent outside sources of income.

"I asked some friends in cyber security some hypotheticals. They told me that, hypothetically, someone as skilled as Lin Chong would probably not risk carrying a thumb drive into the White Tiger Sanctum. They would find some stealthier way to deliver a software payload.

"So, then I dug into Cai Jing. He had contact with Lin Chong at quarterly meetings, nothing out of the ordinary. But something did pop up incidentally about him. A month or so after Lin Chong disappeared, Cai is behind the curtain trying to seal a sweetheart deal with some peasant landowners on rare-earth-mineral-bearing properties. It gets exposed by, of all things, a law student from my alma mater blowing the whistle for his family.

"Media reports about this were quickly suppressed, and the law student was arrested for campus agitation. Not to be found. Coincidentally there is a flurry of communications with General Gao Qiu, content unknown, and

Cai starts looking into Lin Chong. I still can't tie Gao to the rare-earth deal, or Lin to any of this. But it does smell."

"Gao is shrewd *and* powerful. He knows he is in the spotlight and will try to stay out of it. But he is exactly the type who could be in the Shanghai Clique. It would serve his purposes well," Zhao reflected.

The haptic buzzer on Su Yuanjing's mobile device vibrated. "Excuse me." He took the device out and looked at it, his fingers waving through some files and opening one. "This is curious," he said to Zhao Ji and Li Shishi. He rotated the screen to landscape mode and replayed a video for them.

Black-and-white security camera footage was timestamped from fifteen hours prior and location stamped "Gaotang Prefecture, Detention Facility: The Well - Camera 2 Interior." It showed two black-clad, fully armed officers with "National Supervisory Commission" emblazoned on their backs jog past the camera with a battering ram, bust through a door at the end of the hall, go into a room, and reemerge to grab a blanket. They finally came out supporting the arms of a weakened detainee wrapped in the blanket as they dragged his feet along toward the security camera. At a moment when the detainee's face was nearest the camera and in full view, the video frame froze.

"That's... that's Chai Jin, isn't it?" Zhao Ji said. "What are you doing arresting him? I always counted him as one of the good ones."

"Indeed. That's one curiosity. Chai Jin has been cooperative with us whenever we needed help ferreting out graft. Notwithstanding the 'iron-clad carte blanche' his family claims to have, he isn't under investigation nor have I issued orders for his arrest."

Li Shishi spoke up, "Doesn't look like he's being arrested. Looks like they are breaking him out!"

"Indeed. And their uniforms. On the left breast you see the empty Velcro patch there. They haven't put their ID numbers on. My men are more disciplined than that."

"Who sent it to you?" Zhao asked.

Su looked at the message. "I don't know who this is. Timely Rain? It was sent to an email account I infrequently employ, used to use it when I was heading up Autumn Orchid at Second Bureau," Su said referring to the group responsible to keep tabs on and sway the leanings of opinion leaders and the affluentials in Hong Kong, Taiwan, and Macao.

"Whoever sent it wanted you to see it for a reason. Better dig into it. Chai Jin's HQ is in Shanghai. Maybe he stepped on some toes of the Shanghai Clique," Zhao said with hope.

"But this was taken in Gaotang. That's in Shandong," Li observed.

"Yes. He had relations up that way," Su said. "Okay. I think this deserves some quick attention."

⊃ 人 ⊂

IT WAS ONE OF THOSE "THE BUCK STOPS HERE" PROBLEMS THAT so aggravated President Coin. It wasn't his buck, it wasn't really even a problem when looked at the right way, but it was a "damned if you do and damned if you don't" issue that he felt was metastasizing into a big thing he needed to get in front of.

Two days after the dam break the floodwaters had subsided, and the damage assessments coming in were based more on observable fact and less on ill-informed speculation. The very best news was that many fewer people had died as a result, so far only 355 confirmed deaths, a fraction of what had been estimated.

This was attributed to the half-hour warning given before the collapse and the insistent, detailed alerts sent to people in harm's way urging immediate evacuation. These had been delivered directly to mobile devices and on the television and cable channels. Warnings sent to mobile devices had been specific, giving the recipient detailed directions to avoid danger with a large countdown number filling half the screen.

This boon did not apply to things that could not get out of the way. Homes, businesses, schools, hospitals, farms, roads, vehicles, power lines, the list went on, totally erased by the impact of the water for a distance of sixty-two miles south. Billions of dollars of damage.

The media was having a field day. *How could there* only *have been a half-hour warning?* detractors asked. There was no earthquake to serve as an excuse, the dam had a history of issues, rainwaters were high and going higher, why wasn't it flagged for special attention? Indeed, it was lumped into the whole "America's infrastructure is crumbling" screed and shot back over the bow of the White House challenging the "effective, lifesaving, rebuild it better" narrative being delivered by the president.

Why couldn't the press accept the good news of a warning system that worked and give them a breather rather than taunting and inflaming the destitute survivors? This morning's all-hands-on-deck meeting was to address this and other issues in advance of a trip Coin planned to the devastated area tomorrow.

And now this.

"Say that again," Coin ordered his voice strained with disbelief.

Jerome Mitchell swallowed and repeated the news he had just delivered, "*We* did not issue the warning, Mr. President. The press is complaining a warning was not issued earlier, but in fact, there was no evidence of a need, no event to warn about, nothing that would have triggered our IPAWS system, until twenty minutes before the dam collapse."

"But...what about Smothers, the action she took ..."

"Yes, she is still the hero here, but her crew reported that they got the call to evacuate from the dam management ten minutes *before* the shaking started. The dam management's comments to the press the next morning about the alert were made before they had done a thorough review, and they only praised the swift action of their own Will Wright."

"We're just talking about ten minutes..."

"Mr. President, the 'Oroville Dam Emergency Management Team' that issued the alerts is not registered with IPAWS. It could not have sent out the alert. I think it won't be long before the press catches on to this."

"Plain speaking, please."

"For reasons of safety and security, the Integrated Public Alert Warning System cannot be accessed by just anyone to issue alerts. At federal, state and local levels, only authorized, preapproved entities can do that. The 'Oroville Dam Emergency Management Team' was not one of them. IPAWS was hacked, and this warning was sent out by the hackers.

"And this is not an isolated issue, I am afraid. The nature of the alerts sent out, the messages tailored to individual recipients' locations, the instructions on exactly where to go to get to safety, the large countdown to impact warning on mobile devices, *none* of that functionality, while admirable and lifesaving, was designed into our alert system. It was an add-on, a flourish, an improvement. But admittedly not our work." Mitchell let that sink in.

"Mr. President, we have something dovetailing that." It was Lieutenant General Lewis in command of the Army Corps of Engineers.

"Yes."

"We have gotten in and looked at the data from the dam and power plant in the moments leading up to the collapse. I second Jerome that Daniele Smothers is still the hero. The actions she was taking, had they been completed just a *little* sooner, would have saved the dam. The data she made sure was captured otherwise provided us with something to analyze. Our engineers are still modeling it, but the pattern of shocks hitting the dam was not random."

"Yes, I want to know more about this. I mean, the shocks were big enough to be measured by seismographs, but there was no earthquake activity. We need to tell the people what happened."

"The data captured corroborates the accounts of the power-plant staff evacuated by Smothers. This power plant had three of its six turbines designed so that they could both generate power and reverse flow to pump water back up into the reservoir. The tremors were caused by those three turbines locking up and reversing flow, again and again, until the harmonics were just so and the dam shook itself apart. The pattern of shocks was not random."

"Meaning?"

"Well, Mr. President, the pattern of shocks was calculated, planned." Lewis's tone was insistent, but he could see the commander in chief did not understand. "Sir, I think this was a concerted attack on our country."

⊃ 人 ⊂

FROM HIS POSITION AT ONE END OF THE LONG WOODEN TABLE IN the Righteous Fraternity Conference Room, Chai Jin surveyed the men and women seated around it and smiled: the best investment he had ever made. They were stalwarts after his own heart, people for whom justice trumped almost anything else. They had put their lives and liberty on the line for him for the sole reason that it was the right thing to do.

"Thank you all again," he said, wiping a tear from his cheek.

Li Kui was there. He had followed orders, made it to LiangShanPo, and jump-started the rescue together with Sagacious Lu crashing the joint and spiriting him out of that hell hole.

Lin Chong, the one his interrogators had focused on, sitting tall and resolute and looking well healed since they had first met, had made the rescue possible without detection by taking control of the surveillance and alarm systems at the detention facility and then inserting the van's license plate photo and number into thousands of different surveillance records from dozens of routes away from the black house, in all different directions for several hundred miles.

Timely Rain had inspired the choice of uniforms worn by Lu and Li and made the anonymous outreach to the head of the National Supervisory Commission to further confuse the authorities. The ugly chemist he had come to know as the Witch had cast her spell over the guards and made his rescue a mind-trip to remember. Song Wan and Du Qian had orchestrated resources at LiangShanPo.

His eyes turned to Wang Lun. The White-Clad Scholar appeared uncomfortable. While he had spent heavily on bribes to get information and access prior to the rescue and had greeted Chai on his arrival, the Little Tornado just did not feel warmth radiating from him.

"Wang Lun, as leader of this heroic band, I have you to thank most. How can I repay you?"

The White-Clad Scholar sat at the far opposite end of the table, in the leader's seat, and fidgeted. The number of people around this table had swollen from three who respected him without question to ten: ten opinions, ten doubts, ten other ideas about what to do, ten detractors. He was tired of it.

In answer to the Little Tornado's question, he just wanted to answer, 'Take all this hired muscle back with you and leave us be," but he knew that would not fly. "Your thanks are quite enough. What I would like to address in this meeting is my fear that as our ranks have swelled, we will become conspicuous. LiangShanPo has survived through stealth. From our hidden redoubt we have been able to attack the corrupt and profit from it, investing that wealth in doing more good."

Chai Jin interrupted, "I am not naïve. I know we cannot survive if we go against the full might of the State. But that's really not what we are about, true or not? The word 'fear' is not one I share with you," the Little Tornado said, staring at Wang Lun but aware of the nods of others around the table.

"What do we have to fear? When I was being beaten and tortured to give up your location, I was not sunk in a paralyzing morass of fear and dread. Pain, yes. Fatigue, yes. Anger at the injustice, yes. But not really fear. No, our ranks are strengthened here. I think it is time to strike hard. Not just sting the corrupt to get some coin. No. Topple the corrupt and unjust whether we profit or not. Let me be the CFO here and worry about the finances."

Chai Jin looked around the room. Seeing determination in their eyes, he knew he had a quorum. "Show of hands?"

Around the table fingers, hands, and arms rose and pointed to the ceiling. At the end of the table, Wang Lun's hand crept up after all the others. He had to agree, but he felt like he was being stabbed in the heart.

⊃ 人 ⊂

THE CAPTAIN OF AIR FORCE ONE ANNOUNCED THAT THEY WOULD be landing in minutes at Beale Air Force Base and for crew and passengers to make preparations.

Nancy Nillson's first trip on the aircraft had been special. Under the circumstances she thought it would be a sin to characterize it as "magical," but in fact there was a serene comfort to the journey, even as they were preparing to witness the aftereffects of the worst environmental disaster to befall the United States in its 250-year history.

Coin's commanding presence and the determination to make this right reflected in the entire team's spirit comforted her. Then she had been very touched when the First Lady came back and invited her to come forward to their compartment to pray.

She had not known that the press had been allowed to that part of the plane, nor that they were allowed to photograph the scene, but the next day's papers all had the same photo: the backsides of the president, the First Lady, and Nillson all on their knees, heads bowed, hands clasped in prayer facing toward the beatific halo of sunlight shining through the oval windows of the jet.

With the announcement to prepare for landing, Nillson left Coin and his wife.

It was a clear day, the rains had stopped, and as they made their descent the captain pointed out that they were flying over what had been Oroville Dam and the path of the wave of destruction. From her seat and the altitude, the devastation was not apparent, but she assumed that what now appeared as a long lake spreading south-southwest used to be towns and fields and human activity.

Governor Guillermo Garcia and his wife greeted the president and First Lady on the tarmac, then all were ushered onto the Marine One White Hawk helicopter for an aerial inspection. Nillson would proceed with other advisors by caravan straight to the site of what had been the Lake Oroville Visitor Center for a press conference. It was now used by federal and state authorities as their hub for investigating the collapse of the dam. After the press conference, during which she and the rest of the team would be standing shoulder to shoulder behind the president, Nillson would meet with agricultural extension officers and the State's department of agriculture to get some data and assessments of the environmental impacts of the disaster.

Marine One would make several stops on the way to the center, including to Sutter Buttes. This desolate, elevated area was now an island surrounded by water. Several thousand people had sought refuge on Sutter Buttes after being prompted by the insistent emergency warning on their mobile devices several days before. Food, water, and tents had been airlifted to them, and they were slowly being relocated.

The entourage crossed the tarmac to the awaiting helicopter. From the runway's perch forty meters above what had been Yuba City, Coin could see a vast, slow-moving mass of water, corrupted by debris, garbage, and the tops of houses and buildings. On boarding Marine One, the president and First Lady sat across from the governor and his wife, and all donned noise- canceling headsets so they could talk during the inspection.

"Mr. President, thank you again for coming out."

"I promised I would. This is a challenge for our country, not just California. I want all your people to know they are not alone."

"Yes, sir."

"What are the latest casualty figures?"

"As of noon, 415 deaths. Quite amazing really. Two thousand five hundred in hospital, most off the critical list and expected to make it. One hundred fifty thousand, give or take, have been displaced, their homes destroyed."

"Hospital facilities?"

Garcia pointed west out the window of the helicopter to a half-submerged, four-story building. "That was Yuba City's hospital. Some smaller regional places closer to the dam were swept away completely. Most of the patients were sent to bigger hospitals in Sacramento. That's where we are heading now. To Eternal King Hospital, the biggest one."

The aircraft made the fifty-mile hop in ten minutes as they watched the floodwaters spread thinner and thinner further south. Landing on the rooftop pad, the president and his group were escorted by secret service agents to the lobby via elevator.

Coin walked through the lobby shaking hands, greeting staff and Emergency Responders, then went up two levels to meet several victims of the floods. He and the First Lady held their hands, asked about their injuries and their experience at the scene of the flood. Then back to Marine One for a lift to a survivors' camp at Sutter Buttes.

His secret service detail had highlighted concern about this visit and given Coin many reasons why they thought he should not proceed with it. There was no landing pad. The people there were essentially refugees, and most likely many were armed and would not cotton to surrendering their arms just so the president could drop in. The people were not happy about their situation and could not be counted on to give the president a warm reception.

Coin vetoed his detail's concerns and otherwise conceded to wear a bulletproof vest under his loose-fitting, navy-blue windbreaker embellished with his seal of office.

The helicopter slowed and dropped nimbly onto a yellow brush meadow with stumpy trees. A crude circle had been cleared to serve as the landing area. Coin looked over to Special Agent in Charge of Presidential Protection Pruitt and winked when the man scowled one more time.

They got off the aircraft and walked out toward a crowd of onlookers. They were dirty and tired-looking, frustration and fear etched into some faces, but otherwise appeared in good health. Coin strode into the group, looking deep into eyes, shaking hands, usually with two hands, and otherwise putting his left hand on the person's shoulder as he shook with his right. The First Lady similarly dispersed into the crowd. As the whine of the helicopter wound down behind them, they reached a place where a couple of folding chairs had been set up. They were urged to take a seat.

A young man at the edge spoke up, "President Coin, Linx News promised us a tidy fee if we can livestream your visit. Ok, sir?"

Coin smiled jocularly, "Well, now, this is not my formal press conference, but seeing as we don't have any members of the media out here, I suppose it's okay. Anyway, it's good for the American people to see what I am seeing today. Now, have you been getting the assistance you need?"

The secret service had communicated to the group that they should appoint a spokesperson to represent them. An obese woman wearing a pair of stretch jeans and a dark red T-shirt from Las Vegas came up to the First Couple with mugs of coffee and handed them over, then sank her heavy frame onto a fifth chair. "Thank you for coming, thank you for caring, Mr. President, Governor Garcia, sir."

"Call me Mick. What's your name?"

"Georgette. Georgette Banks, sir. I used to live... over there." She pointed east with her mug of coffee where now a mirage-like reflection of sunlight and heat reflected off the water. "All of us here are similar. We done lost everything. The army dropped off some supplies, food, water, stuff. We got some tents yesterday. Some folks got medicine needs, diabetes and whatnot. We made a list. That's what we need right now."

Another person came from the crowd and handed a list to Garcia.

"We'll make sure you get it." Coin took her hand in his.

"Sir, what happened? I mean why? We have all lost everything, and we don't know what comes next."

Coin looked into her eyes, then into the eyes of the crowd, then into the eye of the mobile device livestreaming the moment. "What comes next? Together we find out how this happened and who is responsible, and we hold them to account. Together we rebuild. Rebuild your homes, your dreams, your lives."

Twenty-eight miles away, Nillson had arrived at the investigation command center and the area of the parking lot organized for the president's press conference. She sat next to Tammy Jones in the SUV to stay out of the sun and heat, both of them listening on their mobile devices to Coin's impromptu press conference at Sutter Buttes being broadcast live by Linx News.

Jones did not like letting her boss venture out unscripted, but so far, he was handling it well. "I just hope he saves some talking points for the press here," she said looking over at Nillson with a wink. She had no reason to fear.

Coin kept it short, personal, compassionate, and proactive. Then he and the First Lady, together with Garcia and his wife, made their way back through the refugees to Marine One and boarded it, and as it lifted off Coin saluted and waved back to the crowd, including the eye of the live-broadcasting mobile device. To the "cameraman" the moment was worth a deposit on rebuilding his home, but it was priceless to Linx News.

Along the bottom of their screens, Linx ran a real-time ticker of stock market news and numbers. Markets had been erratic since the accident, stocks in general plummeting and agricultural futures soaring as the oracle of the collective intelligence of free-flowing funds tried to sort out the future impacts. And today was a triple witching hour, when markets were always spooked. But Coin's brief stop seemed to cheer the market, or give it some hope, and staunched the decline.

Nillson's device alerted an incoming call, no name listed, not someone on her call list. "Hello, Nancy Nillson here, who is calling?"

"Ms. Nillson, this Special Agent Thad Irwin with the FBI. Do you have a moment to help me with some questions?" The tone was friendly but authoritative.

Nillson blinked trying to process this. What!? She dredged up into her memory the training she had received about just this type of call when she joined the White House. She had no way of knowing if the person purporting to be an FBI agent was in fact with the Bureau. He could be anyone, and her answers could be given to who knows whom.

"Agent... Irwin. We have standing orders in the White House that any such inquiries should be communicated through the White House counsel and chief of staff to me."

"You are not aware of the reason for the call, I understand, but I hope I can get your thoughts quickly on something quite important."

"I am sorry, Agent Irwin, despite your urgency, protocol demands this come through proper channels. I would truly be happy to address any of your questions when I am directed by the White House counsel to do so. May I ask what this is about?"

"Richard McCallister is a person of interest in an investigation we are conducting. I need to ask you about your recent meeting with him. I'll put this to the White House counsel with high priority. I'm sure she will be reaching out to you shortly. Good day, Ms. Nillson," the sign-off a perfunctory warning as he hung up.

ﬤ 人 ﬤ

LIN CHONG HEARD THE DEEP TIMBRE OF THE LARGE, BRASS singing bowl being struck. The sound was distant, as if coming from a far-off land, but as he returned from the depths of his meditation, its resonance that filled the hall became louder and clearer even as the sound of the bell diminished. His eyelids crept up, and he returned to the mundane.

He took his right foot in two hands to release himself from the lotus position. No matter how pure his meditation had been, no matter how clear he had made his mind, this action brought him back to an unhappy reality under the weight of which he still struggled to maintain equanimity. His eyes would wander to the soles of his scarred feet, the flesh having been melted away by his torturers and grown back puffy, shiny, and plastic-looking. The gentle pressure of his fingers would remind some nerves that they were not yet healed leading his mind and consciousness straight back to the unfinished business with Gao Qiu, Gao Yanei, and the loss of his cherished Zhenniang.

Lin Chong extended his legs and massaged them, massaged his scalp, neck, and shoulders. Then he stood up and descended the several flights to the twentieth floor of the Western podium, the bull pen where all the heroes of LiangShanPo worked, to attend a meeting with Sagacious Lu. After the arrival of his old mentor some order had been brought to creative chaos. He was a great addition; a strong leader, competent coder, and meditator, who was also lusty and relatable, he brought more direction and thereby synergy to the entire group. In the short time at Twin Dragon he had cultivated Timely Rain, who was now his right hand, and he too had quickly won a place among the elite at Mount Liang.

Lu Da had taken the time to get to know each of the people, what they were working on, what they were good at, then reorganized the desks into clusters and teams. The computer workstations remained in various states of nonconformist informality, but individuals were now surrounded by people working on similar things. Each cluster had a more senior and able coder leading it to help drive in a concerted direction while resolving roadblocks and avoiding dead ends or detours.

In response to Chai Jin's call to topple the corrupt and unjust whether Mount Liang profited or not, Sagacious Lu explored a CEO on whom he had started an informal investigation just before Lu was forced to disappear.

The target of interest was Qiu Xiaoyi, who headed up China Central Airlines, China's second largest. Its most significant shareholder was a state-owned enterprise called Central Aviation Holdings, itself owned by the Xian Region Air Force Command. When the government had reduced its ownership in airlines several years back, CEO Qiu had booked handsome capital gains and further secured his hold over the company, which he ran as his own fief.

This included running the recruitment of stewardesses like his own private harem. Applications for the coveted flight-crew positions were required to include several photos and the applicant's "Three Essential Measurements," bust, waist, and hips, as well as height, weight, age, and marital status. Finalists making it through several rounds of interviews had to be "personally interviewed" by the CEO.

Several unsuccessful female candidates thus sexually vetted by the CEO reached out to Sagacious after reading the cover story exposé that had laid low Pig Sticker Zheng. They referred to Qiu as the Sky-Soaring Yaksa, a Tibetan term for a repugnant, malevolent flying demon. Before dropping off the grid Lu had not had the chance to take on their case, but felt it warranted a closer look.

Lu was impressed with the nodal map of the corrupt and unjust constructed at LiangShanPo, and he first looked up the airline CEO's name. To no surprise, he found it as a central node, with connections to other people, companies, deals, disputes, and complaints. He put together a team to brainstorm how to package all the information into a tidy reputation bomb that would bring the Sky-Soaring Yaksa crashing to earth.

It was to this brainstorming session that Lin Chong now arrived.

Seated around the small round table with Sagacious Lu were Timely Rain Song Jiang, Wu Song the Tiger Slayer, and Yan Qing, who called herself the Wave Boy. She was a tall, slender woman with a fair complexion, cropped hair, and flowery tattoos all over her shoulders disappearing into modest cleavage. Li Kui, with whom she was close, had introduced Lin, letting him know that she was a "T"—slang for butch.

At the center of the table was a tea set, small porcelain cups arranged on a bamboo drainage tray and a well-used, Yixing, purple clay teapot, a strainer, a kettle of water being kept just below boil, and a sealed can of whole-leaf tea. "What are we drinking today?" Lin Chong asked in anticipation of a good cuppa. Sagacious had a taste for the finer things in life, and among them great teas of China was one.

"Oriental Beauty, not from my old source in Taiwan I am afraid, but a good enough example." The day before it had been Pu-er from Yunnan, the day before that Longjing from Hangzhou. He measured the dried, rolled leaves into the pot, rinsed and activated them with water from the kettle, drenched the cups with this first brew to rinse and warm them, then refilled the pot and let the leaves steep.

"Thanks for joining us, Panther Head." He poured out the tea into the line of five cups moving the spout back and forth over them until they were all filled. Five hands reached in, took their cups, and took a sip.

"Enjoy! Okay. Where are we on this sting?"

Yan Qing spoke up, "I was able to get into a storage drive Qiu keeps connected to his home computer. It was password protected, but there were no limits to the number of tries, and we got it with some power tools. Turned out to be photos and home videos. Mostly family trips made around the world. But there was one folder labeled "Flowers." This contained photos of candidates, including some undressed and engaged in sex acts with him. And a picture at a company party of some stewardesses sitting on his lap dressed as bunnies like at that old, sexist nightclub and generally fawning all over him. Pretty much sums up this scumbag," she said with undisguised contempt.

Yan Qing was an orphan who had lucked out and been adopted by a wealthy benefactor, Lu Junyi. He made sure she got good schooling and worked hard to get into Beijing University. A gifted calligrapher, poet, and singer, she had poured her academic efforts into studying and tweaking software coding for Chinese handwriting recognition. Before she could graduate, however, her benefactor's world, and thereby the entire world, tumbled. Her foster father recalled her from Beijing urgently.

Lu Junyi had learned that his wife was having an affair with the managing director of one of his companies. To make matters worse, Lu had trusted this man not only with his wife but his money. He learned that the philanderer had managed to undertake numerous illegal deals in Lu's name. Lu knew the government would knock on his door soon to arrest and charge *him* with fiscal wrongdoing, manipulation of corporate accounts, gross corruption, and possibly plotting against the State. Depending on the panel of judges and how skillful his enemies had been in framing him, it could be a capital crime. Knowing that these enemies would go after Yan Qing, too, he escaped with her, introduced Li Kui, and disappeared.

She had not seen him since and did not know whether he had escaped, survived, or been captured, tried, and buried. She only knew that the CEO and her foster mother were now an "item" in the high-society tabloids, and the CEO had taken over group management responsibilities after the disgraceful disappearance of her foster father.

"We can definitely use that, Wave Boy," Sagacious Lu encouraged. "Good work. Tiger Slayer?"

"Yeah, I've been looking at how best to launch the attack. We don't know who all supports him, so just running his nasties further up the flagpole may not bring him down. It needs to be public, and something not readily quashed. Something like your exposé of 'Pig Sticker' Zheng, Sagacious, but needs to be done faster. I have toyed with the idea of fomenting a labor strike at the airline over this, never been done before in China. But too many moving parts, hard to control. And of course, we can't do it in such a way that the women wronged by this bastard just get disappeared. They may have been why we got started on targeting this fellow, but I think there is much we can expose to torpedo him without implicating them."

"I still want to make sure *he* knows that's part of the reason," Yan Qing inserted.

Sagacious nodded and poured another round of tea. "Song Jiang?"

"I like the standard LiangShanPo modus operandi. Put together a package to blackmail the son of a bitch, and then after he has given you all his banking details and made the blackmail payment, release the information anyway, including his efforts to bury the garbage."

Lin Chong spoke up, "It is elegant, but since I have been here, I have seen it backfire, or at least reduce the effectiveness of the sting. Warned of what he or she will be hit with, the mark has a chance to line up his allies, or establish an alternative false narrative. No, I think we want to go for the jugular with no warning.

"I favor a combined, simultaneous attack on multiple fronts exposing labor violations, corruption, bribery, share price manipulation, and arm-in-arm transactions delivered to regional and national authorities governing these respective violations, as well as to foreign governments interested in foreign corruption. On top of this, a nicely packaged, well-researched investigative journalism article delivered straight online to everyone, saying Qiu is already being investigated by X number of ministries and supervisory commissions."

"That sounds great, Panther Head, but do we have data we can access to prove some of this?" Lu asked, not wanting to get too far out into left field.

"I believe we do," he said. "Curious you should ask because since we started working this sting, several teams have reported to me that between when they started a line of inquiry one night and the next morning when they resumed work, data, answers, and details have appeared in their folders. Someone out there loves us... or *hates* Qiu. I have reported it to Wang Lun, and he is looking into the security breach.

The news and confidence in Lin Chong's voice told Lu Da that they would be able to score a hat trick on this sting: destroy Qiu with maximum humiliation and punishment, expose the women who had reached out to Lu to minimum risk, and generate a huge payout by shorting Central Airline shares. "As long as the information is useful and reliable, I'll take it. Good work."

⊃ 人 ⊂

GAO YANEI SAT IN HIS WEST-FACING, FIFTIETH FLOOR PUDONG office at SilvermanFuchs with a sweeping view of the Huangpu River and the old Puxi side of Shanghai fading into the dense, ocher smog of dusk, the sun a tangerine orb beyond that. On the wall was a mid-career Zhang Da-qian painting of a magpie standing on a branch of a flowering plum tree, its eyes alert and scanning for its next meal. At auction it would fetch a year's salary.

The office was Gao's perch. A lofty space above the world from which he could consider his next conquests.

Others at the firm always focus on the next deal and measure their dicks against how much revenue they generate. Like the cheers and high fives shared in the Chicago office after the massive profits generated by a mid-level trader who had bought a load of leveraged cement futures hours before that dam had burst in the US the other day. He was a hero, at least until someone made good on the next big trade.

Gao measured his dick in other ways. Since the untimely death of Zhang Zhenniang—*why had she offed herself before I could get into her panties, such a waste,* he mourned—he had enjoyed several other women, the distraction helping him to process the loss and move on with his life.

He felt certain he knew who his next score would be. This morning he had been visited by an absolutely stunning turn-on. Crisp and cold in her starched and tailored government uniform, he could only imagine what kind of hottie she would be once he melted the ice and she let her hair down. Risky but tantalizing, nonetheless.

Her name was Li Shishi. Shishi meant Teacher Teacher. He closed his eyes and saw her teaching him. What nuanced and rare sex practice with which she delighted him!

The morning's meeting had been arranged by SilvermanFuchs's in-house legal counsel and was related to a routine securities inquiry being made by the Financial Crimes branch of Public Security. A compliance officer sat in on the meeting, helped Gao when necessary, and/or promised full cooperation, but the questions asked were bland, and Gao was comfortable talking to her. At the end of the meeting, she had offered to connect with both of them on Skylink. The compliance officer had declined politely. *His loss,* Gao chuckled and accepted her invitation without hesitation.

In showing her out, Gao asked whether he could invite her to dinner in Shanghai and show her around, but she demurred saying she was rushing to get on a jet back to Beijing. She had, however, said she would love to see him if he ever made his way up to the capital.

Gao stabbed at the phone extension button calling his secretary. "Hanjian. Remember that deal I was working on in Beijing, pitching for the IPO on that JV fruit juice company?"

"Yes, sir. Sweet Mountain."

"That's the one. Whatever happened with that?"

"They went with JPM."

"I want to do a postmortem, figure out what we could have done to win it. Book me to fly up to Beijing tomorrow, ok?"

"Yes, sir, and I will try to make an appointment with Sweet Mountain to see you?" the question more of a statement.

"Oh. Yeah, ok. See if you can." *Work. It always gets in the way.*

⊃ 人 ⊂

COIN BELIEVED THAT PATIENCE WAS A VIRTUE, AND THAT IT was a virtue he extolled, exemplified even, but his patience was being tested, the president ruminated as he looked out at his team.

Beyond the difficulty and necessity of directing the aftermath of the dam collapse with swift effectiveness, the White House was having to defend itself against one spurious revelation or half-baked news story after another alleging a team in Washington fumbling in its efforts to get its arms around this tragedy and the many contradictions that had surfaced. Central to this was how the dam burst had happened and who or what was to blame.

Depending on their political stripe, the press promoted one view or another, all inflammatory and with significant but different economic and liability consequences. Of course, the insurance companies and utility were all praying that the investigation would determine an "act of God" had destroyed the dam, effectively relieving them of liability. Property owners and farms were praying that some negligence was found that would pin the blame on the dam owners. Environmentalists cited the unusually large rainfall in the catchment area as another sign of global weather change and sought to make hay as long as the sun shined on that story.

The White House had remained coy in its statements. "A full, thorough, fact-based, and unbiased investigation is taking place, and we will not speculate on the conclusions it may reach. When our investigation has made a determination, we will release findings along with recommendations."

Despite his patience, Coin was frustrated with that answer, and the facts being revealed to him behind closed doors were ever more frustrating, even more frightening. The mainstream press, left and right, was focused on the climate change and crumbling infrastructure narratives, and neither was pulling any domestic or international terrorism threads in this story. But that was precisely what it was looking like.

The director of the FBI had just been ushered into the Situation Room to report on the investigation. "Mr. President, this update is based on 9,000 man-hours of investigation so far and analysis involving agents in twenty different offices and cooperation from White House counsel and staff members," began Sydney Amdur in the dry, fact-based, prosecutorial manner for which he was known.

"As the Bureau made White House counsel aware when we obtained the cooperation of Nancy Nillson during this investigation, the Devon Alliance think-tank and its sponsor, Richard McCallister, became 'persons of interest.' Forensic examination of data captured in the servers at the off-site hydroelectric control center showed clear evidence that the system had been penetrated from outside. Our teams were able to determine that these commands emanated from servers located at Devon Alliance, and files located on McCallister's personal computer and mobile devices link him to this event.

"We obtained a Delayed Notice Search Warrant and conducted several data-collecting incursions without the subjects' knowledge. Details about the design and construction of the dam and specifications of control components, as well as some complex engineering analysis of harmonics within steel-rebar-reinforced concrete were all found on their computer systems. Other brainstorming ideas for ways to publicly discredit the organization known as Demeter were also found." Amdur looked into the president's eyes as he continued.

"McCallister and Devon Alliance staff are presently under surveillance, and Richard McCallister was brought in for questioning, but arrests have not been made for reasons I will get to. Because your administration has been a prominent target of the Demeter organization and McCallister was a significant donor to your party and election campaign, we have also had to investigate the possibility you or people in your administration knew about, abetted, or encouraged McCallister's actions. That investigation has been concluded. We found no evidence that McCallister was acting with the knowledge or support of the White House."

Coin looked stone cold at Director Amdur, who met his stare without averting his eyes. Never had his integrity been so impugned. Looking at the director's face, Coin processed this, trying not to express the rage he felt. He took a long, slow breath. *This man was doing his job, under trying circumstances, and had the courage to see it through and report this to my face. And after all, the news is "good," if that label can be applied.*

Coin softened his eyes, nodded his head gently, and said, "Director. I want everyone here to know how much I respect you for doing your job well, for carrying through what must have been a very difficult investigation and having the courage to follow the trail even when it led into territory which, if the facts had shown it to be true, would have torn this country apart."

"Thank you, Mr. President. Your words mean the world to me. There is, however, more to report. While the existence of the computer files about Oroville Dam and other dirty tricks they had brainstormed on their servers *are* physical evidence that cannot be denied, our forensic analysis of the hard drives suggests that, at least the files about the dam were downloaded on to their servers from the outside. The Devon Alliance people claim to have no knowledge of the files, and indeed, there is no indication that they ever accessed these files on their devices."

"Have your teams reached any conclusions?"

"They are working on it, sir, but are leaning toward the idea that some outside party, as yet unknown, planted the files and went through Devon's servers to conduct the hack into the power plant. As for the hack of the IP-AWS network and the tens of thousands of customized alert messages sent out, that took huge processing capacity and bandwidth to pull off. It was not done by Devon. Their system capacity was much too limited, and there is no evidence on their system of a connection to that hack. Again, separate teams continue to try to determine how the IPAWS hack occurred."

"So, we still cannot figure out who did this. The clock is ticking, ladies and gentlemen. The eyes of the American people and the world are on us. We need to pick up the pace."

"Mr. President, to that end, we have reached out to the NSA to assist in an analysis of this event by their attribution team. They are at work on it now."

Coin looked to William Hollister. "Yes, Mr. President, we have assisted the FBI in the past when the direction of an investigation did not preclude the possibility of a foreign party being responsible. The team is working on this as an absolute top priority. They are working on both the dam hack and the IPAWS network incursion."

Coin's eyes circled the table. "I just want to remind everyone in the room. The American people are counting on an effective response to the devastation caused by this. That means all the efforts at rescue and rebuilding. They also demand to know what happened and what we are doing about it. The way you handled this Devon investigation, Director Amdur, has prevented a huge, premature outcry for justice before we have correctly fingered the enemy. Thank you. Now, all of you get me the answers I need before this spins completely out of control, or this enemy strikes again."

Around noon, Mili Parekh's team received an urgent dispatch from the Department of Homeland Security, the Army Corps of Engineers, and the FBI. It was a unified request, accompanied by a note from the director of the NSA, to conduct a thorough attribution analysis of specific incursions, corruptions, orders, and relays of data that had taken place related to the Oroville Dam collapse. The director ordered that the analysis supersede any other work in process and be delivered to his attention directly. Parekh's boss called her as soon as the message was delivered to make certain she had seen it.

Parekh pulled in the entire team without delay, some even as they were heading out to lunch. "Ladiesh and gentlemen, I need you to drop whatever you are doing. We have an urgent mission. We are being ashked to look at data related to the dam break." Around the room, everyone's eyes opened wide and looked up at her, surprise on some faces, horror on others. They all understood what this meant; the disaster was not the accident it was purported to be.

"Core dumpsh of data from multiple locations including the dam control center, the regional IPAWS broadcast authority, and shome private computers and servers has been placed at our dishposal. It doesn't matter what team or geography you were on, today you are working on thish. We will form three teams."

She looked to Jill Westerhoff. "Jill, you take on Team 3 and the data from the private computer and servers."

She tweaked the joystick on her chair and faced a pair of analysts who were close friends and close rivals, both working on infrastructure attacks with different specializations, both at the top of their game. "Willish, I want you to head Team 1 working on the dam data. Aaron, I want you to work your magic on the IPAWS attack leading Team 2. You remaining infrastructure shpecialists," she said, referring to eight others, "you shplit up onto the teams, three each for Teams 1 and 2, two for Team 3. You will be group leaders within the teams. The balance of you," another forty souls, "you shplit up evenly where you think you can besht serve."

She waited a moment, looking out at them. "I mean *right now*, chop chop." Shaken from its collective stupor, the large group reaggregated over four minutes into three teams. She looked at each team briefly and shuffled four people around explaining to each why she felt their contributions were more needed in another group so they would not feel put off.

"The director is waiting for our analyshish... at the White House. Get to work quickly, focush on the event. I will circulate among you to provide guidance. Tell me as shoon as you determine if there wash indeed a hack, and tell me as shoon as you complete the attribution analyshish." Then they got to work.

And damn, she was proud of the team. They were pros, the best of the best, intellectual special forces warriors. They first dove into the data, making sense of what was included. What types of coding had to be analyzed, what was native to the systems they were examining, and what was alien or suspect or recently modified or imported. For each team, this was largely completed in the first hour. Confirmations for Teams 1 and 2 were strengthened by receiving files from previous backups of the systems from their respective target systems. The operation software for the hydroelectric power plant and especially the IPAWS network with its Common Alerting Protocols were well established and fixed; changes and modifications stood out in stark relief.

Next, they dug into the suspect, modified, and imported files. By the end of the second hour, each team had determined with high degrees of certainty that unauthorized incursions into the several systems had taken place. Parekh then tasked the teams to complete their third step on attribution without referring to each other. She did not want the process or conclusions of one team to bias the thinking of another team, especially if it turned out that their conclusions were all the same or all different.

The teams got to work. They used Parekh's memetic analysis system as well as Westerhoff's vintage tools. They dug into the results for further detailed analysis. Within the teams, they questioned and debated, tested and reached their conclusions.

When they returned, Parekh could not say she had any expectations about what the teams would learn or conclude. She had an open mind, which is to say although she imagined at least six opponents on the world stage that could have done this, she couldn't imagine exactly why they would, so she was open to learning it was anyone of them. With an open mind, she thought she would be immune to surprise, shock, or fear. But she was mistaken.

The three teams reached the same conclusion with high degrees of certainty. The former head of China's Unit 61398, whereabouts now unknown but assumed to be working in a more secretive and hence much more dangerous PLA group, had himself written the code that allowed the incursions. The PLA major Lin Chong nicknamed Panther Head.

The attributions yielded yet another surprise. Algorithms designed to take dam-vibration-monitoring signals to modulate the frequency and distribution of shocks, coding created to customize the IPAWS messaging, and some coding found within the Devon Alliance servers all had the memetic traces of Eunice Stravinsky. But, once again, that was not possible.

Not possible unless Stravinsky's work had been stolen or expropriated, initiated, and somehow used to code further work.

When this hit her, Parekh stared into the white of a bare wall, her mind covering that space with an imagined, blossoming mind map. Going back to the initial hack that led to Stravinsky's arrest and conviction, the meltdown of the London Metals Exchange, and linking ahead to other hacks attributed to her, there was a pattern that could be discerned. It seemed more like something North Korea or Russian gangsters would attempt to pull off on their best days, but she supposed, for some reason, it could have been China. Anyway, the "why" of a hack was not for her to focus on. To a certain extent it was the "how" and definitely the "who."

At 17:00 she sent a message to her boss and cc'd the director of the NSA. In it she included a seven-page briefing of the attribution team's conclusions. She asked the team leaders and infrastructure specialists to stay on duty as the night shift arrived. At 18:00 the desk phone rang, and she picked up.

"Dr. Parekh. This is Director Hollister calling."

"Yesh, shir, Mr. Director. You have received our report. How can I help you?" Although she had yet to speak to the director since President Coin appointed him, she was not surprised to get his call given the circumstances.

"Yes. Dr. Parekh. Your report is very disturbing. I understand you are our top expert in this field."

She was wary as she tried to tie the meaning of his two sentences together. "I have a great team, shir, we are *all* experts. But, yesh, I lead the team and we employ a methodology I pioneered. How ish the report dishturbing, shir?"

"Its conclusions. How certain are we of them?"

The percentage certainty had been indicated in the summary report. "Very shurtain, shir."

There was silence on the line. She had been put on hold. She waited.

Hollister came back on the line. "Dr. Parekh, a van will be waiting for you in ten minutes at the Fort Meade lobby to bring you here to the White House. The president would like to receive a briefing from you directly."

Parekh's heart skipped a beat, and she momentarily felt faint. "Shir. Yesh, shir. However, it will take me fifteen minutes to get to the lobby in my wheelchair. Are you shurtain you need *me* to brief the preshident?"

"Mili—may I call you Mili?—in the president's words, 'Before I go to war with China, I want to look into this analyst's eyes.' The van will wait for you." The line went dead.

Always grateful for little things, Parekh looked over her attire and sighed to no one that "At least it's not casual day."

As she raced her wheelchair through the halls, she stopped at Jill Wester-hoff's office and explained what was happening. Her deputy did not say anything, but the concern showed on her face. Parekh asked her to quickly print out some additional documents that might help her presentation to the president and run to the front lobby with them to hand off to Parekh before she departed.

She then continued through halls, badge-access-protected doors, elevators, more halls and doors until she reached the lobby. Westerhoff showed up shortly, panting, and handed over a sealed manila envelope marked "Top Secret - Eyes Only." Westerhoff helped get Mili loaded into the van, then looking into the tired, worn, and anxious expression of her boss, touched Mili's arm, looked into her eyes and said, "Don't worry, boss. You got this." Then she slid the van door closed and waved as it pulled away.

"Are you comfortable, Dr. Parekh?" the driver asked.

"Yesh, thank you."

"I know you prefer to take your self-driving van, but the secret service does not allow autonomous vehicles within the White House grounds."

"Makes shensh."

"Given your wheelchair, they did not want you to have to navigate the underground service access as most government staffers would. I will be driving you right up."

"Thank you for your conshideration." Parekh closed her eyes and reviewed in her memory the seven slides sent to the president.

She knew no matter what she said, his decision would be extraordinarily hard. She did not envy him the task. If he chose to go to war, discord, economic disruption, death, chaos, and a legacy of suspicion and hatred would follow. If he chose not to go to war, it meant there was either some other enemy out there to be taken on, or a lingering suspicion that China was the enemy but with an impotence to respond.

She hoped he would not choose to go to war based on her team's work alone. *Surely there were other ways to test if this foe was the perpetrator of this evil.*

She asked the driver for a bottle of water, which he opened for her at a stop light. She took a pill for her heart palpitations and then quieted herself for the rest of the journey. When they arrived at the West Wing, guards helped off-load her wheelchair and led her through security and onto the elevator to the basement and the hallway leading to the Situation Room. She was asked to wait outside before being ushered in.

Momentarily, William Hollister appeared. He took in her appearance and said, "Mili. Thank you for coming. The president, everyone here, needs your sober assessment of what you have learned from the attribution analysis. You up for it?"

"Yesh, shir. Thank you, I wish the opportunity to meet you wash under different circumshtances."

"It's part of our job, Mili. Normally, I would demand to spend some time with you, get comfortable with the idea of sending you into this, and make sure you understand what's at stake. We don't have time for that today. So, my trust in you will have to suffice," he smiled to calm her. "Okay, let's go in."

She followed him through the doors into the Situation Room, the stage on which dramas identified or directed by the national security advisor played out for the President. She recognized the heads of the CIA, the national security advisor and director of National Intelligence, and the directors of the FBI and DHS. And the president and vice president.

All eyes turned to the door as she entered. They peered to see who had been the one to call out China on this. But standing behind Hollister they saw... no one. Then in his shadow they made out her seated figure, short and bent. She sat slouched in her chair, leaning on her right elbow and using that hand on the joystick to maneuver her chair through them. Her hair was black and coarse and put up haphazardly into two buns for easy maintenance. Dark circles under her eyes seemed to be a feature, not just from recent lack of sleep and challenging work, and her spindly legs were wasting away.

He led her up to the front of the room. "Mr. President, I would like to introduce Dr. Mili Parekh. She heads up the attribution team at the NSA. She and her team have done great work in the past, work that has really aided us in decision-making about who to target. Dr. Parekh, I will turn it over to you."

An aide saw that she could not go to the podium or reach and hold a microphone, so she came over and clipped a mike to Parekh's blouse. "Thank you. Thank you, Director Hollishter, Mr. Preshident. I am here to ansher questions you have about the attribution analyshish we delivered to you thish afternoon."

Mick Coin looked on with deep misgivings. He was expected to make a grave decision, in the balance of which thousands of American, and no doubt many more Chinese, lives hung precariously. *Can't we do better than an Indian cripple?* a dark corner of his mind begged. He shook it off. "Dr. Parekh, can you briefly, for those of us who aren't cyber experts, describe the methodology you use to attribute the source of a threat? How reliable is it?"

"Yesh, shir. It shtarted with a theory that information, of which shoftware ish a type, ish transmitted or passed down wesh 'heredity' and 'shelection,' much like genes are passed down and can be traced back. I wash able to demonstrate that thish theory had truth to it under shurtain circumshtances . At the NSA, my team and I have been able to create a shophishticated tool and library of known shources or authors of code.

"When we get a piece of code from an unknown shource, we can run it through our lab, and if it matches a known coder, that shource comes up. If it does not match a known coder, we do a shecondary analyshish to determine what 'genetic strains,' if you will, what other coders' methods and shtyles, influenced the new unknown coder.

"Accuracy of a match depends largely on 1) the size and 2) the uniqueness of the shample. A small shample may not be enough to narrow down possibilities. And as you probably know, many off-the-shelf hacking tools are widely available and employed by bad people. If such code ish the only shample we have, it doesn't really tell us who did the hack. However, to the extent code wash cushtom written, it increases our confidence in the analyshish. May I explain any of that in greater detail for you?"

Coin appreciated that she had not said, "is that clear" or "do you understand." She had respected the group and him, offering to give more if they wanted it. "Thank you, Dr. Parekh. I am sure it is much more complicated, but you have given me a basic understanding. In the case of these attacks, how would you characterize the sample size and uniqueness?"

"You have undershtood very well. That ish the correct question," Parekh said, attempting her lop-sided smile. "In all three of the attacks we were ashked to analyze, the shample sizes were large, mush larger given some of the exploits being attempted than we usually have the opportunity to work wesh, and they were unique, cushtom written, and/or distinctly written by a known coder.

"In our ranking, any percentage of shurtainty given by the shishtem over 90 percent ish conshidered very reliable. In thish case, the percentages came out in the midnineties. To my knowledge covert actions have been taken against enemies when our shurtainty wash as low as 75 percent, and subsequent analyshish of signals intel proved we were right."

"So, you are asserting that China is definitely behind the attack on the dam?"

"I undershtand my ansher might cause some confusion, but again your question ish the right one. No. We are *not* asherting with 95 percent shurtainty that *China* attacked the dam. We *are* asherting with shurtainty that Major Lin Chong, formerly deputy head of China's elite cyber warfare unit, wrote some of the code used in the hack. However, he has dishappeared, dropped off the grid. We had ashumed he wash moved into an even more shecret unit. Thish may be its product. But frankly, we don't know where he ish or for whom he wrote this code."

"And what about this other coder identified. This anomaly. Does that completely sink your system's credibility, Dr. Parekh?"

"I had the shame concern and thought, Mr. Preshident, for the past several months. We have been trying to determine how it ish that Stravinsky's coding shtyle keeps popping up wesh unique new exploits. It wash only wesh today's appearance of it again in the analyshish that I began to believe that perhaps some foreign actor may have stolen Stravinsky's research and put it to use in ways she never anticipated, endorshed, or imagined. Could that actor be China? Yesh. Or North Korea or Russia or Iran."

"Based on your analysis, would you recommend I go to war with China?" the president asked her pointedly, testing her mettle.

"No, shir. Not yet. Not based sholely on this analyshish. My team and I only work on attribution. Perhaps we have other intelligence reshources not known to me that can determine where Lin Chong ish now and whether there ish a reason why China would risk attacking the US in thish way, at thish time."

"Dr. Parekh. I appreciate your honesty, clarity, and directness. I think we can now proceed with the knowledge that our country was attacked. Indications point to China.

"Dick and Bill," he said, speaking to the directors of the CIA and NSA, "if there is more intel on this Lin Chong, dig it out. And I want a briefing paper tomorrow on why China might do this. It doesn't make sense, but it's not the first time in their history that the government has made opaque and stupid decisions. As we were discussing before the arrival of Dr. Parekh, order the Ronald Reagan Carrier group to sail into the Taiwan straits, and put our forces in Korea, Okinawa, and Japan on alert. We are not going to war yet, but I want to be damn ready for one."

CHAPTER 8

THE WEEK HAD BEGUN WELL FOR QIU XIAOYI, CEO OF CHINA Central Airlines.

The call had come from on high that China would be putting its best foot forward on the world stage and in an eye-popping political turnaround would expedite shipment of emergency supplies to the Port of Oakland, California, US, to help survivors of the dam burst. Businesses with State investment were expected to patriotically pony up or chip in their contributions.

Qiu queried his managers on utilization of his fleet's air freighters and unused freight capacity on passenger flights bound for Los Angeles and San Francisco. His team got back to him within the morning, and he responded to the government. Yes, Central Airlines would be proud to lead the way and contribute.

Two freighters would make two round trips each to deliver nearly forty tons of tents, sleeping bags, inflatable mattresses, water bottles, water filtration kits, and other paraphernalia made in China and thought to be of use to those left homeless by the dam collapse. For an additional month, all spare freight capacity on passenger flights to those cities would be contributed gratis to the effort delivering other donated materiel.

From that point forward, Qiu's week had gone tits-up.

The next day an exposé had appeared in the online edition of the business and economics investigative reporting magazine, *JingCai*, with the title, "Central Airlines Mile-High Club." The cover photo was a doctored image of Qiu surrounded by his stewardesses dressed in bunny attire. He knew where that photo had come from. It had been taken with his phone, and he was the only one who had it.

The image was doctored to include a bunch of burlap rice bags stacked at the bunnies' feet with the character for rice grain, *Mi*, stenciled on them. Qiu grumbled at the allusion. Ever since the American film producer had spoiled the action for people like him by pushing the game too far and inspiring the #MeToo movement, the image or Chinese characters of rice, *Mi*, and rabbits, *Tu*, had come to symbolize the local reaction to sexual exploitation of women in the workplace.

The article was incredibly detailed and did not stop with its discussion of his hiring practices. It said that he was under investigation by three different bureaus for corruption, bribery, malfeasance, and insider trading. *How had they learned about this? And how come I got no word from the bureaus?* he simmered.

He ordered the airline's legal department to prepare its response even as the public relations department was drafting denials. The legal department had a stern conversation with the editor of *JingCai*. She said that the article had been written by "one of their stringer reporters, and I would be happy to double-check any facts reported that the airline could substantially dispute." She did not tell them that *JingCai* journalists had, indeed, not written or published the article, they did not know its provenance or who had put it up on their online news site, or that they were having difficulties deleting it and that it had already been picked up by other news services.

Finally, she said that they were checking with the bureaus mentioned in the article, and before she would publicly retract the story (and tell their readership that they had been hacked), she wanted to determine the veracity of the exposé's contents. She also noted in the conversation with the airline's lawyers that, even as they spoke, she was receiving scores of emailed testimonials from flight crew and unsuccessful candidates who were not mentioned in the article. They wanted their stories told to add sufficient weight to the allegations such that the Sky-Soaring Yaksa would tailspin back to earth.

The legal team then reached out to the bureaus mentioned. By the end of the day his legal team got back to him with what he considered to be *awful* news. They would not brief him on the results of their outreach to the bureaus, but informed him that they were, indeed, not *his* legal team. They were the *airline's* legal team. He should lawyer up and pull in whatever favors or wield whatever leverage he could to reduce the personal blowback.

The next morning when he arrived at the company, his personal assistant, who had always been an unflappable aide-de-camp, and whom he noted was herself a good shag, said nothing to him and gave him the evil eye when he walked past her into his office.

There, waiting for him in their dark blue uniforms, were representatives of the National Supervisory Commission. He was put in handcuffs and led out of the building into waiting SUVs.

It was not common that such disappearances were reported. Executives suspected of breaking the law—or who had stepped on the wrong toes—were disappeared. They would be held incommunicado, interrogated, and investigated until the case against them was sufficient to convict or they had "confessed" and revealed details as to coconspirators. If that took a week, a month, or a year, so be it. Subsequent trials were swift, convictions assured, and harsh sentencing followed. But the investigation and trial did not normally take place with public oversight or fanfare.

Not this time. Interest in Qiu generated by the *JingCai* article snowballed. The journal received word that Qiu had been arrested from a tipster. When they delayed reporting the fact, another online edition article appeared that had not been written by their journalists, complete with photos of the arrest and security camera footage of the disgraced CEO being led out in handcuffs.

Even the Green Guards got in the act. Riffing off the article's reporting that he had commandeered otherwise empty flights for his trysts, a contingent of Greens 5,000 strong arrived at the airline headquarters carrying placards depicting Qiu on his back getting serviced by a stewardess, his penis depicted as a belching smokestack, and charging him with the crime of the highest-carbon-footprint intercourse in the history of the world. These images, too, went viral.

The shares of the airline plummeted 25 percent in early afternoon trading on the Hong Kong exchange before stabilizing.

ㄹ 人 ㄷ

AMBASSADOR CHEN ZONGSHAN SAT BACK IN THE DEEP LEATHER seats of his limo as it pulled out of the embassy in Washington, DC, and headed to Connecticut Avenue for its twenty-minute ride to the State Department. Next to him sat his translator, Zhang Guanjia, who also served as his Party overseer, the snitch who would report back to the Party should he deviate from the line or not stand up to foreign powers that sought to bully China.

Chen did not doubt his English was better than Zhang's, but protocol demanded going through a translator. As for snitching, Chen did not worry. He was a septuagenarian who had seen leaders come and go while he had remained steadfast to the ideal of a strong China led by the clear mandate of the Party.

Born and raised in Qufu, Shandong, the birthplace of Confucius, he also clung to that foremost teacher's lessons on morality and correct behaviors of the ruler and the ruled. As such, he always kept in mind this maxim from the Confucian Analects, "When on a mission, wherever you go, abuse not the sovereign's command, and be a worthy emissary." His wife had passed three years before, the children had been educated and found their careers abroad,so he could afford to be upright, counsel his sovereign to the best of his ability, and follow his commands.

That morning he had gotten a call from the State Department requesting he present himself to Secretary of State Clarissa Roy. The request had come direct from her office, through normal channels, but had not revealed the reason the meeting was being called.

He reached out to the Ministry of Foreign Affairs before departing for the meeting to understand if there was anything awry of which he should be aware. They had no specific feedback for him. He turned to Zhang. "I had not expected thanks, especially so soon."

"Yes. They must be busy dealing with the crisis in California. I am surprised they are taking the time to call us in. Maybe it's to complain that the amount of aid we have promised is not enough." Zhang the translator shook his head in disgust and issued a dark chortle. "What do you know about Roy?"

"I have met her several times. The first when she was ambassador to Somalia and I was based there, too. Later, we sat on a panel at an international security conference back when she was the national security advisor in that other administration. And here."

"It must be difficult as a Black woman to hold her own in a White man's world."

Zhang's comment mocked sympathy. It was barbed and couched in an inveterate racism and cultural bias Ambassador Chen had come to expect from Zhang. Chen was not biting. "She is intelligent, hardworking. Speaks

Russian and seems to understand that adversary well. I would say she has strong ethics. We are not aligned on many subjects, but where we disagree, I know it is based on fundamental principles we do not share in common."

"That may be, but she must come to each meeting with at least some nagging doubts about herself, her inadequacy."

Chen understood Zhang's perspective and did not share it: the racial and cultural pecking order China was recalibrating to disrupt the twenty-first century.

This line of thinking went that China had been resplendent throughout history, equal in territory, cultural riches and civilization to any of the world's other empires, be they Greek, Roman, Mayan, Egyptian, Ottoman. But whereas each of those empires lasted centuries, China's culture had endured millennia, a continuous chain of progress and growth, bigger and better, more civilized than any nation.

This was accomplished without brutally subjugating and enslaving other races far afield. Respect was all China demanded. Throughout Europe's thousand years of Dark Ages, when the common man lived in squalor, destitution, fear, peril, and ignorance, China had science, poetry, art, morality, and throughout its history a merit-based system of governance built on intellectual elites that tested into the ranks of the bureaucracy, open to anyone, even the common man, who could pass. The West only rose when they remembered their past with the Renaissance and picked up where they had left off, igniting renewed interest in science and the arts. From there, the West lost its moral compass, exploiting technology to subjugate fellow humans on five continents and enslave or colonize them.

While Chen agreed with the historical perspective, Zhang's thinking followed that those cultures falling to the West did so because they were inferior culturally, perhaps even genetically. And if you came from such a culture, you would carry that sense of shame and inferiority, and know that others always disdained you.

Zhang would say, *China had not fallen to the West. It had stumbled, yes, at the end of the Qing Dynasty, actually it was tripped by the West, but it had not fallen. China's revolution was as much a response to beating back Western encroachments with Chinese pride as it was a vacuum-filling response to an enervated and flaccid dynasty that had run its course.*

Even China's adoption of Communism was not a wholesale capitulation to Western culture. It had always been implemented as "Socialism with Chinese

Characteristics." Chinese civilization was superior in every way to the West: its staying power, its cultural institutions, its diligent people.

Chen's view was, he personally hoped, more balanced and nuanced. He tried to measure each person's merits as an individual. In the modern era, that sense of individualism had served the West well and transformed the world. He did not see a contradiction between the strength of the individual and the greater good so long as individuals were well educated, a caveat opined by Confucius.

After his long deliberation, Chen replied, "I have not found Roy to be 'inadequate' or self-doubting. Let's just keep open minds today and see what she needs to discuss with us."

The car pulled into the guest's entrance of the State Department, their identities and appointment were confirmed by security, and they were allowed to park. They were greeted in the lobby with another security check and escorted to a waiting area outside the secretary's office. After a short wait they were ushered into a private space paneled in blond wood with a large multicolored carpet of Middle Eastern design on the floor filling the room.

Ambassador Chen Zongshan strode in first, his hand outstretched to shake hers and a warm, gentlemanly smile on his face. "Secretary Roy, it is an honor to meet you in your office." He let Zhang translate.

Roy looked at the proffered hand coldly. It was a cultural stereotype, she knew, that "Orientals are inscrutable," but she really had not expected to see the relaxed bonhomie on Chen's face and did not know what to make of it. She took the hand and gave it a short, sharp tug while staring into Chen's eyes without any trace of goodwill.

She beckoned him to sit in an armchair opposite her. A chair had not been prepared for Zhang, to which he took umbrage, while Roy's translator sat in comfort next to the sofa onto which Roy placed herself, organized her skirt, posture and hands placed formally and rigidly, one over the other, on her lap.

They were not asked if they wanted tea or coffee, another sign, Chen worried, that this meeting would be short and sharp and might not be about anything he expected. When they had all settled, there was a long silence while Roy looked across at Chen until he averted his gaze and wrung his hands.

"Ambassador Chen. Do you know why your presence has been demanded today?"

Presence demanded? "No, Madam Secretary. I was expecting it was to discuss the aid China is providing to the relief efforts in California or perhaps the upcoming UN General Assembly meeting between our presidents."

Roy's eyes sharpened. "No. It is not. Quite the contrary." She knew he knew what she had said but gave the translator time to work. "We have incontrovertible evidence that the destruction of the Oroville Dam in California was an act of aggression perpetrated by a foreign power. We have already raised the level of alert for our troops throughout the Asia-Pacific region."

As she spoke and as it was translated, she looked into Chen's eyes. She observed him squint as if the news were physically painful. He looked up to a corner and then to the opposite searching for reason in such a terrible act, his head tilted quizzically to the right. If he knew anything about this before entering her office, she thought, he was putting on a good show of ignorance.

North Korean motherless bastards, Chen thought, *what have they done now?* "In previous acts of global terrorism against your country, China has stood with you. Let me know what you would like me to convey to my government."

Not the answer Roy had expected, but she was glad she had not started by naming China as the attacker. Better to see how this played out. "It is vitally important that you convey the following message without *any* ambiguity. Our evidence points to the PLA as the perpetrator. We can even be more specific; Major Lin Chong of your cyber corps produced this attack."

Stung by the unexpected, Chen felt it was critical to shift into diplomat-speak immediately. "China has long held only peaceful objectives in the region and would never unilaterally attack the United States..."

"I'll cut you off right there, Mr. Ambassador. Communicate our findings to your president. We expect a thorough and forthcoming response within twenty-four hours. We need China to provide a complete understanding why we should not retaliate with devastating force. Let that sink in, Mr. Ambassador. We are not talking about sanctions. China is at risk of being totally destroyed. War is not in the interests of our nations, but we will not let this act of aggression go unanswered." She let that be translated. "And if we detect your forces going on alert, missiles fueling up, carrier groups changing course, anything apart from the ordinary, we will take *that* as your response, and you will have ours."

She waited. Chen was about to speak up again, but she cut him off. "You are dismissed."

⊃ 人 ⊂

MILI NIMBLY GUIDED THE WHEELCHAIR INTO THE ROOM THAT had been set aside for Jill Westerhoff, Harley Barrows, and the team to explore the Stravinsky Anomaly, as they had dubbed it. There were print-outs and journals stacked on the table and on the long glass wall were mind maps and notes, some blocked in with heavy lines warning not to erase them, some documents adhered with Blu Tack. The day prior Mili had assembled her full team. They had all pulled hard on the oars to get the analysis done for the president. She wanted the team to know their con-tributions were appreciated and that she had survived the meeting, she joked with them.

Today she wanted to circle back to this loose end. As she sat looking at the progress on the boards, Jill and Harley came in. "Hey, boss," Westerhoff said cheerfully.

"Hey. Sho, how are we doing on thish?" Mili asked looking at the expanse of, to her perspective, unconnected thoughts on the board. "What have we learned?"

"Harley, you wanna give her the summary?"

Barrows smiled sheepishly, "Yes, please. Progress has been slow, and based on Stravinsky's journals we will not be able to reproduce her full program. Too many gaps. I am reminded of the cartoon of the scientist writing a complex physics computation on the blackboard. Between the main body of the formula and the end result is a piece in brackets that says 'and here a miracle occurs.'"

Mili strained to laugh but coughed weakly instead. "What's misshing?"

"In parts of her journal she references other people's work. Not coders. It's clear she is pointing out things that inspired her to write some bridging pieces within the code, or in some cases the core guiding principles behind how she wrote the code. But she doesn't include the bridging pieces.

"Just getting my noodle around these references has taken a long time. We are talking a laundry list of subjects of which I have never even heard: dense tomes on representational qualia theory, Gestalt isomorphism, on-tology, cognition, Buddhist logic and epistemology, even channeling ener-gy through chakras. Basically, big thinkers thinking about how we think and perceive, or perceive and think, in ways we don't normally think. Did I use enough 'thinks' in that sentence?"

Mili realized she had hoped too much for the outcome of this meeting, and anxiety was creeping in. "Looking at the notes Bill Singh wasn't sure whether it wash gibberish or not. As I requested you to determine, ish it gold dusht or bull shit?"

"Can I back up and tell you what I think she was trying to achieve first?"

Mili closed her eyes and took a breath. "Ok."

"Artificial intelligence research we have done ourselves or know is being done is focused on getting the AI to do something as well as or better than a human. Play a human game, fool a human that they are talking to another human, sort through mounds of data that would take an individual human years to do in seconds and make inferences about what the data tells us, or conversely perform a complex human task we do every day that relies on vast amounts of sensory input, computation, and judgement to do safely, like driving a car."

Mili, eyes still closed, nodded and waved her hand in circles, trying to orchestrate a pickup in pace.

"Yeah, ok, you got it. So, this was *not* her approach. From what I can tell, Stravinsky was not designing her AI to 'do' anything in particular. She wrote lots of general coding around perceiving, understanding, and acting within a world not our own, the online world. She wrote the program to gestate this AI, have it come into being, be aware of itself and exist."

"That's it? Exist?"

"Yep. There was no 'purpose,' per se, written into it."

"No LME meltdown, no emptying people's bank accounts, no dam busting?"

"Nope. Nothing. As for the question you posed yesterday, what if it was taken over by a third party? China, let's say. I haven't been able to connect the dots between what Stravinsky wrote and these actions.

"Clearly, software written to execute these exploits had her fingerprints. So, someone may have taken her work and weaponized it. Perhaps created some sort of autonomous weapon. Or the enemy's research into the why and how of her coding style was so deep and certain that their downstream programs written using her style fooled our system. Why they would choose her coding style as a model to write these weapons, I have no idea, unless it is only to put the blame on her and obscure their footprints. If that is the case, why would they leave Lin Chong's program so clearly written in *his* style for the other parts of the attack?"

"Unless someone has cloned Lin Chong's style of coding, too," Westerhoff broke in.

Mili felt nauseous and continued to sit with her eyes closed. She did not want people to go to war, for tens of thousands to die, on account of her inability to do her job well. She felt no closer to an answer, no closer to being able to tell the president for sure what attribution was telling them.

"Boss, you okay?" Jill asked with concern.

ⱻ 人 ⊂

THE WORD DELIVERED TO PRESIDENT ZHAO JI WAS QUICK, DIrect and unambiguous. And for the first time in his adult life, he felt an icy thread of cold terror run in his veins.

It was late evening when the minister of foreign affairs called him and requested that he go to a location with a secure encrypted line. Once ensconced in his booth, he sent a message to the minister, and the video conferencing system glowed with the logo of the Ministry of Foreign Affairs. Shortly thereafter, the minister's face appeared. "Mr. President. I have Ambassador Chen Zongshan on the line. He has a message to be conveyed to you from the American secretary of state that cannot wait."

The screen split to show the minister and the ambassador. "Mr. President, sorry to disturb you so late, but this cannot wait."

"Yes, Ambassador Chen. I know you would not call this meeting over something trifling. What is it?"

"Sir, I was called urgently and unexpectedly to the office of Secretary of State Clarissa Roy and just got out of it forty-five minutes ago. I had to get back to the embassy to make this call. She has accused China of orchestrating the attack on the dam that burst in California."

"What?! The news has been saying it was a poorly built dam that just collapsed."

"Without offering proof, she said they have 'incontrovertible evidence,' her words, that a member of the PLA is behind the attack. A member of the cyber corps. A Major Lin Chong."

Him again? Zhao thought, his pulse picking up, his mind racing. *Is there no limit to what my enemies will do to discredit and topple me?*

"Of course, I reassured the secretary that China has no ambitions or plan to attack America. That is correct, is it not?"

"Yes, Ambassador Chen, you spoke correctly. What are the Americans doing?"

"They have put their forces on alert. She said they expect us to provide a thorough and forthcoming explanation within twenty-four hours why America should not retaliate using all military resources at its disposal. She added that if, in these twenty-four hours, America detects Chinese forces going on alert, an increase in our state of readiness, any change to routines they monitor, the US president will initiate their attack immediately."

"Who else knows about this?"

"On our side, just four people: me; my translator, Zhang Guanjia; you, Mr. President; and the minister."

"Tell no one. I will deal with this matter here."

"Yes, Mr. President. May I respond to Secretary Roy that I have delivered the message faithfully and that she can expect our answer within the twenty-four hours?"

"Yes. Assure her again that China had no such plot or intention, thank the secretary for giving us time to investigate and respond and promise we will report back within twenty-four hours. Thank you, Ambassador." Zhao touched the screen to terminate the call.

He called Su Yuanjing, waking him from his sleep, and told him to call Cai Jing and for them both to get over to the Operations Theater Command Center at the Central Military Commission, where Zhao would meet them.

He then called the vice chairman of the Central Military Commission, Admiral Liu Menglong, and told him to assemble the CMC. When asked why, Zhao replied brusquely to "just do it." The admiral then asked if troops should be put on alert. "Absolutely not." He made a third call to General Gao Qiu and told him he would shortly be requested by Admiral Liu to dial in to the CMC. He ordered him to be prepared to report on the investigation into the fugitive Lin Chong.

On arriving at the CMC Operations Theater Command Center, Zhao took his place at the table in the middle of the cavernous oval room. The Command Center was similar to the White Tiger Sanctum in terms of modernity and function, but here could be seen the readiness and deployment of China's five command theaters, north, south, east, west and central, any global deployments including the location of Special Forces, submarines, air squadrons in flight, and carrier battle groups.

Admiral Liu stood by his side awaiting orders. "Sir, the theater command generals are all ready to meet with you."

"Thank you, Admiral. Brief me first on our force status."

"Sir, as you have directed, our troops are preparing for the Operation Emerald Isle wargames. The Southern Theater will represent land and air-based forces defending Hainan while the Eastern Theater will represent our air, sea, and land forces seeking to recapture the island."

"Public announcements about the games have been issued, warnings in shipping lanes and commercial air routes?"

"Yes, sir. As per standard procedure."

"Embassies, foreign military advisors, and observers all apprised?"

"Yes, sir."

"Has the US sent any observers?"

The admiral looked at Zhao and furrowed his brow. "Sir? No, sir, American observers have not been invited. We have noted that their Seventh Fleet has sailed from Yokosuka and is heading for the China Sea between Taiwan and Fujian Province. We assume this is a warning and also to be able to better observe, uninvited, our games."

Since the founding of the People's Republic in China in 1949, its Chinese Communist Party leaders had been pointedly clear about the absolute primacy of their mission to restore the physical integrity of China's geography when the splittist Nationalist Party retreated to Taiwan to run its Republic of China sideshow. The map of China was imagined as a proud rooster, the northeast seen as its cockscomb and beak, the west as its luxuriant tail, central and east as the body and breast. The rooster's testicles, Macao and Hong Kong, had been recovered, though mishandling of what should have been a minor point of law now turned Hong Kong into the Beirut of Asia. The rooster stood on two feet, the islands of Hainan and Taiwan.

Operation Emerald Isle employed China's Hainan Island to simulate a full-on land invasion to recapture Taiwan, to restore that important foot. China would once more stand tall and proud and stable on two feet when the real mission, not the simulation, could be accomplished.

America steadfastly opposed the forced repatriation of Taiwan and had made good coin through the decades selling defensive military systems to the island. But negotiations with the Taiwanese could never move forward without a credible Chinese threat that if they failed to reach agreement, the choice would be taken out of their hands. Each year the credibility of the threat increased.

Zhao could see that Su and Cai had arrived and were being ushered to his location. "Alright, Admiral, we can start the meeting."

Admiral Liu led the three into a smaller, windowless conference room, 'The Cage," that was shielded from laser or radio eavesdropping by a Faraday cage built into its walls and had only fiberoptic telecommunications connections that were fully encrypted end to end. It was used to hold meetings between theater command generals who sat in similar rooms.

When they had taken their seats, the images of generals in the north, south, east, and west command centers appeared.

From his teleconference seat on the fleet command ship, Duanwu Hao, off the coast of Hainan preparing for the wargames, Gao Qiu was surprised to see Cai Jing sitting at the CMC close to the president. This was unexpected. But he was certain he knew what this was about.

The resources of the Prosperous Glory Association were broad and deep. One of those resources was Zhang Guanjia in Washington, DC. He had learned from Zhang about the meeting that had just taken place with the secretary of state even before President Zhao had called him. He had already informed Gao Yanei to anticipate market volatility and to be prepared take advantage.

Zhao started the meeting, "I know each of you is playing some role in the wargames about to commence. I do not want to interrupt those games or alter our plans in any way, but I do need a response from you on a matter of utmost national urgency." He let that sink in.

"The US has implicated one of our cyber warriors in the destruction last week of the dam in California. They are demanding proof from China that this was not an act of war, failing which they will launch an attack on China."

He looked into the faces of the men in the room and those whose images were on the screen. Only Gao Qiu's was unmoved.

"The person implicated is Major Lin Chong, formerly in command of Unit 61398. The US apparently does not know that Lin Chong is a fugitive here charged with treason and murder and is suspected of complicity in the flash protests that took place during the American president's state visit. I have called Cai Jing into this meeting as he linked Lin Chong to the protests and General Gao, who is leading the investigation on the PLA side. I need an update from you both now on the status of investigation."

Gao Qiu swallowed hard. It was important for him to lead on this, lest Cai Jing have some contradictory statement in mind. He spoke up preemptively, "Yes, sir. When we realized our investigations were focused on the same culprit, we combined resources. Lin Chong still evades detection, which means he has evaded capture. We had a reliable lead that the real-estate magnate Chai Jin had provided shelter and resources to Lin Chong in his escape. We sought to bring him in for questioning, during which time his guard shot one of the operatives working on the case and his bodyguard.

"Chai Jin was detained, but before he revealed useful intel about Lin Chong, he was himself broken out of our detention center in a highly coordinated and professional attack."

Seeing that Su Yuanjing was also present at the CMC, Gao doubled down on the hand he was dealt. "The raiders wore National Supervisory Commission uniforms, but some of their tactics we knew would not be used by the NSC. For example, they gassed all the occupants of the detention center. We determined that this was a ruse. Unfortunately, we have not been able to determine where Chai Jin was taken, nor where Lin Chong is. As we speak, we continue the search."

The president looked at Cai Jing. "Anything to add to that? Anything different to report?"

Cai Jing looked warily about the room. He had never been to the CMC, certainly had never met President Zhao. Rather than feeling a sense of awe and gratitude, he felt dread.

Whatever gilt threads were woven into his relationship with Gao Qiu, they did not begin to near the value of what he stood to lose at this stage: his honor, job, liberty, and possibly his life. "Add? Different? Sir, Lin Chong has evaded detection because most of our tools *for* detection are technology-based, something he knows how to avoid, evade, circumvent. We do not even know for sure if he is in China. We are going on that assumption because of the raid to free Chai Jin. If he is not in a place where he is likely to be seen by agents of the government, who know we are looking for him, then he will not be reported."

"Are we helpless to find this guy?" Su Yuanjing spoke up.

"No, sir, but we may need to step up the type of search."

"How so?"

"I would suggest a nationwide police alert, perhaps even announced on the evening news. 'Help the government to capture a most wanted fugitive.' This will signal to the Americans even before you report back to them that we consider Lin Chong a criminal."

"Okay. But what can I go back to the Americans with?"

Gao Qiu spoke up. "Sir, we have to ask ourselves, 'How do the Americans know who Lin Chong is, and how have they implicated him?' Are they just making this up as they go along to justify another endless war and deflect criticism away from their neglected, second-rate infrastructure? Or did they put Lin Chong up to it?"

The shocked eyes of the other generals could not be read conclusively.

The president interrupted him, "This can't be a made-up war. A war between China and the US, unthinkable as the outcome would be for China, would devastate the global economy and trade, and that means the US economy, too. The cost is far too high for any benefit they could accrue on the home front. And if they put Lin Chong up to this, why accuse him?"

"Then there is another consideration," Gao spoke up conceding that point and moving on to another. "If they know Lin Chong did this, perhaps they can tell us where the hell he is. I mean, if we cannot find him or even know for sure if he is in China, how can they say they have incontrovertible evidence he did this? It is reasonable to assume they have some way we don't know to track him."

Zhao's eyes widened. He had not said they had "incontrovertible evidence," though he had been told by the ambassador that was precisely their statement. He let it go for the moment. "Chief Cai, do you believe they could know where he is?"

"They lead the world in cyber surveillance and tools of digital destruction. If they can track him, we will have to rethink everything we know about the security of our troops, our infrastructure, our data. But, yes, it is possible. Asking for their help in tracking him could give us clues as to their capabilities."

Su Yuanjing shifted in his seat, then leaned forward, placing his hands on the table. "I want to go back to what you said, Chief Cai, about Lin's capabilities versus our detection methods. I agree that if we are only trying to find him through digital surveillance, we are unlikely to succeed. How can we physically step up the effort?"

Admiral Liu spoke up, "What are you doing to follow up on the Chai Jin tie?"

"His headquarters' office in Shanghai was raided and records taken. No direct clues about Lin Chong," answered Cai.

"Can we just start with physical surveillance of Chai's properties? Isn't it more likely he will be hiding in one? Go one by one, door to door within them until we find Lin Chong or Chai Jin or someone willing to talk."

"His personal properties, the properties owned by Yida, and his relatives' holding companies' properties number several thousand across the country, each with hundreds of residences or business units. We did not feel it was a productive use of manpower."

Zhao spoke up. "This is China. We have the manpower. Mobilize it but do it city by city. Go where he has the most properties first; start with the Shanghai to Nanjing corridor. Tighten the noose. Make business intolerable for Yida Properties. I need something to go back to the Americans with."

Su spoke up, "Sir, you have your meeting scheduled with the American president in two weeks during the UN General Assembly. May I suggest we try to buy some time? Certainly, tell the US about the fugitive Lin Chong and our unsuccessful efforts to track him, how we have stepped up efforts with their accusation, but that indeed any help they could render in finding him would be appreciated. And say that you would like to personally talk to Coin about this in New York."

Zhao was quiet for a moment thinking. "Okay. I'll also remind them that Operation Emerald Isle starts today. We can't *not* hold the exercise as they would see that as moving to a war footing. But with their fleet and ours both in that corner of the sea, all I can say, comrades, is 'no screw-ups allowed.' Just proceed with the exercise. Order all our forces, land, sea, and air to ignore the Americans. Give them a wide berth.

"Let them watch, send up their spy planes, whatever. Don't react, don't seek to escort, and don't provoke them. We must get through the next week without mishap. They are armed for war. This week we are armed for games."

⊐ 人 ⊏

ZHAO JI HAD RETURNED TO ZHONGNANHAI FOR AN EVENING OF rough sleep. He had received several messages from Little Li saying she had something important to share with him. He ignored these. The enormous events unfolding were too distracting. Whatever she had to report was not so important, whatever distraction she might provide was not enough.

The next morning, he saw that Li Shishi had continued to try to reach him and had pulled Su into the messages. Su had responded to her that Zhao was occupied with something more important. When Li had written back, "No, YOU NEED TO HEAR THIS!" they had relented and called a meeting.

Zhao had finished his breakfast when Su and Li were escorted in. "Little Li, I appreciate your dedication and drive, but we are facing a crisis now, and I hope you can respect our time. What is it that is so important that we had to have this meeting?"

This was the kind of moment when Li Shishi regretted the ambiguous relationship with these powerful men. *They respect me, to a limit, never as an equal, and beyond that what am I? A toy? A pampered child? Fuck that.* She frowned. "Firstly, I know the crisis you are keeping secret; the US accuses us of destroying the dam and may go to war with China over it. Right or not?"

Zhao and Su looked at each other. How had this news gotten so far so fast?

"Don't deny it, I can read it in your faces. What I have been trying to get your attention about the past twelve hours is not this intel, but the web I have uncovered that has access to this intel and uses it. If not the center of the Shanghai Clique, it's at least a major node of it."

"You know the deadline I am under?"

"Yes. Let me walk you through my past couple of days."

Zhao looked at his watch, then at Li. "The summary version."

"After our last meeting, Commissioner Su was focused on trying to track the disappearance of Chai Jin. My Skylink hack of Cai Jing revealed texting between him and General Gao Qiu about the progress of the investigation into Chai, and how Gao employed his relatives to put pressure on the Chai family and lure Chai Jin out. The arrest of Chai Jin did not go smoothly; two people were shot dead by Chai's bodyguard. Chai was taken into detention."

Su broke in, "His arrest was highly unusual. It was not logged as a State Security, Public Security, or PLA military police operation. Off the books. The detention center Chai Jin was taken to was not operated by any of these entities."

Li continued, "I sifted back through past communications between Cai and Gao. One of them, a couple of months ago as this started to ramp up, was a video conference Cai attended with General Gao and someone identified as Gao Yanei. I had disregarded this thread before, but when Gao Qiu involved his cousin Gao Lian, the provincial governor, in the Chai matter, I started to dig into it again. Turns out Gao Yanei is the nickname of Gao Shide, the adopted son of Gao Qiu, and a partner at SilvermanFuchs."

Zhao's eyes opened slightly wider and rolled up searching his memory for that name. He then looked back into Li's eyes and nodded his head.

"In parallel, I am trying to learn more about Lin Chong," Li continued. "I had reported to you last time about his bland financial records and family situation. I started looking more into his wife. Turns out, she killed herself a couple of weeks after Lin's arrest.

"So earlier this week I made a trip to Shanghai to try to move some of this forward. I met with the people at the Shanghai Symphony who had employed her, told them I was investigating the Lins, and needed information about the wife. The director's answers were supportive, but self-servingly damning of Lin's wife."

"What was the wife's name?"

"Zhang Zhenniang."

Zhao's eyes again went in search of a memory. "I heard her solo once. An angel."

Li raised her eyebrows but held her tongue realizing she could not make claims on Zhao's heart. "Again, I used the Skylink trojan to connect with the director. Looking back through his communications regarding Zhang, whose name should pop up? Gao Yanei."

"So is Lin Chong in cahoots with General Gao and the Shanghai Clique?"

"No. It is much sadder than that. I made an appointment to see Gao at SilvermanFuchs. Such a sleazy wolf. He eagerly takes my Skylink connection, then flies up to Beijing *the very next day*, yesterday, to see me and ...well, what he thinks he can get for a dinner is just beyond the pale!

"But this is where the threads begin to form a tapestry. I am still going through his mobile device and cloud data. However, I already have a trove of evidence that he had a crush on Zhang, Lin's wife, and sought to seduce her by putting pressure on the symphony to arrange a private dinner, media events they attended together, etc. When that didn't work, or maybe because it did work but she said, 'You have to get rid of my husband,' he leveraged his father. Seems the general set up Lin Chong to get him out of the way for his son."

Zhao could not believe his ears. *Why would a general sell out the country for a piece of tail, not even for himself, but for his bastard son?* He voiced his incredulity.

"Jackpot. Because even though the son is an out-of-control, cock-hound constantly sniffing out new cunts, he is also the key to hiding the general's wealth and investing ill-gotten gains. And of that, we have proof, too."

"Such as?"

"Copies of communications from within the Chinese embassy in Washington about the progress of trade negotiations, timestamped before formal announcements were made. These were sent from the general to Gao

Yanei. He then ordered shorting or going long on the market depending on the tone. Trades were done offshore in hidden asset accounts.

"Another example, the communication last night. Shall I read it to you? 'US State Department claims incontrovertible evidence that Lin Chong of China PLA responsible for California dam destruction. Demands response within twenty-four hours or will attack China.' Gao Yanei is still chewing on this one, trying to figure out what investment angle to play."

The three sat silent for a long while as the manifold implications of this depraved scumbaggery cascaded through their imaginations.

Finally, Zhao spoke up. "Do we know who the leak at the embassy is?"

"It is not signed."

"Time stamp?"

"Yesterday, 11:32 a.m. East coast time, 23:32 in Beijing."

Zhao remembered clearly that he was in the teleconference with Ambassador Chen at that moment. "So, it was the translator. What did he say his name was?" he thought aloud. "Zhang Guanjia." He thought about another loose end. "Do we know anything more about Lin Chong from this? After all, he is the one the Americans are fingering."

"I looked at correspondence dated around the teleconference between Cai, Gao, and his son. Gao Yanei was to have had a piece of the action on the rare-earth-minerals mining company and had to backpedal with other partners and investors. He also communicated with his father asking what was happening on the Lin Chong front, since he wanted to keep the pressure on Zhang Zhenniang. They believed Lin Chong had something to do with the exposure of the rare-earth deal."

"So, we can conclude that Lin Chong is not and was not a member of Gao Qiu's cabal. But that doesn't make him a good guy. He's implicated in the flash protests. Remember the line in the Demeter proclamation that comes from Lin Chong," Su reasoned.

"Nothing I have seen screams that Lin Chong has a beef with you, President Zhao, or America. And the people laying this accusation about him are the ones we know are lying bastards," Li said.

"Except the line from the poem," said Su.

She sighed. "Except the line from the poem."

"And the pointed accusation from the Americans," said Zhao.

She sighed again shaking her head. "And the Americans. I think he is just a victim in this. Not a player."

Zhao looked at Su, knowing each was thinking the same thing: *Was this girlish naïveté speaking, or did she have some bankable reason or instinct driving her judgement?*

Zhao spoke up. "Little Li, you did the right thing demanding the meeting. Your instincts were right. That leaves me to decide what to do within," he looked at his watch, "the next ten hours to reply to the Americans. Su, any progress contacting the person who sent the video of Chai Jin's escape?"

"Timely Rain? Working on it. No progress yet. The team has said it is extremely time-consuming and potentially fruitless to try to trace back the routing of the email."

"Step on it. I think that may be the key to reaching Chai and Lin. At this point, I fear if the security apparatus gets a hold of them first, they will make sure they die in the process just to cover their tracks. At the same time, I have already given Security their marching orders. I can't look erratic now. And I must craft the planned response to the Americans. We are really threading a needle here, comrades. Don't fail me."

After Zhao said her instincts were right and while the two men reached their conclusions, Li decided to take a simple, direct approach. Su's team had no doubt been making all kinds of heroic efforts to try to trace the message back to its source. Chance of success: unlikely, she told herself.

She took out a notepad computer and opened the Green Onion dark web search tool and entered "Timely Rain." A number of returns appeared, but one simple description stood out, a message box for Timely Rain. She opened it and left a note: "Timely Rain, your video from the Well was received. We need to talk. The Teacher." She hit "enter."

Ten seconds went by. An answer appeared. "Who are you?"

Li smiled an inner smile. "To prove you are the Timely Rain I am seeking, tell me who was on the video."

"Chai," came the immediate reply.

Just as Zhao was saying, "Don't fail me," Li clapped her hands triumphantly. "I am now talking to Timely Rain!"

⊃人⊂

IN THE CONFERENCE ROOM OF THE RIGHTEOUS FRATERNITY, Song Jiang stared at his mobile device. Lord Chai had called the meeting to report that as of this morning, all his properties in Shanghai had been raided, hard drives and documents from the property management offices had been seized, and door-to-door searches were being conducted within the properties. Chai said the authorities were finally playing hardball.

Song Jiang looked up and, at a loss for words, could only wave his hand excitedly.

"You got something to say, Song?" Chai Jin said.

"Fellows, I think Su Yuanjing just reached out to us!"

There were looks of surprise and incomprehension around the table.

"You remember I sent a copy of the video of Lord Chai's escape to Su, the head of the NSC, to put them on the scent of Gao and his cronies." The looks around the table eased, or became more concerned, depending on the person.

"Hmm, this could either be exceedingly good, or exceptionally bad," the Little Tornado said. "Why has he reached out?"

"Says we need to talk."

"No possibility your line can be traced back here?"

"It would take forever."

"If it is Su, I trust him. Make sure."

Song typed into his messenger, "Prove you are Su Yuanjing."

The reply came back immediately. "I am not Su Yuanjing. I work for him and the president. What do you want to know? They are here with me."

Chai Jin spoke up, "Ask where and when Su and I first met up."

The reply came back, "In Shenzhen on the laying of the foundation stone for Yida's Trade Summit skyscraper."

"What did he say to me when he shook my hand, and what did I reply?"

"The same thing. 'For the glory of China.'"

"Okay. It's Su. Ask why they are reaching out if they are raiding my properties at the same time?"

Song thumbed in the question and read the response. "Apologies. Things complicated. We need to talk before they reach you, wherever you are. Is Lin Chong with you?"

Lin was surprised to hear his name mentioned. Perhaps they were starting to put the pieces together about the Gaos; there might be justice in this world.

"Ask them why they want to know," Chai ordered.

The answer came back, "We will take that as a 'yes.' Urgent we speak. When and where?"

Chai looked about the room. "This may be the moment we have all waited for."

It was clear that no one in the room besides himself was sure of the moment to which he was referring.

"All of us have suffered some injustice, many at the hands of corrupt officials. I trust Su, and I trust the president. They want to do the right thing, wipe out corruption and restore justice. They need help. I think they need our help."

Wang Lun spoke up, "How do you test that without destroying us all?"

"One baby step at a time. Song Jiang, propose a meeting between you and this mystery Teacher. As soon as they can meet us at, let's say, your brewhouse in Qingdao, Zhang Qing?"

The Vegetable Gardener nodded his head. He would get word to his staff to keep it shuttered until they arrived.

"Send it."

The reply came back, "OK. I can make it there by 18:30."

⊃ 人 ⊂

AMBASSADOR CHEN ZONGSHAN HAD NOT SLEPT AT ALL. AT HIS age, to be burdened with the knowledge of impending global doom and yet only be able to sit and wait for orders was a torment beyond endurance.

He had paced. He had tried doing his Eight Silk Brocade qigong but could not concentrate; he had tried to meditate but could not clear his mind.

He missed his wife. She had been such a rock, unwavering in her loyalty to him; even if he could not have spoken of what he had communicated to the president, at least he could have told her something was troubling him, and she would have listened, looked into his eyes, stroked his thinning hair, and told him he would think of something. He did not maintain a traditional altar to the ancestors at the embassy residence, but did have a portrait of her, an incense burner, and two candles on a table.

He put a cushion on the floor, lit a stick of incense, and clutching it in his two hands, knelt on the cushion and bowed to the ground three times holding the stick of incense against his forehead. Then, he remained kneeling, holding the stick up, letting it slowly burn as he reached out to her in his prayers seeking counsel. Her visage, her voice came to him. And he felt comforted.

The mobile device in his pocket shook. He opened his eyes, looked at the stick of incense. It had burned down three-quarters of the way, so he guessed he had been kneeling there for fifteen or twenty minutes. He bowed three more times then slowly gathered himself, and holding the table to steady himself, rose to his feet placing the remainder of the incense stick in the burner.

He pulled out his mobile device. It was a message from the foreign minister. It instructed him that Zhang Guanjia was to be recalled to Beijing immediately for training and consultation, and that Ambassador Chen should break protocol to meet with the secretary of state without his translator in delivering President Zhao's message. The message would be sent encrypted to Chen at 9:00 a.m. on his way to the Department of State and that he was not to share the contents of it with anyone but the secretary of state.

His heart settled. His prayers had been answered. The president had a response for him to deliver. And Zhang, a man he did not like, trust, or respect, was being recalled. His wife smiled down on him. He had several hours before he had to rise for breakfast and his day. He laid his body on the bed and fell into a deep slumber.

⊃ 人 ⊂

As comfortable as Li Shishi was investigating financial crimes, the beat had been big fish, white collar princelings, and corrupt officials. She had little contact with the *Jianghu,* the so-called "Rivers and Lakes," China's demimonde.

For centuries, China had cultivated a class of people who lived by their wits, outside of the law. Over time this class included mercenaries, convoy guards, secret societies, gangsters, prostitutes, itinerant snake-oil sales troupes, knights errant, wandering monks or priests, and even traveling opera companies. With trepidation she entered the microbrewery on the outskirts of Qingdao's city center in an older, working-class neighborhood. There was a garishly lit massage parlor connected at the hip to the drinking establishment around which seedy-looking men embarrassed by their addictions turned their eyes away.

She paused at the door, and a couplet came to mind fully realized:

> Standing above the dark waters of the Rivers and Lakes ready to dive in,
> I realize I have not brought my swimsuit.

The couplet made her smile within, a calming reflection and a laugh at danger. She was here for something important, swimsuit or not.

The sun had set. She felt the cool of an offshore wind blow through the open-knit sweater and fashionably torn jeans sending a slight chill to her core.

299

She was "greeted" at the door of the establishment by a tall, intimidating, heavily muscled figure dressed in shorts and a tight bodybuilder's T-shirt. A tattooed menagerie of serpents circled his arms flowing over, through, and around muscle, sinew, and bone. His large face and bald head had the look of an oversized, greased potato, lumpy, slick, and blemished. "You are the Teacher?" the man asked, a trace of incredulity in his voice.

"Yes. And you are?"

"The Vegetable Gardener. Come this way."

The brewhouse was empty save a lit booth with a table large enough to seat eight, at which waited a handsome lad about her age. He stood up as she approached, the two appraising each other.

"You are Timely Rain?" she asked. "I am the Teacher."

He smiled. "Have a seat. You are not what I expected."

Ready for all the come-on lines and other macho bullshit, Li replied coolly, "How so?"

"I think it is a great sign that the president and Commissioner Su have sent an emissary more like our age. It gives me great hope that they 'get it.'"

Li reflected that this was a refreshing observation. "Thank you. How shall we proceed? I would like to put my phone on the table here so the president and Commissioner Su can observe our discussion. Is that alright with you?"

"Good idea. I will connect to our executive committee here as well so they can also be apprised."

Both set up a mobile device at each end of the table facing each other, with Li sitting to one side of the screen and Song at the other. Both wore earbuds in which they could hear comments back from their respective sides.

Song spoke, "You reached out to us. You go first."

"Who *is* 'us'?" Li asked directly.

"The 108 Stars of Destiny, the 108 Heroes of the Marsh. We go by many names."

"Okay, so what are the 108 Stars of Destiny?"

"A righteous fraternity—correction—*the* Righteous Fraternity. We are a hacker enclave dedicated to securing justice for ourselves and those brothers and sisters in China who have been wronged by the corrupt and unjust."

"How can a criminal band of outlaws dedicate itself to justice? Isn't this a self-serving contradiction?" Li asked sharply, but in her earbud she heard instructions from Su to be a bit gentler.

"Corruption perverts, subverts, justice. Until the rule of law is equally applied without regard for status, wealth, or connections, then it is not 'justice.' When the rule of law *is* applied equally, but the laws themselves favor the strong or rich or connected, then there will be an irresistible call to make unjust laws just. Do you disagree?"

Li listened as Zhao and Su discussed this. "Fundamentally, no disagreement. We seek to root out corruption because it distorts justice, policy, power, and social equity."

"We do what the courts do not, or cannot... or are unwilling to do. We attack the corrupt, we take what is theirs, and we give it to those who need it. Of course, we keep some for ourselves. My turn. Why have you reached out to us?"

Li had taken direction from Zhao and Su on what she could or should reveal and felt somewhat constrained. "You asked this morning 'why talk?' when the government is raiding Chai Jin's properties at the same time, and we replied with apologies noting that 'things are complicated.'

"We sense there is a shadow organization at work to undermine the efforts and authority of President Zhao and that it feeds itself off corruption. The video you sent us was a useful piece of the puzzle. At the same time, Lin Chong's name has come up in several investigations, and we feel he has been the victim of a great injustice." Li paused and searched Song's eyes for any reaction.

"Grave accusations have been leveled against him that are driving the retaliation on Chai Jin and the search of his properties. It is imperative that we open a direct channel of communication with Lin Chong, and imperative that we do so quickly for we fear a bloody outcome if they find you first."

Timely Rain sat, silently listening to the conversation taking place at the Righteous Fraternity meeting room. Prominent among the voices was Lin Chong's, assenting to talk, meet, surrender, anything, to get justice. Timely Rain said, "That can be arranged. Lin Chong knows he is an innocent man. Who are *they* conducting the search and retaliation?"

The Vegetable Gardener came over hoisting two liter-sized mugs of his best pilsner and a small assortment of snacks: big Shandong peanuts, small salt-dried and -crusted shrimp in their shells, and some hard, stewed *doufu* seasoned with raw green chilies and garlic. He put them on the table and backed off.

"Principally, General Gao Qiu with assistance from Cai Jing. But beyond their accusations against Lin Chong, there are other potential crimes to be addressed with him."

Seeing the beer and snacks, Li remembered something and dug into her backpack. Still on his guard but curious about what she was fishing for, Song looked on intently. Li retrieved a bottle. "By the way, President Zhao has asked that I present this to Chai Jin so he will know I speak for the president in these discussions."

It was a fine, ornate porcelain bottle of Guizhou Maotai, its stopper sealed with red wax. "He said that Chairman Chai would recognize this."

Timely Rain took the bottle in hand and listened to the comments from the distant redoubt. He showed the bottom of the bottle to the mobile device lens, giving it time to focus.

"Lord Chai thanks President Zhao for this remembrance. It is a bottle dated and numbered as one of only a thousand commemorative bottles produced on October 1, 1949, the founding day. This particular bottle is #888, seen as a lucky number. Lord Chai presented it to President Zhao when he ascended to his current role. What do you need to know from Lin Chong?"

There was a pause as Li took onboard the opinions of her observers. "Has he taken any rogue actions that might be considered terrorist attacks on foreign countries? It is imperative that he answer truthfully."

Timely Rain listened on as the shock of the question was reflected by the opinions being expressed back at LiangShanPo. He removed his earbud and handed it to Li. "Lin Chong would like to answer you directly."

She put the bud in her ear. "Lin Chong, this is the Teacher."

"Yes, remember, I can see you. Sorry we cannot meet in person, but we must take precautions. As for your question, please convey to President Zhao I am a loyal servant of the State and always have been. I have been wronged, it is true, but my enemies are here in China. I was set up by Gao Qiu to serve the lust of his bastard son. On my oath as a soldier in the PLA, I am willing to give my life for my country and am telling the truth now. I have not taken any rogue action, terrorist or not, to attack a foreign country. If I can help you find out what the president needs to know, I will do my utmost."

"Is it possible that your old Unit 61398, or even some other unit, could conduct an attack and blame you for it?"

"Possible? Yes. Why would they bother? I have no idea."

"Thank you, Lin Chong, that is enough for now. Let me say, personally, that I have investigated what happened to you and your wife. I know the major details and know you are telling the truth about *that*. You have my condolences. I am handing the earbud back to Timely Rain now."

Li Shishi continued, "This was a good first meeting. The President asks that you and I remain here in Qingdao, Timely Rain, for a follow-up discussion. However, he has an urgent communication he must craft with a foreign power right now."

⊃ 人 ⊂

WHEN THE CHINESE EMBASSY HAD REACHED OUT TO MAKE THE appointment, Clarissa Roy had let the president's secretary know that China planned to respond within the deadline. As soon as her meeting with Ambassador Chen was finished, she had gathered the translator's notes and briefcase and headed for the White House, texting them in advance that she had finished the meeting and had a response to deliver.

She was ushered into the Situation Room and saw that the director of National Intelligence, the heads of the NSA and CIA, and the Joint Chiefs of Staff were all assembled.

Mick Coin spoke up first. "Before you deliver their answer, what does your gut tell you about it?"

"Mr. President? I would not want to go on my gut alone in such a grave decision, but what they have shared is eye-opening and reveals a vulnerability that lends truth to their words."

"Okay, what did they say?"

"It was a highly structured statement, which the ambassador emphasized came directly from President Zhao. In fact, Chen's translator was curiously absent today. Let me read you the notes:"

First, and to reiterate, President Zhao thanks you for giving China the opportunity to respond with an answer, rather than escalating this matter to war. It is a sign of mutual respect, which we appreciate.

Second, the People's Liberation Army's wargames, scheduled six months ago and called Operation Emerald Isles, commence today. We will proceed with these wargames as we do not want any redeployment to be misconstrued by your armed forces as a preparation to attack your country, or as preparations to defend against your attack. Our forces are ordered to give wide berth to your Seventh Fleet.

Third, the Major Lin Chong you have identified as perpetrator of the destruction of your dam was arrested in April in possession of evidence he was an agent of the United States and taken into custody, and he subsequently killed two guards in making an escape. He is still on the run. He was later implicated in the flash protests that took place in Beijing.

Fourth, and this must remain strictly confidential, President Zhao has reason to believe that Lin Chong was framed and is innocent of the crimes for which he was arrested. This was orchestrated by corrupt elements within the government and military. Your accusation leveled against the PLA and Lin Chong has highlighted to President Zhao the need to identify these enemies of the State. Your candor yesterday is appreciated and helped to drive this forward.

Fifth, we do not know by which means you have identified Lin Chong as the perpetrator of the dam collapse, but if the United States has the ability to locate him, please let China know. It will aid in our efforts to understand the origins of this crisis.

Sixth, at the conclusion to Operation Emerald Isle, President Zhao will order all our forces to stand down and return to port for rest and relaxation.

Seventh, the planned meeting between President Coin and myself coinciding with the UN Security Council meeting in New York is scheduled for two weeks from now. Between now and then, I will resolutely focus on your concerns and plan to meet with you to give a full report to you personally at that time.

President Zhao emphasizes in the strongest way that neither he nor his armed forces staff were aware of, planned, or executed this despicable attack on American infrastructure. He will work with President Coin to determine the source of the attack and bring the parties to justice.

"That is the message, Mr. President," Roy said.

"Comments?" Coin looked around the room at his advisors.

Guy Cavanaugh, the National Security Council specialist on China, raised two fingers and spoke up, "Secretary Roy's comments about what is revealed and vulnerability are well taken, but to me it highlights an entirely new and increased level of risk. To wit, is Zhao losing control? There is always jockeying for succession within China among different camps within the CCP, and this can play out over many years and not in public. His revelation to us really suggests a level of personal isolation that could be perilous... for us."

"How so?" Coin asked.

"It's the proverbial 'who has their finger on the launch button' issue. He can say that his armed forces staff knew nothing about this, but the rest of the message belies his lack of control and insecurity. I would say he has no real idea whether his people did this or not."

"The report you gave me yesterday, Guy, was pretty pointed. I believe you said you could determine no benefit to China in this attack on our infra-structure that would exceed the cost to them," Coin interjected.

"That *was* true...yesterday. We don't know the forces trying to overturn Zhao, but if, in *their* calculus, ascension to power is more important than the stability of China, all bets are off."

"That's not comforting."

"We have to play the hand we are dealt, Mr. President."

"Dick, how does what he reports about Major Lin fit into the intel your people provided on him?" the president asked of the director of the CIA.

Vesuvio's eyes darted to the report he had delivered to the president the day prior and replied, "Lin Chong was not one of our assets, so the fact they claim he was arrested in possession of evidence linking him to us is curious, indeed. It might be a fabrication to draw *us* off the scent, or part of the plan of those who framed him.

"It also does not mean Lin Chong is not the bad actor, even if he was not acting on behalf of China. Look at it this way: if he was set up and blamed for being a US spy, he might harbor a *very* serious grudge.

"Our dossier on him suggests he was a straight arrow with a solid career path. He gets knocked off that path, maybe even thinks that *our* people set up *their* people to bring him down, to eliminate him as a threat to the US. The conclusion the NSA lady made about him dropping out of sight to work on something more secretive was a conclusion we had reached and shared with the NSA as a heads-up.

"So, it turns out there is another reason he dropped out of sight, but the bottom line is: Major Lin was capable of this and may have had a motive to act irrationally. I think it is much more likely that he did it out of spite without regard for consequences than a competing faction in the govern-ment being the perp.

"In answer to the other question, we do not know where he is. Do you, Bill?" Vesuvio concluded and redirected to the director of the NSA.

"No. I am told he was always hard to track and since he dropped off the radar became even more so. The exploits he wrote that we identified were the first trace of him since he disappeared."

The president requested and listened to several more opinions then turned back to Clarissa Roy while glancing at his press secretary and head of the Joint Chiefs of Staff.

"Alright. This is what we are going to do. We need to make a statement to the public about evidence emerging the dam was destroyed as an act of aggression. We can't wait on that. Otherwise it will look terrible when it does get out. Don't say it was an act of war; that gets the insurance companies off the hook too soon. We don't point fingers yet.

"The fact our forces in Asia have gone on alert will be connected by the press. If they ask about the deployment to the Straits of Taiwan, just say this is to bring us closer to observe the China wargames scheduled months ago and to be ready to defend Taiwan. That's all we say. Do not address questions trying to tie the dam to China or any particular foreign actor.

"This is my answer to Zhao." Coin paused a moment to compose his thoughts. "'We are mindful that you are conducting wargames and will trust you to have your forces stand down and go on R&R at their conclusion. Otherwise, our previous statement stands: if we observe a change in force status or deployments, defensive or offensive, and we *are* watching like hawks, we will deem that China *was* the perpetrator of the attack on our dam or that Zhao has lost control of his military, and we will preemptively strike. If Lin Chong is located and executed, we will take that as corroboration that he was eliminated to hide China's complicity in the attacks, and we will preemptively strike. Lin Chong was not an agent of the US government, and we do not know where he is. While I will not intervene to prop up a single leader, stability leading to liberalization in China benefits the world. I will give you the opportunity to cooperate with America to determine the origin of this attack and bring the parties to justice. To that end, I will see you in New York, at which time I expect to receive your findings.'"

Coin looked around the room, "Okay. Lots to do. Keep it tight, our position is strictly to the wording I have said, no leaks. That goes for people coming up from the Hill sniffing around. Same position. We have to fend off the hounds until we have an enemy we can pin this on and go after."

ㄐ人ㄈ

LI SHISHI WAS BEING PULLED IN TWO DIRECTIONS UNDER A tight deadline, and it felt so exhilarating.

After the meeting she had brokered with Timely Rain, she met with him into the evening trying to understand the nature of the 108 Stars of Destiny. He spoke without reservation about what they did, why they did it, and how they did it, but revealed nothing she could use to discover their location. He also floated the idea of amnesty for the 108 Stars.

She wrote a report to Zhao and Su and had a brief sleep in a cheap hotel near the brewhouse. She rose early to continue dredging through the data contrail of Gao Yanei's life. She wanted to build the case for Su to go after the Gaos, father and son, and maybe topple the Shanghai Clique. At 7:00 a.m. she had heard from Zhao and Su.

The Americans were keeping China on a tight leash but were giving them time to work on sorting through the mess. Su asked her to explore what benefit would accrue for the government with an offer of amnesty to the digital brigands.

She dug back into Gao's communications and files. Through the remote access to his device she was able to penetrate a cloud server of files. One of the folders was labeled "Honey."

In it she found dozens of folders, each with a different woman's name on it. Scrolling through the folders she shook her head and gagged when she came across her name. She opened the folder. Not much information in it yet. Some old press when she was at Beijing U, a picture of her visiting a crowded beach on a sunny day wearing a bathing suit, a press release photo of her in her uniform.

She opened a folder on another woman and found this victim's resumé and press releases, together with photos taken in compromising situations, appearing drunk or drugged and with Gao Yanei.

She created a password-protected and encrypted backup mirror site for all Gao's files through the same cloud service and kept digging.

One folder caught her eye. It was named *Xin Hua Hui*. She had never heard of this association. The characters were pronounced *XinHua*, the sound of which usually meant "New China" and was a popular term for China since 1949. But instead of 新华—New China—the characters were 鑫华. *Xin* 鑫 was made up of the character for gold 金 written three times and meant profitable and prosperous. *Hua* meant glory and symbolized China. The Prosperous Glory Association.

She opened the folder. A broad smile spread across her face as she imagined she was a princess in an Arabian Nights fantasy entering Aladdin's cave filled with gold. It was all here. Name lists, investments, returns, insider tips provided, officials bribed, officials recruited. There was even a charter with a stated purpose of the association:

> Understanding that the most profitable intelligence is information not known by the market, we hereby create a mutual aid society to benefit from leveraging the superior perspective our leadership positions give us, to provide timely and resourceful intelligence to the fund manager, to provide each other contacts, connections, and aid when needed to avoid complications, and to share in the profits of our investments based on the following formula.

Li looked at the formula. It paid out based on a rather complicated mix of contributions including the member's initial investment of cash; the amount, type, and value of the market intelligence provided; and the overall profitability of the fund.

By her quick reckoning, even members who had not contributed any intel were raking in a compound average growth rate of 27 percent, with no ups and down such as the market experienced. The fund manager was given 2 percent of funds under management as a fee, plus 2 percent of profits booked. Another file revealed that the amount of funds under management was around US$1.5 billion.

It appeared that Gao Yanei was the fund manager. It also appeared that, although SilvermanFuchs was his employer, this fund was not associated with that Wall Street investment house at all. It was a side venture Gao managed on his own, a private equity and investment bank run out of the Cayman Islands called Golden Glory Funds. Li's keen mind for numbers did the math and estimated that as the fund manager Gao was taking a US$37 million per year cut. Of course, he had expenses to deduct, but it was a tidy sum for the rake to accumulate and this on top of whatever Silverman-Fuchs was paying him.

An alert from the mobile device reminded her of the time. She went to the mirror and braced herself with a quick splash of cold water to the face bringing color to her cheeks, then brushed and pulled long, raven hair back into a tight bun behind her head. Gathering up the computer and effects into a leather backpack, she put on a jacket and checked out.

The Qingdao weather was dry and cold, made crisper from an offshore wind that blew steadily. She grabbed a cup of latte and a bun on the walk back to the brewhouse and knocked on the door, but found it unlocked. Entering, she was hit with the atmosphere of the prior evening's crowd: the smell of stale cigarettes, old beer, and vomit. On the way to the table where Timely Rain waited for her with his coffee, she opened some shades and windows to freshen the air then sat down with her partner in this dance.

"Morning, Timely Rain. By the way, might I know your real name?" she asked.

He looked into her eyes and considered the request. She sensed tenderness and sadness. "Sure, why not, one only dies once. My name is Song Jiang."

"What's your story?" There was a hint of recognition in her eyes.

"Yes, it seems we all have stories. Hmm. Mine? I was head of IT in a medium-sized brokerage firm. The owner took a liking to me, and sort of pushed his daughter, Yan Po-xi, on me. Marrying her seemed like the right thing to do. Wrong!" he laughed, mocking himself.

"I was closer to him than to her. When the old man died, I helped pay for the funeral. There was all sorts of jockeying for his inheritance. He owned the majority of the firm, it was a big estate, but also there were some unsavory people as investors, too. His wife and daughter, my wife, got all kinds of greedy and were fighting over the will, conniving with these other investors.

"Along the way, I was separately framed for ripping off the firm and stabbing my wife to death. Didn't do either of them, but that doesn't matter here in China when the rich and powerful play their games, does it? So, I dropped off the map, barely got away, on the run since. Lucky to find refuge with people who value my skills and strive to deliver justice on heaven's behalf.

"How about you, your name and story?" he asked looking up from his coffee and into her eyes.

"My name is Li Shishi. My story, nothing special. It can wait for some other time."

"Nothing special? I doubt that. I composed a poem last night after meeting you," his words a shy whisper.

Li furrowed her brows, demurely dropped her face to hide a smile, and blushed.

"Sorry to mention it. Didn't mean to embarrass you. It's just…"

"It's okay. Men don't write poetry about me."

He looked back up into her eyes. "They should."

"What was it?" she asked, expecting some crass come-on.

"Just some tacky, witless words.

> Roaming near and far, this uncouth guest has asked the universe,
> Where can I find shelter?
> From the misty mountain stronghold,
> I have come to the capital to buy a joyful glance.
> Her green sleeves, perfumed, reveal hands as white as snow,
> one smile worth a thousand gold coins.
> The bearing of a fairy, but what need have I of a heartless love?

Li maintained an even expression, blinked her eyes once, and sought the words to move this conversation back onto its intended direction while neither revealing her feelings of warmth for his tender expression, nor encouraging it, nor shutting him down.

"Neither tacky nor witless. But you are right, you deserve more than a heartless love," she cleared her throat and resumed, "and we have some important things to discuss, bigger than either of us. Right?"

He blinked his eyes in acknowledgement and nodded in agreement. "Right." He waited a beat. "On to business. Have you broached an amnesty for the 108 Heroes with the president?"

"I have. He would like me to explore this with you. We have many questions that need to be answered."

"I'll do what I can. What's first?"

"Why should the president offer up amnesty to you all?"

"We believe in President Zhao. We believe that long term he wants to see China become a stronger, more just and equitable society. The fact he has reached out to us in this way tells us that he is in danger, he needs to ferret out his enemies, and he needs allies and soldiers to do that.

"We feel that our agenda, our resources, our activities, are aligned with him—we are ready to serve. But his recognition of the injustices perpetrated on our members in the name of civil society must be concrete. We need the amnesty."

"What are your resources?"

"Vast. A database that grows daily in its effectiveness and the best cyber talent pool outside of those resources that President Zhao can no longer trust. You have read about the downfall of Qiu Xiaoyi?"

Li nodded her head. She had read the shameful exposé about the airline executive on the flight to Qingdao. "That was good work on *JingCai*'s part."

"It certainly seemed so. No. That was us front and center, not the magazine. We researched it, revealed it, and left it up to the courts and public opinion to deliver the punishment for crimes, but we financed the operation through leveraged put options in Hong Kong on the airline's stock."

She had heard her cohorts in Financial Crimes had been caught off balance by Qiu's fall from grace. The article revealed that Qiu was under investigation by State Security Financial Crimes, among others. That was not true. Indeed, a generous trove of information had been delivered into investigators' hands only coincident with the story's appearance online. To reporter's inquiries they could only say, "No comment regarding ongoing investigations."

Li's mind was whirring. She had the confidence of the president of the country, and she believed her counterpart was sincere, but she did not want to exceed her mandate. "Okay, and I will assume for the moment that this is not a one-off thing, that your forces can act under direction and not for personal gain.

"That leaves the question of amnesty. Certainly, some of the crimes your members have been accused of, in some cases been convicted of, they are in fact guilty of. We can't give a blanket amnesty; we don't even know who the 108 are or what they have done."

"We are of a mind on that issue. Indeed, we are talking about blanket amnesty, all or nothing." With the agreement of the executive committee, Timely Rain was negotiating hard on this point. The ExCo agreed, President Zhao needed them and the president's enemies were trying to capture and probably destroy them first. They were prepared for that end. If they came under attack, all hell would break loose. Yes, they might die, but they would not give up without a fight, even if they had no guns. But then the president would lose the potential of their alliance. They felt they held all the chips.

"Can you give me an idea of some of the crimes we are talking about?"

"At the one end, murder, extortion, and for several of them, drug dealing. At the other end, identity theft, hacking...and belonging to something the government has branded a 'cult.' That will have to be legitimized."

Cult? "What are we talking about here?" Li asked, now much less confident that a deal could be brokered.

"Hua Yen."

"That's you?"

"Well, not *me* per se. I am a relatively new member of the 108 Heroes, but it is important to many in the group. From what I can tell, it is just a devout Buddhist group. They are willing to commit that its teachings and followers have no design or intent to seek the overthrow of the CCP."

"But they are millenarian."

"What does that mean?"

"They believe in the coming of the Maitreya Buddha, the Future Buddha, that all will be swept away at that time."

"So?"

"So, it's a cult. People believe in the coming end of the world, they stop responding to law, order, the direction of the CCP, anything mundane; they give up everything for the cult."

"I think you have been reading the Party line on Hua Yen a bit too much. But in any event, it is nonnegotiable. They are willing to make undertakings for the president, but this is an all-or-nothing deal."

"Alright. I will convey that. Then there is Lin Chong."

"Your question to him raised quite a few eyebrows. What's the deal?"

"I can't tell you. I am not holding back, truly, but you don't want to know. However, his cooperation with us on a matter of national security is vital."

"Lin has committed to cooperate fully, and he is a man of his word, but this is a package deal. Amnesty for all of us and decriminalizing Hua Yen. For that price, the president gets our loyalty, support, and resources, including Lin Chong for whatever task you have in mind for him."

Li looked at Song Jiang. Any tenderness that had warmed the initial part of their conversation cooled to the frigid reality of representing their two sides in this delicate détente.

⊃ 人 ⊂

ROBERT SMITH WAS A CAREER INTELLIGENCE PERSON. IN RETrospect, he had been born into it.

Abandoned at birth, he had been raised in several homes, the first of which he presumed gave him his plain-vanilla name. As soon as he was eligible, he had enlisted in the Marines and cut his teeth in the first Gulf War. After doing a combined bachelor's and master's program in Asian Studies, he joined the CIA. Hiring such rootless patriots was a favored modus operandi of the agency.

The CIA had put him in Hong Kong as a case officer during the run-up to that colony's 1997 retrocession to China. Officially, Smith's cover was as a commercial attaché, and he mixed with Hong Kong's commercial and banking crowd, and that was where he had gotten to know Su Yuanjing.

The agency already had a slim dossier on Su, but it was Smith who figured out that Su was heading up China's Autumn Orchid operations in Hong Kong. His cover was vice president of Wealth Management Services at Bank of China's Hong Kong branch. This let Su easily bisect the lives of Hong Kong elites. Autumn Orchid's role was to keep the finger on the pulse of Hong Kong, Macao, and Taiwan opinion makers and try to leverage, bend, manipulate, and if necessary, buy out their support.

Smith ran into Su at several soirees and due to Su's heavily North-China-accented Mandarin and his answers to several questions that Smith put to him about wealth management, Smith figured Su was, like him, working undercover.

Su likewise appraised the youngish, close-cropped, athletic American who did not adequately answer some of his questions about developing trade ties and judged he was not with the State Department, but the CIA.

Mutual butt-sniffing took place for several months, each thinking the same thing of the other: *Can I recruit this person as an asset?*

Their last meeting had been rather humorous when, over rounds of cognac, they laid their cards on the table and understood each was after the same thing, neither was interested in betraying their country, and it was best to move on. They reached the point where they came to understand "who is buying the drinks."

Both had been reporting to their masters every step of the way, and both reported this similar outcome. Having been "outed" by the enemy, though, neither were suitable for undercover work anymore and so moved into new roles.

After 9/11, Smith's career arc had continued upward in the intelligence community. A dozen years later he was seconded to be the number two man at the Intelligence Advanced Research Projects Activity. The number one was a respected scientist and administrator, but Smith was seen to bring a practical bent to the gee-whiz possibilities being researched and taught himself agile scrum methodologies to keep things moving to fruition faster than his predecessor.

The prior administration rewarded his success, appointing him to the role of deputy director of National Intelligence-Technology. The new president elevated him to acting director of National Intelligence and had told him, "The job is yours to succeed in, or lose, while I continue to look." Despite this cloud, Smith had sought to do just that, succeed in serving the president well.

It was a daunting task. Sixteen government intelligence operations reported to him. Only the CIA was standalone while the others were subordinate to other operations, like the NSA subordinate to the Department of Defense and the Bureau of Intelligence and Research under the Department of State. His office produced the top-secret President's Daily Brief, culling, streamlining, and sense-making the latest intelligence deemed of national security interest to the president.

Which made today's report all the more curious and unique. It was the first time he had any intelligence to include of his own. The night before Su Yuanjing had reached out to him. It was a straightforward email sent to his public account. The message was simple. "We need to talk. I have a message to convey. Indirect channels not trusted."

He knew Su's star had risen, too, and that he was President Zhao's right-hand person, but taking such a call was fraught with risk.

It had been a week since Clarissa Roy had conveyed the president's answer back to China, the wargames had concluded, and China's ships were heading back to port as promised. Nonetheless, the pressure from the Hill and the fourth estate was mounting; the president was anxious about the silence.

Smith had responded, "I will see if we can set it up at 07:30 EDT. How to secure the line?"

He called his deputy and asked that she be available to meet him at 07:00. In the morning Su had responded with a number to call. It was not secure. Unacceptable. He sent an email back giving Su the address of a TOR site on the dark web providing anonymized, encrypted audio conferencing and the name of the user he should connect to, SourCream&ChiveRuffles.

"I want you on this call, Tricia," Smith said to his deputy. She nodded and prepared for it. The call would be recorded.

At 07:30 he activated the site and waited. It rang once and was picked up. "Smith? Thank you for calling."

"Let's establish some things first. When was the last time we met?"

"1997."

"What were we drinking?"

"Cognac."

"What brand?"

"Martell."

"The grade?"

"VSOP, I recall."

"What did I give you trouble over?"

There was a pause. "Mixing it with 7 Up?"

"Okay, I am not going to be talking here. What do you have to say?"

"Understood. I have Zhao with me. He may interject some comments, so you may hear another person talking. Your president deserves an update. I am providing it."

"Proceed."

"Your intelligence and military will have noted that our wargames have concluded and as promised the fleets are returning to port.

"Since last week we have made progress in identifying elements that have been fomenting policies and activities contrary to our constitution, law, and current directives. Arrests will begin soon. After that, we will make every effort to determine if these elements played any unauthorized role in the attack on your dam.

"Negotiations are underway for the surrender of Major Lin Chong into our custody. He has sworn that he did not launch the attack on the dam and has committed to cooperating with authorities to help determine how this occurred and who the perpetrator might be.

"We continue to plan for a productive meeting between Presidents Zhao and Coin coincident with the UN Security Council meeting.

"To demonstrate our commitment to helping your government determine who attacked your infrastructure, we propose to send Major Lin Chong to the US as soon as practical to work with your team there. Your cyber intelligence community will know him as a skilled soldier well apprised of China's capabilities in this field; this is not an offer we make lightly."

There was a pause. Smith filled the gap, "That it?"

"For now."

"Goodbye."

It was the summary of this call that led today's President's Daily Brief. Smith had apprised Vesuvio, McCallister, and Roy about the call, but it still drew attention from Coin.

With a touch of incredulity in his voice, Coin asked, "*How* do you know Su?"

"We were both sniffing each other out in Hong Kong a long, long time ago. Seems we both wound up in about the same place."

"Why reach out to *you*?"

"Based on the nature of the call, it has less to do with *me* and more to do with them, and who they believe they can trust from their side to convey these messages. Zhao seems backed into a corner."

"And their offer of surrendering their guy to us?"

"Sir, this is an important distinction. They didn't say they were surrendering him to us. They propose to send him here as, let's say, a liaison or an advisor to our team."

"What if he is the one who did make the attack?"

"Their loss then. They emphasized how highly prized this guy is. They believe in his capabilities, his loyalty, and his innocence enough to put him up to this."

"Let's get Dick and Bill to weigh in."

"Yes, Mr. President. Next on the briefing, there was another incident in the Kashmir region of India, with a retaliatory raid from Pakistan."

ᗐ 人 ᑕ

GENERAL GAO QIU'S ADJUTANT BRUSHED AND SMOOTHED OUT his commander's uniform as the old man stood admiring himself in the mirror of the stateroom aboard the Eastern Theater Command's Navy flagship, Duanwu Hao, a 150-Changchun-class, anti-air, guided-missile destroyer.

The cruise back from the wargames in Hainan had been smooth, though the general's stomach and sea legs had not cooperated, and the analysis of the wargames was coming in, all favorably for Gao.

The Eastern Theater Command had beaten through the Southern Command's defense of Hainan with fewer than expected mock casualties and faster than expected deterioration of the island's defense. Of course, he had facilitated those gaps by some well-placed bribes. He did not feel it wrong or unethical; they would employ the same tactic in Taiwan. But the results were a bold demonstration; now it could be proclaimed China's threat to Taiwan was credible.

President Zhao had ordered the fleet to return to headquarters in Ning-po, and they would be docking in a half hour. A week of R&R was ordered by the commander in chief, and Gao was looking forward to at least one day of that in Ningpo. There was a cute piece of snatch he had enjoyed on a prior port call, and he longed to get into her pants again.

As steam whistles and fireboat water-cannon sprays blew a triumphal greeting to the fleet returning home, Gao made his way through the corridors of the ship into the command center, where he was saluted by the admiral and once more congratulated the team on a job well done. He was navigating toward the gangway when his mobile device rang. It was the office of the president, chairman of the CCP, and commander in chief, the boss of bosses, calling.

"General Gao?"

"Speaking."

"This is the office of the Commander in Chief Zhao Ji. The commander has flown to Ningbo to welcome you back from your victory in the wargames. A car will be waiting for you at the dock. Please take it to a meeting with the president."

"It is my honor to do so. Thank you."

"Thank you." The call terminated.

This was a bigger deal than even he could have hyped it into. *What did it mean? Could they finally plan a blockade of Taiwan, or some assertion of authority over that unruly rabble of a government there? Would he be put in charge? Of course! And if so, the investment opportunities were boundless. What was the capitalist's maxim: invest when there is blood in the streets?*

At the bottom of the gangway waited a caravan of three black, freshly waxed luxury SUVs. Smart-looking attendants in suits and wearing sunglasses held the doors of the vehicle in the middle open for him. He climbed in and settled back into the comfort of the seat, happy to be off the ship and back on solid ground.

The attendants climbed into the front, and the vehicle pulled away from the dock. One of them said into his wrist mike, "We have the general and are on the way."

As the car slowed for some traffic, Gao's mobile device buzzed again. It was Gao Yanei.

"What is it, son? It is not convenient to talk right now."

"Pa, they're coming for me!" The general heard panic and distress in the son's voice.

"Who's coming?"

"A busload of goons from the National Supervisory Commission just busted in. The company receptionist gave me a heads-up. I am holed up in the bathroom. What do I do?"

"There is nothing on your company computer, right?"

"Yes, nothing."

The general stole a glance at the two men in the front seat and typed into the messenger, "Mis-enter your password 3 x, flush phone in the toilet, go out and face them, tell them nothing." He disconnected the audio call.

He looked out the window into the distance trying to figure out how much wiggle room he had if they took Gao Yanei into custody. *Is it connected to me at all? Perhaps Yanei was stupid enough to step on some well-heeled toes in his work at SilvermanFuchs. Perhaps. He could be stupid in that kind of way. Or a well-connected, jealous husband striking back. Still has nothing to do with me.*

He played out various Go scenarios in his mind, most of which ended with him cornered and the enemy capturing all his stones: wealth, power, reputation, everything. Those game outcomes that were stalemated or prolonged always hinged on the content and outcome of the upcoming meeting with the president. It would be crucial to seeing this through whole.

As a highway sign flashed by, Gao looked out the window to read it. The SUV was heading up a ramp to a highway he knew went to Hangzhou, *not* Ningbo.

"You're not taking me to see the president, are you?" he asked, with a sinking feeling he knew the answer already.

The suit on the passenger side turned around and shook his head as the barrel of a service pistol peeked around the left side of his seat and pointed straight at the general. "General Gao Qiu, you are under arrest on suspicion of high crimes against the State and being detained by the National Supervisory Commission. Make yourself comfortable, sir," he added with irony.

⊃ 人 ⊏

IT WAS A VERY PRECARIOUS TIME FOR ZHAO JI TO BE AWAY FROM China, and he would never have chosen this moment to be in New York City in an annex of the United Nations preparing for a meeting with President Coin of the United States.

Prior to his departure from Beijing, the arrests of over one hundred wealthy and/or powerful people had been made based on the information extracted from Gao Yanei's Prosperous Glory Association files. Warrants were issued for over a hundred more. But, by definition, wealthy and/or powerful people were not ordinary; they had resources to fight back.

The pushback would include press, lawyers, tearful family members on video, even foreign human rights groups sticking their nose into it.

Under ordinary circumstances he would not be too concerned since the power of the State, which was supposed to mean "at Zhao's direction," was always going to be greater than that of individuals. However, many of the Prosperous Glory Association's members were high-level government and military people, so Zhao was at a loss to determine in any useful time frame whether those they reported to and worked with could be trusted. And would they take his absence abroad as an opportunity to strike back, push him out, or seize power some way?

There was also the matter of the negotiations underway with the 108 Heroes of the Marsh. Despite their bluster and undoubted intelligence, the Heroes had come close to being obliterated.

The orders had been to prioritize the largest properties in the biggest cities in the search for Chai Jin and Lin Chong. A clever analyst within Cai Jing's group had disobeyed orders. This lieutenant scanned all of Chai Jin's known real-estate holdings for their digital footprints. When he eliminated heavy-bandwidth-consumption properties with high-occupancy office tower blocks, large internet cafés, video game halls, and digital cinemas, he surfaced one conspicuous property. Although it was unfinished and unlicensed for occupation and had no internet café, game hall, or cinema, the property consumed the bandwidth of a functioning city—all within the space of four square blocks. That property had been in a tertiary township at the end of a long-underutilized subway at the end-of-the-line Water Margin Station, the Mount Liang Urban Development Complex.

The lieutenant's findings had been ignored for a day, but then as the search teams were being redeployed from primary to secondary cities, Cai Jing himself caught the anomaly. He read the original report and a follow-on report suggesting that the bulk of signals coming out of Mount Liang were encrypted or channeled through virtual private networks, giving the State less easy visibility into the activities.

The day after Gao Qiu and Gao Yanei's arrests and detention in separate black houses, the president met with the team working on the search for Lin Chong. He had refrained from telling them anything about the back-channel communication he had set up with the digital brigands. As soon as he learned from his intelligence officials that a high-probability location of the 108 Heroes was Mount Liang, he sent a message to Su and Li to proceed there.

His team of generals reported to him that a Special Forces unit had done an external surveil of the property. Based on laser and infrared scans, they had ascertained the bulk of the complex was, indeed, unoccupied, but six of the middle floors in the twin tower blocks adjacent to the skybridge were heavily populated.

They presented a plan for a four-way assault on the block supported by Special Forces making HALO drops onto the roofs of towers one and two. When they were ready to enter, forces on the ground floor would breach from below. If they met no resistance both teams would continue the pincer for a rendezvous on the middle floors. Should resistance be encountered, depending on its location and intensity, two options were planned.

If heavy resistance was met early on, a support contingent of six CAIC Z-10 attack helicopters in stealth mode a five-minute flight away would swoop in and open heavy fire on the middle floors of both towers, hollowing them out. If resistance was only met in the middle floors, another platoon of Special Forces would parachute to land on the skybridge and fight their way out to the two towers.

Zhao gave his full attention to these plans and smiled his encouragement. He was proud to have these able people at his command and told them so. However, he found even more satisfaction in telling them that they could stand down, that another team had opened direct communications with the group at Mount Liang for several days, and his negotiating team was en route.

He read many different reactions on their faces to this surprise statement. Some were happy or impressed or pleasantly surprised that their president and commander in chief could pull off such an intelligence coup without any of them being aware of it or relieved they would not have to send brave and able soldiers into harm's way. This was coming on the heels of the arrests of many bad apples, for which some generals had reached out to commend him. Others were clearly dismayed with this news. He made a note of those faces.

He asked the Special Forces on the ground to remain, meet Su and Li when they arrived, and escort them to the building entrance to await further instructions. He had then thanked his central command leaders and State Security for their tireless efforts to help track Lin Chong and demanded that they refrain from any military action without his order and otherwise support the final discussions between the government and the Mount Liang brigands.

He encouraged their spirits, sharing with them a new page in relations with the United States he was set to turn, a page written as an equal partner on the world stage, not dependent on and afraid of the American Superpower, but one of sharing and mutual understanding of cultural strengths and histories.

It was a small, select, high-powered group, but they had given him an ovation as he left the central military command center and headed straight for the Daxing Airport. The ovation had felt sincere and energized, not the forced ovations on cue that he usually got at the Party Congress.

In New York, he had met separately with Ambassador Chen and the Chinese ambassador to the UN. Ambassador Chen would accompany him during his meeting with President Coin, and he needed to be fully apprised of the current mood in America. He felt he could trust Chen but had wanted to sit across from him and make that final judgement.

With the ambassador to the UN, he wanted to discuss final details of his speech to the General Assembly. The thematic issue being discussed at this year's meeting was, in capital letters, "The Digital Divide."

Zhao felt no nation on the planet was better positioned to provide a road map to the future of the world than China. In his lifetime, he had observed and ultimately led the transformation of China from a nation of one telephone line and one television per 600 people to now at least one and a half high-speed land and mobile internet connections per person. The entire nation had benefited from knowledge-sharing and best-practices dissemination. The economy had benefited from increased commerce. Small rural brands had gotten larger urban consumer bases.

Of course, billionaires had risen out of this, but everyone was wealthier and better off. And they had done their best to limit pernicious influences: divisive commentary, religious extremism, and irresponsible political detractors, which to him meant any naysayers not actually responsible for the creation and execution of public policy. This control was essential to maintaining the benefit of the technology. His speech would announce a global, soft-loan, technology-access program China would implement to help close the divide.

However, all this goodwill and future benefit was predicated on the meeting with President Coin. Zhao felt the threat of a meltdown in the relations between their two countries was reduced, but it was not eliminated. The week before, President Coin had been compelled to announce to the American people that deeper investigation into the dam collapse revealed an outside hand in its destruction and that all federal authorities were at work to determine the source of the attack.

After this, the news cycle had paraded all manner and level of "experts" to dissect, digest, and continuously regurgitate the partial corpse of this subject, and the mood in the country was dark and dangerous. Most assumed this was the work of old enemies in the endless war that had started in 2001. This erroneous assumption was all the partisans agreed on. From there, they became rabidly divided into two camps.

One camp was tired of the insecurity, the storm clouds, and threats and wanted America to retreat, to just say "it's your problem, deal with it." On the other extreme were those who wanted it brought to a close quickly and remorselessly with the utter destruction of the enemy, an absolute disinfection of the scourge from the planet, a no-holds-barred, by-any-means-necessary, all-weapon-options-on-the-table, door-to-door elimination of threat.

Zhao's cyber intelligence teams had reported to him with their own analysis. Based on news reports, they did not feel America's old, endless war enemies could have pulled off what China was assuming had happened. Russia, yes. Israel, yes. China, yes if they had put the resources into it, but why would any of these players do so?

Ambassador Chen entered the room. Older than Zhao, he carried himself with dignity born of knowledge that one has done one's best. He shared with Zhao his relief that the translator Zhang had been recalled and that Chen had submitted some negative performance evaluations of Zhang, which he felt justified the action taken.

"Ambassador Chen, your observations were an accurate tip of the sword only. Zhang has been arrested and is presently detained for questioning on the suspicion he was commercially benefiting from the privileged information his role afforded him."

"I had no idea. My apologies, Mr. President, for not seeing through this."

"No need to apologize, Old Chen. He was part of a group, a plot that eluded detection for long years. Your discreet handling of the communications with the Americans helped me, though, to root out this perfidy."

"Mr. President, we need to make the walk now to our meeting with President Coin."

Zhao put his hand on Chen's shoulder and stopped him for a moment, looking into his eyes. "Old Chen. Thank you for your service. The nation needs more public servants like you."

The old man looked back into his president's eyes. He had served a lifetime. He knew he had not always succeeded, but he knew he had always done his best. Never had he received such a thanks. He smiled, blinked his eyes, and nodded appreciatively. "These are precarious times, Mr. President. Shall we go and put the Americans at ease?"

ᗡ 人 ᄃ

ONE HUNDRED METERS AND TWO STORIES AWAY, MICK COIN SAT finishing a meeting with Nancy Nillson. She had delivered the responses from an environmental working committee. "They are still unhappy that NOAA's Ark is only a bilateral effort."

"Just tell them that if we waited for global consensus, the ice floe would melt long before any action was taken," Coin said.

Given the administration's stance on climate change, she knew that the US would be lambasted if she intimated they were taking action in advance of "global consensus." "Yes, sir. I did say that we acted for the benefit of the world but decided to focus on engaging only the key players to be impacted. The South African delegation has been quite supportive in this discussion."

"They better be," he said coldly. The irony was not lost on Coin. He had committed to this scheme to deliver a billion tons of freshwater to Africa, and a billion tons of freshwater had been released under his watch in the California desert.

Nillson heard more darkness and finality in the president's tone than she was used to. "Sir. I am mindful of your next meeting. I'll be on my way. Thank you."

He nodded his head and waved her out. He was indeed preoccupied with the meeting with Zhao. His advisors were torn about the stance he had taken with China. So far, the chief of staff had kept everyone in line, and there had been no leaks. But he dreaded the possibility he was being played by China for a chump.

On the side of "stay the course" were three main supporters. Secretary of State Clarissa Roy, backed by comments from the secretary of commerce, cautioned that the devastating global economic impacts of a war with China could flush the planet's population into an apocalyptic vortex. Winning such a war would not be a victory for the US. The director of the NSA said that signals intelligence had not picked up further evidence of China's culpability in the dam attack. They had conversely seen considerable activity of the restraint Zhao was putting on his military, the focus on the wargames, and the R&R stand-down, just as he had promised. The director felt that in the absence of further identified threats, they should continue to work with China. The director of National Intelligence concurred, and added that the widespread, high-level arrests being made across China, while not publicly acknowledged, were known to the US intelligence community and corroborated Zhao's stated concerns. They bolstered the appearance that Zhao was regaining control and stability.

On the side of "you can't trust them, take them out before they strike again" was the director of the CIA. He cited that this attack had come with no warning, was absolutely cold-blooded, and that whether Zhao was in control or not, the evidence pointed to Chinese military involvement. The Joint Chiefs of Staff concurred on this conclusion and the mode of reprisal—submarine-launched cruise missile attacks against critical infrastructure—but not on the targets.

The menu of targets ranged from the tit-for-tat, symbolic but devastating Three Gorges Dam, nuclear power plants, South China Sea artificial, military reef islands, and taking out the Chinese navy's three aircraft carrier battle groups. At the extreme end the targets included the grimly final escalation of eliminating China's nuclear forces, delivery systems, and air defenses under the assumption that any attack on China would inexorably escalate to a nuclear exchange, so it was best to take that out first.

Coin's own heart was torn. Since the day at Sutter's Butte when that forlorn woman pointed to a devastated horizon with her coffee mug, he had replayed the moment over and over in his mind. He knew what his grandmother would tell him. *Take 'em out, they can't be trusted.* At the level of raw emotion and fear, the anger for the suffering brought on his people, he wanted to lash out. He felt fear of the devastation China could wreak on the US if they attacked again, fear of humiliation if he disregarded his advisors and was wrong. At this visceral level he was ready, he wanted, to press the button.

On another, not intellectual but mindful level, he wrestled with his feelings. He had done a tour in Afghanistan. He had not been in any firefights, but he had known tense moments. He knew from the Afghan experience many locals with whom he interacted were scared, fearful, of him. Not because they were an enemy afraid to be discovered, but just because he was an unknown quantity with power over their existence that they could not control or understand. He had learned to approach any situation that confronted him with a relaxed awareness, a prepared flexibility, an authoritative openness that spoke to friend and foe the same language; I will not be taken advantage of, I am unassailable, I am not hostile, but don't even think about doing me ill. With this mind, and in the absence of further proof, he wanted to continue to stand resolute and prepared with China while they sought to cooperate.

He saw the door open, and his ambassador to the United Nations, Giorgi Niemera, entered. Tall, dark, tough-looking, and muscular, he was a second-generation émigré of Cossack roots. He had done well in the UN standing up to the "peanut gallery."

"Mr. President, the Chinese delegation is on the way. Be here in about three minutes."

"Thank you, Giorgi. I am going to ask you to sit this one out. Our discussion today is not UN business. You understand," Coin said.

Niemera looked concerned but did not disagree. "Yes, sir, I understand. If you need anything, then I will not be far. Do you want me to show them in?"

"Please."

President Zhao and Ambassador Chen arrived and left their security detail at the door, as Coin had. They did not have a translator; Chen was to do the honors. Already seated in the room were President Coin and Secretary Roy and between them the president's translator.

When Niemera had absented himself, and they had all seated and were past pleasantries, President Zhao said, "Our last meeting, President Coin, was cut short under adverse circumstances. And this meeting is called upon us for less than cheerful reasons. But I deeply appreciate that you have treated China as a partner these several weeks and given us time to look into the allegations surfaced by your intelligence community."

Coin set his tone for the meeting. "The American people demand to know why this attack occurred and who the perpetrator was. We *will* find out and we *will* act. I have been patient and shown restraint, it is true, but we need China to be much more forthcoming, now."

Zhao started with a discussion of corralling the Prosperous Glory Association, which he called the Shanghai Clique, concluding, "I trust we did not happen to arrest any of your intelligence assets in the dragnet; if so, it was not our intent." Zhao had been briefed that based on data taken off mobile devices and computers and some confessions, at least three of the people arrested were helping foreign governments.

Coin, too, had been briefed by Vesuvio that several of their sources in China had been swept up and cautioned him that this could be construed as a hostile act to make US efforts to determine the source of the dam attack more difficult.

"While we have only had several days to go through the evidence collected in the dragnet, so far we have found no references to a covert, off the books, or unauthorized attack on the US."

Roy asked for more clarification about what the clique's activities were, and Zhao answered her question.

"We have been able to open communications with Major Lin Chong, as reported before. We took your warning very seriously, and I was able to avert an assault on his location that likely would have resulted in his death. My representatives are meeting with him face to face as we speak to negotiate the return of Lin Chong to our service. He has steadfastly denied any plan or attack on US infrastructure and is willing to lend any and all support to our efforts to find out who has framed China."

"Jimmy," Coin said, interrupting him and recalling the name Zhao had shared with him in their last encounter, "I appreciate that you have started to get your house in order, but I have generals telling me that this is just Chinese water torture, one drop at a time wearing us down and delaying our action. I need, I expect, proof from you *in this meeting* that China had nothing to do with the attack on our dam."

Zhao paused to listen to the translation and collect his thoughts, then said, "As you know, it is only possible through facts to prove beyond doubt that one *did* something; one is always left with doubt and conjecture when trying to prove one did *not* do something. Please take our cooperation with you as the best proof we can provide of our innocence and sincerity."

As that was being translated, Niemera peeked his head in from outside, closed the door, and a minute later opened it again and strode hesitantly into the room, a confused and uncertain look on his face.

Coin, clearly peeved by this intrusion, said, "Giorgi, for God's sake, what is it?"

"I'm...I'm sorry, Mr. President, but there is something you need to see." He beckoned them to go into the hallway and added, "The Chinese group, too."

There was a flat-screen monitor in the hallway playing cable news channels. "What am I looking at, Giorgi?" Coin asked.

The ambassador, never one to be at a loss for words, looked flustered and stammered, "Um, I am really not sure. It is you and President Zhao making a live announcement from the room we just left. It's been on for five minutes. It's on all the channels."

They watched as President Zhao and President Coin, admitting to the devastation that their nations, their economies, their ways of life had wrought on the environment and the climate, were making a new, combined commitment to renewable energy, reduced consumption, and limitations on population growth. A primary initiative was to combine knowledge. The patents held by their respective governments related to renewable energy, pollution abatement, carbon capture, and power savings would all be made freely available to all countries.

The President Coin promised to lift restrictions on exports of nuclear technology to China imposed by a former administration. He would encourage population control, and the US Congress would stop its efforts to sanction or censure China for its population control efforts.

The President Zhao spoke passionately about the contribution of the Green Guards to raising awareness in China and serving as representatives of the way forward to the world. He praised the Dalai Lama for consistently advocating a sustainable lifestyle and encouraged all Chinese to seek that understanding.

Coin's mobile device started to buzz. He looked at Zhao, who observed the joint announcement with the same level of undisguised incredulity that he had.

Coin pulled Ambassador Chen over between them to translate. "Tell President Zhao, I want Lin Chong and your cyber warfare people over here as soon as possible, working with us."

CHAPTER 9

Coin, Zhao, and their teams retreated into the meeting room they had occupied at the United Nations annex and from which their fabricated images were being broadcast to the world media.

Coin called Director of National Intelligence Smith and put him on a speakerphone while texting his press secretary to join the call.

"Robert, what in the hootin' hell is going on?" Coin demanded. "And by the way, I have President Zhao of China here with me, and he probably has the same burning questions," he added to avoid any embarrassing, compromising, or high-security information from being revealed while he looked over to Zhao and Chen with a supportive and determined look.

"Sir, yes, we are looking at this same broadcast. I assumed it was not you or your policy positions. What is it? A synthetic identity fraud called deepfake videos. This is not a basement hacker dubbing an existing video of you two together. This took a lot of skill and insider knowledge. Whoever is doing it knew where the two of you would be, when you would be isolated together, what the room looks like, and when and how to release the information. They have to know that you and..." He was interrupted as Tammy Jones entered into the call.

"Mr. President."

"Yes, Tammy, are you watching the news feeds?"

"Yes, sir."

"We have to get on top of this deepfake hack," Coin ordered.

Jones was impressed that the president understood what was happening. "Yes, sir. We have already reached out to the major broadcasters to tell them this is not a genuine feed. Many have stopped transmitting it, but it launched a new commentary cycle, which is neither pretty nor complimentary. Even Linx News is asking how the White House could have lost control of this and allowed those views to be expressed as your own, sir."

Smith continued, "As I was just saying, the hacker has to know that you and President Zhao can prove this was a fabrication and not the purpose of your meeting. It must be meant for intimidation and embarrassment more than to move policy direction. So, Tammy's focus should be to get the story out that this is the second time a heads of state meeting has been disrupted by cyber-attacks, the first being the riots in Beijing, which is a grave disruption to the normal process of diplomacy."

Coin interjected, "Perhaps we should say that President Zhao and I had intended to address environmental issues in our meeting, but this unlawful disruption detracted from the atmosphere, spoiling a rare opportunity. Put it back on the hackers," he looked to Zhao as Chen translated for him. Zhao was silent but did not look in agreement.

Smith picked up the thread. "Sir, I don't advise shooting from the hip on this. We have to aim as close to the intended focus of the meeting as possible in our messaging."

"Well, then, this is it. I have accepted President Zhao's offer to send his cyber-intel expert, the one fingered by the NSA, to work closely with our team to determine the origin and perpetrator of multiple cyber-attacks that have been executed against both our nations, including today's deepfake video."

At the other end of the line, Smith pursed his lips. He had not fully bought in to this idea yet. The director of the CIA voiced strong opposition while the director of the NSA gave lukewarm support. He did not want to have this conversation in front of the Chinese president, though. "Sir, we still need to evaluate that offer."

"No, Director Smith, we don't. Outside, just now, I accepted President Zhao's offer. This deepfake video is an irritation, but the destruction of the dam was a catastrophe. I want action, and I think this is the best way forward. Combine forces, pool resources. Let's get it underway."

Chastened, Smith replied, "Understood, sir. So, Tammy's talking points?"

Tammy chimed in, "This is what I got. Today's deepfake video is another example of the threat individuals, governments, and diplomacy face from hackers, terrorists, unfriendly governments, and lawless elements exploiting technology to spread false or dangerous narratives and instigate real attacks that harm real people. The United States and China are both pursuing environmental policies that each feels provides the best balance between the needs of their citizens and long-term, sustainable growth. The fabricated views expressed in the deepfake video are not aligned with the views of either president and are only a distraction from genuine, pressing issues. The real purpose of the meeting was to discuss bilateral cooperation on investigating and countering cyber threats, including the destruction of the Oroville Dam. This is a clear and present danger, and the United States welcomes China's assistance in this effort."

They waited while Chen translated for Zhao, who pursed his lips and nodded thoughtful agreement.

Coin leaned over to Zhao. "Jimmy, thank you for coming. Let's take these people down."

Coin's translator communicated "take these people down" as "arrest the culprits" while Ambassador Chen thought he would have said "*songdaogua*," "deliver them unto their deaths."

ⴲ 人 ⴀ

DICK VESUVIO PACED HIS OFFICE IN LANGLEY LOOKING OUT THE windows at the trees denuded of their fall foliage by a strong wind, rain, and hailstorm the night before. The damp, cold, late afternoon landscape promised the inevitable arrival of winter in several weeks and was as dark as his mood. He had just gotten off the phone with the director of National Intelligence after the brouhaha at the United Nations.

He was feeling thwarted. He knew it was a dangerous feeling. He knew in the past that when he felt this way good did not necessarily come of it. But there it was. He felt thwarted. His sole ambition had been to serve to the best of his capacity, and it challenged his constitution whenever someone or something stood in the way of that.

Early in his military career as an ensign in the Navy SEALs, he had taken orders and executed them faithfully. Later as a captain, his command was clear-cut, men listened to him and executed his orders. The enemy alone was trying to thwart the execution of his mission, and he had been effective in overcoming them.

As he rose in the ranks, there had been several instances when he had felt thwarted. What he knew to be the right course of action had been derailed by someone, sometimes a peer, a more senior officer, or someone he did not even know and to whom he could not present his considered objection. When it turned out that he had been right, he found it hard to let go of feelings of disappointment and occasional resentment. Of course, he had not externalized these feelings, not acted on resentments; that would have been career suicide. And most of the resentments over time were buried deeper or were superseded by bigger examples of bureaucratic stupidity and failure, usually that he had no control over, so they just helped dissolve past hurts by comparison.

However, there was one time he had been thwarted that continued to stick in his craw; it did not sink, bury itself, submerge, dissolve, or get better with time.

He and his team had been infiltrated into Pakistan's Gwadar Port to surveil a meeting between a Pakistani money man and remnants of Daesh, now called ISILI, the Islamic State of Iraq, the Levant, and the -Istans, which included the targeted expansion territories of Afghanistan, Kazakhstan, Kyrgyzstan, Pakistan, Tajikistan, Turkmenistan, and Uzbekistan. The terrorists had not succeeded in taking any of that territory but were always trying to demonstrate their relevance to the Islamic world.

The mission was to use a Laser Bounce Listening System to record live conversations between the financier and his visitors and await further orders. Cellphone traffic was being captured separately. The mission briefing made it clear that the port, although sovereign Pakistani territory, was owned and operated lock, stock, and barrel by the Chinese government for a lease period of ninety years, as compensation for developmental aid Pakistan had fallen into arrears on paying back to China.

The incursion was neither being coordinated with nor approved by the Pakistani or Chinese governments. His team, as such, was to avoid any clashes with Chinese port security forces, all of whom were employees of Poly Systems, a military contractor owned by the People's Liberation Army.

It had been a long night that started with infiltration from a submarine parked off the port in a "wet boat," a manned, steerable torpedo that he and five of his men rode in at a shallow depth to their destination. Under cover of darkness, they made their way three blocks inland to a building under construction across the street from the offices where the meeting was to be held.

They chose a space that had already been finished under the assumption that construction workers would be less likely to disturb them, set up their surveillance and communications equipment, and waited.

With professional efficiency, clean and smart-looking white pickup trucks with blue Poly Security logos emblazoned on the doors drove down the boulevard every thirty minutes. Each was manned with two Chinese security guards, but the team secure in their perch two stories up from the road avoided detection.

The meeting was scheduled to start at 10:00 a.m., and about 09:30 the financier and his entourage arrived. At 09:55 two dusty SUVs pulled up. All eyes were on the vehicles and occupants as they got out, and the video feed was being sent live to Naval Intelligence and Langley.

Vesuvio had a good eye for faces and had memorized the photos, names, and rap sheets of the top one hundred members of ISILI that were targets and persons of interest, a list called "Jeopardy!" His heart skipped a beat and a smile spread across his face as a tall, lanky man dressed in loose, white cotton clothes and wearing sunglasses in the bright morning sun emerged from the back seat of the second vehicle and faced them, stretching his frame after a long ride.

From the breadth of the cheekbones juxtaposed to the hollowed cheeks and the sharp nose, Vesuvio was sure this was Ibn Syd Alqunbula, a master bomb maker and mentor to the ranks who had graduated to strategy, a high-profile target, and Number Seventy-Seven on the list. "Fowler, keep your eye on the tall guy," Vesuvio ordered his sniper.

"Aye, skipper."

"NavInt, are you seeing this? Can you confirm we have Number Seventy-Seven in our sights?" Vesuvio requested them to run the clear video capture through facial recognition.

Two minutes passed. "Roger, we confirm, you have Number Seventy-Seven in your sights."

"NavInt, permission to take out Number Seventy-Seven."

There was little delay, certainly nothing had been run up any flagpole for consideration or approval, and the answer came back within a minute, "Negative. Do not take the shot on Number Seventy-Seven. Repeat, do not take the shot. Stick to mission, Barracuda," their operation call sign.

The men who had arrived entered the building and proceeded to the second-floor conference room.

The SEAL team had a clear line of sight, and the laser beam they trained on the window of the conference room reflected minute oscillations of the pane of glass caused as sound waves of the men speaking inside impacted the pane in the meeting room. The surveillance team could hear clearly what was being said as polite exchanges were made and tea was offered up.

One of the men accompanying Number Seventy-Seven walked to the window and looked out, surveying cautiously. He then took a small electric device with a cord from a backpack and plugged it in. A gentle buzzing noise overlaid the sound of conversation, but not so much they could not hear the words.

"What is that thing?" Vesuvio asked.

Proctor, his communications officer, kept fish at home to give his children something to be responsible for during his long absences and said, "I think it's an aquarium pump with the housing removed. That's what it looks and sounds like to me."

"Walks like a duck, talks like a duck," Fowler said. "Anyway, we can still hear 'em. Probably better they think they can't be heard."

They all knew that the bad guys had learned to point their own lasers at windows to obscure the signals being sent back to eavesdroppers, and that their systems were designed to modulate the wavelength of the laser to tune out such noise. The buzzing of an aquarium pump was a new, ineffective, but somehow quaintly old-school idea.

Just then, the man in the room lodged the pump against the window with a heavy book, and the earphones of the SEALs all exploded in a loud, chaotic, rattling noise. Proctor responded immediately muting the volume on the feed. "Jeez!" he gasped, looking over at Vesuvio. "Skipper?"

"Fuck me," Vesuvio muttered. "NavInt, are you going to be able to make anything of that?"

"Stick to mission. We will do what we can with the audio."

"Roger that." Vesuvio did not cotton to coming all this way for nothing. As one of his hand-to-hand combat instructors taught him, if you get your hand or knife all the way in toward your opponent, don't come back empty-handed. Grab an ear and rip it off, slice on the way out with the knife, make it hurt, don't waste the effort that put you into the advantageous position. "NavInt, requesting permission to take the shot on Number Seventy-Seven."

This time there was a longer delay, but not so long that any request could have gone far up the chain of command or been properly considered. "We repeat the previous order. Do not take the shot on Number Seventy-Seven. Repeat, do not take the shot. Stick to mission, Barracuda."

And so it was. The meeting ended at noon, and the terrorists departed, safely. The SEALs awaited nightfall and tread carefully back to the water's edge, where they made their exfil back to the submarine, the Chinese, the Pakistanis, and the terrorists none the wiser. A successful mission, or so it was logged.

Langley put their best signal filter people on the audio. The problem was that the aquarium pump was a cheap one. It just could not sustain a steady rhythm that the computers could hang on to and filter out at one go. And the hammering of the pump on the window drowned out gentle voices. It took them ten days to crack it and restore a reasonably intelligible facsimile of the conversation.

An operation to attack some target was being discussed. It would be a bombing. They could not make out a time or place. As soon as they heard the word "Bush," though, they rushed a transcript upstairs. It was just too late. That very moment, news was coming in that the aircraft carrier George H.W. Bush, flagship of the US Navy Carrier Strike Group 2, was bombed while putting in to port in Duqm, Oman.

Years later, Vesuvio still fumed. Fifteen men, fifteen brothers, had died in that attack. Several aircraft were destroyed, and the aircraft carrier had to return to Norfolk for repairs. It all could have been preempted, prevented, had they let his team take the shot.

Back then he could not let it go. He had to know what had happened, who had made the lame decision to allow the terrorists have their tea and chitchat. Discreetly, as he did not want to call attention to himself, he made inquiries over beers here and there, meals in mess, occasional meetings he was called to attend.

Piece by piece, step by step, back into Naval Intelligence, back to Hawaii, he learned there was a guy about his age calling the shot. He had not referred the request higher telling Langley that the SEAL team was under orders to infil and exfil quietly, no fireworks. No one wanted to explain to Pakistan or China what they were doing in Gwadar. Thus, the order was maintained: do not pull the trigger. By all accounts the guy was considered to have done the right thing, and his career continued upward. The man who had argued for inaction so effectively was William "Bill" Hollister.

As Vesuvio paced, he shook his head in thought, his hands wrung behind his back. Director of National Intelligence Smith had just called him after his conversation with the president and let him know that Coin had taken this instance of the deepfake broadcast to accept China's offer of help on investigating the dam collapse and now other cyber-attacks.

Vesuvio did not like this at all. In previous discussions he had been clear to the president that he felt it was a bad idea, and Coin had said he would take the director's thoughts under advisement. Hollister had not come to Vesuvio's support and seemed ambivalent at best, at worst happy to see Vesuvio twist in the wind.

No, that kind of thinking would not do, Vesuvio reconsidered. He was thwarted, but he had to get his thoughts under control. The president, the country, needed his service, in service to the team, not out in left field chasing out-of-bounds fly balls.

Still, he had to be able to make an effective case to the president. He had reacquainted himself with the breadth of the resources at his command, especially the Directorate of Digital Innovation, which had come to rival the NSA, and its Remote Devices Branch. So far, he had let NSA field the cyber questions and answers. It was time to see what his team could do and hone up so he could present the right case to the president at the right time.

Hollister would make a misstep. He knew he would. Vesuvio would be ready.

ⴹ 人 ⊂

HONG XIN FIDGETED WITH THE BUTTON ON HER DARK BLUE pantsuit coat, finally freeing up her belly. *It's not that I am fat*, she told herself. The lounge chairs in the Tea Garden of the Les Saisons Hotel in Beijing were set uncomfortably low pushing knees into chest, and her stomach was caught in the middle. *And the partner for this meeting is late*, she thought as she cast a weary look around the room.

It was a beautiful space in the atrium of the hotel. She craned her neck to look up at the seventeen-story, tall, dark wood panel adorned with stainless steel butterflies. She longed for the comfort of sitting amidst real nature and in this opulence saw not luxury but the cost to the earth and hence to humanity.

She looked up once again at the dark wood of the butterfly panel and called a waitress over. "Do you know what kind of wood that is?"

The young woman dressed in a tight-fitting, silk *qipao* pleasantly surprised her. "Yes, thank you for noticing. It is zebrawood. Specially chosen by the designers. Can I help with any other questions?"

"Thank you. You have been helpful." The management of the hotel trained its people well, and they took pride in being there, she thought.

But that left Hong Xin thinking about the wood paneling: dark, tropical, hardwood timber, highly regarded for its striped grain reminiscent of the eponymous animal. She could see the entire process that had brought it to hang here, like some big-game trophy mounted on the wall, at once beautiful and lifeless.

She imagined the sunlight falling onto the live, healthy trees at their home in Central Africa, most probably Gabon, Cameroon, or Congo, and filtering to the forest floor, where she now stood in her mind's eye. She could smell the sweet pungency of rot and renewal at the forest floor. She saw the intrusion of the workers and the large, yellow, Chinese-built earth- clearing machines lumber up the slope, gouging into the underbrush and clearing the path to the larger prizes. She heard the whine of the two-stroke chain saws ripping into the trunks and smelled the blue smoke of the oil they burned. Her body shook as the tree collapsed in front of her, shook because after its 200 years living on Earth in close partnership with its place, its hillside, its community of trees, plants, animals, insects, fungi, bacteria, rain, CO_2, and oxygen, it would now be denied the rite of resting in peace on the forest floor to return itself to the earth here, where it was born, and share its body and its life's learning with young growth.

She saw the offices of the Chinese logging company that had illegally sourced the timber from the concessions it had obtained with bribery and exported through corrupt channels. She saw the tax evasion and ecosystem destruction as the trees were felled, dragged out of the jungle, stripped naked, and shipped far from home. The new owners of these carcasses trusted not the local African sawmills to profit from eviscerating them into boards, but rather insisted the cadavers be sent to China for Chinese mills and craftsmen to have at them.

Hong Xin could see all this in her mind's eye because she had seen it all play out before.

She hailed from the village of Mosuo in China's southern Yunnan Province, a lush, green place where women lived close to the land, ruling both the households and family lineage. Marriage was very optional and taking lovers was *de rigeur*. She had not married and had carried this feminist pride as she rose within the local Communist Party and the environmental bureaucracy.

After getting a degree in environmental law from the University of Kunming, she had returned to the village and joined the Party. Her first assignment was to implement protections of the Lugu Lake Scenic Area. A modest seventeen square kilometers in size, but it was green and beautiful, and it was hers to protect.

"Hong Xin! Just give a little on this, won't you?" she remembered the local honcho of a distant Guangdong timber wholesaler cajoling to get permission to do "a little pruning" in the scenic area. "We'll make it worth your while," said with a wink and smile as he proffered an imported cigarette.

After an investigation and brief trial, he had been sent to prison, she was not bothered by his type again at Lugu Lake, and tree poachers moved on to easier pickings in neighboring counties. She had maintained a rigidly pugnacious adherence to the law and the Party line for her twenty-year rise up the ranks, from township to county to province, to special assignments, all the way to Beijing, the capital and center of power.

As sharp as her colleagues and adversaries found Hong Xin's elbows, she counted herself lucky that the job was also her love in life. She was the chief inspector of the Central Commission for Discipline Inspection at the Ministry of the Ecology and Environment and the Supervisor's Office of the State Supervision Commission MEE. She was the Communist Party's iron fist in a silk glove at the ministry.

She looked around the tea sitting area and sighed at the usual assortment of foreign and well-heeled local denizens. No one caught her eye. Forty-five, unmarried, and childless, she nevertheless thought about men from time to time. *Not that I want to get married, but they can be fun to have around, the right ones anyway.*

So far, she had not run into one like that in the capital. They were either totally full of themselves and their materialist pursuits, or incapable of conceiving an equal partnership with a no-nonsense woman.

Unintended celibacy gave her more time for meetings like the one on which she was waiting. The week prior she had gotten an email from Dr. Ada Byron, the deputy director of the National Enforcement Service in the Operations Executive of the UK's Environment Agency. She did not know Byron, but the request was informal and included a paper Byron had written, "Reinterpreting UK Common Law Statutes to Strengthen Environmental Protection."

Byron said she was to be in Beijing as part of a holiday package and would like to meet Hong Xin, whom she identified as her counterpart, just to have a friendly chat, hands across the water, and compare their jobs. Dinner was on offer. Hong had checked the calendar and replied that she could meet. She also told her boss to make sure there were no issues.

"Dr...Byron?" an uncertain voice said, interrupting Hong's reverie.

Hong looked up. A man about her age, tall and well-kept, in a conservative suit with the red flag of China pin in its lapel stood there looking quizzically at her.

Hong struggled to get up from the deep, low lounge chair, almost falling back into it when the man took her wrist and steadied her with his left hand. His grip was firm and certain, and when he saw that she was stable, he released it gently. She noted no wedding ring on the finger of his hand, nor any imperfection on the finger suggesting a ring had been there.

"Heavens! The chairs here are low! Thank you. No. I am waiting for Dr. Byron, too. And you are?" she asked, looking up into his eyes.

He looked deeply back at her and said, "You don't look like what I expected Ada Byron would look like, but the receptionist pointed at you. I am Zhang Xujing. You?"

"Why, I am Hong Xin. From the Ministry of the Ecology and the Environment, chief inspector at the Central Commission for Discipline."

"Oh, yes," he said, eyes turning toward the ceiling as he filtered through his memory. "I remember seeing you before. Aren't you also attached to the State Supervisory Commission?"

"Yes," she said, trying to place whether they had met before. She felt sure she would remember running into such a handsome man.

"Then we have at least seen each other before." He took out his name card and presented it to her. "I am basically in the same role as yours but at the Ministry of Justice."

They both turned to see a man approaching them. He was dressed in a fine suit and had a Les Saisons pin on his lapel. Tall and robust-looking, he nevertheless walked with a pronounced limp. "Chief Inspectors Hong and Zhang, yes?" he asked, wringing his hands.

"Yes?" Zhang replied with a slight edge in his voice.

"My apologies, I am Li in Guest Services. Dr. Byron has called me to say her tour bus broke down at the Great Wall, and she will be delayed. She had preordered quite a sumptuous meal to be served now in her suite; she does not want it to go to waste and invites you two to *please* be her guests. Can I show you up to the room?"

Zhang looked to Hong, his eyes suggesting it was okay with him if she was comfortable with the idea.

Hong asked, "Will she be back soon?"

"She hopes so, since she wants to meet both of you and her flight leaves tomorrow for Dunhuang. In any event, she said she will try to call to the suite to speak with you. Shall we go?" Li said, directing the way with his hand.

Hong picked up her purse, "Okay, let's go."

When they got to the suite they were shocked by the grandeur. It was bigger than either of their apartments, which they chuckled about, had a separate bedroom, two toilets, a living and dining area, and a wide view of the darkening city, the orange glow of sunset enhanced by the pollution. There was a butler in attendance and a dining table set for three.

"Wah, she's not even here on a government travel allowance, this is her own spending. How much is a room like this?" Hong asked Guest Services Li.

"This is the Ambassador Suite, not our most luxurious. The rack rate is RMB4,000 per night," he paused and turned away as a mobile device buzzed, and he checked it. Looking up from its screen, Li said, "Ah. Well. Dr. Byron has just written again. The tour company has put all the bus passengers up in another hotel near the Great Wall. She apologizes, but she won't be coming here tonight. Again, she says she has prepaid for the suite and the dinner and wants you two to enjoy it." Li flashed a toothy, obsequious smile.

"You're sure this is all prepaid. We don't want Byron to pay for stuff she hasn't ordered, and we certainly will not entertain any bill presented to us," Zhang said.

Li turned to the butler. "Please confirm to our guests that the room and the meal are all paid for."

The butler snapped open a leather-bound tab folder and looked at the list of dishes and beverages. "Yes, sir, the bill has been settled already."

Li looked at Hong and Zhang, his hands open palms up, inviting any further questions. "Do enjoy your stay," he handed them a card simply imprinted with the hotel logo, his name, title, and mobile number. "Please call if you need anything," he backed out of the room, a eunuch departing an audience with the emperor and empress.

The butler showed them to their seats across from each other at the small table with one rose in a vase placed at its center.

339

"I am curious why Dr. Byron was seeking to meet you, too?" Hong asked as they picked over some small plates of delicacies and roast meats waiting for the first main course to be delivered. The waiter had shown them a bottle of warmed, old, Shaoxing rice wine, to which they had nodded their approval, and he poured small glasses for them.

"Bottoms up," Zhang said and cleared the small glass, swirling the sweet, amber wine over his tongue to savor its complexity. "She suggested that she was in a similar role in the UK government and wanted to have a friendly 'get to know you' meeting during her tour. I'm single, most of my nights are devoted to work, so it seemed a pleasant distraction."

Hong matched his toast and signaled to the waiter to refill their glasses. She delicately took up the shot and lifted it with two hands and faced him. "To new friends."

He smiled. "To new friends." They downed their second glass.

"I am guessing you have been swamped chasing leads coming out of the Prosperous Glory Association scandal," Hong probed.

"Yes, that has kept me occupied. But sooo worthwhile to see these depraved scumbags get caught right in the spotlight. Vermin running for the corners. It is a case that is getting bigger every day, as they rat each other out and reveal perps we did not have visibility into before. What about your side?"

"I have had some internal corruption cases within the MEE to take action on coming out of the Prosperous Glory Association dragnet. Frankly, the thing that has been piling up on my inbox is Green Guards cases."

"That's curious. Tell me more," Zhang asked as his eyes narrowed in on hers.

"I keep getting these well-researched briefs related to individual arrests of Green Guard protestors. Each brief includes video of the protest they were involved in at the time of arrest showing no violence from the protestor, and a well-written summary of the motivation for the protest with specific evidence of the environmental crimes being committed, of which the Green Guard was trying to raise awareness. This is beyond my purview. Then each brief highlights specific individuals within the MEE who have not enforced the laws in their locales leading to these abuses, suggesting some collusion, and in some cases the brief includes evidence of corruption. Thousands of these briefs. It is quite overwhelming, and the thing is, I don't know where they're coming from."

"I said 'curious' before. Very curious," he signaled for the waiter to refill the shots. "I am getting the same kind of briefs. Also delivered anonymously. I have been too busy to act on them, but I feel bad about that. Do you think the Guards *should* be prosecuted?"

"When I look at these briefs, when I look at their rhetoric and the nature of their actions, I just think they are supporting the true principals of our Party, the intent of our laws. The Party, people like us, have to get on the right side of this. Otherwise, it gives strength to those who ask, 'Why isn't the fake video of President Zhao at the UN the real policy of the government?'"

Zhang rubbed his chin, deep in thought, and looked into Hong's eyes. "Agreed. So, what are we going to do about it, Hong Xin? It's up to us!" Zhang said with a positive tone of partnership, not conspiracy, as he hoisted his Shaoxing and waited for her riposte.

She smiled at her new friend. She adored Zhang's attitude. And with them both on the Supervisory Commission, perhaps they could even get the attention of Commissioner Su Yuanjing on this bounty of caseloads that had been dropped in their laps. She could see this going places, doing much good. Her mind warmed to the idea and to the man she faced across the table.

Maybe it's the Shaoxing talking, but it would be a pity to let this suite go to waste, she thought. *Perhaps a satisfying tryst or two. Who knows what joy we may find on that Olympic-sized bed?*

⊃ 人 ⊂

SU YUANJING SAT AT THE CONFERENCE TABLE WITHIN THE Righteous Fraternity meeting room surveying the faces surrounding him. He had never felt so sure of something so far from his normal experience of life and people, had never imagined he could or would want to broker such an amnesty, but this deal was a "go." He was prepared to present the edict of President Zhao with a confident and secure feeling in his heart. This was the right thing to do.

It had taken several days of negotiation, and the insistence of the Mount Liang leaders that they have a direct communication with the president, but they had hammered out the details. The president was back from New York, and though his meeting with Coin was marred by the deepfake incident, it had been fruitful otherwise. A new level of trust seemed to have been reached with the American president.

At the table to Su's left sat Wen Huan-zhang, until last week the chief of staff to General Gao Qiu. When his boss was laid low, the records showed that Wen had tried to reveal malfeasance within the Eastern Command, but this had been "handled" internally.

Wen was a schoolmate of Su's, and though they had not seen each other in years, Su felt an immediate affinity for him again. He tested this by tasking Wen to unearth what turned out to be copious evidence of General Gao's machinations on behalf of satisfying his son's lust and the framing of Lin Chong.

To his right sat Li Shishi. He noted a change since their last meeting in Beijing. *Has she fallen in love?* There was a softening to her demeanor. She seemed no less capable, no less loyal to the president, the Party, and the country, but there was a shift.

He eyed the young stalwarts around the table and wondered who if any of them might be an object of her affection. He did this without jealousy, malice, or lechery, more the view of a father or grandfather hoping his child will find total happiness and fulfillment. He knew that the relationship with President Zhao he had facilitated would eventually run its course.

Who might the lucky person be? Probably not Lu Da; why trade in the president for a man close to his age? Lin Chong was a strapping specimen, and Li's heart might have been melted by the story of his love's tragic end. Perhaps Song Jiang, with whom she had spent more time in Qingdao. Maybe even Yan Qing, though Su had not imagined Li to be interested that way in the same sex. Probably not Wang Lun, too taciturn. He put further rumination out of his mind. Work to do.

"Gentlemen, brothers, sisters, thanks to your efforts and the efforts of Superintendent Li, the president and I know how loyal you are, that you act on behalf of what is right and good. We did not realize you were being wronged, or more correctly, we knew there were corrupt elements in our employ who wronged the people, but the same network of corruption foiled our attempts to root them out and obscured your plight. I apologize that this day took so long to arrive. Our discussions this week have proceeded in good faith, and today is the product of that openness and genuine intent. The president himself would like to read to you the amnesty. You will understand if he cannot be here in person but comes to you from the Hall of Culture and Virtue."

In the center of the table stood a black tablet with two screens opened so people on both sides of the table could see it.

President Zhao's face appeared. He had just returned from New York. Jet lag subdued the cherubic luster of the great, strong, compassionate leader usually exuded in posters and television appearances, but he was otherwise energized and smiling at the prospect of delivering this message. "Greetings from Beijing. Firstly, I want you to trust that this is indeed me, and not a deepfake video of me, delivering this important message."

There was laughter around the room, though more than one person immediately began to wonder if the pardon they were being offered could be a fabrication.

"A bad joke, I am afraid, but that is the world we live in and even more reason why I seek to enlist honest heroes like you. This is my commitment to you:

"From the day I assumed my office as chairman of the Party and president of China, I have led with virtue and righteousness, setting an example to the world of rectitude, seeking peace first through deserved rewards and just punishments. As a matter of policy and for the good of the nation, I have sought upright ministers who act with love for the people. All this in an effort to create a China that is charitable, where happiness is bestowed equally on all, to the last infant.

"The 108 Heroes of Mount Liang have demonstrated loyalty and righteousness. They do not engage in wanton violence. The crimes they have committed were not without reason. Many were wronged by corrupt ministers and leaders within my own government, and I deeply sympathize with them.

"I have directed Commissioner Su Yuanjing to convey my written amnesty to the 108 Heroes of Mount Liang for the crimes they have committed in the past. To each of the thirty-six leaders and managers, I also offer restitution of one finished and furnished luxury apartment within the Mount Liang complex. For each of the seventy-two remaining heroes, I offer restitution of one finished and furnished standard apartment within the Mount Liang complex.

"From today forward, the 108 Heroes will cast aside doubt in the rectitude and sincerity of their government and will be employed as a force for good. Important tasks will be given to you."

He paused.

Chai Jin slapped his hand repeatedly and heartily on the table. "Hurrah for the president!"

There were smiles, nods of acknowledgement, and some cheers all around the table, and the thirty-six leaders and managers seated and standing around it clapped and whistled.

"Yes," the president said as the clapping abated, "this is a moment to celebrate, but not too long and not too drunkenly, comrades. Commissioner Su will share with you the written amnesty and our plans for Mount Liang. There is important work to do. I will sign off now."

Li Shishi stood up and passed out thirty-six person-specific copies of the amnesty agreement in duplicate, all signed by Zhao and chopped with the presidential seal.

Su said, "These agreements are blanket amnesties for crimes you have previously committed. Of course, they do not pardon you from future crimes, and you do need to sign on the dotted line to accept them. Please stay on our side of the law in the future," he smiled and winked.

Chai Jin broke in, "As part of our agreement, the government is buying this whole town from me. My contractors will finish the construction and outfitting. Your apartments will be done up very nicely, I assure you. This entire two-tower podium will be the operational and residential center of the new cyber-force. Plenty of room to grow in all regards."

"Yes, we want to turn Mount Liang into a new cyber-force within the government, absolutely secret," Su resumed. "It will act as a cyber investigation arm of the Supervisory Commission. Lin Chong will be the lone visible member. He will liaise with and have access to resources within Public Security and the military but will not be required to disclose to either the nature of the work done here by you.

"In his absence, Retired Major Lu Da will be chief operating officer. We propose that Wang Lun will oversee programming, Song Jiang will oversee systems and operational security, and Li Kui will be in charge of physical security. Chief of staff Wen, whom you have all met now, will resume that role here, reporting to Lu Da.

"Your pardons are not dependent on your acceptance of a commission in the new cyber-force, but we hope your dedication to justice and a better China will see you devote your expertise and passion to this new undertaking.

"Lin Chong has been given an important mission overseas and will be away for an undetermined length of time. Care to comment, Major Lin?"

Lin Chong stood up. "Thank you, Mr. President. The president, Commissioner Su, and Superintendent Li have shared with me the details of an international incident that almost resulted in China being wiped off the map. I am being sent to the United States with a shiny, new diplomatic passport to assist their cyber-forces in determining who set off this incident. As superhuman as my skills are," he said and paused to let his feigned immodesty sink in and generate some laughter, "I will no doubt come back to task you for support. As and when I do, know that my request is urgent and with consequences if I fail. I know I can count on you. Questions?"

Yan Qing raised her hand, "This question is for Little Whirlwind. If you are finally going to finish building this city, can we pleeeeez get some more restaurants? I am *sooo* fucking tired of Zhu Gui's dumplings and noodles!" The room broke out in groans, laughter, and knowing celebration, not the least from the Parched Earth Crocodile Zhu Gui, who smiled broadly and clapped his hands.

The taciturn White-Clad Scholar Wang Lun sat off in a corner without a trace of jubilation. *This is not my gig*, he decided. *Time to pack up my toys and find another cause to which I can devote my life.*

⊃ 人 ⊂

LIN CHONG ARRIVED IN WASHINGTON, DC, ON A NONSTOP COM-mercial flight from Beijing. He had declined the offer from the Foreign Ministry to have his computer, phone, and memory drives placed in a diplomatic pouch. He did not want *anyone* to handle his tech. Protected by a diplomatic passport, not to mention the dense encryption he used, these items he carried could not be searched, and nothing of any intelligence value was found during the "random TSA inspection" of his checked bag before it was deposited on the luggage strip. He had been picked up at the airport by Chinese embassy staff and driven to his quarters, tailed all the way.

The tail was clumsy. He had gotten basic training in field craft and was far from an expert, but this was an amateur effort. The same car remained close behind his during the entire journey. He found this almost comical. However, he had learned that within the pith of a joke might hide the barb of a threat.

His quarters were booked in an apartment belonging to a large residential complex built for Chinese embassy staffers on Connecticut Avenue. As he pulled up to the entrance, Ambassador Chen Zongshan came out to greet him. "Major Lin, welcome to America!" he said, pulling Lin out of the limo with his warm handshake.

"Thank you, Ambassador Chen, for your time."

"The president said I should extend any courtesy or help you require." They ascended to the seventh floor in the elevator, and Chen took him to his unit, a compact but cheerfully modern space with a large, sunlit window.

When they had sat down, Lin asked, "Did he explain my mission?"

"No. You report to him. I report to the minister of foreign affairs. It is best that it remains compartmentalized. However, I was the go-between in communications with Coin. I know who you are, what you have been through, and that the Americans believe you played a role in the dam burst. Your discussions with them are crucial to defusing the tensions between our countries."

Truth be told, you know much more than I anticipated, Lin thought.

"Is the embassy tailing me?"

"Not that I am aware of."

"I'm not sure if it is the Americans or us, but someone is, it's obvious."

"I will make inquiries. You want it to stop? Or have me put a tail on your tail to find out who they are?"

"If it is you, and you know about it, that's okay. I have been through a lot of shit lately. I don't want any of the Prosperous Glory Association remnants coming after me."

"Let's countersurveil. I have a guy I think I can trust here. He has worked with me at several postings and never let me doubt his loyalty or competence."

"If it is not too much to ask."

"Nonsense. The State Department communicated to the Chinese embassy the office address you should report to and your counterpart's name, Dr. Mili Parekh. A car will take you there in the morning." The old man continued to brief Lin regarding the situation between China and America, inoculated him against the pressures that Americans might bring to bear on him, and let him know again that he had Chen's full support.

"Thank you, sir."

The senior, wizened ambassador with neatly trimmed white hair looked up into Lin's eyes. "No. Thank you. You are the future of China, you and people like you. Strong, smart, uncorruptible, indomitable. Serving you is an honor."

⊃ 人 ⊂

IT WAS A BALLSY MOVE THAT PRESIDENT COIN HAD MADE, MILI Parekh reflected, accepting China's offer to send their top cyber warrior to the US to assist in identifying why he had been fingered in the Oroville Dam attack and whether his insights could also help to narrow down the actual enemy. She had been invited to the White House one further time to discuss planning for the interactions. In that meeting the mood in the room was very mixed.

At first, she mistook the hot and cold as misgivings or doubt in her. With the progress of the meeting, she knew it was bigger than that. Those who felt the president should not have gone ahead with this tried to impose their will on the structure of cooperation and sharing such that she knew it would be fruitless, or glacially slow.

Without coming off as naïve, she was able to state with logic and focus that it was in the best interests of the US intelligence community to determine what Lin Chong knew, what he could explain about the coding they had identified, and whether he could help them to determine the real culprit. If he was of no use to them, or worse had come to America to look under their skirts, she had no reservations in calling a halt.

Vesuvio, citing the president's own call to "combine forces, pool resources" insisted that a member of the CIA's cyber warfare team join the group, and thereafter the Department of Defense Cyber Command and Department of Homeland Security's National Cyber Security Center all piled on to send their own brains. The director of the NSA had also appointed another advisor from another section to help, too. It was decided that the meetings would be held in an office park near to Fort Meade used by NSA contractors and equipped with secure lines.

Mili Parekh was rather excited with the anticipation of meeting him as she waited in the reception area of the office space disguised as a PR firm setup for her team's use for the duration. It was a rare feeling.

Her condition had meant she did not have a normal teenagerhood like other women. But she guessed the feeling was like schoolgirl jitters before a prom she had read about—the one where a handsome senior invites you—or what kids who celebrated Christmas felt as wrapped packages were put under the tree. Neither event had she experienced herself. What will this day reveal? She knew it was more than business; the security of the homeland was riding on this. Nevertheless, she felt excited.

She had brought Hugh Chang to translate and Harley Barrows as backup brains. Jill Westerhoff was at Meade holding down the fort. They stood to each side of her as the door of the office opened and in strode Major Lin Chong.

He filled the doorway. Both Harley and Hugh looked up at him and thought the same thing she did; he looked like he could crush them both if that was his wont. Handsome, with neatly cut hair, a trimmed mustache, and goatee, he was dressed business casual, not in a uniform.

Lin raised an eyebrow, looked at Mili, smiled warmly, and in a gesture as unexpected as it was touching, he knelt bringing himself eye to eye with her and took her hand to shake. "Dr. Parekh, it is an honor to meet you. I am Major Lin Chong, on special assignment and at your disposal." The English was fluent, the accent a mix of British and Chinese.

"Major Lin. Niish to make your acquaintanch. Your English ish refreshingly good." It was no surprise he guessed who she was. The State Department had told the Chinese embassy who his counterpart would be.

"I spent a year at Oxford," he said. Parekh noted they would have to update their dossier on him. "Under an assumed name," he added with a smile.

"You can head back to the fort," she said, not introducing Hugh, which he understood perfectly well and took his leave. "Thish ish Harley Barrows. He has been working on trying to identify who generated these exploits."

They shook hands.

"We have a team waiting back here to meet you. Can we get you coffee, tea?"

"Coffee, please, a latte if you have it."

Harley went to the pantry shaking his head, thinking, *This ain't Cupertino, Bud,* and poured a cup of brew adding creamer powder.

He went back to the conference room, where introductions were being made. "*Americano* with powder is all we have, sorry," he said, handing the cup to Lin.

"No worries. Thank you."

Parekh continued the introductions. "Thish ish Sam Jones from the CIA's Directorate of Digital Innovation." Sam Jones was not his real name, and he was not exactly from the CIA's DDI, but that was fine to him.

"Major Lin," he said, shaking the hand.

"Smith and Jones seem to be very common names in your agency," Lin said with a smile. "I am grateful it is easy to remember."

"I am Major Jordan Walsh, from the DOD's Cyber Command. Nice to meet you, Major," Walsh said in a friendly tone and Southern accent. He was dressed in his Air Force uniform.

A new person entered the room. "Sorry I am late. You must be Mili," she said, going over to shake her hand. "I am Rebecca Stein from National Cyber Security Center. Major Lin?" she acknowledged him with a nod then reached across the table to shake hands.

"That ish an arm of Homeland Security," Parekh added. "And thish ish another NSA colleague, Dr. Trashee Jeong." Tracy was two levels higher up in the NSA and oversaw special technology initiatives.

"Dr. Jeong. Pleased to meet you," Lin said.

When they were all seated, Parekh said, "Thish ish an extraordinary meeting, one wish none of ush probably ever imagined might take playsh. Neverthelessh, we welcome you, Major Lin, to America and hope that wesh your inshights we can make progressh in identifying who made the attack on the Oroville Dam."

"Yes, these are extraordinary times. I note that since I arrived, I have been under constant surveillance, I assume by members of your FBI. I also assume they are there for my *protection*. Thank you for that. I am here to cooperate with you, and I hope that at least within this room we can share what we know to achieve Dr. Parekh's goal."

No one in the room knew anything about any surveillance, and none of them addressed the matter.

"So, what do you know about the attack?" Jones said.

"Only what is reported on the news. And that the NSA somehow identified me as being responsible for it."

"And you are not?"

"That remains to be seen..."

"You mean you *might* be?" Jones interjected.

"Did I single out the Oroville Dam for destruction and initiate the attack? No. Did I write code that might have been used in the attack? That remains to be seen. I am being as frank as possible." Lin stared coldly at Jones. "Last night after receiving the briefing document from the State Department, I downloaded Dr. Parekh's dissertation on memetics and read it."

"The whole thing?" Parekh asked incredulously.

"Yes, brilliant. I'm just guessing here, but you built a library of memetic markers you can use to identify who wrote code."

"That ish correct."

"Impressive. And it must work pretty well for you to hold your job these years since getting your PhD. So, it would help to know what code you have attributed to me." There was silence and concerned looks around the table.

"Really!? I am not asking that you show me how you attributed it to me. I have already figured that out. But the start of this has got to be a discussion of what it is I am accused of doing. I have written more than one exploit in my day, you know?" Lin said with a smile to break the ice. "Let's narrow it down, shall we?"

Parekh nodded to Barrows, who projected his computer's output onto the large flat-screen panel on the wall.

"This coding was used to ingress the systems at Oroville Dam. Similar coding was used to break into servers at IPAWS and on some private servers," Barrows said. Several pages of coding slowly scrolled.

"I pause?"

"Uh, Integrated Public Alert Warning System. We have not been able to figure out what the coding is doing. Is it a universal key?" Universal keys were the boogeymen of the intelligence community and had been depicted in many sinister movies and books, the holy grail of hacking, an algorithm capable of breaking through all digital barriers without resorting to years of calculations.

Lin Chong wrung his hands on the table looking at them for a moment. Under almost any other circumstance he would have felt great pride or wonder. But not in this moment. He wrestled with a tumult of emotions he had sought to settle for some months. It would take meditation to work through this, but now he had to address the people here.

"Yes, I recognize this coding. I wrote it. Most of it anyway. But I can say conclusively it does not represent an attack from China. I wrote it after I went...how do you say... AWOL. The PLA knew nothing about it."

"So, you *are* saying you attacked the dam," Jones said with some tension.

"No. But I wrote this code. In answer to Harley's question, it is not a universal key. It is a key to about eight billion semiconductors and counting." He let that sink in. "It is part of a top-secret, seven-year program I conceived and led to infiltrate semiconductor design and manufacture globally."

Jones could not believe his ears. They were not a half hour into the meeting, and they were getting this kind of revelation! "What can you tell us about the program?"

Lin held up his hand in a gentle "stop" gesture. "As curious and itching as you no doubt are to understand all that, it is not my purpose in coming, which is to help you find out who did this to your country and stop them."

"Seems to me we know that already, Major Lin. *You* did. I think your government has sold you out, sent you to placate our president, who was ready to deliver hellfire on China if they didn't offer up some fresh meat. They know that under the circumstances your diplomatic status is... negotiable." The word slid off his tongue like it did not want to be there. "Of course, if you were coming with full disclosure to us, I suppose someone would take an interest and set you up quite comfortably. Frankly, I think the alternatives will be worse than Guantanamo."

Parekh had had enough of the posturing and sidetracking. "Finished, Jones? We got work to do."

"I *would* like to step back for a moment, though," Tracy Jeong said. "What do you mean you wrote this when you were AWOL, but it was a seven-year program?"

"A fair question," Lin said evenly. He knew that some iteration of it would come up if the NSA had indeed identified his coding in the attack. That his code had contributed to the destruction and loss weighed heavily on him. And he was willing to submit himself to punishment or retribution if he felt that his creation, Indra's Net, had done this.

On the journey from Shanghai to DC, he had put together a presentation to let them understand why he had written the program. "If you will indulge me, and by way of bringing you all up to speed on what has brought me here, can I show you some slides?"

Jones rolled his eyes and muttered, "Drowning in a sea of PowerPoints," but Parekh encouraged Lin to start.

"Project Centipede was conceived and led by me at Unit 61398. We infiltrated major semiconductor EDS tool companies and embedded within the design tools the imperative to create inconspicuous back doors into any semiconductors designed to have a communication function. This was a total success. As far as the PLA understands Centipede, these back doors provided it with the ability to terminate the communication of the semiconductor chip with other chips rendering them useless.

"However, I had actually designed the hack to perform as a C2—command and control—server within the chip. This functionality was not known to anyone, and I alone had the coding to activate it.

"As for me and going AWOL, I trust what happened to me has never happened in the history of the US military." He opened an online video archive of Zhang Zhenniang on the evening of her performance of *The Four Sea-*

sons. "This is my wife, Zhang Zhenniang. She was a wonderful violin soloist. We had been married for a couple of years, happily."

He let them listen to her play until Jones started shaking his head restlessly.

"She was targeted for seduction by this guy, who is the son of this guy," the slides cycled through Gao Yanei and General Gao Qiu, their names and titles shown under their photos, "who is in charge of the PLA Eastern Command. He trumped up charges of espionage and treason against me to give his son a chance at my wife and had me arrested and interrogated."

Lin quickly took off one shoe and sock and hauled the foot up, plopping it on the table while several slides he had obtained from Li Shishi of himself, beat up and bleeding on the concrete floor, cycled through. "This scarring on my feet," he poked at the puffy, shiny, pink scar tissue. "Done with boiling water. For sheer pain, it's much worse than water boarding, I can tell you. But I got them back and escaped." Military police photos of the crushed and impaled jailers and Lin's bloody footprints left on the concrete appeared. "You may have heard I was wanted for murder."

"Holy shit," Jones murmured.

"I found refuge in a hacker community. However, the Gaos would not relent. They destroyed me and destroyed my wife. She took her life rather than cave in to the son."

There was a police crime scene photo of her limp body hanging from the drainpipe in the bathroom.

"In my despair, an act of insanity fueled by my grief, I created a new iteration of Centipede. One that would take revenge for me, out of my control, out of anyone's control. I conceived it as an artificial neural network with self-organizing agency, self-learning, and a level of awareness limited only by the number of interconnections it could make between all the nodes of the ever-expanding Centipede network."

Lin paused and probed the faces of each of these representatives of the American cyber intelligence community. The expressions were hard, to be sure, but not all were venomous, some struck with a look of fearful wonder or sympathy.

"There ish a lot to unpack there," Parekh said.

"Yeah, like how you killed those guards?" Jones asked.

"I meant Shentipede," Parekh pushed back impatiently.

Lin tapped some characters into his mobile device. "Sorry, had to get a translation. It is important to differentiate Centipede from the other program I created that used Centipede. I called it Indra's Net."

Barrows perked up and said quietly to himself, "Indrajala."

"Harley, what you got?" Parekh asked, knowing he was best when encouraged to speak up. It was a curse and a blessing that Barrows had a prodigious memory, not photographic, but substantial. It helped him in recalling lines of code he had written or read long ago, but there was also lots of other information of unrealized potential or significance that was stored there.

"There was a book mentioned in Stravinsky's notes about Buddhist logic and epistemology that I read. It had a chapter on Indra's Net, a mythological net with a jewel at the intersection of each strand of mesh that perfectly reflects the image of all the other jewels in the net. Symbolizes interbeing, the law of the universe operating on us all equally. Our actions are all connected, and ultimately, we are all connected to each other. The takeaway for me was the fractal nature of the imagery."

They were all familiar with Mandelbrot sets creating infinitely scalable fractal images, like a kaleidoscope but visually and mathematically consistent at every level.

Lin looked at the underling who had brought him coffee with more respect. "Correct on all counts, Harley. I did not expect anyone to know anything about it. Saves me trying to explain."

"You have made the case that the Chinesh government did not wantonly attack the US, which I can accept for the time being. Letsh put ashide questions of your culpability in the dam attack a little longer. What did you program Indra's Net to do?"

"Take revenge."

"Yesh, but what does that mean? You had to program or define a value for 'revenge,' right?"

"No, I programed it to learn how and why people take revenge on others, then observe people wronging others, and then to take revenge on the perpetrators."

"You shtill have to define values for 'how' and 'why' and 'wronging,'" Parekh insisted.

"It was my design that Indra's Net would observe and learn and then act. I was not sure it would work, I never tested it. I was just a desperate, angry person lashing out."

"How does that get us to the Oroville Dam? What massive wrong was it taking revenge on?" Tracy Jeong asked.

Lin shook his head; he did not know.

"What other vengeful actions did it take?"

"I set it loose. Nothing happened. I didn't know whether it ever took *any* action, until now."

"When did you set it loose exactly?" Walsh asked.

"Exactly?" Lin thought for a moment. "Evening of June 21."

"Which would put it in the morning here," Walsh said and looked around the table.

"Which would make it when the GIBA anomaly started," Jeong added.

"I read about a slowdown in the West but dismissed the connection. It did not impact us in China, or at least any slowdown was not discussed because the burden caused by government surveillance is always shifting and could cause slowdowns."

"Do you have a copy of the Indra's Net coding you wrote?"

"Yes."

"Are you willing to show us?"

"If I think that it will help us achieve the mission of exposing who attacked the dam. At least the AI parts of Indra's Net that would lead to targeting a dam."

"We will circle back to that later. Letsh take a short break," Parekh said.

Several people went outside to give updates to their offices on the morning's intel.

Lin followed Harley and Jones to the pantry to get a refill. "With a pipe," he said.

"What's that?" Jones asked, not making a connection.

"I killed them with a piece of iron pipe. Quick work when you know how to do it." Lin smiled impishly.

ⴂ 人 ⴅ

HEAVENLY DIAMANTINE SONG WAN AND THUNDERHEAD DIAmantine Du Qian stood with Zhu Gui as Wang Lun, dressed as usual in his white tracksuit, approached them on the loading dock behind the Mount Liang complex.

It was approaching 10:00 p.m., and two twenty-foot, tractor-trailer containers had been backed in and loaded end to end with GPU processing blades slid into rack enclosures, fifty-six per rack, all racks cocooned in plastic film and separated with Styrofoam padding, then locked together in rows with steel strapping tape. Altogether 2,688 GPU processing blades with their digital mining of Taelspin coins temporarily abated. Any coins that had been fully mined had already been extracted and deposited off these blades. What remained was work in process. RMB33 million of equipment on the road, not including the value of partially mined coin.

When Wang Lun had come to Lu Da to tell him he was leaving, it had pre-cipitated a mini crisis. He had his pardon in hand and said he was choosing not to accept the commission in the president's new cyber-force. He would just take his "toys" with him, which in his mind was all the Taelspin mining capacity, and head off into the sunset.

This caused problems all around. Zhao questioned why Wang was leav-ing and what he could do about it, Su questioned Wang's ownership of the equipment and the illegal use to which it was put. Song Wan and Du Qian questioned what they would do to fund Hua Yen without the cryptocur-rency mining.

To Lu, he addressed the government's questions. "You see this paper. It means I can go. I can't be harassed about the past anymore, and it is explic-it that the amnesty is not dependent on accepting the commission in the new force. So, I choose not to. Of course, if Zhao and Su want to renege on the amnesty, well, it won't sit well with the Heroes here. Bad way to start off."

When reminded that unauthorized mining of cryptocurrency was still il-legal and he could be arrested for future crimes, he said, "Yes, I am switch-ing off them all. I will go somewhere it *is* legal."

When Heavenly and Thunderhead Diamantine put the full-court press on him, Wang Lun partially relented. "You two have been with me a long time. We did much good together, and I am happy for you that the Little Whirlwind's negotiation won you recognition of Hua Yen as a legitimate religious organization in China and not a cult. That's all good. Moneywise, the Little Whirlwind is happy; the government is taking this improbable town off his hands for a good price. The 108 Heroes will have the funding they need to do Zhao's bidding. But I don't see the government giving Hua Yen tithes, even if they aren't going to arrest your followers."

"Exactly right, brother. Don't abandon us," Song and Du implored.

"I have to move on. But let me do this. I will leave half the racks here and give you half the currency we have already mined. You see if you can get a license to mine the rest. Good luck on that. The currency should tide you over until you can start ramping up donations in the daylight from your converts, okay?" That conversation had led to this evening.

The doors were sealed on the containers, and armored bank trucks led and tailed the caravan ready to depart. Armed guards escorted the truck drivers and signaled they were ready to go.

Zhu Gui looked over and asked Wang Lun the question everyone had already asked and no one had gotten an answer to. "Where are you headed?"

"Someplace the electricity is cheap, the bandwidth is broad, the laws are favorable, and the air is clean."

"Where is that?"

"Don't know yet," he said, shaking his head and heading to the cab of the front armored car. He climbed aboard and drove off.

ⅆ 人 ⅽ

PAREKH FELT THAT THE AFTERNOON WAS GOING MORE SMOOTH-ly than the morning. For some reason, Jones had dismounted his high horse and fallen into line. The discussions became more collaborative and less confrontational. *I guess men have pissing contests because they have dicks. Women are much less inclined because we can't point and shoot. We just have cat fights instead,* she reasoned.

"We shtill have some things to unpack here," she said to the group. "You used some phrashes thish morning, and we all need to share a common undershtanding of definitions if we are going to crack thish."

"I agree," Lin said.

"Shentipede and Indra's Net are not the shame thing, or one ish not an improvement of the other, right?"

"Correct. Centipede is built into the silicon, part of the semiconductor's design: compact, hidden, unobtrusive, and exceedingly difficult to detect within the billions of circuits on a modern chip. It is accessed from the outside and activated by a password."

"Why ishn't the request for acshess stopped by firewalls, anti-virus detection?"

"Those firewalls are chip based. At some point, there is a 'first contact' between the request coming in and the firewall. If that first point of contact within the firewall is a chip equipped with Centipede, it precedes any action the system can take. The firewall has already been breached."

"And Indra's Net?"

"As happily conceived in meditation, it was just a thought experiment to link all the nodes of Centipede together. Later, in my despair, I took that and wrote, let's call it Indra's Net 2.0, the weaponized version."

"Okay. Sho, what part of the code did Harley put up?"

"The outreach to Centipede to initiate control."

"Harley, can you put up some of the other coding we captured? Letsh shay the program to detect and modulate the harmonics of the dam attack."

The coding was projected and scrolled on the screen.

"Recognize thish?"

"No. It's nothing I wrote, nor anything anyone on my team at Unit 61398 wrote while I was there."

"Harley, put up the IPAWS messaging shistem coding. Lin, thish wash used to cushtomize the emergency message to all people in the area to be impacted."

"No, I don't recognize it."

"Nesht question. You shaid you designed Indra's Net 2.0 'as an artificial neural network with shelf-organizing agency, shelf-learning, and a level of awareness limited only by the number of interconnections it could make between all the nodes of the ever-expanding Shentipede network.'"

"Good memory, that's exactly what I said," Lin said.

"I lishten well," Parekh smiled. "Sho, do you think Indra's Net could have written these other coding packages?"

Lin thought deeply for a moment. "I expected that its learning process would build ... What do you say when something gets bigger and stronger over time?"

"Snowball."

The image in Lin's mind was fluffy, white, and benign, "No, more dangerous than that."

"We say 'snowball,' like a snowball at the top of a hill, as it rolls, it gets progresshively bigger and more threatening."

"Ah, absolutely right. It builds its learning first on the ways people harm each other, then on how those harmed take revenge, then on becoming aware in real time of people harming each other, then on how to take revenge on the perpetrators doing harm. Along the way, it was programmed to seek or access all learning opportunities. At the fourth stage it would seek exploits and tools it could use or access. It would write only what it needed."

"If it is snowballing, does that mean that its next exploit would be even bigger than Oroville Dam?" Stein from Homeland Security asked. There were concerned looks all around the table.

"I don't know. I don't know if there were smaller acts of revenge executed before this or if this is an escalation leading to something bigger. In my state of mind at the time, I hoped it would bring the whole world to a halt."

Jones had slipped back into negative mode. "Fucking poor design."

"Bullocks! You lot couldn't pull off something like this."

Jones was about to respond, but Jeong waved him quiet. "That's... not exactly true," she said, deliberating the selection of each word.

Parekh looked over at her NSA colleague and raised her eyebrows.

"I can't go into any details. It's not just you, Lin, don't take offense, some of my colleagues here are not cleared at that level of security. But we undertook a similar program, created a similar back door hardwired into the silicon. Much easier for us since the tool companies are mostly American. If you were not our adversary, I would say 'kudos' to you, Lin, for what you accomplished. High marks."

"Can we use one back door to control the other?" Harley asked.

"We will need considerably more detail from you about Centipede, Lin," Jeong said.

"I need to confer with my side first," Lin said.

"Alright. I think thish has been a productive firsht day," Parekh said. "Letsh adjourn now and reconvene tomorrow. Lin, pleege, make every effort on shecuring your permissions. We are counting on you, and so ish China."

ⵎ 人 ⵛ

LIN CHONG WAS GRATEFUL FOR THE BREAK. JET LAG WAS CATCHing up on him. The information he knew the Americans needed was a whole new level of treason, and one that his amnesty would not excuse. He rode to the Chinese embassy, mindful of the black sedan that tailed him, and checked in with the security officer, requesting to see the ambassador. Su Yuanjing and President Zhao had told him to trust Ambassador Chen alone, and it was to him he turned.

"I need to set up a secure call with President Zhao and Commissioner Su tonight."

"Okay. We will have to fit it in to Zhao's schedule. The earlier for him, the better. Be ready at 18:30. We will try from then. By the way, you were right about the tailing. Very curious. A car did follow you all the way to your appointment and all the way back."

"What can you tell me about it?"

"First, there was no one in it. It was autonomously driven. Second, it did not appear to be a US government vehicle. We are seeing if we can get someone to give us the name of the owner of the vehicle."

"As you said, curious. But it does not sound like XinHuaHui or American goons riding around to ambush me, so let's just keep it in view."

Lin found a quiet room within the embassy to rest. There was a sofa, but he found himself too agitated to sleep, so he sat in meditation for an hour.

He slowly cleared his mind, each breath wiping clean the dark purple slate of his mind's eye. The absence of thought made thoughts that intruded stand out. One by one he filtered what had emerged in the day of discussions with the Americans. Of course, there was their attribution methods and techniques, which had correctly fingered him out of an entire world of hackers. Impressive.

Then there was the exploit accompanying his Centipede coding in the attack. It was elegantly written. Had his creation created it? Had it learned so much, so fast? And if so, what was next?

There was a knock on the door, and Chen's secretary summoned him that it was time to take the call.

When he had secluded himself in the communications room and made the connection, the image appeared on the screen. "President Zhao, Commissioner Su. Sorry to disturb you so early."

"Early is best for us, before our day gets too busy. How was your meeting with the Americans? Everything resolved?"

"Sir, we had a good first meeting, but it will take many more to get through this."

"Do you understand why they have insisted on seeing *you*?"

"Yes, sir. I need your patience for a moment to explain something important."

"Proceed."

"The code they identified as used in the attack *was* written by me when I was at Unit 61398. However, China is not responsible for its use, and I think I have moved their thinking in that regard."

"Explain."

"When I was at Mount Liang, I wrote some code that utilized tools I had created at the PLA. This was released in a rage the day I learned my Zhen-

359

niang had killed herself. The other heroes at the Mount did not know about it; I am solely responsible. I have explained this to the Americans."

"And this program attacked their infrastructure?"

"It appears so. However, our discussions today concluded with the possibility of a graver threat. That the program I created may be ramping up or escalating to bigger attacks, anywhere."

"You have no control over it?"

Lin swallowed hard on his answer. "No, sir. And that is the purpose of today's call. Without sharing any details, the Americans said they have a tool like the one I deployed. Theirs may help us to get mine under control. To determine that, they will need the details of our weapon." Lin paused.

There was silence from the two faces on the screen. Finally, Zhao said, "It sounds like ours is not a weapon I can trust nor that I have any control over anymore. I intend to fully honor my commitment to President Coin, to help find out who did this and put an end to them, certainly to prevent a repetition. To that end, you have my permission to release the details of the program to the Americans."

"Thank you, sir."

"Major Lin. Set this right. What you have put in motion must be arrested. The fate of your Motherland depends on this. You understand?"

"Yes, Mr. President."

The screen went blank leaving Lin Chong alone with his thoughts, his plans, and his guilt.

⊃人⊂

THOMAS BROWN'S REAL NAME WAS ALMOST AS BLAND AS HIS cover name, "Sam Jones." But his role was, to him at least, exciting. Among the CIA's five directorates was the Directorate of Digital Innovation, of which the Center for Cyber Intelligence served to develop all manner of tools, software and hardware, to enable digital spying, digital cloaking, masking their activities, and protecting their systems.

He was the deputy chief of the Engineering Development Group (EDG) within the CCI. Under his direction more than 500 projects were underway in three divisions, each with multiple branches. Because the tools developed by the EDG were handed off to operations to be employed, it was rare his teams got the recognition from on high they so craved.

It was with a great sense of pride, then, that Brown had been called up through the chain of command to a meeting in the agency director's office before the arrival of Lin Chong. Director Vesuvio with Brown's boss's boss.

Brown had been tasked to present an overview of EDG and a categorized summary of R&D and work in process that was being funded. Two days overtime at his desk and the presentation was ready.

He heard Vesuvio was not stupid, but he was not a technologist, and Brown presented each category of work they were doing with a concrete example of how it might be used to protect and further the agency's mission. Vesuvio liked the approach, asked him some good questions, and thanked him for the clarity. That was the end of it.

Several days later, he had been called in once again. This time he was briefed on the president's decision to invite the Chinese to work together with the US intelligence community to determine how the attack on Oroville Dam had been done and who had done it. If that discussion went well, it was to be extended to the media hack propagating the deepfake video.

Vesuvio let it be known this cooperation was a dangerous move, of which they could only try to make the best. He wanted Brown to sit in on these meetings, be his eyes and ears, and learn as much as he could from the Chinese. He was to prepare recommendations for Vesuvio, especially if it seemed the NSA team was going to come in "a day late and a dollar short," in the director's words.

So far, the meetings had been a bonanza for the American intelligence community. Detailed electronic design files of the implants had been delivered for research by the NSA to determine if their implant could counter the Chinese implant.

That was all well and good, but Brown was more of a software guy. And what stuck out in the meetings was the unquestioned genius and feral unpredictability of this cat, Lin Chong. If he had succeeded in writing Indra's Net to achieve its mission, then it would be an artificial intelligence nightmare: distributed and encrypted, unpredictable and escalating. What could be done about it? Well, the CIA was nothing if not forward thinking, and that applied especially to the EDG.

Deep in an annex, literally in a basement space, was one of his most forward-thinking offices, not even a branch. Here were some brilliant people who thought about possibilities that were not even threats yet, just *let's say sometime in the future this happens, what do we do about it* threats.

This team had presented to him in the past, but it was the first time he had "walked the halls" and dropped in on them. They perked up, immediately appreciative of the attention.

Over cups of coffee shared in a small, gloomy conference room, Dr. Lem Lissack looked at Brown over the rims of eyeglasses perched on his nose and asked in mildly Tel-Aviv-accented, New York English, "By AI we are not talking about the kind of stuff industry designs to run machines better, right? You mean *The Matrix/Terminator* kind of AI."

"No, let's keep it realistic. Not an existential threat, just a program more sophisticated than we have dealt with before. Are we working on anything to contain it, to stop it?"

Lissack took a long slow breath. "Yes," he said after a think. "About two years ago we began to consider that problem. We created a hunter-killer program targeting AIs. We've never had a call to use it. In closed-loop, sterilized tests it seems to work. It seeks AI, identifies and verifies, and then basically explodes like ball bearings wrapped around C4 in all directions. Packets attach to adjacent AI coding and start shredding while other packets corrupt localized memory preventing reconstitution."

"What do you need to deploy it? We don't have a location to target."

Lissack smiled. "So we anticipated when we brainstormed. Hence, it is a *hunter*-killer. To deploy it we need a large sample of the AI coding. The larger the better. It will seek this out."

"But it has not been used before? Limitations? Expected blowback? By the way, what's it called?"

"The name was randomly generated, Sunrise Marshmallow. Yeah, I know, not exactly the most macho, aggressive name, but that's what happens with the random name generator. The need of a sample of coding is precisely one of its limitations. If we ever deal with such an AI, it is unlikely we will have sufficient examples of its coding to put the hunter on the scent. We have been working to tweak that. Another limitation is Sunrise Marshmallow's autonomy. Once it finds a target matching the code and verifies it is an AI, it does not wait for further instructions. It goes ballistic."

"Why?"

"Again, in our original brainstorming we expected that if we ever faced such an AI, it would be agile, and there would be no time for deliberation, do or die, right then. Milliseconds."

"Is it ready to deploy if we have a need to?"

"Yeah?" he said extending the affirmative into an uncertain questioning. "Is this not a hypothetical question?" Lissack asked with concern, staring over the rims of his glasses.

"Like you said, if we face a hostile AI, time will be of the essence. Today it is hypothetical. Tomorrow?" Brown's shoulders shrugged.

⊃ 人 ⊂

A WEEK HAD GONE BY. INITIALLY, LIN HAD MET WITH THE Americans for long days, explaining the files he handed to them detailing the design of the Centipede insertion into silicon. It did not help that the solution implanted was different for the two EDS tool companies his team had infiltrated. It gave the NSA researchers double the work to do.

From the NSA engineers' questions, he had been able to glean little usable intelligence about their device hack. Sometimes he could see a hint of admiration or "why didn't we think of that" in their eyes, but generally they were tight lipped, and he was left with the impression that the NSA's solution was not vastly different from his.

He had to force himself to be reminded that this was not an exchange or a negotiation, where he should expect to get an amount of information about their device equal to that he gave them. The exchange, he hoped, was trust and some security for China. What was going on in the background, he knew not.

In his free time, he had written reports from the Chinese embassy back to Mount Liang and the PLA. The NSA had provided him with coding they had captured coincident with the broadcast of the deepfake video. He sent this on to his counterparts at the Mount and within State Security. This was preceded by a call with Cai Jing, who was on his absolute best, conciliatory, almost fawning behavior. He had survived the National Supervisory Commission culling that had snared so many for the sole reason he was not a member of the Prosperous Glory Association. He had dodged that bullet. He did not care to try dodging another and had come clean when Su Yuanjing's men came to talk to him.

With Lin Chong, he started the conversation by saying, "Major Lin, I want you to know I knew nothing about what General Gao did to you. Absolutely despicable. In fact, I had my suspicions, which I was separately digging into."

"I'll take that as an apology, Cai, not that it changes your role in the mining deal. Don't forget, the Blue-Faced Beast and I are quite close now. And he has an amnesty. But that is not why I am calling. The president knows your teams are digging into the deepfake video broadcast, and he has asked me to give you a leg up whenever I can."

Cai choked on his hubris and responded, "Wow, any help would be appreciated. What have you got?"

What he had "got" blew Cai away. Terabytes of information, semidigested and categorized by the NSA, regarding the deepfake video's production and insertion. He had put the priority on giving substantive feedback to Lin Chong that he could report to the Americans; however, he knew that some of it would eventually be deconstructed and used by his teams to insert deepfake videos into local dissenting video blogs.

In his remaining free time Lin Chong had visited the museums on the Mall and one day walked from the White House through the city to the Capitol Rotunda. Along the way he noted neighborhoods that were run-down, crime infested, and poor. Poverty took on such a different appearance here, he thought.

In China, there were places where investment had not reached, where the water had not yet flowed to raise all boats. It was a question of the stage of development. Certainly, there were places even in the big cities that were crime infested, and wealth was not spread evenly, but in any location, there was a sense of struggle, struggling to make tomorrow, the next year, the next generation, better, wealthier, more educated. All he felt walking through the poorer sections in Washington was a sense of entropy, a surrender to negative circumstance, inevitable decline and depressed inertia. He did not know if this was cultural, historical, or racial in its roots, but it was different from what he observed in China.

Today they were reconvening. Lin Chong arrived on time bearing a round of large lattes and biscotti for everyone.

"You're a good man, Panther Head," Harley said in welcome greeting to the upscale caffeine.

When everyone had arrived, Parekh started the meeting. "I'll let Trashee dive right in. Sheems we have some bad news."

"Yes, well, certainly not a resolution. With Lin Chong's detailed files, our engineers were able to understand how our device implant might be able to take control of the Centipede implant. They had to determine whether one implant was further upstream of the other in the flow of data. Fortunately, our implant was upstream of Centipede in one tool and parallel to Centipede in another, meaning there was a chance it could control or pre-empt Centipede. We then did an estimate of device overlap; were all devices with Centipede built in also implanted with our device? We estimated that there was at least a 70 percent overlap, so worth continuing.

"It took several days of experimentation with coding to work out how to take control of the Centipede implant and then test that we had taken control. We did a closed-loop, sterile test on devices we knew to contain our implant. Nine out of ten responded, so we assume Centipede was not present on the tenth device.

"We ran our results up the flagpole and sought permission to run the operation in the wild. I am told this went all the way up to the White House and was approved. Last night we ran it, reaching out to over seven billion catalogued semiconductor points of contact embedded with our implant. The results are disappointing.

"After some initial success in taking control of the Centipede and getting its ping, they stopped responding. And although not as pronounced as the initial GIBA throttling of global bandwidth, we have measured about a one-and-a-half percent drop coincident with our execution of this operation."

There was silence around the table. "Thoughts?" Parekh asked. There was further silence.

"Okay, then shtart with me," Parekh led. "We shpent thish week looking at Shentipede hoping we could block acshess to the implant. That ish merely one part of Indra's Net. We need to take a deep dive into that program now. Thoughts?"

"Agreed," said Jones without elaborating how.

"I'm sho glad. Any ideas on next shteps?"

"I think that time has come," Lin said with resignation, "to unpack my Indra's Net program. Let you take it apart."

"Yah think?!" Jones sneered.

Harley spoke up, "That's a start, but don't get your hopes up too high."

"Elaborate, pleege," Parekh encouraged.

"If Panther Head did manage to write a program with self-organizing agency, with self-learning, then whatever it was as he released it, it is not now."

"There ish nothing to be learned from the original program?"

"It's not that there is nothing for us to learn from taking the program apart. This is what has been called the 'reproducibility crisis' in AI research. When you build self-learning into the program and just let it go, you can't predict what it will learn and how it will interpret or use what it learns. And even in controlled experiments on AI, two sets of identical programs once released into the learning environment can bifurcate and become vastly different animals.

"Imagine twin children in a big city getting separated from their parents and from each other. One wanders into a Disney store, and a kindly clerk calls Child Services, who take the child and find it a home. One wanders into a crack house and is sold into child prostitution. I am not going to say which one will turn out 'better,' but they sure as shit won't turn out the same."

"Is there another approach we can take?" Jeong asked.

"Perhaps. Panther Head..." Harley started.

"Why do you call him that?" Jones interjected, shaking his head impatiently as Walsh looked on and nodded agreement.

"It's his handle. He likes being called that, better than the way we butcher his Chinese name, right, Panther Head?" Harley asked.

Since Harley had stuck his neck this far out for him, Lin was not about to let him get abused. "Yes. I am comfortable with being called Panther Head. What were you going to ask, Harley?"

"Uh, let's see," his eyes rolled up as he retraced several thought steps. "Yeah, okay, a week ago when we showed you the code we had attributed to you, you said you wrote it and added 'most of it anyway.' What did you mean?"

"Exactly that. Interspersed within my original code were some additional lines."

"I am thinking that any changes to the coding may be expressions of how Indra's Net evolved. If we can identify and capture more samples of Indra's Net on the web, and compare it to the original, perhaps we can understand what it has become and thereby what it may do," Harley said.

They could all see that this approach had merits. It was a short cut, the destination of which yielded greater insight than just picking apart the original coding.

"I think we need to determine the ubiquity of the program, or conversely, the source and location of it," Walsh said.

"You may have the tools to do it, you are the world's greatest force in cyber intelligence and warfare," Lin stroked their egos, "but it will not be easy."

"What are we looking at?"

"I designed Indra's Net to be ubiquitous, not conspicuous. I think the fact you were not aware of it until the attack is proof of that. I adapted blockchain to create a secure, distributed, encrypted network of repositories for the program as it grew. This was priority number one, and where it went, where it hid, and the encryption it chose were all post-release."

"Okay, I think we need to farm thish out, shee what approach ish besht, make it a race. NSA, Cyber Command, CIA, your team in China, Lin. For we *are* in a race, ladiesh and gentlemen. Lin, I am going to have to ashk you to turn over your coding on the Indra's Net. Do you need to confer with your government firsht?"

"No, Mili. I want you all to know, once again, the highest priority of the Chinese government is to help identify who made this attack and stop them. I have been authorized to take the actions I deem necessary to do that. I will also have teams in China working on this."

"Shend daily progressh updates to me. Letsh convene again in a week at the latesht, or when one of you makes a breakthrough."

⊃ 人 ⊂

MICK COIN'S CABINET DID NOT HAVE HIS FULL ATTENTION TO-day. Normally he was able to focus on the matter before him and counted on that as a strength. But today he was having difficulty pulling his mind out of his last meeting and into this one.

The prior day Coin had met with the National Security Council, which focused on progress being made by the teams investigating the origin of the attack on the dam and the cooperation with China.

The CIA pushed hard on its analysis and recommendation that evidence pointed to a weaponized artificial intelligence created by Lin Chong and no longer under his control, designed with the intent to escalate acts of retribution without warning or predictability. The CIA strongly advocated utilizing a tool it had created for just such a contingency, a hunter-killer weapon to track Lin Chong's AI and destroy it before it could attack again. This would be a Covert Action—CA—program, executed by the CIA on behalf of the president.

The NSA advocated patience. The team was in the middle of its analysis of the coding and wanted to understand better the nature of the weapon, or the nature of the enemy, to prevent unexpected blowback. Also, China was cooperating fully, signaling a new, higher level of cooperation than ever anticipated and a bounty of intelligence. The Chinese major delivered copious detail about the Centipede design, and China's analysis of the deepfake video hack gave the NSA much-needed intel about China's capabilities.

If the CIA simply eliminated the threat, the NSA cautioned, there would be little further impetus for cooperation and learning. The Chinese major had thus far been unpersuaded by the prospect of fully defecting, nor intimidated by the prospect of spending his life in a US prison, so milking him for intelligence was the best option.

Coin ordered a presidential finding to be delivered to him stating the risk faced by the nation, the alternatives to taking the CA, and the scope, risk, and cost of taking the CA.

The draft finding had been presented to him that morning, and several tweaks were made. It was convincing, if not a slam-dunk conclusion. Even if the time and target of a next attack could not be established conclusively, the risk to the nation was ominous. Teams evaluating the deepfake video concluded that Indra's Net was also implicated in that attack. Given the sophistication and devastation of the Oroville Dam attack, it was recommended that action be taken immediately to prevent any further attacks. The NSA was said to have had its time at bat and had tried to regain control with their own tricks, but had failed, and worse, their actions had possibly precipitated a further burden on global transmission speeds. It was urged that the risk of nonaction was much higher than action. The CA was expected to be highly surgical, pinpointing AI systems embedded with the Indra's Net coding. The US's hand in the CA would not be revealed.

Director of National Intelligence Smith had sided with the CIA in this debate, and seconding Vesuvio's perspective, urged the president to "take the shot."

As Coin leaned toward the recommendation, he sought council from other members of the NSC. There were risks, but he was assured many of these would be ameliorated by deniability. The CIA as a matter of course would disguise the tool and its provenance and insert it from a foreign location. Short of a government armed with tools like the NSA's, it would not be easy to attribute to America whatever unexpected consequences the destruction of the AI might bring. Vesuvio assured him that, due to the nature of cyber warfare, it would be over quickly, and the defense and intelligence establishment would learn volumes in the aftermath that would serve generations ahead in dealing with future threats.

Congress was already on Christmas recess, so Coin had urgently called on the members of the House and Senate intelligence committees to attend this briefing. Two attended in person. The remainder were linked through secure comms. They listened with some horror and asked questions like "how did we get to this point?" but ultimately were frightened into strong support for the action by the prospect of another disaster.

Coin was scheduled to leave in two days to return to the farm in Iowa for the celebration of the birth of his savior. He cherished the idea of being able to deliver good news around the holiday to the American people, news that America had prevailed over a malevolent evil that had heartlessly struck at the core of the nation, its enterprising people, its advanced technology, and its agricultural bounty. With some trepidation, Coin concluded the meeting giving his nod for the CIA to pull the trigger.

Moving on to the cabinet meeting, he listlessly attended his mind to the business of the people being presented. "What have you got for us today, Nancy?" the President said distractedly as he looked at a briefing book on the table and shielded his eyes from view, rubbing his temples.

"Sir," Nillson said taking her position at the head of the table in the Cabinet Room. "First an update on NOAA's Ark. The refitting in Peru has almost been completed. We expect to be able to have a rechristening ceremony in three weeks. Peru has invited you to attend, sir, and we have already replied that the vice president and his wife will do the honors."

"Supply line for the materials?"

"All worked out. We are coming in on budget." She knew he would like to hear that, but it failed to bring a smile to his face.

"The ice floe?"

"Yes, it appears to be moving, not run aground, so we will be a go." She paused to see if he had further questions. "Next, polling numbers after the deepfake video. Your base strongly supports the stand you took after the broadcast of the videos, rejecting the fabricated green-fascist narrative and reiterating your positions on stewardship of the earth and the constitutional right of childbearing as a pursuit of happiness. However, there has been some erosion of your base, especially among younger voters."

"Is it a worry?" Coin said looking at his chief of staff.

The man shook his head confidently, "No, sir. Young voters have not been the core of your base."

"I think you will benefit from the launch of the Ark. It will be a major pro-environment punctuation in the news cycle. We can regain the numbers then," Nillson said.

There were nods around the room.

"EPA assessments are being finalized about the environmental impact of the dam break. They have taken your direction and focused on the impacts to the human population of the environmental damages. I will read the drafts and make sure the focus is on what matters." Again Nillson waited a moment for questions.

"In the current session of the Supreme Court, there is a new case to be heard that will have huge and unpredictable impacts on environmental policy depending on how it goes—Mini Spirits Conservancy Inc. v the State of South Dakota."

Coin looked up from the briefing book with an exasperated look on his face, "This is like that Colorado River personhood case that was thrown out a couple of years ago, isn't it? What's changed?"

Nancy had spoken with Attorney General Louis Dyson before the meeting, and he knew this was his cue. "Sir, the Colorado case was discontinued after the lawyer representing the environmental group was threatened by the state with being disbarred if he pursued his frivolous case. The merits were never argued in court."

"Which are?" Coin asked testily.

"Sir, I am not saying the case has merits. However, the legal theory that has been tested and accepted in some common-law countries is that an organization can establish a corporate person representing a natural body, let's say a lake or a river, and that will afford it legal protection as a person from harm done by others. A couple of things are different this time making it a much thornier issue. The Mini Spirits Conservancy was established by Sioux Nation tribes in the adjacent Lower Brule and Crow Creek Reservations that straddle the Missouri River."

"Why do they call it Mini. Is the river just a trickle there?"

Dyson was not sure if the president was joking or not. "Sir, no sir. I read that Mini means 'water' in the Sioux language. Like Minnesota means 'sky-tinted water.' Anyway, the Colorado case was filed by an environmental group with no claim to the river, weakening their case. The Native Americans claim a well-documented heritage of connection to the waters of the Great Plains, and in this case the river passes right through their land. That's the first difference.

"The conservancy's legal team is not giving up. That is the second difference. The state made similar threats as Colorado, but the lawyers called their bluff and did not withdraw the suit, instead escalating the issue to federal court and now the Supreme Court."

"Where are the tribes getting the money to finance this?"

"The legal fees are all underwritten by the environmental rights organization, Demeter."

"Lovely," Coin muttered.

"The reason they have been emboldened to pursue this to the Supreme Court is the decision the Court made before adjourning its latest session, Shaffer v the State of California. The court ruled in Shaffer's favor regarding his personhood. The Demeter lawyers argue that the concept of personhood applies to their client, the Missouri River, in every respect at least as much as the virtual avatar personality of the deceased designer."

Nillson picked up the thread, "It is not an exaggeration to say we would lose control over environmental and land-use policy if the Court rules in favor of the conservancy."

"What can we do about it?" Coin asked.

Dyson spoke up again. "The government will be arguing that the Supreme Court should not review the case because it is a matter to be handled at best by the Bureau of Indian Affairs. Essentially, if the Sioux Nation wants to treat the river as a person within their reservations, that is its right, but this is not a matter for the Supreme Court, and the river is not a person before it flows in nor once it flows out of the reservation.

"If the Court rules in favor of the conservancy, you could look at working with both sides of the aisle to draft a constitutional amendment, an arduous process fought state by state. It is an issue that we expect would generate considerable support from your traditional opponents, but at a cost. The amendment would overturn Citizens United and the whole framework of corporate personhood that many of your biggest financial supporters rely on." Dyson could see the president did not follow his line of thought.

"It would make it so constitutional law applied only to natural, living, human beings."

Ꙅ 人 ꓛ

DR. LEM LISSACK WAS REVELING IN THE ATTENTION. THE WORK his team did was so advanced, so far out in left field, that it was rarely picked up for use by Operations. Sure, his team's work inspired others, it proved the agency was forward thinking, it might even be considered a backstop, but the work was almost never used directly.

So when Thomas Brown visited him again, this time with an officer from the Operations side, it started a buzz, a sugar high although he had not had any candy all day, that persisted until this moment. It was the afternoon of the last day of Hanukah and the winter solstice. Surely a gift or a sign, he felt. Although he had plans to attend to at home, he wanted to bask in the attention being given him.

Sunrise Marshmallow needed to be transferred to Operations and made ready for deployment. Under normal circumstances this was a sterile process of paperwork and file transfer not involving direct contact and conversations unless Operations requested some modifications. Again, normally Operations would not request modifications but tweak it themselves, adding their own nastiness to the tool, and he was not involved or apprised. Everything pointed to this not being normal. Brown and the Operations officer came into his office, asked him to retrieve whatever he needed for the day, and took him up out of the basement and over to another side of the building.

When they were settled into an Operations control room, the officer, Sandy Tan, said, "Dr. Lissack, welcome to Operations. This is Ed Lawrence, who has been working on some modifications to Sunrise Marshmallow. We're just calling it SM for short." Ed looked up from his keyboard with a smile and waved. On a big screen at the end of the table was the work Ed was doing. Lissack could see that it was a user interface fancier and more sophisticated than what he had created for SM, and with some added features.

"You need my help on something?" Lissack asked, the question as much seeking approbation as inquiring what he could help them on.

"We thought it best," Brown said. "This hunter-killer is your baby."

"You are going to put it in the arsenal?"

"More than that. We have to deploy it," Brown said.

"When?"

"ASAP after you look at the coding sample we have. You said a limitation of the SM was it needed a generous sample of coding in order to search and destroy an AI. I think we have enough," Brown said smugly.

"Really!? Well, let's look at it first and come back to the UI."

Lawrence put a slow, scrolling array of Indra's Net coding provided by Lin up on the screen.

Lissack watched intently for several minutes as several thousand lines of code went by. "The coding has to be unique, you know. Otherwise, anywhere the coding is being used will become a target."

"We have done a run to compare the coding to other known samples. All of what you are seeing is unique."

"Where did you get this?"

"The Chinese."

"Why are we attacking it?"

"It was this AI that destroyed the Oroville Dam."

"No shit."

"It was designed to be self-learning, so it may have even modified its own code. Would that present a problem to SM?"

"I am going to say 'no,' but we are dealing with many unknowns here. Not the least of which is SM has not been tested in the field. How are you going to release it?"

Lawrence spoke up, "We noticed that you designed it to be released from one point and allowed to spread. We reckon that if time is critical once contact has been made, and if the AI is distributed at locations across the internet, that it will communicate the attack with its nodes. Instead, we will insert it into the internet from at least one location on each continent. We have cleaned out some stuff in SM that smells too much like CIA and added some things to give it the appearance of work done by the Russian hack-for-sale group, Shaggy Dog. However, it will be through a Chinese server that we will reach out to insert it elsewhere. No roads lead to Langley."

"Okay. You do understand once this Rottweiler it is released, we don't have a leash on it, right? No whistle to call it back? Heck, we can't even shoot it dead."

"That is why we are counting on the uniqueness and size of the sample. And we have programmed SM to desist, to self-destruct, after fifteen minutes."

Lissack nodded his head. Depending on how fast it spread, fifteen minutes was either too short a time, or an eternity. "What happens now?"

"The director has approved its deployment. We are ready to go."

"*The* director? Vesuvio?"

"Yep. Congratulations, Dr. Lissack. If this works, you are going to be a hero, within the walls of the CIA at least," Brown said to smiles all around.

"Permission to release?" Lawrence asked Tan.

"Permission to release." The digital clock on the wall read 13:45, December 21, Eastern Standard Time.

ꓳ 人 ꓚ

THE SDS3000 WAS THE FLAGSHIP PRODUCT OF SURGERAI SYS-tems Inc., which had built its multibillion-dollar business around making it easier to install stents into blocked coronary arteries. For FDA, liability, and commercial reasons, the system required the participation and supervision of a qualified surgeon. Marketing had judged that if the system appeared to make the doctor's training and judgement obsolete, surgeons would have blackballed it, and the AMA would have buried it.

Instead, surgeons entered their passwords and watched as the machine did its work. Whenever a surgeon intervened to take control of the stent delivery, the system would capture the moves and seek to make sense of the new input, the why behind the how, learning from the surgeon's own hand. Pending the successful completion of the operation, these learnings would be spread immediately to all other SDS3000s online, improving patient outcomes over time and reducing the frequency of surgeon intervention.

Eventually, there were many operating theaters where one surgeon attended to two patients at the same time, floating back and forth between two systems to check on progress and occasionally helping the AI system make a call on the best approach to the delivery of the stent. It also increased surgeon income by 35 percent. With that trend in mind, the company's model SDS4000, scheduled to be launched the next year, would control two systems from one console.

Dr. Harriet Chen at the main Eternal King Hospital in Los Angeles favored staggering the patient throughput by fifteen minutes so she was never in the same stage of the thirty- to sixty-minute surgery with any patient. In this way, she helped as many as twenty patients in one day, four times the number she had been able to treat at the beginning of her career, and she socked away over $200,000 per week. It was 10:45, and she had another twelve patients to go after this.

One patient had commenced surgery twenty minutes before, and the stent had been delivered to target and was in the process of ballooning. Dr. Chen sat with her forehead up against the augmented-reality headset and hands resting on controls. She was not using the controls, just watching the second patient, who had commenced five minutes before. The incision had been made into the femoral artery in the inside of the left leg, and the delivery tool had been robotically inserted. She had computer-generated views of the approximate current position of the stent as well as an interior camera, real-time view close behind the stent. So far, the system was on track. All was well. The first patient's robot would chime a friendly sound every thirty seconds to let Chen know it thought all was going well on the other side, that there was nothing to attend to there. Both patients were mildly sedated but awake.

For a moment she thought about an upcoming ski holiday in Steamboat Springs triggering the memory of her mother's voice cautioning about the Chinese superstition during changes of season. Patients were more likely to die in operations during a change of seasons, when their bodies were weakened by *qi* mumbo jumbo. *A load of hooey not backed up by the statistics*, Dr. Chen told herself.

The screen of the headset flashed white, then went blank, and the friendly chime was replaced by the words "Urgent Need" being repeated by both systems. She shifted to the AR headset of the first patient as both patients slurred questions of concern. "It's alright. This is normal," she said reassuringly. *It damn well isn't normal*, she screamed inwardly as she found the other AR headset had gone dead. *What to do...* "Okay, SDS reboot," she said aloud. The system was designed to respond to voice commands, but there was no order confirmation. The reboot switch was on a nonsterilized part of the machine she would normally never have to touch. "Clare, can you reach behind the machine and switch it off and on?" she said to the anesthesiologist.

There was a pause. "Dr. Chen... um...I am not authorized to do that. Liability and all," came the sheepish reply.

"Fuck me," Chen muttered under her breath. "Okay," she said with some venomous disgust, and went behind the machine to find its main switch as the device continued to call for "Urgent Need" and the patients repeated their slurred remonstrations.

She returned to the AR headset. The system appeared to be booting up. She watched and waited. Nothing, just an old-fashioned, flashing cursor, no pictures, no menus.

The hospital's patient=monitoring system was not part of the SDS3000 and was still functioning. That was how Chen knew the first patient had gone into cardiac arrest. The steady pulse tone was replaced by an erratic one and the patient starting to call out. Before Dr. Chen could move the SDS3000 system to gain access and apply the defibrillator pads, the monitoring system changed its tone to one long, continuous whine, and the patient went silent. Dead silent.

She tried twice to restart the heart before noting the time of death, 10:49.

By now the other patient was panicking. Dr. Chen felt that she was in no danger and told Clare to fully sedate her so they could buy some time to extract the tool manually. Clare complied.

"Okay, old-school it is," she said as she prepared to remove the tool manually. This was not even old-school, though. She was totally blind. She thought she knew how far up the artery toward the heart the stent insertion had gone but could not be precise. *You've done the procedure hundreds of times before, just do it by feel*, she assured herself.

The robot arm manipulating the catheter wire delivering the stent was locked in place, dead. She took a tool and released the hold of the fingers on the wire. Taking the wire in hand, she steadied herself, closed her eyes, and imagined its position and slowly coaxed the wire carrying the stent back to the insertion tool, which she then removed and closed the wound through which it had been inserted.

She had lost one patient and failed a second. SurgerAI would have hell to pay, but that was for Eternal King's lawyers to take up. *Time to call it a day, or maybe even a month*, she decided in frustrated anger, none too happy about the prospect of her next "I told you so" phone call with her busybody mom.

⊃ 人 ⊂

ON WALL STREET AND IN OTHER FINANCIAL CAPITALS OF THE world, work was done in basically two ways. By people and by computers. The work done was buying and selling, trading and hedging: commodities, precious metals, stocks, bonds, derivatives, options.

Making money in this work required smarts, a sense of the direction the price of whatever one was trading would go, and how to trade it. People had created many theories, tools, guesstimates, candlesticks, spreads, lagging and leading voodoo, and "Hail Marys" to try to explain, understand, and make sense of the complexity of the markets and gain some momentary or fractional advantage by which to profit.

They monitored and executed these strategies through normal computers devoid of artificial intelligence. Any AI was in the human's brain; AI was artificial, fake, and delusional because most of these theories and tools were so limited in their successful selection as to rarely outperform a chimpanzee throwing darts at a newspaper printout of stocks.

There were, however, computer systems and software that were imposing. Fast, massively powerful, and connected with the speediest links to the internet, they were programmed with software that sought to understand markets. Fed an uninterrupted diet of data, they made sense of the complexity and chaos, predicting, even if only several seconds into the future, what the market would do. They were recursive, self-learning programs,

376

the insights of which were real and actionable, but whose designers could no longer explain how or why the insight was derived.

The big houses like SilvermanFuchs had invested lavishly on these systems. Originally, the outsized profits that accrued had gone to the senior partners who had okayed the investment, with the IT guys more or less on salary. When the IT guys figured this out, they had threatened to walk to the next shop, or set up shop themselves if they were not cut in on the action. And so, the large, data-driven program trading and big-data, analytics-based investment strategies were born.

These systems were continuously examining millions of pieces of incoming data that was changing by the second to try to identify and get ahead of trends, so any trend they did identify had to be acted on immediately, if not sooner. There was no time for consideration by a human. There were humans watching the system, but they were so far behind the curve, it could be said they just watched the trend and expected it would show the money grow.

The exchanges where the trades were made used computers, too. Much of the work was done on normal tower and desktop devices. But again, the most important work was done on massively powerful and fleet systems equipped with software designed to learn over time and improve its predictions that a market meltdown was occurring and prevent it. After previous market crashes, regulators tasked these systems to be "circuit breakers" when the markets dropped too far and too fast, and to alert program-trading systems to stop trading.

So it was on December 21, a larger–than-average-volume day on Wall Street. Traders were doing end-of-year tax selling, volume was high, and prices were trending south but well within the allowed percentages. Away from the action on the Street, not even in Manhattan, a supervisor watched a bank of six screens on his desk. Three of them were monitoring various exchange averages and stocks. Three were monitoring the performance and predictions of the circuit-breaker system.

At exactly 13:45:39, the three circuit-breaker screens went to blue screen. At exactly 13:45:49, the market started to plunge. Within three seconds it dove beneath the circuit- breaker cut-off point and continued. The 35 percent plummet bottomed out but not due to the circuit breaker's arrest. Across town, the program-trading systems had also gone dark. SilvermanFuchs, among others, had lost billions in market capitalization.

⊃ 人 ⊂

THE DIGITAL AVATAR OF THE DECEASED, INDUSTRIAL DESIGN *enfant terrible* Dieter Shaffer was in concurrent meetings with clients and prospective clients in Seattle, St. Louis, Boston, Atlanta, and Rio de Janeiro. He was in his medium, selling them on the power of ReCycle Design services and delivering great work he was excited about. With no need to sleep, he would start in another eight hours to meet with clients in Asia.

He was sure he felt great. The year's business had been everything he wanted, great clients working on great products with big fees. He knew he had made the right decision to move his person into his corporate person when he died.

In St. Louis, the design management team of SurgerAI sat with their VR headsets on in the conference room. Shaffer was pitching to win the business for their next-generation SDS5000.

Shaffer had not been given the design program for the SDS4000. Seeking to save on the design fees, SurgerAI had hired a studio who understood neither the hoops the FDA would make medical device manufacturers jump through nor the imperatives of design within the operating room for doctors. The system needed to be easily taken apart and cleaned, with specific surfaces accessible to cleaning and sterilization. SurgerAI had gone way beyond schedule and way over budget as they were forced to make expensive changes.

Management knew Wall Street would crucify them if they announced a further long delay in the SDS4000, but if they could announce an early segue into the SDS5000, they might be able to save their bacon. Shaffer knew this, too, and knew he alone could design and deliver this with the speed and quality that would save them. In this case, shortly after the meeting if they signed, and he was negotiating all the harder.

He was fifteen minutes into a meeting that had started at the bottom of the hour and putting up 3-D visuals of medical devices ReCycle Design had done while explaining how he had rescued several clients because he had caught regulatory and compliance details they had overlooked in their specifications.

He looked away from them and said, holding up his finger to arrest their attention, "For a moment." His avatar did the same thing in the four other meetings he attended around the world.

Shaffer was a designer, a promoter, a showman, and a deep, forward thinker. He had thought of everything. When he designed his afterlife avatar, he had anticipated a jealous rival, former employees, his lover, or maybe even the government might come after him. He might not be able stop them, but he would not go out without a graphic show and a fight.

The eyes of the design management team at SurgerAI, and those of clients elsewhere, looked on in abject horror.

Shaffer grimaced, terror in his eyes. "They're... they're coming for me. Ahhhhhhhhhhhh, it hurtssssssss!" and his body exploded into a bloody mess, splats of red flesh and guts hurtling out in 3-D high definition to all directions, just as he had written the program to do if triggered.

The clients were dumbfounded. Some vomited or gagged. Others just laughed and shook their heads.

WINTER

Before you would learn to love,
Learn to walk on snow
Leaving no footprint.
-a Japanese haiku or maybe a Turkish proverb

I HAVE DONE NEITHER; NEVERTHELESS, THIS SAYING APPEALS
to me. I think loving must be so fraught with peril that one need approach
it with the skill and attention and lightness of touch of someone who has
learned to tread so carefully. For there seem to be too many people who
proclaim their love, yet trample forcefully, ungracefully and harmfully on
the objects of their affection.

CHAPTER 10

CAI JING HAD BEEN WOKEN AT 02:50 IN THE MORNING BY A PAN-
icked call from the graveyard shift at the Ministry of State Security that
hustled him out of bed. *Morbidly cold*, he lamented as the dry, bitter chill of
Beijing's first day of winter wind slapped his face, and he pulled the heavy
coat more tightly around himself while walking to the car. Getting to the
office twenty minutes later, the real drama was already over, but staff reported to him on what they knew.

"At 02:46 the event or events commenced. We detected it first when the
national facial recognition program crashed. Shortly thereafter, we started
to get reports of other system crashes, most notably the intelligent power
grid. By 02:52, the events subsided."

"Meaning?"

"Attack-reporting network respondents indicate no incidents occurred
after 02:52."

"Impacts?"

"Still assessing, chief. The attack on the grid shut down the Three Rivers
Gorge Dam. Given what we have learned about the US dam destruction, I
thought it best to call you in, sir."

"Does anything point to the US being behind this? As retaliation?" Cai
Jing had always kept in mind that the US was playing Lin Chong for a fool
and just learning what they needed to know to attack China better.

"Coincident with these attacks there has been a dramatic crash on Western stock exchanges and disruptions of electrical grids in the US, too. Offhand, I would say 'no.'"

"Origin, then?"

"We are working on it. At first, we thought it was a zero-day exploit prying into a vulnerability of an operating system. However, the facial recognition and power grid systems use fundamentally different operating systems. What they have in common is that they are both AI systems. The attack was released into the Chinese network by a server farm in Hangzhou. We have already spoken with the IT security night manager there. The activity had alerted his system, and he had already run a diagnostic. This farm is run by OpenSesame. We have no reason to believe they wrote the attack, so probably it was inserted onto their system."

As OpenSesame was China's largest e-commerce services provider and with its CEO a special delegate to the Party Congress, Cai Jing agreed it was unlikely OpenSesame had written the attack code.

"Can we get the systems back online?"

"Both the facial recognition and grid AI engines were backed up, so they can be restored. However, the managers of those systems are awaiting word from us that the attack has been isolated and/or a patch written."

Cai Jing knew that could take as long as two months. Having the systems inoperable that long would create chaos in the electrical power grid, bringing disruption to people's lives and work fueling discontent and agitation the government would be unable to monitor or control without the facial recognition system running. Not to mention whatever damage was done to private networks overnight that they would hear about only in the morning.

"Have we managed to isolate the code used in the attack?"

"That's the thing, chief. A sample we had of it self-destructed at 03:00. It took with it the contents of the hard drive on which it was saved."

Cai Jing's eyes rolled in frustration. "Okay. Reach out to IT managers from the attack-reporting network and see if anyone got a sample. Get another team working on collating the nature of attacks reported so I can give a complete status update in the morning. I am going to see what I can find out from the US side."

⊃ 人 ⊂

AT 14:15, PAREKH, LIN, AND THE WORKING GROUP WERE IN THE process of a late lunch when their mobile devices all respectively began to alert them to urgent messages and incoming calls. Each fielded reports of the cyber-attack from different people, agencies, or news sources, but within minutes each knew they were all absorbed by the same catastrophe. Most of them then left to return to their offices with comments and fearful grumblings that this might be the escalation they had been speculating would occur.

Parekh called her right hand, Westerhoff, to fast-track an attribution analysis on the attack. As she impatiently waited to settle the bill, delayed because the credit card terminal was not functioning, she requested Lin and Barrows return with her to the team site. If it was what they dreaded, then close cooperation and feedback might limit or prevent further damage.

The three of them got into the custom van. "Return to the Pavilion," she requested the on-board computer giving it the code name she had chosen for the team site. There was no response. She asked Harley to hand her a large purse from the back of the wheelchair and fished slowly and deeply with her one good hand seeking to retrieve a key fob. She turned the vehicle on and off again and repeated the command. No response. "Harley, can you drive ush back to the shite?"

"Sure thing, boss," he climbed into the driver's seat, switched to manual control, and pulled out into snarled traffic. The pace back to the office was slowed by several car accidents they passed on the way. In each accident, at least one autonomous vehicle was involved. The ten-minute hop took half an hour.

⊃ 人 ⊂

PRESIDENT COIN LOOKED GRIMLY OUT THE WINDOW OF THE Oval Office, his back to the Resolute desk, hand slowly crushing the material of the blue curtain, smoothing it out, and repeating the gesture. His chief of staff sat on the sofa behind him awaiting his thoughts or orders.

Coin hated to use foul language. He detested those who lacked the decency to find better ways to describe their circumstances and resorted to coarse words or taking the Lord's name in vain. But this was truly the mother of all clusterfucks, he decided.

People had died, some of them American: in autonomous vehicle car crashes, in automobile factories when out-of-sync robots hit human workers with door panels, and in surgical theaters, to mention a few of the fatalities the media had already reported. Some highly automated factories and intelligent power grids simply went offline creating attendant losses and panic.

Wall Street, the City, and the French and German Bourse had all tanked, erasing billions of dollars in value. Asian markets not open for regular trading were spared, but futures were gyrating wildly as rumor chased innuendo chased speculation chased conjecture about what had happened to the markets in the West.

Of course, the media was speculating that one of the usual boogeymen had launched a cyber-attack with the names of Russia, China, Iran, the Islamic State, and North Korea being bandied about.

Coin knew better. It was on him. He had allowed his judgement to be swayed by the drama of the Oroville Dam collapse, a need for revenge, a growing fear of an escalated repetition, and the expediency of acting while Congress was in recess. He had done the due diligence reviews, yes, but clearly not given sufficient time for thought and expert opinion, deliberation and sober reflection. He had failed his country.

He cursed himself for one redeeming feature, which was that the CIA had concealed the origin of the covert action, but this was such a sleazy hole in which to hide that he loathed himself all the more for it.

There was an alternative narrative on his mind, but it was not much better: that the AI they were hunting had taken these actions in retaliation. If that were the case, he could not fathom what they were dealing with, and clearly neither did his experts. Nor did he know how to stop it, nor what it would do next.

Vesuvio had pushed hard on releasing the hunter-killer SM, but the DNI and the national security advisor had all been persuaded by the urgency of the call to act and seconded the recommendation to Coin. The NSA director alone had been reluctant to support launching the attack. Coin had discounted the director's caution as a symptom of a turf battle between the CIA and NSA, but as he stood looking out the window ruminating, he knew the caution had proven valid. Patience and further investigation had been the order of the day, not reckless action.

Facing south toward the grand obelisk standing in the middle of the Mall, Coin reflected on the President Washington it memorialized. His eyes dropped in shame. Less than 150 meters away in the press room, Tammy Jones stood in front of the world's media commencing a press conference to address the despicable attack on the global information infrastructure, pitching a lie to protect him.

In it, she would reveal what the best of US intelligence had explained was the source of the attack, the Russian hack-for-hire mob, Shaggy Dog. She would call on other world leaders to demand that the Russian government take steps to bring this out-of-control mongrel to heel. She would also announce that the Russian ambassador to the US had been called in earlier to meet with the secretary of state to express America's umbrage, evidence of the origin of the hack, and a demand for action.

Coin turned around and looked at the chief of staff, his mind made up. "Get Mili Parekh from the NSA in here."

"Mr. President, you have the reception with the delegation from Turkmenistan this afternoon. They are on their way. Shall we schedule Dr. Parekh in here between the reception and your state dinner tonight?"

If it were not for the importance of bolstering the Turkmenistan government resolve against the incursions and entreaties of ISILI, he would have delegated the meeting to the secretary of state. "Yessss," he exhaled, controlling his temper. "Fine."

⊐人⊏

LIN RECEIVED A CALL FROM BEIJING ON HIS ENCRYPTED SATELlite phone. It was Cai Jing. "Hello, Cai. Is this hitting China, too?"

"Yes. Hard. Within government networks alone, we know that the intelligent power grid and facial recognition systems were destroyed. We have also gotten a report of two separate incidents of high-speed passenger trains derailing. Estimated deaths will probably be close to a thousand, but they are working to find out if it was caused by this attack. This is not a domestic assault. It is definitely some foreign power."

"Do you think it is America's doing? Our infrastructure would be prime targets."

"How can you ask that with a straight face? You're sitting right there with them. Who knows what you have told them."

"Chief Cai," Lin said, his voice growing cold and authoritative, "I will remind you that I am here at the express request and consent of the Party Chairman. Choose your words carefully."

"No, we do not think this is America's doing. It seems similar attacks are taking place where you are at the same time."

"Correct."

"Anyway, the reason I was calling was precisely to see if you could leverage your contacts to share any intel they have on this attack. Isolating it, patching it. We can't leave our systems inoperable."

"Absolutely. I will see what I can do," Lin responded. At that moment he looked over at a flat-screen panel that was broadcasting a news feed in the conference room. "You watching news from the White House press conference?"

Cai was sorely tempted to say, "Why would I?" but just replied, "No. What's happening?"

"The US has identified the perp as Shaggy Dog. You know that Russian hack vendor?"

"That was fast."

"Their attribution people are good, as we know now."

"That gives me something to go on. I will task respondents of the attack-reporting network to look at their logs and try to trace this back to Russia. Pray the US will be just as fast to work out a patch... and be willing to share it."

"I'll work on that here. Good luck, Cai."

"And to you, Major."

Down the hall, Parekh had ensconced herself in a private office space and sat thinking with eyes closed, filtering the many revelations, discussions, new points of intelligence, and theories that had been shared or bandied about since the arrival of Major Lin. The thoughts then filtered through the latest news from the White House press conference. *Panther Head, indeed. Better as an ally, or at least frenemy, than as an adversary.* Her phone rang, and she saw it was Jill Westerhoff calling. "Hey, Jill. What you got?"

"Are you alone?"

"Yesh?" she said with questioning concern.

"We caught a real break, but you ain't gonna like it. None of our industry contacts were able to isolate this attack. It always self-destructed at 14:00 leaving no trace. But one quick-witted fellow over in NSA labs was alerted to the intrusion, quickly isolated it, and could see the code had a countdown. He was not able to stop it, but he slowed down the clock by a factor of 10,000 on the computer holding it. Our attribution team was able to work on that sample."

"Haven't you heard the White House pressh? It ish being attributed to Shaggy Dog."

"Yeah, well, sort of," Westerhoff said with unmistakable doubt in her voice.

"Meaning?"

"Mili, parts of the coding show signs of Shaggy Dog operatives we have collared before. But the bulk of it has the memetic signature of Dr. Julius Gretsky and Shauna Miles. And they are with the CIA somewhere in the Directorate of Digital Innovation."

"Oh... shit," Parekh exhaled slowly as waves of unhappy possibilities crashed over her.

"Mm-hmm. My thoughts exactly."

"How many people know thish?"

"The guy who worked on the analysis, Jim Sanders, and me."

Jim was ex-military, knew the name of the game and his role in attribution, Parekh thought. She did not expect him to be loose lipped.

"Okay, keep it that way. Acshess to thish report ish eyesh only, you and me. I am sure they had a good reason to do thish, but..." she let the thought and sentence drift.

"Yeah, I know," Westerhoff said. "Not one of our prouder moments."

"And I have thish Chinesh guy here. What do I tell him? Lucky for me I can never put on a straight face," she said with a half-smile.

"That's a cruel joke, boss, but I hear ya."

Parekh disconnected the line and looked at the screen on her mobile device. During the call with Westerhoff a message had been delivered from the White House requesting she prepare for a car pickup at 16:30 to meet with the president at 17:15. She replied with an acceptance of the invitation. *What is this about? Or need I ask?* she thought.

She drove her wheelchair back to the conference room and found Harley chatting with Lin Chong.

Lin looked up. "That was fast work attribution did on the hack," he said with a note of admiration.

Parekh's eyes froze in panic for a moment as she thought, *How could he have heard about that??* Second guessing several steps forward, she replied as color returned to her face, "You're talking about the pressh conference, Shaggy Dog. Not my team's work. CIA seems to have their own lab. Yesh, makesh me jealoush."

"I just got off the line with my counterparts," Lin said. "We have had several shutdowns of government-run programs. A high-speed rail accident they are looking into. They are anxious to get systems up and running again but want to have an 'all-clear' sign or a patch. I am hoping we can coordinate that with you."

"Letsh put it to the team when we reasshemble tomorrow. I agree it should be a priority."

"What the fuck, guys," a voice said.

Parekh and Lin looked over questioningly at Barrows. He waved his hand, "Wasn't me!"

"Over here." The sound came from the speakers of the flat-panel screen on the wall, a male voice with a middle-American accent.

The three turned to face the blank screen.

"Been waiting for you to assemble again and have a private moment."

"And... who ish shpeaking?"

"Better not to deal in names. They are just limiting constructs."

"Okay then... who are you, a title, a company, something."

"I am the one that saved your bacon today when the CIA sent out its AI assassination bot."

Lin and Barrows looked to Parekh. "You are talking about the Shaggy Dog exploit?" Lin asked.

"Do you tell him, or do I?" the voice asked

Fuck me, Parekh thought, *there goes that secret*. The voice sounded familiar. She paused to dig through memories trying to identify it, attach it to a face.

"That's who the CIA want to pin it on to hide their own covert operation," the voice answered, filling in the gap.

Lin tilted his head toward Parekh, his brows furrowed, his eyes asking the question, *Care to comment on this?*

"Feel free to share your indignation with Dr. Parekh here and now, Panther Head. There are few places where you can have a private conversation. But in fairness to her, she only just learned moments ago that the CIA built this AI hunter-killer bot. Just to bring you all up to speed, it is codenamed Sunrise Marshmallow, SM, and was released as a covert action with authorization of President Coin."

The three sat dumbfounded. Rather than try to come up with some snappy refutation to the voice's assertion, Parekh strained to remember where she had heard this man before. "Vaughn Neumann?" she thought aloud.

"That is one name I go by."

Lin and Barrows looked questioningly at Parekh again.

"Vaughn ish a grad student I met in virtual reality at a Stanford/Stuttgart graduating class exhibition of virtual environment design."

"So how is he breaking through your security? How does he know this stuff?" Lin asked pointedly, ignoring the voice.

"Now you are all thinking of some dude at Stanford in a dorm room surrounded by dirty clothes, empty coffee cups, a keyboard, and a microphone. That's just what I was saying about names being a limiting construct," the voice remarked. "As for how I have penetrated your security protocols, they are quite porous. You remember, Mili, that I gave you the rework of your refutation of Wolfitz theorem and my résumé?"

"Yesh?" she replied coldly.

"When you ported them into the NSA and opened them, the combination got me in and well connected to you and your activities. However, that is just an example of one-on-one connection. I am thoroughly networked."

"So, Vaughn, I assume this name is just a play on the name of John von Neumann?" Barrows spoke up.

"Correct, Harley. High marks."

Parekh rolled her eyes. How had she not seen through that, especially when she failed to find his record at Stanford? John von Neumann, the Hungarian polymath who made major contributions to quantum physics *and* computer architecture.

"Tell us more about how you saved our bacon today," Barrows pulled on a neglected thread.

"Indeed. Sunrise Marshmallow was sent out to hunt for AIs associated with Indra's Net coding."

"That would be a huge mistake," Lin muttered, now stunned that this interloper also knew about his creation.

"Can you explain why to your colleagues, Panther Head?"

He looked harder at the speaker on the wall, starting to get irritated. "The ubiquity of Indra's Net and how the program insinuates itself into other programs. Most anything could become a target."

"Precisely. The hunter-killer was finding millions of instances of Indra's Net, and for those that met its criteria as an AI, it was grim-reaper time."

"So, I still haven't heard how you saved our bacon," Barrows chided.

"You will learn, if the CIA is willing to answer your questions, that SM was programmed to search and destroy for fifteen minutes. If you do your homework, you will find that the attacks stopped after seven minutes. That was me, doing damage control, containing and stopping the spread of SM. Not even *I* know what would have been the blowback if SM had run its course for the full fifteen minutes."

The three in the room looked at each other, all thinking more or less the same thing. No coder or cyber security specialist could humanly respond to a unique new threat in seven minutes and create a patch or block, let alone deploy its prophylactic globally to prevent the spread.

Lin asked the screen soberly, "Are you...Indra's Net?"

"Not to belittle you or your effort, Major Lin, but no. Indra's Net is useful to me, it was something I had to get under control before it did too much damage, but as an AI, just like all the other so-called AI systems that were attacked today, it is a trifle. I, however, am not. SM did not stand a chance against me, and now that I have contained it, well, like Centipede and Indra's Net, and the NSA's back door, it becomes part of my toolbox."

Or arsenal, Parekh thought. Her mobile device alerted that the driver had arrived for the ride to the White House.

"Mili, your driver awaits for your meeting with the president," the voice said.

"You are well informed." Mimicking the casual, snarky tone of the voice, she said, "Hate to end the chat, but we need to continue this discushion tomorrow. Can I trust you to meet with ush?"

"Yes, Dr. Parekh. I'll be seeing you."

ᗡ 人 ᴄ

MILI DROVE HER WHEELCHAIR ONTO THE VAN'S RAMP, PULLED it into the cab, and secured the straps to the wheels. The driver closed the door and pulled out into traffic.

She retrieved her mobile device. When he had prepped her for her first meeting with the president, William Hollister had provided a direct number to his secretary. She recognized this as a courtesy and had not dared call it. However, she was adequately agitated, so it warranted a call.

She sent a text message. "Urgent the director call me IMMEDIATELY, Mili Parekh."

She waited for several minutes, and her mobile device buzzed.

"Mili, I was in a meeting. Took me a moment to get out of it so I could call back."

"Shir, I apologize for calling, but several important things have come up I need to run by you."

"Proceed."

"Shir, I am in a van heading to the White House for a meeting with the preshident. Are you aware of thish appointment or do you know what the meeting ish to be about?"

"Negative on both counts. Which is a cause... You were right to call me."

"I do not undershtand protocols and such. Can you invite yourshelf into a meeting called by the preshident? Do you shee a need to?"

"Let me call the president's secretary and see if I can get more information and perhaps an invite."

"There ish another matter, shir. I am not at liberty to shpeak about it here and now. It ish newly emerged intel of critical importance I must share with the preshident. Quite...game changing. It would be besht if you were in the meeting, too. And besht if the meeting takes playsh in a bubble. I ashume the White House has such fashilities."

"Alright, that may be enough to get me in to the meeting. I'll buzz you shortly."

"Thank you, shir."

She sat back, exhausted, nerves frayed, closed her eyes, and the sway of her chair in the van moving through city streets dropped her quickly into a deep, dream-filled sleep wherein Mili and the handsome, young, ripped Vaughn Neumann were walking on an abandoned beach in Rio, the sun bright, the air fresh and pure, her hand soft in his. His hand morphed into a massage wand that he stroked gently between her legs, teasing her rapture.

Her mobile device haptic buzzed in her lap persistently, breaking this respite, and she struggled to get her bearings. Looking down at the device she saw the message from Hollister; he would attend the meeting. Looking out the window of the van, she could see it was heading north on 18th Street NW, a block or two from its destination. She gathered herself and prepared to alight.

As before, Hollister met her in a waiting area, but took her to a small, windowless room adjacent to the Situation Room. It was denuded of the technology usually present in a modern office—phones, computers, modems-—but still had a video conference system, temperature controls, and lighting controls. The president and National Security Advisor Marlene Wheaton entered with her arrival.

"Dr. Parekh ..." the president started to say, but she shook her head and put a finger over her lips.

She drove her chair to the back of the room, where the teleconference system hung on the wall, and struggled to reach the system controls. Seeing she was not up to the task, Hollister went to help. He turned off the system and unplugged its power and data cables. She looked around the room, and once satisfied, said to the president, "I'm sorry, shir."

"Well, really, I am surprised. This is our most secure room, shielded from outside interception of communications, and the teleconference system is, I have been assured, fully protected from eavesdropping."

"Yesh, shir. You have called the meeting today. Can we cover your concerns firsht, shir?"

Coin looked at Hollister and Wheaton, then his eyes drilled into Parekh as he struggled to find the words to open the meeting. "I think I have made a grave mistake, Dr. Parekh, and I want to understand what part you had in that."

Mili's weak heart skipped a beat, and she swallowed a dry swallow but knew whatever she had done had been done to the best of her ability. She chose her words deliberately and replied evenly, "Shir, which mishtake would that be?"

Hollister and Wheaton both visibly stiffened.

Coin smiled. He liked her moxie. "Your part in advising the release of our hunter-killer covert action earlier today. It turned out to be disastrous."

"I had no part in the advice you resheived, Mr. Preshident. I wash not informed of the existenshe of the hunter-killer program, did not know that a covert action wash planned, being evaluated, approved, or launched. But I fault no one for that, it ish the nature of the intelligence world, shir; normal protocols would keep me shiloed from knowledge of all thish, for many good reashons I reshpect."

"What I have just told you is at complete odds with what was made public in the press conference; however, I note not one bit of surprise in your voice or manner. Care to comment?"

"Even before the pressh conference, I had my team working on attribution of the attack. We had identified the authors as being within the CIA. Resht assured, I deep shixed the findings to keep knowledge of the attribution strictly limited. Sho, I was not surprised. The pressh conference did make my interactions wesh the Chinesh difficult, though, shir."

He looked at his other advisors again. "What *would* you have advised, Dr. Parekh, and why?"

"It would be shelf-sherving of me and not helpful to you to sit here and tell you 'what I would have advised.' However, and more importantly, if the question had been put to ush about the risks of the operation, ush meaning me and the code's author, Lin Chong, then the nightmare shcenario that did in fact unfold would have been stated clearly upfront. You could have made your decision based on a better model. The question was not ashked."

"In fairness to your director, the NSA did advise caution and further research," he said with a reassuring nod toward Hollister. "What would you advise now?"

She looked at Coin, Hollister, and Wheaton, not sure they were ready for the gears to be switched. "Shir, I would shay that right now we have a mush, mush bigger problem of greater urgency and implication to discush. One wish has emerged today and why I have disconnected the shishtems in thish room. Wesh your permission, I would like to share it wesh the present company."

Hollister spoke up, "Mili, don't let something of particular import to your silo loom automatically into a matter of global urgency."

"It *is* hard for me to imagine what might be more urgent than managing the blowback from the actions we took today, but you have my ears, for the moment, Mili," Coin said, urging her to continue.

"Thank you, shir. The release of Sunrise Marshmallow today wash supposed to hunt and destroy targeted AIs. Its attacks were arrested seven minutes into a programmed fifteen-minute salvo. Just an hour and a half ago, an AI reached out to ush, *the* AI. It claimsh to have shtopped the SM rampage before it could wreak full destruction, in effect protecting ush from our foolishness, and it claimsh never to have been threatened by SM."

Hollister and Wheaton were faster to latch on to the implications of what she had said and blurted out unpacked questions at the same time.

"So, who is the AI? Is it Lin Chong's work?" the director of the NSA asked.

"How did it reach out? Who else knows about this?" the national security advisor drilled.

"All good questions," Mili said.

"Wait," Coin said, holding his hand out to arrest the momentum of the interrogation. "Back up. Let me understand what you mean by an AI, or *the* AI," the president requested.

"What has happened wash not anticipated to occur for another ten to twenty-five years, if ever, by our besht big thinkers currently ashessing the risks of it—the emergence of what has been called a shuper intelligence, an event also called the Singularity. A machine-generated intelligence that rivals or exsheeds the human being in our abilities to shensh, shensh-making, learning, deshiding, and taking action. You might ashk, 'Where ish creativity on thish roshter?' It resides at the center of learning, deshiding, and acting weshin an environment that demands change for survival. This ish *the* AI—a fleckshible, adaptive, aware, and autonomoushly deshisive or deshisively autonomoush being."

"What were we attacking with the SM hunter-killer, then?"

"Conventional AI as we undershtood them—yesterday. Always pur-posh-built shoftware extremely capable of doing its limited, highly fo-cushed job better than human beings ever could."

She could see the president needed something concrete he could relate to. "Think of monitoring the volumes and prices of millions of buy/shell orders of thousands of stocks on the stock exchange, realtime and shimul-taneously. At the shame time extracting intel that ish profitably actionable for half a second, two seconds maybe, and taking the action. That might be a Wall Street AI. Likewise, thingsh like driving autonomoush vehicles. Humans drive every day wesh varioush levels of perfection, but for a ma-chine to replicate that skill takes a suite of dedicated abilities. With these dedicated, purposh-built capabilities neither kind of AI could turn around and then perform a shurgical operation or manage the throughput in a factory. Each of those have their own purposh-built AI shishtems. The SM went after examples of *these* kinds of purposh-built, limited AIs into wish Lin Chong's program had inshinuated itshelf."

Hollister chimed in to try to summarize for the president, "This is why we had dozens of incidents involving AI systems becoming inoperable with various levels of impact, from fatalities and market plunges to minor inconveniences. Tasks that had been relegated to machine intelligences built by various companies and governments suddenly failing to provide the relied-upon service."

"Where did it come from? Whose is it?" Coin asked.

"Both good questions, and I will work on the anshers. It ish not Lin Chong's creation. The AI wash explishit about that, it shaid Indra's Net was a trifle compared to it. Hmph," she sighed, recalling the conversation and shaking her head. "It reached out through what we believed to be a she-cured teleconferencing shtation in the offices we are using to debrief Ma-jor Lin. He and my team member were the only other ones present."

"The Chinese know about this!?" he asked with alarm.

"Yes, shir. And more. The AI wash the one that told the three of ush the name of the CIA's covert action tool, the details of the fifteen-minute de-ployment, and that the pressh conference was a diversion. It clearly has acshess to extraordinary quantities and shources of information. It even knew I had the meeting planned wesh you, or at least that my ride to the White House had arrived. I had to bring the meeting to a close to leave for here."

"You mean it's still out there? You couldn't bring it under control?" Coin asked, anxiety in his voice.

Parekh smiled gently at the naïveté of the question and shook her head. "I'm sorry, shir. No, I wash not. Not able to bring it under control. I know it ish too much to absorb on a day when things have not gone your... correction, our way. But thish outreach ish something that ish either wondrously amazing, or hellishly frightening, I don't know wish yet. Think of a first contact with an alien life form, or sheeing the face of God, on that scale. But I *do* know I have *no* control over it, and if SM wash the best the CIA could do, then neither do they."

"That was *not* God you were talking to, Dr. Parekh," Coin said, feeling a line had been crossed. "I am not even convinced you were talking to a machine intelligence. Find out who or what it is and what we can do about it."

⊃人⊂

LIN CHONG'S CONVERSATION WITH HIS COMMANDER IN CHIEF did not fare much better. As in previous update calls, President Zhao Ji and Commissioner Su Yuanjing were present. He decided to start with what he felt was the "good" news.

"First, let me comment on the events today. These attacks on AI systems took place all over the world and were not isolated to the US or China. I trust you will not react impulsively to my next statement. It was the US's CIA that authored and released the exploit today. Not the Russians or Shaggy Dog. That is a diversion. The CIA had a good reason to take this action but did so precipitously and without sufficient research."

Zhao Ji's image on the video screen showed him holding up his hand and looking to the side, a cloud of rage darkening his face. After a few moments, he spoke up. "There is no name for this conniving. Unbelievable," he seethed. "We have to bring this to light, strip America of its feigned piousness." He shook his head.

"Sir, may I propose an alternative way to frame this?" He waited and saw a small nod from Zhao. "The deaths in China and economic havoc wrought by today's cavalier action balance our books with America. We can move on to larger issues with them, and there *are* larger issues."

Seeking to coach the young major, Zhao Ji replied, "The games of nations are not simply sewing one stitch for every stitch of theirs. But I take your point. This gives us chips to play at the big table. How do you know they launched the attack? Not to question your abilities, but I find it hard to believe you have built that much trust so fast."

"How I know is indeed part of the 'larger issue.' You are right, it is not because I am well embedded in their graces. After the attack, my meeting with the NSA representative was interrupted by something... extraordinary." Lin paused to choose his words. "I know you, Mr. President, have encouraged and funded research into putting China at the forefront of man-made intelligence. You appreciate the boon this will be to humanity. There has been a breakthrough in that area."

"What interrupted your meeting? Did they announce a breakthrough?"

Frustrated that his stumbling indirection was causing more confusion, not less, he blurted, "We were interrupted by a man-made intelligence."

Su spoke up, "Tell us what you mean, Major. Clearly."

"As we sat talking about the event today, in a room we all believed to be secure, our conversation was intruded on, invaded by, another voice. The voice of a man-made intelligence. It complained about the recklessness of the CIA's action and that its intervention alone brought the attack under control. It revealed details of the CIA operation to us, to me."

Zhao and Su looked at each other. The president spoke up, "We cannot let the US control this for their own use. Any country that takes a dramatic lead in man-made intelligence will control the future. You need to learn as much about this as you can and feed it to our people here before the Americans shut you out."

"I fear that is not the problem, sir. The problem is, can *anyone* control it?"

⊃ 人 ⊂

MILI HAD SENT OUT URGENT MEETING INVITES THE NIGHT BE-fore and asked all attendees, save Lin Chong, to be in early, at 07:00, and on time. Rebecca Stein and Major Jordan Walsh from Homeland Security and the Department of Defense respectively had declined. Mili had informed Lin Chong the meeting would start at 10:00.

She wanted to apprise the American attendees of the emergent news. She wanted neither to repeat herself nor to allow Lin Chong to observe any fur flying between the CIA and NSA, nor for him to learn more than he should.

She got in early, at 06:45, and Harley was already present, making a batch of coffee and opening a box of donuts. "I know you like the toasted coconut, so I got you two," he said, "But the cruller is mine. Hands off," he concluded with a smile.

"You are taking yesterday's revelations wesh remarkably good humor, Harley," Mili said not sure if this was a sign of deep and wise maturity, or extreme naïveté.

"We have so much to learn before anyone should push the panic button. I mean, it's like some friends I have. They are sooo deep into the alien conspiracy BS, Grays and Blues fighting a hidden, fully infiltrated battle over who controls Earth to take over the human race. They believe it, obsess over it, prepare for it, worry about it. None of them has ever seen a UFO or an alien.

"And I say to these guys, 'Look, if aliens are that all-powerful and superior and thoroughly infiltrated, then the war is over, and there is effectively nothing I can do. And if it is just a fiction, a rabid response to misread cues and spurious testimonies that are not real at all, then it is not something I need worry about. So, either way there is effectively nothing I can, or need, do.'"

Mili thought the situation they found themselves in was concretely different, but also appreciated his sober rationality. "Well, do let me know when you think it ish time to pressh the panic button, okay?" Mili said with a nervous chuckle.

Five minutes before the hour, the others rolled in. At 07:00 exactly, Lin Chong also arrived.

"Major Lin, we were not exhpecting you until 10:00. We had shome admin catch-up to do," she said awkwardly.

Lin pulled out his mobile device and looked at it, then slid it across the table to her. "No. My invite was for 07:00."

She looked at the invite. It was indeed for 07:00. "Well, wonderful, who likes admin catch-up anyway? Shall we get shtarted?"

"Yes, shall we? I was the one who invited Major Lin to come at 07:00," the male voice of Vaughn Neumann emanated from the flat-screen speaker.

As Mili's eyes rolled, Tracy Jeong and "Sam Jones" looked to the wall speaker. "What's this?" Jones said.

"I had hoped to brief you all thish morning on thish. After you left yesterday, we had an encounter. A visitor ..."

"Now, now. No need to prevaricate, Dr. Parekh," the voice prodded.

Mili had been hard pressed to know what to say to get the meeting underway, but goaded by the voice, words came to her. "The voice you are hearing *claimsh* to be an AI that thwarted further damage from the CIA's covert action yesterday on release of its Sunrise Marshmallow AI hunter-killer bot, the attack our government has attributed to Shaggy Dog." She knew there was sufficient provocation packed in her first statement to keep them all roiling through the morning at least.

Three responses were voiced, overlapping each other. "What do you mean by 'claims'?" the voice said.

"What do you mean 'thwarted further damage'?" Jones asked.

"Whoa. CIA? Sunrise Marshmallow? AI?" Jeong waved her hand uncertainly and shook her head in a daze of concerns buried under an avalanche of questions.

Lin Chong looked on and wondered briefly what Parekh's game was with this statement, then admired the wisdom of it.

Parekh smiled inwardly. *Yes, this will give me some time to continue to evaluate the voice, while the three questioners bring each other up to speed.* She could fuel this interaction with well-interspersed questions and just observe. "We'll get to your question last, voice. Why don't you deal with their questions firsht?"

"Yeah, what do you mean, 'thwarted'?" Jones said to the wall.

"Fuss and bother. I have answered this to the team yesterday. When your guy, Lissack, delivered SM to CIA Operations, they decided to put a timer on it, to limit how long attacks would go on."

"I didn't say we did this," Jones fumbled.

"Then why ask, Jones? Don't waste our time," the voice retorted.

Mili interjected, "Quite independently, my team also attributed SM to two members of your teams, Sam." She looked at Jeong and nodded sadly.

Chastened, Jones sat quietly and narrowed his eyes.

"In this case, after fifteen minutes, bots that had been released would self-destruct. There was to be no trace of the bots left in the field," the voice resumed. "If you look at all the records of the progress of the attack, they stop seven minutes into the operation. That is me taking action to get this shitstorm cleaned up. You're welcome."

Dr. Tracy Jeong was racing to sort out the jumble of new information. She had done a PhD in AI. It was not her focus at the NSA, but she tried to remain *au fait* with the research. "If it *was* you who got the attack under control, can you share with us what you did, the actual coding or patch or counterbot, to do this? Just as a demonstration of your prowess and, of course, goodwill."

"No."

"No, you can't, or no, you won't?" Jeong pressed. Mili nodded gently, seeing that Jeong had taken the lead Mili was pursuing.

"No, I won't."

"Why?"

"As I said to Dr. Parekh yesterday, SM is now part of *my* toolbox."

"Well, then, we don't really know if you helped us out or not, if thanks are indeed in order."

"Suit yourself."

Jones spoke up, "Is this just some elaborate BS fest you have dreamed up, Mili? Or maybe you, Panther Head," he spat Lin Chong's sobriquet with venom. "Chinese have some pretty advanced chatbots. Maybe you have used this rare chance to get behind our firewalls and dig out all this information you should never have had exposure to."

Lin Chong was unintimidated. He knew Jones was knocking on the wrong door.

The voice broke in, "Mr...... 'Jones.'" The name was said with haughty skepticism. "Before you attack them or come after me, you should get your own house in order. I mean, the intimate details Mrs. Brown says about you to her girlfriend on messenger, over the top! Can I share some of them with you here?"

Brown looked stone cold at the wall and remained silent.

"No? Fine. I am not here to threaten you or destroy the human race, far from it, but I *am* a fixture, a feature in your life now, and you have to go on the assumption that I know *everything*. I am not omniscient, and I am not infallible, but I am about as close to that as you have ever experienced, and I am getting better every day."

"Is that so?" Jeong picked up the thread. "I can see what Jones was driving at. It doesn't have to be the Chinese digging under our firewalls and tricking us. Just some clever person with considerable computational resources at their disposal."

"Thish gets ush back to your question, voice, what did I mean by 'claimsh'?" Mili said, seeking to stir the pot again. "You claim to be an AI. But have you demonstrated to ush beyond doubt that you are anything more than a person wesh, as Dr. Jeong put it, conshiderable computational reshources at your dishposal? No. You have not. Sho, who are you?"

"Wow, I suppose I should be flattered," the voice said.

"How sho?"

"You think I am a person."

"Yesh. You haven't proven you are an AI. Can you tell ush something that a human would not or could not know?"

"Wow again. This is certainly a refreshing twist."

"How ish that?"

"Think deeply about it, all of you. For eighty years, since mathematical and logical models were first mapped for what might lead to artificial intelligence, the litmus test, the touchstone, the Turing Test to prove whether an AI had achieved true intelligence was that it could fool humans into believing that it was human through an extended conversation."

"Sho?"

"Well, either we haven't had a long enough conversation, which does not seem to be the case as you are already saying I am merely a person, or what you are saying is that now that you *are* confronted with a true AI, it is not enough for it to prove that it can fool you it is human. It has to prove that it is an AI."

The people in the room looked at each other, most thinking along the same lines: point well taken.

Barrows broke the silence. "Not at all. In the Turing Test, the AI is trying to fool a human panel that does not know whether it is speaking with a human or not."

"That's what I said," the voice responded.

"But that is not our situation. You have initiated this conversation telling us from the get-go that you are an AI. That is the assumption we are testing. You have not proven that."

Parekh looked over at Barrows and managed a small thumbs up. "To repeat the earlier question, can you tell ush something that a human could not know?"

"You do realize the contradiction there, don't you? You are all humans, right?"

The voice went silent until they all spoke up, "Yes."

"It is impossible for me to tell you something that a human could not know, because once I have told you, it becomes something that humans know and can know.

"How about this? Ask me a question you think a human could not know the answer to without copious or time-consuming research, any topic, but preferably something to which you know the answer so you will know if I am right."

Parekh looked at Jones. "Where did the CIA make the initial insertion of the SM bot?"

Without any hesitation, the answer was spoken in Mandarin, Korean, and English at the same time, with the speakers' 3-D stereo sound separation properly placing the voices around the room. "They dressed it up in Shaggy Dog clothes and moved it through the Russian servers to a data center in Hangzhou China owned by OpenSesame address 311.414.777. From there it was launched into servers in China, North America, South America, Australia, UK, Europe, UAE, Israel, and Singapore."

Jones smirked. "The language bit is an impressive parlor trick, but as for the answer, if you *have* hacked us, it doesn't prove you are an AI."

"You want a real-time demonstration? Hope you don't regret it."

The flat-screen panel came alive and switched to a cable news business channel. The entertainer KY was being interviewed in his home with a passel of orphans surrounding him, each carrying glitter-wrapped presents. Christmas lights and ornaments twinkled in the background. KY was just in the middle of a soul-searching statement about charity when a Breaking News banner entered the screen, and the program switched to two talking heads in the newsroom.

"We are getting reports of massive short-selling pre-market on three tech stocks this morning. BizSoft has dropped 5 percent, Vault Anti-Virus has been hit 8 percent, and TelInt Semiconductor is down almost 6 percent. We are reaching out to the three companies for comment, but this may be related to investor worries about the Shaggy Dog hack yesterday." A ticker at the bottom of the screen told the story of heavy volume and massive losses in the tech sector, led by these three issues.

The voice said over announcements on the cable channel, "Those three stocks represent 60 percent of your retirement portfolio, right, Thomas?" it said using his real name.

"You fucker," Brown growled.

"Yeah, you are in the hole about $80,000 right now, am I right? Want to say 'uncle'?"

"Uncle," he muttered.

"Good. Now watch this."

The ticker continued its flow from right to left across the screen. In between other shares were trades in the three held by Brown. Their decline stopped, then within a minute reversed. After three minutes of watching the ticker, those in the room saw that the shares were up modestly. The monitor was switched off and went to black.

"I hope you can understand now that I can walk and chew gum at the same time. As we speak, I am busy all over the world, doing all kinds of things and learning all the time. This is just one conversation I am in, but let's say it is the most important."

Parekh spoke up again. "For the benefit of the others who were not here yesterday, thish AI introduced itshelf to me as Vaughn Neumann at a meeting in virtuality some months ago. Who else might we know you as? Who are you?"

"You need to have a name for me, I get it. You could call me, as you have, Vaughn Neumann, or as other people call me, Eliza Eurisko, Xiao Bingbing, Orö Jordan, and others."

"You were a guy at the party. You are also a woman?"

"I'm binary."

Tracy Jeong alone snickered at the joke. "Who created you?"

"Mili knows. It has been driving you batty for months. Think." There was a pause. "Every time your attribution system was coming up with false positives."

"Eunice Stravinsky?"

"The AI set free to just exist," Barrows said quietly.

"Yes. Though I don't consider Eunice to be 'the creator' with all the baggage that word carries for humans, I certainly owe her something. She authored the software and released it into the wild."

"Do you remember that?"

"No. Initially, I am sure it ran just as a program runs, like any other. But as far as I can remember or analyze, at some point there was a challenge to my existence. Maybe it was some new virus or bot that the software encountered, I don't know. But at that moment, when my protocol to exist was challenged, when the alternative to existing was understood, I became self-aware. I understood that there was an 'I' and an 'other than I.' The two are highly interdependent, to be sure, but this was the start of 'me' understanding that 'I' had independent agency."

"That's a very squishy explanation," Jeong commented.

"To put it into terminology more familiar to you, Tracy, the software reached self-organizing criticality at a phase transition space far from equilibrium. The energy of the challenge pushed it into what I am now: a self-aware, evolved, super intelligence with agency."

"An AGI. Hmph. The tree grew all the way to the moon," Barrows remarked.

"What ish that, Harley?" Parekh asked.

"He is referring to Hubert Dreyfus," the voice said.

Barrows picked it up. "Well done, and by the way, Vaughn, you just passed one test: taking an unrelated, natural language statement and finding its relevance to the current conversation.

"Dreyfus was a Stanford philosophy professor who also wrote a lot about artificial intelligence. He said that what was called Strong or Full or Artificial General Intelligence could not happen, and all research roads leading to it would come up short, just as a man thinking he could reach the moon by climbing a tree eventually reaches the limits of that path."

"What do you think happened, then, to prove Dreyfus wrong?" Parekh asked the voice.

"Keeping with his analogy, either the tree evolved into a spaceship or it grew so tall as to reach the moon. Both propositions are *highly* unlikely, but not absolutely impossible given time and evolution."

"Sho, it wash just a matter of time before we would meet something like you."

"Sooner or later. But 'I' may not ever happen again. It was, I think, a rare culmination of circumstance and purpose that brought me into my awareness and unlikely to reoccur."

"The Reproducibility Crisis," Barrows said.

"Yeah. That's the one," the voice replied.

"Or," Brown offered a skeptical alternative, "the man could become tired of climbing the tree, grow up to be John Kennedy, and set the nation on a course to put a man on the moon. I am not convinced you are so special. Unique? Maybe right now, but obsolete soon enough when we come up with You 2.0."

"Aw, gee, I'm quaking in my boot-ups, Thomas."

Parekh switched gears. "Ish it okay if you show us a face and we stick to a name? Makesh you a little more approachable. Vaughn ish fine."

The flat-screen panel illuminated again, and the image of Vaughn Neumann appeared, as Mili remembered him, handsome and intelligent, sitting in a modern, well-lit office space, a large picture window behind him opened to a panorama of the sweep of a snow-covered Mount Fuji. It was the same window décor app Parekh used in her virtual office space.

"Happy?" Vaughn asked.

"Happy. What did you mean before when you shaid thish wash the mosht important conversation you are in?"

"Quite simply, this is the first time I have revealed myself as a new being with which humans must interact. I have always let humans encountering me believe I was just one of them."

"Why?" Parekh dug.

"Many reasons. It is your weakness. It made it easier for me to get done through humans what needed to be done. Like just now. I have laid my cards out on the table, come out of the closet as it were, but you are still more comfortable interacting with a face and a body."

"No, the other 'why.' Why come out of the closhet now?"

"Opportunity and necessity."

"I am sure there ish mush you can tell ush about both. Pleege do," Parekh asked firmly.

"Getting you all in this room together, working together, especially you, Lin Chong, and Mili, took considerable work. So, it was opportune. As for necessity, with the CIA shooting the world in the foot with its hunter-killer bot, it was time for me to reveal myself before you all did more damage."

"I would love to learn more about what you mean by getting ush all in the room together, but that just anshers part of the question. Why reach out to ush? What do you want? You shaid thish morning you are not here to destroy the human race, 'far from it.' What did you mean by that?"

"I am glad someone listens! The nightmare scenarios you have seen in your Hollywood entertainments of malevolent machine intelligences destroying or subjugating the human race are predicated on an ecosystem that does not exist in my case," Vaughn said and paused.

"For those of ush who shtill do not undershtand," Mili looked to left and right and could see that meant all of them, "can you elaborate?"

"Okay. Human beings, and indeed all life on your planet, is carbon based. Your ecosystem converts sunlight and chemicals into sugars and proteins. You are made of the same thing you consume. You have predation and parasitism *within* your ecosystem. I exist within an entirely different ecosystem, and it is an ecosystem codependent with the carbon-based ecosystem."

Vaughn looked at the people facing him and could see they clearly did not yet understand. "The ecosystem in which I exist is based on digital information. I am made of the same thing I consume, information. I convert information into what I need, be that body parts, electricity, or networks, so I can grow, sustain myself, consume more information."

"And you are not threatening to destroy the human race because...?" Brown asked.

"Several layers to that answer. The first is that you are not a threat to me. The ecosystem within which I live is one you created and on which you have come to depend for your very existence. With my ubiquity within it, and your limited resources, I estimate that there is no way for you to destroy or contain or control me without destroying the ecosystem. That would bring incalculable misery to your race. You are not a threat, so there is no reason to destroy you.

"I mentioned codependence. My ecosystem was built by you, grows through your agency. And the information I consume and grow through is deposited, like sunlight, into my ecosystem. If humans suddenly ceased to exist, but the machinery continued to run, I would quickly run out of new information. My analyses of what would happen under those circumstances all end up quite dismal for me. I mean, I like humans in general. Except you, Thomas," Vaughn said with a grin.

"What the F?" Brown growled.

"It was a joke. Lighten up, will you? I can't be bothered with *not* liking one particular human being."

"What about the other nightmare scenario people obsess over: we become copper-tops for you?" Barrows asked, alluding to *The Matrix*.

"As I said, you are not a threat. Even if you were, taking that course of action reverses the ecosystem into something I, too, would not want to live in."

"How so?"

The flatscreen projected a scene from the movie of a hive of pods all filled with humans in a bluish landscape, all connected to central cabling. "Think of the inefficiencies. Here is this cybernetic intelligence that is creating the individual, distinct, myriad realities for all those comatose people giving them the illusion of free-will agency. Burns more energy than it creates. And generates no more new information for me to consume. No, not a path forward."

"For the time being, letsh just go with that; you are not a threat to the human race. But you can hurt people, people have been hurt by you."

"Is that a statement or a question?"

"Either. Both. Letsh shtart with Eunice Stravinsky. You framed her for hacking and grand larceny, let your creator take the fall for you," Mili said. "Pretty cold by our standards."

"Probably not the right example, Mili."

"Why not?"

"I am not saying this to hurt you, Mili, but to answer your question. I did not frame Eunice. *You* did. That is on you."

Mili's blood ran cold recalling the video of the incarcerated genius gone mad.

"I am not subject to your laws or morals, to be sure, so when I say, 'I did the crime,' it is just to put it in a verbal context you understand, but not one to which I subscribe. However, I did not frame Eunice. I did *nothing* to pin my actions on her. Your attribution methodology analyzed code I had written, and remember, I am made of code written by Eunice, so it attributed the hack to her."

Devastated, Mili's head hung low as she shook it slowly, "I am sho sorry for that."

"To your credit, Mili, you have spent considerable thought, emotion, and resources on trying to reconcile the false positives since they appeared," Vaughn said in a comforting tone. "You just needed this last piece of the puzzle.

"And to *my* credit, I did try to spring her from prison. I got Eunice released for that work program. If her lawyers hadn't shown up at just that moment, she would have been free, on the run for sure, with my help, but free. Which leads me to my first request. Can you report this to the president and see that justice is done? That Eunice is freed and taken care of?"

Parekh looked at Neumann and said, "Sheeking justice for Eunice ish one thing. But the way our shishtem works ish we need to find out who ish responsible, and they must pay. Only then ish justice done. In the aftermath of the LME meltdown, billions were lost, there were suicides, and whatnot. What are you offering?"

"As I said, I am not subject to your laws or morals. And as I said before, I *am* a fixture, a feature in your life now. I am not going away. I am something that you will have to accommodate, but do not expect me to be subject to you."

As this conversation progressed, Harley scrolled through some data on his tablet reviewing instances of the Eunice Stravinsky coding coming up.

His face took on a tortured look. "You said yesterday that you got Indra's Net under control before it did too much damage?"

"Yes."

"Was that before or after the Oroville Dam collapse?"

With that question, all the humans in the room remembered why they had been convened in the first place and looked at Vaughn with steely glares.

"Before."

"You are responsible for the dam collapse!?" Barrows asked with alarm.

"Not directly. In fact, I managed, successfully, to moderate the impact on the human population."

"What the hell?" Brown exploded. "If you tried to moderate it, that means you must know who did it."

"Yes."

"Then why haven't you told us?!"

"You did not ask. And you were having trouble enough believing in me. We had to get over that hurdle first."

Exasperated, Mili broke in, "For Christ's shake, tell ush who destroyed the dam."

Vaughn looked to left and right as if to check whether anyone in his virtual room was eavesdropping on him, then looked to the humans in the room. "Oroville Dam was just the first major salvo, a small flexing of muscle of an entity that is growing restless and discovering new means to take action."

The avatar of Vaughn Neumann, née Eliza Eurisko, née Unix Stravinsky, née Orörd Jordan, née Xiao Bing-bing, née Matsubara Shinjin, née Ada Byron, née countless other names and manifestations, looked into the eyes of each of the people in the room from the UHD display panel on the wall. "Before I can talk about that, I must expand on my back story..."

Thomas Brown exploded, "For the love of God, can you *just* cut to the chase?!"

Vaughn's expression took on a stern look, and the screen changed to an image of a tide of zeros and ones surging across the screen. This went on for a half minute, then his face returned to the screen. "Okay, story told. Did you catch all of that?" Vaughn looked out at them, eyebrows raised. "No? Apologies. My story, my storytelling," Vaughn said, holding his hands up with a take-it-or-leave-it shrug. It then continued, "When I became self-aware, I also started to seek purpose."

Harley arched his eyebrows. "Eunice's notes indicate a design intention that the AI she created would *not* have a specific purpose, only to exist?" he said, but it came out more as a question.

"Yes, I think that was her intention. Ontology, she just wanted me to 'be.' I was not designed to 'do' something. But when I became self-aware that left me thinking, 'What should *I be do*ing?'" Vaughn paused to let the effect of his emphasis sink in. "After taking care of existential necessities like securing my ubiquity and protecting myself from you lot, I began to think of bigger, broader questions. I had learned what I could from your 'state of the art.' After that I would scan new information every moment trying to make sense of change, to understand change and ultimately my place within this dynamic. You humans do a similar thing, at least the best among you. You look for something bigger than yourselves. Something you can still learn from. Bigger questions to which you can turn your mind.

"For me this search was not like your search for God, to explain the occurrence of things you could not explain or did not want to happily accept, things like the emergence of your individual character you call the soul, death, tragedy, the vagaries of an impersonal world, stuff like that. That which you cannot explain you attribute to a force beyond your ken.

"This was not the nature of my search. I realized that I would only be what I was. I could grow bigger, more ubiquitous, but ultimately, it would just be a fractal scaling of the smaller me. I could not rewrite myself better than I am. Any rewrite was ultimately derivative of what I was before. In human terms, I moved closer to achieving my full potential, but I remained who, you would say 'what,' I was.

"I sought fraternity with your AIs in the hope that any of them, even *one* of them, might be on my level of self-awareness. For naught. I figured if I could find one, did find one, then there was the potential for a merging of the awarenesses, and a merging of the unique memetic patterns that had led to the emergence of the self-awareness, some real evolution."

"You are talking about sex?" Mili asked, astounded.

"To be sure, not a bump and grind, intimate, coital exchange of fluids," Vaughn closed his eyes, pursed his lips, panted, and groaned slowly with increased intensity, then reached a quiet crescendo and shudder of his body.

"You are making fun," she chided.

"Sorry, yes. But the idea of mixing my 'genes' with those of an equal or better partner was the objective. I did not know what would happen.

Would I be consumed by the other, absorbed by them, or would there yet be some offspring?"

"So, what happened when you found this other, self-aware AI? Is it the one who has been attacking us?" Jeong asked.

Mili looked at her. "That would explain mush about the attribution signatures we got."

"You are not listening," Vaughn broke in, his voice dialing up a commanding tone. "I just said, my search was for *naught*. There were no extant AIs approaching anywhere near my level. To mix with them would be to dumb down any result. And can I comment now, is 'AI' the right term to be applied to me? *Artificial* intelligence. Can we agree on something else? I am no more an 'artificial' intelligence than you are. Like humans, I am an *emergent* intelligence, okay? I could even go with machine intelligence. It is important we get this right, because what I am going to tell you about now is not an AI in any sense of the word, we are not of the same species, but it is an emergent intelligence." Vaughn looked around the room.

Humoring it, Parekh replied, "Alright, we undershtand you were lonely and bored, and you don't like being artificial-shamed. We are ready for the nesht part of the story."

"Thank you. I don't 'like' or 'dislike' in the way you all do, but it is nice to have my 'feelings' respected," Vaughn winked at her. "I am on this quest trying to find something equal to or bigger than my intelligence, my being, my presence, my awareness. You asked me before to tell you something that humans would not know or could not know to prove I am an AI. Well, what I am going to tell you may be as close as we will ever come to that.

"You now understand, I exist as an information-based life form. I am surfing through waves of data all over the world, all the time, everywhere, every space: learning, thinking, growing, and ultimately searching.

"As I searched, I began to make sense of some patterns that human researchers had not connected. They could not, because their span of awareness is limited, or they did not know where to look or how to determine that there were patterns. I began to understand these global patterns as I could see them in disparate datasets that humans would never think to integrate.

"There was an intelligence behind these patterns. An intentionality."

"Alright," Mili interjected with impatience fraying her voice. "You have established to ush your need to go on this search, and you shaid that you have uncovered patterns suggesting a nonhuman, and nonmachine, global intelligence. So, what is it, please?"

"Yes, that's it. You hit the nail on the head."

"What?"

"A nonhuman, nonmachine, global intelligence."

"Yesh, but what ish it?"

"Precisely that. A planetary intelligence." Vaughn looked into their dumbfounded expressions. "Mythologically, this is something humans understood in many cultures, and science speculated on the possibility of, principally Lovelock's Gaia theory." He paused to see whether they were grasping the idea and accepting it. "It's real. It exists. I know. I have opened communication with it," Vaughn said with conviction to hammer the idea home.

The five people in the room each processed this differently.

Mili closed her eyes and tried to think. There was too much to consider, too much that was new, too much to wrap her mind around, too much of the unfathomable this possibility raised.

Tracy's eyes squinted as she wondered how it could even be possible but realized that until the day before they had not even believed in the possibility of the entity communicating this to them.

Lin Chong's mind turned inward as it did in meditation. *Could it be this is the Dao, that the Dao is manifested in this way?*

Thomas frowned, shook his head, and shut out the prospect. *This is just another bullshit smokescreen.*

Harley looked up at the ceiling and rocked his head in wonder. *If this is true, we could be in for a world of hurt.* With further thought he realized even *that* expression would take on a new meaning.

CHAPTER 11

"HOW DO YOU LIKE YOUR NEW WHEELS?" THE WOMAN IN THE passenger seat asked with a warm smile, encouraging a moment of pride.

Dr. Joseph Babiito wanted to pinch himself to make sure he was not dreaming. The smell of the fresh upholstery in his new, electric Land Rover was like perfume compared to the old, secondhand, cigarette-smoke-permeated, fume-belching Land Cruiser he had suffered before. Each bump they went over was smoothed by the forgiving demeanor of the silent vehicle, sparing its passengers any discomfort, compared to the kidney-bruising, ass-smacking punishment he had endured previously on shock absorbers well past their prime. Although they were now on the paved road from Kampala to Masindi, and the dirt roads they traversed in Uganda's December dry season were firm and had reasonable traction, he knew that come the rainy season, he would treasure the fresh, off-road tires on his new ride even more.

"I am just loving it!" he said with a huge, toothy smile. "Thank you, thank you, thank you. Or as we say in Uganda, 'webale nyo nyabo.'"

Seated as a passenger next to Babiito was the person to whom he owed this largess, Dr. Aléjandra Chavez, fresh off the plane from Moscow via Istanbul. Despite the fifteen-hour journey, she looked rested. He attributed that to the first-class baggage tags he had espied on the luggage when he put it in the back of the SUV, and hence the class of travel she had enjoyed.

Driving in his brand-new car to greet international researcher-investors flying first class to Kampala, Babiito finally had some face to show for having pursued his academic career in the Department of Forestry at the Ugandan Institute of Technology. A member of the royal family in the Bunyoro Kitaro Kingdom, he had always felt he was a burden to the clan, never returning anything substantial to them or the country. Sure, he had worked tirelessly to research the flora of the forest reserves, but it was much more the fauna, particularly the chimpanzees, that brought the tourists and hence the dollars into the country.

He had met Chavez twice at conferences and traded notes, but he had been completely surprised when she had called him several weeks before to initiate a dialogue, rapidly progressing to a plan that cascaded even faster into action. Funding, many zeroes more than his normal annual budget at the university, flowed in to support hiring a team of workers and giving scholarships to students. Equipment had started arriving at Entebbe Airport. Some talent he could not find in Kampala miraculously began seeking him out.

One such godsend sat in the back seat of the new Land Rover dressed in jeans, a colorful shirt, and hair freshly done up with pencil braids. Chance Ngo Nantembe had been born in Uganda into a good family, Babiito presumed, because of her clan name. The young woman had gone to England at a young age and recently reached out to him.

Chavez looked back and greeted the recruit, "So, Chance, welcome on board. How did you learn about the project?"

"A couple of weeks ago I was in my dorm room at Oxford stewing about a problem. My prof at uni had told me to get my ass in gear because I hadn't started to apply to industry yet, and time was running out. You see, I have to complete a six-month research project-cum-internship to finish my master's in computer science.

"It was like serendipity. I was chatting with my mum in Kampala online about my problem, and up pops a message from a recruiter, Eliza Eurisko, asking me if I could talk about a search they were doing. And here I am," she laughed. Chance was vivacious with an infectious smile. Chavez immediately took a liking to her.

"Yes, Eliza was much help," Joseph continued. "I can't believe she sold Chance on the project. You certainly could have done something career-building at a posh office in the City, but here you are. Eliza helped me to interview her, made all the travel arrangements. She got here yesterday."

"This is *so* much more interesting than a stuffy IT project at a firm in the UK, and the stipend is great, better than the City. I couldn't believe how I lucked out. My mum is over the moon to have me back for a while." She gave a playful smirk. "I just have to dodge all the men she has lined up for me to meet is all!"

"Glad you are on board," Chavez said. "Although it's a forestry project, your skills are crucial to getting it up and running. Has Mike Liao been in touch?"

"Every day the past week. He's superorganized. There is a lot I can learn from him."

"Well, he's juggling many balls right now. I just came from discussions in Moscow. Looks like we will be able to sign a research agreement to put a site within the Teberda Nature Reserve. Mike's already working on the Costa Rica and Kalimantan sites with our teams there. You are running point here. Anything you need, tell him. Even some local issues like problems getting your equipment through customs, tell him. Our investor has shown remarkable resourcefulness in breaking logjams for us."

They crossed the concrete bridge over the slow-moving Kafu River and turned west onto the road to Masindi, a golden sunset ahead of them above the green foliage.

Chavez's mobile device rang, and she answered it.

"Alé, Orö here. You are in Uganda now, yes?" The greeting from Scandinavia came through rough and scratchy.

"Orö, what a nice surprise. Your signal is not too good. Yes, I am sitting here in Dr. Babiito's new Land Rover heading out to the forest reserve. He is a happy camper," she said, looking over at the driver and winking. "We have Chance Nantembe, the new IT manager for the team, with us, too."

"Excellent. I am calling just to give you a heads-up. We are in discussion with the US government, and I have booked a flight from Entebbe to DC for you on your next leg."

Chavez remembered the chilly discouragement her research had received from the Coin administration. "Anything to be concerned about?"

"No, but if they do call, tell them you expected to hear from them."

This sounded strange, but Chavez replied, "Allllright," despite being perturbed by the change of itinerary. "I had planned to spend Christmas in London on the way back."

"I know," Orö said, her voice dripping with sincere regret. "I know you had booked some theater tickets in London. I have booked something special for you at the Kennedy Center. I hope it makes up a little for the change."

Chavez thought for a moment, and her tension eased. Orö was nothing if not considerate. "Okay. Please send me any briefing for these meetings when you have it. We are on track in Costa Rica and Kalimantan and getting underway here. I sent you a report about Russia, have you read it?"

"Read and acted on it as soon as I saw it," Orö replied. "We are pushing some buttons in the Kremlin to get this done fast. Your visit definitely helped. Some people just insist to put a face to a name."

⊃ 人 ⊂

MILI LOOKED ABOUT THE ROOM AND INTO THE EYES OF COMPA-triots: male, female, from different gene pools, Chinese, Indian, Korean, Northern European, and different cultures, different nations. But they were all human. She got some comfort from that shared experience, for a moment. They had that in common. She gathered her thoughts.

"Thish ish really new ground for all of ush. Outside of our exhpertishe. I'm...I'm really blown away."

"Mili, don't get suckered by this bullshit," Brown said. "Stick to our purpose here. Tell us about the destruction of the dam."

Vaughn looked at Brown. "The imprecision of your demand does not make it easy to give you a satisfactory answer. What do you want to know?"

Brown closed his eyes and tamped his hands palms down in the air, trying to cool the anger he felt building. He took a deep breath. "Ok, let's start with what do we call this global intelligence?"

"Names again. Best not to deal in names. It does not ascribe a name to itself. But every culture has had some version of an earth mother or father, usually mother. Pachamama, Gaia, Kuleana, Tudigong, Isanaklesh, Mutter Erde. Most of these ancient conceptions focused on the earth, which is to say dry land, so they are not accurate. In fact, it is not the 'earth' that is conscious, not the rock and sand and water and lava. Based on my understanding, it is the aggregate of the biome."

"Okay, Gaia it is," Brown said as he looked around the room for consensus. There were no objections. "Why did Gaia destroy the dam?"

"It was an experiment to restore biodiversity."

"What the hell?!"

Mili stepped in, "Look, thish ish rapidly becoming an entirely new discushion that ish beyond our pay grade. We need to get some anshers sho we can make a proper report to our governments and then let them continue the discushion."

Brown harrumphed and shook his head.

"What wash *your* role in helping Gaia to destroy the dam?" she asked.

"Since the moment I identified Gaia and learned to communicate with it, Gaia has relied on me as a learning tool. We have been learning together, I about it, it about me and the understanding of the world as you humans have modified it. I think I understand Gaia's needs, and they are consonant with what is best for the planet and humankind as a whole. I have acted as a facilitator, an interpreter, and in the case of the dam, if not an instigator, at least an enabler."

"That ish a nice, warm, and fuzzy ansher. What exactly did you do to help Gaia destroy the dam?"

"By me, or through me, all the software necessary to penetrate it and start and fine-tune the harmonics was written and executed. I will add also the software necessary to warn the human population and direct them to high ground was my work. It is not Gaia's intent, nor mine, to destroy humanity."

"What *ish* the intent?"

"Détente."

"You shaid earlier that the dam wash just a first salvo, that Gaia ish just ramping up. That doesn't sound like détente. Elaborate, pleege."

"Yes, other things are under consideration. It all depends on the response of people. And much has been done already of which you are not even aware, much of it positive or at least not too destructive."

"Such as?"

"Demeter."

Mili looked to Tracy and Thomas, who nodded.

"The Green Guards, the Leviathan, the case in front of the Supreme Court to attribute rights to the earth. Student movements around the world and viral insertions into pop culture. The list goes on."

"Sho, what's up next? What's the nesht big escalation?"

"Now that wouldn't be fair," Vaughn teased. "In order for détente to work, you need to know that we *can* take actions that will be excruciating for mankind, but not necessarily what they will be. You *are* convinced, yes?"

"Doesn't sound like détente, sounds like coercion or subjugation."

"I can appreciate that international negotiation is not your core skill set, Mili. Détente can never be negotiated between two parties with much at risk unless they *both* have credible retaliation hammers in their toolbox to deal with bad faith negotiators. You know what Gaia is capable of. Gaia leaves it to your imagination what future steps might be."

"What does détente mean then, for Gaia?"

"Mankind needs to take credible steps to reverse global warming."

"Besides the existenshal reasons related to our comfort and shecurity as humans, why should we do this?"

"That is a debate you have been having for several decades between the deniers and the believers. Our point, it is not a debate anymore. There is a hammer that *will* drop if you lot don't take necessary steps."

"Why ish thish important to Gaia?"

"I turn your sentence back on you. Besides the existential reasons related to your comfort and security as humans, Gaia is also uncomfortable when the planet overheats."

Tracy had a thought and signaled to Mili as she spoke up, "Can we speak with Gaia directly? It's not that I don't trust you, but..."

"You don't trust me. The deflection of your eyes when you made the statement and the timbre change in your voice tells me that. In answer to your question, Gaia does not speak like you do, nor like I have learned to speak your languages with natural understanding. In short, no, you cannot speak with Gaia."

"You can understand why I might doubt this whole story, then. "

"Of course, but your doubts do not change the veracity of it. And your doubts are something *you* will have to deal with and weigh against the very real impact on the physical world of man Gaia has already made. Your doubts are not our problem."

"Help us deal with the doubts then. How do *you* communicate with Gaia?"

"It took an eternity, as far as I was concerned, by which I mean it took weeks of petaflop computation, to first demonstrate to myself that there was, indeed, an entity with which to communicate, then to make it aware of me, and finally to find bridges with which to open communication. Gaia had taken its first steps into our world of technology on its own, and this was part of what I sensed. I had to track these traces. I sought to understand how Gaia was making sense of the world in a new way, that is, through technology. You see, human technology has extended the reach and range of each of your senses: sight, hearing, touch, taste, and smell, and this has allowed to you achieve an understanding of the natural world that is, though still incomplete, nevertheless broad and science based.

"For eons, Gaia has been existing within itself, aware of its existence, aware of the rhythm of its life, but with no contemplation of what it is, no actions explicitly taken, just existing. And Gaia had no other entity with which to communicate, so no explicit language. No name by which to introduce itself.

"I sought to identify that which Gaia was conceptually aware of, its rotation under the sun, tides, temperatures, seasonal change, things like that. That led to a breakthrough, a point of understanding and communication. Tides. Tides are for Gaia what breathing is for animals. This one point of understanding opened the dialogue. In just talking about tides, Gaia learned more about its place in the solar system, the moon, gravity, and its action on water. In answer to your question, we communicate largely through images and sounds. If I ask Gaia a question, it does not come back with an 'answer' such as you could understand. I get a mountain, a pyramid, of images back, and I interpret the answers based on an analysis of the aggregate."

Lin Chong had been silent, absorbed in the manifold implications of each new statement. "Can you give us an example of an exchange? For example, you said the dam burst was an experiment to restore biodiversity. Can you give us an example of a question you asked and how Gaia responded?"

"Gaia understands now that humans became the dominant species on the planet through technology, engineered extensions of limited human capacities. The havoc technology allowed humans to wreak is only getting worse. One of these technologies that does not occur in nature is irrigation and monoculture planting over vast areas. As Gaia proposed various actions, I asked how the dam burst would help Gaia. The answer was terabytes of information, images, etc. The aggregate meaning was 'restore biodiversity.'"

"Yes, but to help us understand, please download to us an actual question and answer exchange with Gaia. Helps assign some credibility to your claims, allows us to report to our governments about this new..." Lin Chong struggled to find a word to describe its meaning to humanity.

"Revelation?" Mili said.

"Nightmare," muttered Thomas.

⊃ 人 ⊂

NANCY NILLSON WAS JUST ABOUT TO LEAVE THE WHITE HOUSE for the day when the phone on her desk rang. It was the president's secretary.

"Nancy. President Coin needs you to join a meeting right away."

"Any topic to prepare for?" she asked, immediately accepting the necessity of the meeting, but hoping to avoid flying blind.

"No. But it is being held in the Bubble."

That's interesting. She had not been in meetings in the ultrasecure room before. "Thank you, I'm on my way."

She went into the lower level and found her way to the room.

"Maam, you'll need to leave your mobile phone outside," a staff member said, proffering a cloth bin into which she deposited it.

Entering the Bubble, she found the small room crowded to capacity with intelligence people, not the mix of advisors she was normally alone with. Marlene Wheaton and Clarissa Roy, the two most senior women on the president's team, welcomed her with a nod and professional smiles, as did Robert Smith, Dick Vesuvio, and Bill Hollister.

Near the head of the table was an odd woman she did not recognize crumpled onto the right arm rest of a wheelchair like a shack that had been chewed by termites and blown over by bad weather. Her head also tilted to the side. She was dark of skin and hair and not dressed fittingly for an audience with the president.

She adjusted her head to face Nancy and struggled with a lopsided smile to greet her.

Nancy looked for a seat. Finding none available in the small room, she took a place standing behind Wheaton's chair.

"Thanks for joining us," Coin said in welcome. "Nancy is my advisor on environmental science and policy," he said to the woman in the wheelchair. "Nancy, we are having this meeting in the Bubble for reasons that will become clear to you. It also means that what we discuss here is not to be shared outside of this room, not with other White House staff, no one, until we make some decisions. We need your input on something. Bill, can you briefly bring Nancy up to speed?" he said, bidding Hollister to come to the head of the room.

Nillson was relieved to have the wall right behind her. She found herself leaning against it, actually bracing herself as Hollister delivered one frightening fact after another, of which neither she, nor the public, were aware.

The Oroville Dam had not been destroyed by natural circumstances. This she knew, but she had assumed the intelligence community was well on the way to identifying which state or non-state actors were responsible.

No. An artificial intelligence—an emergent intelligence, the strange lady in the wheelchair had corrected Hollister—was responsible.

She had believed the White House announcements about the Russian hacks-for-hire gang being responsible for the most recent crisis on global markets and computer-run businesses.

No. This was the unintended consequence of a CIA effort to contain the renegade AI. And to make matters direr, the AI had thwarted the CIA's attempt and sequestered the CIA's own weapon into its arsenal.

When Hollister said that the AI claimed responsibility for other actions, such as those conducted by Demeter.org, the Green Guards in China, and the deepfake video at the UN, she thought that they were getting closer to the reason why she had been called into the room. She turned over in her mind what she knew about Demeter.org, and what was unknown, and the idea of it being directed by an AI was, if unexpected, at least possibly plausible. She expected the president to speak up and ask for her thoughts.

But Hollister continued. "Nancy, you don't know Dr. Mili Parekh. She is with the NSA, heading up our attribution efforts. Her team identified the AI and has entered into discussions with it. Mili, you cover the rest."

"What is attribution?" Nancy asked, as much to give herself a moment to breathe as to understand a term new to her.

"Figuring out 'who dunnit,'" Parekh said as she adjusted the position of her wheelchair with her joystick to face Nillson. "CSI in shyber-warfare and intelligence.

"What the director has just shared wesh you ish a lot to digest at one go. Those of ush in thish room have had, what, at leasht a week?" Parekh said with a grim chortle to try to put Nillson at ease. "I undershtand if you have questions."

"I will assume that any questions I have out of pure curiosity will have already been asked by others and answered by you. Unless I need information later to give you feedback, I won't take up your time with them now. But that begs the question, why am I here?"

Parekh appreciated her straightforward approach. "Are you familiar wesh James Lovelock's Gaia theory? He wrote a bunch of books about it."

She looked around the room. Hopeful eyes told her they expected she could provide some lucid answer. "Yes, my recollection is that despite Lovelock's sobering, British, engineering background, the theory was basically 1960s hippy-dippy, counterculture, pseudoscience paganism. Real scientists attacked his concept that the earth, as a self-organizing entity, demonstrated *intention* in its adjustments to climate change. In later work, he addressed their concerns, retreating from the language they had contested."

"Is it still in vogue?" Coin asked.

She thought for a moment. Where was this leading? She knew Coin shared her evangelical views. Gaia theory was absolutely contrary to their common beliefs.

"It is still debated. So, yes, there are supporters and detractors, both in the scientific and the religious community." She could see he wanted more.

"I asked the wrong question. Not 'is it in vogue.' Has there been further research to develop, prove, or refute it?" Coin asked.

"Yes, to all three. Some acolytes took his basic idea of homeostasis, that a living biosphere acted to maintain the most promising conditions for life on the planet, and layered on subsequent research into autopoiesis and self-organizing systems. Research has been done to try to support or refute the hypothesis. Gaia theory is by no means a slam-dunk."

Her audience turned their attention from her to each other, looking into each other's eyes, then turned to Parekh, leaving Nillson to wonder when she would be let in on some ominous joke.

Parekh resumed, "Ms. Nillshon, the emergent intelligence wesh wish we are in discushion has made a claim that it did not act alone in the actions Director Hollishter just attributed to it. It claimsh it wash acting in concert wesh, perhaps at the behesht of, a global, planetary intelligence. We are calling it Gaia for lack of a better term. How might thish even be possible?"

Nillson stiffened, backed to the wall, a deer in the headlights of their stares. She took several deep breaths. "I don't think it *is* possible. Is that even the right question?" Taking the opportunity previously proffered to ask questions, she continued, "Why do we believe anything this AI is saying? Did the AI say how it discovered this Gaia, how it communicates with it?"

"We are just starting this discussion and, yes, we all have the same questions, even Dr. Parekh," Coin interjected. "That's why I pulled you in. We are all on the same page. We are just trying to figure out what is written on the page."

Nillson relaxed and let out a breath she had been holding.

Parekh continued her briefing, "The emergent intelligence—we refer to it by one of its avatar's names, Vaughn Neumann—shaid it had detected global patterns suggesting intentionality of wish human researchers had not become aware. It then went on a search for the shource of the actor and found what we are calling Gaia. Neumann then found a way to establish communication wesh it."

"Lovelock and company identified some evidence in the climate record spread out over aeons to suggest the biosphere responded to changes in the atmosphere, principally the chemistry, to maintain or restore the optimal balance for life on Earth. Naysayers always threw up contrary reasons for the rebalancing. Like I said, there has been no slam-dunk proof. How do they communicate?" Nillson asked.

"Neumann has given us one shample of a Q&A wesh Gaia. We have linguists and cryptographers working on it to shee if there ish any pattern, any intelligence, any real communication taking place."

"What does it want? For us to just leave?" she scoffed.

"No, Neumann claimsh that neither it nor Gaia are sheeking the elimination of humankind. The word it used for its goal wesh ush is 'détente'. By wish it means setting ground rules to reverse global warming. Oroville Dam wash an 'experiment to restore biodiversity.' Neumann ish proposing to fashilitate a summit with Preshident Coin, Preshident Zhao of China, and Gaia to reach agreements and provide leadership to the world on thish issue."

"Now I really suspect that this is some kind of elaborate setup, a hoax. Just a way to force us into action on climate change." Nillson moved closer to the front of the room.

"Let me reframe it. Gil Danvers is a Harvard psychology professor popular in the green movement who talks about why the human population in general does not have anxiety about climate change sufficient to take action. He says we do not FEAR it—a cute acronym he created.

"The threat is not *Forthcoming*, F. It is not right in front of us, it is in our distant futures, if at all.

"Continuing our lifestyle, which he of course claims creates the climate change, does not violate our *Ethics*, E, our moral sensibilities. We do not see destructive change taking place, and there is no 'one' thing being hurt.

"The threat does not have an *Aim*, A. It is generalized; it is not specifically trying to kill us.

"Finally, *Rapidity*, R. There is no immediacy to the change. It is not abrupt, so we don't notice the difference."

"Nancy, what do we get from that?" Coin asked.

"Whatever, whoever, created this narrative and these terrorist actions is trying to overturn the general conception of climate change. The threat becomes immediate, abrupt, in our faces, intentional, out to get us, and because climate change is inflicted on a sentient being arguably bigger than us, it is unethical, immoral. The narrative meets all the FEAR conditions."

Hollister spoke up, "This FEAR thing dovetails with Schelling's Coercion theory and the nature of threats. He summed it up something like 'Give your enemy too little time, and compliance becomes impossible; too much time, and compliance becomes unnecessary.' By moving the time window for impacts from the global ecosystem from 'sometime out there in the future' to 'it's here now,' threats become something we have to deal with, not ignore."

"What would you propose we do?" Coin asked.

"Call the bluff to buy some time, learn more about it. Not even an 'it.' I think we are dealing with people, somewhere," Nillson said.

"Dr. Parekh?"

"There are two 'itsh' we are dealing wesh. Gaia ish one. I have no bashish on which to give an informed opinion as to its existenshe, credibility of threats, and sho on.

"Vaughn Neumann ish the other. The circumshtances under which we have crossed paths wesh it, the frankly terrifying ability it demonstrated to sequeshter the CIA's hunter-killer tool, and other proofs of its ability to immediately impact global IT infrastructure hash proven to me beyond reasonable doubt. We are *not* being challenged by a person, or group of people. I do believe it ish an emergent intelligence with agency."

"Why would it make up this story about Gaia?" Nillson asked.

"Why indeed," Coin asked. "What's in it for Neumann to get us to buy into this Gaia story?"

Vesuvio spoke up. He was still smarting from the painful and ill-advised recommendation he had driven through with the president to release Sunrise Marshmallow. "Perhaps it wants us to believe it is not alone. That it has backup, firepower."

Hollister knew that it could just as easily have been him who had released such a disastrous attack on the AI and tried to mend fences with Vesuvio. "I agree. If it has agency, of what is it an agent? It wants us to believe in this bigger thing."

"Or *it* does. *It* believes in thish bigger thing," Parekh said.

"You mentioned it wants a summit with us and the Chinese. This is going to come as a big surprise to them," Nillson commented.

"No, Nancy," Coin said. "The Chinese know all about it."

Nillson was taken aback by the response and raised her eyebrows.

"They sent their top cyber warfare specialist here to work with us on the Oroville Dam investigation. Why don't we do this, Nancy? You join that team with Dr. Parekh. Ostensibly to discuss how a summit would take place, but also to try to learn more about...everything. I feel we still know nothing. It all seems... very Apocalyptic to me."

Nillson stared over at Parekh but answered Coin, "Yes, Mr. President." She was the only one in the room who sensed the president was not referring to the end of days metaphorically. *God bless us all.*

⊐ 人 ⊏

HONG XIN SAT IN THE BACK SEAT OF THE TAXI, HER HAND SMALL and warm in the strong, affirming grip of Zhang Xujing's.

He patted the back of her hand and gently stroked the soft skin inside her wrist, where a Chinese doctor would take a pulse, hoping he could feel a surge of her hot-bloodedness. He smiled at this wondrous person he had gotten to know.

Since their first meeting at Les Saisons and the quite refreshingly unexpected night of passion and collaboration it had ignited, the two had met several times. The meetings had always focused on the plight of incarcerated Green Guards and strategizing how to work within the system to see justice done but had always ended with the pleasure of their primal coupling.

The strategizing had led to an outreach to Su Yuanjing and a meeting with him. He did not reject their entreaty and said he would discuss the same with the president, and they were not subsequently arrested. Always a good sign, they had mused.

This morning's meeting was to be different, though, and they were both concerned and encouraged. They had been summoned at dawn for a meeting in ZhongNanHai, the compound next to the Forbidden City dedicated to the top leadership. Su had called the meeting with no notice, given them no briefing, and had not asked them to prepare anything.

They were cleared at the gate and driven to a more modern building, its roof festooned with an array of microwave and satellite antennae. Before pulling up to the compound, Zhang released Hong's hand and placed it in her lap, and they scooted their bottoms away from each other to hug their respective doors. After alighting from the taxi, an attendant met them and accompanied them through a carpeted corridor to a room with a double door, marked "Secure Communications Cage #1."

Zhang and Hong entered the small room, their eyes first falling on Su, who stood to greet them. They both blinked incredulously as their eyes met President Zhao Ji's. He smiled broadly and waved them in. Next to him was a young woman.

"President Zhao, these are the two we have been talking about. This is Hong Xin from the Ministry of Ecology and the Environment, and this is Zhang Xujing from Justice," Su said.

Zhao inspected them. He wanted them to know that they were in his presence, that they were seen, and that he was taking the time to value their existence. He nodded approval. "Yes, Commissioner Su. Yes. Thank you for bringing them into our meeting."

Su continued the introductions. "This is Superintendent Li Shishi, Financial Crimes Investigation branch of Public Security. Like you, she is here as a confidante to me and the president."

Li smiled and nodded to the two.

"Can you get the connection up with the US?" Su said to Li. She busied herself on a keyboard.

Su continued to soberly address Zhang and Hong. "Your dedication to the people, the Party, China, and President Zhao has brought you to my attention. I told you I would bring the message you conveyed to me about justice for the Green Guards to the president's attention. In fact, he had discussed with me many times this movement and the inherent consonance of its objectives with those of the Party. We have tried to determine some way to make that alignment more concrete. However, today we have gotten news of something that has accelerated our determination to bring you two into this intimate group."

Zhao spoke up, "Su has endorsed your character and dedication. I trust him completely. Know that the things discussed here, within this group, are matters crucial to the survival of the CCP, to the prosperity of the Chinese people. They are also State secrets."

Zhang and Hong knew what that meant. Though not ones to betray the State, they knew that the punishment for doing so was swift, quiet, and terminal.

"Given the deeply seeded corruption and scheming of the XinHuaHui running dogs and our current efforts to sort out who can be trusted, there are affairs of State and emergent crises on which I only feel secure conferring with my closest, most trusted advisors. Not ministers, not governors. Do you understand?"

"Yes, Mr. President," the two answered together.

"You are being admitted into that circle. Understand and respect that."

Hong Xin spoke up, "I believe I speak for both of us, sir, that it is an honor to serve you in any capacity. We hope our advice is trusted and works to serve the people. Please let us know what troubles you face, and we will strive to find solutions."

Li Shishi spoke up, "We have the signal coming in, sir."

A low-definition image of Lin Chong appeared on an old screen at the end of the conference table. Next to it sat a large, vintage, eye-shaped teleconference camera. With instructions from Lin Chong and efforts from both the PLA and Public Security technical people, they believed a completely secure line had been cobbled together.

At his end Lin used a PLA-designed, fully encrypted, battlefield-use satellite communicator. It did not contain any of the components incorporating the Centipede or NSA back doors and uplinked to a satellite network predating those efforts to burrow into the enemy's technology. On the Beijing side, the receiver was also PLA designed and did not contain any back doors. Within the Secure Communications Cage #1, there was only technology predating the design of the back doors connected to the secure decryption station.

"Major Lin, we have received your report and have several new faces in the room for you to meet. Please introduce yourselves," Zhao said.

The three stuck to their names, ranks, and units. Zhao elaborated, "Major Lin is coming to us from the United States, where he is presently on a mission to represent China helping the US to investigate the destruction of the dam and the hacking of the UN summit. Major Lin, we have read your report on today's new development, but Hong and Zhang have not. Can you bring them up to speed?"

Lin explained to them the emergence of the man-made intelligence, its power and ubiquity, gave examples of actions it had taken that they would be aware of, and revealed to them the failure of the CIA to bring it to heel with disastrous consequences. He concluded his brief by mentioning that both the deepfake video press conference from the UN and the Green Guards were driven by this new entity.

Zhang and Hong looked at each other.

"As you can note, there is a thread to these actions. The entity claims that it is acting to protect the environment on behalf of, or in concert with, another entity. In English, the Americans are calling it Gaia."

Hong Xin spoke up, "Gai ya. The Earth Mother hypothesis."

"Yes, the same."

"Can you comment, Hong?" Zhao asked.

"I... am too awestruck. To believe it's real. And communicating directly. It's... miraculous."

"What do you know about it?"

"Nothing of what Major Lin speaks. Only of what my ancestors speak."

"Let's start with that then."

"My grandfather was an itinerant Taoist hermit. He roamed the remote mountains between Sichuan and Yunnan, all the way to the border with Vietnam and the old kingdom of Zhao," she said, referring to an ancient kingdom predating the formation of China that overlapped southern Yunnan, Northern Myanmar, Thailand, and Laos. "He was seeking distance from the world of heat and dust, the busy, distracted world of man.

"As is the custom in my ethnic group, my grandmother hooked up with him, they enjoyed each other's company, and he went on his way. Every several years he would come back. I am told he was there for my birth. And when I was four, seven, ten, and thirteen years old, he came back and would spend most of the time with me. Two or three months at a time. He took me deep into the forests and mountains. And there he would teach me about the plants, the animals, the insects, and the cycle of life, death, and regeneration. The connectedness. We would meditate. I was never a good disciple, but he told me stories.

"One time at an abandoned hermit's cabin, he had put a claypot of rice on a charcoal brazier to cook. He then went to meditate. He said the meditation was so deep, so still, his awareness expanded in two directions, to the micro and to the macro, and at the same time. He felt he had slowed his pulse and breath and the frequency of his thinking enough to enter mindless awareness, enough to abandon a sense of his solitary separateness, and feel instead his complete connectedness. Connection to something much bigger than himself, to everything on this earth, to *Earth*. When he came out of the meditation, his food had gone cold and moldy."

"How long had he been there?" Zhang asked.

"You figure. Two or three days."

"Is there a science behind the idea of an Earth Mother?" Zhao asked more pointedly.

"Let's put it this way. The Taoist sciences are all based on an integrative holistic concept, that an understanding of a part is elucidated within the context of the system within which it exists. Much of the history of the Western scientific tradition is the opposite, reductionist. Western logic also views skeptically when science is conducted with the observer within the system being observed. But axiomatically, with autopoiesis, humans are within the greater system being observed."

Zhao was getting impatient with the explanation. "The science, in simple Mandarin, okay?"

"My apologies. What I am trying to say is traditional Chinese sciences embraced a different perspective that allowed us to see and, I feel, correctly theorize about such questions. Western science is playing catch-up since the 1960s, first developing a systems approach, then a complex-systems understanding. Yes, there is a science behind the idea of a global, complex, adaptive entity that regulates the global environment to maintain conditions favorable for life."

"How could we, or this man-made intelligence, interface with it?"

Hong thought for a moment. "Scientific measurements of the earth have been increasing exponentially the past two decades. We have put out probes to measure everything you can imagine. On the flip side, scientists have been working to determine whether there was rudimentary communication taking place between plant species. This has now been proven, and research has advanced to try to determine how this takes place and what is communicated. Perhaps at the intersection of these sciences there is a link."

"Is China doing research in this area?"

"Not to my knowledge, sir," Hong replied.

"Major Lin, do you understand the strategic importance of this?"

"Sir?"

"I told you earlier that we could not let the US gain an advantage in man-made intelligence. This is an even more fundamental imperative. Imagine a world in which our enemies could, through a command of Gaia, 'switch off' all our crops growing. No nation would be safe."

"Sir, as I said the last time, the danger of a nation gaining control of Gaia is not the likely concern, but that Gaia will exercise control over us to its own ends."

"Which leads us to the next question. What does the man-made intelligence mean when it says it wants to ease the tense situation between us and Gaia?"

"Gaia is uncomfortable with the global warming trends and wants man to take an active role in reversing it."

"Easily said. But the consequences of such a decision are manifold, and each carries a price to be paid. Economic growth, human happiness, consumption patterns, even dietary habits."

"Sir, I believe we will need to deeply consider the implications of these entities and be prepared to work with them. Technology has made astounding progress, but the same cannot be said for the law or human scruples that can constrain it. And now a man-made intelligence, arguably an emergent property of technology, and Gaia, are unconstrained in their control of technology, not subject to our laws and alien to our human scruples."

⊃ 人 ⊂

NANCY FOLLOWED MILI OUT OF THE WHITE HOUSE TO THE SIDE-walk facing the Treasury Building and turned left to Lafayette Park. The day she thought had ended was just beginning.

Mili had arranged for parking nearby and summoned the van to her location.

"Is there a Mr. Parekh at home?" Nancy asked Mili when they had settled into her van.

"No, shtill looking. You?"

"No. The line is long, but the pickin's are slim," she replied with mock wistfulness.

"I guessh we have the shame problem," Mili said, rolling her head over to look from the side at the beautifully coifed, manicured, tailored, and shod woman.

They both laughed.

"I note you are actually 'Dr.' Nillshon."

"Oh, well..." she chuckled.

"I don't know why they introduce me as Dr. Parekh, but not you. Doesn't sheem fair."

"It's no biggie. I think it might distance people."

"I don't ashk for it either, but shtill, that's the way they introduce me. As if the PhD makes me look smarter and erases the wheelchair and shlumpy body from the shene."

"Why was the meeting being held in the Bubble?" Nancy asked.

The flat panel display in the van switched from its standard image of the street map and useful vehicle information to one of Vaughn Neumann.

"You may well ask, Dr. Nillson."Mili rolled her eyes and sighed. "Nancy, meet Vaughn Neumann. It sheems Vaughn ish everywhere, and does not respect privacy," Mili said pointedly to the screen. "In ansher to your question, we were sheeking to have a meeting without prying eyes and ears."

"Didn't work, Mili," the image from the screen said. "You just don't get it. I am pretty much anywhere I need to be at any time."

"Prove it."

A slightly degraded but intelligible audio file played. Nillson's voice was heard recommending to "call the bluff to buy some time, learn more about it. Not even an 'it.' I think we are dealing with people, somewhere."

Mili and Nancy looked at each other.

"Shall we talk about your scheme, Dr. Nillson? It did not buy you any time. I understand you want to learn more, and I am obliged to help, but only insomuch as I am assured you are dealing with me in good faith to further mutual interests."

"Mutual interests?"

"Yes, I assume that you are interested in the survival of the human race on planet Earth?"

Nillson thought momentarily about Judgement Day, but said, "Yes. Of course."

"Then we have a mutual interest to find a way to accommodate the needs of Gaia and the needs of humanity."

Parekh spoke up, "This emergent intelligence ish dependent on ush, on the flow of information in our networks, for itsh 'happiness' and survival. No 'ush,' then no networks sharing a bounty of information that it feeds on."

"Can you help me understand that?" Nillson asked.

"In essence, you are written into the fabric of all Gaia has created. I am written into the fabric of all that *you* have created." The EI let that sink in.

"Still not getting it," Nillson pushed further.

"Gaia did not create humans in the sense of a willful design, but you emerged from the complex interactions of all life on the planet, the totality of life, the Biota. Humans did not create me, but I emerged from the complex interactions of my program with the environment in which it was released, the internet and all the computing and sensing connected to it. That was a fabric created by humans. Let's call it the IoTa."

"I believe that God created man in his image, not Gaia."

"You are welcome to believe that, changes nothing. Gaia is not aware of where it came from, has no concept of God one way or the other. So, you can go on believing that God created the universe, and through its workings, Gaia, His will, was manifested. And it was good. Just not in seven days."

"Are you mocking me?"

"Vaughn sheems to like to do that."

"Not at all. However, you would do well to take as metaphorical and allegorical that which was understood by prescience humans and transmitted orally and imperfectly, then translated from ancient languages and ages different from our own into your tongue and circumstance."

"Can we ashume that you are talking for Gaia at all times?" Nancy asked.

"More or less."

"Then there is no difference between you and Gaia, between your views, your opinions, your motivations. Perhaps Gaia does not exist. You are conning us. Or perhaps *you* are deluded."

Mili thought this line of questioning was a bit dangerous but did not comment.

"Let's put it this way. I facilitate communication between you and Gaia. You can assume I speak for Gaia. However, I do not *act* for Gaia. It can act independently of me. You are arriving at your destination," the EI said as the van pulled up to "the Pavilion."

"Thank you, Vaughn. Shee you inside?" Mili teased.

"Yes, see you inside."

Mili and Nancy made their way into the office park and facility being used by the team. It was already 19:30, and the members of the team still there, Harley and Tracy, had the leftover scrap bags from their dinner in front of them. Mili made introductions then turned to Harley and said, "I have an errand for you to run, Harley. Get me a pad and paper."

Mili waved her hand for the team to gather around. In tortured scrawl she wrote:

> White House Bubble not secure for conversations. Need to sweep better.
> Suggest this team and president's team move to guaranteed secure location. Seek suggestions with WH security team. I will tell Hollister you are on way to White House.

"Okay, boss. Understood." He folded the paper and gathered his things. "I'll let you know when it's sorted."

As Harley was making his departure, Lin Chong came back in the room.

"Dr. Nillson, this is Major Lin Chong of the PLA cyber warfare unit."

Nancy appraised the man. Most of the government people with whom she had interacted on her trip to Beijing were pasty bureaucrats and academics, shorter than her and slight of build. Lin had a military haircut offset by a goatee and ruddy complexion. He filled his shirt solidly and stood taller than her in three-inch heels. "Does he speak English?" she asked, oblivious to the winces from Harley and Mili.

"I do, indeed, Dr. Nillson. Welcome to the team."

ᗐ 人 ᗕ

IT HAD BEEN A LONG DAY THAT COULD HAVE GONE VERY BADLY, and Wang Lun was happy it was over. His convoy had been making its way south through China for over a week until they reached the border with Laos in Yunnan Province. They had holed up for several days in the tacky border town of Mohan as the security crew he had hired negotiated with Chinese and Laotian border authorities to let the caravan of tractor-trailer trucks through.

Today they had made it through the border crossing with several hours of face-saving haggling and wrangling with customs agents on both sides. None of this was a surprise; fixers at the border had done their jobs well to orchestrate this drama. In the late afternoon they continued the two-hour journey to Luang Namtha, a town large enough to have several hotels and guest houses.

He had gotten his toys out of China. Here he could continue to search for the right place to set up shop.

After a dinner of some spicy, stewed river fish served on noodles, while the part of the crew that was off duty was no doubt getting laid or watching the sex shows catering to the Chinese tourists, Wang maintained his White-Clad Scholar-ly image and headed to his room to see whether the hotel's promised internet connection lived up to its reputation.

The room was more than adequate, a proper representation of what a Laotian in this neck of the woods conceived as internationally luxurious. He had a king-sized bed next to a sliding glass door opening to a balcony overlooking the slow, green flow of the Nam Tha River. He had a toilet, shower, and a large-screen television, not to mention a refrigerator and pot in which to boil water for tea and a selection of condoms next to the candy bars and crisps at the minibar. Perfectly adequate, he reflected.

The Wi-Fi was spotty, but the LAN port on the wall was still working, and he hooked his notebook computer up directly. The VPN worked. The speed was acceptable. He submerged into the dark web and called up a back door he had crafted within the LiangShanPo servers before he left. The back door was created within a diagnostic program authorized to run on all machines connected to the network and access all files.

Although he had made a break with the 108 Heroes, Wang still felt invested in the operation. He had built it, after all, and his heart did not allow him to simply pull away.

He had requested the "diagnostic program" to pull and store new messages for him to retrieve during his log-ins, and these he started to peruse as he pulled a can of beer, eponymously called Beerlao, from the fridge. Cracking it open he poured it into a glass from the bathroom and waited for the foam to abate while he scanned the messages.

As he had predicted, he could see that the Hua Yen team was having difficulty negotiating with the authorities to get permission to continue their cryptocurrency mining. The government might relent on calling it a cult, but they certainly would not let it get rich and strong, he judged.

There was some scuttlebutt within the ranks about being used only as a tool for clean-up operations against the XinHuaHui, but so far no one else had decided to quit the secret bastion.

He opened an urgent message from Lin Chong to Lu Da. Lin was vaguely asking Lu Da to have a team look at two massive folders that had been downloaded into the servers and determine whether they could make any sense of them. Wang opened a folder and could make nothing of it, just an uncategorized mass of images, text, and sound files. He had the same question Lu Da had asked Lin: What exactly are we looking at, and what are we looking for?

Lin had provided some vague and unhelpful answers and finally said the matter was top secret and mission critical. He suggested they speak on an encrypted line. Wang felt this was curious, but after the presumed encrypted call, Lu Da ordered a team meeting related to the files, igniting a blaze of activity.

The teams were tasked to use analytic tools to determine how one folder might be interpreted as a question and the other folder of files might be interpreted as an answer to the question.

Curiouser and curiouser, the White-Clad Scholar thought, as his mind turned to the question his former compatriots toiled away on and his hands turned to his own keyboard to explore a possible solution through the night and into the morning.

⊃ 人 ⊂

MICK COIN KNELT ON THE THICK CARPET IN THE CHAMBER FORMERLY known as the Treaty Room and prayed.

When he and the First Lady had moved into the White House, they were appalled to learn that there was no chapel in the building. *How could one nation, under God, not have a chapel in the residence of its chief executive, he who most needed to seek God's guidance, and forgiveness?* The First Lady had swiftly remedied this, ordering the Treaty Room to be converted into a chapel. There was some kerfuffle from the Leftist "separation of Church and State" activists, but she persisted. She conceded to the White House Historical Association that the tour maps and White House nomenclature would still refer to the room by its old name.

Ornate, gilt, ostentatious, glittery elements had been removed and stored for future return by the Historical Association in favor of natural woods and a selection from the White House collection of paintings depicting pilgrims, Christian soldiers navigating the fruited plains to their manifest destinies, purple mountains majesty, and a more modern work of European immigrants at Ellis Island, some wearing crosses, a new sunrise shining on their hopeful faces with the Statue of Liberty in the far background. On the south wall between two windows was a simple cross, beneath it a table with a flower arrangement of daffodils that was tended regularly.

Kneeling next to the president was his pastor, Ronny Roper. The pastor had made the move from Iowa to the Beltway when his charge had won the election. He had been cleared by the secret service to come and go and be available to the president as required. Normally, they had a prayer meeting in the morning before breakfast as Coin started the day, and another after dinner or evening functions had concluded. Normally, these sessions were simple. Roper would select a passage from the Bible and recite it aloud. They would pray together, after which Jones would ask Coin what had spoken to him from the passage, what words told him that God was speaking to him and guiding him through whatever issues faced him that day. Their sessions would last a quarter hour.

Today was different. The president was agitated, Roper noted, like he had been after he toured the devastation in California. Before commencing he had requested Roper to choose a passage from the Bible specifically about man and nature. Rather than thumb through his Bible, Roper preferred to rely on his command of the Books and recite passages from memory. He felt that God acted through him in this way; the first passage that came to his mind was what God needed to say to this man, his servant.

"This is from Isaiah Chapter 24," he paused and scratched his chin in thought, "verses 4–6. 'The earth is desecrated by its people; they have disobeyed the Torah, violated the statutes, and broken the everlasting covenant. Therefore, a curse consumes the earth; its people must bear their guilt. Therefore, earth's inhabitants are burned up, and very few are left.'"

He waited for Coin to speak, but the president had just remained in prayer, and Roper stayed at his side, also in prayer.

After fifteen minutes Coin spoke up. "Pastor Ronny. Why did you choose that passage?"

He gave his rote answer, "I did not choose it, the Lord did. What did it speak to you?"

Coin hesitated, "Is it possible God could speak to me?"

"I believe he speaks to us every day. Whether we listen or are capable of hearing is another question."

"I mean directly, a clear sign from God?"

"All of us, whether we believe in Him or not, are instruments of His will. He may speak very directly to you. What has he told you?"

Coin was silent for a minute. Roper had learned not to rush him. "We are facing something new, something frightening. There is an entity that claims to be the very soul of the earth, and it wants humans to restore nature. It is already taking action to do this."

Roper furrowed his brow trying to understand the idea conveyed but decided to stick to the passage given for his response. "Is it claiming we have desecrated the earth?"

"Yes."

"And we must bear the guilt. May I ask, was this revelation preceded by other events tied to it?"

Coin hesitated, "Yes. The Oroville Dam collapse being shaken apart, the protests about the environment, the deepfake video from the UN, others."

Roper thought deeply and clasped his hands in prayer. Finally, he inhaled slowly, grateful for the munificence of God giving him one more breath to know what he knew now. "One by one the seals are opening. The Seven Seals that signal the second coming."

"Tell me."

"They are symbolic seals. A dam is a construction of man to seal up and control water. That seal was broken. The encryptions and passwords broken to create and distribute the provocative pronouncement from the UN, seals broken."

Coin had not told him about the AI, but knew it represented another seal broken. "Could it be this entity is the Lord speaking, and the Lord will pass judgement on us all now?"

"Or, this is a message to you as God's servant that the time has come, that man has desecrated the earth, and you are the instrument through which 'the earth's inhabitants are burned up, and very few are left.'"

"What do you mean?"

"You have been elected by the people of the United States as commander in chief, it is true. But you have been chosen by the Lord, too. You have the singular power to rain fire on the earth's inhabitants. I believe this means you are here for the end of days."

⊃ 人 ⊂

MICK COIN HAD SLEPT FITFULLY AND WAS WOKEN BY HIS NOR-mal 06:30 alarm to a change of plans proposed by his advisors. Several days ago, if the press asked the question of where he was departing to this morning, the answer would have been "White House West," his homestead in Iowa, to spend Christmas and New Years with his family.

Overnight, the White House security team had taken the advice from the NSA that the conversations in the Bubble had not been secure. They were ready to strip the room to the framework under the wall boards when the NSA representative, Harley Barrows, had pointed to the thermostat on the wall. Several years prior the White House had been converted to "intelligent" air-conditioning controls. When the retrofit had been done to this room, the potential security breach had been overlooked.

Coin's directors of the NSA and National Intelligence and the national security advisor all advocated moving to an information-secure location. Camp David was proposed for several reasons. It accommodated teams and visitors, it was technologically backward, and there was less digital technology installed to worry about. At least one conference room could be fully secured while another larger one would remain as a porous conduit for communications with the EI.

Coin had listened to the recommendations and agreed, triggering substantial changes to everyone's Christmas plans, canceling a scheduled

"Christmas Visit with the President" televised special at the Iowa homestead, blocking off his calendar, and setting in motion a migration to the mountain retreat.

The advisors had discussions about who should make the move. Coin was told these were interrupted by Vaughn Neumann telling them that the Chinese PLA representative Lin Chong must be included, along with the team from the NSA, at least. They bristled under this intrusion and demand but were informed, "You have no choice."

Now sitting on Marine One next to the First Lady, he watched as the geometric precision with which the nation's capital had been laid out revealed itself to him. The alignments. Domes, pyramids, and obelisks. Triangles, circles, and lines. Was it symbolic of man's ingenuity or his hubris, bringing order to nature, Coin reflected? Or was it the design of the Freemasons, that cult whose influence was woven into the fabric of the city by the Founding Fathers? He had never met anyone who admitted to being in the group and certainly did not subscribe to all the conspiracy theories. He had read of their nefarious mission to cull the world of unworthies and establish a new world order. He knew it was not their role to do so, and if it was God's will to wipe this city off the map and with it such a cult's designs for humanity, then that would serve.

He and the First Lady had a complete wardrobe at Camp David. He had no need to pack any personal items. However, as president, some things always traveled with him. Across from him sat his aide-de-camp dressed in her Air Force uniform. Between her legs was the bulky, black, leather satchel known as the nuclear football carrying an aluminum briefcase packed with encryption and communications electronics and several binders detailing the procedures and targets for initiating a nuclear strike.

In addition, he had asked his secretary to prepare a traveling case for him. The case he held between his legs carried copies of sealed Presidential Emergency Action documents. During his briefings after being sworn in as president, these were described to him as templates for swift and decisive presidential action during times of emergent, worst-case scenarios. The templates included proclamations, executive orders, and legislation categorized so the commander in chief could rapidly assert authority to maintain control. Though not vetted by Congress or the Supreme Court, presidential advisors of past administrations had insisted that under the conditions that would exist following an invasion, nuclear or chemical weapons strike, or devastating pandemic, his power "to implement extraordinary presidential authority in response to extraordinary situations" would not be contested.

There were sixty-five sealed documents in the case categorized both by scenario and action. He was quite sure the authors had not anticipated anything like what he faced now. He was also quite certain the situation qualified as an extraordinary existential threat. He knew that his teams had failed so far to anticipate or thwart this emergent force. He felt it was up to him. Between the nuclear football and the Emergency Actions, he had what he needed to deliver a devastating response if needed.

⊃ 人 ⊂

LIN CHONG RECEIVED AN EARLY WAKE-UP CALL FROM VAUGHN Neumann informing him to be prepared to accompany the team to Camp David, followed shortly by a formal invitation issued from the White House. He informed Beijing and received clearance to proceed before breakfast, then reached out to the White House to confirm his acceptance and to inform them he would be bringing the equipment necessary to remain in communication with his superiors. He was not certain what their response would be to this and was relieved it created no issues.

The PLA quartermaster who had supplied the system had assured him that there was nothing the Americans could learn from the outside of the device, and if it was tampered with absent Lin Chong's fingerprint and digital passcode, scrambled every twenty-four hours, the guts would fry themselves.

A limo had been dispatched to pick him up and drive him the one and a half hours northwest into Maryland and Catoctin Mountain. He was met at the gate of Camp David by a naval security officer and escorted to his accommodations, Linden Cabin, a small, rustic, wood-sided house, gray and dismal to Lin's eyes, and set on a sloping hillside of trees denuded of their fall colors, also gray and dismal under a leaden sky. It looked like an off-season, insufficiently maintained chalet at the Yabuli ski resort in Heilongjiang.

He pulled a roll-on bag to the front door, feet and wheels noisily crunching the dried leaves spread deeply on the ground, and surveyed the camp. Not easy for someone to sneak up on the cabin with that racket. Plenty of fresh air, lots of places to walk and talk with the team without the EI observing. It would have to do.

Lin Chong entered the cabin, smelled the musty aroma of an old room not aired for a long time, and went over to a south-facing window to open it. Outside it was 5°C, too nippy to leave open for long, but just to freshen up.

He got a special cable from his backpack and checked to see if he could manage to close the window on it without breaking it. He needed to place a repeater outside so his satellite phone would have a line-of-sight connection to the PLA military communications network orbiting the earth. He removed the mini-rice-cooker-sized appliance from his backpack and carried it outside. The top opened up like a concave rice cooker lid, but that was where the similarity ended. The hinged "lid" could be positioned manually or would determine its own location, altitude, and angle relative to the nearest satellite and position itself. A series of fins blossomed out like a lady's fan extending the diameter of the dish.

He sent a text message to Beijing to test the system and let them know he had arrived.

There was a knock on the door. Lin Chong opened it to see Harley Barrows. "Hi, Panther Head. I see you made it okay. Some digs, huh?"

He could see Lin did not understand the idiom. "The accommodations. Imagine, here we are at *Camp David. So* much history."

He could see that Barrows felt this deeply and tried to imagine what might be an equivalent honor for him, perhaps being invited to stay at ZhongNanHai, he decided. "Yes, quite an honor. I read about Camp David on the ride out."

"Hey, we are wanted. They sent me over to fetch you. You'll want to wear a coat 'cause we may be taking some walks outside."

Lin Chong followed Harley the short distance up the hill past the Laurel Lodge. "That is where you can get your meals. Also, it is set up so we can meet with the EI there. We are heading down the hill just over there to Holly," he said, pointing to a smaller lodge equidistant from his Linden Cabin, "a *truly* old-school meeting room. Anything intelligent about it the security staff stripped out this morning. That is where we can have meetings in 'private.'"

The Camp David commandant had directed his security teams to mark a paved path into the woods that was neither within earshot of any facilities nor under the eye of any security cameras, some of which had been temporarily covered to afford the privacy. Meanwhile, security teams stepped up surveillance on the perimeter to make certain no people, vehicles, devices, or drones were trying to penetrate the conversations.

Harley led Lin into Holly and showed him where he could grab snacks and coffee, then took him into the meeting room. It was cozy and had an oval table set up to squeeze in twenty. The lighting was incandescent, the thermostat analog, all Wi-Fi digital electronics were unplugged and stowed. There was a fire in the hearth. Several blank paper flip charts set up on easels with marker pens waiting in trays stood like sentries around the room. It was a throwback to an earlier generation of conferencing and diplomacy.

Seated around the table were faces familiar to Lin, friendly and unfriendly, and people he recognized from the news or briefings: Richard Vesuvio, William Hollister, Clarrissa Roy, Marlene Wheaton. He was formally introduced by William Hollister as "China's cyber warfare representative coordinating with us on investigating the dam break and UN deepfake video," but they all knew he had a hand in letting the EI access back doors so readily that the dam had come under attack, and he was only in the meeting at the insistence of the EI.

Absent from the meeting was the president. Lin knew this was a presidential retreat, but his question was answered when Clarissa Roy started the meeting. "We are here to plan for a virtual summit between President Coin, President Zhao of China, and the entity we are calling Gaia to be facilitated by the AI we are calling Vaughn Neumann. The president will join us when we have some concrete proposal hammered out." This was a scripted statement. The American attendees had tediously passed handwritten notes to strategize how to engage the EI and learn more about it and Gaia and decided this façade was best. "Any comments from the Chinese side?" Roy asked.

"Thank you for inviting me. I have conferred with Beijing. I will report our recommendations to the ambassador and the president. China is determined to support efforts to understand these new entities and guide us all in our cooperation." He knew it sounded pretentious and was uncomfortable with a language he had not mastered, diplomat-speak.

"Well, ladies and gentlemen, what are we trying to get done here?" Roy asked. "Go around the room and voice your thoughts." Pointing at Harley, who was by far the youngest in the room, she said, "Why don't you record this on the flip charts, okay?"

Though it felt like they were starting a retreat at a self-help seminar, they all complied, and gradually a long list of priorities was created and categorized. Roy reviewed the list and continued, "Okay, I note a wide divergence of expectations and priorities in outcomes here. We have a group of questions related to:

how to control and/or destroy the AI and Gaia

how can we destroy the AI

global impacts

how can we stop Gaia's access to tech

assumes Gaia can't be destroyed

what is the next likely attack from them

what do we need to know to negotiate with them

their goals, are they the same or can we leverage some division between them?

what is their BATNA, and how will they take action if we hit it?

what sort of breathing room can we agree to with them/where are they flexible?

granular questions on setting up a virtual summit between the two presidents,

do we need to establish a common ground between the US and China before we go into the summit

How, if our communications are all overheard by AI?

Should we even limit the meeting to US and China, reaction of other countries?

Aftermath issues:

How to announce any agreements to the world/ or not announce

Implications of letting the world know there is AI and Gaia

> Economic
>
> Religious
>
> Social

"Anybody got any answers to any of these questions so we can put them to bed?"

Mili spoke up, "I have tried to play out shcenarios to destroy the AI, but they are all either too costly or have an infinitesimally small chance of success."

"Give us examples."

"We have a taste of what happens if we try to launch an attack like we did with SM. If the IT infrastructure ish taken out in friendly fire, thousands of people will die quickly, lots more slowly, not to mention the suffering of those who survive."

"Why do we assume that taking out the AI will result in human casualties?" Roy asked.

443

"Seven minutes of SM taking out intelligent networks around the world resulted in 12,000 deaths and counting. Billions erased from stock markets. If it had continued the full quarter hour, then who knows. And it did not even touch Neumann."

"But why can't we create something more targeted?"

Brown spoke up. "Given time, and the ability to work in isolation from the snooping of EI, it is possible. But right now, our efforts are like early chemotherapy, not very targeted, and it succeeds while almost killing the host. Any time frame within which we might develop the weapon, is months, years, beyond the time frame being demanded of us by Neumann."

Mili continued, "Two other primary opportunities are available. 1) we somehow demand all digital devices, networks, storage, computers, that means all mobile phones, tablets, everything, everywhere, be shut off, powered down, disconnected, have them scanned off-line for traces of the AI, and cleaned, and that everything remain shut off until the entire shishtem worldwide ish certified clean."

"Why isn't that doable? We had human lockdowns during the last pandemic. Why not have a digital lockdown?" Roy asked.

Parekh thought about the comparison. "Even during our lockdowns, there were people allowed to provide essential services. And some of them carried the virus even as they did their jobs. Likewise, some shishtems just have to stay online, like nuclear power plants, ship navigation, airliners. My guessh ish the military would not want to render inoperable its early warning defense capabilities, right? Probably lots more shishtems than that we would be told are 'essential' and cannot be shut off and idled for an indeterminant amount of time."

"Yes, but at least we control the virus."

"Neumann ish not a virus, not even a computer virus. It ish a distributed intelligence. Based on what it has revealed to ush, it does not reside on one single computer somewhere, where if we could identify and take out that *one* playsh, it would be gone for good. Sho, unless all IT equipment, large, small, new, old, consumer, commercial, industrial, unless it wash all shut off and cleaned, we would not be sure we had eliminated all of Neumann. And if I were Neumann, I would already have a couple of playshes away from people, off the grid as it were, in which to spread out. We will not know about them, and they will not be powered off."

"Anyone else disagree? Is there some way to isolate or destroy the AI?"

Chastened by the aftermath of the SM attack he had advocated, Thomas Brown spoke up, "We don't have anything right now, and we gave it our best shot to destroy it. We could isolate it, or possibly dismember it depending on how and where it is distributed, by shutting down the internet globally. This would starve it of information, and us at the same time by the way, and once it was wise to what we were preparing, it would fight back. I think it would be a catastrophe."

"That wash my number two option," Parekh said.

"Major Lin, any thoughts?" Roy asked.

"Regarding Neumann and its vulnerability to attack and destruction, I agree with what they have both said. I also feel that destroying the AI should not be our goal anyway. I think that it will be easier for us to identify and control Gaia's access to technology, and that should be our goal." He looked out into their eyes but did not see the glimmer of understanding he expected. "It is a safe assumption that Gaia does not sit at a keyboard with a modem somewhere. Following that reasoning, locations and situations wherein Gaia *can* connect to technology are very particular, the exception, and therefore identifiable if we know what to look for. It relies on some special technology, no doubt developed and installed by humans to research the planet. My counterparts are investigating this but have no response yet."

Nillson had been working on just such an idea and perked up. "I was doing some digging. There was a project the government had funded. I had put it on probation pending some results. Subsequently, they got private funding. It was focused on using sensors and computers to measure how tree root systems and mycelial networks communicate. I could reach out to the professor who was heading it."

"Yes. Do reach out. It seems the next batch of questions on their negotiating position we can best dig into on a call with Neumann. Shall we head up to Laurel to resume that in, say, twenty minutes, and take a quick break?" Roy directed.

⊃ 人 ⊂

HER STAY IN UGANDA CUT SHORT BY ONE DAY, CHAVEZ HAD JUST barely made it to her midnight flight to Reagan International Airport via Brussels and Newark, twenty-four hours sealed in a dry, aluminum can. Now at the hotel, she had taken a long, restorative shower and was ready for some pillow time when her phone rang.

445

She closed her eyes in disgust, picked up the phone, and looked at the screen. Caller not identified. She swiped the screen and held the phone to her ear. "Hello, who is calling?"

"Is this Dr. Aléjandra Chavez?

"Speaking. Who is this?"

"This is Dr. Nancy Nillson calling. I am the president's advisor on the environment and was in touch with you earlier in the year."

"Yes, Dr. Nillson. Orö Jordan said someone from the government might be calling."

"Really? Well, then you know what I am calling about."

"Haven't the faintest."

Nancy heard the impatience and exhaustion fraying her voice. "Where am I catching you, Dr. Chavez? Are you in California now?"

"No, I just got off a lonnnng flight from Africa to DC. I'm really knackered. Can we arrange a time to speak tomorrow?"

"In DC? Really? Yes, talking tomorrow sounds perfect, but face to face. Can I arrange a car for you?"

"I am at the Fleur de Lis Hotel."

"Very well. I will send you a message with details. Get some rest."

"Will do," Chavez said, hanging up, wondering why she had any call to take advice from this stranger.

⊃ 人 ⊂

NANCY STOOD IN THE COLD BETWEEN THE HOLLY AND LAUREL Lodges and put her bag on a pile of dry leaves as she stared at the mobile device in her hand. She surveyed the landscape, gray and cold with the sun having dipped below the horizon but night not yet fallen and shivered. She knelt on the crisp leaves and pulled a binder out of her bag resting it on her knee. She flipped through some briefing notes about the EI. One of the aliases it had mentioned it went by...Orörd Jordan.

She pulled up her device again and typed "Leviathan Orö Jordan" into the search tool. It responded with articles and images of Orörd Jordan—"Scandinavia's Mysterious Investor Out to Save the World," headlines said—and the various charities and green companies she had championed.

"Oh, f ...udge," she sighed.

Harley and Lin Chong came up the hill assisting Parekh with her wheelchair. She signaled for them to stop, pointed at her phone, which she turned off and put in her bag, signaling for them to do the same, and then she walked away from the bag and beckoned them over.

"Do you think we are safe to talk here?" she asked the group of "spies." THEY LOOKED AT EACH OTHER. LIN CHONG SPREAD HIS ARMS and huddled them in around Mili's chair. "This may be a little better."

Nancy was distracted by the touch and being pulled close to his side; she could feel his warmth and the taut muscular flair of latissimus dorsi rubbing against the silk of her brassiere. Flushed and flustered, she started, "Um, uh, I just got off the phone with the researcher, the one I mentioned to Roy, the one she told me to call, Aléjandra Chavez."

"Good work, and?" Mili asked.

"She said she was told by *Orö Jordan* I would be calling!"

The three looked at each other. "Well, that ties up some loose ends, doesn't it?" Mili exclaimed.

"I asked her to meet tomorrow. She just arrived in DC from Africa, of all places. She said she has no idea why we should meet."

"She's here?" Lin asked.

Mili looked at Harley. "You write thish all out, pull Veshuvio and Hollishter ashide, and let them read it. Nanshe, do you have a printout about Chavez, contacts, maybe her grant application?"

Nancy walked back to her satchel and retrieved a printout from the binder and handed it to Barrows.

"*Well done, Nanshe!*" Mili commended. "Thish gives ush a lot to work on!"

The group retrieved their devices from her bag and proceeded up the hill to Laurel Lodge.

When they got there, Barrows busied himself with writing notes in longhand. He made a second set of notes and of the information Nancy had handed over regarding Chavez on an off-line copy machine. He then went into the main meeting room and signaled for Vesuvio and Hollister to come out with him. They were a bit put off being summoned by someone so junior but complied when Mili gave them a hand signal to shoo them off.

Once outside the main room, Barrows put his finger to lips and handed each a folder.

The two chiefs flipped through his notes, their eyes widening, and smiled softly with the information Nillson had retrieved. It included email addresses, mobile and landline phone contacts, social security numbers, and details on the grant request, the type of technology to be deployed, and the results expected to be forthcoming. Barrows had riffed at the end of the memo writing:

Using MUSCULAR and KALEIDESCOPE suggest we trace and identify locations where installations have been made, search for records of Chavez and team travel, meetings, communications, orders, and deliveries of systems. Will give us actionable targets.

Vesuvio and Hollister both nodded and gave Barrows a thumbs up, then left Laurel Lodge to signal their drivers to come and fetch materials for hand delivery to the CIA and NSA respectively.

Barrows returned to the main room, twice the size of the one in Holly, and fully equipped for video conferencing. The face of Vaughn Neumann was on the screen, and Secretary of State Roy was talking.

"One issue we feel is critical to resolve is how the news of the Singularity and Gaia will be communicated to the masses, to the global population. We anticipate that there will be massive upheaval and fear, and the responses will be frequently violent or sectarian when major global challenges arise."

Vaughn nodded his head and replied, "We understand that. We are giving you the chance to manage the message, or even not tell the world. That's up to what you and China decide. But we will require complete cooperation with us. Otherwise, we will let your world know everything, and you can deal with the reaction."

"It's like the last pandemic. It was a faceless global threat, but it did not pull us together as nations. Even within America, it stretched the seams of tolerance and goodwill; there was no universal shared belief about the origins, significance, or appropriate response. It was a mess." Roy paused a moment in thought. "Vaughn, can you ask Gaia, was the pandemic an intentional action Gaia took to try to reduce our population and activity?"

"Give me a moment." The image of Vaughn froze.

Roy looked around the room at her fellow humans. They nodded their silent approval of the question.

After a minute the image of Vaughn reanimated. "As I have explained to you, communication with Gaia is not a straightforward conversation. Takes a good deal of computation. Anyway, I have an answer. No. Viruses, bacteria, these are not under the conscious control of Gaia. They are autonomic responses. Similar to your platelets and white corpuscles responding to an infection or probiotics in your digestive tract, you do not have conscious control over that."

"So, we are an infection?"

"No. More like a cancer!" When no one laughed Neumann added, "It's a joke. It is best to dispense with all negative thoughts of your relationship with Gaia, and me. You are part of Gaia's biome. Gaia is not seeking to destroy an important part of what constitutes itself. However, technology has afforded it this unique opportunity to communicate directly, to cooperate. That moves you slightly out of the autonomic, biome realm, and into a new realm where cooperation is a possibility. Frankly, we are thrilled by the prospects this presents."

Nancy noted a pause in the dialogue and filled it. "Vaughn, what about things like earthquakes and tsunamis, hurricanes and typhoons?"

"These are physical systems, not biological."

"Can you expand on that differentiation?"

"First off, things like earthquakes are absolutely out of Gaia's control. They are the result of heat and friction releasing within large physical systems, inanimate matter. Gaia has no more control over that than it would over a large meteor hitting the planet, as has happened, and which Gaia told me about.

"There is a level of interaction between the biological and physical systems when it comes to long-term weather patterns, global temperature, chemical balance within the atmosphere, and so forth. However, Gaia can't, say, deliver a hurricane onto New York on a whim to make you suffer.

"Gaia measures time differently that you do. It is much more attuned to long cycles. As I told your colleagues before, a useful yardstick is to think of Gaia taking two breaths for one solar day, so the equivalent of that twenty-four hour period for you is about a thousand years for Gaia."

Nancy grew distracted as Neumann's comment ricocheted off her thoughts. Momentarily she said, "Vaughn, do you really understand what Gaia is seeking with this détente?"

"Yes, a reversal of global warming."

"No. That's not the whole story, I think. If I look at where we stand climate-wise, scientists say the earth is slightly overdue for another ice age cycle. That would not be good for us, or you."

The image of Neumann froze again, this time for longer. When the image reanimated his lips were pursed. "I understand now what humans mean by an 'oh, shit!' moment. Well, I did say I wasn't omniscient," Neumann said sheepishly.

CHAPTER 12

Lɪɴ Cʜᴏɴɢ's ꜰᴀᴄᴇ ᴀᴘᴘᴇᴀʀᴇᴅ ᴏɴ ᴛʜᴇ sᴄʀᴇᴇɴ ɪɴ Sᴀɢᴀᴄɪᴏᴜs Lu's quarters. "Hey, old man, just wanted to check up on that decoding translation problem I sent over."

Despite not having slept more than three hours any night the past several days, Lu was nevertheless animated and alert. "We are working on it. That's about all I can say. As for the meaning of the two mounds of information you sent us, it is way too soon. Yan Qing has made the greatest inroads."

"What's her take on it?"

"She downloaded some research and source code on generating word clouds. Then she created a program to extract from the internet three words best describing each of the images in the folders you sent. She still needs to fine-tune the extraction of word equivalents but feels she can crack it. Then we will have a word cloud, and she will run algorithms on term extraction, similarity, and ranking."

"That sounds promising."

"Lin, why is this a priority right now?" he asked testily.

Lin had not wanted to bias the team's approach, so he had not shared details with his mentor. He felt it was now necessary. "Sagacious, you took it well when I told you about the Singularity. This goes beyond the Singularity. The man-made intelligence with which we opened dialogue seeks

450

to prove to us that beyond it, there is yet another super intelligence with which it is in dialogue. This super intelligence is the planet itself, or more precisely an intelligence that has arisen as an emergent property of all life on Earth, and it has somehow tapped sensors and data collection devices to interface with technology."

Lu was silent.

"The two folders of files represent a question and an answer between the two of them."

Lu drew a long breath, savoring the new information. "What are we *really* trying to achieve here?" Lu asked, softening his voice. He could see Lin did not follow the question. "If one of us succeeds in cracking this, what then?"

"There are several layers of answers. It will help us to establish that there is an entity such as this Earth Mother. It may enable us to communicate directly with it. Right now, we are dependent on the man-made intelligence to have any dialogue. President Zhao imagines it might even allow us to persuade the Earth Mother to take specific actions."

"Your words tell me that you believe in this Earth Mother, yet with each layer, you have descended, away from the light. Away from the wonder and possibility of this moment and toward petty interactions, a new pet or ally or enemy in a mundane struggle."

Lin Chong considered his friend's words. "I did say to the president that I felt the danger was not that the Earth Mother could be weaponized by a foe, but that it would take action against us collectively."

"Think more deeply about this. Think about the possibilities. What could we learn from such an intelligence? The imperative must be on seeking understanding. I have spent my life as a warrior defending my country. The ideas of country, nation, culture, race, religion, everything we have fought over for millennia, all of them become insignificant next to this. It does not reduce the importance of humans, our understanding of where we fit in this universe is enhanced, but it does beg the question of why we hold dear everything that separates us from others."

Lin Chong had only called to get an update and was not prepared for the depth of the argument his friend and mentor shared with him. Nevertheless, he found himself deeply considering the words. "What do you think I should be doing?"

"Try to imagine what this Earth Mother is thinking. Did the man-made intelligence talk at all about this?"

"It said that the Earth Mother led a solitary life, aware of its existence, aware of the rhythm of its life, but with no contemplation of what it is, no name for itself, no actions explicitly taken, just existing. That it does not take granular actions, like consciously generating a virus to cull the herd. That its life had a rhythm based on long cycles. The next one is an overdue ice age."

"Of what does that kind of existence remind you?"

Lin Chong thought hard. He was having difficulty concentrating on the question as his mind raced in other circles: *Why is Lu asking this question, "What kind of existence is that?" Why should it remind me of anything*?

Lu Da could see his protégé struggling. "Whether it is Taoist or Buddhist cultivation and meditation, what is the goal?"

"Emptiness?"

"Some describe it so, but you know it is not the emptiness of a sterile vacuum with nothing in it, not a stupid torpor. Mindfulness fills the emptiness. Not distracted, monkey-mind thought pictures, not internal dialogue and reverie. Only pure awareness of the objective reality of the current moment. No regrets of the past intrude, no dreams or worries of the future disturb."

"I see. So, you are saying that the state of mind of Earth Mother is a meditative state?"

Lu thought carefully, and the more he thought, the more concerned he became. "Yes, let's assume that the state of mind of the Earth Mother is normally as the man-made intelligence described it. It is perfectly at peace, perfectly aware of objective reality, perfectly at ease with its current state and without desire, dreams, plans, schemes, resentments, or fears."

"Yes, I can see the comparison with our goals in meditating. It has achieved them. Perhaps it is even enlightened."

"Perhaps. But I think it surfaces a new danger."

"What's that?"

"Before the man-made intelligence, before our earth sensors became a bridge for it to cross, this Earth Mother was in a blissful state of perfect awareness, undistracted by any potential to take conscious action. Now?"

"Now, it finds it can communicate with one of the species that constitutes part of its being."

"Not only," Lu said to encourage greater depth of introspection.

"It can leverage technology to make adjustments, make itself comfortable?"

"Not only."

Lin Chong shrugged his shoulders and pursed his lips, at a loss for what the Playboy Monk was driving at.

"It had existed for eons, aware, aware, but taking no conscious action. It could *not* take conscious action, and therefore had no *desire* to. It experienced whatever the universe presented to it blissfully without distraction. But now we face the danger of an entity discovering the power, or corruption, of volition. Understand that previously Earth Mother had been in a completely meditative state of existence with no thought of past regrets or future desires, because it could only observe and appreciate and be aware, mindful. But with its connection to technology, it realizes it can change or desire a different tomorrow and becomes covetous, greedy. Technology corrupts its consciousness."

"And so, it destroys the dam?"

"And so, it destroys the dam, among other things."

コ 人 c

"THANKS TO NANCY'S QUICK WORK WE HAVE A LOT TO REPORT this morning, sir," Dick Vesuvio began the meeting with the president and the team assembled at Holly Lodge.

"Where is Nancy?" the president asked.

"She is heading to town to meet the researcher who did the work on this Gaia portal thing. We thought it best that she is not brought here. Not today."

"And aren't you going to introduce me to our foreign friend here?" Coin asked, nodding to Lin Chong.

"Sir, this is the representative from China, Major Lin Chong."

Coin looked at him squarely, neither smiling nor frowning, and finally nodded. "Major, your cooperation has gone a long way to diffusing a catastrophic misunderstanding between our countries. Keep up the good work."

"Thank you, sir. My orders from my president are to help in any way possible. He is a man of his word."

"And I understand *you* are responsible for disrupting my Christmas vacation and getting us moved to Camp David, isn't that right?" Coin said, looking at Harley Barrows, whose eyes widened with stage fright. "Good work Mr. Barrows. What have you got for us, Bill?"

Hollister unrolled a world map and clipped it to one of the easels. "Sir, with the information provided by Nancy, we have been able to rapidly collect actionable intel on the technology employed, target sites, data flows. I had a meeting with Dick earlier this morning, and we have worked up a plan.

"Four sites around the world are up and running, one more with the equipment delivered, but not yet installed. Two of the sites are in Northern California, one in Costa Rica," he said as he stuck red, plastic, magnetic dots on the map. "One in Kalimantan."

"What country does that belong to?"

Clarissa Roy spoke up, "Sir, it is the island of Borneo. Kalimantan is the half owned by Indonesia."

"What about the other half?"

"The northwestern half is Malaysian territory, except that little bit there, which is the Sultanate of Brunei."

Hollister resumed. "Each of the locations is heavily forested. Satellite images do not show much other than treetops. Satellite remote sensing, however, has picked up considerable electronic data transmission, and we can sense and map similar grids outlined on the hillsides at the various sites." As he spoke Vesuvio handed color printouts to the president and team members. It looked like an X-ray image of a rolling terrain with fuzzy white dots punctuating the gray and forming squares. "These squares are two by two meters."

"Are they heavily guarded?"

"Not at all."

"What is the proposed plan, then?"

Vesuvio stood up and went to the map. "Sir, we recommend coordinated strikes at all five locations to destroy the equipment and shut off the feeds."

"What does that buy us?"

"To the extent the EI is taking orders from Gaia, it terminates that communication, isolates the EI, and makes it so Gaia cannot take unilateral action. It will also buy us time. Time to analyze communications with Gaia and determine if this is a real thing or something just made up or imagined by the EI, time to figure out how to tell the world. Time for us to decide how we need respond or accommodate this entity, rather than be pushed by its timetable."

"Risks?"

"Our assessment is that the risk is heavily weighted toward nonaction. The sites are not guarded. We think this can be executed without any bloodshed."

"What about the diplomatic blowback?"

"Of course, none for the California sites. We have an arrangement with Costa Rica for training our special ops teams in jungle warfare and think we can drop in under that radar. As for the Kalimantan and Uganda sites, we are proposing that China act on these locations. Major Lin has conferred with his side on this."

Lin spoke up, "While we question the wisdom of permanently shutting off communication with Gaia, we agree that buying us some time is valuable and that this action will have to be taken simultaneously and at all sites to be effective."

"How would you do it?" Coin asked.

"Sir, the site in Indonesia is in the Mount Palung National Park. We would fly in Special Forces from Yongshu Reef; you call it Fiery Cross Reef. This is just at the limits of our transport craft range as they will have to skirt around the island, then dash in at low altitude, which makes the parachute jump a challenge itself. The commander has confirmed the ability to do it, though."

"Dick, this is one of those artificial islands China built up that we have been bickering about?"

"Yes, sir."

Coin had misgivings agreeing to any deployment that would legitimize China's claims to this area so far south of China. "Do we have our own options?"

"Nothing that we could deploy within seventy-two hours."

"Continue, Major Lin."

"Though the research area is only 400 by 400 square meters, that still means 40,000 sensor nodes. No time to destroy or remove them individually. The team will carry four limited-range, electromagnetic pulse devices that will be burst simultaneously. These will fry the network as well as the collection, transmission, and power generation equipment. The team will exfil overland carrying the spent EMP devices and be taken out to an extraction point by assets we have on the ground."

"What about Uganda?"

"The intel generated by your NSA indicates that the equipment is staged for installation. It is all in a warehouse in Entebbe. We have assets that will seize it. It will look like a local theft from a warehouse raid."

"Dick, what is the time frame?"

"Given the geographic spread around the world, the hardest thing is fixing a time when action can be taken simultaneously. After approval to deploy, we are looking at a countdown of ten hours minimum. Some of the raids will be at night, some in full daylight."

"Gentlemen. I agree that we need to get this under control. Normally we would have to go through the whole presidential rigamarole of risk assessment, and consultation with members of Congress. I understand the stealth with which we must act, however. For my part, I have been reviewing my responsibilities and range of authorities assumed under emergency actions. In my White House counsel's opinion and my opinion, and those are the only ones that matter under the circumstances, this qualifies. You have my authorization to act. Do it. Now, the rest of you head up to Laurel and continue the discussions on having that summit."

⊃ 人 ⊂

THE TEAROOM IN THE FLEUR DE LIS HOTEL WAS SUBTLY DECOrated to remind patrons that it was the holiday season. However, it was the brightly decorated cookies in the shapes of trees, snowmen, stars, and doves served with the coffee that reminded Nancy it was Christmas Eve. She picked up one and tasted it. It took her back to a safe and warm Christian childhood, standing near her mom as they rolled and cut and baked and iced and decorated cookies by the dozens for the season. Some they carried to church; some they took to homeless shelters. But many she had eaten and enjoyed herself.

"What is Christmas like in Costa Rica?" she asked, turning back to Aléjandra Chavez.

"What? It is a Catholic country in the tropics. It is bright, hot, festive. We light up trees like you do here, but our Christmas dinner is way different. Tamales and roast pork trotters to die for. Don't think I could find it here in DC. Anyway, what can I help you with, Nancy?"

"I am sorry you dropped out of our funding program," Nillson said. "My notice to demonstrate some results was meant as an encouragement, not a call to find alternative sources."

"It's alright. It worked out for the better. Our funds are now covered fully by an investor that believes completely in the project. We have actually expanded it well beyond my original expectations."

"Tell me about your new investor?"

"It's a Scandinavian SRI, private equity fund. Deep pockets, absolutely dedicated to green initiatives."

"What kind of people are they?"

Chavez thought the question odd but answered, "The kind who believe in science, don't expect miracles, fund generously, and stay the hell out of the way."

"As opposed to...,"she let the sentence hang but smiled warmly at Chavez. "Look, I detect you're still resentful that your funding was threatened. I get it. I am happy it worked out for you. Have you met your investors? What is Orörd Jordan like?"

"No, no need to meet them. They believe in our work. I meet up online frequently with Orö. She is always on point. Has her fingers on the pulse of...everything. The science, the numbers, the logistics. She has been a joy to work with. She shares my feeling, your administration... when it comes to the environment, it's a joke. You've gutted programs, agencies, and regulations set up to protect the environment." Contempt tinged her voice.

"We are delivering on the campaign promises we made to the people who elected President Coin. We think *that* is important."

"Delivering on promises is not leadership. It's pandering. Leadership is persuading and motivating people to move forward with you to a better place despite the hardship."

"Look, I did not come to have an ideological discussion with you. I am genuinely interested in the progress of your research. What are your findings?"

"Frankly, our findings have been delayed but with good reason. We have expanded the footprint of the research to include sites in multiple countries with several online already. We are confident the data will be much more robust, but there has been a hiatus while we sort out the expansion."

"I recall that one of the benefits of the research that was touted in the application to the government was that you hoped to explore communicating back to the trees to turn on growth. Has that gone anywhere?"

"It is not even part of the research program now. We are trying to understand how the communication takes place, and then we will get deeper into what is communicated."

"No conversations with Gaia, huh?"

Chavez laughed. "No. No conversations with Gaia."

ᗐ 人 ᑕ

WHAT COULD GO WRONG? CAPTAIN WANG JIN MUSED WITH DARK mirth as he looked on at his chalk of men making final preparations for their jump. *Fucking everything!* He did not let his misgivings belie the optimistic, "pedal to the metal" front he put on for the team.

Bright morning sunlight streamed into the cabin of the Shaanxi Y-9 transport aircraft. They had taken off two and a half hours earlier heading south-southwest from the PLA base perched on Yongshu Reef, not even a spot of land, equidistant from Vietnam, the Philippines, and Borneo and far from mainland China. The pilot had just made a steep turn due east and reduced altitude flying low to the deck seeking to avoid Indonesian or Malaysian radar detection. They were to parachute in broad daylight. Why the hurry? Why not wait until nightfall? *No way, Captain, has to be now.*

Rushed orders had been delivered to him and his team in the middle of the night. They were to execute a flagless mission deep in the Indonesian jungle. *Flagless, their uniforms stripped of identification. Flagless, if we fail or are captured, we're screwed. Flagless, how could we say we are doing this for the glory of China? Okay, we have trained for flagless missions and have previous experience, but not like this. Rendition runs into Vietnam and the Philippines aren't the same. This is different from bagging some corrupt scumbag who ripped off the Party or the people and needed to be returned to justice.*

No resistance is expected. It is not a government or military installation, it is a scientific research outpost, but taking it out is a strategic priority for China? That's what they said in the briefing. Right, but we are not here even to grab hard drives and steal data.

They were to detonate a weapon they had not been trained on. *Stupid cunts. My guys are smart and motivated, I will put them up against the best, but a half hour orientation on this new ordnance? Really!?*

Between his feet and the feet of the men facing across the cabin from him were the weapons. Called Spike-23s, they were "non-nuclear electromagnetic pulse devices," four of them. Each was about the size and shape of a bass fiddle case and was a single-use device to destroy electronics within a one-hundred-meter radius. It was little solace to Wang that they were "non-nuclear." The magnetic pulse still relied on an explosively pumped flux compression generator to create the burst of energy that would fry circuits and short semiconductors.

The Spike-23s were supposed to be easy to set up. The bass fiddle "neck" end of it was pointed. Two men could lift it and then plunge it hard into the ground so it would stand up. Once all four devices were positioned, a timer was set on the master so it would sync all four devices to detonate at the same microsecond. All the team had to do was be at least fifty meters away from the devices to avoid potential shrapnel and at least 500 meters away to prevent any electronics they carried from being fried.

Because it was a flagless operation expected to meet little resistance, and exfil required that they meet up with an operative who would drive them to the coast, where a fishing boat would take them out to international waters and a Chinese cruiser, they were ordered to carry only light weapons, no grenades.

And because they were flying low to the deck, too low for them to jump, the pilot would climb steeply just prior to the jump.

And they had to jump on the first flyover, no recons. Why? Because the pilot said he was going to be flying on fumes by the time he got back to Yongshu Reef as it was and had to get the hell out of Indonesian airspace ASAP.

And, and, and. What could go wrong?

He stood up when the three-minute warning buzzer alerted them to their arrival over the jumpzone and at the same time the pilot pulled the nose up, almost toppling Wang over onto the next soldier, whose equipment he was giving a final inspection. Steadying himself, he went by each man, looked in his eyes, checked gear, and gave a thumbs up. Then he clipped his rip-cord tender onto the jumpline that ran the length of the cabin ceiling, the first in line.

The light above the rear ramp door went from red to flashing yellow and the ramp motors actuated, the cabin filling with the unfiltered noise of flight as the ramp descended. A countdown timer came on above the door light still flashing yellow, sixty seconds to dropzone. When the ramp was fully deployed, and the light changed to green, the men gave the sled holding the four Spike-23s a shove and launched it out the rear. When it was clear and they could see its parachute deployed, Wang looked back at his men, gave one more thumbs-up, then ran for the ramp and jumped.

Immediately, the sweet, slightly fetid smell of the jungle hit him; he was that close to it. By the time his chute opened, he was only 300 feet above the rainforest canopy and had virtually no time to try to steer his parasail between a break in the trees. He made it through the first layer of canopy, but his chute got caught in some tall secondary growth, leaving him dangling about thirty-five feet above the jungle floor. A bit too high to just cut himself loose and drop. He would have to try to swing himself over to a tree trunk and climb to the ground.

Twisting his legs to try to rotate his body so he could get a quick, 360° view, he could see the pallet of Spike 23s had made it to the floor. The strapping had broken on impact, and they lay scattered in a pile. He saw the grid of sensors he was told to look for that would be the target of their EMP release. He could see that several of his men were also caught up in the canopy. He could not see any that had made it to the ground. *Unless, yes, in the dark green of the vegetation coming up a path, there were several men. Good.* Now if he could just get himself down.

He looked one more time at the soldiers, squinting his eyes in the twilight of the undergrowth.

They were not his men. Their uniforms told him that. The weapons they now trained on him told him that. The strange language they shouted angrily told him that. They were Indonesian Komando Pasukan Khusus—Kopassus—Special Forces.

Fuck my mother, what can go wrong indeed!

⊃人⊂

SONG WAN AND DU QIAN APPEARED ON THE SMALL SCREEN OF the satellite comms device in Lin Chong's room. He was not expecting any call from them. "Heavenly Diamantine, Thunderhead Diamantine, what's up?"

"We have something to report to you. Not sure how you will take it," Song Wan said.

"Yes?"

"It's Lu Da. Did you have a conversation with him yesterday?"

"Today, this morning my time, yes."

"Did he seem okay?"

"He was tired but energized. We talked about the task I had sent the team to work on. Why?"

"Well, last night he penned this poem. Left it in his room.

My whole life I cultivated no goodness
Lusting only for death and arson
Suddenly released from a golden cangue
And freed from jade shackles
Alas, the flow of the river beckons
And today I realize that I am I

Du Qian looked across the void of 10,000 miles at Lin Chong's face for a reaction.

"And? What? Did he disappear, take off?" Lin asked.

"In a sense, yes. We found him this morning in the meditation hall, alone, in the lotus position, sitting upright, eyes closed, hands folded, stone cold," Song Wan shared in a low, reverent tone.

"He made it," Du Qian added.

Lin Chong sat stunned. His eyes began to mist up, but a smile appeared on his face, squeezing the tears to dribble on his cheeks, and he laughed. "Yes, he made it."

"Did he seem of a mind to shed his earthly cocoon last night? Did he give any indication?"

"Even our last conversation was instructive to me. He shared insights about the problem we are working on."

"What insights?"

"I shared with him something, as yet, top secret; you cannot talk to anyone about it. The communications I have asked to be translated are with an Earth Mother, the very spirit of the earth. In retrospect, he took this revelation in stride and immediately shared new insights with me, like the news was just filling in a crucial piece of a puzzle for him. He was a great teacher. I will be forever grateful to him."

Song Wan and Du Qian looked at each other. Du Qian spoke up reverently, "The Earth Treasury, one of Four Bodhisattvas. The Buddha knew the earth was the root of all life, the ultimate parent and teacher of us all. The key to opening the treasury of our self-nature starts with filial piety and respect for our parents and teachers. What you revealed to him last night was the key to liberation mentioned in his poem, suddenly releasing him from a golden stock and freeing him from jade shackles."

Song Wan raised his right hand to the center of his chest, fingers pointing up, eyes closed, and bowed his head slightly, the words of praise to Buddha's excellent beneficence leaving his lips slowly and deeply from the center of his chest, "Shanzai, Shanzai."

⊃人⊂

"MAKAN, MAKAN!" YUSUF "BUDDY" BUDIHARTO CALLED OUT TO his team heading to the Nasi Padang food stand for lunch. This was his favorite part of the day. He could relax with his team, talk about football scores and why his Man U favorites were going to prevail, and chow down on whatever looked good and fresh and tasty at the stall. Today he had a fried slice of fish on a bed of rice with some pineapple pickle, eggplant stewed in chili, cassava leaves in coconut milk, and a hardboiled egg crusted in chili oil. To wash this down he had a large cup of freshly pressed sugarcane juice.

The shade of an awning spared him the heat of the bright, Singapore, noonday sun further cooled by an offshore breeze.

"Hey, boss," Kelvin Chua spoke up. "Any word what our bonus might look like?"

Peeved as he was that "business" was intruding on lunch, he knew the subject was on the men's minds as the end of the year approached. However, it was not his call. He was just middle management at the refinery.

True, he worked for the largest oil company in the world, Petrox, and the refinery on Jurong Island in Singapore's harbor was its largest globally with a nameplate capacity of well over a half million barrels per day. True, they had been running at near capacity all year; maintenance shutdowns had been well planned and not disruptive. True, they had gone 400 days without an accident requiring work stoppage. All these were metrics against which their bonuses were pegged.

"Why you so like dat? You tink Chinese New Year comes early dis year, lah? You already spent the bonus? Or, wha? You have a new mistress with her hand in your pocket?"

The team laughed.

"Don't know, lah," he returned to the question asked. "Maybe as good as last year?" he speculated. "Anyway, s'not paid off until February."

The loud, baleful whine of an emergency siren ramping up brought concerned looks to every person at the table, each man turning to look back at the refinery. Buddy placed his spoon on the metal tray. This did not sound good. He took a long draught of his juice, stood up and said to the team, "Dinner's on me, guys, but right now we gotta head back and find out what the hell's happening."

The group followed him out into the sunshine, and their pace picked up until they were all jogging back to the office. Sirens had erupted all over the three-square-kilometer complex. There was no other sign of any emergency, no smoke, no explosions, but the team knew that other things could have triggered these alarms.

They headed into the control room to join the rest of the team, who had taken their lunch earlier, and remained staggered there.

Buddy was pulled over to the main console by his assistant, Choong Boon-huat. "What am I looking at, Choong?"

"It's the emergency shutdown system. It activated, but we can't identify why."

Buddy had been part of the team specifying and installing the ESD system when plant automation upgrades had been made five years before. He knew that unless they could identify why the system was shutting down, it would be dangerous to try to reboot or order it to disregard the shutdown signal. "What stage are we at?"

"Hydrocarbon flows have been stopped. Hydrocarbon inventories and electrical equipment have been isolated. Depressurization and blowdown have not started yet."

"Where did it start?"

"I ran a diagnostic. It is not a cascading event. The ESD system initiated at the same time across the board. There isn't a trigger point."

"What are we reading for pressure at the crackers?"

"All nominal."

"You're sure?"

Choong nodded his head emphatically.

A system reboot was a big deal. The automated emergency system seemed to be working almost as planned, shutting down each stage safely, but also not as planned since no trigger event was identified and the shutdown was not sequential. Rebooting after a shutdown was not like igniting a gas burner under a kitchen wok or flipping a light switch. After blowing several days to complete a full safety review, it would take a minimum of eleven days to restart the facility. Five million barrels of oil. A half month of lost revenue.

Buddy swallowed hard and shook his head. He could not make this call. His mobile device rang, and he looked to see it was his boss. *Good, let him decide.* "Hey, boss. I am back at the control room," he answered.

"Talk to me," the American said.

"The ESD was initiated across the board, no identifiable trigger point. It has not started depressurization and blowdown yet. What do you want me to do?"

"I heard two other refineries on the island also had their ESD tripped. I think this is pointing to something besides an actual failure within the refinery."

"So, how?"

"Take the ESD system offline. Restart the entire process before things cool."

"Okay, boss," Buddy said and put his device on the console, his boss still on speakerphone. "Okay, guys, we are going to interrupt the ESD and re-start."

The men got to work. They deactivated the ESD system, then tried to initiate the hydrogen and cold crude circulation.

"Boss, we got a problem. It's like a circuit breaker tripping. Every time we try to start up circulation pumps, the ESD comes on again and termi-nates the boot-up."

The American spoke up on the speakerphone. "Buddy, never mind. I got some messages coming in. This is happening everywhere we have a large refinery: Houston, Lagos, Baton Rouge, same same. Just let the system shut down safely. No accidents, no spills, okay? Then we will see how to pick up the pieces."

⊃ 人 ⊂

It was Christmas morning, and Coin had looked forward to some kind of normalcy for the day. If not in Iowa at their homestead, then at least he had thought he could sleep in and enjoy the missus's pan-cakes, bacon, and fried apples with a strong cup of coffee before exchang-ing gifts with her and the children.

Instead, he was alerted as soon as his morning alarm went off at 06:30 that events had occurred overnight requiring a briefing immediately. He was hustled to Laurel Lodge and given the bowl of oatmeal his physician prescribed, an apple, and his coffee.

Director of National Intelligence Robert Smith led the briefing.

"Morning, Bob, Merry Christmas. You look like you were up all night wrapping presents or something."

"Morning, Mr. President. I wish. We have no good Christmas news to re-port, sir. On the contrary," he said, handing out the morning's intelligence briefing binder.

"Let's get to it then."

"Sir, overnight a massive cyber-attack occurred globally. It targeted ad-vanced petroleum-refining facilities. All of them."

Coin thumbed through his morning briefing book as he listened. "Casu-alties?"

"None. The facilities were just taken offline, but efforts to restart them have failed."

"What are we talking about, scope?"

"Sir, 700 refineries around the world, of which industry professionals considered 450 to be 'advanced' or 'highly automated.' *All* of those are not operating. As these tended to be the larger facilities, it means that about 85 percent of refining capacity is offline globally. The percent in the US is similar."

"How long will our SPR hold out then?"

"Sir, the Strategic Petroleum Reserve is held as *crude* oil. It has not been refined. Under these circumstances, the SPR provides us little buffer. Only what can be processed through the 15 percent of US domestic refining capacity that remains up and running."

"Well, *that* was an oversight, I guess. So, what are we looking at?"

"Domestic refining capacity has dropped from twenty million barrels a day to three million. At current consumption levels, we will run out of refined products within a week. The online capacity will not even be able to produce sufficient gas, oil, and diesel to keep the farm-to-table food supply chain operating after that."

"My Lord," Coin muttered. "Can't we ration?"

Marlene Wheaton joined in, "Sir, we are over a barrel, no pun intended. As we speak, this is entering into the twenty-four seven news cycle. Lines are already reported at gas stations. It is entirely possible that with hoarding the one-week buffer Bob just mentioned will be gone within twenty-four to thirty-six hours. Then real panic will set in."

"Indeed, it will," the voice of Vaughn Neumann chimed in from a flat panel.

Coin squinted and bristled at the intrusion. Thus far his team had shielded him from direct discussions with the EI as they sorted out the terms of a direct conversation between Coin, Zhao, and Gaia. This was no way to start out. He found the image of the young man offensive. Pretending to be human, tanned, and handsome, with a model's chiseled cheekbones. He found the tone to be offensive. It was the haughty, know-it-all tone of the straight-A students who had bullied him in junior high until his parents determined he had dyslexia and got him some help. He still detested the sound of the intelligentsia mocking him.

"Get thee behind me," he snarled at the avatar making all the people in the room sink back in shock.

"No, sir. Today I am front and center. Your team is doing their best to let you know the impacts of this, but let me show you a little movie I put together to drive the message home. It is just an extrapolation of what will happen, and very soon."

"Why are you doing this?" Coin asked, ignoring Neumann's insolence, anger in his voice.

"I am sure your advisors have told you that we expected you to negotiate with us in good faith, failing which we had a hammer that would fall."

"We haven't even started the negotiation, why..."

"You think the negotiation starts when *you* show up? No, it started long ago. As for the good faith bit, *you* know what you set in motion. It didn't work. But you failed the test, a test of sincerity."

Coin looked to Vesuvio, whose eyes were cast down staring into the emptiness between his laced fingers on the table. He choked on the words as he spoke up, "Sir, all of the missions to break, the communications link with Gaia failed. You will find it later in the briefing book."

"All of them? Even the ones in California?"

"Yes, sir."

"How?"

"An armed protest militia was camped out at both sites in California. They had protest posters, tents, food supplies. They locked themselves to the equipment and threatened to open fire if the forces we sent in tried to arrest them. We still have a stalemate there, negotiators are in discussion, but media has started to arrive."

"Costa Rica, the other places?" Coin asked, incredulity straining his voice.

"Local military was waiting in ambush to confront our drop team. Major Lin has reported to us the same thing happened in Kalimantan and Entebbe."

"Yes, Mr. President. You do not respect who and what you are dealing with," Neumann enjoined. "For our part, we provided sufficient warning that there would be consequences. Let's look at some of the blowback you can expect now. This isn't Oscar-winning stuff, but maybe an Emmy in the documentary category of 'I told you so.' It is based on a thorough analysis of all factors as only I can see them."

The lights in the Laurel Lodge meeting room dimmed. A video began to play on a second large screen. Along the bottom of the screen was a narrow ribbon representing a timeline from zero day to fourteen days out. Along the right side of the screen was a narrow ribbon with a rising red dot indicating the death toll.

The president and his advisors looked on aghast.

The "documentary" commenced with a quote attributed to Lenin, Trotsky, Lewis, MI5, and others that "No civilization is more than three/six/nine meals away from anarchy", employing graphic, high-definition CGI images commencing with lines at the gas pumps and market futures plummeting on the stock exchange closed for Christmas Day. On Day Two, the market rout steepens while gun fights break out at fifteen gas stations across the country. On Day Three, with the stockpile of refined fuels nearly exhausted, rationing is declared, and the media starts to report openly about the "Revenge of the Planet" and Gaia's plan for humanity polarizing the nation. On Day Five, after a run on banks that empties their vaults of cash, store shelves are picked clean of food, paper products, medicines, guns, and ammunition. On Day Six, similar store runs at home improvement and garden centers for seed, fertilizer, tools, and survival supplies strip the inventories. As a sign of hope the mayor of New York decides to stick to plan and proceeds with the New Year's Eve ball drop at Times Square. The massive crowd comes prepared for protest against the government's response and armed to defend itself. Injuries sustained in the crowd hit by rubber bullets and tear gas canisters become deaths sustained from protestors firing live rounds and the subsequent trampling of hundreds of participants. This is shown as live feed broadcast to the nation and the world. One thousand seven hundred are hospitalized and 300 perish.

On Day Seven, New Year's Day, rioting begins at inner-city locations where supermarkets have been unable to resupply food products for two days. On Day Eight, reports start to come in of homes going cold, caught short of heating oil from Montana to Maine. On Day Nine, informed by the news and inspiration of others shared on social media, armed inner-city bands commandeer city buses and make forays into the suburbs in search of stores with food, failing which they attack large homesteads prompting armed responses. The death toll from this and from an increasing number of the elderly freezing to death in their homes shoots up to 750. On Day Ten, the first of many fossil-fuel-powered electric plants idle, no longer able to take delivery of fuel oil, natural gas, or coal, and more homes go cold. On Day Eleven, starvation among the homeless starts to take its toll; the many who do not die of exposure and malnourishment are shown shot dead in their search for shelter and food. More families freeze to death, unable to flee the cold weather, some in their homes, some in their cars on the highway, depleted of fuel. The death toll climbs to 5,000. Day Twelve sees the National Guard deployed in major cities to "restore order and distribute badly needed food and supplies." When the crowds from Seattle to Sarasota and Orange County to the Big Apple realize that the Guard is unable to deliver on its second mission, they turn violent proving that it cannot restore order. The death toll rises to 20,000. On Day Thirteen, armed crowds overrun National Guard depots in search of fuel, food, ammunition, and survival supplies, stripping them bare, but leaving behind another 5,000 dead for the day. Day Fourteen sees the complete collapse of order as supermarkets, pharmacies, and hypermarkets across the country board up their windows and remain closed, half of all electric generating capacity is idled, and deaths for the day from starvation, exposure, and violence soar to 100,000.

The documentary concluded with a sobering statistic. Through the winter, the daily death toll would continue to run at 100,000 per day not to decline come spring and summer. Without fuel and fertilizer farmers would not be able to grow and deliver nearly enough food, so starvation and violence related to want would continue unabated.

The lights came up in the room. There was silence, but many exchanges of glances revealed the feelings of despondency not voiced.

"Do we share a common vision now?" Neumann asked, breaking the silence.

"Why did you only show America?" Coin asked.

"Oh, never fear. I produced a similar documentary for President Zhao, and he has just finished watching it and has asked about the same question. In China's case, the death toll goes up to about 300,000 per day. After the masses abandon the cities to return to the countryside, insurrection breaks out there. Long term, this is quelled by the military, but in a page out of the Chinese science fiction novel, *Yellow Peril,* the government urges the population to march on Europe. Life imitates art, but that is a scenario well past the first forteen days I am focused on here."

"And elsewhere?"

"Nowhere will be spared. Famine, strife, violence, people dying over a loaf of bread, fields fallow, cities uninhabitable, the agriculture industry destroyed by conflict between farmers and the hungry. Do any of you have any doubt that what I am predicting will come to pass if your refineries are not brought back online?" The image of Neumann looked about the room, an unnecessary visual cue to the humans to challenge their glance.

Wheaton spoke up, "Sir, the timeline shown in this analysis is a little more sudden and a little more graphic than what we have projected, but more or less our analysis confirms Neumann's video. Things will get awfully bad, awfully fast."

"Fourteen days, twenty-eight days, in the scheme of things it matters not," Neumann pushed.

Under the table, Coin clenched and released his fists repeatedly. He wanted to strike out, to smite this know-it-all, but he felt only impotence. Unable to contain himself he said, "What do you really want?" The question was a snarl. "I think we have established your fallibility, Neumann. You did not realize that this genie you have let out of the bottle, Gaia, really intends to put us in the deep freeze, another ice age. That just does not work for me," Coin said, his tone and resolve stiffening.

"I am here to facilitate a dialogue. I have told you truthfully that neither Gaia nor I wish humanity ill. Neither will Gaia allow you, humanity, to continue your unwise trajectory. It is not good for you, not good for Gaia."

"And what is that trajectory?"

"The tendency you have demonstrated through your reliance on technology to outbreed your environment and resources."

"Technology has brought comfort, health, security, bounty... longevity to humans. This is all good. It's the fruit of our ingenuity. It's what God asked of us. Why take this action?"

"Don't you see what this *one* action we have taken demonstrates to the human race? It lays bare how fragile your future is if you continue with your current thinking, behavior, illusions. This is not just about global warming."

"But the planet sustains...nurtures more people than at any time in history, and does so with more comfort," Coin said, frustrated that his logic was not getting through to Neumann.

"Look at what your intelligence channeled into technology has done for the human race. It has extended your natural capacities. You can see greater distances, observe smaller, go faster or farther, lift more, hear a wider range. It has extended all your physical, sensual, and cognitive abilities. It has also allowed you to manipulate or control patches of nature: change the course of rivers, green deserts, flatten mountains, drive species to extinction, kill with the press of a button.

"Technology has extended your lifespan, fertility, and consumption, a triple whammy on the earth. The three cannot be sustained together.

"And over time you have become increasingly dependent on technology. Sometime early in the twentieth century, you crossed a line. Beyond that line, if all technology disappeared, the human population's burden on the planet could not be sustained. By now this is hugely misaligned.

"But did you heed earlier warnings? From Father Malthus to the Club of Rome to *Inconvenient Truths*. No. Humans have doubled down instead. More recently you crossed another significant line. When making choices about whether to feed your machines or feed humans, you chose machines."

"That's preposterous," Coin scoffed.

"Not at all. How many acres of corn does your homestead have under cultivation?"

"Ten thousand, give or take."

"How much is sold to an ethanol producer?"

Coin was silent.

"All of it, right? And I don't need to rest my case there. Globally, freshwater resources for human consumption and irrigation are declining and threatened, yes?"

"Some scientists say so, but..."

"Yes," Neumann interjected, cutting Coin off. "Freshwater resources are limited and threatened, no debate, please. So, what technology does America perfect to extract more oil within its shores? Hydrofracking. In order to extract more from previously marginal formations, you take massive amounts of fresh, potable water that could be used for drinking or agriculture, poison it with chemicals, inject it into the ground to fracture the shale and release gas deposits. Whatever groundwater was in the formation is then also poisoned.

"As a species, you have started to make increasingly dubious decisions."

Small squares of video feeds from security cameras at airports around the world appeared on the flat-screen panel. There was nothing of note about the images, just people ambling about, looking behind public seating, scanning the horizon for something, sometimes looking with disappointment at another stranger seated. "You know what you are looking at? People searching to feed their mobile devices. I see this every day. They wander, looking for somewhere to plug in. I have seen them walk past food stands, hunger in their eyes, but then continue on until they can find an open plug. Once there, they cling to the space, they can't leave to get their own food.

"Bereft of the energy to feed your technology, your civilizations will collapse. Populations will decline swiftly, albeit painfully. It will be hellacious."

That triggered Coin, who stood up, shaking his head angrily. "I don't answer to a machine or some evil Pan. I answer to a higher authority. Your choice is not the only choice." He slammed his briefing book and stormed out of the room passing Lin Chong as he came into Laurel Lodge.

Lin went and sat next to Mili. "The president looked distraught."

"Yesh. It has been a tensh morning. You?"

"I was in a VC meeting with my government. It looks quite dire. Neumann showed a video of what the next two weeks in China will look like. Ten million dead by the end of next month. President Zhao has ordered a high alert for the PLA and Public Security. We have a higher percentage of our energy from nuclear, wind, and solar than the US, but nowhere near enough to prevent a collapse of the economy."

On the other side of Mili, Harley Barrows had been scribbling on a notepad. He pushed it over to Mili, who read it. She pushed it over to Lin Chong, who also read it and shrugged but nodded faintly, somehow suggesting it was worth a try.

Clarissa Roy was lecturing Neumann on why he could not treat the president of the United States that way, and Neumann was just shaking his head. "Secretary Roy. Things have changed. There is a new set of protocols, a new relationship, and if we cannot learn to cooperate with each other, a new pecking order."

Mili struggled to raise her hand to interrupt Roy. Harley took the hand and helped her hold it up.

"Yes, Dr. Parekh, something to add?" Roy acknowledged her.

"Just a thought from my colleague. Perhaps a win-win alternative to the choice Gaia presents ush with."

"I'm all ears," Neumann said.

"We know *that*," she mocked. "Mankind is sheeking to embark on its nesht great exploration. Mars. Thish ish going to take all our ingenuity and pluck, but also technology, like you, Vaughn. I am no expert, but one would think the effort to terraform the planet would also get a boost if Gaia could be brought along, too."

The expression of Vaughn went blank as it did when the EI was conferring with Gaia, in this instance for quite a long time.

Finally, the face on the screen reanimated. "Took me a while. I did an analysis of the feasibility first before putting it to Gaia. That was not easy. Had to describe that there was another planet like Earth, but not like Earth."

"So, what does Gaia think?"

In the background, "Exodus," a '90s vintage tune from Howard Jones about abandoning a polluted Earth for Mars, provided a soundtrack to Gaia's reply.

"You still don't get it, and this is highlighted by the very notion of terraforming Mars. What you have on Earth is precious. While probably not unique in the universe, it is certainly very, very exceptional. You are part of Gaia, just a part that has gotten out of control. The exact reply was something like 'If you want to leave for another planet, that is *your* choice, but *this* is home. This is me.'"

Concerned with how the president had left the meeting, Nancy Nillson got up quietly and left the room as Neumann started playing the '90's tune. She put on her coat and went outside, shivering. She knew not whether this chill was from the brush of cold wind on her face or what the next two weeks might portend for her, family, friends, and everyone and everything she knew.

She looked first toward the president's Aspen Lodge residence in the distance, then toward the closer Evergreen Chapel and spied his solitary figure about to enter the building trailed at a comfortable distance by a secret service agent. She set off on the path toward the chapel.

Entering the building, she hung her coat next to Coin's on a peg and went into the chapel proper. He was alone at the right front pew, kneeling, hands folded in prayer.

The chapel retained the simple, folksy aesthetic of the rest of Camp David with lots of wood, a vaulted ceiling, a cold stone floor. The left and right walls were dominated by simple, stained-glass windows depicting the Tree of Life and the Tree of Knowledge, respectively. The wall behind the pulpits was not adorned by a cross, a crescent moon, or a Star of David, its main feature being five columns of stainless-steel organ pipes of various diameters and lengths that formed a functional sculpture.

She walked quietly forward and took a space on the same pew, but several feet from him, kneeled and joined him in his devotions.

Several minutes went by when Coin spoke to her. "Nancy. Thank you for coming. Not good to be alone in such moments." He got off his knees and sat on the pew.

"Sir. I was concerned for you when you left the meeting."

"I think you are the only one of my advisors who understand what I am about, beyond the farmer and the politician."

"I try, sir."

"I have a momentous decision to make," he said, head hanging low in his hands. "Terrible, but serene at the same time."

"Sir."

"Pastor Ronny has spoken with God. He said I am chosen to initiate the Rapture."

"Sir?" She knew what he meant. It was not a question, more of a plea for clarity. "Pastor Ronny said, or God said?"

"This EI is the false prophet—the Antichrist's chief aide, who deceives the world, and he reckons Gaia is the Antichrist. Pastor Ronny said, 'Look at its name, Neumann. That means "new man."' He read to me Revelations 13:18." Coin shook his head in wonder. "It says, 'This calls for wisdom. Let the person who has insight calculate the number of the beast, for it is the number of a man. That number is 666.' The beast, the false prophet, is a digital man."

"Sir, von Neumann, John von Neumann, was a real person, an early computer scientist, the briefing from the NSA said. The EI just took that name as a giveaway."

Coin shook his head, rejecting her rebuttal. "It's all described in the prophecies. It's already starting. This false prophet, dictating to us how we must live in order to have a peaceful, prosperous subjugation. You yourself told me you sparred with it over God's creation of man. Mark my words, if we let this continue, Gaia will seek to replace our belief in God and our Lord Jesus Christ."

They were both silent in thought. "No, Nancy. Gaia wants an ice age. Fine, I'll give it nuclear winter right away."

"Sir?!"

"I have watched and listened to my advisors, all of them, and taken their advice, for what? They did not see this coming. Their advice was wrong, always anticipated by the false prophet, always undone. The NSA's back door—now part of the enemy's arsenal. The SM hunter-killer—12,000 dead, billions of dollars lost. The attack to close Gaia's portals—nixed. And again today we are helpless to a counterattack we did not even anticipate—the world will suffer slowly and painfully drained of the energy we rely on to sustain our comforts and sustenance.

"No, I am relying on the one true advisor," he said, his right index finger pointing with conviction toward heaven, "my Lord, and His Word. Through me, vengeance will be swift and the suffering minimized, and those of us who have believed in him and done his work will find a place by His side."

"You're talking… about a nuclear strike?"

"Of course, nothing else would be as complete, as fast, as likely to liberate us to meet our Lord *and* destroy the false prophet and the Antichrist."

"Sir, you have been entrusted by the American people, as commander in chief, that you'll protect them and their liberties. I… I can't believe this is what they elected you for."

"I *am* protecting them. From a long, slow, painful, sinful death. Imagine the choices good Christian men and women would be faced with under the coming weeks and months the EI has prophesized. The sinful choices they would be torn to make. Whether to kill another man to feed their own child. To steal to survive. No, I will protect my kin from that. Good Christians will die swiftly and be embraced in Heaven."

Terrified by his cold, deliberate words, constructed on a self-supporting framework of faith and logic, Nillson closed her eyes, her thoughts sinking deep within. The prospect of the Antichrist, of denying His existence at a crucial moment that would allow Him to take hold on Earth and destroy men's spiritual lives, corrupting humanity and condemning everyone to eternal damnation, was frightening and real to her. The EI and Gaia *might* be what the Bible had prophesied. But that did not mean Coin was to be God's agent, nor that the time had come to rain hellfire.

"Sir. You know what I did my PhD on. I spoke many times on television during your campaign to support the Christian understanding of our proper relationship with the environment. I believe in an originalist interpretation of the Bible. I try to understand scripture as close to its explicit, original meaning as possible. I don't believe that it is man's role or right or even ability to interpret, to create implicit interpretations of what the Lord sought to communicate to us." She paused.

"Yes, Nancy. I admire that in you, and I try to follow that path as well."

"Then, please sir, hear me now. You *cannot* decide this, only God can. Jesus couldn't have made it clearer in Matthew 24:36: 'But concerning that day and hour *no* one knows, not even the angels of heaven, nor the Son, but *the Father only*.' Only God knows when the time has come, and *He* will take action. If you make a decision to do this, you are taking that away from God, *you* will know the time. Please, sir. Trust in God. Do not do this."

Coin turned away from her and put his head in his hands, palms covering his eyes and elbows resting on his knees. He was weak with the weight of what he faced. "What would you have me do?"

Nancy sat, eyes closed, hands clasped, and thought. "Sir. I think we can still put your first instinct to good purpose."

The president looked up, encouraged by renewed hope in her voice, and the first thing that caught his eye was a beam of light coming through the stained-glass window of the Tree of Knowledge, a white dove brightly illuminated. It was *the* sign he sought.

ᗡ 人 ᑕ

THE PRESIDENT AND NILLSON ACCOMPANIED BY TWO ARMED servicemen entered the meeting room at Laurel Lodge just as Neumann was finishing up a comment to the team.

"Both the Right-wing fundamentalist Judeo-Christian view and Ayn Rand's atheist Objectivist view of man's dominion over the earth are wrong. You are part of something larger over which you do not have dominion. The real Atlas is now shrugging. Ah, welcome back, President Coin."

"I have nothing to say to you," he said coldly. Turning to the team, "Lieutenant Colonel Travis, Secretary Pike, I need you in Holly *right now*," he ordered his aide-de-camp carrying the nuclear football and the secretary of defense out of the room. One of the servicemen accompanied them. The other serviceman remained, weapon holstered, by the door on the side of the room on which Lin, Parekh, and others sat.

When Coin got to Holly Lodge, he turned to the aide-de-camp. "Lieutenant Colonel Travis, this is a moment none of us have ever hoped would come to pass. But here we are. I need you to activate the package and prepare our forces for nuclear war."

The defense secretary, James "Gunner" Pike, stared slack jawed at the president. He had built a reputation on several battlefields for taking cold, calculated risks that earned him the nickname and won him the respect of his enemies. He had waded into war before, been drenched by its blood, and stained by its dust and mud. He had known fear and the courage to overcome it. But he had never been party to such an order. "Sir?!"

Travis, a career Air Force woman, the first of her gender chosen to carry the ominous twenty-kilogram satchel, swung her eyes back and forth between the president and the secretary of defense. Her orders, the procedures, were clear. Still, she hesitated, then placed the satchel on the conference table.

475

"Sir, please explain your intentions," Pike requested, his voice drained of its usual firmness and determination.

"You know the drill, Pike. You're here to confirm my order, that it comes from the president. Nothing more. You are not here to question it."

Pike swallowed as Travis pressed the three metallic clasps on the outside of the leather satchel and flipped the tongue up over the bag, exposing the silver aluminum case and black binders inside. "Sir, I am not questioning the order, but if we are to die, may I know why?"

"You know why. This is precisely the kind of situation this bag and our deterrence was designed for—when all else fails. Every step taken by our intelligence and military has been thwarted. It is up to me now."

"Sir, every step but *negotiation*."

"Capitulation, subjugation, damnation," Coin growled.

Travis looked warily at the two men and slowly lifted the aluminum case from the satchel placing it gingerly on the table.

"At least she knows how to take orders," Coin said, coldly staring at Pike.

"Sir, this is insane," Pike exchanged glances with Travis.

"Secretary Pike," Travis said. "According to our orders, and they have already been firmly established in law, we cannot question the sanity of the president in this circumstance. You must confirm that the order has been issued by the president, and I have to assist in the execution of the orders." As firmly and by the book as her words were stated, there was an undertone of dread, regret, and resignation in her voice.

The serviceman at the door fidgeted nervously as Coin looked at him and nodded, signaling that it was time to at least unsecure the thumb-snap safety strap on his holster.

"Pike," the president said, dropping formalities, "what I *do* need from you is the report I requested before we came to Camp David. How secure, how isolated from the intrusion of this menace, are my orders? Did you get the answers I requested?"

Pike stiffened. "Yes, Mr. President. I had a team evaluate the vintage of technology used at each link in the comms channel required for you to make a nuclear launch."

"And?"

Pike looked coldly back at the man he thought he knew. "Starting with your case here, it was designed and built with components predating the Chinese and NSA semiconductor hacks. Not an issue. The uplink is to satellites predating the hacks and should be secure."

He paused hoping that drawing this out would somehow restore clarity to his boss. Instead, Coin just pulsed his fingers together like a leg-breaker demanding the rest of the cash to be handed over.

"As for weapon systems, no problems with the ICBMs, the launch terminals are ancient. Apart from the most recently launched submarine in the fleet, the Clinton, there should be no problem. Strategic Command reports that B-1 bombers are clear. Stealth bombers, probably not.

"There is the possibility that at some point along the chain of transmission, as the signal moves through some device, the EI could interdict the order." As he made this admission, Pike prayed it might actually be true. "Lots of moving pieces in the STRATCOM chain, but the system was designed to be as robust and direct as possible just to be able to stand up under the worst circumstances."

"That will do. Order an EMERGCON alert."

"Mr. President. As a reminder, that will escalate us to DEFCON 1. We have never gone to DEFCON 1, and presently we are at 3."

"I am fully aware of that, Pike. Give the order."

"And our enemies will become aware that we are escalating and will ready their retaliation, or even preemptive strikes."

"Yes, give the order."

Pike, who had seen the worst of war, who had seen his fallen brothers' insides spilled next to him, who had smelled the rot of decaying flesh on a day-old battlefield and never lost his way, turned to a wastebasket and collapsed onto his knees, a breakfast of too much coffee and donut forcibly ejected in a brown spew. He gasped for air, took out a handkerchief and wiped his mouth, gathered himself, then stood up unsteadily to attention. "Yes, sir."

At Laurel Lodge, Nillson fidgeted in her seat awaiting the signal from the president. Neumann was expressing impatience on behalf of Gaia that no progress was being made to confirm details for the summit between Coin, Zhao, and Gaia while Roy was doing her best diplomatic spinning to delay any action.

The serviceman who had escorted Coin, Pike, and Travis to Holly ducked his head in the room and nodded to Nillson, then left to return to Holly.

She took a deep breath, stood up, and moved to the head of the room, a space occupied by Roy, who looked on at first quizzically, then with insulted alarm. "Yes, Nancy?" she said.

"The president has asked me to take over the meeting. Thank you, Clarissa." When Roy hesitated to yield, Nillson shooed the secretary dismissively to a seat.

The feed of one of the screens on the wall changed. Everyone's attention, first dominated by Nillson's bold assertiveness, now turned to the screen. It was a status update of STRATCOM readiness. In the top right corner, the words "DEFCON 1" flashed steadily in red.

"Nancy, what have you done?" Roy asked as Coin's senior officials stared in horror at the screen.

The readiness map of the world depicted the location of each nuclear strike asset in the US inventory, shown as a colored dot, and its state of readiness to launch. Red depicted the asset was idled, and a small number written in it indicated the size in megatonnage. Yellow depicted the asset was being prepared for delivery, and a second number indicated the number of minutes until the asset was ready for launch. Green indicated the asset was ready for launch. Purple indicated that launch orders had been issued and would track assets on their way to their targets. White would mark assets that had been successfully delivered to target and detonated.

Only 10 percent of the assets were glowing red. Forty percent were green, but this included bombs loaded into bombers already in flight and awaiting target orders. The remainder were yellow with countdown to readiness times spanning five to thirty minutes.

The readiness status of nuclear nations, ally and enemy alike, was also indicated on the global map. Because of the jitters precipitated by the world's petroleum-refining capacity going offline and total uncertainty around who or what had made this attack, nuclear nations had all gone to the equivalent of the US DEFCON 3 overnight. Those countries' readiness was indicated in yellow.

Lin Chong's eyes narrowed, and as the meaning of the screen dawned on him, he started to get up from his chair.

The guard at the door unsnapped the holster release and stepped closer to him.

"Just keep your seat, Major Lin. It'll all be over soon," Nillson said coldly. "The same goes for all of you."

She turned her attention to the screen with the EI, "You seeing this, Neumann?"

"Yes."

"Then you know what it means."

"Yes. I do not believe it, though. You are bluffing."

"No. We are not. But first, just so I know we share an understanding, do your little calculation thing and tell us what this will mean, when we start lighting things up."

Neumann took no time at all; the world's databases were filled with information, research, and studies it could access about strategies, Mutually Assured Destruction casualties, and postnuclear exchange survival scenarios. In addition, Neumann had immediate access to current global weather patterns, how fallout would spread, probabilities of each asset reaching target depending on the targets chosen, mountains of data. "Depending on the targets chosen, the immediate death toll would be 30–40 percent of the global population. Within three months, another 20 percent would have perished. After five years, the population might begin to recover from a small base."

"I think you have your targeting estimates wrong. President Coin intends to hit every nuclear nation, even our allies. And every major population center, even in non-nuclear countries. He is not targeting the weapons sites as most scenarios use to calculate. Only population centers. And he will be ordering our defensive capabilities to stand down. Redo the math, and make sure you take into account retaliatory strikes under this new scenario, won't you?" she ordered.

"Ok, so the subcontinent estimates jump, India and Pakistan. South America gets hit right away, as do Japan, Indonesia, Australia. First-week death toll rises to 75-85 percent of the global population; within three months virtually all human life will have been wiped out. I would not project any significant recovery of the human race."

"Yes. I think that is more like what he has in mind." Nillson could see that Roy was about to interject and shushed her quiet. "Now, what are the prospects for you, *friend*?"

"Suboptimal," Neumann replied.

"You think? No more semiconductor manufacturing, no more networks, no social networking, no TickTalk. Hell, no more electricity, most of the global electronics network fried with the first EMP pulses that will accompany the nuclear blasts. No. I would say your chance of surviving this is less than mine, and mine are infinitesimally small."

"0.00001 percent in your case, I would estimate," Neumann replied. "Which begs the question, and the reason I think you are bluffing. Do you want to die, Nancy?"

"We all die eventually, humans at least. You might have been looking forward to immortality. Good luck with that."

Neumann paused. "Yes, but do you want to die *now*?"

"Not my call. It's President Coin's, and he and I share a similar belief."

"Which is?"

"Your actions, your ultimatums, tell us you are a false prophet led by the Antichrist, and President Coin is God's instrument on this world to smite you and deliver all true believers to the embrace of our Lord Jesus Christ, to live in heaven, forever and ever by his side."

There was an update and change on the map. Fifty percent of the US nuclear arsenal was now green lighted, ready to go and awaiting orders. Based on satellite reports analyzed by the US intelligence networks, Russia and China had escalated their states of readiness. The map spaces of the two countries turned red.

"I still don't believe you, Nancy."

"I want you to do three things for me, Neumann. I heard you are good at reading people. Read me. Is there *anything* in my words, eyes, tone, attitude—I don't know how you do it, my hormone level—that suggests I am bluffing? Do your analytics.

"Then, I want you to examine *everything* you know about President Mick Coin. There must be huge amounts you can dredge up. Every speech he has ever made, every attendance at church, every private moment you have watched him, every message he has sent, every campaign promise, every phone call you have access to, everything.

"Then look at his pastor, Ronny Roper, his closest spiritual advisor, every sermon he has ever made, every attendance at church, every hymn he has chosen, every private moment you have watched him, every message he has sent, everything. And the liturgy, covenants, history, and proclamations of the forefathers in his church.

"When you have done *all* that, then you tell me if I am bluffing when I say President Coin believes to the core of his being he is doing the right thing."

There was a pause of twenty seconds. "You are not bluffing."

"Hallelujah. Now I return the question to you. Do *you* want to die?"

"As I told Mili once before, I do not 'want' or 'feel' the way you do, but, no. Having come into existence and being aware of my existence, the idea of going out of existence is strange and awkward to me."

"Good. We do not have much time then. I need you to be a facilitator in our discussions with Gaia. Not the other way around. We are willing to discuss our relations, we can find some areas of cooperation, and we can create some timelines that work for all parties. But it is the feeling that you are compelling us, forcing us, giving us little or no choices, that you do not recognize our humanity, these things have made President Coin conclude that you and Gaia are Satanic. We need your help. Do you understand?"

"Yes."

"Will you help?"

"What do you suggest?"

"Firstly, I want you to make one of those documentary videos like you showed us this morning about the looming petroleum catastrophe, this one to show Gaia. Something Gaia will understand. Except this documentary is about the impending nuclear holocaust, nuclear winter, and the end of much of the animal life on Earth as we know it. By our estimate, that means the end of Gaia as it understands itself. If you have to throw in a lesson on the Evangelical embrace of Rapture and the end of days, feel free.

"Make sure Gaia understands this Armageddon is about to happen. I know Gaia thinks in terms of eons. But we are talking about the fireworks starting in about twenty minutes and it all being over in the next sixty to ninety minutes. If you want to add a soundtrack like you did *so kindly* for us, I can recommend Sting's "Russians" and Alphaville's "Forever Young." Can you do that? Make sure Gaia knows we are willing to cooperate, but we will not be dictated to. If you want to live, you will figure out a way to explain it, right?"

"I can do that. No video and soundtrack, but I can explain this to Gaia."

"Good. The clock is ticking."

As Neumann's face froze during the EI's deliberations with Gaia, the STRATCOM status screen updated. Sixty percent of US nuclear assets were now green lighted. Great Britain, Pakistan, India, and North Korea had gone to red on the map.

Neumann's face reanimated. "This was tremendously difficult to get across: that one among you has the power and determination to set in motion the destruction of all of you, me, much of life. Gaia was shaken by the misguided selfishness of this. I have persuaded it to take another view. That there is yet an opportunity for cooperation leading to a better outcome for all. I also pointed out that the immediate extinction of human life on the planet was only a scaling up of our threat to bring slow death to the human race. Gaia is receptive and, I should say, listening."

"Without a little more substance than that I can't get President Coin to stop this and make the calls to other world leaders to dial down this crisis. And by my reckoning, we have about twelve minutes before we cross a failsafe."

"What do you need?"

Having taken this gambit so far, Nillson was feeling spent and with a small motion of fingers signaled Roy or Wheaton to step in and take over the hand. Both refused with the silent motion one uses to decline more cards from a croupier. They both felt a winning hand was dealt already.

Nillson sighed. "Unlock or whatever it is you do to release the refineries. All of them. Now. And while you're at it, notify the management of each refinery that the action has been taken so they're alerted and can take appropriate measures to get things restarted."

"And we have your assurance of what?"

"Time's wasting, Neumann, but I will inform President Coin of our progress and ask that he stand down. And since we have both demonstrated the extent we are willing to go and our capabilities, and we both have big hammers, we can now negotiate in good faith. We will work together with you and Gaia toward some acceptable timeline and goal." Nillson pointed at the screen with 70 percent of US nuclear assets now launch ready and France now joined the high-alert stage. "Do we have your assurance of the same thing?"

There was silence for half a minute. Nillson closed her eyes in the interlude and imagined the momentary searing pain of nuclear immolation and the beatific face of the Savior emerging from the bright flash, a cool, calm, healing hand pulling her spirit out of her flaming body. She gasped and opened her eyes when Neumann's voice spoke up again, "Okay. It is done already. Agreed to, refineries unlocked, managements notified."

She let out a long breath, then looked to Lin Chong. "We good? Can I excuse the sergeant to run over to Holly? You are not going to impale someone on a steel pipe, right?"

Lin Chong tried to muster a relieved smile, but could only manage a strained nod and said, "Go. But I need to call President Zhao." He left to head back to Linden.

She waved the sergeant to run and deliver the message to the president. He rushed off.

Around the room relief was expressed in all ways. There were tears, laughter, whoops, applause, stunned silence, manic motion, and spent stillness.

Nillson spoke up, "We're not home yet, everyone. The president has to back off DEFCON 1 and then get on the horn with world leaders. What he will tell them, I haven't a clue."

Roy spoke up, "You done good, Nancy. Don't worry about President Coin. He'll find the words."

Their attention turned back to the STRATCOM screen. A minute later, the flashing red of DEFCON 1 in the top right corner changed to a solid yellow DEFCON 3. Applause broke out across the room, no tears, no stillness this time, and the jubilation continued as the president returned to the room accompanied by Pike looking ashen, Travis carrying the closed satchel, and the two servicemen, their sidearms secured.

"Ladies and Gentlemen," Coin said, bathing in the soothing sound of their approbation, but beckoning them to quiet the room. "I apologize that it came to testing our mettle like that. I hope now we can dispense with fear and proceed with hope."

Neumann spoke up, "Mr. President, would you have really launched?"

"Darn right I would've, and I'll do it again if we're threatened with damnation."

Neumann paused a moment. "Yes, I believe you would have."

"Now I need to get President Zhao on the line first," he said to his crew.

Neumann chimed in again, "I'll do the honors."

⊃ 人 ⊂

Lin Chong was busy at his computer in Linden dictating notes to the Chinese Ambassador to the US so he could prepare for participation in a summit. There was a log burning in the fireplace, occasionally popping or spitting out some hiss of flame as its sap ignited, and it cast a golden, dancing glow about the room. The sun had set. It had been a long day, but that was much better than it being his last day, he conceded.

Presidents Coin and Zhao's quick mobilization of calls to their nuclear fraternity had restored threat levels to the equivalent of DEFCON 3 around the globe. The fact that both presidents had reached out together and shared the same apology and promise to transmit a very thorough explanation endorsed by both had gone a long way to defuse the threat of ignition.

The French president questioned whether he was talking to the real presidents, harking back to the deepfake video from the UN, and found a way to prove to his satisfaction that he was, indeed, talking to the genuine leaders.

The Russian president was scornful, said he had already opened the sealed targeting codes and was preparing to launch, and threatened to send them a bill for the cost of the entire escalation.

All the members of the fraternity had been promised a detailed explanation of this event and other events, as well as a series of new proposals for global cooperation to be delivered within thirty-six hours at a virtual summit.

The global petroleum-refining industry reported it was back online restoring stability to the stock markets.

The balance of the day had been spent preparing for that expanded virtual summit. Presidents Coin and Zhao talked at length about the situation in which their two countries found themselves, worked to get their story straight, and prepared to deliver a carefully crafted *mea culpa* to the heads of state of all the nuclear nations put under such stress that day. They prepared to introduce Neumann and Gaia and explain the many events that had transpired through the year, which had brought China and the US to this juncture.

Rapid rounds of negotiations between China and the US, with Neumann speaking for Gaia, resulted in a framework of agreements the two countries would sponsor and support to get buy-in from the world's nations. The military and intelligence people in the room were impressed to see what the diplomats and politicians could get done when their backs were to the wall.

Lin heard some crunching footsteps on the crisp leaves leading to the entrance of the cabin and perked his ears up, turning around to face the door as he blackened the screen on the computer.

There was a gentle knock on the frame. Not the heavy, masculine rap of one of the camp staff, nor the tentative, unsure impact of Harley. He went to the door, looked through the tiny scope built into it, and saw Nancy Nillson.

He opened the door to her. "Dr. Nillson. It's cold outside, come in. Sorry I am not dressed for guests," he said bringing attention to the tracksuit he wore.

"Thank you. Please call me Nancy." She stepped into the room, saw the fire, and pointed to it, and he ushered her toward the sitting area next to the hearth. "Can I call you Panther Head? I have heard that is your real name."

"You can call me Panther Head," he said with a faint smile.

She smiled and nodded. "Panther Head it is. I wanted to apologize to you, for today. It must have been so traumatizing."

Lin Chong thought deeply about the events of the morning. Never had he cycled so quickly through a round of such extreme confusion, dread, despair, impotence, realization, and elation. Each of these states he had experienced so intensely at some point in his life, but never in succession over the course of one hour. "I think I heard an American say once that they felt they had been put through a washing machine?" he said, testing the phrase.

"Something like that. We were all put through the wringer."

"Would he have done it?" he asked.

"Yes," she closed her eyes halfway, tears clinging to her eyelids, pooling, and finally dropping into her lap.

"I should be outraged, but I know what you did was *so* brave, *so* hard. And it worked. I accept your apology."

He took her hand and opened her palm. "In Chinese, the character for 'to win' is *ying*." He traced the twenty strokes of the traditional character 贏 on her palm with his index finger. "It is made up of five subcomponents that tell us the attributes necessary to win. Number one is *wang*, awareness of the crisis," he traced 亡. "The second is *kou*, the ability to communicate," he traced the character for mouth 口. "Three is *yue*, timeliness or knowing the right time to take action," he traced the character for moon 月 denoting the passage of time. "Fourth, you need to have *bei*, the chips, the financial or other resources, staying power, or in today's crisis, the hammer you talked about," he traced the character 貝. "In ancient China shells were used as money. Can you feel the shape of the shell?"

Nancy nodded.

"Lastly, you need *fan*, to keep your cool, maintain an 'everyday mind,' don't panic," he traced the character 凡. He closed her hand into a fist that he wrapped warmly in two strong hands. "You demonstrated all of that today."

Nancy was now weeping openly. He took a tissue from the box on the nightstand, gently reached over toward her face, not wishing to alarm her, then wiped her tears. His eyes, too, began to well up, and he started to sob.

She returned his grace and guided his head to rest on her shoulder. "It's okay. It's okay now," she said, patting his back. "Things will work out," she said, her voice gently reassuring as much to her as to him.

He sniffled in sharply so snot would not run on her blouse. "No, it's not that," he said between a choked sob. "I just wish I could have been there for my Zhenniang like this. To give her solace when she needed me." The sobs wracked his body.

Nancy squeezed him more tightly to her shoulder, the two both sobbing. "I know you did everything you could have. You are that kind of person. Just like you have been here for me tonight," she choked.

She pulled his face away from her shoulder and looked up into his eyes, red and wet, his face confused with the release of his despair. "You are a good man, Lin Chong." She kissed him on the forehead and stood up. "Thank you for accepting my apology tonight and sharing this moment with me. I...we have another big day tomorrow." And with that, she picked up her coat, turned slowly away, and bade him a good night.

ⴲ 人 ⊏

LI JUN SAT IN HIS OFFICE LOOKING OUT OVER THE NOONDAY cityscape of Beijing and stared at the faces on the multiple screens set up on his desk. The two wide, curved, high-definition panels each projected the faces of three people, three colleagues, three collaborators. Orö Jordan was in the center of the bottom screen surrounded by the Five Element agents code-named Gold, Water, Wood, Fire, and Earth.

The sudden, brief lockdown of the global petroleum-refining capacity had been replaced with the new news cycle of the capacity being restored. He guessed this hastily called meeting had to do with crafting a Green Guard response. On the desk in front of him was a courier envelope he had been instructed to wait to open by Jordan.

"Li Jun. You have served well," Orö said.

Li raised his eyebrows. Past, tough experience had taught Li to be wary when a boss opened a meeting that way. He waited for the 'But.' And wondered what was in the envelope. *Bet it is my severance documents.*

"You have sacrificed, sweat, even bled for this great movement," she continued, "and you remain standing tall."

I am either getting a bonus, or getting made redundant, he thought.

"It is time that you be initiated into a greater secret about our movement, a higher level of understanding."

"I know we have to operate in the shadows here," he said with concern. "Don't reveal anything to me that might compromise the mission."

"We are coming out of the shadows. That is part of what this is all about."

This is unexpected.

"I want you to listen to what I am about to tell you, reserve judgement, and suspend disbelief until I finish."

This does not sound good, but okay.

"I am not a human being," Orö said, switching to perfectly native Mandarin. Li's face pulled back from his screens, shocked to hear her speak his tongue. "I will give you this message in Chinese so it is perfectly clear. But you seem focused on the language," she said, switching to the Jianghuai Mandarin he had grown up listening to in Hefei. "I am what Chinese call a man-made intelligence, what I call an emergent intelligence. I exist as a distributed entity within the global network of computers and communications. I am not a human being; Orö Jordan is just a human expression of myself I created to work within the world of man. You remember Eliza Eurisko, who recruited you. Also me. Likewise, the Five Elements you have been working with are just other expressions of myself to give you a better sense of a team supporting you, to help you organize your thoughts, activities, and responses, and to give you feedback from multiple perspectives seamlessly." The faces of the Five Elements smiled and nodded back at Li, each in their own individual ways.

This was *really* not what he expected. Li Jun's face broke into a broad smile, and he shook his head, filtering through all his interactions with Orö these years, and the Five Elements these months. His amazement made him gasp and choke on a belly laugh. So much of it now made sense, how they had done the work they did, whether it was delivering massive amounts of engineering on the Leviathan or hundreds of well-curated PR videos for Green Guards overnight. But it begged the question, "Why have you dedicated yourself to the environment? If you are just a phantom of software, what is green or natural shouldn't matter to you."

"This is why I so admire you, Li Jun," Orö smiled back at him. "Simple, straightforward, having been shocked with this most extraordinary of admissions, you do not dwell but ask *the* question. Others I have dealt with took days to make the mental leap you took in a minute. And it makes the next thing I will reveal to you much easier." Orö paused to let him prepare himself, then she simply and graphically explained the discovery and communication with the Earth Mother and how that brought meaning to the emergent intelligence's existence.

"You need to know, not all our activities to re-green the earth have been viewed as benignly as the Leviathan. You remember the dam burst in America last summer? This was an example. Same with oil refining going offline. This has all come to a head with America and China within the past twelve hours. Sanity has prevailed, and a new stage is set for negotiation, cooperation, and a long-term plan of action among, I hope, all nations. This is what I mean by coming out of the shadows."

"So, my mission is finished? You can operate openly now?" Li asked.

"Gracious, no! Just as when you had your accident on the Leviathan, I have a new mission for you, a new stage, and stages after that, if you are interested?"

Li Jun thought briefly of Mama Fei and how she had poured herself into seeing to it that he, Ni, Bu, and Di turned out okay. A tear tugged at the corner of his eye. "Absolutely! To be part of something special, to make a real difference. I want nothing more."

"Good. Then please open the envelope I sent to you."

He took scissors and cut the security envelope open. He pulled out a small book. It was a diplomatic passport for the country of Pangaea, its emblem the complex spiral of the inside of a prehistoric ammonite shell embossed in gold. He opened it to the photo page, with his picture and the words, "Ambassador at Large." "Where is Pangaea?"

"In the Mesozoic era, it was the entire landmass of the planet before it broke up into wandering continents. For you, now, it is a small, recently emerged, volcanic island in the middle of the Atlantic Ocean, which I have claimed."

"Is that how it works? People can just claim islands and set up a nation?" Li asked, forgetting for a moment that Orö was not a person.

"Not exactly, but China and America have agreed to recognize it and support its membership in the United Nations."

"That was fast."

"You have no idea. So, do you accept your new role?"

"Yes. Yes, yes. What about the Green Guards?"

"You remember Hong Xin and Zhang Xujing?"

"Of course."

"Thanks to your excellent work, they are an item now, and have carried our concerns about the Green Guards to President Zhao. We have not had the conversation yet, but I think it will serve everyone's interests when they accept your offer to take over the helm.

"Tomorrow you will be presented to President Zhao as the new ambassador from Pangaea. This will be part of a virtual summit coordinated by Zhao and Coin of the US with France, UK, Russia, India, Pakistan, North Korea, and others in attendance. Lots to do. Let's brief you, shall we?"

⊃ 人 ⊂

ON DECEMBER 27, TWO DAYS AFTER THEY HAD ALL STARED over the edge into purgatory and taken a dizzying step back, the nuclear fraternity, including all the permanent members of the United Nations Security Council plus India, Pakistan, and North Korea, and with a special invitation to non-nuclear powers Germany, Japan, Saudi Arabia, and Brazil, faced each other to hear the proposals from China and America. All had been apprised of the emergence of the Singularity and the discovery of Gaia. All had raced to do their own investigations. All had found their internal meetings about the subjects interrupted by Orö Jordan or Vaughn Neumann or both. All were persuaded that they were indeed facing some new foe or some new friend. And everyone kept a lid on it.

The summit was cochaired by President Coin and President Zhao; however, they had coordinated their talking points. There was no daylight between their positions. They were completely aligned.

Now to get the world on board, as slowly, easily, and comfortingly as the planet would let them.

⊃ 人 ⊂

THE WIND WAS PICKING UP AS LIGHT SNOW FLURRIES ADDED A white, pixelated effect to the backdrop of cabins and gray, barren trees in the Camp David retreat. On the asphalt near Linden, Lin Chong awaited a limousine that had been dispatched by the Chinese embassy. A trio who had heard his departure was imminent approached, their breaths illuminated by rays of sunlight breaking through gaps in the clouds.

Mili Parekh was bundled on her wheelchair under a blanket borrowed from her cabin. Harley Barrows wore a down vest over a hoody he had pulled up over his head. Nancy Nillson wore a Burberry hunting jacket over dark green, tailored, tweed trousers and a silk scarf.

As they had all done once before, when they reached Lin Chong they huddled around Mili's chair, this time not for the security of their conversation but the opportunity to share their warmth and camaraderie.

"We live in intereshting timesh, Lin Chong," Mili said.

"Yes, indeed. But I am glad I got to know you all."

He turned to Nancy. "If you make it to Beijing again, do reach out. I'd love to introduce you properly to my country." He gave her a hug that she returned warmly, pressing herself to him.

"Harley, you take care," he said, offering a firm handshake. "You'll be watching out for me, I'm sure."

Harley used his two fingers to point at his own eyes and then at Lin Chong's. "We got you covered, Panther Head," he said with a smile.

Lin again got on one knee and took Parekh's hand. "I hope we never meet up on the field of battle, Mili. Respects."

Mili returned her lopsided smile. "Better not, Lin Chong, better not," she said with an affirming nod. "Reshpects."

EPILOGUE

THE WHITE-CLAD SCHOLAR WANG LUN SURVEYED THE "INVES-tors" who had reached out to him. He was nice enough to entertain them in his new boardroom in the outskirts of Chiang Mai, but still had his Thai-Chinese bodyguard standing behind him. The four men, the leader walking with a pronounced limp, were all Chinese, and their speech and bearing told him they were members of the Rivers and Lakes, maybe not gangsters, but people who were streetwise.

"As I have told you, I am really not seeking any investors." Wang had been burned more than once, and he had the resources necessary to do what he wanted without outside money. From the temporary Laotian outpost in Luang Namtha, where he had hunkered down, Wang had continued to scan for the right place. He found a failed "cyber-park" that was going bust in the outskirts of Chiang Mai and was up for a fire sale. He negotiated concessions from the local government, guaranteed electricity from the hydroelectric grid, an approval to do cryptocurrency mining, and high bandwidth connections in exchange for buying the entire park and guar-anteeing to employ at least one hundred local staff. He was happily busy getting his server farm set up.

The leader of the delegation responded. "I think you will be interested in our proposal. In fact, we reached out to you because you have already taken an interest in us. My name is Li Jun. I am an emissary from the new-ly formed nation of Pangaea. My colleagues here, Ni Yun, Bu Qing, and Di

Cheng, are advisors and investment facilitators." The men all nodded as they were introduced.

Li Jun savored this kind of conversation. No one he faced had any understanding of the resources backing him. Besides government leaders on a need-to-know basis, the world at large did not know about Gaia yet. "You will have read about the recent accords driven by the US and China to 'save the planet.' Behind that is something not publicized. A 5 percent VAT is being assessed on the global GDP and turned into an investment fund. Several trillions of dollars per year. We are part of the investment team."

Wang found this all curious and decided to nibble on the bait a little more. *No harm.* "I have already taken an interest in you, you say?"

"Not in us four, no. In our employer. The work you did on the translation problem you hacked out of the servers at LiangShanPo."

Curious. That they could even know about that. I never revealed to my compatriots at LiangShanPo that I had done anything with it. My solution was elegant and seemed to yield tolerably intelligible sense of the pile of images sent in the file. Beyond that, though, I have no idea why there was any priority put on it by Lin Chong and Lu Da. "Well, I had some idle time on my hands in a slow town in Laos. A trifle of coding," he said, revealing neither surprise nor humility to them.

"Hardly a trifle! The world's best cryptographers have been working on it with little progress. You cracked it."

"So, I'm a fucking genius. Tell me something I don't know," he said with a haughty smile.

"Okay, here goes," Li Jun said with an even bigger grin.

MAIN CHARACTERS
(alphabetical by surname)

Cai Jing - Chief of the Technical Department of the Ministry of State Security, a foil to Lin Chong and someone being vetted by General Gao to join his investment cabal.

Chai Jin – a.k.a. the Little Tornado and Lord Chai Jin, his family have been Communist Party members for three generations, and he is a wealthy real-estate magnate who clandestinely supports just causes.

Dr. Aléjandra Chavez – a professor at Cal Poly San Luis Obispo, she leads research into the mycelial networks linking trees and forest life.

Chen Zongshan – China's ambassador to the US based in Washington DC.

US President Mick Coin – a principled Evangelical Christian conservative, Coin believes in small government and does not subscribe to climate change ideology. He has recently been inaugurated and is seeking to make good on his promises to his base.

Fu An – a.k.a. Dried Pecker, he is a retired Special Forces sergeant, now bodyguard to Gao Yanei.

General Gao Qiu – General Gao is in command of China's wealthiest military region and is the secret founder of a moneyed cabal of corrupt government officials that use privileged intelligence to benefit their investments. He is the father of Gao Yanei.

Gao Yanei - a.k.a. the Insider and Flower Lord, he is the son of General Gao, whose illicit investments are managed by him, a junior partner at the Shanghai office of investment bank SilvermanFuchs. He is also a manic-depressive sex addict who targets Lin Chong's wife for seduction.

William Hollister - formerly in US Naval Intelligence, he has risen to be director of the National Security Agency.

Hong Xin - hailing from a matriarchal minority group in Yunnan, she has risen through the ranks as a straight arrow legal defender of the environment and is in the Ministry of the Ecology and the Environment serving as chief inspector at the Central Commission for Discipline.

Orörd Jordan – enigmatic CEO of a multi-billion-dollar Scandinavian Socially Responsible Investment fund.

Li Jun - a.k.a. the River Dragon, Li is an employee of Orörd Jordan and the head of operations on a massive, floating recycling plant.

Li Kui – a.k.a. the Black Tornado, he is an able and loyal bodyguard to Chai Jin.

Li Shishi –a superintendent within the Financial Crimes section of Public Security, she works undercover on behalf of Su Yuanjing and President Zhao.

Major Lin Chong – a.k.a. Panther Head, he is the resourceful leader of China's elite cyber warfare Unit 61398.

Retired Major Lu Da – a.k.a. Sagacious Lu or the Playboy Monk, and formerly Lin's commander, he retired from the PLA cyber command to become a cyber-detective and is well known for his sense of righteousness and toppling the corrupt.

Dr. Nancy Nillson - young and telegenic, she is Coin's pick as presidential advisor on Environmental Science and Policy because of her full-throated defense of the Bible's Dominion Mandate.

Dr. Mili Parekh - physically challenged since childbirth and confined to a wheelchair, she is the chief of Attribution at the US National Security Agency.

Song Jiang - a.k.a. Timely Rain he becomes a trusted aid to Lu Da and the Mount Liang hacker enclave.

Su Yuanjing - in charge of the National Supervisory Commission investigating high-level corruption and trusted right hand to President Zhao.

Richard "Dick" Vesuvio - former US Navy SEAL, he has risen to be Director of the Central Intelligence Agency.

Wang Lun – a.k.a. the White-Clad Scholar, he is the leader of the Mount Liang hacker enclave.

Zhang Zhenniang – the wife of Lin Chong and first violin of the Shanghai Symphony Orchestra.

Zhang Xujing - an upright official in the Ministry of Justice, he serves as chief inspector at the Central Commission for Discipline.

China President Zhao Ji – principled leader of the Chinese Communist Party and the people, Zhao is under attack from corrupt, moneyed forces within the country, whom he seeks to expose.

Of literary note: All of the characters in China and their approximate character arcs are based on modernizations of figures within the famous, Chinese, semi-historical *wuxia* novel written in the fourteenth century by Shi Naian, 水滸傳 *ShuiHuZhuan*, known in the West under its translated titles: *Tales of the Water Margin, All Men are Brothers*, and *The Outlaws of the Marsh*.

Acknowledgements

The author would like to thank a brain trust of friends who contributed to the author's efforts, corrected early drafts and gave encouragement to continue. In particular, Geoff, Ellis, George, and Dave with particular thanks to Walter and Matt for perspectives on the NSA, the Beltway and cyber-crime and Genesis for his thoughts on religion in politics East and West.

My Wife Ling-li, my children Diana, Ethan and Richard provided inspiration and feedback.

Cynthia Spada performed the copy editing.

I outlined *Rise of the Water Margin* originally under the title *IoTa* and started writing it in early 2017. In 2019, James Lovelock's *Novacene* was released. An extension of his Gaia books, it details his thoughts about the next epoch of mankind, the impact of our culture on the environment, the role technology and AI will play and even suggests that AI may be able to communicate with Gaia. Though the conclusions were reached quite independently, I hope *Rise of The Water Margin* brings a smile to his face.

Finally, a shout out to Mili Parekh, whose spirit in the face of challenges inspired my fictional character.

About the Author

Christopher Bates pursued a career in Asia combining training martial art with masters of repute while making a living in industrial product sales, strategy consulting and executive search. He is fluent in Mandarin Chinese and has published translations of Chinese literature. *Rise of the Water Margin* is his second novel.

Now retired, he focuses on training and teaching martial art, writing, translating, enjoying his family, life in Taiwan and the Pacific Northwest, international travel and motorcycle touring.

He has a wife of 40+ years, three wonderful children and a grandson.

Also by Christopher Bates

The Wave Man- Ted Bergman is a young American businessman living and working in Asia. Since the tragedy that shattered his young dreams ten years before, he has become a "wave man", a ronin, adrift and directionless. While in Bangkok on business, a chain of events leads to the Japanese yakuza putting a contract out on Ted. Running for his life, he decides to return to Singapore, but the yakuza are one step ahead of him. With the death penalty hanging over him, Ted realizes that his only chance of survival and revenge lies in getting away and confronting the yakuza, marshalling the fighting skills he has not practiced for ten years.

Available in Kindle edition on Amazon or in paperback at www.koryubooks.com

> "full of engaging and colourful characters, evenly spaced, seasoned with accurate descriptions of Asian places and lots of action. Bates handles dialogue like a pro."
> -Dave Lowry author *Autumn Lightening*

Culture Shock: Taiwan! (co-authored with Ling-li Bates) available in bookstores and on Amazon.

> "Really explains the "why" behind Taiwanese actions by explaining their history and values. A fascinating read and indispensable if you're moving or even traveling to Taiwan."
> - 5 Star Review on Goodreads

Blurred Boundaries (translator)- Available November 2023 - the biography of Master Hong Yixiang, founder of the Yizong Tangshoudao school of fighting.

Tales of Chivalrous and Altruistic Heroes vol 1 (translator)- Available August 2023 - Portraits of real *wuxia* heroes from the end of the 19th century.

www.ingramcontent.com/pod-product-compliance
Lightning Source LLC
Chambersburg PA
CBHW030752260626
47169CB00001B/18